Mike Ashley is a full-ti r with almost a hundred books t er fifty Mammoth Books includi *ctreme Science Fiction, The Mamm* d *The Mammoth Book of Perfec* *es*. He has also written the biogra, y or Aigernon Blackwood, *Starlight Man*, and a comprehensive study *The Mammoth Book of King Arthur*. He lives in Kent with his wife and three cats and when he gets the time he likes to go for long walks.

THE MAMMOTH BOOK OF MINDBLOWING SF

Edited and with an Introduction by

Mike Ashley

ROBINSON

RUNNING PRESS
PHILADELPHIA · LONDON

Constable & Robinson Ltd
3 The Lanchesters
162 Fulham Palace Road
London W6 9ER
www.constablerobinson.com

First published in the UK by Robinson,
an imprint of Constable & Robinson, 2009

A copy of the British Library Cataloguing in Publication
Data is available from the British Library

UK ISBN 978-1-84529-891-3

1 3 5 7 9 10 8 6 4 2

First published in the United States in 2009 by
Running Press Book Publishers
All rights reserved under the Pan-American and
International Copyright Conventions

9   8   7   6   5   4   3   2   1
Digit on the right indicates the number of this printing

US Library of Congress number: 2008944131
US ISBN 978-0-76243-723-8

Running Press Book Publishers
2300 Chestnut Street
Philadelphia, PA 19103-4371

Visit us on the web!
www.runningpress.com

Printed and bound in the EU

CONTENTS

ACKNOWLEDGMENTS

Permission to use the stories in this anthology has been granted as follows:

"The Pevatron Rats" © 2009 by Stephen Baxter. First publication, original to this anthology. Printed by permission of the author.

"A Dance to Strange Musics" © 1998 by Gregory Benford. First published in *Science Fiction Age*, November 1998. Reprinted by permission of the author.

"The Hole in the Hole" © 1994 by Terry Bisson. First published in *Asimov's Science Fiction*, February 1994. Reprinted by permission of the author.

"Bridge" © 1952 by James Blish. First published in *Astounding Science Fiction*, February 1952. Incorporated in *They Shall Have Stars* (Faber, 1956) and subsequently in *Cities in Flight* (Avon, 1970), currently in print from Victor Gollancz. Reprinted by permission of the author's estate, the estate's literary agent, Heather Chalcroft, and Orion Publishing, Ltd.

"Hotrider" © 1991 by Keith Brooke. First published in *Aboriginal Science Fiction*, December 1991. Reprinted by permission of the author.

"The Rest is Speculation" © 2009 by Eric Brown. First publication, original to this anthology. Printed by permission of the author.

"Out of the Sun" © 1957 by Arthur C. Clarke. First published in *If*, February 1958. Reprinted by permission of the author's agents, Scovil Chichak Galen Literary Agency, Inc., New York.

"The Edge of the Map" © 2006 by Ian Creasey. First published in *Asimov's Science Fiction Magazine*, June 2006. Reprinted by permission of the author.

"Palindromic" © 1997 by Peter Crowther. First published in *First Contact*, edited by Martin H. Greenberg & Larry Segriff (New York: Daw Books, 1997). Reprinted by permission of the author.

INTRODUCTION

THAT SENSE OF WONDER

What was it that first attracted you to science fiction? Or, if this is the first time you've thought of checking out a science-fiction anthology, what are you hoping for?

I'll tell you what first hooked me on science fiction: its ability to evoke a sense of wonder. Science fiction is a good medium for a number of things – satire, prediction, adventure, invention . . . but these can also be delivered by other forms of fiction. If there's one thing that science fiction has that towers above all other types of fiction, it is that sense of wonder.

But what is the "sense of wonder". If you've experienced it, you'll know exactly what it is, but it isn't so easy to put into words. To me, it's that moment when the story flicks a switch in your mind and opens new doors and perceptions, allowing you to appreciate things in a different and remarkable way. It's especially pertinent in demonstrating the potential of science or technology, the wonders that may be discovered in the depths of space or in the far future or deep within the human spirit.

That sense of wonder once defined science fiction: the wonders that science might bring. Unfortunately, as we all learned with the coming of the nuclear age, science could bring as much horror as it could wonder, and, for some, science fiction lost that glow. These days it tends to be associated with the earliest forms of science fiction, particularly in the American pulp magazines, when the spirit of science fiction was still young. But, while the spark of wonder may have dimmed in certain regions of science fiction, it has not expired. It's still there, if you know where to look.

And that's what I wanted to do in this anthology: to show that the spirit of wonder can still be discovered in the science fiction of the recent years.

This anthology brings together twenty-one mindblowing stories – two of them full-length novellas – that will allow you, once more, to experience that sense of wonder. Much like beauty is in the eye of the beholder, I can't guarantee that every story will ignite that spark for you, as they do for me, but I'd be surprised if most don't. Here are some of the concepts you will encounter:

- a discovery on the Moon that allows us to revisit our past
- distances across the world suddenly expand and people vanish in between
- explorers trapped under the surface of an alien world where the only way out is down
- a future where death has been eradicated but returns to fulfil its destiny
- the very last moments on planet Earth and the fate of the last inhabitants

And a lot more besides. For the most part I've selected stories from the last ten or twenty years, but I chose two older stories, both from the 1950s, to show how that sense of wonder compares with more recent material. Those stories are by Arthur C. Clarke and James Blish, two authors whose work was always vibrant with wonder. There are also five new stories, written specially for this anthology, which bring new twists and turns to the wonders of science and humanity.

One side-effect, indeed a major benefit, of that sense of wonder, is that these stories are, for the most part, uplifting and positive. They may at first seem to deal with difficult subjects and problems, but opening the mind allows new ideas and solutions to be generated. Science fiction at its best makes you think about the world and ourselves, and when it does it in a positive way, it encourages us to look beyond. So in selecting these stories I wanted ones that not only blew the mind, but left us with a glow of satisfaction and delight and, of course, wonder.

Here's science fiction doing what it does best.

Mike Ashley

OUT OF THE SUN

Arthur C. Clarke

*If there is one writer whose work epitomizes that sense of
wonder, it is without doubt, Arthur C. Clarke. It's almost
impossible to read any of his stories or novels without
experiencing that trigger-moment when the mind
expands to take in an awe-inspiring concept. Along with
Stanley Kubrick, he achieved it magnificently in the film
2001: A Space Odyssey. It's there in his novels
Childhood's End, The City and the Stars, Rendezvous
with Rama and his short stories "The Star", "Jupiter V"
and "The Nine Billion Names of God" – possibly the
definitive "sense-of-wonder" story. For this anthology I
wanted to choose a lesser known story, but one that still
packs a considerable punch – even though it's the shortest
story in the book. (Well, the last story is the same length.)
Clarke had that ability to develop a remarkable, near
transcendental idea, in just a few words – and deliver an
idea that will remain with you ever after.*

*I was much saddened upon learning of Clarke's death
in March 2008, while I was assembling this volume. His
death brought to an end a significant chapter in the
history of science fiction – but it was only a chapter.
Clarke would be the first to emphasize that the story
continues – and that's why he opens this anthology.*

IF YOU HAVE ONLY LIVED on Earth, you have never seen the sun.
Of course, we could not look at it directly, but only through
dense filters that cut its rays down to endurable brilliance. It hung

there forever above the low, jagged hills to the west of the Observatory neither rising nor setting, yet moving around a small circle in the sky during the eighty-eight-day year of our little world. For it is not quite true to say that Mercury keeps that same face always turned toward the sun; it wobbles slightly on its axis, and there is a narrow twilight belt which knows such terrestrial commonplaces as dawn and sunset.

We were on the edge of the twilight zone, so that we could take advantage of the cool shadows yet could keep the sun under continuous surveillance as it hovered there above the hills. It was a full-time job for fifty astronomers and other assorted scientists; when we've kept it up for a hundred years or so, we may know something about the small star that brought life to Earth.

There wasn't a single band of solar radiation that someone at the Observatory had not made a life's study and was watching like a hawk. From the far X rays to the longest of radio waves, we had set our traps and snares; as soon as the sun thought of something new, we were ready for it. So we imagined . . .

The sun's flaming heart beats in a slow, eleven-year rhythm, and we were near the peak of the cycle. Two of the greatest spots ever recorded – each of them large enough to swallow a hundred Earths – had drifted across the disk like great black funnels piercing deeply into the turbulent outer layers of the sun. They were black, of course, only by contrast with the brilliance all around them; even their dark, cool cores were hotter and brighter than an electric arc. We had just watched the second of them disappear around the edge of the disk, wondering if it would survive to reappear two weeks later, when something blew up on the equator.

It was not too spectacular at first, partly because it was almost exactly beneath us – the precise center of the sun's disk – and so was merged into all the activity around it. If it had been near the edge of the sun, and thus projected against the background of space, it would have been truly awe-inspiring.

Imagine the simultaneous explosion of a million H-bombs. You can't? Nor can anyone else but that was the sort of thing we were watching climb up toward us at hundreds of miles a second, straight out of the sun's spinning equator. At first it formed a narrow jet, but it was quickly frayed around the edges by the magnetic and gravitational forces that were fighting against it. The central core kept right on, and it was soon obvious that it had escaped from the sun completely and was headed out into space – with us as its first target.

Though this had happened half a dozen times before, it was always exciting. It meant that we could capture some of the very substance of the sun as it went hurtling past in a great cloud of electrified gas. There was no danger; by the time it reached us it would be far too tenuous to do any damage, and, indeed, it would take sensitive instruments to detect it at all.

One of those instruments was the Observatory's radar, which was in continual use to map the invisible ionized layers that surround the sun for millions of miles. This was my department; as soon as there was any hope of picking up the oncoming cloud against the solar background, I aimed my giant radio mirror toward it.

It came in sharp and clear on the long-range screen – a vast, luminous island still moving outward from the sun at hundreds of miles a second. At this distance it was impossible to see its finer details, for my radar waves were taking minutes to make the round trip and to bring me back the information they were presenting on the screen. Even at its speed of not far short of a million miles an hour, it would be almost two days before the escaping prominence reached the orbit of Mercury and swept past us toward the outer planets. But neither Venus nor Earth would record its passing, for they were nowhere near its line of flight.

The hours drifted by; the sun had settled down after the immense convulsion that had shot so many millions of tons of its substance into space, never to return. The aftermath of that eruption was now a slowly twisting and turning cloud a hundred times the size of Earth, and soon it would be close enough for the short-range radar to reveal its finer structure.

Despite all the years I have been in the business, it still gives me a thrill to watch that line of light paint its picture on the screen as it spins in synchronism with the narrow beam of radio waves from the transmitter. I sometimes think of myself as a blind man exploring the space around him with a stick that may be a hundred million miles in length. For man is truly blind to the things I study; these great clouds of ionized gas moving far out from the sun are completely invisible to the eye and even to the most sensitive of photographic plates. They are ghosts that briefly haunt the solar system during the few hours of their existence; if they did not reflect our radar waves or disturb our magnetometers, we should never know that they were there.

The picture on the screen looked not unlike a photograph of a spiral nebula, for as the cloud slowly rotated it trailed ragged arms of gas for ten thousand miles around it. Or it might have been a terrestrial hurricane that I was watching from above as it spun through the atmosphere of Earth. The internal structure was extremely complicated, and was changing minute by minute beneath the action of forces which we have never fully understood. Rivers of fire were flowing in curious paths under what could only be the influence of electric fields; but why were they appearing from nowhere and disappearing again as if matter was being created and destroyed? And what were those gleaming nodules, larger than the moon, that were being swept along like boulders before a flood?

Now it was less than a million miles away; it would be upon us in little more than an hour. The automatic cameras were recording every complete sweep of the radar scan, storing up evidence which was to keep us arguing for years. The magnetic disturbance riding ahead of the cloud had already reached us; indeed, there was hardly an instrument in the Observatory that was not reacting in some way to the onrushing apparition.

I switched to the short-range scanner, and the image of the cloud expanded so enormously that only its central portion was on the screen. At the same time I began to change frequency, tuning across the spectrum to differentiate among the various levels. The shorter the wave length, the farther you can penetrate into a layer of ionized gas; by this technique I hoped to get a kind of X-ray picture of the cloud's interior.

It seemed to change before my eyes as I sliced down through the tenuous outer envelope with its trailing arms, and approached the denser core. "Denser", of course, was a purely relative word; by terrestrial standards even its most closely packed regions were still a fairly good vacuum. I had almost reached the limit of my frequency band, and could shorten the wave length no farther, when I noticed the curious, tight little echo not far from the center of the screen.

It was oval, and much more sharp-edged than the knots of gas we had watched adrift in the cloud's fiery streams. Even in that first glimpse, I knew that here was something very strange and outside all previous records of solar phenomena. I watched it for a dozen scans of the radar beam, then called my assistant away from the radiospectrograph, with which he was analyzing the velocities of the swirling gas as it spun toward us.

"Look, Don," I asked him, "have you ever seen anything like that?"

"No," he answered after a careful examination. What holds it together? It hasn't changed its shape for the last two minutes."

"That's what puzzles me. Whatever it is, it should have started to break up by now, with all that disturbance going on around it. But it seems as stable as ever."

"How big would you say it is?"

I switched on the calibration grid and took a quick reading.

"It's about five hundred miles long, and half that in width."

"Is this the largest picture you can get?"

"I'm afraid so. We'll have to wait until it's closer before we can see what makes it tick."

Don gave a nervous little laugh.

"This is crazy," he said, "but do you know something? I feel as if I'm looking at an amoeba under a microscope."

I did not answer; for, with what I can only describe as a sensation of intellectual vertigo, exactly the same thought had entered my mind.

We forgot about the rest of the cloud, but luckily the automatic cameras kept up their work and no important observations were lost. From now on we had eyes only for that sharp-edged lens of gas that was growing minute by minute as it raced toward us. When it was no farther away than is the moon from Earth, it began to show the first signs of its internal structure, revealing a curious mottled appearance that was never quite the same on two successive sweeps of the scanner.

By now, half the Observatory staff had joined us in the radar room, yet there was complete silence as the oncoming enigma grew swiftly across the screen. It was coming straight toward us; in a few minutes it would hit Mercury somewhere in the center of the daylight side, and that would be the end of it – whatever it was. From the moment we obtained our first really detailed view until the screen became blank again could not have been more than five minutes; for every one of us, that five minutes will haunt us all our lives.

We were looking at what seemed to be a translucent oval, its interior laced with a network of almost invisible lines. Where the lines crossed there appeared to be tiny, pulsing nodes of light; we could never be quite sure of their existence because the radar took almost a minute to paint the complete picture on the screen – and between each sweep the object moved several thousand miles. There was no doubt, however, that the network itself existed; the cameras settled any arguments about that.

So strong was the impression that we were looking at a solid object that I took a few moments off from the radar screen and hastily focused one of the optical telescopes on the sky. Of course, there was nothing to be seen – no sign of anything silhouetted against the sun's pock-marked disk. This was a case where vision failed completely and only the electrical senses of the radar were of any use. The thing that was coming toward us out of the sun was as transparent as air – and far more tenuous.

As those last moments ebbed away, I am quite sure that every one of us had reached the same conclusion – and was waiting for someone to say it first. What we were seeing was impossible, yet the evidence was there before our eyes. We were looking at life, where no life could exist . . .

The eruption had hurled the thing out of its normal environment, deep down in the flaming atmosphere of the sun. It was a miracle that it had survived its journey through space; already it must be dying, as the forces that controlled its huge, invisible body lost their hold over the electrified gas which was the only substance it possessed.

Today, now that I have run through those films a hundred times, the idea no longer seems so strange to me. For what is life but organized energy? Does it matter *what* form that energy takes – whether it is chemical, as we know it on Earth, or purely electrical, as it seemed to be here? Only the pattern is important; the substance itself is of no significance. But at the time I did not think of this; I was conscious only of a vast and overwhelming wonder as I watched this creature of the sun live out the final moments of its existence.

Was it intelligent? Could it understand the strange doom that had befallen it? There are a thousand such questions that may never be answered. It is hard to see how a creature born in the fires of the sun itself could know anything of the external universe, or could even sense the existence of something as unutterably cold as rigid nongaseous matter. The living island that was falling upon us from space could never have conceived, however intelligent it might be, of the world it was so swiftly approaching

Now it filled our sky – and perhaps, in those last few seconds, it knew that something strange was ahead of it. It may have sensed the far-flung magnetic field of Mercury, or felt the tug of our little world's gravitational pull. For it had begun to change; the luminous lines that must have been what passed for its nervous system were clumping together in new patterns, and I would have given much to know their meaning. It may be that I was looking into the brain of a mindless beast in its last convulsion of fear – or of a godlike being making its peace with universe.

Then the radar screen was empty, wiped clean during a single scan of the beam. The creature had fallen below our horizon and was hidden from us now by the curve of the planet. Far out in the burning dayside of Mercury, in the inferno where only a dozen men have ever ventured and fewer still come back alive, it smashed silently and invisibly against the seas of molten metal, the hills of slowly moving lava. The mere impact could have meant nothing to such an entity; what it could not endure was its first contact with the inconceivable cold of solid matter.

Yes, *cold*. It had descended upon the hottest spot in the solar system, where the temperature never falls below seven hundred degrees Fahrenheit and sometimes approaches a thousand. And that was far, far colder to it than the antarctic winter would be to a naked man.

We did not see it die, out there in the freezing fire; it was beyond the reach of our instruments now, and none of them recorded its end. Yet every one of us knew when that moment came, and that is why we are not interested when those who have seen only the films and tapes tell us that we were watching some purely natural phenomenon.

How can one explain what we felt, in that last moment when half our little world was enmeshed in the dissolving tendrils of that huge but immaterial brain? I can only say that it was a soundless cry of anguish, a death pang that seeped into our minds without passing through the gateways of the senses. Not one of us doubted then, or has ever doubted since, that he had witnessed the passing of a giant.

We may have been both the first and the last of all men to see so mighty a fall. Whatever *they* may be, in their unimaginable world within the sun, our paths and theirs may never cross again. It is hard to see how we can ever make contact with them, even if their intelligence matches ours.

And does it? It may be well for us if we never know the answer. Perhaps they have been living there inside the sun since the universe was born, and have climbed to peaks of wisdom that we shall never scale. The future may be theirs, not ours; already they may be talking across the light-years to their cousins in other stars.

One day they may discover us, by whatever strange senses they possess, as we circle around their mighty, ancient home, proud of our knowledge and thinking ourselves lords of creation. They may not like what they find, for to them we should be no more than maggots, crawling upon the skins of worlds too cold to cleanse themselves from the corruption of organic life.

And then, if they have the power, they will do what they consider necessary. The sun will put forth its strength and lick the faces of its children; and thereafter the planets will go their way once more as they were in the beginning – clean and bright . . . and sterile.

THE PEVATRON RATS

Stephen Baxter

Stephen Baxter (b. 1957) collaborated with Arthur C. Clarke on four novels, starting with The Light of Other Days *(2000). In some ways, he might be seen as the natural successor to Clarke, as both share similar visions of the potential of technology. Baxter's own work began in 1987 with "The Xeelee Flower", a story that introduced Baxter's future history series, which includes the novels* Raft *(1991),* Flux *(1993) and* Ring *(1994). He attracted a wider readership with* The Time Ships *(1995), his sequel to H. G. Wells'* The Time Machine, *and went on to establish himself as one of Britain's most innovative and entertaining science fiction writers.*

"MR HATHAWAY, it's Amanda Breslin. Ms Breslin from the high school?"

A call from Penny's teacher wasn't particularly welcome in the middle of the working day. I kicked shut the office door. "Yes, Ms Breslin. Is something wrong?"

"Not exactly . . ."

That hesitation triggered memories of meeting her at the last parent-teacher night: a slim woman, intense, shy, eyes that drew you in. Penny, twelve years old, was on a school field trip to Harwell today, the nuclear lab. I had lurid imaginings of what might have gone wrong. "Go on."

"Penny found some rats."

"What?"

"Two rats, to be precise. Babies. The problem is, the rats

shouldn't have been where they were. Couldn't have been, in fact. The lab authorities suspect this is some kind of hoax played by the kids. And since it was Penny who found them – "

Ever since the cancer that had taken her mother three years before, I had fretted continually about Penny's welfare. Now Ms Breslin's prevaricating about what seemed a trivial matter irritated me. "What's this all about? Where exactly did she find these damn rats?"

I heard Ms Breslin take a breath. "In a particle accelerator."

"I'll be there." And I hung up, rudely. I made some excuses to old Harrison, the senior partner, and went to get my car.

That was the start of it for me. Soon, of course, the whole county was going to be getting calls and emails about rats turning up where they shouldn't be. I suppose it's my peculiar distinction to have been the very first.

Harwell is only a couple of miles west of Didcot, where we lived. It didn't take me long to drive out.

Penny was doing fine at school, as far as I could tell. That was the trouble – I was increasingly unsure that I *could* tell. The school itself was very alien to a 1990s relic like me, with more laptops than teachers, who all had job titles like "motivational counsellor". Penny and I had muddled through the first couple of years after we lost her mother, when she was still essentially a child. Now, at twelve, I knew she was moving into a more complex phase of her life – still fascinated by horses, but increasingly distracted by bad-boy soccer players with dirty hair.

I was an office manager for a firm of solicitors. I can handle people reasonably well, I think – crusty old lawyers and their clients anyhow. How well I could handle the moods and dilemmas of a teenage daughter I was much less sure. Maybe today was going to be a test.

The facility that everybody calls Harwell Laboratory, in Oxfordshire, was founded after World War II as a nuclear fission laboratory, on an old RAF airfield close to Oxford University. Some good work was done there, in fission reactor designs and fusion experiments. But as the decades wore away the slowdown of government science and the reduced threat of nuclear war saw the place go through complicated sell-offs. RAL, the Rutherford

Appleton Laboratory, still operates within what is now known as the Harwell Science and Innovation Campus. This year, 2018, RAL had briefly made the headlines when the public were first allowed to see the revolutionary new Pevatron, a new breed of particle accelerator, which was due to come online in a couple more years. And that was why Penny's school party had gone there that day.

As I approached the gate I had to drive through a sullen picket line of protestors. They were calm and sane-looking, and their placards, leaning against the outer fence, were wordy warnings about the dangers of doing high-energy physics in the middle of the English countryside: black holes might be created, or wormholes, or "vacuum collapses" might be triggered, none of which meant very much to me.

Ms Breslin met me at the security gate, as I signed bits of paper and submitted to retinal and DNA scans. I even had to pass through a Geiger counter trap, as if I might try to smuggle radio-active materials *into* a nuclear laboratory. Then we walked across the laboratory campus, side by side, her pace rapid, edgy. "Harwell's a major local employer, of course," she said, talking too fast, "and for the kids to be able to see a world-class science facility in development right on their doorstep is a great oppor-tunity – it helps that I know a couple of the scientists on staff here personally . . ."

It was a bright spring day, late April, with a bit of wind that blew Ms Breslin's hair around her face. She was a slim woman, tall, in her late thirties a bit younger than me, with hints of grey in her tied-back brown hair. She struck me as wistful, a woman at the end of her youth – and, I guessed, alone; she wore no rings.

The lab buildings were blocky and old-fashioned, laid out in a rough grid pattern, like a military base. But every so often I glimpsed a fission-reactor dome, silent and sinister, rising beyond the tiled rooftops, or the glistening hulk of a cooling plant or oxygen store, and much of the site was sealed off by fences plastered with warning signs and radiation symbols. The facility we were approaching was a kilometre across, but unprepossessing, like a ring of garden sheds set out across the scarred runway of the old airfield.

"The Pevatron," I prompted her.

"It is a fantastic development," she said. "Called the Pevatron because it can reach energies of peta-electron volts – that's ten to power fifteen, a million billion. Orders of magnitude more even than the big new International Linear Collider in Japan, and at a fraction of the cost and scale thanks to the new methods they've developed here. It's all to do with room-temperature superconductors controlled at the femtosecond scale by a new quantum computer – I have a physics PhD myself and I barely understand it . . ." I wondered how she had ended up teaching high school kids.

"And it's infested by rats," I said.

"Apparently." Ms Breslin's nervousness was overwhelming her now. "I'm sorry to have caused you so much trouble."

I smiled at her. "Don't be. Stuff happens. You should try running elderly solicitors. And thanks for bringing me out so quickly."

She seemed surprised to be thanked. Her eyes widened, those eyes I remembered, seawater green.

Schoolkids, teachers, white-coated lab workers and a couple of management suits gathered by an entrance. I recognized Penny, slim and small in her school uniform. Penny was actually cradling the two baby rats that were the cause of all the trouble, pink slivers of flesh. She smiled at me in the wry, almost adult way she had. "Hello, Dad. Look what I found."

It was where she had found the animals that was the problem. An apologetic site manager showed me a ball of glass and steel a couple of metres across, sealed save for vents to either side. "When the Pevatron is operational the particle beams will run through this sphere." The manager was about fifty, greying, a scientist turned administrator. He used his fists to mime particles colliding. "Electrons and positrons will slam into each other at a whisker below the speed of light. Because they're elementary particles, you see, unlike the protons they use in the LHC in Switzerland, we can control the energies of collision very precisely . . . Well. The point is this chamber will be evacuated when the facility is in use."

"A vacuum."

"And so it's entirely sealed off, save for the valves to either side."

"There must be air in it today, or these baby rats wouldn't have survived."

"There's nothing wrong with the rats, Dad," Penny said

brightly. "In fact they were nice and warm when I picked them up, warm little bellies."

"But," said the manager, "there's no way the rats could have got in there in the first place . . ."

I inspected the cage for myself. A hermetically sealed sphere, two baby rats, no sign of a mother or nest. It was a locked-room mystery, with rats. When Penny found the rats the junior technician who had been hosting the school party immediately got suspicious.

"Which is why we called you," said the site manager apologetically. "Ben's guess that Penny had planted the rats did make sense. Occam's razor, you know. The simplest hypothesis is likely to be correct. We have to take such allegations seriously – terrorism and all that. But in this case Occam let us down. We looked over the sphere; there's simply no way the brightest child, and I'm sure Penny is bright as a button, could have set this up. Well, we got into the sphere and saved the baby rats. Didn't want a gaggle of traumatized school-children on our hands." He sighed. "Of all the issues I've had to wrestle with over this project – academic rivalries, funding cuts, anti-science protestors – I never expected to have to deal with vermin! Well. I do apologise for your trouble. Of course we'll take care of those two beasts for you." He reached out for the baby rats.

Penny clutched them to her chest. "What will you do, destroy them?"

"Well – "

"Oh, Dad, can't we keep them? They've already been locked up in a particle accelerator. And they're only babies."

"Penny, be serious."

"Lots of people have rats for pets," Penny said, more in hope than belief.

Ms Breslin said, "Actually that's true. We keep a few at the school. I could help you get set up if you like. They're so young they might need mother's milk for a while . . . Oh." She glanced at me. "I'm not helping, am I?"

What she had said had made no difference; I had already seen there was only one positive outcome from what might have been a very difficult day. I said to Penny, "OK, you can keep them. But you're responsible for cleaning them out. Clear?"

Ms Breslin asked, "What will you call them?"

Penny, beaming, held up the rats. "Rutherford and Appleton – ow! Rutherford just *bit* me."

"Let me hold them for you – I've gloves."

So Ms Breslin held them carefully in her gloved hands as the party walked out of RAL, all the way back to the gate. And as we passed back out through security, that Geiger gate bleeped. Ms Breslin held up the little animals and inspected them curiously.

We saw a lot of Ms Breslin in the weeks after that – although we became "Amanda" and "Joe" when she started to visit us at home. The house I had bought with Mary, Penny's mother, was too big for the two of us, but neither of us had wanted to move away from the memories. I could see Amanda working some of this out as she glanced around the place.

She found a big old parrot's cage for our rats, and she and Penny worked on making runs and providing toys and litter. Amanda helped us "rat-proof" our home, as she put it. I had to lift my piles of books off the floor and up onto shelves, and we put covers over the soft furnishings as a guard against territory-marking urine spurts, and I slit lengths of old hosepipe to cover electric flex. We kept the rats in a corner of our dining room, close by a window. I didn't mind the little beasts save for a lingering stink of urine. And I enjoyed Amanda's visits.

After a few weeks the rats were very active, with jet black hair and bright, glittering little eyes. Amanda said they were growing unusually fast. She was also curious about the way they'd triggered the RAL Geigers. She asked if she could bring some instruments home from the school's physics lab to test them.

She showed up on a rainy May day, about four weeks after we had acquired the rats, with instruments that turned out to be advanced forms of radiation detectors. My own physics GCSE was in the dim past. "In my day we didn't have this kind of stuff – just crackling Geiger counters."

"Fantastic, isn't it? Instrumentation has gotten so cheap. Now schoolkids can detect cosmic rays . . ." Penny and Amanda manipulated the rats, holding them up before the detectors, while Amanda inspected them. "They *are* growing fast," she said. "I mean, they can't have been more than a few days old when Penny found them, but their eyes were already open." And though they should have been dependent on their mother's milk until they were four weeks old, from the beginning they'd been able to take solid food – high-protein puppy food, recommended by Amanda.

Appleton, it turned out, was a female – a doe, as Amanda put it. "And she's pregnant," Amanda said now, feeling the rat's tiny belly.

Penny stared. "By her brother? *Eughh*."

"She's young to be fertile but it's not impossible . . . You generally try to separate siblings, always assuming Rutherford *is* her sibling." One of her sensor boxes bleeped.

I asked, "And she's giving off cosmic rays?"

"Dad," Penny said, "cosmic rays come from supernovas and stuff. Rats do *not* give off cosmic rays."

"OK, so why is Amanda's box bleeping?"

Amanda was downloading a record onto a laptop. "There is some kind of high-energy radiation. Just a trace." She passed a plastic wand over Appleton's stomach. "A source, around here."

"Inside her?" Penny asked.

"Is it dangerous?" I asked immediately. "For us, I mean."

"Oh, no, it's the merest trace – you have more energetic particles lacing through your body all the time, from all sorts of natural sources. This would make no difference. Odd, though."

Penny said, "Maybe the rats ate some plutonium in that atomic lab. They were just babies. They must have been hungry. They'd have eaten anything."

But there is no plutonium in a particle accelerator. "Another mystery," I said.

"Ow!" Penny pulled her hands back and dropped Rutherford, who scampered off behind a radiator. "That little bugger nipped me again!"

"Language," I said. This time the rat had made her hand bleed. "That one's getting vicious."

"Some do," Amanda said. "He's probably just being macho. Like a teenage boy." She put Appleton back in her cage. "Joe, I'll fetch some TCP if you round up Rutherford."

"OK. You sit still, Penny, and try not to bleed on anything."

I picked up a hearth brush and fish net and went after Rutherford. After a month we were working out a routine. I was confident the beast couldn't get out of the room; the trick was to shepherd him with the brush, and then swipe him gently with the net. I soon backed him into a corner of the room. He stood on his haunches looking back at me, and I thought I saw traces of Penny's blood around his mouth. I dropped the brush to block his exit to my left, and when he made a run for it I dropped the net in his path to my right.

And missed him. He ended up running between my legs as if I was a nutmegged goalkeeper, following a course a good thirty degrees away from the one I'd thought he'd chosen. I couldn't believe I'd managed to miss him so badly.

I tried again. I chased him down to a corner of the room's blocked-off fireplace, and tried the same routine: brush in one hand, net in the other. But again he ran off on a course very different from the one I *saw* him choose.

"Curiouser and curiouser," Amanda said. She'd returned and was dabbing at Penny's bitten hand. "Joe – do you mind if I webcam you?"

"What for? To give your buddies in the staff room a laugh?"

"I wouldn't do that." She swivelled her laptop so it faced me. "There's something funny going on, I think. Try catching him again."

It took me three more goes to trap him. Each time he fooled me, as if sending me chasing a ghost. I got him in the end by using a rucked-up bit of carpet to create a channel he couldn't escape from.

With both rats safely back in the cage Amanda ran over her webcam footage. "Well, that's very odd. Look. Your second attempt is the clearest . . ."

Rutherford looked as if he had been heading towards my right. That was the way I dropped the net, and as Penny's shoulder happened to be in the frame, I could see from her reaction she thought he was heading that way too. But he headed left, and darted off the screen.

"I'm sure I reacted *after* he made his move."

"You did, every time I watched you." Amanda said carefully, "Each time it's as if he got another chance. As if, knowing what you would do, he went back and made a second choice."

"'Went back'? What's that supposed to mean?"

Amanda might have been careful in her choice of words, but

Penny wasn't. "We did fish them out of an atomic lab, Dad. What did you expect? Time-travelling mutant radioactive rats! Brilliant," she said gleefully.

We continued to see a good deal of Ms Amanda Breslin as the rats grew into two big, heavy, hungry, snappy animals. Amanda devised tests to try to establish the truth of the mysterious "time-hopping". She and Penny built elaborate mazes of cardboard and plastic, baited with cheese and timed locks, but their results were inconclusive. Penny, designing experiments and keeping notes, loved all this. Amanda must be a hell of a teacher, I thought.

And every so often I was reminded of that doctorate in physics.

"I mean, think what an evolutionary advantage it would be," she said. "When you're chasing your lunch, or trying to keep from being somebody else's lunch – if you make a mistake you can *go back*, even just a few seconds, and choose the option that keeps you safe, or fed. Once such a facility rose in a population you'd expect it to propagate fast."

"If they're changing the past," Penny said, "why would we remember? Our memories should be changed too."

"Good question," Amanda said respectfully. "Maybe any changes to the time stream are localized – the effects travelling no wider than the rats need them to be. After all time travel must be energy-consuming. In general it ought to be a last resort. Maybe the time-travel reflex cuts in only as an emergency option when the rat is cornered. We might be able to use that to test them . . ."

But Penny absolutely vetoed doing any kind of experiment that would put her rats under stress.

I couldn't really have cared less about rats, even time-travelling rats. But it was a pleasure to come home after another dull day with dusty solicitors, to help Penny with the rats' feed or with cleaning them out, and to talk over their latest exploits. "Who would have thought," as Penny said, "that a pair of glow-in-the-dark rodents would bring us together?"

And then there was Amanda. At first it was odd to have a woman of my age around the house again. Even after weeks she was awkward, oddly shy, but with that sharp brain and a healthy dose of empathy she was always good company.

I did try to find out more about her. "You said you did a PhD.

Wouldn't you rather be working in a place like RAL, than with rats and schoolkids?"

"Not me." She pushed back her hair. "Academia is a pretty brutal world, you know. Petty bullying when you're junior, and lifelong rivalries when you're older."

"Like a rat pack," Penny said.

"Oh, academics make rats look civilized."

"All that conflict wasn't for you," I suggested. "And I'm guessing you don't enjoy stress."

"Well, that's true. We evolved as hunter-gatherers, which is generally a low-stress lifestyle. Children and animals around all the time too. Maybe I'm a throwback." She smiled.

She seemed to enjoy our company, as long as we had the rats as neutral ground between us. She evidently had nobody at home, no partner or kids. Penny clearly hoped that some kind of relationship was going to bloom between us, that her mother would be replaced in her life's hierarchy of security by a favourite teacher. It wasn't impossible. I was drawn into those seawater eyes. But I could see nothing but complications, and held back, taking it slowly.

Too slowly, in the event. In the brief time we had left, I learned little more about Amanda's past and her private life, and nothing about her few sad, failed love affairs. For in the end, of course, the rats got in the way.

On the day Appleton gave birth Amanda stayed with us late into the evening, as the rat suckled her babies, a dozen of them. Then it was about seven weeks since we'd brought the rats home from RAL. It was early June now, and the evening was long, the air through the open window fresh and full of the scent of cut grass. Didcot's not an exciting place, but on a warm summer evening, with the birds singing and the lawns green, middle England is as pretty a place as you'll find anywhere. The baby rats had made Penny happy. It was a good day, and by about eleven p.m., hours after the rat had given birth, I felt pretty mellow, and was vaguely wondering how I could arrange for some time alone with Amanda.

Then Penny broke the mood with a sudden scream. Amanda and I rushed to see what was wrong. Of the dozen babies, only two remained in the cage with Appleton, who seemed to be sleeping soundly.

Penny was distressed. She thought the babies must have been eaten by their mother, a gruesome thought, and I hugged her.

But Amanda calmly pointed out there was no evidence of such cannibalism. "If Appleton had eaten all those babies," she said reasonably, "we'd have heard, and we'd see the by-products. The mess."

"Then where are the little beggars?" I snapped. "We've been sitting by this damn cage all day. Baby rats don't just disappear – "

"Baby rats just *appeared*," Penny pointed out. "Inside the accelerator, remember? Maybe they time-travelled out."

Now, given what had gone before, that was a reasonable suggestion. But with my mood shattered I'd had enough of mutant rats. I snorted, and as Amanda and Penny exchanged glances, I turned up the lights and started a more conventional search around the room. I soon found a hole, gnawed through the skirting board. When I dug into the hole with a probing finger, I found bits of paper, stinking of urine. A rat nest.

I sat back on my heels, looking at the hole, and Penny and Amanda joined me.

"Baby rats can't gnaw holes that size," Penny said.

"Adults can," said Amanda. She ran a finger around the rim of the hole. "The nest looks weeks old to me. Three or four?"

"The thing is," I said reluctantly, "I checked this board this morning. I checked the whole room. I usually do. There was no hole here. I'm sure of it. And certainly not a three-week-old nest."

Penny grasped the situation immediately. "The babies travelled back in time, three or four weeks. They went back in time, and built a nest here and grew up."

Amanda nodded. "They changed the past. So a nest exists here now where it didn't before."

"Oh, come on," I said. "How about Occam's razor? Isn't it simpler to suppose that we've just got another bunch of rats, that just happened to show up now – or were drawn by the scent of Rutherford and Appleton?"

Penny shook her head. "Won't wash, Dad. That doesn't explain the way the hole just magically appeared."

Amanda, kneeling down, was still inspecting the hole. "I wish I had a torch . . . I can't see evidence of more than a couple of animals here. Three at the most? But we lost maybe ten of our dozen babies. So where are the rest?"

Penny ran to her laptop and immediately began scanning news sites, blogs, police and health resources, for unusual sightings of rats. That night there were four sightings in the Didcot area – four encounters with rats where no rats had been seen before, big, aggressive animals that were hard to catch. One report claimed a rat had attacked an infant in her cot. Penny looked at us, her eyes shining in the screen's silver light. "Oops," she said.

Amanda stood up. "I think it's time we took this a bit more seriously. Penny, do you mind if I take one of these babies into RAL for some tests? I have contacts there . . ."

That was week seven, as we started to count it later: the seventh week since Penny first spotted those baby rats in their sealed-up sphere at RAL.

The sightings of the rats continued through spring and summer, spreading out through Oxfordshire and Berkshire, the range increasing by roughly a couple of kilometres every three weeks. Penny and I set up an Ordnance Survey map on the wall of the dining room, and tracked the sightings with sticky coloured dots. By the beginning of September – week twenty – our dots had got as far as Abingdon, about eight kilometres away. The attacks on food stores, pets, livestock and, unfortunately, people, were getting more serious, and there were reports of the creatures causing other problems by gnawing through power lines, telephone optic-fibre cables and plastic water pipes. The rats were ferociously difficult to kill or contain, baffling the vermin controllers. The health authorities and the police were considering quarantining off an infected zone to try to stop the spread of the tabloids' "super-rats".

Amanda came to visit us on the first Saturday in September, the last weekend before school started again – although it wasn't yet clear if the schools would open, because of the continuing rat problem – and brought back the baby she had borrowed for testing in a cat box; it was now fully grown. Rutherford, Appleton and their unnamed babies, now separated by sex, watched impassively.

Amanda professed admiration for our map.

"Look," Penny said. "We used a different colour code for each week since I found the first two at RAL. See how it spreads out?

And there's more of them all the time. I counted it up with Dad. There were four nests sighted that first night when the babies were born. Three weeks later there were twenty-six. Three weeks after that 128 . . ."

"Show her your graph," I told her.

Penny brought up a graph of the number of reports of independent nests versus time, plotted on logarithmic scales. There was a scatter of points around a neat straight-line trend. "Dad showed me how to do this. See that? It's a power-law line. That's what Dad says. Every three weeks the nests seem to multiply by about five. That kind of multiplication grows quickly. This is week twenty and we're up to over 1,300, spread across a circle with a diameter about sixteen kilometres."

Amanda nodded. "You should show this to Mr Beauregard. He keeps saying you're underachieving at maths."

She pulled a face. "This isn't maths. This is *real*."

Amanda raised her eyebrows at me. "Which tells you all you need to know about Bob Beauregard's teaching methods. That fivefold increase maybe makes sense. You get typically ten or a dozen babies per litter. Maybe five breeding pairs each generation? But the generations are coming too close together, though, even for these rats . . . I'll have to think about that. Do some mathematical modelling."

I went to put the kettle on. "So how's the youngster? Survived its tests at RAL?"

"Oh, yes." She leaned down to look at the rat in its cat box. "Although my friends in there couldn't agree on an interpretation of their scan results."

Penny said, "Tell us what you think."

Amanda said slowly, "Well – I think this rat has got a wormhole in its stomach. A flaw in spacetime. And I think it was born that way, born with the wormhole." She smiled at us. "Isn't that a wonderful idea?"

Penny clapped her hands.

I poured out mugs of tea for me and Amanda, handed Penny a soda, and we sat at the table. "'A flaw in spacetime.' I'm not sure what that means."

"The classical description of a wormhole is the Einstein-Rosen bridge, which – "

"Einstein didn't keep rats, as far as I know. This, this *flaw* in its stomach, is how the rat can travel back in time. Is that what you mean?"

She nodded. "But not voluntarily, I don't think. It must be connected to the rat's nervous system somehow – like a muscular reflex. When it's cornered, it flexes this spacetime spring, and flips back."

"Just a few seconds," Penny said.

"Yes. That would be enough to escape most entrapment situations. But I'm speculating that a deeper reflex can work when the rats are very young. What if some babies in a litter can hop back *weeks*? It would be a random jump into the unknown, but they would be safe from any predators who might be attracted to the nest."

"Or the vermin controllers."

"Well, yes. And we know this strain of rat is able to survive precociously young – especially if it finds some kind human like Penny to look after it."

Penny frowned. "They'd be separated from their mother. For *ever*."

"But rats don't have the same kind of parental bond as we do, Penny. We, with our ape lineage, only have a few children whom we cherish. The rats have lots of babies, expecting to lose most of them to predators. Being able to throw at least some of your babies back to the safety of the past is a valid survival option."

I said, "And this is what the RAL people wouldn't believe."

"Well, would you? Although you'd think by now others would have noticed something odd. The police and the rest keep saying they're just an extreme strain of ordinary rat."

"So how did spacetime wormholes get into the bellies of rats?"

"It started – or will start – in the place we found the first pair."

"The Pevatron?"

"You'll recall those anti-science protesters outside the facility. They may have a point. The Pevatron will work at unprecedented high energies, and even some of the RAL people are expecting it to create extremely exotic objects . . ."

Objects such as wormholes and black holes. The energies released by the Pevatron's colliding electrons and positrons could be enough to rip the fabric of spacetime and leave it stitched back together again *wrong*, with points that should be separated in space or in time unnaturally connected together.

"Miniature time machines," Penny said.

"Yes. The RAL people are actually figuring out ways to detect such things. If a particle got trapped in such a wormhole it might bounce back and forth so you'd see multiple copies of it. Or, you might see a flash as all the light that fell in the wormhole in the future, as long as it existed, was sent back to the instant of its creation and emerged all at once."

I nodded, half-understanding, not quite believing. "And if such a wormhole did form, at high energy –"

Amanda spread her hands on the table. "I'm speculating. You'd get not one but a whole population of the things. The wormholes would interact and self-select – I think we might see a kind of evolution, a physical evolution, as the wormholes spiralled into stable, low-energy modes that could persist even outside the Pevatron, in our low-energy environment."

"Until one got swallowed by a rat," I said sceptically.

"Well, something like that. After that we're talking about biological evolution. It's obvious what a competitive advantage an ability to time-travel would confer. And, remember, if these creatures are somehow looping back in time, a lot of generations could be compressed into a short interval. Evolution could work very quickly, the time-travel gene spreading fast."

"OK. But even if I buy all that, the Pevatron doesn't work yet. It isn't due to come online for two whole years! So how did those first time-travelling rats end up back in April?"

"That's obvious, Dad," Penny said, admonishing. "They just got thrown further back in time than usual. Their origin is in the future. They are infesting the past." She smiled at the idea. "Cool."

Amanda and I shared a glance.

That didn't seem so cool to me. Mankind has waged war against rats since we became farmers. Even before the Pevatron rats came along, there were thought to be more rats than all the other mammals put together; and rats and the diseases they brought were thought to have killed more humans in the second millennium than all our wars. If this new strain really did have the ability to time-travel – even to plant their young in the deep past – how could humanity stop them?

We weren't about to alarm Penny, who clearly hadn't thought it through that far. I raised the pot. "More tea?"

A population increasing fivefold expands fast. By the end of September there were over six thousand nests, being spied as far out as Wantage. That was when we were evacuated out of the expanding infestation zone. It broke Penny's heart when Rutherford and Appleton were taken away.

Amanda sent us a video clip. It had been caught by chance, by a webcam in a bird's nesting box: it was the arrival of a baby rat, apparently sent from the future into its past, our present. At first you saw a sort of outline, flattened like roadkill, that gradually filled up to a living, breathing, three-dimensional rat. Amanda said it was as if the rats were using their wormhole muscles to *fold* up into a higher spacetime dimension, and then back down into ours. She had hacked this footage out of data being gathered by government science units at the heart of the infected zone. The scientists didn't know what to make of it – or if they did, they weren't admitting it.

By week twenty-nine, mid-November, the rats were being seen in Wallingford, around thirteen kilometres from Harwell. In our government-issue caravan we kept up our map, and the centre of it was covered with dots; the rats weren't just spreading outward but were filling in the spaces they had already colonized. The authorities estimated there were over 150,000 nests in the area. Penny extrapolated her graph and made lurid predictions of how quickly the rats would reach Birmingham, London, the Channel Tunnel. "It's the end of the world, Dad, for humans anyhow," she said, thrilling herself by half-believing it.

By the end of November, the authorities were making provisional plans to evacuate Oxford. That was when Amanda called me and asked me for help. "We need to sort this out before it's too late."

I met her at the edge of the control zone, near Wallingford. She had requisitioned an NHS ambulance, rat-hardened with cages over its tyres and netting over its doors. She was already wearing her spacesuit, as she called it, a coverall of tough Kevlar fabric with thick gloves and a hood like a nuclear engineer's. She had one for me; I had to put it on as she drove us briskly into the zone. I was impressed by the resources she'd assembled, leaning on her contacts within Harwell itself. She was always far smarter, more resourceful than she appeared, and was rising to this challenge. She was having a good war. That's one reason why I'll miss her.

Inside the infected zone the towns and villages were deserted of people. The rats were everywhere, swarming out of doorways and windows and over the streets in a black tide. Even out in the country I could hear their heavy bodies thumping against the body of the ambulance as we drove.

"They've eaten everything there is to eat," Amanda said. "The supermarkets, larders, granaries, fields, all stripped. The population must be near its peak. Soon they'll turn on each other, if they haven't already . . ."

As we neared Harwell we passed the hub of the emergency control, a heavily fenced-off group of trailers, vehicles and comms masts – Gold Command, as it was called, under the control of the local chief constable, and patrolled by squaddies armed with rifles and flame-throwers. Rats scurried across the ground even inside the soldiers' perimeter. That was the nature of them.

At Harwell itself we left the ambulance at RAL's security gate, were passed through the unmanned security barriers by Amanda's retinal scans, and walked across a campus deserted save for the shadowy black forms of rats. Amanda wore a canvas pack on her back that looked suspicious even to me, but none of the campus's security measures impeded us.

We passed through the rough ring of the Pevatron accelerator, and came to a group of more finished buildings at its centre. The area was heavily fenced off and the ground dosed with poison; this billion-pound facility had not yet been abandoned to the rats.

"In fact," Amanda said, "you could say the Pevatron's development is continuing, even now, as *that* works its way through its own, slow, superhuman calculations."

That was the quantum computer. Contained within one of the largest of the central buildings and held behind a glass wall, it was a translucent ball maybe three metres across that hovered in the air, suspended by magnetic fields and contained in a perfect vacuum. Walking back and forth in its hall I thought I saw hints of deeper structure, glimmering. Even aside from its engineering quality, that computer was one of the most beautiful pieces of sculpture I have ever seen.

"Nobody knows how it works," Amanda said. "Not in detail anyhow. It bootstrapped itself. It finished its own physical design, and now is working out its own programming for the task of running the Pevatron."

"That is one smart machine."

"But vulnerable." And she took off her pack, and pulled out pretty much what I expected: a lump of pale plastic, an explosive. I didn't ask her where she had got this from. She slapped the plastic against the glass window, where it stuck easily, and attached a detonator charge. This would be controlled by a radio switch. She showed me what to do, just in case: it was a gadget like a TV remote, with a big red button to push. "We need some distance," she said, and led me out of the building to the open air.

"The quantum computer is the heart of the Pevatron – and where most of the money has been spent. If we destroy it there's a good chance the project will be derailed enough to be cancelled altogether, especially given it's in the middle of a disaster zone. Of course others might build equivalent facilities somewhere else, but at least we'd buy time to prove the reality of the time loops, and to protect against the danger."

We stood near the edge of the ring, looking back at the unprepossessing control buildings. "Do we really have to do this? To smash such a beautiful machine – "

"I know," she said, smiling at me. "I feel it too. But, yes, we have to do this. Look . . ." She pulled a handheld out of her pack, and showed me how she had modelled the spread of the supervermin. "These rats are fertile at four weeks old, and have a gestation time of about three weeks. When a litter is born, a percentage of it is thrown back in time *four* weeks. So they are mature just at the point they were born – if you see what I mean. That's why we see this jump in the spread with each three-week generation.

"But I'm speculating that under conditions of extreme stress – such as the overcrowding we're already seeing here – some individuals, or their offspring, can be thrown back further still. Just as Penny suggested."

"To escape the population crash."

"That's it. Because if you dive deep enough into the past, you always find virgin territory: you are the first of your kind, and your offspring can fill their boots. Think about it. The first boom will start when the Pevatron comes on line. Forty weeks later, crash . . ." The authorities were predicting a crash for us around week forty, when the rats would have overrun Oxford, and there would be tens of millions of nests – hundreds of millions of rats, swarming over an area thirty or forty kilometres across. Amanda went on, "A few extreme individuals escape back, say, a hundred weeks into the past, into the virgin time *before* the Pevatron was even turned on. Forty weeks later, their ancestors are still ahead of the first origin. But there's another crash –"

"And another leap into the past, even deeper."

"Yes. And back they go, crash and leap, crash and leap, working their way ever deeper into history. Every time it will start as it did for us, with just a handful of cute-looking babies in a virgin world. Every time it will end with a crash. You know, maybe this is the only way a species as smart as us could be eradicated. We fought back against predators and plagues; we'd probably survive everything short of the planet being destroyed altogether. But not this." Those seawater eyes were grave behind her scuffed faceplate. "There's *nothing* ahead of us, Joe. Nothing but rats swarming and fighting and dying; whatever human future existed has been *eaten*." She waved a hand. "And soon none of this will exist either. We won't just be dead; we will never even have existed. Our history, our very existence, consumed by the rats."

I touched the hand that held the bomb control. "And you think this will put it right."

"This must be where it started. I can't think of anything else to do." I would never have believed that the timid teacher I had got to know only months before would ever have been capable of setting up an operation like this, which shows how much I know about people. But she was trembling inside her suit. "I'm scared, Joe."

I squeezed her gloved hand. "Don't be. To have figured this out, to have got this far – I could kiss you."

She looked away, shy even in that extreme moment. There were rats running around our feet. "We shouldn't risk it."

"I guess not," I said. I will regret that choice forever.

She held up her control, the button under her gloved thumb. "I hope this works. Three, two, one – "

A flash of light.

It took me a long time to recover from the injuries I suffered in the next few seconds, and even longer to figure it all out.

Amanda and I had talked about what the rise of the rats would mean for humanity – that is, our extinction. What we didn't talk about was what it would mean for the rats themselves.

Rats breed fast, and compete hard. In a world empty of mankind there would be a quick radiation of forms; I imagined slavering wolf-like rats preying on big grazing antelope-like beasts. And I imagined intelligence advancing. Why not? Rats are already smart and highly social, and the stuff we left behind would give a start to any tool-users. Whatever society they built would surely be quite unlike ours, however. Rats, with their different breeding strategy, show little loyalty to their many offspring; there will be no rodent Genghis Khan. And natural time travellers would wage wars of a qualitatively different kind from ours. All this in a rat future.

But that future was always contingent. Suppose Amanda was right – suppose her one action in aborting the Pevatron was enough to stop the rise of the rats. Maybe a smart enough super-rat of the future would know that. And maybe he or she would come back in time to avert the extinction of its kind before it existed – or to confirm the defeat of mankind. But for the rat, it was a leap across time too far.

This is all speculation. But it would explain what I saw.

"Three, two, one – "

I saw Amanda's thumb press down on that red button.

And in the same instant I saw a vertical line appear in space before us, and fold out, like a cardboard cut-out rotating.

I've tried to describe it, even to draw it, for the doctors and policemen who have questioned me since. It was a rat, but a *big* rat, maybe a metre tall, upright, with some kind of metal mesh vest over its upper body, and holding a silvery tube, unmistakeably a weapon, that it pointed at Amanda. Even as it appeared it opened its mouth wide – I saw typical rat incisors, just like Rutherford's – and it screamed.

And it started to glow.

Amanda had told me how the scientists had hoped to detect the Pevatron's miniature time machines by flashes of light: all the radiation that would ever fall on those wormholes, as long as they lasted, all pouring out at the moment of their formation. And right at the beginning of the affair Penny said the babies she found in the vacuum sphere were warm too, warm in their little bellies where the wormholes lay like tumours. Maybe there's a limit to how much of that gathered radiation an organic time machine can stand – a limit to how far a much-evolved rat thing can throw itself back in time.

I think the post-rat that tried to attack Amanda knew this. It was sacrificing itself in a hopeless attempt to save its timeline. If so, it was a hero of its kind.

I saw it die. Light shone out of its mouth, its boiling, popping eyes, and then out through its flesh and singed fur, as if it exploded from within. I closed my eyes, thus probably saving my sight. When its body detonated I was knocked to the ground, burned. Amanda, closer, did not survive.

But she had pressed that damn button, and I felt a second concussion as her plastic explosive went up, and the quantum computer died.

When the Harwell security officers found us, shouting, cocking pistols, there was not a trace of that damn rat to be seen – and none of its swarming ancestors who had been under my feet moments before – nothing but the body of Amanda, and me with a head full of memories of the Pevatron rats that nobody else shares, not even Penny.

THE EDGE OF THE MAP

Ian Creasey

---

*I'm a sucker for stories of lost worlds and lost races.
There are still a few remote places on Earth that are
unexplored, but the great stories of explorers encounter-
ing lost races in the Amazon jungle or in the centre of
Australia or on a remote island are pretty much a thing
of the past – though the TV series* Lost *is doing its bit in
keeping the spirit alive. With a dearth of such stories you
can imagine my delight when I first read this one. It's not
really a lost world story, not in the traditional sense. But
that's what's so wonderful about it.*

*Yorkshire born-and-bred, Ian Creasey (b. 1969) has
been selling stories to magazines and anthologies since
2002 but has yet to have a book of his own published –
though surely that is only a matter of time. He is one of
the most original and exciting talents to emerge in science
fiction in recent years. This story was inspired by
Creasey's interest in Fortean phenomena and what might
still survive in the wilds of the world.*

SUSANNA LISTENED resentfully to the helicopters spraying nanocams over the foothills. She kept her gaze locked on the plantation, rubbing her tense neck as she waited to get the shot. It was a
long time since she'd filmed her own footage. She fiddled with the
controls on her ancient glasses, practising framing the scene,
zooming in, panning back for a wide angle.

"How long will this take?" asked Ivo. "This isn't what I'm here
for. We need to head off soon." In her peripheral vision, she saw

him twitch restlessly as he kept glancing in all directions, like a nervous bird in a garden full of cats.

"I want to film a few things before I'm finally obsolete," Susanna said. "It shouldn't be long now." She saw no sign of movement downhill. The cannabis plants, which had grown four metres tall in the African sun, might still harbour a few defiant hippies. Should she move along the ridge for a better angle?

A bar of green light split the sky in two. The *crack* of ionized air rolled across the mountain like a manmade thunderbolt. Susanna adjusted her glasses, zooming in to focus on the flames. The smell of burning cannabis rose up the hillside.

She gave the glasses to Ivo, then walked a few steps down the hill. "Keep looking at me, but film as much fire behind me as you can."

Ivo donned the glasses with little enthusiasm. He brushed aside the fringe of his ash-blond hair, then gave her a perfunctory thumbs-up sign.

Susanna stood up straight, took two deep breaths, and raised her voice over the crackle of flames. "As the Blind Spot shrinks, more secrets are revealed." Another zap echoed around the hills. "When the nanocams found a drugs plantation, American satellites fried it."

A gust of wind fanned aromatic smoke toward her, and Susanna suppressed a tickle in her throat. She wiped her brow with a sponsored sweatband. "I can smell the burning from here. With the sun and the fire and the lasers from the sky, I'm roasting like an ant under a magnifying glass." She included these sensory details to emphasize that she reported from the spot, unlike all the bloggers who'd comment on the nanocam footage from the comfort of their own homes.

"In the last few days, soldiers have arrested dozens of terrorists as soon as the cams spotted them. But who else – and what else – is still out there?" She left a dramatic pause before signing off. "This is Susanna Munro reporting from Zaire."

Now she let herself cough volcanically. Her eyes watering, she stumbled up the bare slope, following Ivo to his battered Land Rover.

The vehicle, parked in the shade of a huge rock, was a blessed harbour from the heat and smoke. Ivo started the engine and turned up the air-conditioning, then returned her glasses with a grimace of distaste.

"Thanks," said Susanna, smiling. "They won't bite you."

"It's not me I'm worried about," Ivo said, and she felt that he only barely refrained from adding "old chap". Despite the heat, he wore a formal shirt and waistcoat as if he were starring in a twentieth-century movie about a nineteenth-century explorer.

Susanna played the recording. The obsolete glasses pixellated the image on zoom shots, and Ivo had jiggled his head while filming her. But the segment was usable. Watching her spiel, she winced at the sight of her grey hair. The last time she had used these glasses – or their backup system – her hair had been Pre-Raphaelite red. And in those days, simple moisturiser had kept wrinkles at bay. Throughout the past week she had felt the tropical sun beating through her high-factor sunblock, scouring crevasses in her skin, tanning it like old leather.

But that hardly mattered now. There would be no more stories after this one, no more despatches from the field. The advancing nanocams made images accessible to everyone, and frontline journalism redundant.

A black helicopter roared overhead, spraying its invisible cargo. Inside the Land Rover, both their comps beeped to signal Net access. Susanna plugged in her glasses, uploading all the footage recorded this morning and last night – when the doomed hippies had got high for the last time, vowing that the Man could have their joints when he pried them from their cold dead hands. She sent the update to various channels she freelanced for, then began scanning her mail.

Ivo interrupted. "That's where we're going," he said, pointing to a map on his laptop screen. An overlay showed nanocam coverage at ninety-eight per cent, and the Blind Spot shrank by a few more pixels as she stared. "Are you ready?" he asked. "Forward, forward, let us range."

Susanna hesitated, thinking of the desperate criminals who could still be out there, hiding from the advancing cameras. If she met them, she might be giving them their last chance to commit rape, torture, murder.

And yet this was her last chance too, her last opportunity for an old-fashioned scoop, here in the continent where scoops began when *New York Herald* reporter Henry Stanley said, "Dr Livingstone, I presume?"

She nodded. "Let's go."

Ivo revved the engine, and the Land Rover shot forward into the glare of the sun. Susanna's comp chirped indignation as they left the Net behind and re-entered the Blind Spot. She read the mail she'd downloaded. Her husband had sent a Happy Birthday message, in case she stayed out here another week. Her daughters were baking cookies – chocolate for Michelle, and almond for Vanessa. In the background the kitchen looked like chaos, as always, and she saw Toby scooping chocolate dough from an abandoned mixing bowl.

Susanna took off her glasses, and put them in the pocket of her once-white blouse, now stained with sweat and smoke and dust. The children, she thought. The children were one reason she had stopped chasing stories across the globe. But it wasn't just that. It had seemed a promotion to become the anchorwoman in the studio, to become an armchair pundit filing expert opinions from home. And yet as the nanocams spread, everyone became a pundit. Anyone could bookmark footage and post comments, edit montages and record a voiceover. Susanna had once been proud to call herself a journalist, but the label meant nothing now.

Well, the bloggers weren't out here, breathing the parched air, clutching a broken seat-belt as the Land Rover bumped over stones and fallen branches. There was hardly any trail, just a network of goat tracks and dry stream-beds. Ivo zigzagged up the mountain, leaving the contour-hugging helicopter behind. The nanocams could only advance slowly and methodically, needing to knit together in a network. From their inception as an anti-terrorist measure in the USA, they had spread remorselessly across the world. War and disease had kept this remote corner of Africa clear, a haven for the hunted, but now the last Blind Spot would disappear – Ivo's laptop predicted – in less than two days.

She watched Ivo drive. Every few minutes he turned his head for a sudden glance out of the side window, as though trying to catch something by surprise.

"What are you looking for?" she asked.

"We've been through this already," he said. "I'm not telling you what could be out there. The power of suggestion might make you imagine anything I mentioned. I'm bringing you because I need an independent pair of eyes. You're the journalist – shouldn't you see for yourself?"

Susanna thought of pressing him, but decided to wait. Sometimes silence created its own pressure. People gripped by an obsession – and Ivo's had brought him to the remotest corner of the Earth – could rarely shut up for long.

But he didn't speak again until the Land Rover crunched to a halt. Susanna hopped out and helped Ivo heave a dead shrub from their path. She swallowed hard, trying to relieve the pain in her left ear. They had climbed many hundreds of metres, but even in the thin air, the midday sun still broiled the landscape. The rocky hillside, pockmarked with tufts of dry grass, felt hot through her shoes, as if the long-extinct volcano plotted a comeback.

Ivo said, "Can you see anything?"

She paused and looked around. Bar the Land Rover, she saw no sign of human presence. The only movement came from a single bee darting between small purple flowers.

"Can you see anything in the corner of your eye?" Ivo asked. "Can you feel anything brushing past you – running from the nanocams 'like ghosts from an enchanter fleeing'?" He spoke with the intensity of a true believer, though she still hadn't figured out precisely what he believed in.

"Maybe you inhaled too much of that burning dope," said Susanna. She hoped this might sting him into saying more, but he only shrugged and joined her back in the Land Rover.

They crawled on, stopping more frequently as the slope grew rugged. Eventually a huge jumble of boulders halted their progress.

"From here, we walk," said Ivo.

Susanna rummaged in her holdall. "Coke?" she offered.

Ivo stared in disbelief. "Where did you get this? There's not a bar or a vending machine in 200 kilometres." When he opened the can, froth spurted out and soaked him with cola.

They both laughed. "Sorry," said Susanna. "I guess we're pretty high up. And you just wasted about a hundred dollars worth of Coke, by the way. Some guy airlifted it all in and charged me $1000 for a six-pack." She tried to ease open her own can, and relieve the pressure gradually, but she only succeeded in spraying foam out of the window. Bubbles hissed as they fell on the Land Rover's sun-heated metal.

"Unless the forex markets just exploded, that's a lot of money for Coke." Ivo wagged a finger in mock disdain. "And it's not even chilled!"

"Yeah . . ." She sighed. "It was my little nostalgia trip. Back in the old days, when there were dozens of reporters chasing every story, we used to compete to see who could get the most outrageous item through expenses." She remembered Pink-Slip Pete, the BBC veteran who'd mentored her through early assignments. He would have applauded the $1000-Coke, and topped it with some ludicrously expensive taxi or minibar tab. Pete had died before the newsroom started sourcing all their pictures from the nanocams.

Ivo clinked his can with hers. "Cheers." He started checking the contents of his rucksack. "Are you going to hump your bag up the rest of the hill?" he asked.

Susanna frowned. "How far is it?"

"The more you carry, the farther it'll feel."

She hefted the holdall, which contained exactly what she used to pack in the old days. "I'll give it my best shot."

"Fair enough." Ivo pointed to her blouse pocket. "But you're leaving those behind."

Susanna pulled out the thick-framed glasses. "These? Why?"

"Because they're a camera. Okay, they're not the nanocams, but they're a camera nonetheless. Why do you think I'm here in the Blind Spot?"

"I don't know. You won't tell me what you're looking for."

"No . . . but the reason I'm looking *here* is that there are no cameras. Not yet, anyway." Ivo looked up, as if to check for helicopters, but silence shrouded the mountain. "And that's why you can't bring your glasses."

"But I'm a journalist," Susanna said. "When I find the story, I need to film it."

"Ah, but what I'm looking for can't be filmed."

She turned to stare at him. "Run that by me again."

Ivo drained his can of warm Coke. "In ancient times," he began, "when people made maps, they wrote 'Here Be Dragons' at the edge, and drew sea-monsters in the ocean. Over the centuries the dragons got pushed back and back.

"Even in the scientific era, people still saw strange sights. Giant apes, rains of frogs, lights in the sky, fairies at the bottom of the garden. All sorts of stuff, but with one thing in common – they didn't show up too well on film. When the nanocams blanketed North America, you didn't hear much about Bigfoot any more.

"So there are two possibilities. Anyone who ever saw anything weird was mistaken or lying – or all those weird things retreated from the cameras, just as expanding civilization has always made wildlife retreat."

"Or die out," Susanna said.

"Cheery soul, aren't you?" said Ivo. "Yes, many creatures have died out. But wildlife isn't all extinct. And there were so many different weird things, they can't all have died, just as those witnesses can't all have been wrong."

"So we're looking for Bigfoot?" she said, pleased to have finally winkled out Ivo's obsession, and a little amused by it.

He shook his head. "I knew I shouldn't have mentioned anything specific. No, unless Bigfoot managed to swim all the way across the Atlantic, it seems unlikely he's here – if he ever existed. The same applies to most of what used to be called the unexplained, before the nanocams showed exactly how rains of frogs occurred.

"But if there's anything left, if there's just one single weird thing left in the world, it's right here. The nanocams have driven it back and back, and now the Blind Spot is the edge of the Earth. And that's why you can't bring your camera-glasses. The weird is like a superimposed state in quantum mechanics – when you record it, you destroy it." He said the last sentence as if it made sense.

"So you invited a journalist along, and now you're asking her to leave her camera behind?"

"'Full many a flower is born to blush unseen' – but what if it can *only* blush unseen by mechanical eyes?"

"Then I wonder what it has to hide." Yet Susanna felt sympathetic to Ivo's bizarre request. Journalism wasn't just about taking pictures, otherwise she could have stayed home and let the nanocams get the footage. Journalism was about being on the spot, talking to the locals, getting the real story rather than just a picture of it. Yes, she could leave her glasses behind.

After all, she still had her backup system.

"Okay," she said, putting her glasses into the Land Rover's glove compartment. "Let's go."

They clambered over the boulders that had blocked the vehicle's ascent, and then began trudging the rest of the way up the mountain. Susanna kept transferring her holdall from one shoulder to the other, in ever-diminishing intervals as the weight grew harder to bear. She wanted to rush to the top, to get the climb over with, but found herself panting for breath in the thin air. She felt dizzy, and saw black spots floating in her vision.

Were they what Ivo was looking for? When she asked, he smiled and shook his head. "You're just trying too hard, using too much energy. It's easier if you take small steps." He demonstrated walking with tiny heel-to-toe steps that Susanna remembered from childhood games.

"Let's catch a yeti, hitch a ride," she said.

Ivo disdained to reply, and climbed onward. She followed him, grateful for the nanobots maintaining her osteoporosis-stricken bones. The sun descended the empty sky.

Susanna only noticed that Ivo had stopped when she bumped into him. "Take a rest," he said. "From here it's easier."

They'd reached the rim of the ancient volcano. Before them a vast lake stretched as far as Susanna could see. She sat on her holdall, too tired to even speak. Ivo, ten years younger, looked just as glad to take a breather. She watched him staring out into the lake, and wondered what he had expected to find. Only wind-blown ripples broke the surface.

They couldn't afford to rest long; the sun hung low, with twilight brief in the tropics. Ivo led them round the shore of the lake, crunching grey sand underfoot. Ahead stood a small hut, built from mortarless stones and roofed with reeds.

"I scouted out a few places," Ivo explained. "When the nanocams began their final push, I didn't know exactly where the last Blind Spot would be, but I thought the lake was a likely spot." He paused. "Um . . . you might want to wait here for a minute."

Ivo approached the doorway cautiously, and Susanna remembered that terrorists might be hiding beyond. But he gave her a reassuring wave, and she joined him inside.

A few folding chairs surrounded a picnic table full of mouldy styrofoam cups and empty Rizla packets. "Some of the hippies used to come up here for the fishing," Ivo said. "They had lots of stories about the things that got away."

Susanna thought he referred to drug-inspired tales, until she realized that he meant *weird* things. What monsters might be wandering outside the stone walls? Was it safe up here?

The hell with it, she thought. Bigfoot could scare off the terrorists – or vice versa. She was too tired to worry. She looked for a bed, but saw only a pile of dry reeds. From her holdall she took some spare clothes for a pillow.

"Good thinking," said Ivo. "We need to start early tomorrow, to beat the helicopters."

If he said anything else, Susanna didn't hear it before she fell asleep.

In the morning they walked further round the lake to a stretch of tall reeds growing in the shallows. A thin layer of cloud veiled the sun, but did little to restrain its heat from baking the landscape.

Ivo splashed through the reeds until he shouted in triumph. Susanna stepped into the water – finding it colder than she expected – and joined Ivo as he heaved aside a faded tarpaulin. Underneath bobbed a motor-boat, its off-white interior colonized by nesting spiders. Susanna threw in her holdall and clambered onto a bench, brushing arachnids aside. *Oh, the joys of location reporting.* She towelled off her wet feet while Ivo struggled to start the engine.

The boat roared into the lake, flattening reeds on its way. Ivo throttled back to a gentler pace. He kept glancing from port to starboard, bow to stern. Susanna saw only birds wading near the shore, taking to the air when the boat came too close.

She looked away from the shore, out into the lake. Beyond the boat's wake, the still water reflected the sky. She barely saw any boundary between them. No farther shore darkened the horizon.

Susanna blinked, and peered into the distance. She still couldn't see anything.

"How big is this lake?" she asked.

Ivo shrugged. "I haven't been round it."

"I thought we were in a volcano crater. Shouldn't we be able to see the other side?"

"I'll check the map." Ivo delved into his rucksack. But when he tried to boot up the laptop, nothing happened. He shook his head. "Batteries must have run out. They don't last long out here."

"You don't have any spares?"

"Sure, back in the Land Rover."

Ivo looked more excited than concerned. "Let's get across and have a look," he said, revving the boat like a boy racer.

Susanna glanced back and watched the hut dwindle into an imperceptible speck. The loss of her only landmark disturbed her on a visceral level.

You wanted to chase a story, she reminded herself. In the old days she'd survived dozens of disturbing moments. Back then she had almost relished being scared, because the most uncomfortable stories sometimes turned out to be the best.

In those days, of course, she didn't have a family waiting back home.

The engine cut out.

"Shit!" said Ivo. He yanked the starter. The engine coughed and grunted, but wouldn't fire. "We must be out of gas. Stupid hippies! They promised me there was loads left."

Susanna bent down to peer under her bench. She rejoiced at the sight of a red canister, but when she grabbed it, she could feel it was empty.

Below the other bench, Ivo retrieved two long paddles. "I guess this is the emergency engine."

"It's a long time since I did any canoeing," said Susanna. *Or anything much*, she thought.

The motor-boat was no canoe. Susanna found the benches uncomfortably placed for paddling, as did Ivo. Nevertheless, after several minutes of splashing and swearing, they found they could move the boat if they had to. This made Susanna feel a little better, though she reflected that the few minutes the engine had driven them out would take a whole lot longer to paddle back.

And where was "back", exactly? In struggling to co-ordinate their paddling, they'd spun the boat so many times that Susanna had no idea which way they'd come.

All directions looked the same, an expanse of water stretching to the hazy sky. The heat made her scalp itch with sweat. She opened a Coke and swigged the whole can.

"Laptop down; engine stopped," she said. "Do you reckon gremlins did it? Are they part of the weird?" She wanted to bait him, to get him to talk about what he was looking for.

"If gremlins existed, they'd sabotage the nanocams. They haven't managed that yet," said Ivo.

He raised an ancient pair of binoculars to his eyes. For long minutes he slowly turned, scanning all angles. He peered into the depths of the lake, then shrugged and sat down.

For a few minutes, no one spoke. The occasional call of a faraway bird sounded as distant as if it came from another world.

Susanna decided to test her backup system. She fixed her gaze upon Ivo and asked, "What made you start chasing the weird? Did you once have an encounter with it?"

"No," said Ivo. "Quite the opposite." He paused to put on more suncream, then continued, "When I was a child, I used to lie a lot. I would make up stories, tell people I'd seen strange things. My parents thought I just wanted attention, that I'd say anything to make people listen to me. Maybe it started out that way.

"But I didn't *want* to lie. I really wanted to have stories to tell, true stories of marvellous things, inexplicable sights, strange meetings. I hated living in a suburb where nothing ever happened except bikes disappearing and pets being run over. I made up stories about bicycle-napping aliens, and monsters who emerged from the woods to gnaw the corpses of roadkill."

Susanna nodded sympathetically. Ivo went on, "To get ideas, I read old books about strange phenomena. And I began to wonder why those things didn't happen any more – not in the suburbs, anyway. That's when I realized that maybe all the surveillance was pushing back the unexplained, driving it away."

When he halted for a moment, Susanna rewound the last few seconds in her eyes. She saw Ivo speaking; she didn't hear him, because she didn't have an ear implant. But her camera-eyes included a tiny microphone to capture sound. When she uploaded the footage, she'd have full sound and vision.

She remembered the day she'd finally topped Pink-Slip Pete, when she told him how she'd persuaded the network to pay for cyber-eyes as a covert backup for her glasses. The expense claim was so huge, it had to be authorized by a vice-president. But her eyes had secretly captured some great stories.

Then the nanocams came along, and left her with a head full of obsolete hardware. This would be the last time she'd ever use it.

She filmed Ivo talking about all the years he'd spent in ever more remote parts of the world. The oppressive heat made his Arctic adventures sound almost cosy. They both splashed themselves with water from the lake to cool down.

"What about you?" Ivo asked at last. "Is this the story you anticipated when you came to Zaire?"

Susanna shrugged. "I was just looking for someone to take me into the Blind Spot. I didn't know what the story would be, and I still don't. Yours isn't the only theory about what's out here, you know. I've heard conspiracy types claim there's a secret government base beyond the cameras. There's plenty of other theories, too. Whatever people want to believe in, they find a place for. And this is the only hidden place left."

Ivo scanned the horizon yet again. "The occupants are staying hidden so far." He took a monogrammed snuffbox from his waistcoat pocket, extracted a mint and ate it.

"What are you expecting, the last UFO to turn up and beam you away?"

"I already said, I'm not telling you what I'm expecting. You're the independent witness – just keep watching."

Susanna wondered if Ivo refused to specify his goal because he didn't know what it was, and only had a blind faith in *something* out there.

Years of failing to find it, of being narrowed down to this one final spot, must have shaken that faith. Maybe he knew in his heart that he'd been chasing a mirage. Why invite a journalist, then forbid her to bring cameras? Was he planning a hoax?

She didn't see how he could manage it, unless he had an accomplice somewhere out on the lake. Susanna sighed. Professional paranoia was all very well – Pete's journalistic motto had been "Why is this bastard lying to me?" – but Ivo's sincerity had convinced her that he believed in what he searched for. She admired his commitment, his unwavering pursuit. He'd spent years in the field, chasing his goal, while she'd stayed home with the Teletubbies.

Ivo gazed at the lake like a patient fisherman, absently twiddling with his cufflinks. "'Once by men and angels to be seen,'" he muttered to himself. "'In roaring he shall rise and on the surface die.'"

Susanna recognized the cadence of poetry, but without a Net

connection she couldn't identify it. Who memorized verse nowadays?

A breath of wind blew across the lake, a welcome breeze in the furnace of the volcano crater. Susanna stared at the water, waiting for Atlantis to appear or Nessie to start frolicking, or whatever might manifest in front of her recording eyes. To pass the time, she mentally rehearsed voiceovers. For the Nostalgia Channel, "Remember Bigfoot and the Loch Ness Monster? You don't hear so much about them these days, but one man reckons he can track them down . . ." For the Conspiracy Channel, "The government captured Bigfoot and friends, and is holding them in a secret reserve in remotest Africa. What sinister experiments are they performing on harmless yetis?"

The searing heat had given her a headache. She swallowed an aspirin along with her lunch of a low-fat cereal bar. "Should we make a move?" she asked at last. "We're not seeing a damned thing sitting here."

"We're certainly not," said Ivo, frowning. "The weird flees from cameras. Yet here we are, in a camera-free zone – the only camera-free zone on Earth – and it still hasn't showed up. I wonder why that is? You left the glasses behind, but you wouldn't happen to have brought any *other* cameras, would you?"

Susanna stared at him, her cyber-eyes filming twenty-four frames per second. A surge of fear made her tremble. If she admitted that her eyes were cameras, what would he do? Ivo's single-minded quest might make him do anything to reach his goal, anything to someone who threatened it. She felt acutely vulnerable, alone on the lake with this burly stranger. Years of living under the nanocams had made her feel safe; crime had plummeted under their surveillance. And now she had abandoned their protection for someone with a weird obsession.

She pondered whether to lie to him, to say she had no other cameras. And yet as a journalist, she hated being lied to. She was committed to finding the truth. So how could she lie?

All these thoughts whirled through her mind while Ivo waited for her to answer. At last, she nodded. "Yes, I've been using a backup camera. I'll turn it off if I have to, I promise."

Ivo stared at her. Susanna realized that he wanted to see her turn off the camera, so he knew she'd done it, so he knew where it was.

She couldn't bear to tell him that the cameras were her eyes. He might rip them out of her head.

"Look! Out there!" she shouted.

He turned round and squinted at the calm surface of the lake. "What?" he demanded. "What did you see?"

"I'm not telling you," she replied. "The power of suggestion, remember? We're making independent observations."

"Indeed we are," said Ivo, his voice full of scepticism.

By not claiming to see anything in particular, Susanna hadn't actually lied. She'd heard so much spin as a journalist, she could spin herself when she had to.

And yet . . . "Look," she said again. This time she pointed.

A faint patch of mist hung over the water.

"'The game's afoot,'" Ivo said. "We need to get over there. You ready to paddle?"

"Er . . . yeah." Susanna didn't feel quite as much enthusiasm as the prospect ought to inspire. The fog seemed to thicken as she gazed at it. What was out there anyway – the Flying Dutchman?

"Then let's go," Ivo said impatiently.

Susanna sat port and aft, with Ivo diagonally opposite. Together they slowly paddled across the lake. The mist approached faster than their paddling speed, as if the fitful wind blew it toward them. Now a whole bank of fog stretched across the water, like a cloud fallen from the sky.

Just before they reached the whiteness, Susanna shipped her paddle. Ivo swore as his strokes, now unbalanced, sent the boat spinning. They slipped sideways into the fog.

The cool mist made Susanna grateful for a respite from the heat. Inside the fog, visibility fell to a few metres. They floated in a cotton-wool cocoon, silence pressing down upon them.

Susanna peered around to see what might be looming in the mist. The minutes passed slowly. Ivo drummed his fingers on the side of the boat, then stopped. Susanna saw nothing, heard nothing. She sniffed the air, but smelled only their own sweat.

She remembered her promise to turn off her backup camera. But she hadn't filmed with her eyes for years, and had forgotten exactly how they worked. Now she recalled that they recorded continuously on a seven-day loop. Was her gaze repelling weirdness? Ivo certainly thought so.

There was probably nothing out there, she thought. But if there was, right now it didn't even have a chance to show up. She felt sorry for Ivo, about to have his dreams shattered when the nanocams finally covered the whole Earth. All his years of dedication would be wasted – all those years he'd spent out in the field, while she sat at home spouting punditry and interviewing spin doctors. Didn't Ivo deserve a chance at his story? Didn't he deserve it more than she, who had abandoned journalism for a decade and even now hadn't fulfilled the promise she'd just made?

Her cameras had been staring for hours and not seen a damned thing anyway.

Susanna took two deep breaths. Then she closed her eyes.

Immediately, the silence developed texture. She heard the faint swish of water around the boat, the quiet creak of her bench as tension made her muscles twitch. She smelled dampness in the air, tasted moisture on her tongue. Her skin crawled; or maybe it was just the spiders. After barely a minute, the urge to open her eyes grew so strong that she had to clap her hands over her face. She began counting seconds under her breath, trying to calm down. But she kept imagining the fog closing in, crushing the boat.

When I get to a hundred, she promised herself, *I'll do something*.

At a hundred, she set herself the goal of reaching 200.

At 157, she couldn't stand it any more. "Can you see anything?" she asked, trying not to sound like a gibbering wreck. "Ivo?"

He didn't answer. Susanna counted more rapidly, gabbling through the rest of the numbers. At 200 she opened her eyes.

Her companion had vanished.

"Ivo?" she shouted. Her voice sounded thin and muffled. The mist had surged – no, it had only thickened, Susanna told herself desperately – so that she could barely see past the end of the boat. She peered over the side, wondering if Ivo had fallen into the lake, though she would surely have heard a splash. Frantically, she scoured the water with the paddle, half-hoping and half-fearing to prod his body. But all around as far as she could reach, she only disturbed the smooth dark depths of the lake.

"Ivo!"

She strained her ears for any reply. Ripples slapped the boat with a whispery susurration.

"Lift not the painted veil which those who live Call Life – "

Was that Ivo's voice, or just her remembrance of his dusty quotations?

"Where are you?" she cried.

The fog swallowed her voice, as it had swallowed him. He had found the weird at last. Maybe they had fled to another world, and he had managed to follow them. Or maybe they had resented his long chase, and dealt with him.

As the mist swirled around the boat, Susanna felt that if it came any closer, it would envelop her and take her away. If it touched her, she would disappear like Ivo.

No! Her eyes would protect her. Hadn't Ivo said that the weird couldn't appear on camera? All she had to do was keep looking, and she'd be safe.

And yet – she didn't have eyes in the back of her head. The fog could creep up behind her. Something could reach out and grab her.

She whirled round. Nothing there, of course. Just more fog. Was it closer? She turned her head from side to side, trying to cover all angles. She heard the harsh sound of her own panting breath.

Then she heard something else, a muffled roar high in the sky. A monster was –

And then she recognized the sound of a distant helicopter. She had never been happier to hear any noise in her life. She waited for it to come closer, for the nanocams to save her.

The drone faded. The fog was growing stronger, swallowing all sound, swallowing everything within it.

Susanna started paddling frantically, chasing the faint whirr of the helicopter. The boat moved, but kept slewing to port. "Ivo!" she shouted again. Yet she knew he had gone.

She struggled to recall her canoeing lessons, to remember how a single person could steer a straight line, even paddling on one side of a boat. How? How?

J-shaped strokes. Susanna paused, took two deep breaths, and paddled furiously but with more effect. She followed the helicopter's siren song. Tendrils of fog brushed across her face, then dissipated. She could see further ahead. Looking up to the sky, she thought she glimpsed the copter. Or maybe something else was out there –

Susanna paddled faster, gasping with exertion. A noise inside the boat made her heart skip. Then she realized it was her comp, beeping to indicate Net access.

The nanocams had arrived. She stopped paddling, knowing she had reached safety. Looking back, she saw only thin wisps of fog, shredding and fading in the wind. No sign of Ivo.

How had he disappeared? Had there ever been anything weird out there? If so, she hoped he was happy to join his friends – his large, hungry, monster friends.

But maybe Ivo had just searched for weirdness so hard that finally, in disappearing, he *became* the mystery that he had longed for.

Susanna smiled. Certainly she had got one final old-fashioned scoop, an epitaph for the end of strangeness in the nanocams' world. *The mysterious disappearance of Ivo the weird-hunter.*

The Conspiracy Channel would love it.

CASCADE POINT

Timothy Zahn

Here's the first of the two novellas in this anthology, clocking up close on 20,000 words. First published in 1983, this story went on to win the Hugo Award as that year's best novella. It was subsequently collected in Cascade Point and Other Stories *(1986), but the length of the story means it does not get reprinted that often and it is long overdue for another outing. It takes us far into deep space on ships that are able to travel vast distances by taking advantage of "cascade points", which allow a leap through hyperspace, but which are also moments of severe danger when individuals can become aware of their alternate selves.*

Timothy Zahn (b. 1951), is probably best known for his contributions to the Star Wars universe that began with Heir to the Empire *(1991). His work there has rather distracted him from the wider science-fiction world where, in the 1980s, he was one of the most innovative and inspiring contributors to the magazines. His intriguing concepts will be found in his first novel,* Spinneret *(1985) and other story collections,* Time Bomb and Zahndry Others *(1988),* Distant Friends *(1992) and* Star Song *(2002).*

IN RETROSPECT, I suppose I should have realized my number had come up on the universe's list right from the very start, right from the moment it became clear that I was going to be stuck with the job of welcoming the *Aura Dancer*'s latest batch of passengers aboard. Still, I suppose it's just as well it was me and not Tobbar who let Rik Bradley and his psychiatrist onto my ship. There are some things that a captain should have no one to blame for but himself, and this was definitely in that category.

Right away I suppose that generates a lot of false impressions. A star liner captain, resplendent in white and gold, smiling toothily at elegantly dressed men and women as the ramp carries them through the polished entry portal – forget all of that. A tramp starmer isn't polished anywhere it doesn't absolutely have to be, the captain is lucky if he's got a clean jumpsuit – let alone some pseudo-military Christmas tree frippery – and the passengers we get are the steerage of the star-traveling community. And look it.

Don't get me wrong; I have nothing against passengers aboard my ship. As a matter of fact, putting extra cabins in the *Dancer* had been my idea to start with, and they'd all too often made the difference between profit and loss in our always marginal business. But one of the reasons I had gone into space in the first place was to avoid having to make small talk with strangers, and I would rather solo through four cascade points in a row than spend those agonizing minutes at the entry portal. In this case, though, I had no choice. Tobbar, our master of drivel – and thus the man unofficially in charge of civilian small talk-was up to his elbows in grease and balky hydraulics; and my second choice, Alana Keal, had finally gotten through to an equally balky tower controller who wanted to bump us ten ships back in the lift pattern. Which left exactly one person – me – because there was no one else *I'd* trust with giving a good first impression of my ship to paying customers. And so I was the one standing on the ramp when Bradley and his eleven fellow passengers hove into sight.

They ranged from semi-scruffy to respectable-but-not-rich – about par for the *Dancer* – but even in such a diverse group Bradley stood out like a red light on the status board. He was reasonably good-looking, reasonably average in height and build; but there was something in the way he walked that immediately caught my attention. Sort of a cross between nervous fear and something I couldn't help but identify as swagger. The mix was so good that it was several seconds before it occurred to me how mutually contradictory the two impressions were, and the realization left me feeling more uncomfortable than I already did.

Bradley was eighth in line, with the result that my first seven greetings were carried out without a lot of attention from my conscious mind – which I'm sure only helped. Even standing still, I quickly discovered, Bradley's strangeness made itself apparent, both in his posture and also in his face and eyes. Especially his eyes.

Finally it was his turn at the head of the line. "Good morning, sir," I said, shaking his hand. "I'm Captain Pall Durriken. Welcome aboard."

"Thank you." His voice was bravely uncertain, the sort my mother used to describe as mousy. His eyes flicked the length of the *Dancer*, darted once into the portal, and returned to my face. "How often do ships like this crash?" he asked.

I hadn't expected any questions quite so blunt, but the fact that it was outside the realm of small talk made it easy to handle. "Hardly ever," I told him. "The last published figures showed a death rate of less than one per million passengers. You're more likely to be hit by a chunk of roof tile off the tower over there."

He actually cringed, turning halfway around to look at the tower. I hadn't dreamed he would take my comment so seriously, but before I could get my mouth working the man behind Bradley clapped a reassuring hand on his shoulder. "It's all right, Rik – nothing's going to hurt you. Really. This is a good ship, and we're going to be perfectly safe aboard her."

Bradley slowly straightened, and the other man shifted his attention to me. "I'm Dr Hammerfeld Lanton, Captain," he said, extending his hand. "This is Rik Bradley. We're traveling in adjoining cabins."

"Of course," I said, nodding as if I'd already known that. In reality I hadn't had time to check out the passenger lists and assignments, but I could trust Leeds to have set things up properly. "Are you a doctor of medicine, sir?"

"In a way," Lanton said. "I'm a psychiatrist."

"Ah," I said, and managed two or three equally brilliant conversational gems before the two of them moved on. The last three passengers I dispatched with similar polish, and when everyone was inside I sealed the portal and headed for the bridge.

Alana had finished her dickering with the tower and was running the pre-lift computer check when I arrived. "What's the verdict?" I asked as I slid into my chair and keyed for helm check.

"We've still got our lift slot," she said. "That's conditional on Matope getting the elevon system working within the next half-hour, of course."

"Idiots," I muttered. The elevons wouldn't be needed until we arrived at Taimyr some six weeks from now, and Matope could practically rebuild them from scratch in that amount of time. To insist they be in prime condition before we could lift was unreasonable even for bureaucrats.

"Oh, there's no problem – Tobbar reported they were closing things up a few minutes ago. They'll put it through its paces, it'll work perfectly, they'll transmit the readout, and that'll be that." She cleared her throat. "Incidentally . . . are you aware we've got a skull-diver and his patient aboard?"

"Yes; I met – *patient*?" I interrupted myself as the last part of her sentence registered. "Who?"

"Name's Bradley," she said. "No further data on him, but apparently he and this Lanton character had a fair amount of electronic and medical stuff delivered to their cabins."

A small shiver ran up my back as I remembered Bradley's face. No wonder he'd struck me as strange. "No mention at all of what's wrong – of why Bradley needs a psychiatrist?"

"Nothing. But it can't be anything serious." The test board bleeped, and Alana paused to peer at the results. Apparently satisfied, she keyed in the next test on the checklist. "The Swedish Psychiatric Institute seems to be funding the trip, and they presumably know the regulations about notifying us of potential health risks."

"Um." On the other hand, a small voice whispered in my ear, if there was some problem with Bradley that made him marginal for space certification, they were more likely to get away with slipping him aboard a tramp than a liner. "Maybe I should give them a call, anyway. Unless you'd like to?"

I glanced over in time to see her face go stony. "No, thank you," she said firmly.

"Right." I felt ashamed of the comment, not really having meant it the way it had come out. All of us had our own reasons for being where we were; Alana's was an overdose of third-degree emotional burns. She was the type who'd seemingly been born to nurse broken wings and bruised souls, the type who by necessity kept her own heart in full view of both friends and passersby. Eventually, I gathered, one too many of her mended souls had torn out the emotional IVs she'd set up and flown off without so much as a backward glance, and she had renounced the whole business and run off to space. Ice to Europa, I'd thought once; there were enough broken wings out here for a whole shipload of Florence Nightingales. But what I'd expected to be a short vacation for her had become four years worth of armor plate over her emotions, until I wasn't sure she even knew anymore how to care for people. The last thing in the universe she would be interested in doing would be getting involved in any way with Bradley's problems. "Is all the cargo aboard now?" I asked, to change the subject.

"Yes, and Wilkinson certifies it's properly stowed."

"Good." I got to my feet. "I guess I'll make a quick spot survey of the ship, if you can handle things here."

"Go ahead," she said, not bothering to look up. Nodding anyway, I left.

I stopped first at the service shafts where Matope and Tobbar were just starting their elevon tests, staying long enough to satisfy myself the resulting data were adequate to please even the tower's bit-pickers. Then it was to each of the cargo holds to double-check Wilkinson's stowing arrangement, to the passenger area to make sure all their luggage had been properly brought on board, to the computer room to look into a reported malfunction – a false alarm, fortunately – and finally back to the bridge for the lift itself. Somehow, in all the running around, I never got around to calling Sweden. Not, as I found out later, that it would have done me any good.

We lifted right on schedule, shifting from the launch field's grav booster to ramjet at ten kilometers and kicking in the fusion drive as soon as it was legal to do so. Six hours later we were past Luna's orbit and ready for the first cascade maneuver.

Leeds checked in first, reporting officially that the proper number of dosages had been drawn from the sleeper cabinet and were being distributed to the passengers. Pascal gave the okay from the computer room, Matope from the engine room, and Sarojis from the small chamber housing the field generator itself. I had just pulled a hard copy of the computer's course instructions when Leeds called back. "Captain, I'm in Dr Lanton's cabin," he said without preamble. "Both he and Mr Bradley refuse to take their sleepers."

Alana turned at that, and I could read my own thought in her face: Lanton and Bradley had to be nuts. "Has Dr Epstein explained the reasons behind the procedure?" I asked carefully, mindful of both my responsibilities and my limits here.

"Yes, I have," Kate Epstein's clear soprano came. "Dr Lanton says that his work requires both of them to stay awake through the cascade point."

"Work? What sort of work?"

A pause, and Lanton's voice replaced Kate's. "Captain, this is Dr Lanton. Rik and I are involved in an experimental type of therapy here. The personal details are confidential, but I assure you that it presents no danger either to us or to you."

Therapy. Great. I could feel anger starting to churn in my gut at Lanton's casual arrogance in neglecting to inform me ahead of time that he had more than transport in mind for my ship. By all rights I should freeze the countdown and sit Lanton down in a corner somewhere until I was convinced everything was as safe as he said. But time was money in this business; and if Lanton was glossing things over he could probably do so in finer detail than I could catch him on, anyway. "Mr Bradley?" I called. "You agree to pass up your sleeper, as well?"

"Yes, sir," came the mousy voice.

"All right. Dr Epstein, you and Mr Leeds can go ahead and finish your rounds."

"Well," Alana said as I flipped off the intercom, "at least if something goes wrong the record will clear us of any fault at the inquest."

"You're a genuine ray of sunshine," I told her sourly. "What else could I have done?"

"Raked Lanton over the coals for some information. We're at least entitled to know what's going on."

"Oh, we'll find out, all right. As soon as we're through the point I'm going to haul Lanton up here for a long, cosy chat," I checked the readouts. Cascade point in seventeen minutes. "Look, you might as well go to your cabin and hit the sack. I know it's your turn, but you were up late with that spare parts delivery and you're due for some down time."

She hesitated; wanting to accept, no doubt, but slowed by considerations of duty. "Well . . . all right. I'm taking the next one, then. I don't know, though; maybe you shouldn't be up here alone. In case Lanton's miscalculated."

"You mean if Bradley goes berserk or something?" That thought had been lurking in my mind, too, though it sounded rather ridiculous when spoken out loud. Still . . . "I can lower the pressure in the passenger deck corridor to half an atmosphere. That'll be enough to lock the doors without triggering any vacuum alarms."

"Leaves Lanton on his own in case of trouble . . . but I suppose that's okay."

"He's the one who's so sure it's safe. Go on, now – get out of here."

She nodded and headed for the door. She paused there, though, her hand resting on the release. "Don't just haul Lanton away from Bradley when you want to talk to him," she called back over her shoulder. "Try to run into him in the lounge or somewhere instead when he's already alone. It might be hard on Bradley to know you two were off somewhere together talking about him." She slapped the release, almost viciously, and was gone.

I stared after her for a long minute, wondering if I'd actually seen a crack in that heavy armorplate. The bleep of the intercom brought me back to the task at hand, Kate telling me the passengers were all down and that she, Leeds, and Wilkinson had taken their own sleepers. One by one the other six crewers also checked in. Within ten minutes they would be asleep, and I would be in sole charge of my ship.

Twelve minutes to go. Even with the *Dancer*'s old manual setup there was little that needed to be done. I laid the hard copy of the computer's instructions where it would be legible but not in the way, shut down all the external sensors and control surfaces, and

put the computer and other electronic equipment into neutral/
standby mode. The artificial gravity I left on; I'd tried a cascade
point without it once and would never do so again. Then I waited,
trying not to think of what was coming . . . and at the appropriate
time I lifted the safety cover and twisted the field generator control
knob.

And suddenly there were five of us in the room.

I will never understand how the first person to test the Colloton
Drive ever made it past this point. The images silently surrounding
me a bare arm's length away were life-size, lifelike, and – at first
glance, anyway – as solid as the panels and chairs they seemed to
have displaced. It took a careful look to realize they were actually
slightly transparent, like some kind of colored glass, and a little
experimentation at that point would show they had less substance
than air. They were nothing but ghosts, specters straight out of
childhood's scariest stories. Which merely added to the discomfort
. . . because all of them were me.

Five seconds later the second set of images appeared, perfectly
aligned with the first. After that they came more and more quickly,
as the spacing between them similarly decreased, forming an ever-
expanding horizontal cross with me at the center. I watch – forced
myself to watch – knew I *had* to watch – as the lines continued to
lengthen, watched until they were so long that I could no longer
discern whether any more were being added.

I took a long, shuddering breath – peripherally aware that the
images nearest me were doing the same – and wiped a shaking
hand across my forehead. *You don't have to look*, I told myself,
eyes rigidly fixed on the back of the image in front of me. *You've
seen it all before. What's the point?* But I'd fought this fight before,
and I knew in advance I would lose. There was indeed no more
point to it than there was to pressing a bruise, but it held an equal
degree of compulsion. Bracing myself, I turned my head and gazed
down the line of images strung out to my left.

The arm-chair philosophers may still quibble over what the
cascade point images "really" are, but those of us who fly the small
ships figured it out long ago. The Colloton field puts us into a
different type of space, possibly an entire universe worth of it –
that much is established fact. Somehow this space links us into a
set of alternate realities, universes that might have been if things

had gone differently . . . and what I was therefore seeing around me were images of what I would be doing in each of those universes.

Sure, the theory has problems. Obviously, I should generate a separate pseudo-reality every time I choose ham instead of turkey for lunch, and just as obviously such trivial changes don't make it into the pattern. Only the four images closest to me are ever exactly my doubles; even the next ones in line are noticeably if subtly different. But it's not a matter of subconscious suggestion, either. Too many of the images are . . . unexpected . . . for that.

It was no great feat to locate the images I particularly needed to see: the white-and-gold liner captain's uniforms stood out brilliantly among the more dingy jumpsuits and coveralls on either side. Liner captain. In charge of a fully equipped, fully modernized ship; treated with the respect and admiration such a position brought. It could have been – *should* have been. And to make things worse, I knew the precise decision that had lost it to me.

It had been eight years now since the uniforms had appeared among my cascade images; ten since the day I'd thrown Lord Hendrik's son off the bridge of the training ship and simultaneously guaranteed myself a black-balling with every major company in the business. Could I have handled the situation differently? Probably. Should I have? Given the state of the art then, no. A man who, after three training missions, still went borderline claustrophobic every time he had to stay awake through a cascade point had no business aboard a ship, let alone on its bridge. Hendrik might have forgiven me once he thought things through. The kid, who was forced into a ground position with the firm, never did. Eventually, of course, he took over the business.

I had no way of knowing that four years later the Aker-Ming Autotorque would eliminate the need for *anyone* to stay awake through cascade maneuvers. I doubt seriously the kid appreciated the irony of it all.

In the eight years since the liner captain uniforms had appeared they had been gradually moving away from me along all four arms of the cross. Five more years, I estimated, and they would be far enough down the line to disappear into the mass of images crowded together out there. Whether my reaction to that event would be relief or sadness I didn't yet know, but there was no doubt in my mind that it would in some way be the end of a chapter in my life. I gazed at the figures for another minute . . . and then, with my ritual squeezing of the bruise accomplished, I let my eyes drift up and down the rest of the line.

They were unremarkable, for the most part: minor variations in my appearance or clothing. The handful that had once showed me in some non-spacing job had long since vanished toward infinity; I'd been out here a long time. Perhaps too long . . . a thought the half-dozen or so gaps in each arm of the pattern underlined with unnecessary force. I'd told Bradley that ships like the *Dancer* rarely crashed, a perfectly true statement; but what I hadn't mentioned was that the chances of simply disappearing en route were something rather higher. None of us liked to think about that, especially during critical operations like cascade point maneuvers. But the gaps in the image pattern were a continual reminder that people still died in space. In six possible realities, apparently, I'd made a decision that killed me.

Taking another deep breath, I forced all of that as far from my mind as I could and activated the *Dancer*'s flywheel.

Even on the bridge the hum was audible as the massive chunk of metal began to spin. A minute later it had reached its top speed . . . and the entire ship's counterrotation began to register on the gyroscope set behind glass in the ceiling above my head. The device looked out of place, a decided anachronism among the modern instruments, control circuits, and readouts filling the bridge. But it was the only way a ship our size could find its way safely through a cascade point. The enhanced electron tunneling effect that fouled up electronic instrument performance was well understood; what was still needed was a way to predict the precise effect a given cascade point rotation would generate. Without such predictability, readings couldn't even be given adjustment factors. Cascade navigation thus had to fall back on gross electrical and purely mechanical systems: flywheel, physical gyroscope, simple on-off controls, and a non-electronic decision-maker. Me.

Slowly, the long needle above me crept around its dial. I watched its reflection carefully in the magnifying mirror, a system that allowed me to see the indicator without having to break my back looking up over my shoulder. Around me, the cascade images did their own low dance, a strange kaleidoscopic thing that moved the images and gaps around within each branch of the cross, while the branches themselves remained stationary relative to me. The effect was unexplained; but then, Colloton field theory left a lot of things unexplained. Mathematically, the basic idea was relatively straightforward: the space we were in right now could be described by a type of bilinear conformal mapping – specifically, a conjugate inversion that maps lines into circles. From that point it was all downhill, the details tangling into a soup of singularities, branch points, and confluent Riemann surfaces; but what it all eventually boiled down to was that a yaw rotation of the ship here would become a linear translation when I shut down the field generator and reentered normal space. The *Dancer*'s rotation was coming up on two degrees now, which for the particular configuration we were in meant we were already about half a light-year closer to our destination. Another – I checked the print-out – one point three six and I would shut down the flywheel, letting the *Dancer*'s momentum carry her an extra point two degree for a grand total of eight light-years.

The needle crept to the mark, and I threw the flywheel switch, simultaneously giving my full attention over to the gyro. Theoretically, over- or undershooting the mark could be corrected during the next cascade point – or by fiddling the flywheel back and forth now – but it was simpler not to have to correct at all. The need to make sure we were stationary was another matter entirely; if the *Dancer* were still rotating when I threw the field switch we would wind up strung out along a million kilometers or more of space. I thought of the gaps in my cascade image pattern and shivered.

But that was all the closer death was going to get to me, at least this time. The delicately balanced spin lock worked exactly as it was supposed to, freezing the field switch in place until the ship's rotation was as close to zero as made no difference. I shut off the field and watched my duplicates disappear in reverse order, waiting until the last four vanished before confirming the stars were once again visible through the bridge's tiny viewport. I sighed; and fighting the black depression that always seized me at this point, I turned the *Dancer*'s systems back on and set the computer to figuring our exact position. Someday, I thought, I'd be able to afford to buy Aker-Ming Autotorques and never, *never* have to go through this again.

And someday I'd swim the Pacific Ocean, too.

Slumping back in my chair, I waited for the computer to finish its job and allowed the tears to flow.

Crying, for me, has always been the simplest and fastest way of draining off tension, and I've always felt a little sorry for men who weren't able to appreciate its advantages. This time was no exception, and I was feeling almost back to normal by the time the computer produced its location figures. I was still poring over them twenty minutes later when Alana returned to the bridge, "Another cascade point successfully hurdled, I see," she commented tiredly. "Hurray for our side."

"I thought you were supposed to be taking a real nap, not just a sleeper's worth," I growled at her over my shoulder.

"I woke up and decided to take a walk," she answered, her voice suddenly businesslike. "What's wrong?"

I handed her a print-out, pointed to the underlined numbers. "The gyroscope reading says we're theoretically dead on position. The stars say we're short."

"Wumph!" Frowning intently at the paper, she kicked around the other chair and sat down. "Twenty light-days. That's what, twice the expected error for this point? Great. You double-checked everything, of course?"

"Triple-checked. The computer confirmed the gyro reading, and the astrogate program's got positive ident on twenty stars. Margin of error's no greater than ten light-minutes on either of those."

"Yeah." She eyed me over the pages. "Anything funny in the cargo?"

I gestured to the manifest in front of me. "We've got three boxes of technical equipment that include Ming metal," I said. "All three are in the shield. I checked that before we lifted."

"Maybe the shield's sprung a leak," she suggested doubtfully.

"It's supposed to take a hell of a break before the stuff inside can affect cascade point configuration."

"I can go check if you'd like."

"No, don't bother. There's no rush now, and Wilkinson's had

more experience with shield boxes. He can take a look when he wakes up. I'd rather you stay here and help me do a complete programming check. Unless you'd like to obey orders and go back to bed."

She smiled faintly. "No, thanks; I'll stay. Um . . . I could even start things alone if you'd like to go to the lounge for a while."

"I'm fine," I growled, irritated by the suggestion.

"I know," she said. "But Lanton was down there alone when I passed by on my way here."

I'd completely forgotten about Lanton and Bradley, and it took a couple of beats for me to catch on. Cross-examining a man in the middle of cascade depression wasn't a terrifically nice thing to do, but I wasn't feeling terrifically nice at the moment. "Start with the astrogate program," I told Alana, getting to my feet. "Give me a shout if you find anything."

Lanton was still alone in the lounge when I arrived. "Doctor," I nodded to him as I sat down in the chair across from his. "How are you feeling?" The question was more for politeness than information; the four empty glasses on the end table beside him and the half-full one in his hand showed how he'd chosen to deal with his depression. I'd learned long ago that crying was easier on the liver.

He managed a weak smile. "Better, Captain; much better. I was starting to think I was the only one left on the ship."

"You're not even the only one awake," I said. "The other passengers will probably be wandering in shortly – you people get a higher-dose sleeper than the crew takes."

He shook his head. "Lord, but that was weird. No wonder you want everyone to sleep through it. I can't remember the last time I felt this rotten."

"It'll pass," I assured him. "How did Mr Bradley take it?"

"Oh, fine. Much better than I did, though he fell apart just as badly when it was over. I gave him a sedative – the coward's way out, but I wasn't up to more demanding therapy at the moment."

So Bradley wasn't going to be walking in on us any time soon. Good. "Speaking of therapy, Doctor, I think you owe me a little more information about what you're doing."

He nodded and took a swallow from his glass. "Beginning, I suppose, with what exactly Rik is suffering from?"

"That would be nice," I said, vaguely surprised at how civil I was being. Somehow, the sight of Lanton huddled miserably with his liquor had taken all the starch out of my fire-and-brimstone mood. Alana was clearly having a bad effect on me.

"Okay. Well, first and foremost, he is *not* in any way dangerous, either to himself or other people. He has no tendencies even remotely suicidal or homicidal. He's simply . . . permanently disoriented, I suppose, is one way to think of it. His personality seems to slide around in strange ways, generating odd fluctuations in behavior and perception."

Explaining psychiatric concepts in layman's terms obviously wasn't Lanton's forte. "You mean he's schizophrenic? Or paranoid?" I added, remembering our launch field conversation.

"Yes and no. He shows some of the symptoms of both – along with those of five or six other maladies – but he doesn't demonstrate the proper biochemical syndrome for any known mental disease. He's a fascinating, scientifically annoying anomaly. I've got whole bubble-packs of data on him, taken over the past five years, and I'm convinced I'm teetering on the edge of a breakthrough. But I've already exhausted all the standard ways of probing a patient's subconscious, and I had to come up with something new." He gestured around him. "This is it."

"This is what? A new form of shock therapy?"

"No, no – you're missing the point. I'm studying Rik's cascade images."

I stared at him for a long moment. Then, getting to my feet, I went to the autobar and drew myself a lager. "With all due respect," I said as I sat down again, "I think you're out of your mind. First of all, the images aren't a product of the deep subconscious or whatever; they're reflections of universes that might have been."

"Perhaps. There *is* some argument about that." He held up a hand as I started to object. "But either way, you have to admit that your conscious or unconscious mind *must* have an influence on them. Invariably, the images that appear show the results of *major* decisions or events in one's life; never the plethora of insignificant choices we all make. Whether the subconscious is choosing among actual images or generating them by itself, it *is* involved with them and therefore can be studied through them."

He seemed to settle slightly in his chair, and I got the feeling this wasn't the first time he'd made that speech. "Even if I grant you all that," I said, "which I'm not sure I do, I think you're running an incredibly stupid risk that the cascade point effects will give Bradley a shove straight over the edge. They're hard enough on those of us who *haven't* got psychological problems – what am I telling you this for? *You* saw what it was like, damn it. The last thing I want on my ship is someone who's going to need either complete sedation or a restraint couch all the way to Taimyr!"

I stopped short, suddenly aware that my volume had been steadily increasing. "Sorry," I muttered, draining half of my lager. "Like I said, cascade points are hard on all of us."

He frowned. "What do you mean? You were asleep with everyone else, weren't you?"

"Somebody's got to be awake to handle the maneuver," I said.

"But . . . I thought there were autopilots for cascade points now."

"Sure – the Aker-Ming Autotorque. But they cost nearly twenty-two thousand apiece and have to be replaced every hundred cascade points or so. The big liners and freighters can afford luxuries like that; tramp starmers can't."

"I'm sorry – I didn't know." His expression suggested he was also sorry he hadn't investigated the matter more thoroughly before booking aboard the *Dancer*.

I'd seen that look on people before, and I always hated it. "Don't worry; you're perfectly safe. The manual method's been used for nearly two centuries, and my crew and I know what we're doing."

His mind was obviously still a half kilometer back. "But how can it be that expensive? I mean, Ming metal's an exotic alloy, sure, but it's only selenium with a little bit of rhenium, after all. You can buy psy-test equipment with Ming metal parts for a fraction of the cost you quoted."

"And we've got an entire box made of the stuff in our number one cargo hold," I countered. "But making a consistent-property rotation gauge is a good deal harder than rolling sheets or whatever. Anyway, you're evading my question. What are you going to do if Bradley can't take the strain?"

He shrugged, but I could see he didn't take the possibility seriously. "If worse comes to worse, I suppose I could let him sleep while I stayed awake to observe his images. They *do* show up even in your sleep, don't they?"

"So I've heard." I didn't add that I'd feel like a voyeur doing something like that. Psychiatrists, accustomed to poking into other people's minds, clearly had different standards than I did.

"Good. Though that would add another variable," he added thoughtfully. "Well . . . I think Rik can handle it. We'll do it conscious as long as we can."

"And what's going to be your clue that he's not handling it? The first time he tries to strangle one of his images? Or maybe when he goes catatonic?"

He gave me an irritated look. "Captain, I *am* a psychiatrist. I'm perfectly capable of reading my patient and picking up any signs of trouble before they become serious. Rik is going to be all right; let's just leave it at that."

I had no intention of leaving it at that: but just then two more of the passengers wandered into the lounge, so I nodded to Lanton and left. We had five days before the next cascade point, and there would be other opportunities in that time to discuss the issue. If necessary, I would manufacture them.

Alana had only negatives for me when I got back to the bridge. "The astrogate's clean," she told me. "I've pulled a hard copy of the program to check, but the odds that a glitch developed that just happened to look reasonable enough to fool the diagnostic are essentially nil." She waved at the long gyroscope needle above us. "Computer further says the vacuum in the gyro chamber stayed hard throughout the maneuver and that there was no malfunction of the mag-bearing fields."

So the gyroscope hadn't been jinxed by friction into giving a false reading. Combined with the results on the astrogate program, that left damn few places to look. "Has Wilkinson checked in?"

"Yes, and I've got him testing the shield for breaks."

"Good. I'll go down and give him a hand. Have you had time to check out our current course?"

"Not in detail, but the settings look all right to me."

"They did to me, too, but if there's any chance the computer's developed problems we can't take anything for granted. I don't want to be in the wrong position when it's time for the next point."

"Yeah. Well, Pascal's due up here in ten minutes; I guess the astrogate deep-check can wait until then. What did you find out from Lanton?"

With an effort I switched gears. "According to him, Bradley's not going to be any trouble. He sounds more neurotic than psychotic, from Lanton's description, at least at the moment. Unfortunately, Lanton's got this great plan to use cascade images as a research tool, and intends to keep Bradley awake through every point between here and Taimyr."

"He *what*? I don't suppose he's bothered to consider what that might do to Bradley's problems."

"That's what *I* wanted to know. I never did get an acceptable answer." I moved to the bridge door, poked the release. "Don't worry, we'll pound some sense into him before the next point. See you later."

Wilkinson and Sarojis were both in the number one hold when I arrived, Sarojis offering minor assistance and lots of suggestions as Wilkinson crawled over the shimmery metal box that took up the forward third of the narrow space. Looking down at me as I threaded my way between the other boxes cramming the hold, he shook his head. "Nothing wrong here, Cap'n," he said. "The shield's structurally sound; there's no way the Ming metal inside could affect our configuration."

"No chance of hairline cracks?" I asked.

He held up the detector he'd been using. "I'm checking, but nothing that small would do anything."

I nodded acknowledgment and spent a moment frowning at the box. Ming metal had a number of unique properties inside cascade points, properties that made it both a blessing and a curse to those of us who had to fly with it. Its unique blessing, of course, was that its electrical, magnetic, and thermodynamic properties were affected only by the absolute angle the ship rotated through, and not by any of the hundred or so other variables in a given cascade maneuver. It was this predictability that finally had made it possible for a cascade point autodrive mechanism to be developed.

Of more concern to smaller ships like mine, though, was that Ming metal drastically changed a ship's "configuration" – the size, shape, velocity profile, and so on from which the relation between rotation angle and distance traveled on a given maneuver could be computed. Fortunately, the effect was somewhat analogous to air resistance, in that if one piece of Ming metal were completely enclosed in another, only the outer container's shape, size, and mass would affect the configuration. Hence, the shield. But if it hadn't been breached, then the cargo inside it couldn't have fouled us up . . .

"What are the chances," I asked Wilkinson, "that one of these other boxes contains Ming metal?"

"Without listing it on the manifest?" Sarojis piped up indignantly. He was a dark, intense little man who always seemed loudly astonished whenever anyone did something either unjust or stupid. Most everyone on the *Dancer* OD'd periodically on his chatter and spent every third day or so avoiding him. Alana and Wilkinson were the only exceptions I knew of, and even Alana got tired of him every so often. "They couldn't do that," Sarojis continued before I could respond. "We could sue them into bankruptcy."

"Only if we make it to Taimyr," I said briefly, my eyes on Wilkinson.

"One way to find out," he returned. Dropping lightly off the shield, he replaced his detector in the open tool box lying on the deck and withdrew a wand-like gadget.

It took two hours to run the wand over every crate in the *Dancer*'s three holds, and we came up with precisely nothing. "Maybe one of the passengers brought some aboard," Sarojis suggested.

"You've got to be richer than any of *our* customers to buy cases with Ming-metal buckles." Wilkinson shook his head. "Cap'n, it's got to be a computer fault, or else something in the gyro."

"Um," I said noncommittally. I hadn't yet told them that I'd checked with Alana midway through all the cargo testing and that she and Pascal had found nothing wrong in their deep-checks of both systems. There was no point in worrying them more than necessary.

I returned to the bridge to find Pascal there alone, slouching in the helm chair and gazing at the displays with a dreamy sort of expression on his face. "Where's Alana?" I asked him, dropping into the other chair and eyeing the pile of diagnostic print-outs they'd thoughtfully left for me. "Finally gone to bed?"

"She said she was going to stop by the dining room first and have some dinner," Pascal said, the dreamy expression fading somewhat. "Something about meeting the passengers."

I glanced at my watch, realizing with a start that it was indeed dinnertime. "Maybe I'll go on down, too. Any problems here, first?"

He shook his head. "I have a theory about the cascade point error," he said, lowering his voice conspiratorially. "I'd rather not say what it is, though, until I've had more time to think about it."

"Sure," I said, and left. Pascal fancied himself a great scientific detective and was always coming up with complex and wholly unrealistic theories in areas far outside his field, with predictable results. Still, nothing he'd ever come up with had been actually dangerous, and there was always the chance he would someday hit on something useful. I hoped this would be that day.

The *Dancer*'s compact dining room was surprisingly crowded for so soon after the first cascade point, but a quick scan of the faces showed me why. Only nine of our twelve passengers had made it out of bed after their first experience with sleepers, but their absence was more than made up by the six crewers who had opted to eat here tonight instead of in the duty mess. The entire off-duty contingent . . . and it wasn't hard to figure out why.

Bradley, seated between Lanton and Tobbar at one of the two tables, was speaking earnestly as I slipped through the door. ". . . less symbolic than it was an attempt to portray the world from a truly alien viewpoint, a viewpoint he would change every few years. Thus *A Midsummer Wedding* has both the slight fish-eye distortion *and* the color shifts you might get from a water-dwelling creature; also the subtleties of posture and expression that such an alien wouldn't understand and might therefore not get right."

"But isn't strange sensory expression one of the basic foundations of art?" That was Tobbar – so glib on any topic that you were never quite sure whether he actually knew anything about it or not. "Drawing both eyes on one side of the head, putting nudes at otherwise normal picnics – that sort of thing."

"True, but you mustn't confuse weirdness for its own sake with the consistent, scientifically accurate variations Meyerhäus used."

There was more, but just then Alana caught my eye from her place at the other table and indicated the empty seat next to her. I went over and sat down, losing the train of Bradley's monologue in the process. "Anything?" she whispered to me.

"A very flat zero," I told her.

She nodded once but didn't say anything, and I noticed her gaze drift back to Bradley. "Knows a lot about art, I see," I commented, oddly irritated by her shift in attention.

"You missed his talk on history," she said. "He got quite a discussion going over there – that mathematician, Dr Chileogu, also seems to be a history buff. First time I've ever seen Tobbar completely frozen out of a discussion. He certainly seems normal enough."

"Tobbar?"

"Bradley."

"Oh." I looked over at Bradley, who was now listening intently to someone holding forth from the other end of his table. *Permanently disoriented*, Lanton had described him. Was he envisioning himself a professor of art or something right now? Or were his delusions that complete? I didn't know; and at the moment I didn't care. "Well, good for him. Now if you'd care to bring your mind back to ship's business, we still have a problem on our hands."

Alana turned back to me, a slight furrow across her forehead. "I'm open to suggestions," she said. "I was under the impression that we were stuck for the moment."

I clenched my jaw tightly over the retort that wanted to come out. We were stuck; and until someone else came up with an idea there really wasn't any reason why Alana shouldn't be down here relaxing. "Yeah," I growled, getting to my feet. "Well, keep thinking about it."

"Aren't you going to eat?"

"I'll get something later in the duty mess," I said.

I paused at the door and glanced back. Already her attention was back on Bradley. Heading back upstairs to the duty mess, I programmed myself an unimaginative meal that went down like so much wet cardboard. Afterwards, I went back to my cabin and pulled a tape on cascade point theory.

I was still paging through it two hours later when I fell asleep.

I tried several times in the next five days to run into Lanton on his own, but it seemed that every time I saw him Bradley was tagging along like a well-behaved cocker spaniel. Eventually, I was forced to accept Alana's suggestion that she and Tobbar offer Bradley a tour of the ship, giving me a chance to waylay Lanton in the corridor outside his cabin. The psychiatrist seemed preoccupied and a little annoyed at being so accosted, but I didn't let it bother me.

"No, of course there's no progress yet," he said in response to my question. "I also didn't expect any. The first cascade point observations were my baseline. I'll be asking questions during the next one, and after that I'll start introducing various treatment techniques and observing Rik's reactions to them."

He started to sidle past me, but I moved to block him. "Treatment? You never said anything about treatment."

"I didn't think I had to. I *am* legally authorized to administer drugs and such, after all."

"Maybe on the ground," I told him stiffly. "But out here the ship's doctor is the final medical authority. You will *not* give Bradley any drugs or electronic treatment without first clearing it with Dr Epstein." Something tugged at my mind, but I couldn't be bothered with tracking it down. "As a matter of fact, I want you to give her a complete list of all drugs you've brought aboard before the next cascade point. Anything addictive or potentially dangerous is to be turned over to her for storage in the sleeper cabinet. Understand?"

Lanton's expression stuck somewhere between irritated and stunned. "Oh, come on, Captain, be reasonable – practically every medicine in the book can be dangerous if taken in excessive doses." His face seemed to recover, settling into a bland sort of neutral as his voice similarly adjusted to match it. "Why do you object so strongly to what I'm trying to do for Rik?"

"I'd hurry with that list, Doctor – the next point's scheduled for tomorrow. Good day." Spinning on my heel, I turned and stalked away.

I called back to Kate Epstein as soon as I reached my cabin and told her about the list Lanton would be delivering to her. I got the impression that she, too, thought I was overreacting, but she nevertheless agreed to cooperate. I extracted a promise to keep me informed on what Lanton's work involved, then signed off and returned once more to the Colloton theory tapes that had occupied the bulk of my time the past four days.

But despite the urgency I was feeling – we had less than twenty hours to the next cascade point – the words on my reader screen refused to coalesce into anything that made sense. I gritted my teeth and kept at it until I discovered myself reading the same paragraph for the fourth time and still not getting a word of it. Snapping off the reader in disgust, I stretched out on my bed and tried to track down the source of my distraction.

Obviously, my irritation at Lanton was a good fraction of it. Along with the high-handed way he treated the whole business of Bradley, he'd now added the insult of talking to me in a tone of voice that implied I needed his professional services – and for nothing worse than insisting on my rights as captain of the *Dancer*. I wished to hell I'd paid more attention to the passenger manifest before I'd let the two of them aboard. Next time I'd know better.

Still . . . I had to admit that maybe I *had* overreacted a bit. But it wasn't as if I was being short-tempered without reason. I had plenty of reasons to be worried: Lanton's game of cascade image tag and its possible effects on Bradley, the still unexplained discrepancy in the last point's maneuvers, the changes I was seeing in Alana –

Alana. Up until that moment I hadn't consciously admitted to myself that she was behaving any differently than usual. But I hadn't flown with her for four years without knowing all of her moods and tendencies, and it was abundantly clear to me that she was slowly getting involved with Bradley.

My anger over such an unexpected turn of events was not in any way motivated by jealousy. Alana was her own woman, and any part of her life not directly related to her duties was none of my business. But I knew that, in this case, her involvement was more than likely her old affinity for broken wings, rising like the Phoenix – except that the burning would come afterwards instead of beforehand. I didn't want to see Alana go through that again, especially with someone whose presence I felt responsible for. There was, of course, little I could do directly without risking Alana's notice and probable anger; but I could let Lanton know how I felt by continuing to make things as difficult for him as possible. And I would.

And with that settled, I managed to push it aside and return to my studies. It is, I suppose, revealing that it never occurred to me at the time how inconsistent my conclusion and proposed course of action really were. After all, the faster Lanton cured Bradley, the faster the broken-wing attraction would disappear and – presumably – the easier Alana would be able to extricate herself. Perhaps, even then, I was secretly starting to wonder if her attraction to him was something more than altruistic.

"Two minutes," Alana said crisply from my right, her tone almost but not quite covering the tension I knew she must be feeling. "Gyro checks out perfectly."

I made a minor adjustment in my mirror, confirmed that the long needle was set dead on zero. Behind the mirror, the displays stared blankly at me from the control board, their systems having long since been shut down. I looked at the computer's print-out, the field generator control cover, my own hands – anything to keep from looking at Alana. Like me, she was unaccustomed to company during a cascade point, and I was determined to give her what little privacy I could.

"One minute," she said. "You sure we made up enough distance for this to be safe?"

"Positive. The only possible trouble could have come from Epsilon Eridani, and we've made up enough lateral distance to put it the requisite six degrees off our path."

"Do you suppose that could have been the trouble last time? Could we have come too close to something – a black dwarf, maybe, that drifted into our corridor?"

I shrugged, eyes on the clock. "Not according to the charts. Ships have been going to Taimyr a long time, you know, and the whole route's been pretty thoroughly checked out. Even black dwarfs have to come *from* somewhere." Gritting my teeth, I flipped the cover off the knob. "Brace yourself; here we go."

Doing a cascade point alone invites introspection, memories of times long past, and melancholy. Doing it with someone else adds instant vertigo and claustrophobia to the list. Alana's images and mine still appeared in the usual horizontal cross shape, but since we weren't seated facing exactly the same direction, they didn't overlap. The result was a suffocatingly crowded bridge – crowded, to make things worse, with images that were no longer tied to your own motions, but would twitch and jerk apparently on their own.

For me, the disadvantages far outweighed the single benefit of having someone there to talk to, but in this case I had had little choice. Alana had steadfastly refused to let me take over from her on two points in a row, and I'd been equally insistent on being awake to watch the proceedings. It was a lousy compromise, but I'd known better than to order Alana off the bridge. She had her pride, too.

"Activating flywheel."

Alana's voice brought my mind back to business. I checked the print-out one last time, then turned my full attention to the gyro needle. A moment later it began its slow creep, and the dual set of cascade images started into their own convoluted dances. Swallowing hard, I gave my stomach stern orders and held on.

It seemed at times to be lasting forever, but finally it was over. The *Dancer* had been rotated, had been brought to a stop, and had successfully made the transition to real space. I slumped in my seat, feeling a mixture of cascade depression and only marginally decreased tension. The astrogate program's verdict, after all, was still to come.

But I was spared the ordeal of waiting with twiddled thumbs for the computer. Alana had barely gotten the ship's systems going again when the intercom bleeped at me. "Bridge," I answered.

"This is Dr Lanton," the tight response came. "There's something very wrong with the power supply to my cabin – one of my instruments just burned out on me."

"Is it on fire?" I asked sharply, eyes flicking to the status display. Nothing there indicated any problem.

"Oh, no – there was just a little smoke and that's gone now. But the thing's ruined."

"Well, I'm sorry, Doctor," I said, trying to sound like I meant it.

"But I can't be responsible for damage to electronics that are left running through a cascade point. Even something as simple as an AC power line can show small voltage fluc – *oh, damn it!*"

Alana jerked at my exclamation. "What – "

"Lanton!" I snapped, already halfway out of my seat. "Stay put and *don't touch anything*. I'm coming down."

His reply was more question than acknowledgment, but I ignored it. "Alana," I called to her, "call Wilkinson and have him meet me at Lanton's cabin – and tell him to bring a Ming metal detector."

I caught just a glimpse of her suddenly horrified expression before the door slid shut and I went running down the corridor. There was no reason to run, but I did so anyway.

It was there, of course: a nice, neat Ming-metal dual crossover coil, smack in the center of the ruined neural tracer. At least it *had* been neat; now it was stained with a sticky goo that had dripped onto it from the blackened circuit board above. "Make sure none of it melted off onto something else," I told Wilkinson as he carefully removed the coil. "If it has we'll either have to gut the machine or find a way to squeeze it inside the shield." He nodded and I stepped over to where Lanton was sitting, the white-hot anger inside me completely overriding my usual depression. "What the *hell* did you think you were doing, bringing that damn thing aboard?" I thundered, dimly aware that the freshly sedated Bradley might hear me from the next cabin but not giving a damn.

His voice, when he answered, was low and artificially calm – whether in stunned reaction to my rage or simply a reflexive habit I didn't know. "I'm very sorry, Captain, but I swear I didn't know the tracer had any Ming metal in it."

"Why not? You told me yourself you could buy things with Ming-metal parts." And I'd let that fact sail blithely by me, a blunder on my part that was probably fueling ninety percent of my anger.

"But I never see the manufacturing specs on anything I use," he said. "It all comes through the Institute's receiving department, and all I get are the operating manuals and such." His eyes flicked to his machine as if he were going to object to Wilkinson's manhandling of it. "I guess they must have removed any identification tags, as well."

"I guess they must have," I ground out. Wilkinson had the coil out now, and I watched as he laid it aside and picked up the detector wand again. A minute later he shook his head.

"Clean, Cap'n," he told me, picking up the coil again. "I'll take this to One Hold and put it away."

I nodded and he left. Gesturing to the other gadgets spread around the room, I asked, "Is this all you've got, or is there more in Bradley's cabin?"

"No, this is it," Lanton assured me.

"What about your stereovision camera? I know some of those have Ming metal in them."

He frowned. "I don't have any cameras. Who told me I did?"

"I – " I frowned in turn. "You said you were studying Bradley's cascade images."

"Yes, but you can't take pictures of them. They don't register on any kind of film."

I opened my mouth, closed it again. I was sure I'd known that once, but after years of watching the images I'd apparently clean forgotten it. They were so lifelike . . . and I was perhaps getting old. "I assumed someone had come up with a technique that worked," I said stiffly, acutely aware that my attempt to save face wasn't fooling either of us. "How *do* you do it, then?"

"I memorize all of it, of course. Psychiatrists have to have good memories, you know, and there are several drugs that can enhance one's basic abilities."

I'd heard of mnemonic drugs. They were safe, extremely effective, and cost a small fortune. "Do you have any of them with you? If so, I'm going to insist they be locked away."

He shook his head. "I was given a six-month treatment at the Institute before we left. That's the main reason we're on your ship, by the way, instead of something specially chartered. Mnemonic drugs play havoc with otherwise reasonable budgets."

He was making a joke, of course, but it was an exceedingly tasteless one, and the anger that had been draining out of me reversed its flow. No one needed to remind me that the *Dancer* wasn't up to the Cunard line's standards. "My sympathies to your budget," I said briefly. Turning away, I strode to the door.

"Wait a minute," he called after me. "What are my chances of getting that neural tracer fixed?"

I glanced back over my shoulder. "That probably depends on how good you are with a screwdriver and solder gun," I said, and left.

Alana was over her own cascade depression by the time I returned to the bridge. "I was right," I said as I dropped into my seat. "One of his damned black boxes had a Ming-metal coil."

"I know; Wilkinson called from One Hold." She glanced sideways at me. "I hope you didn't chew Lanton out in front of Bradley."

"Why not?"

"Did you?"

"As it happens, no. Lanton sedated him right after the point again. Why does it matter?"

"Well . . ." She seemed embarrassed. "It might . . . upset him to see you angry. You see, he sort of looks up to you – captain of a star ship and all – "

"Captain of a struggling tramp," I corrected her more harshly than was necessary. "Or didn't you bother to tell him that we're the absolute bottom of the line?"

"I told him," she said steadily. "But he doesn't see things that way. Even in five days aboard he's had a glimpse of how demanding this kind of life is. He's never been able to hold down a good job himself for very long, and that adds to the awe he feels for all of us."

"I can tell he's got a lot to learn about the universe," I snorted. For some reason the conversation was making me nervous, and I hurried to bring it back to safer regions. "Did your concern for Bradley's idealism leave you enough time to run the astrogate?"

She actually blushed, the first time in years I'd seen her do that. "Yes," she said stiffly. "We're about thirty-two light-days short this time."

"Damn." I hammered the edge of the control board once with my clenched fist, and then began punching computer keys.

"I've already checked that," Alana spoke up. "We'll dig pretty deep into our fuel reserve if we try to make it up through normal space."

I nodded, my fingers coming to a halt. My insistence on maintaining a high fuel reserve was one of the last remnants of Lord Hendrik's training that I still held onto, and despite occasional ribbing from other freighter captains I felt it was a safety precaution worth taking. The alternative to using it, though, wasn't especially pleasant. "All right," I sighed. "Let's clear out enough room for the computer to refigure our course profile. If possible, I'd like to tack the extra fifty light-days onto one of the existing points instead of adding a new one."

She nodded and started typing away at her console as I called down to the engine room to alert Matope. It was a semimajor pain, but the *Dancer*'s computer didn't have enough memory space to handle the horribly complex Colloton calculations we needed while all the standard operations programming was in place. We would need to shift all but the most critical functions to Matope's manual control, replacing the erased programs later from Pascal's set of master tapes.

It took nearly an hour to get the results, but they turned out to be worth the wait. Not only could we make up our shortfall without an extra point, but with the slightly different stellar configuration we faced now it was going to be possible to actually shorten the duration of one of the points further down the line. That was good news from both practical and psychological considerations. Though I've never been able to prove it, I've long believed that the deepest depressions follow the longest points.

I didn't see any more of Lanton that day, though I heard later that he and Bradley had mingled with the passengers as they always did, Lanton behaving as if nothing at all had happened. Though I knew my crew wasn't likely to go around blabbing about Lanton's Ming metal blunder, I issued an order anyway to keep the whole matter quiet. It wasn't to save Lanton any embarrassment – that much I was certain of – but beyond that my motives became uncomfortably fuzzy. I finally decided I was doing it for Alana, to keep her from having to explain to Bradley what an idiot his therapist was.

The next point, six days later, went flawlessly, and life aboard ship finally settled into the usual deep-space routine. Alana, Pascal, and I each took eight-hour shifts on the bridge; Matope, Tobbar, and Sarojis did the same back in the engine room; and Kate Epstein, Leeds, and Wilkinson took turns catering to the occasional whims of our passengers. Off-duty, most of the crewers also made an effort to spend at least a little time in the passenger lounge, recognizing the need to be friendly in the part of our business that was mainly word of mouth. Since that first night, though, the exaggerated interest in Bradley The Mental Patient had pretty well evaporated, leaving him as just another passenger in nearly everyone's eyes.

The exception, of course, was Alana.

In some ways, watching her during those weeks was roughly akin to watching a baby bird hacking its way out of its shell. Alana's bridge shift followed mine, and I was often more or less forced to hang around for an hour or so listening to her talk about her day. *Forced* is perhaps the wrong word; obviously, no one was nailing me to my chair. And yet, in another sense, I really did have no choice. To the best of my knowledge, I was Alana's only real confidant aboard the *Dancer*, and to have refused to listen would have deprived her of her only verbal sounding board. And the more I listened, the more I realized how vital my participation really was . . . because along with the usual rolls, pitches, and yaws of every embryo relationship, this one had an extra complication: Bradley's personality was beginning to change.

Lanton had said he was on the verge of a breakthrough, but it had never occurred to me that he might be able to begin genuine treatment aboard ship, let alone that any of its effects would show up en route. But even to me, who saw Bradley for maybe ten minutes at a time three times a week, the changes were obvious. All the conflicting signals in posture and expression that had bothered me so much at our first meeting diminished steadily until they were virtually gone, showing up only on brief occasions. At the same time, his self-confidence began to increase, and a heretofore unnoticed – by me, at least – sense of humor began to manifest itself. The latter effect bothered me, until Alana explained that a proper sense of humor required both a sense of dignity and an ability to take oneself less than seriously, neither of which Bradley had ever had before. I was duly pleased for her at the progress this showed; privately, I sought Lanton out to find out exactly what he was doing to his patient and the possible hazards thereof. The interview was easy to obtain – Bradley was soloing quite a bit these days – but relatively uninformative. Lanton tossed around a lot of stuff about synaptic fixing and duplicate messenger chemistry, but with visions of a Nobel Prize almost visibly orbiting his head he was in no mood to worry about dangerous side effects. He assured me that nothing he was using was in the slightest way experimental, and that I should go back to flying the *Dancer* and let him worry about Bradley. Or words to that effect.

I really *was* happy for Bradley, of course, but the fact remained that his rapid improvement was playing havoc with Alana's feelings. After years away from the wing-mending business she felt herself painfully rusty at it; and as Bradley continued to get better despite that, she began to wonder out loud whether she was doing any good, and if not, what right she had to continue hanging around him. At first I thought this was just an effort to hide the growth of other feelings from me, but gradually I began to realize that she was as confused about what was happening as she sounded. Never before in her life, I gathered, had romantic feelings come to her without the framework of a broken-wing operation to both build on and help disguise, and with that scaffolding falling apart around her she was either unable or unwilling to admit to herself what was really going on.

I felt pretty rotten having to sit around watching her flounder, but until she was able to recognize for herself what was happening there wasn't much I could do except listen. I wasn't about to offer any suggestions, especially since I didn't believe in love at first sight in the first place. My only consolation was that Bradley and Lanton were riding round trip with us, which meant that Alana wouldn't have to deal with any sort of separation crisis until we were back on Earth. I'd never before had much sympathy for people who expected time to solve all their problems for them, but in this case I couldn't think of anything better to do.

And so matters stood as we went through our eighth and final point and emerged barely 800,000 kilometers from the thriving colony world Taimyr . . . and found it deserted.

"Still nothing," Alana said tightly, her voice reflecting both the remnants of cascade depression and the shock of our impossible discovery. "No response to our call; nothing on any frequency I can pick up. I can't even find the comm satellites' lock signal."

I nodded, my eyes on the scope screen as the *Dancer*'s telescope slowly scanned Taimyr's dark side. No lights showed anywhere.

Shifting the aim, I began searching for the nine comm and nav satellites that should be circling the planet. "Alana, call up the astrogate again and find out what it's giving as position uncertainty."

"If you're thinking we're in the wrong system, forget it," she said as she tapped keys.

"Just checking all possibilities," I muttered. The satellites, too, were gone. I leaned back in my seat and bit at my lip.

"Yeah. Well, from eighteen positively identified stars we've got an error of no more than half a light-hour." She swiveled to face me and I saw the fear starting to grow behind her eyes. "Pall, what is going *on* here? Two hundred million people can't just disappear without a trace."

I shrugged helplessly. "A nuclear war could do it, I suppose, and might account for the satellites being gone as well. But there's no reason why anyone on Taimyr should *have* any nuclear weapons." Leaning forward again, I activated the helm. "A better view might help. If there's been some kind of war the major cities should now be big craters surrounded by rubble. I'm going to take us in and see what the day side looks like from high orbit."

"Do you think that's safe? I mean – " She hesitated. "Suppose the attack came from outside Taimyr."

"What, you mean like an invasion?" I shook my head. "Even if there are alien intelligences somewhere who would want to invade us, we stand just as good a chance of getting away from orbit as we do from here."

"All right," she sighed. "But I'm setting up a cascade point maneuver, just in case. Do you think we should alert everybody yet?"

"Crewers, yes; passengers, no. I don't want any silly questions until I'm ready to answer them."

We took our time approaching Taimyr, but caution turned out to be unnecessary. No ships, human or otherwise, waited in orbit for us; no one hailed or shot at us; and as I turned the telescope planetward I saw no signs of warfare.

Nor did I see any cities, farmland, factories, or vehicles. It was as if Taimyr the colony had never existed.

"It doesn't make any sense," Matope said after I'd explained things over the crew intercom hookup. "How could a whole colony disappear?"

"I've looked up the records we've got on Taimyr," Pascal spoke up. "Some of the tropical vegetation is pretty fierce in the growth department. If everyone down there was killed by a plague or something, it's possible the plants have overgrown everything."

"Except that most of the cities are in temperate regions," I said shortly, "and two are smack in the middle of deserts. I can't find any of those, either."

"Hmm," Pascal said and fell silent, probably already hard at work on a new theory.

"Captain, you don't intend to land, do you?" Sarojis asked. "If launch facilities are gone and not merely covered over we'd be unable to lift again to orbit."

"I'm aware of that, and I have no intention of landing," I assured him. "But something's happened down there, and I'd like to get back to Earth with at least *some* idea of what."

"Maybe nothing's happened to the colony," Wilkinson said slowly. "Maybe something's happened to us."

"Such as?"

"Well . . . this may sound strange, but suppose we've somehow gone back in time, back to before the colony was started."

"That's crazy," Sarojis scoffed before I could say anything. "How could we possibly do something like that?"

"Malfunction of the field generator, maybe?" Wilkinson suggested. "There's a lot we don't know about Colloton space."

"It *doesn't* send ships back in – "

"All right, ease up," I told Sarojis. Beside me Alana snorted suddenly and reached for her keyboard. "I agree the idea sounds crazy, but whole cities don't just walk off, either," I continued. "It's not like there's a calendar we can look at out here, either. If we *were* a hundred years in the past, how would we know it?"

"Check the star positions," Matope offered.

"No good; the astrogate program would have noticed if anything was too far out of place. But I expect that still leaves us a possible century or more to rattle around in."

"No, it doesn't." Alana turned back to me with a grimly satisfied look on her face. "I've just taken signals from three pulsars. Compensating for our distance from Earth gives the proper rates for all three."

"Any comments on that?" I asked, not expecting any. Pulsar

signals occasionally break their normal pattern and suddenly increase their pulse frequency, but it was unlikely to have happened in three of the beasts simultaneously; and in the absence of such a glitch the steady decrease in frequency was as good a calendar as we could expect to find.

There was a short pause, then Tobbar spoke up. "Captain, I think maybe it's time to bring the passengers in on this. We can't hide the fact that we're in Taimyr system, so they're bound to figure out sooner or later that something's wrong. And I think they'll be more cooperative if we volunteer the information rather than making them demand it."

"What do we need *their* cooperation for?" Sarojis snorted.

"If you bothered to listen as much as you talked," Tobbar returned, a bit tartly, "you'd know that Chuck Raines is an advanced student in astrophysics and Dr Chileogu has done a fair amount of work on Colloton field mathematics. I'd say chances are good that we're going to need help from one or both of them before this is all over."

I looked at Alana, raised my eyebrows questioningly. She hesitated, then nodded. "All right," I said. "Matope, you'll stay on duty down there; Alana will be in command here. Everyone else will assemble in the dining room. The meeting will begin in ten minutes."

I waited for their acknowledgments and then flipped off the intercom. "I'd like to be there," Alana said.

"I know," I said, raising my palms helplessly. "But I *have* to be there, and someone's got to keep an eye on things outside."

"Pascal or Sarojis could do it."

"True – and under normal circumstances I'd let them. But we're facing an unknown and potentially dangerous situation, and I need someone here whose judgment I trust."

She took a deep breath, exhaled loudly. "Yeah. Well . . . at least let me listen in by intercom, okay?"

"I'd planned to," I nodded. Reaching over, I touched her shoulder. "Don't worry; Bradley can handle the news."

"I know," she said, with a vehemence that told me she wasn't anywhere near that certain.

Sighing, I flipped the PA switch and made the announcement.

They took the news considerably better than I'd expected them to

– possibly, I suspected, because the emotional kick hadn't hit them yet.

"But this is absolutely unbelievable, Captain Durriken," Lissa Steadman said when I'd finished. She was a rising young business administration type who I half-expected to call for a committee to study the problem. "How could a whole colony simply vanish?"

"My question exactly," I told her. "We don't know yet, but we're going to try and find out before we head back to Earth."

"We're just going to leave?" Mr Eklund asked timidly from the far end of the table. His hand, on top of the table, gripped his wife's tightly, and I belatedly remembered they'd been going to Taimyr to see a daughter who'd emigrated some thirty years earlier. Of all aboard, they had lost the most when the colony vanished.

"I'm sorry," I told him, "but there's no way we could land and take off again, not if we want to make Earth again on the fuel we have left."

Eklund nodded silently. Beside them, Chuck Raines cleared his throat. "Has anybody considered the possibility that *we're* the ones something has happened to? After all, it's the *Aura Dancer*, not Taimyr that's been dipping in and out of normal space for the last six weeks. Maybe during all that activity something went wrong."

"The floor is open for suggestions," I said.

"Well . . . I presume you've confirmed we *are* in the Taimyr system. Could we be – oh – out of phase or something with the real universe?"

"Highly poetic," Tobbar spoke up from his corner. "But what does *out of phase* physically mean in this case?"

"Something like a parallel universe, or maybe an alternate time line," Raines suggested. "Some replica of our universe where humans never colonized Taimyr. After all, cascade images are supposed to be views of alternate universes, aren't they? Maybe cascade points are somehow where all the possible paths intersect."

"You've been reading too much science fiction," I told him. "Cascade images are at least partly psychological, and they certainly have no visible substance. Besides, if you had to trace the proper path through a hundred universes every time you went through a cascade point, you'd lose ninety-nine ships out of every hundred that tried it,"

"Actually, Mr Raines is not being all *that* far out," Dr Chileogu put in quietly. "It's occasionally been speculated that the branch cuts and Riemann surfaces that show up in Colloton theory represent distinct universes. If so, it would be theoretically possible to cross between them." He smiled slightly. "But it's extremely unlikely that a responsible captain would put his ship through the sort of maneuver that would be necessary to do such a thing."

"What sort of maneuver would it take?" I asked.

"Basically, a large-angle rotation within the cascade point. Say, eight degrees or more."

I shook my head, feeling relieved and at the same time vaguely disappointed that a possible lead had evaporated. "Our largest angle was just under four point five degrees."

He shrugged. "As I said."

I glanced around the table, wondering what avenue to try next. But Wilkinson wasn't ready to abandon this one yet. "I don't understand what the ship's rotation has to do with it, Dr Chileogu," he said. "I thought the farther you rotated, the farther you went in real space, and that was all."

"Well . . . it would be easier if I could show you the curves involved. Basically, you're right about the distance-angle relation as long as you stay below that eight degrees I mentioned. But above that point there's a discontinuity, similar to what you get in the curve of the ordinary tangent function at ninety degrees; though unlike the tangent the next arm doesn't start at minus infinity." Chileogu glanced around the room, and I could see him revising the level of his explanation downward. "Anyway, the point is that the first arm of the curve – real rotations of zero to eight point six degrees – gives the complete range of translation distance from zero to infinity, and so that's all a starship ever uses. If the ship rotates *past* that discontinuity, mathematical theory would say it had gone off the edge of the universe and started over again on a different Riemann surface. What that means physically I don't think anyone knows; but as Captain Durriken pointed out, all our real rotations have been well below the discontinuity."

Wilkinson nodded, apparently satisfied; but the term "real rotation" had now set off a warning bell deep in my own mind. It was an expression I hadn't heard – much less thought about – in years, but I vaguely remembered now that it had concealed a seven-liter can of worms. "Doctor, when you speak of a 'real' rotation, you're referring to a mathematical entity, as opposed to an actual, physical one," I said slowly. "Correct?"

He shrugged. "Correct, but with a ship such as this the two are for all practical purposes identical. The *Aura Dancer* is a long, perfectly symmetrical craft, with both the Colloton field generator and Ming-metal cargo shield along the center line. It's only when you start working with the fancier liners, with their towers and blister lounges and all, that you get a serious divergence."

I nodded carefully and looked around the room. Pascal had already gotten it, from the expression on his face; Wilkinson and Tobbar were starting to. "Could an extra piece of Ming metal, placed several meters off the ship's center line, cause such a divergence?" I asked Chileogu.

"Possibly," he frowned. "Very possibly."

I shifted my gaze to Lanton. His face had gone white. "I think," I said, "I've located the problem."

Seated at the main terminal in Pascal's cramped computer room, Chileogu turned the Ming-metal coil over in his hands and shook his head. "I'm sorry, Captain, but it simply can't be done. A dual crossover winding is one of the most complex shapes in existence, and there's no way I can calculate its effect with a computer this small."

I glanced over his head at Pascal and Lanton, the latter having tagged along after I cut short the meeting and hustled the mathematician down here. "Can't you even get us an estimate?" I asked.

"Certainly. But the estimate could be anywhere up to a factor of three off, which would be worse than useless to you."

I nodded, pursing my lips tightly. "Well, then, how about going on from here? With that coil back in the shield, the real and physical rotations coincide again. Is there some way we can get back to our universe; say, by taking a long step out from Taimyr and two short ones back?"

Chileogu pondered that one for a long minute. "1 would say that it depends on how many universes we're actually dealing with," he said at last. "If there are just two – ours and this one –

then rotating past any one discontinuity should do it. But if there are more than two, you'd wind up just going one deeper into the stack if you crossed the wrong line."

"Ouch," Pascal murmured. "And if there are an infinite number, I presume, we'd never get back out?"

The mathematician shrugged uncomfortably. "Very likely."

"But don't the mathematics show how many universes there are?" Lanton spoke up.

"They show how many Riemann surfaces there are," Chileogu corrected. "But physical reality is never obliged to correspond with our theories and constructs. Experimental checks are always required, and to the best of my knowledge no one has ever tried this one."

I thought of all the ships that had simply disappeared, and shivered slightly. "In other words, trying to find the Taimyr colony is out. All right, then. What about the principle of reversibility? Will that let us go back the way we came?"

"Back to Earth?" Chileogu hesitated. "Ye-e-s, I think that would apply here. But to go back don't you need to know . . . ?"

"The real rotations we used to get here," I nodded heavily. "Yeah." We looked at each other, and I saw that he, too, recognized the implications of that requirement.

Lanton, though, was still light-years behind us. "You act like there's still a problem," he said, looking back and forth between us. "Don't you have records of the rotations we made at each point?"

I was suddenly tired of the psychiatrist. "Pascal, would you explain things to Dr Lanton – on your way back to the passenger area?"

"Sure." Pascal stepped to Lanton's side and took his arm. "This way, Doctor."

"But – " Lanton's protests were cut off by the closing door.

I sat down carefully on a corner of the console, staring back at the Korusyn 630 that took up most of the room's space. "I take it,' Chileogu said quietly, "that you can't get the return trip parameters?"

"We can get all but the last two points we'd need," I told him. "The ship's basic configuration was normal for all of those, and the Korusyn there can handle them." I shook my head. "But even for those the parameters will be totally different – a two-degree rotation one way might become a one or three on the return trip. It depends on our relation to the galactic magnetic field and angular momentum vectors, closest-approach distance to large masses, and a half-dozen other parameters. Even if we *had* a mathematical expression for the influence Lanton's damn coil had on our first two points, I wouldn't know how to reprogram the machine to take that into account."

Chileogu was silent for a moment. Then, straightening up in his seat, he flexed his fingers. "Well, I suppose we have to start somewhere. Can you clear me a section of memory?"

"Easily. What are you going to do?"

He picked up the coil again. "I can't do a complete calculation, but there are several approximation methods that occasionally work pretty well; they're scattered throughout my technical tapes if your library doesn't have a list. If they give widely varying results – as they probably will, I'm afraid – then we're back where we started. But if they happen to show a close agreement, we can probably use the result with reasonable confidence." He smiled slightly. "*Then* we get to worry about programming it in."

"Yeah. Well, first things first. Alana, have you been listening in?"

"Yes," her voice came promptly through the intercom. "I'm clearing the computer now."

Chileogu left a moment later to fetch his tapes. Pascal returned while he was gone, and I filled him in on what we were going to try. Together, he and Alana had the computer ready by the time Chileogu returned. I considered staying to watch, but common sense told me I would just be in the way, so instead I went up to the bridge and relieved Alana. It wasn't really my shift, but I didn't feel like mixing with the passengers, and I could think and brood as well on the bridge as I could in my cabin. Besides, I had a feeling Alana would like to check up on Bradley.

I'd been sitting there staring at Taimyr for about an hour when the intercom bleeped. "Captain," Alana's voice said, "can you come down to the dining room right away? Dr Lanton's come up with an idea I think you'll want to hear."

I resisted my reflexive urge to tell her what Lanton could do with his ideas; her use of my title meant she wasn't alone. "All right," I sighed. "I'll get Sarojis to take over here and be down in a few minutes."

"I think Dr Chileogu and Pascal should be here, too."

Something frosty went skittering down my back. Alana knew the importance of what those two were doing. Whatever Lanton's brainstorm was, she must genuinely think it worth listening to. "All right. We'll be there shortly."

They were all waiting quietly around one of the tables when I arrived. Bradley, not surprisingly, was there too, seated next to Alana and across from Lanton. Only the six of us were present; the other passengers, I guessed, were keeping the autobar in the lounge busy. "Okay, let's have it," I said without preamble as I sat down.

"Yes, sir," Lanton said, throwing a quick glance in Pascal's direction. "If I understood Mr Pascal's earlier explanation correctly, we're basically stuck because there's no way to calibrate the *Aura Dancer*'s instruments to take the, uh, extra Ming metal into account."

"Close enough," I grunted. "So?"

"So, it occurred to me that this 'real' rotation you were talking about ought to have some external manifestation, the same way a gyro needle shows the ship's physical rotation."

"You mean like something outside the viewports?" I frowned.

"No; something inside. I'm referring to the cascade images."

I opened my mouth, closed it again. My first thought was that it was the world's dumbest idea, but my second was *why not*? "You're saying, what, that the image-shuffling that occurs while we rotate is tied to the real rotation, each shift being a hundredth of a radian or something?"

"Right," he nodded, "although I don't know whether that kind of calibration would be possible."

I looked at Chileogu. "Doctor?"

The mathematician brought his gaze back from infinity. "I'm not sure what to say. The basic idea is actually not new – Colloton himself showed such a manifestation ought to be present, and several others have suggested the cascade images were it. But I've never heard of any actual test being made of the hypothesis; and from what I've heard of the images. I suspect there are grave practical problems, besides. The pattern doesn't change in any mathematically predictable way, so I don't know how you would keep track of the shifts."

"I wouldn't have to," Lanton said. "I've been observing Rik's cascade images throughout the trip. I remember what the pattern looked like at both the beginning and ending of each rotation."

I looked at Bradley, suddenly understanding. His eyes met mine and he nodded fractionally.

"The only problem," Lanton continued, "is that I'm not sure we could set up at either end to do the reverse rotation."

"Chances are good we can," I said absently, my eyes still on Bradley. His expression was strangely hard for someone who was supposedly seeing the way out of permanent exile. Alana, if possible, looked even less happy. "All rotations are supposed to begin at zero, and since we always go 'forward' we always rotate the same direction."

I glanced back at Lanton to see his eyes go flat, as if he were watching a private movie. "You're right; it *is* the same starting pattern each time. I hadn't really noticed that before, with changes and all."

"It should be easy enough to check, Captain," Pascal spoke up. "We can compute the physical rotations for the first six points we'll be going through. The real rotations should be the same as on the outbound leg, though, so if Dr Lanton's right the images will wind up in the same pattern they did before."

"But how – ?" Chileogu broke off suddenly. "Ah. You've had a mnemonic treatment?"

Lanton nodded and then looked at me. "I think Mr Pascal's idea is a good one, Captain, and I don't see any purpose in hanging around here any longer than necessary. Whenever you want to start back – "

"I have a few questions to ask first," I interrupted mildly. I glanced again at Bradley, decided to tackle the easier ones first. "Dr Chileogu, what's the status of your project?"

"The approximations? We've just finished programming the first one; it'll take another hour or so to collect enough data for a plot. I agree with Dr Lanton, though – we can do the calculations between cascade points as easily as we can do them in orbit here."

"Thank you. Dr Lanton, you mentioned something about *changes* a minute ago. What exactly did you mean?"

Lanton's eyes flicked to Bradley for an instant. "Well . . . as I told you several weeks ago, a person's mind has a certain effect on the cascade image pattern. Some of the medicines Rik's been taking have slightly altered the – oh, I guess you could call it the *texture* of the pattern."

"Altered it how much?"

"In some cases, fairly extensively." He hesitated, just a bit too long. "But nothing I've done is absolutely irreversible. I should be able to recreate the original conditions before each cascade point."

Deliberately, I leaned back in my chair. "All right. Now let's hear what the problem is."

"I beg your pardon?"

"You heard me." I waved at Bradley and Alana. "Your patient and my first officer look like they're about to leave for a funeral. I want to know why."

Lanton's cheek twitched. "I ddn't think this is the time or the place to discuss – "

"The problem, Captain," Bradley interrupted quietly, "is that the reversing of the treatments may turn out to be permanent."

It took a moment for that to sink in. When it did I turned my eyes back on Lanton. "Explain."

The psychiatrist took a deep breath. "The day after the second point I used ultrasound to perform a type of minor neurosurgery called synapse fixing. It applies heat to selected regions of the brain to correct a tendency of the nerves to misfire. The effects *can* be reversed . . . but the procedure's been done only rarely, and usually involves unavoidable peripheral damage."

I felt my gaze hardening into an icy stare. "In other words," I bit out, "not only will the progress he's made lately be reversed, but he'll likely wind up worse off than he started. Is that it?"

Lanton squirmed uncomfortably, avoiding my eyes. "I don't *know* that he will. Now that I've found a treatment – "

"You're about to give him a brand-new disorder," I snapped. "*Damn* it all, Lanton, you are the most cold-blooded – "

"Captain."

Bradley's single word cut off my flow of invective faster than anything but hard vacuum could have. "What?" I said.

"Captain, I understand how you feel." His voice was quiet but firm; and though the tightness remained in his expression, it had been joined by an odd sort of determination. "But Dr Lanton wasn't really trying to maneuver you into supporting something unethical. For the record, I've already agreed to work with him on this; I'll put that on tape if you'd like." He smiled slightly. "And before you bring it up, I *am* recognized as legally responsible for my actions, so as long as Dr Lanton and I agree on a course of treatment your agreement is not required."

"That's not entirely true," I ground out. "As a ship's captain in deep space, I have full legal power here. If I say he can't do something to you, he can't. Period."

Bradley's face never changed. "Perhaps. But unless you can find another way to get us back to Earth, I don't see that you have any other choice."

I stared into those eyes for a couple of heartbeats. Then, slowly, my gaze swept the table, touching in turn all the others as they sat watching me, awaiting my decision. The thought of deliberately sending Bradley back to his permanent disorientation – *really* permanent, this time – left a taste in my mouth that was practically gagging in its intensity. But Bradley was right . . . and at the moment I didn't have any better ideas.

"Pascal," I said, "you and Dr Chileogu will first of all get some output on that program of yours. Alana, as soon as they're finished you'll take the computer back and calculate the parameters for our first point. *You* two – " I glared in turn at Bradley and Lanton "– will be ready to test this image theory of yours. You'll do the observations in your cabin as usual, and tell me afterward whether we duplicated the rotation exactly or came out short or long. Questions? All right; dismissed."

After all, I thought amid the general scraping of chairs, *for the first six points all Bradley will need to do is cut back on medicines. That means twenty-eight days or so before any irreversible surgery is done.*

I had just that long to come up with another answer.

We left orbit three hours later, pushing outward on low drive to conserve fuel. That plus the course I'd chosen meant another ten hours until we were in position for the first point, but none of that time was wasted. Pascal and Chileogu were able to program and run two more approximation schemes; the results, unfortunately, were not encouraging. Any two of the three plots had a fair chance of agreeing over ranges of half a degree or so, but there was no consistency at all over the larger angles we would need to use. Chileogu refused to throw in the towel, pointing out that he had another six methods to try and making vague noises about statistical curve-fitting schemes. I promised him all the computer time he needed between point maneuvers, but privately I conceded defeat. Lanton's method now seemed our only chance . . . if it worked.

I handled the first point myself, double-checking all parameters beforehand and taking special pains to run the gyro needle as close to the proper angle as I could. As with any such hand operation, of course, perfection was not quite possible, and I ran the *Dancer* something under a hundredth of a degree long. I'm not sure what I was expecting from this first test, but I *was* more than a little surprised when Lanton accurately reported that we'd slightly overshot the mark.

"It looks like it'll work," Alana commented from her cabin when I relayed the news. She didn't sound too enthusiastic.

"Maybe," I said, feeling somehow the need to be as skeptical as possible. "We'll see what happens when he starts taking Bradley off the drugs. I find it hard to believe that the man's mental state can be played like a yo-yo, and if it can't be we'll have to go with whatever statistical magic Chileogu can put together."

Alana gave a little snort that she'd probably meant to be a laugh. "Hard to know which way to hope, isn't it?"

"Yeah." I hesitated for a second, running the duty arrangements over in my mind. "Look, why don't you take the next few days off, at least until the next point. Sarojis can take your shift up here."

"That's all right," she sighed. "I – if it's all the same with you, I'd rather save any offtime until later. Rik will . . . need my help more then."

"Okay," I told her. "Just let me know when you want it and the time's yours."

We continued on our slow way, and with each cascade point I became more and more convinced that Lanton really would be able to guide us through those last two critical points. His accuracy for the first four maneuvers was a solid hundred percent, and on the fifth maneuver we got to within point zero two percent of the computer's previous reading by deliberately jockeying the *Dancer* back and forth until Bradley's image pattern was exactly as Lanton remembered it. After that even Matope was willing to be cautiously optimistic; and if it hadn't been for one small cloud hanging over my head I probably would have been as happy as the rest of the passengers had become.

The cloud, of course, being Bradley.

I'd been wrong about how much his improvement had been due to the drugs Lanton had been giving him, and every time I saw him that ill-considered line about playing his mind like a yo-yo came back to haunt me. Slowly, but very steadily, Bradley was regressing back toward his original mental state. His face went first, his expressions beginning to crowd each other again as if he were unable to decide which of several moods should be expressed at any given moment. His eyes took on that shining, nervous look I hated so much: just occasionally at first, but gradually becoming more and more frequent, until it seemed to be almost his norm. And yet, even though he certainly saw what was happening to him, not once did I hear him say anything that could be taken as resentment or complaint. It was as if the chance to save twenty other lives was so important to him that it was worth any sacrifice. I thought occasionally about Alana's comment that he'd never before had a sense of dignity, and wondered if he would lose it again to his illness. But I didn't wonder about it all that much; I was too busy worrying about Alana.

I hadn't expected her to take Bradley's regression well, of course – to someone with Alana's wing-mending instincts a backsliding patient would be both insult *and* injury. What I wasn't prepared for was her abrupt withdrawal into a shell of silence on the issue which no amount of gentle probing could crack open. I tried to be patient with her, figuring that eventually the need to talk would overcome her reticence; but as the day for what Lanton described as "minor surgery" approached, I finally decided I couldn't wait any longer. On the day after our sixth cascade point, I quit being subtle and forced the issue.

"Whatever I'm feeling, it isn't any concern of yours," she said, her fingers playing across the bridge controls as she prepared to take over from me. Her hands belied the calmness in her voice: I knew her usual check-out routine as well as my own, and she lost the sequence no fewer than three times as I watched.

"I think it is," I told her. "Aside from questions of friendship, you're a member of my crew, and anything that might interfere with your efficiency is my concern."

She snorted. "I've been under worse strains than this without falling apart."

"I know. But you've never buried yourself this deeply before, and it worries me."

"I know. I'm . . . sorry. If I could put it into words – " She shrugged helplessly.

"Are you worried about Bradley?" I prompted. "Don't forget that, whatever Lanton has to do here, he'll have all the resources of the Swedish Psychiatric Institute available to undo it."

"I know. But . . . he's going to come out of it a different person. Even Lanton has to admit that."

"Well . . . maybe it'll wind up being a change for the better."

It was a stupid remark, and her scornful look didn't make me feel any better about having made it. "Oh, come *on*. Have you *ever* heard of an injury that did any real good? Because that's what it's going to be – an injury."

And suddenly I understood. "You're afraid you won't like him afterwards, aren't you? At least not the way you do now?"

"Why should that be so unreasonable?" she snapped. "I'm a damn fussy person, you know – I don't like an awful lot of people. I can't afford to . . . to lose any of them." She turned her back on me abruptly, and I saw her shoulders shake once.

I waited a decent interval before speaking. "Look, Alana, you're not in any shape to stay up here alone. Why don't you go down to your cabin and pull yourself together, and then go and spend some time with Bradley."

"I'm all right," she mumbled. "I can take my shift."

"I know. But . . . at the moment I imagine Rik needs you more than I do. Go on, get below."

She resisted for a few more minutes, but eventually I bent her sense of duty far enough and she left. For a long time afterwards I just sat and stared at the stars, my thoughts whistling around my head in tight orbit. What *would* the effect of the new Bradley be on Alana? She'd been right – whatever happened, it wasn't likely to be an improvement. If her interest was really only in wing-mending, Lanton's work would merely provide her with a brand-new challenge. But I didn't think even Alana was able to fool herself like that any more. She cared about him, for sure, and if he changed too much that feeling might well die.

And I wouldn't lose her when we landed.

I thought about it long and hard, examining it and the rest of our situation from several angles. Finally, I leaned forward and keyed the intercom. Wilkinson was off-duty in his cabin; from the time it took him to answer he must have been asleep as well. "Wilkinson, you got a good look at the damage in Lanton's neural whatsis machine. How hard would it be to fix?"

"Uh . . . well, that's hard to say. The thing that spit goop all over the Ming-metal coil was a standard voltage regulator board – we're bound to have spares aboard But there may be other damage, too. I'd have to run an analyser over it to find out if anything else is dead. Whether we would have replacements is another question."

"Okay. Starting right now, you're relieved of all other duty until you've got that thing running again. Use anything you need from ship's spares – " I hesitated – "and you can even pirate from our cargo if necessary."

"Yes, sir." He was wide awake now. "I gather there's a deadline?"

"Lanton's going to be doing some ultrasound work on Bradley in fifty-eight hours. You need to be done before that. Oh, and you'll need to work in Lanton's cabin – I don't want the machine moved at all."

"Got it. If you'll clear it with Lanton, I can be up there in twenty minutes."

Lanton wasn't all that enthusiastic about letting Wilkinson set up shop in his cabin, especially when I wouldn't explain my reasons to him, but eventually he gave in. I alerted Kate Epstein that she would have to do without Wilkinson for a while, and then called Matope to confirm the project's access to tools and spares.

And then, for the time being, it was all over but the waiting. I resumed my examination of the viewport, wondering if I were being smart or just pipe-dreaming.

Two days later – barely eight hours before Bradley's operation was due to begin – Wilkinson finally reported the neural tracer was once again operational.

*   *   *

"This better be important," Lanton fumed as he took his place at the dining room table. "I'm already behind schedule in my equipment set-up as it is."

I glanced around at the others before replying. Pascal and Chileogu, fresh from their latest attempt at making sense from their assortment of plots, seemed tired and irritated by this interruption. Bradley and Alana, holding hands tightly under the table, looked more resigned than anything else. Everyone seemed a little gaunt, but that was probably my imagination – certainly we weren't on anything approaching starvation rations yet. "Actually, Doctor," I said, looking back at Lanton, "you're not in nearly the hurry you think. There's not going to be any operation."

That got everyone's full attention. "You've found another way?" Alana breathed, a hint of life touching her eyes for the first time in days.

"I think so. Dr Chileogu, I need to know first whether a current running through Ming metal would change its effect on the ship's real rotation."

He frowned, then shrugged. "Probably. I have no idea how, though."

A good thing I'd had the gadget fixed, then. "Doesn't matter. Dr Lanton, can you tell me approximately when in the cascade point your neural tracer burned out?"

"I can tell you exactly. It was just as the images started disappearing, right at the end."

I nodded; I'd hoped it was either the turning on or off of the field generator that had done it. That would make the logistics a whole lot easier. "Good. Then we're all set. What we're going to do, you see, is reenact that particular maneuver."

"What good will *that* do?" Lanton asked, his tone more puzzled than belligerent.

"It should get us home." I waved towards the outer hull. "For the past two days we've been moving toward a position where the galactic field and other parameters are almost exactly the same as we had when we went through that point – providing your neural tracer is on and we're heading back toward Taimyr. In another two days we'll turn around and get our velocity vector lined up correctly. Then, with your tracer running, we're going to fire up the generator and rotate the same amount – by gyro reading – as we did then. *You* – " I leveled a finger at Lanton – "will be on the bridge during that operation, and you will note the exact con-figuration of your cascade images at that moment. Then, *without shutting off the generator*, we'll rotate *back* to zero; zero as defined by your cascade pattern, since it may be different from gyro zero. At that time, I'll take the Ming metal from your tracer, walk it to the number one hold, and stuff it into the cargo shield; and we'll rotate the ship again until we reach your memorized cascade pattern. Since the physical and real rotations are identical in that configuration, that'll give us the real angle we rotated through the last time – "

"And from *that* we can figure the angle we'll need to make going the other direction!" Alana all but shouted.

I nodded. "Once we've rotated back to zero to regain our starting point, of course." I looked around at them again. Lanton and Bradley still seemed confused, though the latter was starting to catch Alana's enthusiasm. Chileogu was scribbling on a notepad, and Pascal just sat there with his mouth slightly open. Probably aston-ished that he hadn't come up with such a crazy idea himself. "That's all I have to say," I told them. "If you have any comments later – "

"I have one now, Captain."

I looked at Bradley in some surprise. "Yes?"

He swallowed visibly. "It seems to me, sir, that what you're going to need is a set of cascade images that vary a lot, so that the pattern you're looking for is a distinctive one. I don't think Dr Lanton's are suitable for that."

"I see." Of course; while Lanton had been studying Bradley's images, Bradley couldn't help but see his, as well. "Lanton? How about it?"

The psychiatrist shrugged. "I admit they're a little bland – haven't had a very exciting life. But they'll do."

"I doubt it." Bradley looked back at me. "Captain, I'd like to volunteer."

"You don't know what you're saying," I told him. "Each rotation will take twice as long as the ones you've already been through. *And* there'll be two of them back to back; *and* the field won't be shut down between them, because I want to know if the images drift while I'm moving the coil around the ship. Multiply by about five what you've felt afterwards and you'll get some idea what it'll be like." I shook my head. "I'm grateful for your offer, but I can't let more people than necessary go through that."

"I appreciate that. But I'm still going to do it.'

We locked eyes for a long moment . . . and the word *dignity* flashed through my mind. "In that case, I accept." I said. "Other questions? Thank you for stopping by."

They got the message and began standing up . . . all except Alana. Bradley whispered something to her, but she shook her head and whispered back. Reluctantly, he let go of her hand and followed the others out of the room.

"Question?" I asked Alana when we were alone, bracing for an argument over the role I was letting Bradley take.

"You're right about the extra stress staying in Colloton space that long will create," she said. "That probably goes double for anyone running around in it. I'd expect a lot more vertigo, for starters, and that could make movement dangerous."

"Would you rather Bradley had his brain scorched?"

She flinched, but stood her ground. "My objection isn't with the method – it's with who's going to be bouncing off the *Dancer*'s walls."

"Oh. Well, before you get the idea you're being left out of things, let me point out that *you're* going to be handling bridge duties for the maneuver."

"Fine; but since I'm going to be up anyway I want the job of running the Ming metal back and forth instead."

I shook my head. "No. You're right about the unknowns involved with this, which is why *I'm* going to do it."

"I'm five years younger than you are," she said, ticking off fingers. "I also have a higher stress index, better balance, and I'm in better physical condition." She hesitated. "And I'm not haunted by white uniforms in my cascade images," she added gently.

Coming from anyone else, that last would have been like a knife in the gut. But from Alana, it somehow didn't even sting. "The assignments are non-negotiable," I said, getting to my feet. "Now if you'll excuse me, I have to catch a little sleep before my next shift."

She didn't respond. When I left she was still sitting there, staring through the shiny surface of the table.

*   *   *

"Here we go. Good luck," were the last words I heard Alana say before the intercom was shut down and I was alone in Lanton's cabin. Alone, but not for long: a moment later my first doubles appeared. Raising my wrist, I keyed my chrono to stopwatch mode and waited, ears tingling with the faint ululation of the Colloton field generator. The sound, inaudible from the bridge, reminded me of my trainee days, before the *Dancer* . . . before Lord Hendrik and his fool-headed kid . . . Shaking my head sharply, I focused on the images, waiting for them to begin their one-dimensional allemande.

They did, and I started my timer. With the lines to the bridge dead I was going to have to rely on the image movements to let me know when the first part of the maneuver was over; moving the Ming metal around the ship while we were at the wrong end of our rotation or – worse – while we were still moving would probably end our chances of getting back for good. Mindful of the pranks cascade points could play on a person's time sense, I'd had Pascal calculate the approximate times each rotation would take. Depending on how accurate they turned out to be, they might simply let me limit how soon I started worrying.

It wasn't a pleasant wait. On the bridge, I had various duties to perform; here, I didn't have even that much distraction from the ghosts surrounding me. Sitting next to the humming neural tracer, I watched the images flicker in and out, white uniforms dos-à-dosing with the coveralls and the gaps.

Ghosts. *Haunted*. I'd never seriously thought of them like that before, but now I found I couldn't see them in any other way. I imagined I could see knowing smiles on the liner captains' faces, or feel a coldness from the gaps where I'd died. Pure autosuggestion, of course . . . and yet, it forced me for probably the first time to consider what exactly the images were doing to me.

They were making me chronically discontented with my life.

My first reaction to such an idea was to immediately justify my resentment. I'd been cheated out of the chance to be a success in my field; trapped at the bottom of the heap by idiots who ranked political weaselcraft higher than flying skill. I had a *right* to feel dumped on.

And yet . . .

My watch clicked at me: the first rotation should be about over.

I reset it and waited, watching the images. With agonizing slowness they came to a stop . . . and then started moving again in what I could persuade myself was the opposite direction. I started my watch again and let my eyes defocus a bit. The next time the dance stopped, it would be time to move Lanton's damn coil to the hold and bring my ship back to normal.

My ship. I listened to the way the words echoed around my brain. *My ship.* No liner captain owned his own ship. He was an employee, like any other in the company; forever under the basilisk eye of those selfsame idiots who'd fired me once for doing my job. The space junk being sparser and all that aside, would I *really* have been happier in a job like that? Would I have enjoyed being caught between management on one hand and upper-crusty passengers on the other? Enjoyed, hell – would I have *survived* it? For the first time in ten years I began to wonder if perhaps Lord Hendrik had known what he was doing when he booted me out of his company.

Deliberately, I searched out the white uniforms far off to my left and watched as they popped in and out of different slots in the long line. Perhaps that was why there were so few of them. I thought suddenly; perhaps, even while I was pretending otherwise, I'd been smart enough to make decisions that had kept me out of the running for that particular treadmill. The picture that created made me smile: my subconscious chasing around with secret memos, hiding basic policy matters from my righteously indignant conscious mind.

The click of my watch made me jump. Taking a deep breath, I picked up a screwdriver from the tool pouch laid out beside the neutral tracer and gave my full attention to the images. Slow . . . slower . . . stopped. I waited a full two minutes to make sure, then flipped off the tracer and got to work.

I'd had plenty of practice in the past in the past two days, but it still took me nearly five minutes to extricate the coil from the maze of equipment surrounding it. That was no particular problem – we'd allowed seven minutes for the disassembly – but I was still starting to sweat as I got to my feet and headed for the door.

And promptly fell on my face.

Alana's reference to enhanced vertigo apart, I hadn't expected anything that strong quite as soon. Swallowing hard, I tried to ignore the feeling of lying on a steep hill and crawled toward the nearest wall. Using it as a support, I got to my feet, waited for the cabin to stop spinning, and shuffled over to the door. Fortunately, all the doors between me and One Hold had been locked open, so I didn't have to worry about getting to the release. Still shuffling, I maneuvered through the opening and started down the corridor, moving as quickly as I could. The trip – fifteen meters of corridor, a circular stairway down, five more meters of corridor, and squeezing through One Hold's cargo to get to the shield – normally took less than three minutes. We'd allowed ten; but already I could see that was going to be tight. I kept my eyes on the wall beside me and concentrated on moving my feet . . . which was probably why I was nearly to the stairway before I noticed the kaleidoscope dance my cascade images were doing.

While the ship was at rest.

I stopped short, the pattern shifts ceasing as I did so. The thing I had feared most about this whole trick was happening: moving the Ming metal was changing our real angle in Colloton space.

I don't know how long I leaned there with the sweat trickling down my forehead, but it was probably no more than a minute before I forced myself to get moving again. There were now exactly two responses Alana could make: go on to the endpoint Lanton had just memorized, or try and compensate somehow for the shift I was causing. The former course felt intuitively wrong, but the latter might well be impossible to do – and neither had any particular mathematical backing that Chileogu had been able to find. For me, the worst part of it was the fact that I was now completely out of the decision process. No matter how fast I got the coil locked away, there was no way I was going to make it back up two flights of stairs to the bridge. Like everyone else on board, I was just going to have to trust Alana's judgment.

I slammed into the edge of the stairway opening, nearly starting my downward trip headfirst before I got a grip on the railing. The coil, jarred from my sweaty hand, went on ahead of me, clanging like a muffled bell as it bounced to the deck below. I followed a good deal more slowly, the writhing images around me adding to my vertigo. By now, the rest of my body was also starting to react to the stress, and I had to stop every few steps as a wave of nausea or fatigue washed over me. It seemed forever before I finally reached the bottom of the stairs. The coil had rolled to the middle of the corridor; retrieving it on hands and knees, I got back to the wall and hauled myself to my feet. I didn't dare look at my watch.

The cargo hold was the worst part yet. The floor was swaying freely by then, like an ocean vessel in heavy seas, and through the reddish haze surrounding me, the stacks of boxes I staggered between seemed ready to hurl themselves down upon my head. I don't remember how many times I shied back from what appeared to be a breaking wave of crates, only to slam into the stack behind me. Finally, though, I made it to the open area in front of the shield door. I was halfway across the gap, moving again on hands and knees, when my watch sounded the one-minute warning. With a desperate lunge, I pushed myself up and forward, running full tilt into the Ming-metal wall. More from good luck than anything else, my free hand caught the handle; and as I fell backwards the door swung open. For a moment I hung there, trying to get my trembling muscles to respond. Then, slowly, I got my feet under me and stood up. Reaching through the opening, I let go of the coil and watched it drop into the gap between two boxes. The hold was swaying more and more violently now; timing my move carefully, I shoved on the handle and collapsed to the deck. The door slammed shut with a thunderclap that tried to take the top of my head with it. I hung on just long enough to see that the door was indeed closed, and then gave in to the darkness.

I'm told they found me sleeping with my back against the shield door, making sure it couldn't accidentally come open.

I was lying on my back when I came to, and the first thing I saw when I opened my eyes was Kate Epstein's face. "How do you feel?" she asked.

"Fine," I told her, frowning as I glanced around. This wasn't my cabin . . . With a start I recognized the humming in my ear. "What the hell am I doing in Lanton's cabin?" I growled.

Kate shrugged and reached over my shoulder, shutting off the neural tracer. "We needed Dr Lanton's neural equipment, and the tracer wasn't supposed to be moved. A variant of the mountain/Mohammed problem, I guess you could say."

I grunted. "How'd the point maneuver go? Was Alana able to figure out a correction factor?"

"It went perfectly well," Alana's voice came from my right.

I turned my head, to find her sitting next to the door. "I think we're out of the woods now, Pall – that four-point-four physical rotation turned out to be more like nine point one once the coil was out of the way. If Chileogu's right about reversibility applying here, we should be back in our own universe now. I guess we won't know for sure until we go through the next point and reach Earth."

"Is that nine point one with or without a correction factor?" I asked, my stomach tightening in anticipation. We might not be out of the woods quite yet.

"No correction needed," she said. "The images on the bridge stayed rock-steady the whole time."

"But . . . I saw them shifting."

"Yes, you told us that. Our best guess – excuse me; Pascal's best guess – is that you were getting that because you were moving relative to the field generator, that if you'd made a complete loop around it you would've come back to the original cascade pattern again. Chileogu's trying to prove that mathematically, but I doubt he'll be able to until he gets to better facilities."

"Uh-huh." Something wasn't quite right here. "You say I told you about the images? When?"

Alana hesitated, looked at Kate. "Actually, Captain," the doctor said gently, "you've been conscious quite a bit during the past four days. The reason you don't remember any of it is that the connection between your short-term and long-term memories got a little scrambled – probably another effect of your jaunt across all those field lines. It looks like that part's healed itself, though, so you shouldn't have any more memory problems."

"Oh, great. What sort of problems will I have more of?"

"Nothing major. You might have balance difficulties for a while, and you'll likely have a mild migraine or two within the next couple of weeks. But indications are that all of it is very temporary."

I looked back at Alana. "Four days. We'll need to set up our last calibration run soon."

"All taken care of," she assured me. "We're turning around later today to get our velocity vector pointing back toward Taimyr again, and we'll be able to do the run tomorrow."

"Who's going to handle it?"

"Who do you think?" she snorted. "Rik, Lanton, and me, with maybe some help from Pascal."

I'd known that answer was coming, but it still made my mouth go dry. "No way," I told her, struggling to sit up. "You aren't going to go through this hell. I can manage – "

"Ease up, Pall," Alana interrupted me. "Weren't you paying attention? The real angle doesn't drift when the Ming metal is moved, and that means we can shut down the field generator while I'm taking the coil from here to One Hold again."

I sank back onto the bed, feeling foolish. "Oh. Right."

Getting to her feet, Alana came over to me and patted my shoulder. "Don't worry," she said in a kinder tone. "We've got things under control. You've done the hard part; just relax and let us do the rest."

"Okay," I agreed, trying to hide my misgivings.

It was just as well that I did. Thirty-eight hours later Alana used our last gram of fuel in a flawless bit of flying that put us into a deep Earth orbit. The patrol boats that had responded to her emergency signal were waiting there, loaded with the fuel we would need to land.

Six hours after that, we were home.

They checked me into a hospital, just to be on the safe side, and the next four days were filled with a flurry of tests, medical interviews, and bumpy wheelchair rides. Surprisingly – to me, anyway – I was also nailed by two media types who wanted the more traditional type of interview. Apparently, the *Dancer*'s trip to elsewhere and back was getting a fair amount of publicity. Just how widespread the coverage was, though, I didn't realize until my last day there, when an official-looking CompNote was delivered to my room.

It was from Lord Hendrik.

I snapped the sealer and unfolded the paper. The first couple of paragraphs – the greetings, congratulations on my safe return, and such – I skipped over quickly, my eyes zeroing in on the business portion of the letter:

As you may or may not know, I have recently come out of semi-retirement to serve on the Board of Directors of TranStar

Enterprises, headquartered here in Nairobi. With excellent contacts both in Africa and in the so-called Black Colony chain, our passenger load is expanding rapidly, and we are constantly on the search for experienced and resourceful pilots we can entrust them to. The news reports of your recent close call brought you to my mind again after all these years, and I thought you might be interested in discussing –

A knock on the door interrupted my reading. "Come in," I called, looking up.

It was Alana. "Hi, Pall, how are you doing?" she asked, walking over to the bed and giving me a brief once-over. In one hand she carried a slender plastic portfolio.

"Bored silly," I told her. "I think I'm about ready to check out – they've finished all the standard tests without finding anything, and I'm tired of lying around while they dream up new ones."

"What a shame," she said with mock sorrow. "And after I brought you all this reading material, too." She hefted the portfolio.

"What is it, your resignation?" I asked, trying to keep my voice light. There was no point making this any more painful for either of us than necessary.

But she just frowned. "Don't be silly. It's a whole batch of new contracts I've picked up for us in the past few days. Some really good ones, too, from name corporations. I think people are starting to see what a really good carrier we are."

I snorted. "Aside from the thirty-six or whatever penalty clauses we invoked on this trip?"

"Oh, that's all in here too. The Swedish Institute's not even going to put up a fight – they're paying off everything, including your hospital bills and the patrol's rescue fee. Probably figured Lanton's glitch was going to make them look bad enough without them trying to chisel us out of damages, too." She hesitated, and an odd expression flickered across her face. "Were you really expecting me to jump ship?"

"I was about eighty per cent sure," I said, fudging my estimate down about nineteen points. "After all, this is where Rik Bradley's going to be, and you . . . rather like him. Don't you?"

She shrugged. "I don't know *what* I feel for him, to be perfectly honest. I like him, sure – like him a lot. But my life's out there" – she gestured skyward – "and I don't think I can give that up for anyone. At least, not for him."

"You could take a leave of absence," I told her, feeling like a prize fool but determined to give her every possible option. "Maybe once you spend some real time on a planet, you'd find you like it."

"And maybe I wouldn't," she countered. "And when I decided I'd had enough, where would the *Dancer* be? Probably nowhere I'd ever be able to get to you." She looked me straight in the eye and all traces of levity vanished from her voice. "Like I told you once before, Pall, I can't afford to lose *any* of my friends."

I took a deep breath and carefully let it out. "Well. I guess that's all settled. Good. Now, if you'll be kind enough to tell the nurse out by the monitor station that I'm signing out, I'll get dressed and we'll get back to the ship."

"Great. It'll be good to have you back." Smiling, she disappeared out into the corridor.

Carefully, I got my clothes out of the closet and began putting them on, an odd mixture of victory and defeat settling into my stomach. Alana was staying with the *Dancer*, which was certainly what I'd wanted . . . and yet, I couldn't help but feel that in some ways her decision was more a default than a real, active choice. Was she coming back because she wanted to, or merely because we were a safer course than the set of unknowns that Bradley offered? If the latter, it was clear that her old burns weren't entirely healed; that she still had a way – maybe a long ways – to go. But that was all right. I may not have had the talent she did for healing bruised souls, but if time and distance were what she needed, the *Dancer* and I could supply her with both.

I was just sealing my boots when Alana returned. "Finished? Good. They're getting your release ready, so let's go. Don't forget your letter," she added, pointing at Lord Hendrik's CompNote.

"This? It's nothing," I told her, crumpling it up and tossing it toward the waste basket. "Just some junk mail from an old admirer."

Six months later, on our third point out from Prima, a new image of myself in liner captain's white appeared in my cascade pattern. I looked at it long and hard . . . and then did something I'd never done before for such an image.

I wished it lots of luck.

A DANCE TO STRANGE MUSICS

Gregory Benford

Two of the great core themes of science fiction are the first-contact story and the problem story. In this story, you get both. It's one thing trying to solve a seemingly unsolvable or intractable problem, but when that problem takes place on an especially unusual alien world, the solution – if there is one – is even more complex, but no less fascinating.

Gregory Benford (b. 1941) is a professor of physics at the University of California, Irvine, specializing in plasma turbulence and astrophysics. He advises NASA on national space policy and has been heavily involved in the Mars exploration programme. His novels, The Martian Race *(1999) and* The Sunborn *(2005), are generally regarded as amongst the most authentic considerations of the race to and exploration of Mars. In 1995 he received the prestigious Lord Foundation award for scientific achievement.*

In the world of science fiction, Benford has received many awards including the Nebula for Timescape *(1980), still one of the most realistic time-travel novels. Among his more recent novels is* Cosm *(1998), involving an artificially created micro-universe, while some unusual worlds will be found in* Worlds Vast and Various *(2000), which contains this story.*

1

THE FIRST CREWED STARSHIP, the *Adventurer*, hung like a gleam-ing metallic moon among the gyre of strange worlds. Alpha Centauri was a triple-star system. A tiny flare star dogged the two big suns. At this moment in its eternal dance, the brilliant mote swung slightly toward Sol. Even though it was far from the two bright stars it was the nearest star to Earth: Proxima.

The two rich, yellow stars defined the Centauri system. Still prosaically termed A and B, they swam about each other; ignoring far Proxima.

The *Adventurer*'s astronomer, John, dopplered in on both stars, refreshing memories that were lodged deep. The climax of his career loomed before him. He felt apprehension, excitement, and a thin note of something like fear.

Sun B had an orbital eccentricity of 0.52 about its near-twin, with the extended axis of its ellipse 23.2 astronomical units long. This meant that the closest approach between A and B was a bit farther than the distance of Saturn from Sol.

A was a hard yellow-white glare, a G star with 1.08 the Sun's mass. Its companion, B, was a K-class star that glowed a reddish yellow, since it had 0.88 times the Sun's mass. B orbited with a period of 80 years around A. These two were about 4.8 billion years of age, slightly older than Sol. Promising.

Sun A's planetary children had stirred *Adventurer*'s expedition forth from Earth. From Luna, the system's single Earth-class planet was a mere mote, first detected by an oxygen absorption line in its spectrum. Only a wobbly image could be resolved by Earth's kilometer-sized interferometric telescope, a long bar with mirror-eyes peering in the spaces between A and B. Just enough of an image to entice.

A new Earth? John peered at its shrouded majesty, feeling the slight hum and surge of their ship beneath him. They were steadily moving inward, exploring the Newtonian gavotte of worlds in this two-sunned ballroom of the skies. Proxima was so far away, it was not even a wall-flower.

The Captain had named the fresh planet Shiva. It hung close to A, wreathed in water cirrus, a cloudball dazzling beneath. A's simmering yellow-white glare. Shimmering with promise, it had beckoned to John for years during their approach.

Like Venus, but the gases don't match, he thought. The complex tides of the star system massaged Shiva's depths, releasing gases and rippling the crust. John's many-frequency probings had told him a lot, but how to stitch data into a weave of a world? He was the first astronomer to try out centuries of speculative thinking on a real planet.

Shiva was drier than Earth, oceans taking only forty per cent of the surface. Its air was heavy in nitrogen, with giveaway tags of eighteen per cent oxygen and traces of carbon dioxide; remarkably Earth-like. Shiva was too warm for comfort, in human terms, but not fatally so; no Venusian runaway greenhouse had developed here. How had Shiva escaped that fate?

Long before, the lunar telescopes had made one great fact clear: the atmosphere here was far, far out of chemical equilibrium. Biological theory held that this was inevitably the signature of life. And indeed, the expedition's first mapping had shown that green, abundant life clung to two well-separated habitable belts, each beginning about thirty degrees from the equator.

Apparently the weird tidal effects of the Centauri system had stolen Shiva's initial polar tilt. Such steady workings had now made its spin align to within a single degree with its orbital angular momentum, so that conditions were steady and calm. The equatorial belt was a pale, arid waste of perpetual tornadoes and blistering gales.

John close-upped in all available bands, peering at the planet's crescent. Large blue-green seas, but no great oceans. Particularly, no water links between the two milder zones, so no marine life could migrate between them. Land migrations, calculations showed, were effectively blocked by the great equatorial desert Birds might make the long flight, John considered, but what evolutionary factor would condition them for such hardship? And what would be the reward? Why fight the jagged mountain chains? Better to lounge about in the many placid lakes.

A strange world, well worth the decades of grinding, slow, starship flight, John thought. He asked for the full display and the observing bowl opened like a flower around him. He swam above the entire disk of the Centauri system now, the images sharp and rich.

To be here at last! *Adventurer* was only a mote among many –
yet here, in the lap of strangeness. Far Centauri.

It did not occur to him that humanity had anything truly vital to
lose here. The doctrine of expansion and greater knowledge had
begun seven centuries before, making European cultures the inher-
itors of Earth. Although science had found unsettling truths, even
those revelations had not blunted the agenda of ever-greater
knowledge. After all, what harm could come from merely looking?

The truth about Shiva's elevated ocean only slowly emerged. Its
very existence was plainly impossible, and therefore was not at
first believed.

Odis was the first to notice the clues. Long days of sensory
immersion in the data-streams repaid her. She was rather proud of
having plucked such exotica from the bath of measurements their
expedition got from their probes – the tiny speeding, smart
spindle-eyes that now cruised all over the double-stars' realm.

The Centauri system was odd, but even its strong tides could not
explain this anomaly. Planets should be spherical, or nearly so;
Earth bulged but a fraction of a percent at its equator; due to its
spin. Not Shiva, though.

Odis found aberrations in this world's shape. The anomalies
were far away from the equator; principally at the 1,694-
kilometer-wide deep blue sea, immediately dubbed the Circular
Ocean. It sat in the southern hemisphere, its nearly perfect ring
hinting at an origin as a vast crater. Odis could not take her gaze
from it, a blue eye peeking coyly at them through the clouds: a
planet looking back.

Odis made her ranging measurements, gathering in her data like
number-clouds, inhaling their cottony wealth. Beneath her,
Adventurer prepared to go into orbit about Shiva.

She breathed in the banks of data-vapor, translated by kinesthetic
programming into intricate scent-inventories. Tangy, complex.

At first she did not believe the radar reflections. Contours leaped
into view, artfully sketched by the mapping radars. Calibrations
checked, though, so she tried other methods: slow, analytical,
tedious, hard to do in her excitement They gave the same result.

The Circular Ocean stood a full 10 kilometers higher than the
continent upon which it rested.

No mountains surrounded it. It sat like some cosmic magic trick, insolently demanding an explanation.

Odis presented her discovery at the daily Oversight Group meeting. There was outright skepticism, even curled lips of derision, snorts of disbelief. "The range of methods is considerable," she said adamantly. "These results cannot be wrong."

"Only thing to resolve this," a lanky geologist said, "is get an edge-on view."

"I hoped someone would say that." Odis smiled. "Do I have the authorised observing time?"

They gave it reluctantly. *Adventurer* was orbiting in a severe ellipse about Shiva's cloud-wrack. Her long swing brought her into a side view of the target area two days later. Odis used the full panoply of optical, IR, UV, and microwave instruments to peer at the Circular Ocean's perimeter, probing for the basin that supported the round slab of azure water.

There was none. No land supported the hanging sea.

This result was utterly clear. The Circular Ocean was 1.36 kilometers thick and a brilliant blue. Spectral evidence suggested water rich in salt, veined by thick currents. It looked exactly like an enormous, troubled mountain lake, with the mountain subtracted.

Beneath that layer there was nothing but the thick atmosphere. No rocky mountain range to support the ocean-in-air. Just a many-kilometer gap.

All other observations halted. The incontrovertible pictures showed an immense layer of unimaginable weight, blissfully poised above mere thin gases, contradicting all known mechanics. Until this moment Odis had been a lesser figure in the expedition. Now her work captivated everyone and she was the center of every conversation. The concrete impossibility yawned like an inviting abyss.

Lisa found the answer to Shiva's mystery, but no one was happy with it.

An atmospheric chemist, Lissa's job was mostly done well before they achieved orbit around Shiva. She had already probed and labeled the gases, shown clearly that they implied a thriving biology below. After that, she had thought, the excitement would shift elsewhere, to the surface observers.

Not so. Lissa took a deep breath and began speaking to the Oversight Group. She had to show that she was not wasting their time. With all eyes on the Circular Ocean, few cared for mere air.

Yet it was the key, Lissa told them. The Circular Ocean had intrigued her, too: so she looked at the mixture of oxygen, nitrogen, and carbon dioxide that apparently supported the floating sea. These proved perfectly ordinary, almost Earth-standard, except for one oddity. Their spectral lines were slightly split, so that she found two small spikes to the right and left of where each line should be.

Lissa turned from the images she projected before the Oversight Group. "The only possible interpretation," she said crisply, "is that an immensely strong electric field is inducing the tiny electric dipoles of these molecules to move. That splits the lines."

"An *electric* shift?" a grizzled skeptic called. "In a charge-neutral atmosphere? Sure, maybe when lightning flashes you could get a momentary effect, but – "

"It is steady."

"You looked for lightning?" a shrewd woman demanded.

"It's there, sure. We see it forking between the clouds below the Circular Ocean. But that's not what causes the electric fields."

"What does?" This from the grave captain, who never spoke in scientific disputes. All heads turned to him, then to Lissa.

She shrugged. "Nothing reasonable." It pained her to admit it, but ignorance was getting to be a common currency.

A voice called, "So there must be an impossibly strong electric field *everywhere* in that 10 kilometers of air below the ocean?" Murmurs of agreement. Worried frowns.

"Everywhere, yes." The bald truth of it stirred the audience. "Everywhere."

Tagore was in a hurry. Too much so.

He caromed off a stanchion but did not let that stop him from rebounding from the opposite wall, absorbing his momentum with his knees, and springing off with a full push. Rasters streaked his augmented vision, then flickered and faded.

He coasted by a full-view showing Shiva and the world below, a blazing crescent transcendent in its cloud-wrapped beauty. Tagore ignored the spectacle; marvels of the mind precccupied him.

He was carrying the answer to it all, he was sure of that. In his haste he did not even glance at how blue-tinged sunlight glinted from the Circular Ocean. The thick disk of open air below it made a clear line under the blue wedge. At this angle the floating water refracted sunlight around the still-darkened limb of the planet. The glittering azure jewel heralded dawn, serene in its impudent impossibility.

The youngest of the entire expedition, Tagore was a mere theorist. He had specialized in planetary formation at university, but managed to snag a berth on this expedition by developing a ready, quick facility at explaining vexing problems the observers turned up. That, and a willingness to do scutwork.

"Cap'n, I've got it," he blurted as he came through the hatch. The captain greeted him, sitting at a small oak desk, the only wood on the whole ship – then got to business. Tagore had asked for this audience because he knew the effect his theory could have on the others; so the captain should see first.

"The Circular Ocean is held up by electric field pressure," he announced. The captain's reaction was less than he had hoped: unblinking calm, waiting for more information.

"See, electromagnetic fields exert forces on the electrons in atoms," Tagore persisted, going through the numbers, talking fast. "The fields down there are so strong – I got that measurement out of Lissa's data – they can act like a steady support."

He went on to make comparisons: the energy density of a hand grenade, contained in every suitcase-sized volume of air. Even though the fields could simply stand there, as trapped waves, they had to suffer some losses. The power demands were *huge*. Plus, how the hell did such a gargantuan construction *work*?

By now Tagore was thoroughly pumped, oblivious to his audience. Finally the captain blinked and said, "Anything like this ever seen on Earth?"

"Nossir, not that I've ever heard."

"No natural process can do the stunt?"

"Nossir, not that I can imagine."

"Well, we came looking for something different."

Tagore did not know whether to laugh or not; the captain was unreadable. Was this what exploration was like – the slow anxiety of not knowing? On Earth such work had an abstract distance, but here . . .

He would rather have some other role. Bringing uncomfortable truths to those in power put him more in the spotlight than he wished.

Captain Badquor let the Tagore kid go on a bit longer before he said anything more. It was best to let these technical types sing their songs first. So few of them ever thought about anything beyond their own warblings.

He gave Tavore a captainly smile. Why did they all look so young? "So this whole thing on Shiva is artificial."

"Well, yeah, I suppose so . . ."

Plainly Tagore hadn't actually thought about that part very much; the wonder of such strong fields had stunned him. Well, it was stunning. "And all that energy, just used to hold up a lake?"

"I'm sure of it, sir. The numbers work out, see? I equated the pressure exerted by those electric fields, assuming they're trapped in the volume under the Circular Ocean, the way waves can get caught if they're inside a conducting box – "

"You think that ocean's a conductor?" Might as well show the kid that even the captain knew a little physics. In fact, though he never mentioned it, he had a doctorate from MIT. Not that he had learned much about command there.

"Uh, well, no. I mean, it is a fairly good conductor, but for my model, it's only a way of speaking – "

"It has salt currents, true? They could carry electrical currents." The captain rubbed his chin, the machinery of his mind trying to grasp how such a thing it could be. "Still, that doesn't explain why the thing doesn't evaporate away, at those altitudes."

"Uh, I really hadn't thought . . ."

The captain waved a hand. "Go on." *Sing for me.*

"Then the waves exert an upward force on the water every time they reflect from the underside of the ocean – "

"And transfer that weight down, on invisible waves, to the rock that's 10 kilometers below."

"Uh. yessir."

Tagore looked a bit constipated, bursting with enthusiasm, with the experience of the puzzle, but not knowing how to express it. The captain decided to have mercy on the kid. "Sounds good. Not any thing impossible about it."

"Except the size of it, sir."

"That's one way to put it."

"Sir?"

A curious, powerful feeling washed over the captain. Long decades of anticipation had steeled him, made him steady in the presence of the crew. But now he felt his sense of the room tilt, as though he were losing control of his status-space. The mind could go whirling off, out here in the inky immensities between twin alien suns. He frowned. "This thing is bigger than anything humanity ever built. And there's not a clue what it's for. The majesty of it, son, that's what strikes me. Grandeur."

John slipped into his helmet and Shiva enclosed him. *To be wrapped in a world* – His pov shifted, strummed, arced with busy fretworks – then snapped into solidity, stabilized.

Astronomy had become intensely interactive in the past century, the spectral sensoria blanketing the viewer. Through *Adventurer*'s long voyage he had tuned the system to his every whim. Now it gave him a nuanced experience like a true, full-bodied immersion.

He was eager to immerse in himself in the feel of Shiva, in full 3-D wraparound. Its crescent swelled below like a ripe, mottled fruit. He plunged toward it. A planet, fat in bandwidth.

For effect – decades before he had been a sky-diver – John had arranged the data-fields so that he accelerated into it. From their arcing orbit he shot directly toward Shiva's disk. Each mapping rushed toward him, exploding upward in finer detail. *There* –

The effect showed up first in the grasslands of the southern habitable belt. He slewed toward the plains, where patterns emerged in quilted confusions. After Tagore's astonishing theory about the Circular Ocean – odd, so audacious, and coming from a nonscientist – John had to be ready for anything. Somewhere in the data-fields must lurk the clue to who or what had made the ocean.

Below the great grassy shelves swelled. But in places the grass was thin. Soon he saw why. The natural grass was only peeking out across plains covered with curious orderly patterns – hexagonals folding into triangles where necessary to cover hills and valleys, right up to the muddy banks of the slow-moving brown rivers.

Reflection in the UV showed that the tiles making this pattern were often small, but with some the size of houses, meters thick . . . and moving. They all jostled and worked with restless energy, to no obvious purpose.

Alive? The UV spectrum broke down into a description of a complex polymer. Cross-linked chains bonded at many oblique angles to each other, flexing like sleek micro-muscles.

John brought in chemists, biologists in an ensemble suite: Odis and Lissa claimed in the scientific choir. In the wraparound display he felt them by the shadings they gave the data.

The tiles, Lissa found, fed on their own sky. Simple sugars rained from the clotted air, the fruit of an atmosphere that resembled an airy chicken soup. *Atmospheric electro-chemistry seems responsible, somehow*, Lissa sent. Floating microbial nuggets moderated the process.

The tiles were prime eaters. Oxidizing radicals the size of golf balls patroled their sharp linear perimeters. These pack-like rollers attacked invader chemicals, ejecting most, harvesting those they could use.

Lissa brought in two more biologists, who of course had many questions. *Are these tiles like great turtles?* one ventured, then chuckled uneasily. They yearned to flip one over.

Diurnal or nocturnal? *Some are, most aren't.*

Are there any small ones? A *few*.

Do they divide by fission? *No, but* . . . Nobody understood the complicated process the biologists witnessed. Reproduction seems a tricky matter.

There is some periodicity to their movements, some slow rhythms, and particularly a fast Fourier-spectrum spike at 1.27 second – but again, no clear reason for it.

Could they be all one life form? – could that be?

A whole planet taken over by a tiling-thing that co-opts all resources?

The senior biologists scoffed. How could a species evolve to have only one member? And an ecosystem – a whole world! – with so few parts?

Evolution ruled that out. Bio-evolution, that is. But not social evolution.

John plunged further into the intricate matrices of analysis. The endless tile-seas cloaking mountains and valleys shifted and milled, fidgety, only occasionally leaving bare ground visible as a square fissioned into triangles. Oblongs met and butted with fevered energy.

Each hemisphere of the world was similar, though the tiles in the north had different shapes – pentagonals, mostly. Nowhere did the tiles cross rivers but they could ford streams. A Centauri variant of chlorophyll was everywhere, in the oceans and rivers, but not in the Circular Ocean.

The ground was covered with a thin grass, the sprigs living off the momentary sunlight that slipped between the edges in the jostling, jiggling, bumping, and shaking. Tiles that moved over the grass sometimes cropped it, sometimes not, leaving stubs that seemed to have been burned off.

The tiles' fevered dance ran incessantly, without sleep. Could these things be performing some agitated discourse, a lust-fest without end?

John slowed his descent. The tiles were a shock. Could these be the builders of the Circular Ocean? Time for the biologists to get to work.

The computer folk thought one way, the biologists – after an initial rout, when they rejected the very possibility of a single entity filling an entire biosphere – quite another.

After some friction, their views converged somewhat. A biologist remarked that the larger tiles came together like dwarf houses making love . . . gingerly, always presenting the same angles and edges.

Adventurer had scattered micro-landers all over the world. These showed only weak electromagnetic fringing fields among the tiles. Their deft collisions seemed almost like neurons in a two-dimensional plan.

The analogy stirred the theorists. Over the usual after-shift menu of beer, soy nuts, and friendly insults, one maven of the digital realm ventured an absurd idea: could the planet have become a computer?

Everybody laughed. They kidded the advocate of this notion . . . and then lapsed into frowning silence. Specialists find quite unsettling those ideas that cross disciplines.

Could a species turn itself into a biological computer? The tiles did rub and caress each other in systematic ways. Rather than carrying information in digital fashion, maybe they used a more complex language of position and angle, exploiting their planar geometry. If so, the information density flowing among them was immense. Every collision carried a sort of Euclidean talk, possibly rich in nuance.

The computer analogy brought up a next question – not that some big ones weren't left behind, perhaps lying in wait to bite them on their conceptual tail. Could the tiles know anything more than themselves? Or were they strange, geometroid solipsists? Should they call the tiles a single It?

Sealed inside a cosmos of its own making, was It even in principle interested in the outside world? Alpha Centauri fed It gratuitous energy, the very soupy air fueled It: the last standing power on the globe. What reason did it have to converse with the great Outside?

Curiosity, perhaps? The biologists frowned at the prospect. Curiosity in early prehumans was rewarded in the environment The evolving ape learned new tricks, found fresh water, killed a new kind of game, invented a better way to locate those delicious roots and the world duly paid it back.

Apparently – *but don't ask us why just yet!* the biologists cried – the game was different here. What reward came from the tiles' endless smacking together?

So even if the visiting humans rang the conceptual doorbell on the tile-things, maybe nobody would answer. Maybe nobody was home.

Should they try?

John and Odis and Lissa, Tagore and the captain, over a hundred other crew – they all pondered.

2

While they wrestled with the issue, exploration continued.

A flitter craft flew near the elevated ocean and inspected its supporting volume with distant sensors and probing telescopes. Even Shiva's weather patterns seemed wary of the Circular Ocean. Thunderclouds veered away from the gap between the ocean and the rugged land below. In the yawning height clouds formed but quickly dispersed as if dissolved by unseen forces.

Birds flew through the space, birds like feathery kites.

Somehow they had missed noticing this class of life. Even the microlanders had not had the speed to capture their darting lives. And while the kite-birds did seem to live mostly on tiny floating balloon-creatures that hovered in the murky air of the valleys, they were unusually common beneath the Circular Ocean.

John proposed that he send in a robo-craft of bird size, to measure physical parameters in the heart of the gap. Captain Badquor approved. The shops fabricated a convincing fake. Jet-powered and featuring fake feathers, it was reasonably convincing.

John flew escort in a rocket-plane. The bird-probe got seventeen kilometers inside and then disappeared in a dazzling blue-white electrical discharge. Telemetry showed why: the Circular Ocean's support was a complex weave of electrical fields, supplying an upward pressure. These fields never exceeded the breakdown level of a megavolt per meter, above which Shiva's atmosphere would ionize. Field strength was about a million volts per meter.

The robo-craft had hit a critical peak in the field geometry. A conductor, it caused a flashover that dumped millions of watts into the bird within a millisecond.

As the cinder fell, John banked away from his monitoring position five kilometers beyond the gap perimeter. There was no particular reason to believe a discharge that deep within the gap would somehow spread, engulfing the region in a spontaneous discharge of the enormous stored energies. Surely whoever – no, whatever – had designed the Circular Ocean's supports would not allow the electromagnetic struts to collapse from the frying of a mere bird.

But something like that happened. The system responded.

The burned brown husk of the pseudo-bird turned lazily as it fell and sparks jumped from it. These formed a thin orange discharge that fed on the energy coursing through the now-atomized bird. The discharging line snaked away, following unerringly the bird's prior path. It raced at close to the speed of light back along the arc.

The system had *memory*, John realized. He saw a tendril of light at the corner of his vision as he turned his flitter craft. He had time only to think that it was like a huge, fast finger jabbing at him. An apt analogy, though he had no time to consider ironies. The orange discharge touched the flitter. John's hair stood on end as charge flooded into the interior.

Ideally, electrons move to the outer skin of a conductor. But when antennae connect deep into the interior, circuits can close.

Something had intended to dump an immense charge on the flitter, the origin of the pseudo bird. Onboard instruments momentarily reported a charge exceeding seventeen coulombs. By then John had, for all intents and purposes ceased to exist as an organized bundle of electrical information.

John's death did yield a harvest of data. Soon enough Lissa saw the true function of the Circular Ocean. It was but an ornament, perhaps an artwork.

Ozone fizzed all around it. Completely natural-seeming, the lake crowned a huge cavity that functioned like a steady, standing laser.

The electrical fields both supported the Ocean and primed the atoms of the entire atmosphere they permeated. Upon stimulus – from the same system that had fried John – the entire gap could release the stored energy into an outgoing electromagnetic wave. It was an optical bolt, powerful and complex in structure – triggered by John.

Twice more the ocean's gap discharged naturally as the humans orbited Shiva. The flash lasted but a second, not enough to rob the entire ocean structure of its stability. The emission sizzled out through the atmosphere and off into space.

Laser beams are tight, and this one gave away few of its secrets. The humans, viewing it from a wide angle, caught little of the complex structure and understood less.

Puzzled, mourning John, they returned to a careful study of the Shiva surface. Morale was low. The captain felt that a dramatic gesture could lift their spirits. He would have to do it himself.

To Captain Badquor fell the honor of the first landing. A show of bravery would overcome the crew's confusions, surely. He would direct the complex exploring machines in real-time, up close.

He left the landing craft fully suited up, impervious to the complex biochem mix of the atmosphere.

The tiles jostled downhill from him. Only in the steep flanks of this equatorial mountain range did the tiles not endlessly surge. Badquor's boots crunched on a dry, crusty soil. He took samples, sent them back by runner-robo.

A warning signal from orbit: the tiles in his area seemed more agitated than usual. A reaction to his landing?

The tile polygons were leathery, with no obvious way to sense him. No eyes or ears. They seemed to caress the ground lovingly, though Badquor knew that they tread upon big crabbed feet.

He went forward cautiously. Below, the valley seemed alive with rippling turf, long waves sweeping to the horizon in the twinkling of an instant. He got an impression of incessant pace, of enthusiasm unspoken but plainly endless.

His boots were well insulated thermally, but not electrically; thus, when his headphones crackled he thought he was receiving noise in his transmission lines. The dry sizzle began to make his skin tingle.

Only when the frying noise rose and buried all other signals did he blink, alarmed. By then it was too late.

Piezoelectric energy arises when mechanical stress massages rock. Pressure on an electrically neutral stone polarizes it at the lattice level by slightly separating the center of positive charge from the negative. The lattice moves, the shielding electron cloud does not. This happens whenever the rock crystal structure does not have a center of structural symmetry, and so occurs in nearly all bedrock.

The effect was well known on Earth, though weak. Stressed strata sometimes discharged, sending glow discharges into the air. Such plays of light were now a standard precursor warning of earthquakes. But Earth was a mild case.

Tides stressed the stony mantle of Shiva, driven by the eternal gravitational gavotte of both stars, A and B. Periodic alignments of the two stars stored enormous energy in the full body of the planet. Evolution favored life that could harness these electrical currents that rippled through the planetary crust. This, far more than the kilowatt per square meter of sunlight, drove the tile-forms.

All this explanation came after the fact, and seemed obvious in retrospect. The piezoelectric energy source was naturally dispersed and easily harvested. A sizzle of electric micro-fields fed the tiles' large, crusted footpads. After all, on Earth fish and eels routinely use electrical fields as both sensors and weapons.

This highly organized ecology sensed Badquor's intrusion immediately. To them, he probably had many of the signatures of a power-parasite. These were small creatures like stick insects that Badquor himself had noticed after landing; they lived by stealing electrical charge from the tile polygons.

Only later analysis made it clear what had happened. The inter-linked commonality of piezo-driven life moved to expel the intruder by overpowering it – literally.

Badquor probably had no inkling of how strange a fate he had met, for the several hundreds of amperes caused his muscles to seize up, his heart to freeze in a clamped frenzy, and his synapses to discharge in a last vision that burned into his eyes a vision of an incandescent rainbow.

Lissa blinked. The spindly trees looked artificial but weren't.

Groves of them spiraled around hills, zigzagged up razor-backed ridges and shot down the flanks of denuded rock piles. Hostile terrain for any sort of tree that earthly biologists understood. The trees, she noted, had growing patterns that bore no discernible relation to water flow, sunlight exposure, or wind patterns.

That was why Lissa went in to see. Her team of four had already sent the smart-eyes, rugged robots, and quasi-intelligent proces-sors. Lightweight, patient, durable, these ambassadors had dis-covered little. Time for something a bit more interactive on the ground.

That is, a person. Captain Badquor's sacrifice had to mean something, and his death had strengthened his crew's resolve.

Lissa landed with electrically insulated boots. They now under-stood the piezoelectric ecology in broad outline, or thought they did. Courageous caution prevailed.

The odd beanpole trees made no sense. Their gnarled branches followed a fractal pattern and had no leaves. Still, there was ample fossil evidence – gathered by automatic prospectors sent down earlier – that the bristly trees had evolved from more traditional trees within the past few milllon years. But they had come so quickly into the geological record that Lissa suspected they were "driven" evolution – biological technology.

She carefully pressed her instruments against the sleek black sides of the trees. Their surfaces seethed with electric currents, but none strong enough to be a danger.

On Earth, the natural potential difference between the surface and the upper atmosphere provides a voltage drop of a hundred volts for each meter in height A woman two meters tall could be at a significantly higher potential than her feet, especially if her feet had picked up extra electrons by walking across a thick carpet.

On Shiva this effect was much larger. The trees, Lissa realized, were harvesting the large potentials available between Shiva's rocky surface and the charged layers skating across the upper reaches of the atmosphere.

The "trees" were part of yet another way to reap the planetary energies – whose origin was ultimately the blunt forces of gravity, mass and torque – all for the use of life.

The potential-trees felt Lissa's presence quickly enough. They had evolved defenses against poachers who would garner stray voltages and currents from the unwary.

In concert – for the true living entity was the grove, comprising perhaps a million trees – they reacted.

Staggering back to her lander, pursued by vagrant electrical surges through both ground and the thick air, she shouted into her suit mike her conclusions. These proved useful in later analysis.

She survived, barely.

3

When the sum of these incidents sank in, the full import become clear. The entire Shiva ecology was electrically driven. From the planet's rotation and strong magnetosphere, from the tidal stretching of the Centauri system, from geological rumblings and compressions, came far more energy than mere sunlight could ever provide.

Seen this way, all biology was an afterthought. The geologists, who had been feeling rather neglected lately, liked this turn of events quite a bit. They gave lectures on Shiva seismology which, for once, everybody attended.

To be sure, vestigial chemical processes still ran alongside the vastly larger stores of charges and potentials; these were important for understanding the ancient biosphere that had once governed here.

Much could be learned from classic, old-style biology: from

samples of the bushes and wiry trees and leafy plants, from the small insect-like creatures of ten legs each, from the kite-birds, from the spiny, knife-like fish that prowled the lakes.

All these forms were ancient, unchanging. Something had fixed them in evolutionary amber. Their forms had not changed for many hundreds of millions of years.

There had once been higher forms, the fossil record showed. Something like mammals, even large tubular things that might have resembled reptiles.

But millions of years ago they had abruptly ceased. Not due to some trauma, either – they all ended together, but without the slightest sign of a shift in the biosphere, of disease or accident.

The suspicion arose that something had simply erased them, having no further need.

The highest form of life – defined as that with the highest brain/body volume ratio – had vanished slightly later than the others. It had begun as a predator wider than it was tall, and shaped like a turtle, though without a shell.

It had the leathery look of the tile-polygons, though.

Apparently it had not followed the classic mode of pursuit, but rather had outwitted its prey, boxing it in by pack-animal tactics. Later, it had arranged deadfalls and traps. Or so the sociobiologists suspected, from narrow evidence.

These later creatures had characteristic bony structures around the large, calculating brain. Subsequent forms were plainly intelligent, and had been engaged in a strange manipulation of their surroundings. Apparently without ever inventing cities or agriculture, they had domesticated many other species.

Then, the other high life forms vanished from the fossil record. The scheme of the biosphere shifted. Electrical plant forms, like the spindly trees and those species that fed upon piezoelectric energy, came to the fore.

Next, the dominant, turtle-like predators vanished as well. Had they been dispatched?

On Shiva, all the forms humans thought of as life, plant and animal alike, were now in fact mere . . . well, maintenance workers. They served docilely in a far more complex ecology. They were as vital and as unnoticeable and as ignorable as the mitochondria in the stomach linings of *Adventurer*'s crew.

Of the immensely more complex electrical ecology, they were only beginning to learn even the rudiments. If Shiva was in a sense a single interdependent, colonial organism, what were its deep rules?

By focusing on the traditional elements of the organic biosphere they had quite missed the point.

Then the Circular Ocean's laser discharged again. The starship was nearer the lancing packet of emission, and picked up a side lobe. They learned more in a millisecond than they had in a month.

A human brain has about ten billion neurons, each connected with about 100,000 of its neighbors. A firing neuron carries one bit of information. But the signal depends upon the path it follows, and in the labyrinth of the brain there are 1,015 pathways. This torrent of information flows through the brain in machine-gun packets of electrical impulses, coursing through myriad synapses. Since a single book has about a million bits in it, a single human carries the equivalent of a billion books of information – all riding around in a two-kilogram lump of electrically wired jelly.

Only one to ten per cent of a human brain's connections are firing at any one time. A neuron can charge and discharge at best a hundred times in a second. Human brains, then, can carry roughly 1,010 bits of information in a second.

Thus, to read out a brain containing 1,015 bits would take 100,000 seconds, or about a day.

The turtle-predators had approximately the same capacity. Indeed, there were theoretical arguments that a mobile, intelligent species would carry roughly the same load of stored information as a human could. For all its limitations, the human brain has an impressive data-store capabililty, even if, in many, it frequently went unused.

The Circular Ocean had sent discrete packets of information of about this size, 1015 bits compressed into its powerful millisecond pulse. The packets within it were distinct, well bordered by banks of marker code. The representation was digital, an outcome mandated by the fact that any number enjoys a unique representation only in base 2.

Within the laser's millisecond burst were fully a thousand brain equivalent transmissions. A trove. What the packets actually said was quite undecipherable.

The target was equally clear: a star 347 light years away. Targeting was precise; there could be no mistake. Far cheaper if one knows the recipient, to send a focused message, rather than to broadcast wastefully in the low-grade, narrow bandwidth radio frequencies.

Earth had never heard such powerful signals, of course, not because humans were not straining to hear, but because Shiva was ignoring them.

After Badquor's death and Lissa's narrow escape, *Adventurer* studied the surface with elaborately planned robot expeditions. The machines skirted the edge of a vast tile-plain, observing the incessant jiggling, fed on the piezoelectric feast welling from the crusted rocks.

After some days, they came upon a small tile lying still. The others had forced it out of the eternal jostling jam. It lay stiff and discoloured, baking in the double suns' glare. Scarcely a meter across and thin, it looked like construction material for a patio in Arizona.

The robots carried it off. Nothing pursued them. The tile-thing was dead, apparently left for mere chemical processes to harvest its body.

This bonanza kept the ship's biologists sleepless for weeks as they dissected it. Gray-green, hard of carapace, and extraordinarily complex in its nervous system – these they had expected. But the dead alien devoted fully a quarter of its body volume to a brain that was broken into compact, separate segments.

The tile-creatures were indeed part of an ecology driven by electrical harvesting of the planetary energies. The tiles alone used a far higher percentage of the total energetic wealth than did Earth's entire sluggish, chemically driven biosphere.

And deep within the tile-thing was the same bone structure as they had seen in the turtle-like predator. The dominant, apparently intelligent species had not gone to the stars. Instead, they had formed the basis of an intricate ecology of the mind.

Then the engineers had a chance to study the tile-thing, and found even more.

As a manifestation of their world, the tiles were impressive. Their neurological system fashioned a skein of interpretations, of lived scenarios, of expressive renderings – all apparently for communication outward in well-sculpted bunches of electrical information, intricately coded. They had large computing capacity and ceaselessly exchanged great gouts of information with each other. This explained their rough skins, which maximized piezo connections when they rubbed against each other. And they "spoke" to each other through the ground, as well, where their big, crabbed feet carried currents, too.

Slowly it dawned that Shiva was an unimaginably huge computational complex, operating in a state of information flux many orders of magnitude greater than the entire sum of human culture. Shiva was to Earth as humans are to beetles.

The first transmissions about Shiva's biosphere reached Earth four years later. Already, in a culture more than a century into the dual evolution of society and computers, there were disturbing parallels.

Some communities in the advanced regions of Earth felt that real-time itself was a pallid, ephemeral experience. After all, one could not archive it for replay, savor it, return until it became a true part of oneself. Real-time was for one time only, then lost.

So increasingly, some people lived instead in worlds made totally volitional – truncated, chopped, governed by technologies they could barely sense as ghostlike constraints on an otherwise wide compass.

"Disposable realities," some sneered – but the fascination of such lives was clear.

Shiva's implication was extreme: an entire world could give itself over to life-as-computation.

Could the intelligent species of Shiva have executed a huge fraction of their fellow inhabitants? And then themselves gone extinct? For what? Could they have fled – perhaps from the enormity of their own deeds?

Or had those original predators become the tile-polygons?

The *Adventurer* crew decided to return to Shiva's surface in force, to crack the puzzles. They notified Earth and descended.

Shortly after, the Shiva teams ceased reporting back to Earth. Through the hiss of interstellar static there came no signal.

After years of anxious waiting, Earth launched the second

expedition. They too survived the passage. Cautiously they approached Shiva.

Adventurer still orbited the planet, but was vacant.

This time they were wary. Further years of hard thinking and careful study passed before the truth began to come.

4

{— John/Odis/Lissa/Tagore/Cap'n —}
—all assembled/congealed/thickened —
—into a composite veneer persona—
—on the central deck of their old starship,
—to greet the second expedition.
Or so they seemed to intend.

They came up from the Shiva surface in a craft not of human construction. The sleek, webbed thing seemed to ride upon electromagnetic winds.

They entered through the main lock, after using proper hailing protocols.

But what came through the lock was an ordered array of people no one could recognize as being from the *Adventurer* crew

They seemed younger, unworn. Smooth, bland features looked out at the bewildered second expedition. The party moved together, maintaining a hexagonal array with a constant spacing of four centimeters. Fifty-six pairs of eyes surveyed the new Earth ship, each momentarily gazing at a different portion of the field of view as if to memorize only a portion, for later integration.

To convey a sentence, each person spoke a separate word. The effect was jarring, with no clue to how an individual knew what to say, or when, for the lines were not rehearsed. The group reacted to questions in a blur of scattershot talk, words like volleys.

Sentences ricocheted and bounced around the assembly deck where the survivors of the first expedition all stood, erect and clothed in a shapeless gray garment. Their phrases made sense when isolated, but the experience of hearing them was unsettling. Long minutes stretched out before the second expedition realized that these hexagonally spaced humans were trying to greet them, to induct them into something they termed the Being Suite.

This offer made, the faces within the hexagonal array began to show separate expressions. Tapes of this encounter show regular facial alterations with a fixed periodicity of 1.27 seconds. Each separate face racheted, jerking among a menu of finely graduated countenances – anger, sympathy, laughter, rage, curiosity, shock, puzzlement, ecstasy – flickering, flickering, endlessly flickering.

A witness later said that it were as if the hexagonals (as they came to be called) knew that human expressiveness centered on the face, and so had slipped into a kind of language of facial aspects. This seemed natural to them, and yet the 1.27 second pace quickly gave the witnesses a sense of creeping horror.

High-speed tapes of the event showed more. Beneath the 1.27 frequency there was a higher harmonic, barely perceptible to the human eye, in which other expressions shot across the hexagonals' faces. These were like waves, muscular twitches that washed over the skin like tidal pulls.

This periodicity was the same as the tile-polygons had displayed. The subliminal aspects were faster than the conscious human optical processor can manage, yet research showed that they were decipherable in the target audience.

Researchers later concluded that this rapid display was the origin of the growing unease felt by the second expedition. The hexagonals said nothing throughout all this.

The second expedition crew described the experience as uncanny, racking, unbearable. Their distinct impression was that the first expedition now manifested as like the *tile-things*. Such testimony was often followed by an involuntary twitch.

Tapes do not yield such an impression upon similar audiences: they have become the classic example of having to be in a place and time to sense the meaning of an event. Still, the tapes are disturbing, and access is controlled. Some Earth audiences experienced breakdowns after viewing them.

But the second expedition agreed even more strongly upon a second conclusion. Plainly, the *Adventurer* expedition had joined the computational labyrinth that was Shiva. How they were seduced was never clear; the second expedition feared finding out.

Indeed, their sole, momentary brush with {— John/Odis/Lissa/ Tagore/Cap'n . . . —} convinced the second expedition that there was no point in pursuing the maze of Shiva.

The hostility radiating from the second expedition soon drove the hexagonals back into their ship and away. The fresh humans from Earth felt something gut-level and instinctive, a reaction beyond words. The hexagonals retreated without showing a coherent reaction. They simply turned and walked away, holding to the four centimeter spacing. The 1.27 second flicker stopped and they returned to a bland expression, alert but giving nothing away.

The vision these hexagonals conveyed was austere, jarring . . . and yet, plainly intended to be inviting.

The magnitude of their failure was a measure of the abyss that separated the two parties. The hexagonals were now both more and less than human.

The hexagonals left recurrent patterns that told much, though only in retrospect. Behind the second expedition's revulsion lay a revelation: of a galaxy spanned by intelligences formal and remote, far developed beyond the organic stage. Such intelligences had been born variously, of early organic forms, or of later machine civilizations which had arisen upon the ashes of extinct organic societies. The gleam of the stars was in fact a metallic glitter.

This vision was daunting enough: of minds so distant and strange, hosted in bodies free of sinew and skin. But there was something more, an inexpressible repulsion in the manifestation of {— John/Odis/Lissa/Tagore/Cap'n . . . —}.

A nineteenth-century philosopher, Goethe, had once remarked that if one stared into the abyss long enough, it stared back. This proved true. A mere moment's lingering look, quiet and almost casual, was enough. The second expedition panicked. It is not good to stare into a pit that has no bottom.

They had sensed the final implication of Shiva's evolution. To alight upon such interior worlds of deep, terrible exotica exacted a high cost: the body itself. Yet all those diverse people had joined the *syntony* of Shiva – an electrical harmony that danced to unheard musics. Whether they had been seduced, or even raped, would forever be unclear.

Out of the raw data-stream the second expedition could sample transmissions from the tile-things, as well. The second expedition caught a link-locked sense of repulsive grandeur. Still organic in their basic organization, still tied to the eternal wheel of birth and death, the tiles had once been lords of their own world, holding dominion over all they knew.

Now they were patient, willing drones in a hive they could not comprehend. But – and here human terms undoubtedly fail – they loved their immersion.

Where was their consciousness housed? Partially in each, or in some displaced, additive sense? There was no clear way to test either idea.

The tile-things were like durable, patient machines that could best carry forward the first stages of a grand computation. Some biologists compared them with insects, but no evolutionary mechanism seemed capable of yielding a reason why a species would give itself over to computation. The insect analogy died, unable to predict the response of the polygons to stimulus, or even why they existed.

Or was their unending jostling only in the service of calculation? The tile-polygons would not say. They never responded to overtures.

The Circular Ocean's enormous atmospheric laser pulsed regularly, as the planet's orbit and rotation carried the laser's field of targeting onto a fresh partner-star system. Only then did the system send its rich messages out into the galaxy. The pulses carried mind-packets of unimaginable data, bound on expeditions of the intellect.

The second expedition reported, studied. Slowly at first, and then accelerating, the terror overcame them.

They could not fathom Shiva, and steadily they lost crew members to its clasp. Confronting the truly, irreducibly exotic, there is no end of ways to perish.

In the end they studied Shiva from a distance, no more. Try as they could, they always met a barrier in their understanding. Theories came and went, fruitlessly. Finally, they fled.

It is one thing to speak of embracing the new, the fresh, the strange. It is another to feel that one is an insect, crawling across a page of the *Encyclopedia Britannica*, knowing only that something vast is passing by beneath, all without your sensing more than a yawning vacancy. Worse, the lack was clearly in oneself, and was irredeemable.

This was the first contact humanity had with the true nature of the galaxy. It would not be the last. But the sense of utter and complete diminishment never left the species, in all the strange millennia that rolled on thereafter.

PALINDROMIC

Peter Crowther

Peter Crowther (b. 1949) is a writer, editor, anthologist and publisher – he runs the small press PS Publishing and produces the quarterly magazine Postscripts. *Despite his British origins, and northern British at that, Crowther sets most of his stories in the United States, and writes in an American idiom. His stories have been collected in* The Longest Single Note *(1999),* Songs of Leaving *(2004) and* The Space Between the Lines *(2007).*

Alien invasion stories may seem all too common and not immediately a theme to evoke that sense of wonder, but the opening paragraph of this story will soon change all that.

> *What seest thou else,*
> *In the dark backward and abysm of time?*
> William Shakespeare, *The Tempest*

IT WAS ON THE THIRD DAY after the aliens arrived that we made the fateful discovery which placed the future of the entire planet in our hands. That discovery was that they hadn't arrived yet.

There were three of us who went over to the vacant lot alongside Sycamore . . . that's me, Derby – like the hat – McLeod, plus my good friend and local genius Jimmy-James Bannister and Ed Brewster, Forest Plains' very own bad boy . . . except there was nothing bad about Ed. Not really.

We went up into that giant tumbleweed cloud thing that served

as some kind of interstellar flivver – it had been at the aliens'
invitation, or so we thought: our subsequent discovery called that
particular fact into some considerable dispute – purely to get a
look at whatever this one alien was doing. Jimmy reckoned – and
he was right, as it turned out – he was keeping tabs on what was
going on and recording everything in some kind of 'book'.

Not that he – if the alien *was* a 'he': we never did find out –
was writing the way you or I would write, because he wasn't. We
didn't even know if he was writing at all until later that night,
when Jimmy-James had taken a long look in that foam-book of
theirs.

Not that this book was like any other book you ever saw. It
wasn't. Just like the ship that brought them to Forest Plains wasn't
like any other ship you ever saw, not in *Earth vs The Flying
Saucers* or even on *Twilight Zone* – both of which were what you
might call 'current' back then. And the aliens themselves weren't
like any kind of alien you ever saw in the dime comic books or
even dreamed about . . . not even after maybe eating warmed-over
two-day-old pizza last thing at night on top of a gut full of
Michelob and three or four plates of Ma Chetton's cheese
surprises, the small pieces of toasted cheese flapjack that Ma used
to serve up when we were holding the monthly Forest Plains Pool
Knockout Competition.

It was during one of those special nights, with the moon hanging
over the desert like a crazy Jack o'Lantern and the heat making
your shirt stick to your back and underarms, that the whole thing
actually got itself started. That was the night that creatures from
outer space arrived in Forest Plains. Then again, it wasn't.

But I'm getting way ahead of myself here . . .

So maybe that's the best place to start the story, that night.

It was a Monday, the last one in November, at about 9 o'clock.
The year was 1964.

Ma Chetton was sweeping the few remaining cheese surprises
from her last visit to the kitchen down onto a plate of freshly-made
cookies, their steam rising up into the smoky atmosphere of her
husband Bill's Pool Emporium over on Sycamore, when the place
shook like jello and the strains of The Trashmen's *Surfin' Bird*,
which had been playing on Bill's pride-and-joy Wurlitzer, faded
into a wave of what sounded like static. Only thing was we'd never

heard of a jukebox suffering from static before. Then the lights went out and the machine just ground itself to a stop.

Jerry Bucher was about to take a shot – six-ball off of two cushions into the far corner as I recall . . . all the other pockets being covered by Ed Brewster's stripes: funny how you remember details like that – and he stood up ramrod tall like someone had just dropped a firecracker or something crawly down the back of his shorts.

"What the hell was that?" Jerry asked nobody in particular, switching the half-chewed matchstalk from one side of his mouth to the other while he glanced around to put the blame on somebody for almost fouling up his shot. Ed was never what you might call a calm player and he was an even worse loser.

Ed Brewster was crouched over, his shoulders hunched up, watching the dust drifting down from the rafters and settling on the pool table, his girlfriend Estelle's arms clamped around his waist.

Ma was standing frozen behind the counter, empty plate in her hand, staring at the lights shining through the windows. "Felt like some kind of earthquake," she ventured.

Bill Chetton's head was visible through the hatch into the kitchen, his mouth hanging open and eyes as wide as dinner plates. "Everyone okay?"

I leaned my pool cue against the table and walked across to the windows. By rights, it should have been dark outside but it was bright as a night-time ballgame, like someone was shining car headlights straight at the windows, and when I took a look along the street I saw sand and stuff blowing across towards us from the vacant lot opposite.

"Some kind of power failure is what it is," Estelle announced, her voice sounding even higher and squeakier than usual and not at all reassuring.

Leaning against the table in front of the window, my face pressed up against the glass, I saw that the cause of that power failure was not something simple and straightforward like power lines being down between Forest Plains and Bellingham, some thirty-five miles away. It was something far more complicated.

Settling down onto the empty lot across the street was something that resembled a cross between a gigantic metal canister and an equally gigantic vegetable, its sides billowing in and out.

"Is it a helicoptor?" Old Fred Wishingham asked from alongside me, his voice soft and nervous. Fred had ambled over from the booth he occupied every night of the year and was standing on the other side of the table staring out into the night. "Can't be a plane," he said, "so it must be some kind of helicoptor." There sounded like a good deal of wishful thinking in that last statement.

But wishful thinking or not, the thing descending on the spare ground across the street didn't look like any helicoptor I'd ever seen – not that I'd seen many, mind you – and I told Fred as much.

"It's some kind of goddam hot air balloon," Ed Brewster said, crouching down so's he could get a better look at the top of the thing – it was tall, there was no denying that.

"Looks more like some kind of furry cloud," Abel Bodeen muttered to himself. I figured he was speaking so softly because he didn't feel like making that observation widely known because it sounded a mite foolish. And it did, right enough. The truth of the matter was that the thing *did* look like a furry cloud . . . or maybe a giant lettuce or the head of a cauliflower, with lights flashing on and off deep inside it.

Pretty soon we were all gathered around the window watching, nobody saying anything else as the thing settled down on the ground.

Within a minute or two, the poolroom lights came back on and the shaking stopped. "You going out to see what it is?" Fred asked. Nobody responded. "I guess *some*body should go out there to see what it is," he said.

Right on cue, the screen door squeaked behind us and we saw the familiar figure of Jimmy-James Bannister step out onto the sidewalk. He glanced back at the window at us all and gave a shrug. Then he started across the street.

"Hope that damn fool knows what he's doing." Ed Brewster was a past master at putting everyone's thoughts into words.

The truth of the matter was Jimmy-James knew a whole lot of things that none of the rest of us had any idea at all about. And anything he didn't know about he just kept on at until he did. Jimmy-James – born James Ronald Garrison Bannister (he'd made his first name into a double to go partways to satisfying his father and partways to keep the mickey-taking down to an acceptable minimum) – was the resident big brain of Forest Plains. Still only twenty-two years old – same age as me, at the time – he was finishing up his Master's course over at Princeton, studying languages and applied math.

Jimmy-James could do long division problems in his head and cuss in fourteen languages which, along with the fact that he could drink anyone else in town – including Ed – under the table, made him a pretty popular member of any group gathering . . . particularly one where any amount of liquor or even just beer was to be consumed. He was home for Thanksgiving, taking the week off, and there's a lot of folks owe him a debt of gratitude for that fact.

Anyway, there went Jimmy-James, large as life and twice as bold – though some might say 'stupid' – walking across the street, his hands thrust deep into his trouser pockets and his head held high, proud and fearless. There were a couple of muted gasps from somewhere behind me and then the sound of shuffling as folks tried to get closer to the window to get a good look. After all, we'd all seen from the *War Of The Worlds* movie what happened to people who got a little too close to these objects . . . and we'd all pretty much decided that the thing across the street was about as likely to have come from anyplace on Earth as it was to have flown up to us from Vince and Molly Waldon's general store down the street. Nobody actually came right out and said it was from another planet but we all knew that it was. But why it was here was another matter, though we weren't in any great rush to find out the answer to that question. None of us except Jimmy-James Bannister, that is.

"Go call the Sheriff," Ma Chetton whispered.

I could hear Bill Chetton pressing the receiver and saying *Hello? Hello?* like his life depended on it. It didn't come as any surprise when Bill announced to the hushed room that the line seemed like it was dead. Then the jukebox kicked in again with a loud and raucous *A papapapapapa* . . ., the needle somehow having returned to the start of The Trashmen's hit record.

The street outside seemed like it was holding its breath in much the same way as the folks looking out of the window were holding their breath . . . both it and us waiting to see what was going to happen.

What happened was both awesome and kind of an anticlimax.

Just as Jimmy-James reached the sidewalk across the street, the sides of the giant vegetable balloon canister from another world dropped down and became a kind of shiny skirt reaching all the way to the ground. No sooner had that happened than a whole group of smaller vegetable things – smaller but still twice the size of Jimmy-James . . . and, at almost six-four, JJ is not a small man – came sliding down the platform onto terra firma . . . and into the heart of Forest Plains.

We could hear their caterwauling from where we were, even over the drone of The Trashmen telling anyone who would listen that *the Bird was the Word* . . . and, as we watched, we saw the vegetable-shapes come to a halt on the sidewalk right in front of Jimmy-James where they kind of spun around and then gathered around him in a tight circle. Then all but one of them moved back a few feet and then the last one moved back, too.

At this point, Jimmy-James turned around and waved to us. "Come on out," he yelled.

"You think it's safe?" Ed Brewster asked.

I shrugged. "Doesn't seem to be they mean any harm," Ma Chetton said softly, the wonder in her voice as plain as the streaks of grey colouring the hair around her ears and temples.

"They come all the way from wherever it is they come from, seems to me that if they'd had a mind to do us any harm they'd have done it by now," said Old Fred Wishingham. "That said, mind you," he added, "I'm not about to go charging out there until we see what it is they *have* come for."

"Maybe they haven't come for nothing at all," Estelle suggested.

Somebody murmured that such an unlikely scenario could be the case but they weren't having none of it. That was the way folks were in Forest Plains in those days – the way folks were all over this country, in fact. Nobody (with the possible exception of Ed Brewster, and even he only did it for fun) wanted to make anyone look or feel a damned fool and hurt their feelings if they could get away without doing so. With Estelle it could be difficult. Estelle had turned making herself look a damned fool into something approaching an art form.

"You mean, like they're exploring . . . something like that?" Abel Bodeen said to help her out a mite.

"Yeah," Estelle agreed dreamily, "exploring."

"Well, I'm going out," Ma said. And without so much as a second glance or a pause to allow someone to talk her out of it, she rested the empty plate on the counter-top and strode over to the door. A minute or so later she was walking across the street. It seemed like the things had sensed she was going to come out because they'd moved across the street like to greet her, swivelling around at the last minute – just as Ma came to a stop – and ringing her just the way they had done with Jimmy-James.

They seemed harmless enough but I felt like we should have the law in on the situation. "Phone still out, Bill?" I shouted. Bill Chetton lifted the receiver and tried again. He nodded and returned it to the cradle.

"Okay Ed," I said, "let's me and you scoot out the back and run over to the Sheriff's office."

Ed said okay, after thinking about that for a second or two, and then the two of us slipped behind the counter and into Bill's and Ma's kitchen, then out of the back door and into the yard, past the trashcans towards the fence . . . and then I heard someone calling.

"What was that?" I whispered across to Ed.

Ed had stopped dead in his tracks on the other side of the fence. He was staring ahead of him. When I got to the fence I looked in the direction Ed was looking and there they were. Three of them. Right in front of us, wailing. I'll never forget that sound . . . like the wind in the desert, lost and aimless.

The door we'd just come out of opened up again behind us and Fred Wishingham's voice shouted, "Hold it right where you . . ." and then trailed off when Fred saw the things. "I was just going to tell you that some of those things had just turned around and headed over to where you'd be appearing . . . and, well, you already saw that." Fred had lowered his voice like he'd just been caught shooting craps in Church.

Ed nodded and I told Fred to get back inside.

As I heard the lock click on the door, I whispered to Ed. "You think maybe they can read our minds?"

Ed shrugged.

The things were about ten, maybe twelve feet high and seemed to float above the ground on a circular frilled platform. I say "floated" because they didn't leave any marks as they moved along, not even in the soft dirt of the alleyway that ran behind Bill's and Ma's store.

The platform was about a foot deep and, above that, the thing's body kind of tapered up like a glass stem until it reached another frilly overhang – like a mushroom's head – at the top. Halfway between the two platforms a collar of tendrils or thin wings – like the gossamer veils of a jellyfish – stuck out from the stem a foot or so and then drooped down limply about three feet. These seemed to twitch and twirl of their own accord, no matter whether a wind was blowing or not, and it didn't take me too long to figure out these were what passed for arms and hands on the things' own world.

I looked up at the first creature's top section, trying to see if there were any kind of air-holes or eyes but there was nothing, although the texture of the skin-covering was kind of translucent . . . see•through, for want of a better phrase, and I could see things moving around in there, shifting and re-forming. Where the noise they made came out, I couldn't tell. And we never did find out.

We watched as the creatures moved closer. Suddenly, the one at the front turned around real fast and the hand-arm things fluttered outwards, like a sheet settling on a bed, and, just for a moment, they touched my shoulder. There was something akin to affection there. At the time, I thought I was maybe imagining it . . . maybe reading the creature's thought-waves or something, but I was later to discover that there was, if not an outright affection, then at least a feeling of familiarity on the creature's part.

This confrontation lasted only a few seconds, a minute at the most, and then the creatures moved back away from us in the direction of the Sheriff's office, the wing things outstretched towards us as they went.

"What did you make of that?" Ed Brewster said, his voice a little croaky and hoarse.

"I have absolutely no idea at all," I said.

I kept watching because one of the creatures intrigued me more then the others. This one carried what seemed to be some kind of foam box, thick with piled-up layers of what looked like cotton candy. All the time we'd been 'meeting' with the leader – we supposed the thing that had touched me *was* the leader – this other creature was removing small pieces of foam which it seemed to absorb into its tendrils. It was still doing it as the three of them moved down the alleyway. Just as they reached the back of the Sheriff's office, the leader put down its wings, turned around and, leaving the other two behind, moved up onto the sidewalk and out of sight.

I turned at the sound of hurried footsteps behind me and saw Jimmy-James running along the alleyway, his face beaming a wide smile. Ma Chetton was following him, her head still turned in the direction of the street to see if any of the creatures were following *her*.

"What about *that*!" JJ said. Then, "What *about* that!"

I nodded and when I turned to look at Ed, he was nodding too. There didn't seem much else to do.

"Did they say anything?" Jimmy-James asked. "Did they say where they've come from?"

"Nope," I said. "Not a word. Just that mournful wailing. Gives me the creeps . . . sounds like a coyote."

"Or a baby teething," Ma said breathlessly.

"Same here," said JJ. "I tried them with everything I know . . . English, French, German, Spanish, Russian . . . quite a few more. And I tried out a couple of hybrids, too."

"Like standing in the United Nations," Ma Chetton muttered testily, her breath rasping. "Or hanging atop the Tower of Babel come Doomsday."

"What the hell are hybrids?" Ed Brewster asked.

"Mixtures of two or three languages," JJ explained. "In the old days, that was the way most folks communicated . . . I mean before any one single language or dialect had gained enough of a footing to be commonplace. And I tried them with all kinds of signs and stuff but they didn't seem to know what I was doing. I thought maybe they would have known all about our language by listening to our radio waves out there in outer space. But it was no-go. I can't figure out how they communicate with each other at all," he said. "Unless it's that wailing noise or maybe through that thing that one of them's carrying around."

"You mean the box-thing? The thing that looks like a pile of cotton candy?"

JJ nodded. "He's messing with that thing all the time, changing it even as I'm trying to talk to them."

"Yeah," I agreed, "but did you notice he's taking things *out* instead of adding to what's already in there."

"I'd noticed that," JJ said. "I was wondering if that stuff is absorbed into him and enables him to communicate to the others. Like a translator."

I shrugged. It was all too much for me.

Ed glanced around to make sure none of those creatures had sneaked up on him and said, "We figure they can read our minds."

"Really?" said JJ. "How's that?"

"Well," Ed said, matter-of-factly, "they knew we were coming out here into the alleyway."

JJ frowned and glanced at me before returning his full attention to Ed.

Ed gave a characteristic shrug. "Why else would they come on down here from the street if they didn't know we were coming out?"

While JJ mulled that over, I said, "What do you figure they want, JJ?"

The back door to the poolroom opened and Abel Bodeen peered out. "Is there any of those things out there?"

"Nope, they've gone down to see the Sheriff," I said.

Abel pulled a face and gave a wry smile. "That should please Benjamin no end," he said with a chuckle.

The fact was that the creatures *did* please Sheriff Ben Travers, as it turned out. Or they didn't *dis*please him anyway. The truth of the matter was that the aliens didn't do anything to upset or irritate anyone. In fact, they didn't do anything at all.

"Why the hell did they come, Derby?" Abel Bodeen asked me a couple of days after they'd . . . after we'd first seen them.

"Beats me," I said.

We were sitting out on the old straight-backed chairs Molly Waldon had left out in front of her and Vince's General Store, watching the creatures wander around the town, just as they had been doing all the time. But I was watching a little more intently than I had done at first. The folks around town had become used to the aliens after two full days and nobody seemed to care much *what* they were there for. So it's probably fair to say that people hadn't picked up that the attitude of the creatures was changing. It wasn't changing by much, but it *was* changing.

"You've noticed, haven't you?"

I shielded my eyes from the glare of the late afternoon November sunshine and looked across at Jimmy-James. "Noticed what?"

He looked across at two of the creatures gliding along the other side of the street. "They're slowing down."

I followed his gaze and, sure enough, the creatures did seem to be slower than they had been at first. But it was more than that. They seemed to be more cautious. I mentioned this to JJ and Abel, and to Ed and Estelle who were leaning on what remained of an old hitching rail at the edge of the sidewalk.

Ed snorted. "That don't make no sense at all," he said. "Why would they be cautious now, when they've been here two goddam days."

"Ed, watch your mouth," Estelle whined in her high-pitched voice.

"He's right," agreed Jimmy-James.

"Who?" Ed asked. "Me or him?"

"Both of you." JJ got to his feet and strode across to the post behind Ed and leaned. "They *are* getting slower and they do seem to be more . . . more careful," he said, choosing his words. "And, no, it doesn't make any sense for them to be more careful the longer they're here."

"Nothing for them to be nervous about, that's for sure," Abel said. "They've got us wrapped up neat as a Christmas gift."

The aliens had effectively cut off the town. There were no phone lines and the roads were . . . well, they were impassable. It was Doc Maynard had seen it first, trying to get his old Ford Fairlane out to check on Sally Iaccoca's father, over towards Bellingham. Frank Iaccoca had taken a bad fall – cracked a couple of ribs, Doc said – and Doc had him trussed up like Boris Karloff in the old *Mummy* movie.

The car had cut out three miles out of Forest Plains and there was nothing Doc could do to get it going again. So he'd come back into town for help, without even taking a look under the hood, and Abel, Johnny Deveraux and me had gone out there to give him some help. Johnny, who works at Phil Masham's garage, had taken some tools and a spare battery in case it was something simple he could fix out on the road. Doc Maynard was not renowned for looking after his automobile.

When we got out there, Johnny tried the ignition and it was dead. But when he made to move around to the front of the car to open the hood he suddenly started floundering and dropped the battery. That's when we found the barrier.

A "force field" is what Jimmy-James called it.

Everything looked completely normal up ahead in front of Doc Maynard's Fairlane but there was no way for us to get to it. It felt like cloth but not porous. JJ said it was an invisible synthetic membrane – whatever *that* was – and he reckoned the creatures had set it up around the town to protect their spaceship. Sure enough, the same barrier travelled all the way around town . . . or so we figured. We tried different points on farm tracks and woodland paths and each one came to a complete halt.

Like it or not, we were caught like fish in a bowl. But that didn't seem to matter . . . at least not until JJ took a look in the creatures' "book".

"There he goes, if it is a 'he'," said Jimmy-James, pointing to the creature with the box of cotton candy. The funny thing was that the box now looked to have a lot less of the stuff in it than it had done at first. The first time we'd seen it, the thing had looked to be almost full.

"The other thing," said JJ in a soft voice that made you think he was realizing what he was about to say at exactly the same time as he said it, "is they seem not to be touching people with those . . . those veil-things."

"Yeah," I agreed. "I guess that was what I meant about them being more cautious. Part of it, anyway."

Ed snorted. "Maybe it's a case of the more they see of us the less they like."

Estelle rubbed Ed Brewster's oiled hair and puckered up her mouth. "I'm sure they like what they see of you, honey," she trilled without changing the shape of her mouth. "Anyone would." It sounded as though Estelle was talking to a newborn babe sitting in a stroller. Ed must've thought so, too, because he told her to can it while he readjusted his quiff.

"We need to get a look in that box-thing," JJ said.

"How we going to do that?" I asked. "And what good is it going to do us anyway? Just looks like a load of gunk to me."

JJ stepped away from the rail and out onto the street. "That's just it," he shouted over his shoulder as he strode across to the creature with the box. "None of us has seen what's in there, not up close."

We watched the confrontation.

Jimmy-James stopped right in front of the creature and it turned around. Almost immediately, the little veil-arms wafted out as though blown by a breeze and settled on JJ's shoulders, the wailing sound rising a pitch or two in the process. Then it started to back away, its arms still blowing free.

JJ shouted over to me to come on along. Ed Brewster stood up and moved alongside me. "I'm coming, too," he said.

"Now you be careful what you're doing, Ed, honey," Estelle warbled.

"I will, Estelle, I will," Ed said, with maybe just a hint of a sigh. And the two of us walked onto the street to join JJ. Which was how we got into the creatures' spaceship.

The alien with the book kept on backing away from the three of us and we just kept on walking after it. Eventually, we reached the ship where we discovered two more of the creatures standing by the ramp.

The creatures then backed on up into the ship. We kept on following.

A few minutes later the three of us were standing amidst a whole array of what looked to be lumps of foam, all of various size, piled up on or stuck against other lumps. Some of the lumps were circular – cylindrical, JJ said – and others looked like tears of modelling clay thumbed into place by a gigantic hand without design or reason.

Up inside the ship, the things' wing-arms were fluttering faster and more frequently than ever . . . and the alien that we reckoned to be recording the whole visit was mightily busy, removing small pieces of foam with the tendrils and absorbing them. When I glanced inside the box, I saw there was hardly anything in it.

Over to one side of the crowded room a wide lamp-thing stood by itself. Standing beneath the lamp, two aliens were seemingly absorbed in another of the boxes, their wings-arms fluttering like a leaf caught in a draught. This particular box was completely full, a collection of multi-coloured shapes and lumps and pieces, all pressed into each other or standing alone.

"We need to get a look at that," JJ whispered to Ed and me.

"Leave it to me," Ed Brewster said. He walked across to the box and lifted it with both hands. "Okay if I borrow this for a while, ol' buddy?" he said, waving the box in front of the two creatures.

The things didn't seem to do anything as Ed stepped back and moved back alongside us, although their arms were fluttering faster than ever. Then, suddenly, the little arm-wings dropped limp and the two creatures turned around. As they did this, the creature standing in front of the other two in the centre of the room waved its arms and then it, too, spun around.

"Let's get out of here," Jimmy-James said. "I'm starting to get a bad feeling about this."

As we ran down the platform leading back onto Sycamore Street I asked Jimmy-James what he'd meant by that last remark. But he just shook his head.

"It's too fantastic to even think about," was all he'd say. "Just let me take a look at the box and then maybe I'll be able to get an idea."

We high-tailed it back to Jack and Edna Bannister's house down on Beech Avenue and, while me and Ed drank cup after cup of JJ's mom's strong coffee, JJ himself pored over the contents of the alien box. It was almost three in the morning when a wild-eyed Jimmy-James rushed into the Bannisters' lounge and slammed the box onto the table. Ed was asleep, curled up like a baby on the sofa, and I was reading the TV Guide.

"I have to look at the other box," he said. "Now!"

Ed smacked his lips together loudly and shuffled around on the sofa.

I looked up from a feature on *Gilligan's Island* and was immediately surprised to see how much Jimmy-James resembled that hapless shipwreck survivor. "What's up?"

JJ shook his head and ran his hands through his hair. I noticed straight away that they were shaking. "A lot, maybe . . . maybe nothing. I don't know."

"You want to – "

"I've been through all of the usual coding techniques," JJ said, ticking off on his outstretched fingers. "I've applied the Patagonian Principle of repeated shapes, colour motifs, spacing . . . I've run the

Spectromic Law of shading relationships and the old Inca constructional communication dynamics . . ."

I held up a hand and waved for him to stop. "Whoa, boy . . . what the hell are you talking about?"

JJ crouched down in front of me and looked up into my eyes. "It makes sense," he said. "I've made it work . . . made the patterns fit."

"You *understand* it?" I glanced across at the box of jumbles shapes. "*That*?"

JJ nodded emphatically. "Yes!" he said. Then, "No! Oh, God, I don't know. That's why I need to check. And I need to do it tonight. Tomorrow may be too late."

"I still don't know what you're – "

The resident genius of Forest Plains placed a hand on my knee. "No time," he said. "No time to talk. It has to be *now*."

I studied his face for a few seconds, saw the look in his eyes: there was an urgent need there, sure . . . but there was something else, too. It was fear. Jimmy-James Bannister looked as scared as any man could be. "Okay, let's go do it."

He stood up and looked at Ed. "What about him?"

"He'll be fine. We expecting any trouble in there?"

"I don't think so."

"Okay. Let's go."

And we went.

The ship was silent and dark. JJ borrowed his old man's flashlight and the two of us crept up that platform and into the depths of the creatures' rocketship. The place was deserted, which was just as well. It didn't take too long before JJ found the second box – the one the creature had been using all the time – and he scooped it into his arms and rushed back out of the ship.

We were back in the house almost as soon as we had left. The whole thing had taken less than ten minutes.

I watched as JJ sat in front of the new box – now containing but a few lumps and dollops of that clay-stuff – wringing his hands and muttering to himself. I couldn't stand it any more and I grabbed a hold of JJ and shook him until I could hear his teeth clattering. "What the hell *is* it, JJ . . . why don't you tell me for God's sake."

He seemed to come to his senses then and he quietened down. Then he said, softly, "It's the aliens."

"What about them?" I said.

"They're . . ." He seemed to be trying hard to find the right words. "They're palindromic."

"They're *what*?"

"They run backwards . . . their time is different to ours."

"Their time is *different* to ours? Like *how* different?"

"It moves in a different direction . . . backwards instead of forwards – except to them it *is* forwards. But to us it's – " JJ waved his arms around like he was about to take off. "Well, it's ass-backwards is what it is."

"What the hell is all the goddam noise about?" Ed said, turning over on the sofa. He reached for his pack of Luckies and shook one into the corner of his mouth, lit it with a match.

I didn't know what to say and looked across at Jimmy-James. "Maybe you'd better tell him – *us*!"

JJ sat down at the table next to the two boxes, one full and one almost empty. He smiled and said, calmly, "It's this way.

"I've broken the basics of their language. It wasn't really too difficult once I'd eliminated the obvious no-go areas." He pointed to the almost empty box. "This is the 'book' they're using now . . . the one that's recording everything that happens *here* . . . here on Earth."

"Looks like a mound of clay to me," Ed said, blowing smoke across the table and shuffling one edge of the box away from him.

"That's because you're you," JJ said impatiently, "because you're from Earth. To them, it's the equivalent of a diary . . . a ship's log, if you like."

Ed settled back on the sofa. "Okay. What's it say?"

"It starts at the very moment they opened the doors. It says they found a group of creatures standing outside watching them disembark . . . get out. These creatures, their record says, held instruments . . . they thought at first the things might be gifts."

I frowned. "When was that? I never held no instrument."

JJ leaned forward. "That's just it. You didn't. It didn't happen. At least it didn't happen yet." He lifted the box onto his knee and pointed at the shapes inside. "See, it's all arranged in a linear fashion, with each piece linking to others, building across the box in waves and doubling back to the other side. It's like layers of pasta furled over on itself. But see the way that it's arranged . . .

you can pull pieces out of place and the gap stays. It's an intricate constructional form of basic communication. I say 'basic' because I've only been able to pick up the very basic fundamentals. There's much much more to it . . . but I don't have the time to work it out. Not now, anyway."

Ed tapped his cigarette ash onto the carpet and rubbed it in with his free hand. "*Why* don't you have the time? What's the panic?"

"The panic is that the record goes on to say how surprised they all were to find creatures – "

"Not half a surprised as we were to see them!" I said.

JJ carried on without comment. "It goes on to say how they came out and stood in front of us and nobody – none of *us* – moved or did anything. We just stood there. Then we all moved away and went to some structures. They walked around and looked at the outside of these structures and then went back into their ship. They were concerned that they had somehow created the situation by their ship's power."

"Huh?"

JJ waved for Ed to keep quite and continued.

"Listen. Then it says that, after some early investigations – they say that much more research has to be carried out – after these early investigations, we came on board the ship and borrowed their log."

"Yeah, well, we've got the log," I said. "For what good it's doing us."

"But none of that other stuff happened," JJ said. "This stuff in here . . ." He pointed at the individual pieces of clay . . . lifted one end of the carefully interwoven sheet of linked pieces and tiny constructions. "This only amounts to less than one single day. The creatures have been here almost three days now. There's no mention of all the other things that have happened. And bear this in mind . . . the stuff in here is what's *left*, as far as we're concerned."

I figured someone had to ask so it might as well be me. "How do you mean 'what's left'?"

"I mean, we've been watching the creature remove stuff from this box all the time he's been here, right?" I nodded and saw Ed Brewster do the same. "*And*," JJ continued, emphasizing the word, "what we have here, *now* – and which represents what's left in the

box after he's been removing the clay stuff for almost three days –
is a record of when they first *arrived*. The creature has been
removing the stuff from the *top* – I've watched him . . . so have
you, Derby; you, too, Ed – and leaving the stuff at the bottom
completely intact. And that stuff records them *arriving*."

Ed and I sat silently, watching Jimmy-James. I didn't have the
first idea of what to say and I was sure Ed didn't either. JJ must
have sensed it because he started speaking again without giving us
much of a chance to comment.

"Derby, the creatures . . . have you noticed how they seem
always to be turned away from you when you go up to speak to
them?"

We'd already figured that the clear part of the mushroom tops
more or less worked as the things' faces. And it was true, now that
Jimmy-James mentioned it, that the things always had that part of
themselves turned away whenever you went up to them.

"That's because at the moment you start trying to communicate
with them, they've actually just finished trying to do the same with
you."

"That sounds like horseshit," Ed said. "Not even Perry Mason
could convict somebody on that evidence."

"And have you noticed how they keep facing you when they
move away? That's because, in their time-frame, they're
approaching you."

Some of it was beginning to make some kind of sense to me and
JJ noticed that.

"And we've all commented on how their attitude to us is
changing," he said. "You said they seemed to be getting slower . . .
more cautious."

"That I did," I remembered.

"Well, they're getting more cautious because where they are
now is they've just *arrived*. Where they were when we first saw
them was in their third or fourth day around us. They were *used*
to us then . . . they're not now."

"Okay, okay, I hear what you say, JJ," I said. "Maybe the
creatures' time does move in reverse, if that's what you're saying.
I don't understand it, but then I don't understand a lot of things.
The thing that puzzles me is why you're getting so hot under the
collar about this. Everything's going to go okay: we saw them

'arrive' – which you say is when they left – and nothing happened in the meantime. All we have to worry about is our future which is their past . . . and they've come through that okay haven't – "

I saw JJ's face screw up like he'd just sucked on a lemon. He reached over and pulled the full box across to the edge of the table, held up another of those interlaced jigsaw puzzles of multi-coloured clay pieces. "This is the previous diary," he said, "the one before the one they started after they had arrived.

"You remember I said there was an entry in the current ship's log about the creatures being concerned that they had somehow created the situation they found when they arrived?" We both nodded. "Well, that situation is explained in a little more detail in the previous record." At this point, Jimmy-James sat back on his chair and seemed to draw in his breath.

"Okay: the log says that they were following the course taken by an earlier ship – one that had disappeared a long time ago – when they experienced some kind of terrible space storm the like of which had never previously being recorded. For a time, it was touch and go that they would survive, though survive they did. But when the storm subsided, they were nowhere that they recognized. After a few of their time periods – which, based on the limited information in the new book, I would put at quarter days . . . give or take an hour – there was a sudden blinding flash of light and a huge explosion. When they checked their instruments, they discovered that the ship was about to impact upon a planet which had apparently appeared out of nothingness."

Ed looked confused. "So this explosion went off *before* they hit the planet?"

JJ nodded.

"I don't get it," Ed said.

I said to let Jimmy-James finish.

"There hadn't been any planet there at all until then," JJ said. "Then, there it was. And that planet was Earth.

"They narrowly averted the collision," JJ went on, "and settled onto the planet's surface. After checking atmospheric conditions they prepared to go outside. The log finished with them wondering what they'll find there."

While JJ had been talking I'd been holding my breath without even realizing it. I let it out with a huge sigh. "Are you sure?"

The owner of the best mind in town shook his head sadly.

"But you *think* you're right."

"I think I'm right, yes."

"And they found us, right?"

"Right, Ed," JJ said. "They found us." He waited.

I thought over everything I had heard and knew there was something there that should bother me . . . but I couldn't for the life of me figure out what it was. Then it hit me. "The blinding flash," I said. "If before that blinding flash there was nothing and after it there was the Earth . . . then, if the creatures' time *does* move backwards, and their version of their arrival is – or *will* be – our version of their departure, that means the aliens will destroy the planet when they leave."

JJ was nodding. "That's the way I figure it, too," he said.

I looked across at Ed and he looked across at me. "What are we going to do?" I asked JJ.

JJ shrugged. "We have to stop them leaving . . . in terms of our *own* time progression."

"But, in their terms, that would be to stop them *arriving* . . . and they're already here."

"Yes, that's true. In just the same way, if we do something to stop them – and I see only one course of action there – then, again in our time, they never actually 'arrive' . . . though, of course, they've arrived already as far as we're concerned. What we do, is prevent their departure in our terms."

Ed Brewster shook his head and pushed himself off the sofa onto the floor. "Jesus Christ, I'm getting a goddam headache here," he said. "Their arrival is our departure . . . their departure is our arrival . . . but if they don't do this, how could they do that . . . and as for *palindoodad* . . ." He stood up and rubbed his hands through his hair. "This all sounds like something off *Howdy Doody*. What does it all mean? How can we play about with time like that? How can *any*body play about with time like that?"

"I think it may have been the space storm," JJ said. "I think, maybe, their time normally progresses in exactly the same way as our own . . . although Albert Einstein said we shouldn't allow ourselves to be railroaded about time being a one-way linear progre – "

"Jesus, Jimmy-James!" Ed shouted, and JJ winced . . . glancing upwards towards his parents' bedroom while we all waited for sounds of people moving around to see what all the noise was about. "Jesus," Ed continued in a hoarse whisper, "I can't keep up with all of this stuff. Just keep it simple."

"Okay," JJ said. "I figure one of two things: either the aliens always move backwards in time or they don't.

"If we go for the first option, then we have to ask how they found their way into our universe."

"The space storm?" I suggested.

"I think so," said JJ. "If we go for the second option – that they *don't* normally travel backwards in time – then we have to ask what might have caused the change." He looked across at me again and gave a small smile.

I nodded. "The space storm."

"Kee-rect! So either way, the storm did the deed. But whatever the cause, the fact remains that they're here and we have to prevent whatever it was that caused the explosion."

We sat for a minute or so considering that. I didn't like the sound of what I'd heard but I liked the sound of the silence that followed even less. I looked at Ed. He didn't seem too happy either. "So how do we do that, JJ?" I said.

JJ shrugged. "We have to kill them . . . kill them *all*," he said. He pulled across the almost empty box that we all reckoned was the alien's current ship's log and lifted up the few lace-like constructions of interwoven clay pieces. "And we have to do it *tonight*."

I don't remember the actual rounding up of people that night. And I don't recall listening to JJ telling his story again and again. But tell it he did, and the people got rounded up. There was me, Sherriff Ben, Ed, Abel, Jerry and Jimmy-James Bannister himself. We walked silently out to the spaceship and weren't at all surprised to see faint wisps of steam coming out from the sides or that the platform was up for the first time since . . . well, the first time since three days ago. As the platform lowered itself slowly to the dusty ground of the vacant lot across from Bill's and Ma's poolroom, I heard JJ call out my name.

"Derby . . ."

I turned around and he held up his rifle, then nodded to the others standing there on Sycamore Street, all of them carrying the same kind of thing. "Instruments," he said.

By then it was too late. The bets were placed.

As soon as they appeared we started firing. We moved forward as one mass, vigilantes, firing and clearing, firing and clearing. The creatures never knew what hit them. They just folded up and fell to the ground, some inside the ship and others onto Sycamore Street. When they were down, Sheriff Ben went up to each one and put a couple of bullets into its head from his handgun.

We continued into the ship and finished the job.

There were sixteen of them. We combed the ship from top to bottom like men in a fever, a destructive killing frenzy, pulling out pieces of foam and throwing them out into the street . . . in much the same way as you might rip out the wires in the back of a radio to stop it from playing dance band music. God, but we were scared.

When the sun came up, we put the aliens back on the ship and doused the whole thing in gasoline. Then we put a match to it. It burned quietly, as we might have expected of any vehicle operated by such gentle creatures. It burned for two whole days and nights. When it had finished, we loaded the remains onto Vince Waldon's flatbed truck and took them out to Darien Lake. The barrier – or "force field", as JJ called it – had gone. Things were more or less back to normal. For a time.

It turned out that JJ found more of those ship's logs that night, when the rest of us were tearing and destroying. Turned out that he sneaked them off the ship and kept them safe until he could get back for them. I didn't find that out right away.

He came round to my house about a week later.

"Derby, we have to talk," he said.

"What about?"

"The aliens."

"Oh, for crissakes, I – " I was going to tell him that I couldn't stand to talk about those creatures any more, couldn't stand to think about what we'd done to them. But his face looked so in need of conversation that I stopped short. "What about the aliens?" I said.

That was when Jimmy-James told me he'd taken the old diaries from inside the ship.

Walking along Sycamore, he said, "Have you ever thought about what we did?"

I groaned.

"No, not about us shooting the aliens . . . about how we changed their past?" Someone had left a soda bottle lying on the sidewalk and JJ kicked it gently into the gutter. The clatter it made somehow set off a dog barking and I tried to place the sound but couldn't. It did sound right, though, that mixture of a lonely dog barking and the night and talking about the aliens . . . like it all belonged together. "I mean," JJ went on, "we changed our future – which is okay: anyone can do that – but we actually changed things that, as far as they were concerned, had already happened. Did you think about that?"

"Nope." We walked in silence for a minute or so, then I said, "Did you?"

"A little – at first. Then, when I'd read the diaries, I thought about it a lot." He stopped and turned to me. "You know the big diary, the full box? The one that ended with details of the explosion?"

I didn't say anything but I knew what he was talking about.

"I went into more of the details about the missing ship . . . the one that had disappeared? The last message they received from this other ship was at these same co-ordinates."

"So?"

He shrugged. "The message said they'd been moving along when they suddenly noticed a planet that was not there before."

"Do I want to hear this?"

"I think the Earth is destined for destruction. The aliens were fulfilling some kind of cosmic plan."

"JJ, you're starting to lose me."

"Yeah, I'm starting to lose *me*," he said with a short laugh. But there was no humour there. "This other ship – the first one, the one that the diary talks about – I've calculated that it's about forty years in their past. Or in our future."

I grabbed a hold of his arm and spun him around. "You mean there's more of those things coming?"

JJ nodded. "In about forty years, give or take. And they're going to be going through this section of the universe and BOOM! . . ." He clapped his hands loudly. "'Hey, Captain,'" JJ said in an accent that sounded vaguely foreign, "'there's a planet over there!' And there's no kewpie doll for guessing the name of that planet."

"So, if they're moving backwards, too . . . then that means they'll destroy us." The dog barked again somewhere over to our right.

"Yep. But if the aliens we just killed were going to do the job, how could the others have done it, too?"

"Another planet?"

JJ shook his head. "The co-ordinates seemed quite specific . . . as far as I could make out. That's another problem right there."

"What's that?"

"The diaries are gone. They liquified . . . turned into mulch."

"All of it?"

"Every bit. But it *was* Earth they were talking about. I'd bet my life on it . . . hell, I'd even bet yours."

That was when I fully realized just how much of a friend Jimmy-James Bannister truly was. He placed a greater value on my life than on his own.

"Which means, of course," JJ said, "that we were destined to stop the aliens the way we did."

"We were *meant* to do it?"

"Looks that way to me." He glanced at me and must have seen me relax a little. "That make you feel better?"

"A little."

"Me too."

"What is it? What is it that's causing the destruction?"

"Hey, if I knew *that* . . . Way I figure it, they're maybe warping across space somehow – kind of like matter transference. The magazines have been talking about that kind of thing for years: they call them black funnels or something.

"But maybe they're also warping across time progressions, too . . . without even realizing they're doing it. Then, as soon as they appear into our dimension or plane, one that operates on a different time progression . . . it's like a chemical reaction and . . ."

I clapped my hands. "I know," I said. "BOOM!"

"Right."

"So what do we do?"

"Right now? Nothing. Right now, the balance has been restored. But the paradox will be repeated . . . around 2003, 2004." He smiled at me. "Give or take."

We went on walking and talking but that's about all I can remember of that night.

The next day, or maybe the one after, we told Ed Brewster. And we made ourselves a pact.

We couldn't bring ourselves to tell anyone about what had happened. Who would believe us? Where was the proof? A few boxes of slime? Forget it. And if we showed them the blackened stuff at the bottom of Darien Lake . . . well, it was just a heap of blackened stuff at the bottom of a lake.

But there was another reason we didn't want to tell anyone outside of Forest Plains about what we'd done. Just like nobody else in town wanted to tell anyone. We were ashamed.

So we made a pact. We'd keep our eyes peeled – keep watching the skies, as the newspaperman said in *The Thing* movie . . .

And when something happens, we'll know what to do.

What really gets to me – still, after all this time – is not just that there's a bunch of aliens somewhere out there, maybe heading on a disaster course with Earth . . . but that, back on their own planet or dimension there's another bunch of creatures listening to their messages . . . a bunch we killed on the streets of Forest Plains almost forty years ago.

CASTLE IN THE SKY

Robert Reed

Robert Reed (b. 1956) has been one of the more prolific writers of science fiction since he first appeared in 1986. His work is diverse but he is probably best known for his more extreme concepts, such as that found in Marrow *(2000), about a group of aliens and genetically changed humans who travel through the universe in a ship that is so huge that it contains its own planet. Most of his short stories remain to be collected into book form but some will be found in* The Dragons of Springplace *(1999) and* The Cuckoo's Boys *(2005). This story, which is published here for the first time, is a little more down to Earth, or at least the Moon, but contains a far-reaching concept with untold consequences.*

WHEN I WAS EIGHT years old, my best friend lived a few doors down the street – a little black-haired kid named Donnie Warner. Donnie was about as shy as anybody I've ever known, and he was desperately sweet. I always enjoyed my time with him. His toys were different from my toys, which is a major selling point among kids. We didn't fight about anything, which means one of us probably got his way more often than not. And that was probably me, I should confess. But I don't remember being particularly bossy, and I'm halfway sure that Donnie equally enjoyed my company. There was a long stretch during third grade when he came up to my house almost daily, to visit me and to escape from his own difficult home.

My parents and other gossipy adults talked about Donnie's

family. The Warners didn't have much money, it seemed, and I'd heard words like "weird" and "crazy" to define life under their roof. Nobody sat me down to explain why that was, but I always assumed it was because the mother was stuck home alone with four kids: Donnie was the oldest, and there were two baby sisters. There were also various cats and a young golden retriever rescued from the pound – a dog meant for Donnie, though my friend rarely showed interest in the beast. There was a father too, but he frequently traveled for work. On those rare occasions when I played at the Warner house, things seemed noisy but not exceptionally strange. The only genuine oddity, at least to my mind, was that both of the adults were into religion. Every room had at least one crucifix watching over it, and on Sunday mornings the entire family dressed up in their best clothes and piled into an elderly Oldsmobile station wagon, driving off to visit their church and demanding God.

One evening – a Monday evening – Donnie walked to my house and rang the bell, then with his usual shy politeness asked my mother if I could play for a little while. But Mom had other ideas. I was sitting in the kitchen, using a glue stick and plain cardboard to erect a spectacularly ugly castle. My assignment was due at eight-thirty in the morning, sharp. "Tell your buddy hello and goodbye," Mom barked at me. "Then get back in here. I'm not doing any piece of this work."

I stepped onto our little concrete porch to explain things.

Donnie was never angry. He had deer-like eyes, big and always edging into depression. And since eight-year-old boys usually don't notice things like sadness, he must have been pretty miserable to get my empathy flowing. On that particular night, his voice was softer than usual. His father had just flown to Memphis, he explained. Gone until the end of the week. I couldn't see why that mattered, but I said, "Okay," and then, "Huh". Donnie listened while I described my castle. Then I asked if he had his project done, and he said, "Yeah." Except it didn't sound like an answer to my question. It was polite noise, and I could tell that he wasn't really listening to me. Which made me a little angry. Then he asked if he could hang out in my room and play with my Gameboy. It didn't seem to matter what he was doing, so long as he was close to me. But I just kept telling him that I shouldn't and he couldn't, sorry, my school project was the only thing that mattered now, and I was really tired of my mother staring at us through the storm door.

"I'll see you tomorrow. Okay, Donnie?"

He just nodded, gave me a weak smile and wandered off.

I returned to the kitchen and finished the castle's brown walls and a couple of tilted towers, and sticking a pennant or two on top, I called it quits.

Maybe I felt bad about brushing him off, or maybe I just wanted help lugging my project to school. Either way, I stopped by Donnie's house that next morning, ringing the bell until I was sure nobody was going to answer. Then I picked up my castle again and carefully went down the steps, pausing on the driveway for a few seconds, finally noticing the warm, faintly damp smell of car exhaust.

Fumes were pushing their way out from under the garage door, although I didn't realize it at the time. I thought it was funny, smelling a car but not seeing one. Then I turned and marched off toward third grade. Which saved me. I didn't have to discover something truly awful. And because I was saved from one horrific pain, the rest of my life has been spent struggling with a relentless, almost unbearable sense of guilt.

Lifting the garage door would have done nothing, of course.

By then, it was too late, and I'm an idiot to blame myself. Donnie and his mother and his four-year-old brother and the twin baby sisters were sitting in the station wagon that was parked in that darkened garage, all dead, along with that dog that he didn't care about and a bunch of cats too.

On occasion, inauspicious beginnings lead to large accomplishments.

As I grew older, I cultivated an unsuspected talent for designing castles and other fortifications. Most of my early projects can't be discussed, since they involved military bunkers hiding at undisclosed locations. But a few public buildings wear my handiwork, each structure brawny yet elegant, special concretes and reinforced stone peppered with a minimum of windows, all wrapped around internal skeletons designed to withstand fertilizer bombs and baby nukes.

After retiring from government work, I made a tidy fortune

building mansions for wealthy clients. My largest job was never finished. Just a few months after we broke ground on the King's new palace, there was a sudden shift in Arabian politics. But then the Israelis came to my rescue, snatching me up as a consultant, wanting my help with their constantly evolving East Wall. It was lucrative work, challenging and endless, and that was one of the reasons why I said, "No thank you," when my government showed up at my door.

"But you haven't heard the offer," their representative said. Then she smiled winsomely, adding, "I think you'll find it intriguing."

"All right. Try me," I said.

Her name was Colonel Sutter, although she had given me permission to call her Katherine. With a crisp, practised tone, Katherine mentioned a significant project, and then she offered an address that was sure to pique my interest.

Most definitely, I heard the word, "Moon".

Six bases were established on our sister planet. China and the EU, Japan and Russia each had their one. And there were two American facilities, one dedicated to science while the other was being built by the military.

"Craig," she said, "we would love your help." Katherine used my name with that false familiarity salesmen employ while praying for a commission. "You're one of the finest structural engineers in the world," she told me. "You're first on my list, and frankly, I don't even know who I'd rank number two."

She was lying. I learned that soon afterwards. Two former colleagues had already been approached. But one had a young family he didn't want to abandon, while the other poor man was freshly diagnosed with liver cancer.

"Let me get this straight," I said. "You want to hire me – "

"At a very competitive rate, Craig. Yes."

"And to earn my money, I'll live at the lunar base . . . and do what? Help finish the base construction, I'm guessing."

"And what would be wrong with that?"

I couldn't see anything wrong. But she hadn't answered my question either, which set off alarms.

"Here's the problem," I explained. "Much as I'd love to travel in space, and in particular, bounce across another world, I also know that building habitats on the moon is relatively simple work. You drag prefabricated structures up where you want them and then bury your new city under the regolith. A few meters of packed ground protect people and machines from the solar and cosmic radiation, which are the important hazards. Basically, you need to be about as sophisticated as a kid with a plastic shovel and beach full of sand. And that's why I have to ask: Why would you have any use for me?"

Katherine said nothing, but she smiled in a certain way. And that's when I noticed that she was handsome, at least for a woman who had spent her vital years inside a uniform.

Finally, I admitted, "Of course, I've heard some interesting rumors."

"About?"

"Our new base."

"Really?" she replied, feigning surprise.

I nodded. "We've got some stubborn international treaties down here. Nations aren't free to test whatever new and theoretical weapon systems they want to test. But those rules might not apply on the moon. At least according to certain government lawyers, they don't."

"Is that what you've heard?"

Looking at Katherine's gray eyes, I admitted, "I still know a few bodies at the Pentagon. One or two have mentioned plans to melt mountains and blast new craters. With gamma-ray lasers or super-clean nukes. Or we've developed an easy way to make antimatter bombs, and you're digging some very deep holes to set them off in safe, out-of-view places."

Only the gray eyes smiled.

"Is that what you want from me? You want help building secret, robust test chambers?"

"Not at all," she promised.

"Really?" I was honestly surprised.

Once again, Katherine said, "Craig," with that best-of-friends voice. "You're an exceptionally qualified structural engineer."

"And you're still not making much sense," I complained.

"Maybe we don't want you to build anything."

"Then what good am I?"

The smiling eyes waited.

"Okay, how's this." Then I fired the last round in my arsenal. "I know how to construct strong, durable structures. So maybe you're hoping that I can make my expertise run backwards."

"Which means what?"

"It's happened in the past," I confessed. "Military boys come to me wanting clues how to destroy a Korean or Pakistani bunker. Is that the kind of game we're playing? Are you deciding how best to hit the Chinese facilities?"

"An interesting speculation, and no." Katherine shook her head while grinning. "We don't necessarily want to attack anybody. But we would appreciate your help gaining access to a particularly difficult structure."

"What structure?"

"But now how can I tell you that?" she asked. Then she leaned close enough to feel too close, saying, "Some secrets are too large, even to somebody with your security clearance."

My heart was hammering, my breath quickening.

"When?" I asked.

"You'll leave for the moon as soon as you pass your physical."

"No. I mean when do I get told the truth?"

Katherine sat back, her eyes filling that handsome, early-middle-aged face. "When you're standing beside your target . . . then we'll tell you everything we know. Which, I have to warn you, is not very much at all . . ."

My religious upbringing was decidedly minimal. In our household, Christ wasn't a religious figure so much as a political one, and my parents would never have voted for Him. Religious holidays were either ignored, or in the case of Christmas, drained of their history and passion – with a few presents thrown at my sister and me as a bribe. Other cultures seemed to have their own ideas about God, but it was hard to hold opinions when you doggedly ignored everyone else. Only in exceptional cases did we visit churches. Weddings were one excuse, but only if they involved close friends or the immediate family. And with funerals, the same restrictions applied. Plus my parents had to actually like the deceased. Which meant that a peculiar family living down the block, and even the boy who was briefly my best friend, were not worthy of suits and nice dresses and a visit to anyone's house of worship.

I wanted to attend the service. "We can sit in back, like we did at my cousin's wedding," I promised. "And we don't even have to pretend to pray, or talk in tongues, or anything."

But my folks shared a different opinion.

"Do you know why she did what she did?" my father asked. "Donnie's mother . . . do you know what she wrote in her suicide note . . . ?"

"God," Mom snapped. "She wrote that God wanted her and her children to come live in Heaven. That's why she killed everybody."

Dad said, "The woman was profoundly depressed."

"There's nothing profound about any of this," Mom told us.

"Well, I won't go inside their stupid, stupid church," my sister piped in. She was sixteen and relentlessly opinionated, assuring everyone at the dinner table, "I hate everything about that idiot religion of theirs. The paternalistic tone, and all that mind-control crap . . . I don't want anything to do with those crazy people . . ."

"You're talking about my friend," I mentioned.

Mom noticed the discomfort on my face. "I'm sorry, Craig. This is an awful situation, and Donnie was just unlucky. Nothing was his fault. He just had the misfortune of being born to a couple exceptionally crazy parents."

I used to think my folks were crazy. But in the midst of negotiations, I knew better than mention that possibility.

"Do you know what his dad's doing now?" my sister asked.

I'd heard that Donnie's father returned to town on the next flight, but I hadn't seen him yet.

"He's living inside that awful house," she reported. "Can you believe it? With all those ghosts running around?"

"There's no such thing as ghosts," Father corrected her.

"You know what I mean." Then she shook her head scornfully, adding, "I read it in the paper. He says everything that happened was God's will. Everything everywhere is God's will. He's a creature of faith, and he can't question God's design, and since he knows that his family is in a better place . . ."

"Underground," Mom blurted. "In boxes."

"He can sleep, and he can pray, and he feels God's good hand."

On her mellowest day, my sister was a passionate creature. Eight years my senior, we were never confused for being close. Yet there was something about that moment – listening to her words, feeling her barely restrained rage – that makes the rest of her life even more memorable, ominous and ironic.

Two years later, during her freshman year at college, my atheistic sister converted to a West Coast cult. Our parents promised themselves it was a rebellious stage – her blatant, clumsy attempt to hurt them in the worst possible way. For years and years, they maintained that dogged faith of theirs. My sister contacted them only when she needed money, and they always gave her some lesser amount. That's how they convinced themselves they were strong, solid people. And just to be safe, they kept one bedroom waiting for my sister, since someday, sure as the sun comes and goes, she was going to realize her mistake and break free of that evil, money-grubbing sect.

Our parents died before I turned forty, within weeks of each other.

My middle-aged sister was still avoiding the funerals, it seemed. But shortly after the final scattering of ashes, she called me. She needed an infusion of cash. There were vague living expenses and ill-defined debts, and when that particular hymn didn't work, she claimed that she was seriously ill and desperate for an unmentionable operation.

My response was a godly silence, and after a few blistering curses, she hung up. After several more failed solicitations, the calls ceased.

As far as I know, my sister still wears the odd robes of her contrived faith, living as part of a thriving commune tucked into the backmost portion of Wyoming. Though perhaps I'm the fool here and the mother ship finally arrived, the Believers now streaking happily towards the holy temple orbiting Alpha Centauri.

My own journey into space was spellbinding – as close to transcendence as this old atheist will ever achieve, I kept telling myself – and the moon proved to be a wonderland, spectacularly dead and gorgeously drab. Within the hour, my hosts took me out to see their mysterious structure. Katherine drove the buggy with me sitting beside her, Pentagon suits plus three of the mission's top scientists filling the seats behind us. The others were speaking with familiar, slightly bored voices. Our destination was a low lump of some exceptionally smooth material that happened to wear the same general grayness as the surrounding moonscape. Most of the object was subsurface – a spherical body a little less than a kilometer in diameter, resembling a child's toy ball buried and forgotten on a very dry beach. It was by no means an impressive sight, but what amazed me was the array of tools and weapons that had been left scattered across the scene. I saw broken drills and burnt-out lasers, at least two plasma guns, plus abandoned railguns and their shattered projectiles, and rocket casings, and an assortment of bomb-making supplies. There was even somebody's broken ball peen hammer lying on the sterile dust. Judging by the boot prints and wheel marks, every person who lived at the base had taken his or her crack at the target, and everybody eventually gave up, standing aside while others wasted their inventiveness and all that useless muscle trying to crack a shell that refused to break.

Katherine parked beside the slick gray body, and with a nod, she signaled the team's leader to come forward.

Dr Nathan Peck was half my age – a tall gawky and unhandsome polymath. On his worst day, he was relentlessly brilliant. I soon learned enough about the man to feel sure that I'd never met anyone with half his intellectual gifts. He was a world-class physicist with a strong grounding in both information technologies and biology, and he knew enough mathematics to teach it to professors in the Ivy League. And make no mistake about it, Peck saw no need to bring a simple nuts-and-bolts engineer into his playground. He told me as much. Kneeling beside me, he began by shaking my hand and remarking, "Of course you aren't my idea. I really don't see how you could even hope to help us."

"Maybe I'll surprise you," I offered.

His response was a rolling of the eyes and a hard stare at our shared conundrum.

I asked him for details, but it was Katherine who supplied answers. She recited the object's dimensions and total volume, plus some very broad estimates of its mass and density. Meteorites had left no mark in its surface. Human beings had pumped fabulous amounts of energy onto its face, oftentimes in the same few square centimeters; yet the only credible result was a slight increase in the body's overall temperature.

"The entire structure warms up?" I asked.

"It's highly conductive to heat, we think." She risked a glance in Peck's direction. "Isn't that what you told me, Doctor?"

"Something like that." The young man nodded, and with a grudging tone added, "Maybe you've got ideas about this thing's composition. A fresh perspective would be helpful. Unless it isn't, of course."

Usually it takes me an entire day to dislike somebody. But Peck wasn't a creature who wasted time.

I asked obvious questions.

"We can't analyse what we can't sample," he responded.

"We haven't even gotten a taste?"

He shook his head.

Lasers and plasma beams should have kicked loose individual atoms. I brought this up, and with a palatable frustration, Peck said, "Don't you think we'd have thought of that?"

"Sorry," I said with a distinctly unsorry tone. Then aiming for humor, I asked, "So what do you call it? The Sentinel?"

It was an old joke apparently. "That would be a poor official name," Katherine warned. "Since it contains what might be useful information."

Standard military thinking.

"Castle Rock," said the resident general. "That's its official designation, at least for moment. And we're actively leaking misinformation, keeping people thinking about weapons tests and that sort of bullshit."

Everybody was pressed against the windows, watching an object that refused to notice our existence.

"What about the surrounding ground?" I asked nobody in particular. "Does the land tell us anything about the object's age? Or give clues about who could have placed it here?"

"We've used every available tool," Katherine promised. "Nothing about the regolith is unusual. Or the bedrock beneath it, for that matter. There is no credible trace of excavations or disruptions of any significant kind."

"We're still doing a full survey of the deepest rock," Peck added. "Half a dozen angled shafts are being dug, as manpower and machinery allow. And we're naturally studying the sphere's surface – "

"In case you find a doorway," I interjected.

Peck had a grating way of lifting one side of his mouth, snarling at the world. But his voice was soft and hopeful when he admitted, "That would be nice. Or if not a doorway, at least some kind of guidepost."

Another fifteen minutes were spent retracing the project's brief, frustrating history. Then we drove back to the buried base. I have gone for rides on nuclear submarines, and they offer their crews more spacious quarters than we enjoyed in that camp. I was escorted to a tiny cabin that I'd share with three military boys, each of whom fortunately worked staggered twenty-hour shifts. For the moment, I was alone. So I took the chance to lie down. Drifting toward sleep, my head began playing with the information that I'd been fed. There were little moments when it seemed as if intuition was working. Some creative portion of me was feeling confident that I'd soon figure this problem out. Fate or my own relentless talent would decipher the perfect solution, I kept telling myself, and of course as a consequence I would earn a hero's pleasures.

Then I was asleep, dreaming about nothing important.

A hand shook me awake, and my first thought was that one of my bunkmates was home. But as I sat up, a woman's voice said my name. I heard, "Craig," wrapped inside an important tone. And then Katherine knelt closer, happily telling me, "You brought us luck, Craig. We just found our doorway. It's not large, but it's not that difficult to reach, either. And from what we can tell, it leads all the way inside."

While Donnie was alive, his father didn't enjoy any real presence in the neighborhood. But after his family was dead, the man quit his traveling job. For two years, he lived alone inside that ghostly house. I occasionally saw him mowing his weeds or dragging his garbage can to the curb and back again. In unsettling ways, the man resembled my dead friend. They both had the same black hair and a similar wiry build, and sometimes there was shyness in Mr Warner's stance and the way he didn't quite look anybody in the eye. But one day he forced himself to stare into my eyes. I was walking home from school, and he stopped his mower and strode down to the street to ask me with a flat, simple voice, "Did you know my son?"

I nodded, an invisible hand clamped over my throat.

"I thought so," he said. Then he conjured up a big smile, telling me, "Donnie had some nice games. Toys. So I was wondering . . . if you'd like to take a few of them home with you?"

I was ten years old, which meant that beneath my skin was a rich instinctive greed. The man was offering free trinkets, and I couldn't find any worthy reason to say, "No thank you." So I nodded, and he said, "Come on then," and led me up to his house.

Without pets or a family, the little split-level felt spacious. The furniture hadn't changed, and judging by appearances, Donnie's father was a fairly determined housecleaner. Smiling in a big way, he asked if I wanted water or maybe some milk. I told him, "No thank you," and instantly felt thirsty. We walked down the brief hallway while he asked what kinds of toys I preferred. "All kinds," I said, although an unexpected doubt was waiting inside me. What was I doing here? How did I agree to this? Then he opened the first door on the left, ushering me into a darkened little bedroom once shared by two small boys.

Suddenly I was sad and a little sick, standing in the middle of that gloomy quiet. Donnie's father hovered behind me. I heard him muttering and turned to find his hands together and his head dipped, his wide thick-lipped mouth whispering a prayer or two to our Holy Father.

Donnie had slept in the top bunk. Thorough hands had put away every toy, wicker boxes and various shelves jammed full. I studied the assembled pleasures, but then realized that my greed had abandoned me.

The prayers stopped.

Kneeling beside me, Mr Warner said, "Take whatever you want. I'm sure my boy would approve."

But I was ten years old, and nothing that I saw would entertain a wise worldly man like me.

"Here," he said, handing me a drawing tablet. The tablet looked old – second- or third-hand old. Its face had been wiped clean innumerable times with the built-in magnet, but I could still make out faint gray lines that Donnie, or somebody, had drawn years ago.

"No thank you," I muttered.

"Or this," he said, offering me a toddler's plastic puzzle.

It hadn't belonged to my friend. Unless Donnie had played with it before I knew him, then surrendered it to his younger brother. But I took the simple object in my hand and held tight, and then I felt the kneeling man pushing his shoulder against my shoulder. Quietly, he said, "I am very sorry for you."

I made a vague chirping noise.

"Sorry for you and your family," he told me. "When you die, the four of you will be transported directly to Hell."

I let the puzzle drop to the floor, unnoticed.

The man put an arm around my shoulder and said, "Join me."

My stomach hurt and every breath burned.

"Pray," he said to me. "Accept our Savior into your life."

I said nothing, but the ensnaring arm was pressing me toward the floor. In another moment or two, I would have found myself trapped in the most difficult circumstances. I imagined being coaxed to say a few kind words about Jesus, and even if I didn't mean them, the floodgates would open. Against my will, I would begin an inexorable fall into the clutches of the Christian faith.

That's why I used my elbow, popping the man on his chin.

And then I jumped away, and with the gracelessness of youth, I told him that he was a crazy bastard, and he fucking well better leave me alone.

Beneath Katherine's navel lay the neat, almost lovely arc of a C-section scar, softened by time but still discernable under careful fingers. We spoke often about it, but never with words. There were my touches and curious looks, to which she replied with a hard gaze that left no doubt this was one topic that my current lover refused to discuss. Then came a purposeful silence and mutual discomfort, the sense of some taboo being avoided, and I think she hoped that I would feel ashamed. Or maybe something awful was shaming her. Either way, the emotions would fill her tiny cabin, leaving us almost no air to breathe.

Being female among a hundred youngish males, Katherine had been granted a princess's life. At least as far as possible on the Spartan moon. She and the other six ladies on the base each had their own quarters – tiny cubicles physically removed from the male habitats. Vague troubles at the other American base had brought about this inadequate arrangement, I was told. I was also informed that I was handsome and a fine lover, and she assured me that she was grateful for having a friend such as me – her word, "friend" – and she appreciated decent older gentlemen who had experienced life yet somehow retained their humor.

Yet my age and alleged wisdom kept me from feeling too proud. I was rumored to be wealthy, which no doubt made me attractive. And unlike most of the males kicking around the place, I had no uniform or rank to mess up the career of a female officer. By accepting my company, Katherine had an ally who was grateful and compliant, and who also had ample time on his hands. My government job had come to an end even before I began to work; the Castle's door, it seemed, had been open all along. But freighting my old body home again would cost too much in terms of fuel and effort, not to mention raise a few security concerns, and that's why I was marooned here. I was trapped. And I had nothing to do with my days but act pleasant, keep out of the way, and wait for my lover's return.

We avoided uncomfortable talk about scars and psychic wounds. Our old lives were on a left-behind world, and they didn't matter here. What mattered was the latest news from Castle Rock. What secrets had been discovered during the last hours? How was the mapping of passageways going? And had they found more of the indescribable machines? Dozens of contraptions were set inside the deepest chambers, silently doing nothing . . . except of course creating a host of unanswerable questions that were frustrating everyone involved.

"What's the latest wrong theory?" I would ask.

That was our little joke. These great minds that were sharing our air had been generating hypotheses at a staggering rate, only to toss them aside when they proved wrong, or even worse, untestable.

"What is Peck's head thinking today?" I wondered aloud. "Is it an old castle, or a very young one?"

"Old," she reported. "Nearly as old as the moon. Which explains why it's buried as it is. The object fell to the surface while the crust was still liquid, nearly four and a half billion years ago. Fell here and floated until the world froze up around it."

The hypothesis had potential. I mentioned several tests to

Katherine, who nodded and said, "Yes, I know. They're going over the data from the biggest kinetic blasts right now, hunting for definite numbers."

In other words, Peck was trying to weigh his conundrum.

But the next day, Katherine shook her head, halfway laughing when she admitted, "The numbers didn't work out."

"The Castle's too dense," I guessed. "It should have sunk into any magma sea."

"That's the reasonable assumption," she replied.

Again, that was one of our jokes. What sounded reasonable never seemed to apply in these situations. "You mean it isn't a big lump of gold?"

"According to several scales," she admitted, "the sphere is about half as dense as water."

Meaning that it would have floated on the molten moon like a child's inflated ball.

"Erosion covered it up," I offered.

"Peck has both of our geologists looking at that possibility. But to him and to me and just about everybody else . . . it seems more likely that someone took a giant spoon and carved out a round hole just big enough to bury the object most of the way . . ."

"Which somebody?" I asked.

Every day, in fashion or another, one of us brought up that salient question.

"He doesn't want anyone using the 'A' word," she warned. "If you see him, don't mention it."

Don't say, "Alien," she meant.

"Peck doesn't want our perceptions contaminated," Katherine explained, her voice wearing a slightly mocking tone. "If we assume little green starfarers, then that's all we're going to see. Which would be a mistake, he claims."

"But who else could have done this?" I asked.

Shrugging her bare shoulders, she admitted, "I have no idea."

After some hard consideration, I said, "Well I do." Then I mentioned another candidate. "God."

She surprised me, saying, "Maybe," with a pleased, even relieved tone.

But of course I was joking. Ancient extraterrestrials were completely credible next to the Almighty. Taking a breath, I steered our conversation to safer, smaller matters. "Have they found more tunnels?"

"Not this week, no."

"Or any new machines?"

For a few moments, she put on a wary expression. I was pushing too hard, and Katherine suddenly remembered her rank and pledges and the secret nature of this very important business. She was very high in our local pecking order. It was her duty to properly chasten me. So I said nothing for the next several minutes, one arm wrapped around her stocky waist, my free hand touching a few favorite places. I knew the woman wanted to tell somebody what she knew. And who else was available to absorb her gossip?

"No new machines," she reported.

"The map's finished?"

"And you can't see it," she warned. "Just Peck and his people and the top officers have access."

Yet I had a pretty fair version of it sitting in my head. I'd drawn it from Katherine's descriptions and stories overheard in the galley, and none of those important souls were allowed to see my map, either.

She told me, "Those machines, or whatever they are . . . they're our main focus for now . . ."

Again, I let silence ask my questions.

"And Peck believes one of them is working."

She said those words, and when I didn't reply, she asked, "Craig? Are you asleep?"

Not at all.

"One of the machines is awake?" I whispered.

"Peck says so. Station Gamma is."

I was breathing faster, my mouth and throat turning dry. "Does anybody happen to agree with him?"

"Some do. But not everybody, no."

"Why not?"

"Because the energy levels are tiny." She named a group of lesser researchers – an alliance had formed around this single issue – and she repeated their arguments as if they were her own. "The power usage is minuscule, and there doesn't seem to be a pattern. And nobody, not even Peck, has a clue about how to talk to the machine, or control whatever it's doing just now."

Yet I had faith in Peck. I'd spent one hour of my life with the man, enjoying none of it; but I knew his mind was as relentless and sharp as any could be. And his word outweighed the judgment of a million skeptics, so far as I could tell.

"What are you thinking?" Katherine asked.

By chance, I had just touched her belly, fingers skimming along the crease of the old scar. For every good reason, I said, "Nothing important. I'm not thinking anything."

She probably assumed that I was wondering about her vanished child. And grateful that I didn't pursue the matter, she swung a leg over me and took the initiative, giving this old man ten or fifteen minutes of fun.

Three days after that, Katherine said, "Another theory dies."

"Which one?"

"The one where the alien machinery is working," she reminded me. "Now Peck says he was wrong, he was fooled. 'Transient propagations of electricity,' he says it is. Was. 'I just made a mistake. The Castle's dead as dead can be.'"

I imagined him saying those exact words, in various voices.

Pulling her close, I whispered, "Too bad."

"I don't think it's too bad," Katherine replied. "I don't want alien machines doing mysterious jobs, thank you . . . !"

Another eleven days passed before I could corner Peck.

If swagger was something you wore, then the man had been stripped naked. I could tell as much from across the galley. He shuffled to an empty table, and he set down his tray, then his body, and his head bowed as he spent the next long while using his nylon fork, punching holes in the helpless veal.

I wasn't the only one to notice. A couple of the base mechanics were sitting beside me – good-natured boys who didn't mind an old engineer hanging around their shop when he was bored. Empathy wasn't their strong suit, but one of them astutely observed, "Our resident Hawking looks kind of blue."

"Kind of blue?" his buddy laughed. "I'd keep him away from guns, if it was my call. Know what I mean?"

Too well, I understood the implications.

"I hear he got his ass chewed pretty well today," said the first boy.

"A real mastication," said the other, sounding infinitely pleased.

"When was that?" I asked.

"A few hours back," the first mechanic said. "You were visiting your daughter's room. You probably didn't hear that other screaming."

They liked teasing me about Katherine. And I liked to believe that they were jealous.

"Who did the screaming?" I asked.

"The Pentagon suits. Then the general. Then the suits again." The kid made a show of shrugging his shoulders, explaining, "This isn't a big place, and you don't have private meltdowns."

"Our prick-genius isn't performing," said the second boy. "Billions spent and nothing to show for it."

Just then, I made my choice and acted on it.

"Where you going?" both asked, in a rough chorus.

"I'm going to have a chat with Peck." Then I threw them a wink, adding, "I'll sit with him until he insults me."

"See you in thirty seconds," the first mechanic kidded.

But really, the man didn't have enough energy for abusing anyone, except for himself. He barely looked up when I settled across the table, and after a lot longer than thirty seconds, he finally managed to ask, "What?"

"So the Castle's dead, is it?"

Nothing.

"Katherine told me. You thought you had something big at Gamma, but you didn't. And then you had to announce to everybody you were wrong."

His face lifted. His expression was drunken tired and sorry, with a strangeness gathered up behind the eyes. I couldn't tell what I was seeing, much less what it meant. Even when I made guesses, they fell miles short.

"I was surprised," I admitted.

"With what?" He spoke in a dry whisper.

"I can imagine you admitting to an error, sure. I can see that happening. But it's the phrasing. Katherine quoted you: 'I just made a mistake.' Which didn't sound like you. Those aren't your normal words, and the tone in her voice didn't seem like you, either."

"What tone?"

I took a moment. "Suppose we're playing cards."

"Okay."

"And you make a lot of noise when you push your chips into the middle. Then you lay back in your chair and smile too much."

"What are you talking about?"

"Bluffing," I said.

Peck might have been one of the world's great minds, but at a poker table, I would have destroyed him. He heard me say, "Bluffing," and shrank down a little bit, eyes bouncing left and then right, hunting for a friendly place to hide.

"The Castle isn't dead. Is it?"

He tried silence.

"Katherine didn't pick up on it. But to me, you sounded a little too confident about your failure. A guy like you . . . being wrong should have chewed at you, and just to prove that you could, I would expect you to generate ten new hypotheses in the next little while."

He maintained his uneasy silence.

"Were you bluffing, Doctor?"

Then he chewed his bottom lip, saying everything.

I made a show of grabbing my tray but not rising. Then with a voice that I hoped nobody else could hear, I asked, "Do you want me to go to the General and give him a poker-player's observation?"

"And what would you tell him? What's your best guess here?"

"You did discover something. I don't know what, but you did. And you don't want to share your news with anybody."

"Why wouldn't I?"

"Because you want it for yourself. By nature, you're a greedy soul. Somehow you pieced together some corner of this puzzle, and you're acting like the little boy who can't share his toys."

Peck almost laughed.

Then he caught himself, and after a moment's hard reflection, he admitted, "I do hate sharing the limelight. That's true."

I started to nod, glad to be right.

"Except that's not the problem here," he said.

With the tray still in both of my hands, I started to push back my chair.

"Stay," he told me.

I relaxed my back, then my fingers.

"You think I'm a bastard. I know. Arrogant and self-absorbed, and all the rest."

"What of it?"

"You were a government man once, Craig. Well, in my case, I've never been. I'm just a hired hand brought here because of my talent, and because they knew I would agree to almost anything to be involved in this work."

"The first scientist to peer inside an alien treasure box," I offered.

With a gesture, he pushed my words aside. Then with an even quieter voice, he said, "I doubt that the Castle is alien, Craig. At least not alien in the ways most people envision it."

"What do you know?" I pressed. "And why aren't you sharing your inspirations with these other children?"

"I'm not government, and I'm certainly not military," Peck told me. "And sure, I am a prick. I've got two ex-wives that will say the same thing. But that doesn't mean I lack ideals, or that I lack limits. When something huge comes my way – like the A-bomb came to Oppenheimer – I feel morally obligated to ask myself, 'What is the right thing to do?'"

"Okay," I said. "And what makes the Castle so awful?"

Peck's mouth opened, but no words wandered out.

"And why the miserable act today?" I gave my question several moments to work at him, and then I saw an obvious answer. "The big boys are trying to take you out of the game, aren't they? You can't give them the answers they want, and they're threatening to steal away your precious bauble."

His old pride bubbled again. "And who'd replace me? You?"

I let his insult slide.

"But they are threatening to cut my powers and rein me in."

"So you found a new A-bomb?" I asked.

Then he shrank down again, and with a tight sorrowful voice, Peck said, "I wish it was a bomb. A world-killing weapon. Because then I would know exactly what to do next."

I was thirteen when Donnie's father remarried. The lucky woman was younger than him – young enough that their union just missed becoming a scandal – and the newlyweds lived down the block from an outraged teenager. By then, my sister was lost to her mysterious, money-grubbing cult. By then, my parents were emotional wrecks, and the kindest words about religion in our household were cranky statements about people being certified idiots, eating any lie so long as it made them feel less miserable.

A few days after turning fourteen, I saw a cheap cardboard sign planted on Donnie's yard. "IT'S A BOY," I read.

The birth was no surprise, since the young wife had been showing for what seemed like half a year. But even today, I can recall my gut-wrenching horror when I heard that the infant child had been named Donald and that my dead friend's bedroom had been transformed into Donald's nursery.

For a couple of years, I managed to avoid that house and its insane inhabitants. My habit was to walk or ride my bike in inconvenient directions, and if I saw one or more Warner in public, I used every trick to escape notice.

Looking back, I'm appalled at my behavior.

Really, they made a sweet, silly couple. Donnie's father was angular middle-aged man with a tidy, somewhat drab face that seemed grateful for every good thing in his life. He had survived the death of his first family, and now he was working hard to convey a sense of peace. To a glowering adolescent, he looked altogether too happy. His laughter was cheap. He made too much of a show of loving his young wife, holding her hand or keeping a long arm over her pudgy little shoulder, kissing her on the ears whenever I saw them at the grocery store or in the park. And she seemed like any happy, fertile mother, pregnant twice again before I could finally abandon the old neighborhood.

Once I was in college, I would come home for only a few weeks in summer and a few days around Christmas. On a snowy afternoon in December, I drove in from the inconvenient direction, according to my habit, and while getting out of my car I noticed a new sign propped up in Donnie's front yard.

"FOR SALE," I read, at least three times.

"Oh, the Warner's are divorcing," my mother explained. Then she quickly added, "It's Polly's doing. Not his."

"Polly?" I asked, momentarily uncertain who that was.

"Her. The second wife." Mom laughed at my ignorance. "He can't let go, Polly says. And she's sick of it. He's always praying to his dead family, and he won't let Tom be called Tom – "

"And who's Tom?"

"The boy. Donald Thomas."

The gossip had a good rich flavor in the mouth. But another question begged to be asked. "How do you know what he does and what she wants?"

"Oh, Polly's one of our best friends," my mother reported.

Then my father, who was standing in the wings, burst in to report, "She's coming to dinner, by the way. With the kids." Slapping me on the back, he added, "You know, she's been asking about you, Craig."

I was outraged, but trapped.

"What does she want to know about me?" I muttered.

"Nothing special," Mom assured. Then she dropped plates into my hands, telling me, "Set the table now. Seven spots, okay?"

It didn't escape my notice that the famous Polly wasn't many years older than my vanished sister. And it didn't take long to realize that she was nothing like what I had assumed her to be. She didn't pray before dinner, and she didn't once mention God or Christ as a personal friend. Her missing husband was discussed – in code, if the kids were present, and if they were downstairs tearing apart the base-ment, she was more open about their ongoing problems.

"I knew it was dangerous, foolish, silly," Polly confessed, looking in my general direction even when she was speaking to my parents. "I should have run away when he insisted that we live inside his house."

I couldn't agree more.

"He always says that he's happy and at peace. But really, he's barely begun grieving. Regardless what he says and God says, he still a miserable mess."

I wanted to escape, but I couldn't dream up any useful excuse. So I sat in the living room with a thirtyish woman – pudgy and plain, but with bright sensible eyes and a knowing voice that I found oddly appealing.

I finally asked, "So are you Christian?"

Both of my parents smiled in a sly fashion.

"I was," she said. Then with her own buoyant grin, she said, "Maybe I still am. But I hope not. And I know for a fact that I've never been half the believer my husband is."

"That must piss him off," I offered.

She nodded and sighed, and with some satisfaction, she said, "In so many ways." Then she stared at me, and out of nowhere, she asked, "You knew Donnie well. Didn't you?"

Hardly at all, I could have said. And that would have felt like an honest answer: I knew him years ago, and we weren't close for very long. But instead of that, I admitted, "He was a friend," and dipped my head.

"By far, he was my husband's favorite," she mentioned. "My own son is a pale shadow next to his Donnie. Just wait until we reach heaven, I've been told. Then we'll meet him and understand what a saint that boy was. And is."

I felt sick and tired, and under everything else, furious.

Polly studied me for a long moment. Then she took the trouble to touch me on my hand, saying, "It was difficult for you. Of course."

"Not really," I lied.

"Do you believe you'll see Donnie in heaven?"

I laughed bitterly. Then in a crisp fashion, I described my journey to his bedroom and his father's praying beside me.

My parents hadn't heard that story, and they were predictably outraged.

But Polly absorbed my news without surprise. She knew the man better than any of us, and that was in his character. After I was done telling my story, she leaned in closer, asking, "Do you believe that you will see your friend again?"

Until that moment, I didn't even suspect that I wanted to see Donnie. But I did, desperately. All at once I was sobbing like a little kid, and the wise young mother threw her arms around me, hugging me while my parents sat apart from us, stunned by their boy's secret grief.

And that was the moment, after too many delays, when I finally began the slow business of getting over Donnie.

Lights were burning up ahead. As we approached the brilliance, I saw two physicists wearing spacesuits, hunkering over a bizarre piece of apparatus. The object looked like a box bristling with senseless holes and random black wires. Naturally I assumed it was one of the Castle's mysterious machines, but then one of the physicists cursed and threw a punch at the plastic housing.

"Careful," Peck remarked.

In the hard vacuum, it was impossible to tell a voice's direction. Both men first looked down the long passageway, and then they turned together, seeing us bearing down on them.

Again, Peck told them, "Be careful."

The less-angry researcher stood up straight and named the apparatus – a nonsensical string of syllables, as far as I could make out. I had no clue what the marvelous device was supposed to do, but according to the fellow's testimony, it wasn't working. Everything checked out fine, but for some damnable reason, they couldn't even do a calibration run.

"Keep at it," was Peck's advice.

The two men nodded, and suddenly they noticed me trailing behind.

"I want Craig's input on something," Peck offered, explaining nothing. "We're going to be at Gamma for a while. I want you to try everything before you give up here. Understand?"

We bounce-walked past before either man could respond, the lamps on our helmets casting a single bobbing light.

"Some of our equipment works fine inside the Castle. Which is damned fortunate." My companion had switched to a private, heavily scrambled frequency, holding a steady pace. There was a slight downward tilt to the gray-white hallway, but the footing was reliable. He skipped along, telling me, "I suppose the Castle could be tinkering selectively, screwing up sensors that might tell us something useful."

"Does the Castle think?" I asked.

"Probably not." Peck slowed a little and turned his shoulders to look back at me, his lamp making me blink. "Somebody else does the thinking. That's my current hypothesis."

"Who's that 'somebody'?"

"I'm not naming names," he said.

"Sure."

"But what we've been seeing here can be explained, at least to a degree." He turned forward again, bouncing along even faster. "That box of widgets they're kicking? It studies forces that operate across fantastically tiny distances. Our guess of the moment is that one or more hidden dimensions have been expanded inside the Castle. Or twisted down to where we can see it, maybe. How gravity operates here is going to give us a good clue, if they can collect meaningful data."

"And what do the new dimensions mean?"

"Well, for one thing . . . they could explain the incredible strength of this place. If the Castle extends far out into the multiverse – into realms we normally can't see or interact with – then our normal forces might bleed off in harmless directions. These walls could weather the worst abuse humans are capable of producing. Maybe."

"But who could build such a thing?"

The passageway had reached an abrupt end, a human-built door standing in our way. Peck punched at an oversized keypad with the fat fingers of his glove, and the airlock's outer door pulled opened. We stepped into the vacuum beyond, and again he offered up a code. The door closed and air began pouring in from some hidden reservoir. We stood as close as shy dancers, and once again, I asked, "Who could manage this kind of work? Do you have candidates?"

Peck looked straight ahead. "Oh yeah."

I kept quiet.

The outside air stopped whistling. As soon as I had a green light, I pulled off my helmet, hanging it beside my new friend's helmet. Then we stepped into a surprisingly large chamber – the biggest space I had enjoyed since arriving on the moon. Permanent lights came to life as we moved. The air was dry and a little too warm, but clean. Near the airlock was a small hill of supplies – food and bottled water, computer pads and paper pads, plus several top-grade digital cameras, each wearing a label that said, "MALFUNCTIONED". At the far end of the room was a portable thorium reactor, tucked inside a sleeve of regolith concrete and ready to power any job. And in the room's center, maybe twenty lunar strides away from me, was an object that could have been a machine, unless it was a piece of sculpture. Or it was neither, of course.

Katherine had prepared me for a black mystery, but the truth was, I felt disappointed. I'd imagined a rich velvety blackness that would swallow my gaze and threaten to engulf my soul. But instead, the machine was glossy, almost shiny – a complicated set of flat obsidian surfaces forming an odd doughnut surrounding a spherical object that looked large at a distance and quite small up close. Without sound, the ball hovered above the gray-white floor – a slight reddish cast to its blackness – and from every point of view, that strange ball occupied the same space in my eye.

If I pushed my face up against it, the ball would turn into a speck.

That was one of the early experiments performed by the polymath standing beside me. Against the wishes of colleagues and the General, Peck had said, "I want a closer look," and clambered over the doughnut's sides.

He was a brave soul; I'd grant him that.

"Nobody can see us here," the brave soul reported, taking what seemed to be his usual position before one of the flat black surfaces. "They tried installing cameras. Thermal sensors and microphones. 'Security tools' they call them. But they never worked very long."

"You're sure?" I asked.

"Absolutely. Since I'm the culprit who disabled each one of them." Peck had unsealed and removed his glove, and now he set his bare palm against the doughnut's shiny surface. A set of controls appeared. Suddenly I saw simple buttons and numbers and some kind of projection of what looked like a tiny point highlighted inside a much larger sphere.

"What made that happen?"

"Not my hand, if that's what you're asking." A smile softened his normal intensity. "Other people touched this surface, plenty of times. But the key seems to be here." He tapped his own forehead. "If you know enough, or at least if you make the right assumptions, the display is built for you. And it's designed to perfectly match your knowledge as well as your limitations."

I stared at his controls, a thousand questions begging to be asked.

"Suppose you can escape our four constrictive dimensions," Peck began, anticipating my first query. "That's what I was asking myself: from outside our space-time, wouldn't everything be visible? The omniscient observer could examine every location in the universe, every instant in time."

"You were thinking that?"

"I was considering the possibility," he explained. "Sitting here,

I was making various assumptions and calculations, trying to find the sense in this conundrum . . . and when I touched the surface, the controls appeared. Perfectly comprehensible to me, which is only reasonable since they match my brain's expectations and its finite abilities."

I glanced at the next empty surface on the obsidian doughnut.

"Think of Time," Peck suggested. "And think of the Castle as if it exists outside of Time and our flat little neighborhood."

With my bare hand, I touched what felt like cold glass.

Nothing appeared.

"You're not quite there," he remarked. Then after a moment's consideration, he said, "Make a guess: who would want to build this contraption?"

"Martians."

Peck shrugged his shoulders. "Do you want to know the plain truth, Craig? I can't imagine any kind of alien that would go to this trouble. Not for human beings, they wouldn't."

"So who?"

He didn't reply.

"How about God?" I asked.

"That's what your ladyfriend believes. This is all God's doing."

My eyes instantly grew huge. "Don't act surprised, Craig. After our conversation, the other day in the galley, I came here and did research. I wanted to understand you better, to see if I could trust you. I've been replaying your last several weeks, watching you and Katherine discussing me – "

"You looked into our bed?"

"If it's any consolation," he said, "I focused on faces and voices. Because frankly, I'll tell you . . . I'm not eager to see either one of you naked."

"You looked back in time?"

"Yes."

"Goddamn," I whispered.

He calmly waved my consternation aside, adding, "If there is a God, Craig, I cannot find Him. And believe me, I've been sitting here for days, searching. With this amazing tool, I've hunted up each of the old prophets. I've watched them preach and eat, screw and cheat, and I've seen all of them eventually die. And I'll tell you this too: not one of them accomplished a single credible miracle.

Not that I can find. They were ordinary men and extraordinary salesmen. They convinced other people to follow them, and after death, they did nothing but rot."

That was exactly what I had always believed – what I had been taught since birth – yet a distinct disappointment arrived with that sorry news.

"If God lives," Peck continued, "he's even less likely to intrude in human lives than aliens would be. Which leaves us with one viable candidate, Craig. The only entity that truly cares about human beings. Which would have to be us." He laughed, shaking his head slowly. "Only people care enough about people to make such an enormous investment."

"Humans built this?" I whispered.

"Humans will build it. In some remote future, or in a parallel universe. Who can say for sure when?"

I felt numb.

"Think about it this way, Craig: to our future selves, Time is just another malleable dimension. Whatever their reasons, our descendants will build this amazing object, and they will set it where we won't find it until we are ready."

I shook my head. "Aren't there some mighty paradoxes on the prowl?"

"You mean because if they sent it back through Time, that should the change the future and maybe destroy them in the process? No, Craig, that's old-thinking about temporal matters. The universe is defined by quantum mechanics. Reality is constantly dividing into a multitude of pathways. As soon as their gift arrived here, from whenever and wherever that was, an entirely new history was created, separate from the existence our benefactors experienced."

"So what exactly is their gift?"

"Maybe it's a blessing, and they're offering us a portion of their enormous power. Or maybe it's some kind of elaborate, horrible curse. At this point, I don't have opinions, one way or the other."

Again, I touched the glassy flat surface.

Simple controls appeared, and it happened so quickly that my mind half-believed they had always been there, begging to be noticed. The display showed me a specific date and hour, and a location that I recognized immediately. I did the math, and my belly tightened into a knot. Then almost as a reflex, I touched the broad green button, and when I looked up I discovered that from my perspective, the black sphere had vanished. In its place I could see my mother, exceptionally alive and young, lying naked in a rumpled bed, while my father, wearing only a sweaty T-shirt, lay panting beside her, muttering something like, "Okay," and then, "That was pretty nice."

The newly pregnant woman coughed into a tiny fist. Then she pulled the covers over herself, and with a voice that I knew better than my own asked, "By the way, did you remember to lock the front door?"

The front door of my childhood home was latched and securely locked. But fat good that does when you're trying to stop voyeuristic entities that exist outside time and space.

Entities such as me.

Peck muttered gibberish in my direction. I turned toward him, my expression perplexed and enthralled.

"Human history," he said to me, his face betraying a humbled, undiminished astonishment. "From this vantage point, you and I can observe everything that has ever happened to our species. I've watched the first *Homo sapiens* running across an African valley, and I've seen pyramids built on two continents, and I've seen wars and concentration camps and nuclear blasts. Wherever humans have stood, we can stand. We can witness every act that people have unleashed and hear every sound that we have made, and there's even an effective translator function." He pushed closer, whispering, "Languages no living man has heard . . . they can be turned into functional, mid-century American . . ."

I stepped back away from the doughnut, legs shaking. My postcoital parents lingered, but their features softened and their spent voices fell away into soft, incoherent murmurs.

"How long have you known?" I asked.

"Thirteen days."

"Nobody else – ?"

"No."

So I offered the obvious question: "Why me?"

"Because you've got experience with the world, and you seem skeptical by nature. And most important, you aren't genuine military." Whispering again, he asked, "Can you imagine what kind of intelligence weapon this would make? Armed with a tool of this magnitude, a person or government would have an open window over everybody's life."

I nodded, imagining possibilities both grim and wondrous.

"I don't really know you, Craig. But what I've seen of you . . . it tells me that I can trust you to help . . ."

"What have you seen of me?"

Peck hesitated, his crooked smile wavering.

"Have you watched my life?"

"It's remarkably easy, picking up a person's existence, following it through its high points."

I was embarrassed and I was thrilled. It took me several moments to find my voice again, warning him, "They'll learn what you're doing here. Tomorrow or next week, one of your colleagues down in Alpha or Beta is going to figure this puzzle out. Or the General's going to follow through with his threats, curbing your little freedoms."

"Oh, everybody's suspicious," he admitted. "I've been keeping close tabs on their conversations. I doubt if I have two days left to work however I want."

"So what were we talking about here?"

"Telling the world what we know. Obviously. Otherwise, there will be people who will shut a heavy lid over this place. Button it up and keep it to themselves. For decades, maybe for centuries."

"And maybe that would be best," I allowed.

Panic took hold. With a quick worried voice, he tried to sweeten the prospects. "Imagine, Craig. A world where the past is just as visible and immediate as the present is. Sure, I agree. It's going to cause a huge upheaval. Twenty upheavals, maybe. People are going to lose all their ancient ideas about human origins and God and our mythic heroes. But after a few years . . . in a generation or two, at the very most . . . we'll find ourselves with a new society. An honest, enlightened society. There won't be any awful secrets anymore. And this will be the only holy site: scholars from every nation will come to the Castle to study and learn, and the lessons of a 100,000 years will be shared equally with every citizen. Or at least that's how it should be."

"Maybe," I allowed. "So do you have a plan here, Dr Visionary?"

"With your help." Using a conspirator's voice, Peck said, "Every message I send home is being vetted. And it's the same for you. Did you know that? They don't trust either one of us. But if we can get our news to the other bases on the moon, or even just the civilian-run US settlement – "

"And how do we manage that?"

He grinned, thrilled by my interest. "Almost everything I've seen here, plus my explanations for the Castle . . . several hundred hours of files in all . . . I've them copied into a dozen null-sink hard-drives." From a food bin, he pulled out a camera that actually worked, then handed me one of the bullet-shaped devices. "They're very durable and wonderfully small. But what I can't do and you can . . . since you're an engineer and all . . . you can step outside and play with the hardware that's scattered on the surface. The stuff we used trying to crack the Castle's walls. My plan . . . and you'll appreciate this, Craig . . . is to cobble together a railgun. I'll supply the plausible excuse. I'll want you to shoot a hole in this panel, maybe. But instead of using it down here, you're going to wrap my hard-drives inside iron slugs and mark them with alarm beacons, then launch them in five carefully calibrated suborbital arcs."

"Clever," I offered.

"It's an elegant solution," Peck agreed, shamelessly applauding his scheme. "People will eventually find one or all of those hard-drives. And do you think that China or the French will let our Pentagon hold the Castle for themselves?"

I had to admit, "It might work."

"And if you want, launch the extra hard-drives toward the earth. The biggest railguns have enough kick, and if we wrap the iron inside ceramic envelopes to serve as heat shields . . ." He hesitated before admitting, "This is your expertise more than mine, Craig. I should leave it in your capable hands to decide."

I nodded, saying nothing.

Peck glanced at my controls. "I'm going to walk back up and help my staff with their little experiment. I'll be gone two hours. As soon as you hear the airlock cycling through again, blank everything. That red button at the bottom should do the trick. At least that's how mine works."

Just to make sure, I kicked the button, replacing my parents with the plain black ball.

"And what do you want me to do until then?" I asked.

"Play," Peck told me, as if nothing could be plainer. "Go whenever and wherever you want. Walk your life. Eavesdrop on the great moments in history. But whatever you do, I promise this much: after the first hour, you'll be an expert. That's how well built this system is."

"Okay," I whispered.

Then with a voice unaccustomed to trusting words, Peck told me, "I've got my faith in you." And he let me keep the hard-drive, showing me his hopeful smile before he turned and bounced toward the airlock.

I needed less than an hour to see everything I needed to see. Another twenty minutes, and I was finished with my work. Pushing the red button, I cleared the last scene; I pulled a fresh hard-drive from the camera and put the camera back in its hiding place; then I sealed my gloves and helmet, and with two hard-drives hidden inside a pocket, I passed through the airlock and marched up the long unlit hallway.

Fortunately Peck was where he had promised to be, working on the balky machine with his back toward me. Nobody noticed my presence until I was past, and except for a casual wave with my hand, I didn't signify their presence.

A supply rover carried me back to base.

I didn't bother trying to seem at ease. In a rush, I pulled off the suit and hurried underground, and at a certain door, I paused and knocked, wishing for a small measure of luck.

Katherine said, "Yes?"

I entered her small cabin and set the lock.

She was in uniform, minutes away from going on-duty. Something about my mood and looks alarmed her. "Sit," she advised. And then with a mixture of tenderness and revulsion, she asked, "Are you sick?"

I produced the fresh hard-drive and plugged it into her notebook. There was only one file on it, but before I punched PLAY, I stared at her while saying, "Peck has the mystery solved. And he wants to tell the world before he tells you."

Her surprise was far from total. She sat up in her chair, nodded for a moment while coming to terms with some old suspicions. And then very quietly, she said, "Thanks for coming forward – "

"Don't thank me," I interrupted.

She glanced at the glowing screen, curious now.

In the briefest possible terms, I outlined what I had just learned. Then I told her, "If you want, report both of us. Do it this minute. Or you can sit there for the next fifteen minutes and watch your daughter while she plays in a dirty little sandbox. She's six years old, and I know for a fact she won't make seven."

Katherine shrank down.

I hit PLAY and let the video run for nearly ten minutes. Then Peck was at the door, knocking on it while saying our names over and over, his voice tense and urgent, trying hard not to sound desperate but moving very much in that direction.

I froze the image of a pretty child burying her own legs under brown sand. Then I leaned close to her weeping mother, saying, "This isn't just a video. It's a piece of your daughter's entire life. Good and not, her whole life is waiting for you. But ask yourself this: if you report what you know now, what are the odds that you'll see any more of this girl? Ask yourself that, Katherine. And now, make up your mind."

I'm not the biggest name in this story. Peck made the discovery, after all. And Katherine effectively ended her career when she used her rank to evade the normal vetting procedures, uploading Peck's hard-drive straight home to the Internet – in effect, announcing this unexpected news to a thoroughly unprepared species. But people still have to ask me, "Why didn't you just do what Peck suggested? Why not use a railgun and send off the hard-drives like bullets?"

Because you're never sure where a bullet will end up, and you can't know what the person who finds it will actually do. What if another base or its government simply decided to take the Castle for itself? A war would break out on the moon, hundreds dying for a prize like none other . . . and who could envision what miserable future that would bring . . . ?

No, I tell people. I did what I thought was quickest and safest, and more than most ways, smartest.

"But Katherine was a believer," people like to remind me. "And the Castle has made a lot of Believers crazy."

The ugly upheavals are still gaining momentum, sure. Every faith feels threatened by the Castle, as well it should be. But I didn't approach Katherine with her God. I brought her daughter to her. And I would argue that when given the chance, people believe mostly in people. Gods and souls are inventions to make us feel better about those we have lost . . . but what if nobody is truly lost, if every who is born is always alive . . . if only in a different slice of time . . . ?

"And where did you figure that out?" people have to ask.

My final epiphany occurred after Peck left me alone. "What do I want to watch?" I asked myself. Then my mind jumped back to that long-dead friend and the horrible suffering that he must have endured on his last night. When I started playing with the controls, I meant to watch the tragedy: Donnie would come to my house and get turned away. Then somehow his depressed mother would manage to coax everyone into the car. Between her prayers and threats, what did she say to the older boys to keep them calm and compliant? How long did it take for the fumes to build up and for everyone to lose consciousness? Did Donnie weep? Did he call for me? And what was I doing at that moment when his little body turned into nothing but mindless, lost meat?

Yet when I had my chance, I found myself searching out a different moment.

Death is a very small part of life. And if you have only a little time to look at anyone's existence – yours or some shy kid from third grade – you would have to be pretty sick to seek out that kind of nightmare.

I spent an hour doing nothing but watch Donnie playing with me in my bedroom. I stared at that little black-haired boy, and I cried hard, and somewhere in the midst of that bland normalcy and those pleasantly wasted minutes, I realized nothing dies because nothing ever ceases.

To me, that's what the Castle means.

I saw this child that was once me pushing a toy battleship across the shag carpeting while his best friend maneuvered a thousand-foot robot over the ocean's golden surface, each making those silly little sounds of cannons and ray guns blazing away . . . Those boys are there now, safely contained in that impregnable, eternal moment . . . and if you ever have the chance to see my old self watching that scene, here is all that you need to know:

I told myself that if a mother didn't want to risk her rank and career for the chance to see her daughter again, then she was never much of a mother. And we probably wouldn't be much of a species, either. And if I were wrong about Katherine, I decided that we surely deserved our ignorance and idiocy, now and to the last of our sorry, perishable days . . .

THE HOLE IN THE HOLE

Terry Bisson

Terry Bisson (b. 1942) caused quite a stir with his short story "Bear Discovers Fire" (Asimov's Science Fiction, August 1990) which went on to win both the Hugo and Nebula awards. It's a deliberate tongue-in-cheek satire with chilling overtones about the discovery that bears have evolved to master fire. The story will be found in Bear Discovers Fire (1993). Although Bisson has written a number of novels, including the alternate world Fire on the Mountain (1988), he remains best known for his idiosyncratic and often anarchic short stories. "The Hole in the Hole", first published in Asimov's in February 1994, was the first of three stories he wrote about the brilliant but socially challenged Wilson Wu and his friends, which has fun with one of science fiction's basic concepts – the space-time portal. All three stories were collected as Numbers Don't Lie (2005).

TRYING TO FIND Volvo parts can be a pain, particularly if you are a cheapskate, like me. I needed the hardware that keeps the brake pads from squealing, but I kept letting it go, knowing it wouldn't be easy to find. The brakes worked okay – good enough for Brooklyn. And I was pretty busy, anyway, being in the middle of a divorce, the most difficult I have ever handled, my own.

After the squeal developed into a steady scream (we're talking about the brakes here, not the divorce, which was silent), I tried the two auto supply houses I usually dealt with, but had no luck. The counterman at Aberth's just gave me a blank look. At Park

Slope Foreign Auto, I heard those dread words, "dealer item". Breaking (no pun intended) with my usual policy, I went to the Volvo dealer in Bay Ridge, and the parts man, one of those Jamaicans who seems to think being rude is the same thing as being funny, fished around in his bins and placed a pile of pins, clips, and springs on the counter.

"That'll be twenty-eight dollars, mon," he said, with what they used to call a shit-eating grin. When I complained (or as we lawyers like to say, objected), he pointed at the spring which was spray-painted yellow and said, "Well, you see, they're gold, mon!" Then he spun on one heel to enjoy the laughs of his co-workers, and I left. There is a limit.

So I let the brakes squeal for another week. They got worse and worse. Ambulances were pulling over to let me by, thinking I had priority. Then I tried spraying the pads with WD-40.

Don't ever try that.

On Friday morning I went back to Park Slope Foreign Auto and pleaded (another legal specialty) for help. Vinnie, the boss's son, told me to try Boulevard Imports in Howard Beach, out where Queens and Brooklyn come together at the edge of Jamaica Bay. Since I didn't have court that day, I decided to give it a try.

The brakes howled all the way. I found *Boulevard Imports* on Rockaway Boulevard just off the Belt Parkway. It was a dark, grungy, impressive-looking cave of a joint, with guys in coveralls lounging around drinking coffee and waiting on deliveries. I was hopeful.

The counterman, another Vinnie, listened to my tale of woe before dashing my hopes with the dread words, "dealer item". Then the guy in line behind me, still another Vinnie (everyone wore their names over their pockets) said, "Send him to Frankie in the Hole."

The Vinnie behind the counter shook his head, saying, "He'd never find it."

I turned to the other Vinnie and asked, "Frankie in the Hole?"

"Frankie runs a little junkyard," he said. "Volvos only. You know the Hole?"

"Can't say as I do."

"I'm not surprised. Here's what you do. Listen carefully because it's not so easy to find these days, and I'm only going to tell you once."

There's no way I could describe or even remember everything this Vinnie told me: suffice it to say that it had to do with crossing over Rockaway Boulevard, then back under the Belt Parkway, forking onto a service road, making a U-turn onto Conduit but staying in the centre lane, cutting a sharp left into a dead end (that really wasn't), and following a dirt track down a steep bank through a grove of trees and brush.

I did as I was told, and found myself in a sort of sunken neighbourhood, on a wide dirt street running between decrepit houses set at odd angles on weed-grown lots. It looked like one of those leftover neighbourhoods in the meadowlands of Jersey, or down South, where I did my basic training. There were no sidewalks but plenty of potholes, abandoned gardens, and vacant lots. The streets were half-covered by huge puddles. The houses were of concrete block, or tarpaper, or board and batten; no two alike or even remotely similar. There was even a house trailer, illegal in New York City (so, of course, is crime). There were no street signs, so I couldn't tell if I was in Brooklyn or Queens, or on the dotted line between the two.

The other Vinnie (or third, if you are counting) had told me to follow my nose until I found a small junkyard, which I proceeded to do. Mine was the only car on the street. Weaving around the puddles (or cruising through them like a motorboat) gave driving an almost nautical air of adventure. There was no shortage of junk in the Hole, including a subway car someone was living in, and a crane that had lost its verticality and took up two back yards. Another back yard had a piebald pony. The few people I saw were white. A fat woman in a short dress sat on a high step talking on a portable phone. A gang of kids was gathered around a puddle killing something with sticks. In the yard behind them was a card table with a crude sign reading MOON ROCKS R US.

I liked the peaceful scene in the Hole. And driving through the puddles quieted my brakes. I saw plenty of junk cars, but they came in ones or twos, in the yards and on the street, and none of them were Volvos (no surprise).

After I passed the piebald pony twice, I realized I was going in circles. Then I noticed a chainlink fence with reeds woven into it. And I had a feeling.

I stopped. The fence was just too high to look over, but I could see between the reeds. I was right. It was a junkyard that had been "ladybirded".

The lot hidden by the fence was filled with cars, squeezed together tightly, side by side and end to end. All from Sweden. All immortal and all dead. All indestructible, and all destroyed. All Volvos.

The first thing you learn in law school is when not to look like a lawyer. I left my tie and jacket in the car, pulled on my coveralls, and followed the fence around to a gate. On the gate was a picture of a snarling dog. The picture was (it turned out) all the dog there was, but it was enough. It slowed you down; made you think.

The gate was unlocked. I opened it enough to slip through. I was in a narrow driveway, the only open space in the junkyard. The rest was packed so tightly with Volvos that there was barely room to squeeze between them. They were lined up in rows, some facing north and some south (or was it east and west?) so that it looked like a traffic jam in Hell. The gridlock of the dead.

At the end of the driveway, there was a ramshackle garage made of corrugated iron, shingleboard, plywood, and fibreglass. In and around it, too skinny to cast shade, were several ailanthus – New York's parking-lot tree. There were no signs but none were needed. This had to be Frankie's.

Only one living car was in the junkyard. It stood at the end of the driveway, by the garage, with its hood raised, as if it were trying to speak but had forgotten what it wanted to say. It was a 164, Volvo's unusual straight six. The body was battered, with bondo under the taillights and doors where rust had been filled in. It had cheap imitation racing wheels and a chrome racing stripe along the bottom of the doors. Two men were leaning over, peering into the engine compartment.

I walked up and watched, unwelcomed but not (I suspected) unnoticed. An older white man in coveralls bent over the engine while a black man in a business suit looked on and kibitzed in a rough but friendly way. I noticed because this was the late 1980s and the relations between blacks and whites weren't all that friendly in New York.

And here we were in Howard Beach. Or at least in a Hole in Howard Beach.

"If you weren't so damn cheap, you'd get a Weber and throw these SUs away," the old man said.

"If I wasn't so damn cheap, you'd never see my ass," the black man said. He had a West Indian accent.

"I find you a good car and you turn it into a piece of island junk."

"You sell me a piece of trash and . . ."

And so forth. But all very friendly. I stood waiting patiently until the old man raised his head and lifted his eyeglasses, wiped along the two sides of his grease-smeared nose, and then pretended to notice me for the first time.

"You Frankie?" I asked.

"Nope."

"This is Frankie's, though?"

"Could be." Junkyard men like the conditional.

So do lawyers. "I was wondering if it might be possible to find some brake parts for a 145, a 1970. Station wagon."

"What you're looking for is an antique dealer," the West Indian said.

The old man laughed; they both laughed. I didn't.

"Brake hardware," I said. "The clips and pins and stuff."

"Hard to find," the old man said. "That kind of stuff is very expensive these days."

The second thing you learn in law school is when to walk away. I was almost at the end of the drive when the old man reached through the window of the 164 and blew the horn: two shorts and a long.

At the far end of the yard, by the fence, a head popped up. I thought I was seeing a cartoon, because the eyes were too large for the head, and the head was too large for the body.

"Yeah, Unc?"

"Frankie, I'm sending a lawyer fellow back there. Show him that 145 we pulled the wheels off of last week."

"I'll take a look," I said. "But what makes you think I'm an attorney?"

"The tassels," the old man said, looking down at my loafers. He stuck his head back under the hood of the 164 to let me know I was dismissed.

Frankie's hair was almost white, and so thin it floated off the top of his head. His eyes were bright blue-green, and slightly bugged out, giving him an astonished look. He wore cowboy boots with the heels rolled over so far that he walked on their sides and left scrollwork for tracks. Like the old man, he was wearing blue gabardine pants and a lighter blue work shirt. On the back it said –

But I didn't notice what it said. I wasn't paying attention. I had never seen so many Volvos in one place before. There was every make and model – station wagons, sedans, fastbacks, 544s and 122s, DLs and GLs, 140s to 740s, even a 940 – in every state of dissolution, destruction, decay, desolation, degradation, decrepitude, and disrepair. It was beautiful. The Volvos were jammed so close together that I had to edge sideways between them.

We made our way around the far corner of the garage, where I saw a huge jumbled pile – not a stack – of tyres against the fence. It was cooler here. The ailanthus trees were waving, though I could feel no breeze.

"This what you're looking for?" Frankie stopped by a 145 sedan – dark green, like my station wagon; it was a popular colour. The wheels were gone and it sat on the ground. By each wheel well lay a hubcap, filled with water.

There was a hollow thud behind us. A tyre had come over the fence, onto the pile; another followed it. "I need to get back to work," Frankie said. "You can find what you need, right?"

He left me with the 145, called out to someone over the fence, then started pulling tyres off the pile and rolling them through a low door into a shed built onto the side of the garage. The shed was only about five feet high. The door was half-covered by a plastic shower curtain hung sideways. It was slit like a hula skirt and every time a tyre went through it, it went *pop*.

Every time Frankie rolled a tyre through the door, another sailed over the fence onto the pile behind him. It seemed like the labours of Sisyphus.

Well, I had my own work. Carefully, I drained the water out of the first hubcap. There lay the precious springs and clips I sought

– rusty, but usable. I worked my way around the car (a job in itself, as it was jammed so closely with the others). There was a hubcap where each wheel had been. I drained them all and collected the treasure in one hubcap. It was like panning for gold.

There was a cool breeze and a funny smell. Behind me I heard a steady *pop, pop, pop*. But when I finished and took the brake parts to Frankie, the pile of tyres was still the same size. Frankie was on top of it, leaning on the fence, talking with an Indian man in a Goodyear shirt.

The Indian (who must have been standing on a truck on the other side of the fence) saw me and ducked. I had scared him away. I realized I was witnessing some kind of illegal dumping operation. I wondered how all the junk tyres fit into the tiny shed, but I wasn't about to ask. Probably Frankie and the old man took them out and dumped them into Jamaica Bay at night.

I showed Frankie the brake parts. "I figure they're worth a couple of bucks," I said.

"Show Unc," he said. "He'll tell you what they're worth."

I'll bet, I thought. Carrying my precious hubcap of brake hardware, like a waiter with a dish, I started back toward the driveway. Behind me I heard a steady *pop, pop, pop* as Frankie went back to work. I must have been following a different route between the cars – because when I saw it, I knew it was for the first time.

The 1800 is Volvo's legendary (well, sort of) sports car from the early 1960s. The first model, the P1800, was assembled in Scotland and England (unusual, to say the least, for a Swedish car). This one, the only one I had ever seen in a junkyard, still had its fins and appeared to have all its glass. It was dark blue. I edged up to it, afraid that if I startled it, it might disappear. But it was real. It was wheelless, engineless, and rusted out in the rocker panels. But it was real. I looked inside. I tapped on the glass. I opened the door.

The interior was the wrong colour – but it was real, too. It smelled musty, but it was intact. Or close enough. I arrived at the driveway, so excited that I didn't even flinch when the old man looked into my hubcap (like a fortune teller reading entrails) and said, "Ten dollars."

I raced home to tell Wu what I had found.

*   *   *

Everybody should have a friend like Wilson Wu, just to keep them guessing. Wu worked his way through high school as a pastry chef, then dropped out to form a rock band, then won a scholarship to Princeton (I think) for math (I think), then dropped out to get a job as an engineer, then made it halfway through medical school at night before becoming a lawyer, which is where I met him. He passed his bar exam on the first try. Somewhere along the line he decided he was gay, then decided he wasn't (I don't know what his wife thought of all this); he has been both democrat and republican, Catholic and Protestant, pro and anti gun-control. He can't decide if he's Chinese or American, or both. The only constant thing in his life is the Volvo. Wu has never owned another kind of car. He kept a 1984 240DL station wagon for the wife and kids. He kept the P1800, which I had helped him tow from Pennsylvania, where he had bought it at a yard sale for $500 (a whole other story), in my garage. I didn't charge him rent. It was a red 1961 sports coupe with a B18. The engine and transmission were good (well, fair) but the interior had been gutted. Wu had found seats but hadn't yet put them in. He was waiting for the knobs and trim and door panels, the little stuff that is hardest to find, especially for a P1800. He had been looking for two years.

Wu lived on my block in Brooklyn, which was strictly a coincidence since I knew him from Legal Aid, where we had both worked before going into private practice. I found him in his kitchen, helping his wife make a wedding cake. She's a caterer. "What are you doing in the morning?" I asked, but I didn't wait for him to tell me. I have never been good at surprises (which is why I had no success as a criminal lawyer). "Your long travail is over," I said. "I found an 1800. A P1800. With an interior."

"Handles?"

"Handles."

"Panels?"

"Panels."

"Knobs?" Wu had stopped stirring. I had his attention.

"I hear you got your brakes fixed," Wu said the next day as we were on our way to Howard Beach in my car. "Or perhaps I should say, 'I don't hear.'"

"I found the parts yesterday and put them on this morning," I told him. I told him the story of how I found the Hole. I told him about the junkyard of Volvos. I told him about stumbling across the dark blue P1800. By then, we were past the end of Atlantic Avenue, near Howard Beach. I turned off onto Conduit and tried to retrace my turns of the day before, but with no luck. Nothing looked familiar.

Wu started to look sceptical; or maybe I should say, he started to look even more sceptical. "Maybe it was all a dream," he said, either taunting me or comforting himself, or both.

"I don't see P1800s in junkyards, even in dreams," I said. But in spite of my best efforts to find the Hole, I was going in circles. Finally, I gave up and went to Boulevard Imports. The place was almost empty. I didn't recognize the counterman. His shirt said he was a Sal.

"Vinnie's off," he said. "It's Saturday."

"Then maybe you can help me. I'm trying to find a place called Frankie's. In the Hole."

People sometimes use the expression "blank look" loosely. Sal's was the genuine article.

"A Volvo junkyard?" I said. "A pony or so?"

Blank got even blanker. Wu had come in behind me, and I didn't have to turn around to know he was looking sceptical.

"I don't know about any Volvos, but did somebody mention a pony?" a voice said from in the back. An old man came forward. He must have been doing the books, since he was wearing a tie. "My Pop used to keep a pony in the Hole. We sold it when horse-shoes got scarce during the War."

"Jeez, Vinnie, what war was this?" Sal asked. (So I had found another Vinnie!)

"How many have there been?" the old Vinnie asked. He turned to me. "Now, listen up, kid." (I couldn't help smiling; usually only judges call me "kid" and only in chambers.) "I can only tell you once, and I'm not sure I'll get it right."

The old Vinnie's instructions were completely different from the ones I had gotten from the Vinnie the day before. They involved a turn into an abandoned gas station on the Belt Parkway, a used car lot on Conduit, a McDonald's with a dumpster in the back, plus other flourishes that I have forgotten.

Suffice it to say that, twenty minutes later, after bouncing down a steep bank, Wu and I found ourselves cruising the wide mud streets of the Hole, looking for Frankie's. I could tell by Wu's silence that he was impressed. The Hole is pretty impressive if you are not expecting it, and who's expecting it? There was the non-vertical crane, the subway car (with smoke coming from its makeshift chimney) and the horse grazing in a lot between two shanties. I wondered if it was a descendant of the old Vinnie's father's pony. I couldn't tell if it was shod or not.

The fat lady was still on the phone. The kids must have heard us coming, because they were standing in front of the card table waving hand-lettered signs: MOON ROCKS THIS WAY! and MOON ROCKS R US! When he saw them, Wu put his hand on my arm and said, "Pull over, Irv," – his first words since we had descended into the Hole.

I pulled over and he got out. He fingered a couple of ashy-looking lumps, and handed the kids a dollar. They giggled and said they had no change.

Wu told them to keep it.

"I hope you don't behave like that at Frankie's," I said, when he got back into the car.

"Like what?"

"You're supposed to bargain, Wu. People expect it. Even kids. What do you want with phoney moon rocks anyway?"

"Supporting free enterprise," he said. "Plus, I worked on Apollo and I handled some real moon rocks once. They looked just like these." He sniffed them. "Smelled just like these." He tossed them out the window into the shallow water as we motored through a puddle.

As impressive as the Hole can be (first time), there is nothing more impressive than a junkyard of all Volvos. I couldn't wait to see Wu's face when he saw it. I wasn't disappointed. I heard him gasp as we slipped through the gate. He looked around, then looked at me and grinned. "Astonishing," he said. Even the inscrutable, sceptical Wu.

"Told you," I said. (I could hardly wait till he saw the 1800!)

The old man was at the end of the driveway, working on a diesel this time. Another customer, this one white, looked on and kibitzed. The old man seemed to sell entertainment as much as expertise. They were trying to get water out of the injectors.

"I understand you have an 1800," Wu said. "They're hard to find."

I winced. Wu was no businessman. The old man straightened up, and looked us over. There's nothing like a six-foot Chinaman to get your attention, and Wu is six-two.

"P1800," the old man said. "Hard to find is hardly the word for it. I'd call it your rare luxury item. But I guess it won't cost you too much to have a look." He reached around the diesel's windshield and honked the horn. Two shorts and a long.

The oversized head with the oversized eyes appeared at the far end of the yard, by the fence.

"Two lawyers coming back," the old man called out. Then he said to me: "It's easier to head straight back along the garage till you get to where Frankie is working. Then head to your right, and you'll find the P1800."

Frankie was still working on the endless pile (not a stack) of tyres by the fence. Each one went through the low door of the shed with a *pop*.

I nodded, and Frankie nodded back. I turned right and edged between the cars toward the P1800, assuming Wu was right behind me. When I saw it, I was relieved – it had not been a dream after all! I expected an appreciative whistle (at the very least), but when I turned, I saw that I had lost Wu.

He was still back by the garage, looking through a stack (not a pile) of wheels against the wall.

"Hey, Wu!" I said, standing on the bumper of the P1800. "You can get wheels anywhere. Check out the interior on this baby!" Then, afraid I had sounded too enthusiastic, I added: "It's rough but it might almost do."

Wu didn't even bother to answer me. He pulled two wheels from the stack. They weren't exactly wheels, at least not the kind you mount tyres on. They were more like wire mesh tires, with metal chevrons where the tread should have been.

Wu set them upright, side by side. He slapped one and grey dust flew. He slapped the other. "Where'd you get these?" he asked.

Frankie stopped working and lit a cigarette. "Off a dune buggy," he said.

By this time, I had joined them. "A Volvo dune buggy?"

"Not a Volvo," Frankie said. "An electric job. Can't sell you the wheels separately. They're a set."

"What about the dune buggy?" Wu asked. "Can I have a look at it?"

Frankie's eyes narrowed. "It's on the property. Hey, are you some kind of environment man or something?"

"The very opposite," said Wu. "I'm a lawyer. I just happen to dig dune buggies. Can I have a look at it? Good ones are hard to find."

I winced.

"I'll have to ask Unc," Frankie said.

"Wu," I said, as soon as Frankie had left to find his uncle, "there's something you need to know about junkyard men. If something is hard to find, you don't have to tell them. And what's this dune buggy business, anyway? I thought you wanted interior trim for your P1800."

"Forget the P1800, Irv," Wu said. "It's yours. I'm giving it to you."

"You're what?"

Wu slapped the wire mesh wheel again and sniffed the cloud of dust. "Do you realize what this is, Irv?"

"Some sort of wire wheel. So what?"

"I worked at Boeing in 1970," Wu said. "I helped build this baby, Irv. It's off the LRV."

"The LR what?"

Before Wu could answer, Frankie was back. "Well, you can look at it," Frankie said. "But you got to hold your breath. It's in the cave and there's no air in there."

"The cave?" I said. They both ignored me.

"You can see it from the door, but I'm not going back in there," said Frankie. "Unc won't let me. Have you got a jacket? It's cold."

"I'll be okay," Wu said.

"Suit yourself." Frankie tossed Wu a pair of plastic welding goggles. "Wear these. And remember, hold your breath."

It was clear at this point where the cave was. Frankie was

pointing toward the low door into the shed, where he rolled the tyres. Wu put on the goggles and ducked his head; as he went through the doorway he made that same weird *pop* the tyres made.

I stood there with Frankie in the sunlight, holding the two wire mesh wheels, feeling like a fool.

There was another *pop* and Wu backed out through the shower curtain. When he turned around, he looked like he had seen a ghost. I don't know how else to describe it. Plus, he was shivering like crazy.

"Told you it was cold!" said Frankie. "And it's weird. There's no air in there, for one thing. If you want the dune buggy, you'll have to get it out of there yourself."

Wu gradually stopped shivering. As he did, a huge grin spread across his face. "It's weird, all right," he said. "Let me show my partner. Loan me some extra goggles."

"I'll take your word for it," I said.

"Irv, come on! Put these goggles on."

"No way!" I said. But I put them on. You always did what Wu said, sooner or later; he was that kind of guy.

"Don't hold your breath in. Let it all out, and then hold it. Come on. Follow me."

I breathed out and ducked down just in time; Wu grabbed my hand and pulled me through the shed door behind him. If I made a *pop* I didn't hear it. We were standing in the door of a cave – but looking out, not in. The inside was another outside!

It was like the beach, all grey sand (or dust) but with no water. I could see stars but it wasn't dark. The dust was greenish grey, like a courthouse hallway (a colour familiar to lawyers).

My ears were killing me. And it was cold!

We were at the top of a long, smooth slope, like a dune, which was littered with tyres. At the bottom was a silver dune buggy with no front wheels, sitting nose down in the grey dust.

Wu pointed at it. He was grinning like a maniac. I had seen enough. Pulling my hand free, I stepped back through the shower curtain and gasped for air. This time I heard a *pop* as I went through.

The warm air felt great. My ears gradually quit ringing. Frankie was sitting on his tyre pile, smoking a cigarette. "Where's your buddy? He can't stay in there."

Just then, Wu backed out through the curtain with a loud *pop*.

"I'll take it," he said, as soon as he had filled his lungs with air. "I'll take it!"

I winced. Twice.

"I'll have to ask Unc," said Frankie.

"Wu," I said, as soon as Frankie had left to find his uncle, "let me tell you something about junkyard men. You can't say 'I'll take it, I'll take it' around them. You have to say, 'Maybe it might do, or . . .'"

"Irving!" Wu cut me off. His eyes were wild. (He hardly ever called me Irving.) He took both my hands in his, as if we were bride and groom, and began to walk me in a circle. His fingers were freezing. "Irving, do you know, do you realize, where we just were?"

"Some sort of cave? Haven't we played this game before?"

"The Moon! Irving, that was the surface of the Moon you just saw!"

"I admit it was weird," I said. "But the Moon is a million miles away. And it's up in the . . ."

"Quarter of a million," Wu said. "But I'll explain later."

Frankie was back, with his uncle. "That dune buggy's one of a kind," the old man said. "I couldn't take less than five hundred for it."

Wu said, "I'll take it!"

I winced.

"But you've got to get it out of the cave yourself," the old man said. "I don't want Frankie going in there anymore. That's why I told the kids, no more rocks."

"No problem," Wu said. "Are you open tomorrow?"

"Tomorrow's Sunday," said the old man.

"What about Monday?"

I followed Wu through the packed-together Volvos to the front gate. We were on the street before I realized he hadn't even bothered to look at the 1800. "You're the best thing that ever happened to those two," I said. I was a little pissed off. More than a little.

"There's no doubt about it," Wu said.

"Damn right there's no doubt about it!" I started my 145 and headed up the street, looking for an exit from the Hole. Any exit.

"Five hundred dollars for a junk dune buggy?"

"No doubt about it at all. That was either the Hadley Apennines, or Descartes, or Taurus Littrow," Wu said. "I guess I could tell by looking at the serial numbers on the LRV."

"I never heard of a Hadley or a Descartes," I said, "but I know Ford never made a dune buggy." I found a dirt road that led up through a clump of trees. Through the branches I could see the full Moon, pale in the afternoon sky. "And there's the Moon, right there in the sky, where it's supposed to be."

"There's apparently more than one way to get to the Moon, Irving. Which they are using as a dump for old tyres. We saw it with our own eyes!"

The dirt road gave out in a vacant lot on Conduit. I crossed a sidewalk, bounced down a curb, and edged into the traffic. Now that I was headed back toward Brooklyn, I could pay attention. "Wu," I said. "Just because you worked for NAPA – "

"NASA, Irv. And I didn't work for them, I worked for Boeing."

"Whatever. Science is not my thing. But I know for a fact that the Moon is in the sky. We were in a hole in the ground, although it was weird, I admit."

"A hole with stars?" Wu said. "With no air? Get logical, Irv." He found an envelope in my glove compartment and began scrawling on it with a pencil. "No, I suspected it when I saw those tyres. They are from the Lunar Roving Vehicle, better known as the LRV or the lunar rover. Only three were built and all three were left on the Moon. Apollo 15, 16, and 17. 1971. 1972. Surely you remember."

"Sure," I said. The third thing you learn in law school is never to admit you don't remember something. "So how did this loonie rover get to Brooklyn?"

"That's what I'm trying to figure out," Wu said. "I suspect we're dealing with one of the rarest occurrences in the universe. A neotopological metaeuclidean adjacency."

"A non-logical metaphysical what?"

Wu handed me the envelope. It was covered with numbers:

$$\int_0^\infty x e^{-\Delta_3 \frac{1}{g^2}} F^2 \sqrt{\frac{\Delta \cdot dx}{1420 \, nhz} \cdot \frac{CTL}{}} \cdot \frac{17\pi}{4\sum c_i c_i} = \frac{H}{h}$$

"That explains the whole thing," Wu said. "A neotopological metaeuclidean adjacency. It's quite rare. In fact, I think this may be the only one."

"You're sure about this?"

"I used to be a physicist."

"I thought it was an engineer."

"Before that. Look at the figures, Irv! Numbers don't lie. That equation shows how space-time can be folded so that two parts are adjacent that are also, at the same time, separated by millions of miles. Or a quarter of a million, anyway."

"So we're talking about a sort of back door to the Moon?"

"Exactly."

On Sundays I had visitation rights to the big-screen TV. I watched golf and stock-car racing all afternoon with my wife, switching back and forth during commercials. We got along a lot better now that we weren't speaking. Especially when she was holding the remote. On Monday morning, Wu arrived at the door at nine o'clock sharp, wearing coveralls and carrying a shopping bag and a toolbox.

"How do you know I don't have court today?" I asked.

"Because I know you have only one case at present, your divorce, in which you are representing both parties in order to save money. Hi, Diane."

"Hi, Wu." (She was speaking to him.)

We took my 145. Wu was silent all the way out Eastern Parkway, doing figures on a cocktail napkin from a Bay Ridge nightclub. "Go out last night?" I asked. After a whole day with Diane, I was dying to have somebody to talk to.

"Something was bothering me all night," he said. "Since the surface of the Moon is a vacuum, how come all the air on Earth doesn't rush through the shed door, along with the tyres?"

"I give up," I said.

We were at a stoplight. "There it is," he said. He handed me the napkin, on which was scrawled:

$$\frac{H}{h} = \int_{WAP}^{\infty} 1920 \Big) dx \frac{1}{4} \Big|_{\Delta 33} \sqrt{\int_{4\Delta(\pi^0)}^{32} \sqrt{RHT}} \cdot \sum_{K\cos^2} \frac{dx}{} = \frac{h}{H}$$

"There what is?"

"The answer to my question. As those figures demonstrate, Irv, we're not just dealing with a neotopological metaeuclidean adjacency. We're dealing with an *incongruent* neotopological metaeuclidean adjacency. The two areas are still separated by a quarter of a million miles, even though that distance has been folded to the width of a centimetre. It's all there in black and white. See?"

"I guess," I said. The fourth thing you learn in law school is to never admit you don't understand something.

"The air doesn't rush through, because it can't. It can kind of seep through, though, creating a slight microclimate in the immediate vicinity of the adjacency. Which is probably why we don't die immediately of decompression. A tyre can roll through, if you give it a shove, but air is too, too . . ."

"Too wispy to shove," I said.

"Exactly."

I looked for the turn off Conduit, but nothing was familiar. I tried a few streets, but none of them led us into the Hole. "Not again!" Wu complained.

"Again!" I answered.

I went back to Boulevard. Vinnie was behind the counter today, and he remembered me (with a little prodding).

"You're not the only one having trouble finding the Hole," he said. "It's been hard to find lately."

"What do you mean, 'lately'?" Wu asked from the doorway.

"Just this last year. Every month or so it gets hard to find. I think it has to do with the Concorde. I read somewhere that the noise affects the tide, and the Hole isn't that far from Jamaica Bay, you know."

"Can you draw us a map?" I asked.

"I never took drawing," Vinnie said, "so listen up close."

Vinnie's instructions had to do with an abandoned railroad track, a wrong-way turn onto a one-way street, a dog-leg that cut across a health club parking lot, and several other ins and outs. While I was negotiating all this, Wu was scrawling the back of a car-wash flyer he had taken from Vinnie's counter.

"The tide," he muttered. "I should have known!"

I didn't ask him what he meant; I figured (I knew!) he would tell me. But before he had a chance, we were bouncing down a dirt track through some scruffy trees, and onto the now-familiar dirt streets of the Hole. "Want some more moon rocks?" I asked when we passed the kids and their stand.

"I'll pick up my own today, Irv!"

I pulled up by the gate and we let ourselves in. Wu carried the shopping bag; he gave me the toolbox.

The old man was working on an ancient 122, the Volvo that looks like a '48 Ford from the back. (It was always one of my favourites.) "It's electric," he said when Wu and I walked up.

"The 122?" I asked.

"The dune buggy," the old man said. "Electric is the big thing now. All the cars in California are going to be electric next year. It's the law."

"No, it's not," I said. "So what, anyway?"

"That makes that dune buggy worth a lot of money."

"No, it doesn't. Besides, you already agreed on a price."

"That's right. Five hundred," Wu said. He pulled five bills from his pocket and unfolded them.

"I said I couldn't take *less* than five hundred," the old man said. "I never said I couldn't take more."

Before Wu could answer, I pulled him behind the 122. "Remember the second thing we learned in law school!" I said. "When to walk away. We can come back next week – if you still want that thing."

Wu shook his head. "It won't be here next week. I realized something when Vinnie told us that the Hole was getting hard to find. The adjacency is warping the neighbourhood as well as the cislunar space-time continuum. And since it's lunar, it has a monthly cycle. Look at this."

He handed me the car wash flyer, on the back of which was scrawled:

$$T = \frac{\alpha \sqrt{\frac{L}{G}}}{H(\lambda)} = \frac{1}{\theta^2} F^2$$

"See?" said Wu. "We're not just dealing with an incongruent neotopological metaeuclidean adjacency. We're dealing with a *periodic* incongruent neotopological metaeuclidean adjacency."

"Which means . . ."

"The adjacency comes and goes. With the Moon."

"Sort of like PMS."

"Exactly. I haven't got the figures adjusted for daylight savings time yet, but the Moon is on the wane, and I'm pretty sure that after today, Frankie will be out of the illegal dumping business for a month, at least."

"Perfect. So we come back next month."

"Irv, I don't want to take the chance. Not with a million dollars at stake."

"Not with a what?" He had my attention.

"That LRV cost two million new, and only three of them were made. Once we get it out, all we have to do is contact NASA. Or Boeing. Or the Air & Space Museum at the Smithsonian. But we've got to strike while the iron is hot. Give me a couple of hundred bucks and I'll give you a fourth interest."

"A half."

"A third. Plus the P1800."

"You already gave me the P1800."

"Yeah, but I was only kidding. Now I'm serious."

"Deal," I said. But instead of giving Wu two hundred, I plucked the five hundred-dollar bills out of his hand. "But you stick to the numbers. I do all the talking."

We got it for six hundred. Non-refundable. "What does that mean?" Wu asked.

"It means you boys own the dune buggy – whether you get it out of the cave or not," said the old man, counting his money.

"Fair enough," said Wu. It didn't seem fair to me at all, but I kept my mouth shut. I couldn't imagine a scenario in which we would get our money back from the old man, anyway.

He went back to work on the engine of the 122, and Wu and I headed for the far end of the yard. We found Frankie rolling tyres through the shed door: *pop, pop, pop*. The pile by the fence was as big as ever. He waved and kept on working.

Wu set down the shopping bag and pulled out two of those spandex bicycling outfits. He handed one to me, and started taking off his shoes.

I'll spare you the ensuing interchange – what I said, what he said, objections, arguments, etc. Suffice it to say that, ten minutes later, I was wearing black and purple tights under my coveralls, and so was Wu. Supposedly, they were to keep our skin from blistering in the vacuum. Wu was hard to resist when he had his mind made up.

I wondered what Frankie thought of it all. He just kept rolling tyres through the doorway, one by one.

There were more surprises in the bag. Wu pulled out rubber gloves and wool mittens, a brown bottle with Chinese writing on it, a roll of clear plastic vegetable bags from the supermarket, a box of cotton balls, a roll of duct tape, and a rope.

Frankie didn't say anything until Wu got to the rope. Then he stopped working, sat down on the pile of tyres, lit a cigarette, and said: "Won't work."

Wu begged his pardon.

"I'll show you," Frankie said. He tied one end of the rope to a tyre and tossed it through the low door into the shed. There was the usual *pop* and then a fierce crackling noise.

Smoke blew out the door. Wu and I both jumped back.

Frankie pulled the rope back, charred on one end. There was no tyre. "I learned the hard way," he said, "when I tried to pull the dune buggy through myself, before I took the wheels off."

"Of course!" Wu said. "What a fool I've been. I should have known!"

"Should have known what?" Frankie and I both asked at once.

Wu tore a corner off the shopping bag and started scrawling numbers on it with a pencil stub. "Should have known this!" he said, and he handed it to Frankie.

Frankie looked at it, shrugged, and handed it to me:

$$\frac{t_\nu \approx \frac{1}{c} \times \frac{e^4}{m_p m_e^2 c^3}}{h(H)}$$

"So?" I said.

"So, there it is!" Wu said. "As those figures clearly indicate, you can *pass through* a noncongruent adjacency, but you can't *connect* its two aspects. It's only logical. Imagine the differential energy stored when a quarter of a million miles of space-time is folded to less than a millimetre."

"Burns right through a rope," Frankie said.

"Exactly."

"How about a chain?" I suggested.

"Melts a chain," said Frankie. "Never tried a cable, though."

"No substance known to man could withstand that awesome energy differential," Wu said. "Not even cable. That's why the tyres make that *pop*. I'll bet you have to roll them hard or they bounce back, right?"

"Whatever you say," said Frankie, putting out his cigarette. He was losing interest.

"Guess that means we leave it there," I said. I had mixed feelings. I hated to lose a third of a million dollars, but I didn't like the looks of that charred rope. Or the smell. I was even willing to kiss my hundred bucks goodbye.

"Leave it there? No way. We'll drive it out," Wu said. "Frankie, do you have some twelve-volt batteries you can loan me? Three, to be exact."

"Unc's got some," said Frankie. "I suspect he'll want to sell them, though. Unc's not much of a loaner."

Why was I not surprised?

Half an hour later we had three twelve-volt batteries in a supermarket shopping cart. The old man had wanted another hundred dollars, but since I was now a partner I did the bargaining, and we got them for twenty bucks apiece, charged and ready to go, with the cart thrown in. Plus three sets of jumper cables, on loan.

Wu rolled the two wire mesh wheels through the shed door. Each went *pop* and was gone. He put the toolbox into the supermarket cart with the batteries and the jumper cables. He pulled on the rubber gloves, and pulled the wool mittens over them. I did the same.

"Ready, Irv?" Wu said. (I would have said no, but I knew it wouldn't do any good. So I didn't say anything.) "We won't be able to talk on the Moon, so here's the plan. First, we push the cart through. Don't let it get stuck in the doorway where it connects the two aspects of the adjacency, or it'll start to heat up. Might even explode. Blow up both worlds. Who knows? Once we're through, you head down the hill with the cart. I'll bring the two wheels. When we get to the LRV, you pick up the front end and – "

"Don't we have a jack?"

"I'm expecting very low gravity. Besides, the LRV is lighter than a golf cart. Only 460 pounds, and that's here on Earth. You hold it up while I mount the wheels – I have the tools laid out in the tray of the toolbox. Then you hand me the batteries, they go in front, and I'll connect them with the jumper cables, in series. Then we climb in and – "

"Aren't you forgetting something, Wu?" I said. "We won't be able to hold our breath long enough to do all that."

"Ah so!" Wu grinned and held up the brown bottle with Chinese writing on it. "No problem! I have here the ancient Chinese herbal treatment known as (he said some Chinese words), or 'Pond Explorer'. Han dynasty sages used it to lie underwater and meditate for hours. I ordered this from Hong Kong, where it is called (more Chinese words), or 'Mud Turtle Master' and used by thieves; but no matter, it's the same stuff. Hand me those cotton balls."

The bottle was closed with a cork. Wu uncorked it and poured thick brown fluid on a cotton ball; it hissed and steamed.

"Jesus," I said.

"Pond Explorer not only provides the blood with oxygen, it suppresses the breathing reflex. As a matter of fact, you *can't* breathe while it's under your tongue. Which means you can't talk. It also contracts the capillaries and slows the heartbeat. It also scours the nitrogen out of the blood so you don't get the bends."

"How do you know all this?"

"I was into organic chemistry for several years," Wu said. "Did my master's thesis on ancient Oriental herbals. Never finished it, though."

"Before you studied math?"

"After math, before law. Open up."

As he prepared to put the cotton ball under my tongue, he said, "Pond Explorer switches your cortex to an ancient respiratory pattern predating the oxygenation of the Earth's atmosphere. Pretty old stuff, Irv! It will feel perfectly natural, though. Breathe out and empty your lungs. There! When we come out, spit it out immediately so you can breathe and talk. It's that simple."

The Pond Explorer tasted bitter. I felt oxygen (or something) flooding my tongue and my cheeks. My mouth tingled. Once I got used to it, it wasn't so bad; as a matter of fact, it felt great. Except for the taste, which didn't go away.

Wu put his cotton ball under his tongue, smiled, and corked the bottle. Then, while I watched in alarm, he tore two plastic bags off the roll.

I saw what was coming. I backed away, shaking my head –

I'll spare you the ensuing interchange. Suffice it to say that, minutes later, we both had plastic bags over our heads, taped around our necks with duct tape. Once I got over my initial panic, it wasn't so bad. As always, Wu seemed to know what he was doing. And as always, it was no use resisting his plans.

If you're wondering what Frankie was making of all this, so was I. He had stopped working again. While my bag was being taped on, I saw him sitting on the pile of tyres, watching us with those blue-green eyes; looking a little bored, as if he saw such goings-on every day.

It was time. Wu grabbed the front of the supermarket cart and I grabbed the handle. Wu spun his finger and pointed toward the shed door with its tattered shower curtain waving slightly in the ripples of the space-time interface. We were off!

I waved goodbye to Frankie. He lifted one finger in farewell as we ran through.

From the Earth to the Moon – in one long step for mankind (and in particular, Wilson Wu). I heard a crackling, even through the plastic bag, and the supermarket cart shuddered and shook like a lawnmower with a bent blade. Then we were on the other side, and there was only a huge cold empty silence.

Overhead, a million stars. At our feet, grey dust. The door we had come through was a dimly lighted hole under a low cliff behind us. We were looking down a grey slope strewn with tyres. The flat area at the bottom of the slope was littered with empty bottles, wrappers, air tanks, a big tripod, and of course, the dune buggy – or LRV – nose down in the dust. There were tracks all around it. Beyond were low hills, grey-green except for an occasional black stone. Everything seemed close; there was no far away. Except for the tyres, the junk and the tracks around the dune buggy, the landscape was featureless, smooth. Unmarked. Untouched. Lifeless.

The whole scene was half-lit, like dirty snow under a full moon in winter, only brighter. And more green.

Wu was grinning like a mad man. His plastic bag had expanded so that it looked like a space helmet; I realized mine probably looked the same. This made me feel better.

Wu pointed up behind us. I turned, and there was the Earth – hanging in the sky like a blue-green, oversized moon, just like the cover of *The Whole Earth Catalog*. I hadn't actually doubted Wu, but I hadn't actually believed him either, until then. The fifth thing you learn in law school is to be comfortable in that "twilight zone" between belief and doubt.

Now I believed it. We were on the Moon, looking back at the Earth. And it was cold! The gloves did no good at all, even with the wool over the rubber. But there was no time to worry about it. Wu had already picked up the wire mesh wheels and started down the slope, sort of hopping with one under each arm, trying to miss the scattered tyres. I followed, dragging the grocery cart behind me. I had expected it to bog down in the dust, but it didn't. The only problem was, the low gravity made it hard for me to keep my footing. I had to wedge my toes under the junk tyres and pull it a few feet at a time.

The dune buggy, or LRV, as Wu liked to call it, was about the size of a jeep without a hood (or even an engine). It had two seats side by side, like lawn chairs with plastic webbing, facing a square console the size of a portable TV. Between the seats was a gearshift. There was no steering wheel. An umbrella-shaped antenna attached to the front end made the whole thing look like a contraption out of *E.T.* or *Mary Poppins*.

I picked up the front end, and Wu started putting on the left wheel, fitting it under the round fibreglass fender. Even though the LRV was light, the sudden exertion reminded me that I wasn't breathing, and I felt an instant of panic. I closed my eyes and sucked my tongue until it went away. The bitter taste of the Pond Explorer was reassuring.

When I opened my eyes, it looked like a fog was rolling in: it was my plastic bag, fogging up. I could barely see Wu, already finishing the left wheel. I wondered if he had ever worked on an Indy pit crew. (I found out later that he had.)

Wu crossed to the right wheel. The fog was getting thicker. I tried wiping it off with one hand, but of course, it was on the inside. Wu gave the thumbs up, and I set the front end down. I pointed at my plastic bag, and he nodded. His was fogged up, too. He tossed his wrench into the toolbox, and the plastic tray shattered like glass (silently, of course). Must have been the cold. My fingers and toes were killing me.

Wu started hopping up the slope, and I followed. I couldn't see the Earth overhead, or the Moon below; everything was a blur. I wondered how we would find our way out (or in?), back through the shed door. I needn't have worried. Wu took my hand and led me through, and this time I heard the *pop*. Blinking in the light, we tore the bags off our heads.

Wu spit out his cotton, and I did the same. My first breath felt strange. And wonderful. I had never realized breathing was so much fun.

There was a high-pitched cheer. Several of the neighbourhood kids had joined Frankie on the pile of tyres.

"Descartes," Wu said.

"We left it down there," I said.

"No, I mean our location. It's in the lunar highlands, near the equator. Apollo 16. Young, Duke, and Mattingly. 1972. I recognize the battery cover on the LRV. The return was a little hairy, though. Ours, I mean, not theirs. I had to follow the tyres the last few yards. We'll spray some WD-40 on the inside of the plastic bags before we go back in."

"Stuff's good for everything," Frankie said.

"Almost," I said.

It was noon, and I was starving, but there was no question of breaking for lunch. Wu was afraid the batteries would freeze; though they were heavy duty, they were made for Earth, not the Moon. With new Pond Explorer and new plastic bags properly treated with WD-40, we went back in. I had also taped plastic bags over my shoes. My toes were still stinging from the cold.

As we went down the slope toward the LRV site, we tossed a few of the tyres aside to clear a road. With any luck, we would be coming up soon.

We left the original NASA batteries in place and set the new (well, used, but charged) batteries on top of them, between the front fenders. While Wu hooked them up with the jumper cables, I looked around for what I hoped was the last time. There was no view, just low hills all around, the one in front of us strewn with tyres like burnt donuts. The shed door (or adjacency, as Wu liked to call it) was a dimly lighted cave under a low cliff at the top of the slope. It wasn't a long hill, but it was steep – about twelve degrees.

I wondered if the umbrella-antenna would make it through the door. As if he had read my mind, Wu was already unbolting it when I turned back around. He tossed it aside with the rest of the junk, sat down, and patted the seat beside him.

I climbed in or rather "on", since there was no "in" to the LRV. Wu sat, of course, on the left. It occurred to me that if the English had been first on the Moon, he would have been on the right. There was no steering wheel or foot pedals either – but that didn't bother Wu. He seemed to know exactly what he was doing. He hit a few switches on the console, and dials lighted up for "roll", "heading", "power", etc. With a mad grin towards me, and a thumbs up towards the top of the slope (or the Earth hanging above it), he pushed the T-handle between us forward.

The LRV lurched. It groaned – I could "hear" it through my seat and my tailbone – and began to roll slowly forward. I could tell the batteries were weak.

If the LRV had lights, we didn't need them. The Earth, hanging over the adjacency like a gigantic pole star, gave plenty of light. The handle I had thought was a gearshift was actually a joystick, like on a video game. Pushing it to one side, Wu turned the LRV sharply to the right – all four wheels turned – and started up the slope.

It was slow going. You might think the Earth would have looked friendly, but it didn't. It looked cold and cruel; it seemed to be mocking us. The batteries, which had started out weak, were getting weaker. Wu's smile was gone already. The path we had cleared through the tyres was useless; the LRV would never make it straight up the slope.

I climbed down and began clearing an angled switchback. If

pulling things on the Moon is hard, throwing them is almost fun. I hopped from tyre to tyre, slinging them down the hill, while Wu drove behind me.

The problem was, even on a switchback the corners are steep. The LRV was still twenty yards from the top when the batteries gave out entirely. I didn't hear it, of course; but when I looked back after clearing the last stretch, I saw it was stopped. Wu was banging on the joystick with both hands. His plastic bag was swollen, and I was afraid it would burst. I had never seen Wu lose it before. It alarmed me. I ran (or rather, hopped) back to help out.

I started unhooking the jumper cables. Wu stopped banging on the joystick and helped. The supermarket cart had been left at the bottom, but the batteries were light enough in the lunar gravity. I picked up one under each arm and started up the hill. I didn't bother to look back, because I knew Wu would be following with the other one.

We burst through the adjacency – the shed door – together; we tore the plastic bags off our heads and spit out the cotton balls. Warm air flooded my lungs. It felt wonderful. But my toes and fingers were on fire.

"Damn and Hell!" Wu said. I had never heard him curse before. "We almost made it!"

"We can still make it," I said. "We only lack a few feet. Let's put these babies on the charger and get some pizza."

"Good idea," Wu said. He was calming down. "I have a tendency to lose it when I'm hungry. But look, Irv. Our problems are worse than we thought."

I groaned. Two of the batteries had split along the sides when we had set them down. All three were empty; the acid had boiled away in the vacuum of the Moon. It was a wonder they had worked at all.

"Meanwhile, are your toes hurting?" Wu asked.

"My toes are killing me," I said.

The sixth thing you learn in law school is that cash solves all (or almost all) problems. I had one last hundred-dollar bill hidden in my wallet for emergencies – and if this didn't qualify, what did? We gave the old man ninety for three more batteries, and put them on fast charge. Then we sent our change (ten bucks) with one of the kids on a bike, for four slices of pizza and two cans of diet soda.

Then we sat down under an ailanthus and took off our shoes. I was pleased to see that my toes weren't black. They warmed fairly quickly in the sun. It was my shoes that were cold. The tassel on one of my loafers was broken; the other one snapped when I touched it.

"I'm going to have to bypass some of the electrics on the LRV if we're going to make it up the hill," said Wu. He grabbed a piece of newspaper that was blowing by and began to trace a diagram. "According to my calculations, those batteries will put out 33.9 per cent power for sixteen minutes if we drop out the nav. system. Or maybe shunt past the rear steering motors. Look at this – "

"I'll take your word for it," I said. "Here's our pizza."

My socks were warm. I taped two plastic bags over my feet this time, while Wu poured the Pond Explorer over the cotton balls. It steamed when it went on, and a cheer went up from the kids on the pile of tyres. There were ten or twelve of them now. Frankie was charging them a quarter apiece. Wu paused before putting the cotton ball under his tongue.

"Kids," he said, "don't try this at home!"

They all hooted. Wu taped the plastic bag over my head, then over his. We waved – we were neighbourhood heroes! – and picked up the "new" batteries, which were now charged; and ducked side by side back through the adjacency to the junk-strewn lunar slope where our work still waited to be finished. We were the first interplanetary automotive salvage team!

Wu was carrying two batteries this time, and I was carrying one. We didn't stop to admire the scenery. I was already sick of the Moon. Wu hooked up the batteries while I got into the passenger seat. He got in beside me and hit a few switches, fewer this time. The "heading" lights on the console didn't come on. Half the steering and drive enable switches remained unlighted.

Then Wu put my left hand on the joystick, and jumped down and grabbed the back of the LRV, indicating that he was going to push. I was going to drive.

I pushed the joystick forward and the LRV groaned into action, a little livelier than last time. The steering was slow; only the front wheels turned. I was hopeful, though. The LRV groaned through the last curve without slowing down.

I headed up the last straightaway, feeling the batteries weaken with every yard, every foot, every inch. It was as if the weight that had been subtracted from everything else on the Moon had been added to the LRV and was dragging it down. The lights on the console were flickering.

We were only ten yards from the adjacency. It was a dim slot under the cliff; I knew it was bright on the other side (a midsummer afternoon!), but apparently the same interface that kept the air from leaking through also dimmed the light.

It looked barely wide enough. But low. I was glad the LRV didn't have a windshield. I would have to duck to make it through.

Fifteen feet from the opening. Ten. Eight. The LRV stopped. I jammed the joystick forward and it moved another foot. I reached back over the seat and jiggled the jumper cables. The LRV groaned forward another six inches – then died. I looked at the slot under the cliff just ahead, and at the Earth overhead, both equally far away.

I wiggled the joystick. Nothing. I started to get down to help push, but Wu stopped me. He had one more trick. He unhooked the batteries and reversed their order. It shouldn't have made any difference but as I have often noticed, electrical matters are not logical, like law: things that shouldn't work, often do.

Sometimes, anyway. I jammed the joystick all the way forward again.

The LRV groaned forward again, and groaned on. I pointed it into the slot and ducked. I saw a shimmering light, and I felt the machine shudder. The front of the LRV poked through the shower curtain into the sunlight, and I followed, the sudden heat making my plastic bag swell.

The batteries groaned their last. I jumped down and began to pull on the front bumper. Through the plastic bag I could hear the kids screaming; or were they cheering? There was a loud crackling sound from behind the shower curtain. The LRV was only halfway through, and the front end was jumping up and down.

I tore the bag off my head and spit out the cotton, then took a deep breath and yelled, "Wu!"

I heard a hiss and a crackling; I could feel the ground shake under my feet. The pile of tyres was slowly collapsing behind me; kids were slipping and sliding, trying to get away. I could hear glass breaking somewhere. I yelled, "Wu!"

The front of the LRV suddenly pulled free, throwing me (not to put too fine a point on it) flat on my ass.

The ground stopped shaking. The kids cheered.

Only the front of the LRV had come through. It was burned in half right behind the seat; cut through as if by a sloppy welder. The sour smell of electrical smoke was in the air. I took a deep breath and ducked toward the curtain, after Wu. But there was no curtain there, and no shed – only a pile of loose boards.

"Wu!" I yelled. But there he was, lying on the ground among the boards. He sat up and tore the bag off his head. He spit out his cotton and took a deep breath – and looked around and groaned.

The kids were all standing and cheering. (Kids love destruction.) Even Frankie looked pleased. But the old man wasn't; he came around the corner of the garage, looking fierce. "What the Hell's going on here?" he asked. "What happened to my shed?"

"Good question," said Wu. He stood up and started tossing aside the boards that had been the shed. The shower curtain was under them, melted into a stiff plastic rag. Under it was a pile of ash and cinders – and that was all. No cave, no hole; no rear end of the LRV. No moon.

"The cave gets bigger and smaller every month," said Frankie. "But it never did that, not since it first showed up."

"When was that?" asked Wu.

"About six months ago."

"What about my jumper cables?" said the old man.

We paid him for the jumper cables with the change from the pizza, and then called a wrecker to tow our half-LRV back to Park Slope. While we were waiting for the wrecker, I pulled Wu aside. "I hope we didn't put them out of business," I said. I'm no bleeding heart liberal, but I was concerned.

"No, no," he said. "The adjacency was about to drop into a lower neotopological orbit. We just helped it along a little. It's hard to figure without an almanac, but according to the tide table for June (which I'm glad now I bothered to memorize) the adjacency won't be here next month. Or the month after. It was just here for six months, like Frankie said. It was a temporary thing, cyclical as well as periodic."

"Sort of like the Ice Ages."

"Exactly. It always occurs somewhere in this hemisphere, but usually not in such a convenient location. It could be at the bottom of Lake Huron. Or in mid-air over the Great Plains, as one of those unexplained air bumps."

"What about the other side of it?" I asked. "Is it always a landing site? Or was that just a coincidence?"

"Good question!" Wu picked up one of the paper plates left over from the pizza and started scrawling on it with a pencil stub. "If I take the mean lunar latitude of all six Apollo sites, and divide by the coefficient of . . ."

"It was just curiosity," I said. "Here's the wrecker."

We got the half-LRV towed for half-price (I did the negotiating), but we never did make our million dollars. Boeing was in Chapter Eleven; NASA was under a procurement freeze; the Air & Space Museum wasn't interested in anything that rolled.

"Maybe I should take it on the road," Wu told me after several weeks of trying. "I could be a shopping-centre attraction: 'Half a Chinaman exhibits half a Lunar Roving Vehicle. Kids and adults half price.'"

Wu's humour masked bitter disappointment. But he kept trying. The JPL (Jet Propulsion Laboratory) wouldn't accept his calls. General Motors wouldn't return them. Finally, the Huntsville Parks Department, which was considering putting together an Apollo Memorial, agreed to send their Assistant Administrator for Adult Recreation to have a look.

She arrived on the day my divorce became final. Wu and I met her in the garage, where I had been living while Diane and I were waiting to sell the house. Her eyes were big and blue-green, like Frankie's. She measured the LRV and shook her head. "It's like a dollar bill," she said.

"How's that?" Wu asked. He looked depressed. Or maybe sceptical. It was getting hard to tell the difference.

"If you have over half, it's worth a whole dollar. If you have less than half, it's worth nothing. You have slightly less than half of the LRV here, which means that it is worthless. What'll you take for that old P1800, though? Isn't that the one that was assembled in England?"

Which is how I met Candy. But that's another story.

We closed on the house two days later. Since the garage went with it, I helped Wu move the half-LRV to his back yard, where it sits to this day. It was lighter than any motorcycle. We moved the P1800 (which had plates) onto the street, and on Saturday morning, I went to get the interior for it. Just as Wu had predicted, the Hole was easy to find now that it was no longer linked with the adjacency. I didn't even have to stop at Boulevard Imports. I just turned off Conduit onto a likely looking street, and there it was.

The old man would hardly speak to me, but Frankie was understanding. "Your partner came out and gave me this," he said. He showed me a yellow legal pad, on which was scrawled:

$$H\left(M = \frac{E}{c^2}\right)h$$

"He told me this explains it all, I guess."

Frankie had stacked the boards of the shed against the garage. There was a cindery bare spot where the shed door had been; the cinders had that sour moon smell. "I was sick and tired of the tyre disposal business, anyway," Frankie confided in a whisper.

The old man came around the corner of the garage. "What happened to your buddy?" he asked.

"He's going to school on Saturday mornings," I said. Wu was studying to be a meteorologist. I was never sure if that was weather or shooting stars. Anyway, he had quit the law.

"Good riddance," said the old man.

The old man charged me sixty-five dollars for the interior panels, knobs, handles, and trim. I had no choice but to pay up. I had the money, since I had sold Diane my half of the furniture. I was ready to start my new life. I didn't want to own anything that wouldn't fit into the tiny, heart-shaped trunk of the P1800.

That night, Wu helped me put in the seats, then the panels, knobs, and handles. We finished at midnight and it didn't look bad, even though I knew the colours would look weird in the daylight – blue and white in a red car. Wu was grinning that mad grin again; it was the first time I had seen it since the Moon. He pointed over the rooftops to the east (towards Howard Beach, as a matter of fact). The Moon was rising. I was glad to see it looking so – far away.

Wu's wife brought us some leftover wedding cake. I gave him the keys to the 145 and he gave me the keys to the P1800. "Guess we're about even," I said. I put out my hand, but Wu slapped it aside and gave me a hug instead, lifting me off the ground. Everybody should have a friend like Wilson Wu.

I followed the full Moon all the way to Alabama.

HOTRIDER

Keith Brooke

Keith Brooke (b. 1966), like Peter Crowther, wears a variety of hats as editor, writer and publisher. He runs the on-line webzine Infinity Plus, *(www.infinityplus.co.uk) and has been writing science fiction and fantasy for twenty years, as well as horror fiction under the alias Nick Gifford. His novels include the cyber-thriller* Keepers of the Peace *(1990), and the story of a lost Earth colony,* Expatria *(1991) and its sequel* Expatria Incorporated *(1992). Some of his short stories, including this one, were collected in* Head Shots *(2001). This story considers the human desire for danger and thrills, especially in the case of extreme sports. I'm not quite sure you could get much more extreme than this and still see it as a sport.*

TIN MAN HAD LIVED in Malibu for over six years when they told him he'd been for his last ride. I was up on Observation G when he found me. Towering over me, sheened with sweat, his squared-off head hung to one side and his one real eye twitched to some irregular beat. To most people he would have been a scary sight but to me he was Tin Man and he was upset and that was screwing with his neurons where they interfaced with his prosthetic enhancements. It always affected him like that. Tics, couldn't stand still, perspiration. He was my best friend.

"What is it, Tin?" I wiped my part of the view-panel with a sleeve. I don't like to be caught doing nothing, it gives the wrong impression. I'm Ray Siefert, I'm Malibu's fixer, I know all the right people, do all the right things, I've always got myself something on flick-forward, if you follow my drag.

He gripped the hand-rail and pressed his forehead and the bulb of his prosthetic eye against the panel. He was trying to stop the twitching. "It's over," he muttered. "They've dumped me after all I've done for them."

"Who said? What were the terms they used?"

"R & G." He turned to face me. "'No further need of your services' was how they put it – "

"'*They*'?"

"Ruttgers himself. And Gerome's PA. It's final, Ray, the show's over." He couldn't control his twitching any longer so he gave up trying.

It certainly sounded final. I stared past him, up at the streaks of Jupiter, wondering what we could do. Ruttgers and Gerome were part-owners of Malibu. They'd grown from a two-person trip agency into a major force with controlling interests in most of the Jovian system in less than the four years I had lived here on Io.

There was only one answer. We went up to my dom on K and broke out the scotch. Real scotch. The crate had cost me most of the proceeds of a bootleg sim-trip. It was my last bottle – I'd been saving it.

It got to him quickly. Tin Man always said he had a teflon liver, said he could out-drink anybody, but then Tin Man was all talk. My guess is he gets intoxicated so quickly because of how much of his body isn't flesh and juice: the alcohol doesn't have so far to go around. Pretty soon he was doing his party trick of standing on one hand in the middle of my small room. With such big hands and less than a fifth of a gee that's not so great, but you don't tell that to Tin Man when he's had a few slugs of real scotch. I watched him through my alcohol haze. This guy had been the hero of countless hotriding sims, he was looked up to by billions around the solar system, this guy had made the fortunes of Ruttgers and Gerome and now they were dropping him like that.

"No market, they told me," said Tin Man, crumpling slow-mo to the floor, the neurotic twitches finally upsetting his balance. He took another slug. "There's only so much you can do with a sim-trip and then the market's saturated. They say they're winding down the sim side and pumping up on the hands-on, they're going to open Malibu up for the *riches*, build others like it."

"So they're not closing down altogether," I said. My mind was working in parallel, trying to guess how the changes would affect my own position on Io. "Hands-on means people, it means they need guides, stewards – they'll still need hotriders: couldn't you be a guide? You know what the *riches* are like."

That hurt Tin Man. How could he drop from trip star to tour guide?

"Didn't even offer me any pay-off. Just finished, that's all. All I have is enough for a fare to Callisto. *Callisto*. Might as well take a walk out here on Io." Callisto is a stop-over, all caves and transit bars and moving under cover every four days when the place crosses the plane of Jupiter's mag fields – they haven't even installed MP screens to cut out the radiation, it's that run-down a place.

"What's wrong with Callisto?" I said. Tin Man didn't even smile.

"Riding days are over, they say, and I have to accept it!" His tics were pulling his whole head around; he sometimes got like this with drink and stress and raw deals and the like. I skidded the bottle across the floor to him. A pay-off would have been fair, because at least it would have meant he could stay on in Malibu, maybe even buy a share in a buggy. That was all the money would have been to him: a way to carry on hotriding. Riding was more than a way of life to Tin Man, it *was* his life. Without it . . . well, without it I couldn't even imagine him. Tin Man was a rider, that was all.

Maybe I should explain a little about Malibu, about how it all came about. They always said Io was the least hospitable place in the solar system. I can think of worse, but it is true that the inner Jovians were uninhabitable until some Earthbound tecky came up with the MP screen. *Mesoproteic*. Something about mesons and positron moods and the strong nuclear force. I don't know, it's fifty-seven years since my doctorate. A six-year-old could probably explain it better than me now. What it does is it cuts out everything you want, solids, radiation, whatever. MPs let us live on Io, a big one encases all of Malibu. It keeps our air in, keeps the charged particles and the stink of sulphur out where they belong.

Tin Man was one of the first people to set up on Io. Employed by one of the old lunar corporations, he and some others discovered just how useful an MP screen was. Malibu was little more than a small prospectors' dome when a keyboard man called Berg Ruttgers came down and saw Tin Man and his friends skidding around on MP-screened buggies, skimming down a slow-moving channel of molten sulphur, riding the golden surf. Ruttgers had gone back to Callisto to make a deal with Ruby Gerome and raise finance and then, as a newly formed leisure agency, they bought into Malibu and started building.

There were other hotriding stars but Tin Man was always the favourite. With all his alterations and implants he could jack directly into his buggy, link directly with the sim-recorder. The trip technicians could access the raw data from his prosthetic eye, they could trace his tensions through the body-machine interfaces. Others followed, other agencies competed, but Tin Man was the first and best. Tin Man and Malibu had made the fortunes of Ruttgers and Gerome and now they were dropping him.

One time, when the market had apparently peaked, there had been rumours that the sim-trip line would be pared back but Tin Man had managed to revive the interest. Until then hotriding had consisted of skidding around in MP-screened buggies near to Malibu, riding crests of molten sulphur, using low-gee surface effects to go as fast as possible. This time had been like any ordinary trip. R & G hadn't even wanted to bother recording – even then they were shifting their plans towards the tourist trade, the little groups of *riches* that gathered by the view-panels to watch that square-headed trip-star heading out to ride his stick on the liquid brimstone. But R & G had a contract going for a Nutragena ad-operetta and Tin Man had convinced them they needed to re-sim some of the chase sequences. He had headed out on the main drag, not hurrying, just letting the currents take him out onto the sea of golden sulphur, apparently unaware of the two black-shielded buggies closing on him from behind. He had caught the turbulence where his channel joined the sea and ridden it out to where a whirlpool chopped up some real waves, one of his standard moves.

I'm telling all this second hand, up until this point. I wasn't watching, I was too busy cutting a deal with a courier, I think it was one of the lots of trip out-takes I used to sell: she would take them out to a studio where they could be cosmeticized and animated until even Ruttgers would have trouble telling who had originated them. Then a nearby gaggle of *riches* all stopped talking and a man made a bubbly sound in his throat.

I realized something was wrong so I made for a panel, suddenly scared for Tin Man. I knew he had been angry and I didn't like to think what he might have tried.

I looked out and there were the two black chase-buggies, circling slowly, no sign of Tin Man.

Even a magniview only showed whirlpool turbulence where my friend had last been seen. No buggy. I picked up what had happened from the tourists. Tin Man had gone down. The chasers had closed on him, drifting in behind a three metre crest of sulphur. Tin Man had spotted them, hesitated too long and the wave had folded over him, carrying the chasers on past. When the surface had levelled his buggy had vanished. In over sixty years off-Earth I had lost a few friends, some very close, but there was something too terrible to comprehend about going the way I believed then that Tin Man had gone. The MP shielding would protect him from the heat and the pressure, but there would be no way to dissipate his own heat from the buggy or, failing that, he would eventually run out of power or air. I couldn't bear to think about it, but then I couldn't fix my mind on anything else. Maybe he would sink so far that even the MPs would fail, maybe that would be best.

Eventually, the chasers came back in. I saw their faces as they left their buggies. They were creased, shaken. Then a tecky came out and –

"Mega, mega!" said a whining *riche* voice and I looked up and saw Tin Man's buggy skimming back up the drag towards Malibu and, pretty soon, MP screens merging and he was in and home and alive.

He must have been under the brimstone sea for near to forty-five minutes yet he came out of the crowd smiling. People were yelling at him, asking what had happened and all he would do was grin and tap his bulbous plastic eye and say, "It's all in here. Property of R & G. Sorry, you'll have to buy the sim."

That dive had revitalized the hotriding game, but this time it looked like the end was really here. He finished the scotch and cast around for some more. The same Tin Man and now they were dropping him in favour of the tourist trade. He'd never said if he had planned the trip to happen like that, if he'd planned to dive. R & G Publicity had made him up as some kind of hero, trying what nobody had ever even considered, but I couldn't swallow it. "How did you get back to the surface?" I had once asked him.

"You should see it, Ray – not just the sims, but really *see* it. There's all sorts of flows and currents down there. Some of them, it's like a pattern to it, you latch on in the right place, ride the right bubble and it lifts you back up like it was always meant to be. It's really fantastic, Ray, it's a magic kingdom down there. It's beautiful."

Looking at Tin Man's face, I could remember the light in his eye when it had all been new to him. Now it was gone. They were taking it all away from him.

"Tell you one thing," he said, on one hand again, despite the tics. "I'm gonna have one more trip an' ain't nobody gonna stop me." Then he tumbled, slowly, and didn't wake for the next fourteen hours.

Full night on Io would only be dusk anywhere else. The sunlight, reflected red from Jupiter, casts the surface of Io in sepia tones, soft ochres as opposed to the harsh reds and oranges that full sunlight gives.

I left Tin Man asleep in my dom. For some reason I had the idea I could fix him up with something, something better than tour-guide, something better than the resort bum it looked like he was headed for.

On Observation G, like all the ob decks, an entire wall is view-panel. I found Shenet Ra'ath leaning on the hand-rail, staring up at the swirling aurora, our constant link with Jupiter. The flickers and the lightning were building up with the approaching dawn, the build-up that accompanied and fed the volcanic peaks of that time of day, the best for hotriding, the most dangerous for a carbon-based life-form such as myself or Tin Man.

Shenet looked good even if she was well into her fourteenth decade as the records claimed. She worked in Leisure for Ymporial, one of the lunar corporations that had been caught off guard by R & G's sudden onslaught on the sim-trip market. She was a good contact in lots of ways but I could tell from her face that she wouldn't be any help on this occasion.

Regardless, I ploughed in, told her what was happening to Tin Man. "I knew it would happen," she said, when I had finished. She wouldn't meet my eyes. "It's down to Tin that the market's stayed open for so long."

"Will you take him on, Shenet? He deserves better than this."

This time she looked at me. "No, we can't." I like that about Shenet, even when I *don't* like it: she tells you straight. "There may have been some time left in hotriding but if Ruttgers and Gerome pull out then that's a strong signal. I can't persuade Finance to go against a trend like that. You can't fight market forces, Siefert."

That was the kind of line I'd expected but it still dented my shell. Tin Man was going down and there was nothing I could do to help him.

With a brief nod I turned away from Shenet and walked off down the ob deck, wondering if Tin Man was still asleep.

Then I heard the first blast, felt the shock waves under my feet.

I was on my knees when the second blast went off, closer this time. It doesn't take much to take your feet from under you at point eighteen gees, even with grippa flooring.

Silence returned after the sixth blast and I crawled over to the wall, pulled myself up by the handrail, hurried back to confirm that Shenet was okay. Then I saw her eyes widen as she stared over my shoulder, out through the view-panel.

"Jesus," she said, and for a moment I wondered why. Then I saw.

We were moving.

Malibu was edging slowly away from its foundations, sulphurous rock crumpling and crevassing all around. Malibu was an island of rock adrift on a river of liquid sulphur.

Tin Man was having his last ride and he was taking the whole town with him.

"You're his friend: convince him." Ruttgers didn't have any implants to blame for his nervous spasms or his flushed, shining face. He was terrified, that was all.

When we'd realized exactly what Tin Man had done, Shenet and I had headed for Concourse. I guessed that would be where the

action was. There were several routes we could have taken but I
headed down through the ob decks just so I could see what was
happening. *Should be scared*, I kept telling myself, but I stared at
those panels and somehow couldn't manage it.

I'd never been hotriding, myself. Sure, I'd done the sim-trips but
I didn't need Tin Man to tell me how superficial that was. I tried
to think of the stresses on the structure of Malibu, tried to guess if
they would be enough to break up the town's MP screens. They
weren't built for anything like this. But still I couldn't work up any
fear.

By the time I reached Concourse Malibu had found the main
drag, the fastest moving part of the channel. Leaving the last ob
deck, I paused to look out. Soon we would be leaving the drag,
drifting out onto the ochre ocean. Just then green lightning arced
down from Jupiter, colours swirled in the sky and the sun lit the
sea a sudden, bright yellow.

In the middle of Concourse was a cluster of Senior People,
mainly R & G, but there were others too, Ymporial, CalCorp,
Tranche. Shenet joined them and the only reason she stood out
was because she wasn't so scared.

The glass front of Drac's Nite Klub was phasing to a general
view of the brimstone ocean as Ruttgers turned to me, said,
"You're his friend: convince him."

I studied his face. Fear flustered him, but it made him angry, too.
He was a keyboard man, not a hands-on. He was quaking. I didn't
enjoy it, but I can't say his attitude made things appear any worse
at that particular moment.

"Well where in hell is he?" Until then I hadn't even known for
sure that it was Tin Man and I wanted to know more, but I could
see that Ruttgers and his mob weren't in any state to fill me in on
the details. I followed his glance towards the R & G offices and
ignored him after that.

I had to smile when I found Tin Man. Somehow he had found
his way into Ruby Gerome's office and jacked direct into Control,
Malibu's governing mainframe. More than that, he had protected
himself.

No one could get into that office because he had shielded it with
an MP screen.

He'd left a view-panel at the open doorway so we could see in and he out. Jacked in, he was only partly aware of my presence, but he knew who I was because he smiled and mouthed my name. *Ray*.

"Last ride, huh?" I said, not usually so stuck for words.

He nodded, then, after at least a minute, said, "No sim to this trip. Let 'em see it for real. Ray, I tell you: go and jack in. You can't really ride unless you're jacked."

He knew I had illegal access to Control from my dom. I nodded. I'd been planning to anyway, I had to take care of my affairs, hadn't I?

"There's bubbles, Ray, I can feel 'em. I think we might – " the floor lurched and I went down on my hands and knees " – yes! We're going down!" The floor jumped again and when I regained my senses I realized that it was at an angle, maybe ten degrees or more. Then I realized what Tin Man had meant and then I started to be scared.

I found my way back out to Concourse just as the sulphur was closing above us. The big screen on Drac's showed the last tiny disc of Jupiter and then a ripple sealed it off and Malibu was cast in a dim golden glow from the molten sulphur. After a split-second gap, Control cut in with town lighting but that didn't stop the screaming, didn't stop the yells.

Berg Ruttgers had been running around when the lights came on, yelling for somebody to do something. Ruby Gerome had done something. She had hit him with a punch that had carried him metres into the air before he crumpled into a blubbering heap against the view-panel front of Drac's.

I dashed through the crowd, hoping no one would try to stop me, lost my feet a few times as the floor lurched away from under them. I tried not to hear the huge groans and metallic shrieks which I guessed came from the structure of Malibu. Up through the ob decks, I kept getting glimpses of the strangely illuminated world of sulphur. Twists of darker magma spiralling up and around, blobs, bubbles, drifting in an apparently random ballet. I suppose it could have been beautiful but all I could think of was how thin an MP screen really was, how I didn't even know how the damned things worked.

Once in my dom I locked the door, out of habit, I guess. Nobody was likely to just happen by and notice that I had an illegal In-point to Control. Not when we were sinking through a sea of molten sulphur.

I went straight to my view-panel – showing streaming, writhing magma – and yanked it from the wall, reached behind and pulled the access set out into the open. Without another thought I slid the jack into the socket behind my right ear, my one augmentation, a requisite for modern life, the salesperson had told me.

And I was there with Tin Man. I could tell he was there, in Control, but he didn't notice me for a few seconds. Long enough for me to take care of my own insurance.

Ray. His voice was all around me. He'd been thorough, embedded himself deeply in Control. There was no way anyone could corrupt him through the mainframe. If R & G tried anything on they would be attacking Control itself, not a wise option when the only thing that could run Malibu's MP screens was Control.

Here, he said, and my senses were flooded with inputs from all around Malibu's shielded dome. It was overwhelming, the different densities, the magnetic fluxes of the magma, but it did give me a kind of blast-image of where we were.

And that was deep. Deeper than I could remember any hotrider daring to go before.

Tin Man was really doing his best to give the execs a hands-on, as they liked to call the real thing. If he was in control at all.

Bubble's taken us down, chuckled Tin Man in my head. Readings of electrostatic potential scanned through my brain. Slowly, I was getting used to being jacked into a system that was so overwhelmed by another person. There seemed to be some kind of pattern to the readings, some kind of order.

You see it?

Wave patterns, I told myself. Order imposed by universal physical laws.

We're riding the bubbles, said Tin Man. *I told you you had to be jacked before you could see what it's like. Do you see the patterns?*

Tin Man wasn't the only one to talk about patterns in the magma, all the hotriders did it. You catch a good pattern of bubbles and it'll take you back to the surface, it'll jockey you along like you're riding with a mermaid. But Tin Man was the only one to get mystical about it. He talked about bubbles as if they were more than that, as if they weren't just blobs of magma that clung together because of differing densities, differing compositions to the local norm. Sure, I saw the patterns, saw the order to it all, but I'm not one to go mystical like Tin Man.

He flashed me the stresses in Malibu's structure and I wished he hadn't. *Didn't intend to go this far down*, he said. *I only wanted to . . .*

Only I stopped listening at that point because I had noticed something else. I guess that, being closer to the surface than Tin Man, I was more aware of things at that level. That's why he hadn't noticed me as soon as I jacked in. And that's why he didn't notice Magya 38.

Magya 38. That was the handle she was logged under. She was down in the R & G offices, jacked into Control, feeling her way around.

I checked with Tin Man, but he was all taken up by then, part of him off with the bubbles, trying to find a conflux that would get us back to the surface, the rest of him running through with Control, trying to keep Malibu and the MPs from collapsing under the stresses of being in excess of a kilometre under the surface of Io.

Fools. Already Magya was testing Control. Clumsily. Even as I tugged the jack from my skull a power spike made the lights dim and I dived foolishly, reflexively, for the floor.

Down through the ob decks, I could see the magma swirling its golden currents around us, the blobs now scattered evenly, conforming to a strange pattern. Or to my imagination. As I leapt in slow-mo down the steps I kept sensing fluctuations in the electrical energy buzzing around me, kept expecting the MPs to go down. At least it would be a speedy end.

As I hurried across Concourse the big view-panel showed an unmistakable pattern to the blobs and I realized what that meant: Tin Man had found his good flow, we were rising with the bubbles of magma towards the surface.

The lights dimmed again and I cursed the ineptitude of this Magya 38. The execs were by the door of Ruby Gerome's office, craning to look in through the clear panel in Tin Man's defences. They were talking to him – negotiating, they said. And their diversion appeared to have fooled him as he nodded absently in his jacked-in haze.

I passed the end of their corridor, continued to an access corridor and so found my way past them and to the office of Berg Ruttgers. That had to be where Magya 38 was tampering with Control – had to be.

I was right. She was there, jack-leads attached through a sub-occipital lobe, all glittery and awkward-looking. I vaguely recognized her: a teck from Ymporial, one of Shenet's favourites. Why couldn't she see the risk she was taking?

As I crossed the room I wondered how I could stop her, how I could prevent her messing with Tin Man and so with Control and so with the screens that had so far kept us distinct from the sulphurous magma all around.

I knocked her on the head a little. Enough to break some skull, enough to keep her out of Control for a while, but not enough to do anything that couldn't be repaired. Sometimes the simple ways are best. I pulled the jack from her lobe, checked her vitals and then jacked myself back in just in time to get full visuals of us breaking the surface of the sulphur ocean. I tell you: I've never been all that impressed by your everyday scenic beauty but Jupiter sure looked good to me right then. Even *Io* looked okay.

Things were a mess for some time after that. We drifted a while but eventually we came to rest on a newly formed island of black sulphur. They moved Malibu to somewhere more secure a few months later, somewhere more attractive to the touring *riches*. But Tin Man and I had got out of it all by then. He kept his screens up until tempers had cooled and the negotiations were through. You see, when I was jacked in, back in my dom, first thing I did was take out some insurance. Hell, it was almost a reflex action to divert all the sim-data to my own private account within Control. It's how I used to make my living. The way I figured it at the time was that if we ever got out it would all be pretty exciting stuff: we could make a good sim out of it. It turned out that several of the big agencies joined the bidding but in the end we sold it all back to Ruttgers and Gerome. They payed us a lot of money for it and I don't think it was the action sequences that any of them wanted. I think they wanted the crowd scenes, the human interest shots, like the one where Ruby hits Berg, or the one where Berg is running around and screaming like some maniac. A company like Ymporial or CalCorp would have had a great time with a sequence like that. According to Control, Berg and Ruby destroyed all the records as soon as they had paid us for them.

Me and Tin Man are partners now. We have a hotel complex on Io, near to the old site of Malibu. Tin Man takes the guests hot-riding, sometimes in a buggy, sometimes the entire hotel. He shows them the bubbles, shows them the patterns.

I guess that's the end of our story: the two of us on equal footing. I think that's pretty generous of me, seeing as all the trading was done in my name, he had no legal rights or anything. But is he grateful? *Tin Man?* All he can talk about is his bubbles. He gets this stupid grin, tells me it's like swimming with the whales. What's a whale? I say, but he just smiles and goes about his business.

MOTHER
GRASSHOPPER

Michael Swanwick

There will be those of you who may feel this story is a fantasy rather than science fiction. Okay. Maybe it's in the eye of the beholder. Certainly the idea of a planet in the shape of a grasshopper does seem a bit unusual. But then, don't forget Arthur C. Clarke's third law that any sufficiently advanced technology is indistinguishable from magic. What this story has in megaloads, is that sense of wonder. It's the kind of story one might have expected from Ray Bradbury years ago – a sort of Martian Chronicles *for the new age. Michael Swanwick (b. 1950) is no stranger to the bizarre in science fiction and fantasy. He has often blended the two forms, as you'll find in his novels* Stations of the Tide *(1991) and* The Iron Dragon's Daughter *(1993). Some of his short fiction will be found in* Gravity's Angels *(1991),* Tales of Old Earth *(2000) and* A Geography of Unknown Lands *(1997), from which this story comes.*

IN THE YEAR ONE, we came in an armada of a million spacecraft to settle upon, colonize, and claim for our homeland this giant grasshopper on which we now dwell.

We dared not land upon the wings for, though the cube-square rule held true and their most rapid motions would be imperceptible on a historic scale, random nerve firings resulted in premovement tremors measured at Richter 11. So we opted to build in the eyes, in the faceted mirrorlands that reflected infinities of flatness, a shimmering Iowa, the architecture of home.

It was an impossible project and one, perhaps, that was doomed from the start. But such things are obvious only in retrospect. We were a young and vigorous race then. Everything seemed possible.

Using shaped temporal fields, we force-grew trees which we cut down to build our cabins. We planted sod and wheat and buffalo. In one vivid and unforgettable night of technology we created a layer of limestone bedrock half a mile deep upon which to build our towns. And when our work was done, we held hoe-downs in a thousand county seats all across the eye-lands.

We created new seasons, including Snow, after the patterns of those we had known in antiquity, but the night sky we left unaltered, for this was to be our home . . . now and forever. The unfamiliar constellations would grow their own legends over the ages; there would be time. Generations passed, and cities grew with whorls of suburbs like the arms of spiral galaxies around them, for we were lonely, as were the thousands and millions we decanted who grew like the trees of the cisocellar plains that were as thick as the ancient Black Forest.

I was a young man, newly bearded, hardly much more than a shirt-tail child, on that Harvest day when the stranger walked into town.

This was so unusual an event (and for you to whom a town of ten thousand necessarily means that there *will be strangers*, I despair of explaining) that children came out to shout and run at his heels, while we older citizens, conscious of our dignity, stood in the doorways of our shops, factories, and co-ops to gaze ponderously in his general direction. Not quite *at* him, you understand, but over his shoulder, into the flat, mesmeric plains and the infinite white skies beyond.

He claimed to have come all the way from the equatorial abdomen, where gravity is three times eye-normal, and this was easy enough to believe, for he was ungodly strong. With my own eyes I once saw him take a dollar coin between thumb and forefinger and bend it in half – and a steel dollar at that! He also claimed to have walked the entire distance, which nobody believed, not even me.

"If you'd walked even half that far," I said, "I reckon you'd be the most remarkable man as ever lived."

He laughed at that and ruffled my hair. "Well, maybe I am," he said. "Maybe I am."

I flushed and took a step backwards, hand on the bandersnatch-skin hilt of my fighting knife. I was as feisty as a bantam rooster in those days, and twice as quick to take offense. "Mister, I'm afraid I'm going to have to ask you to step outside."

The stranger looked at me. Then he reached out and, without the slightest hint of fear or anger or even regret, touched my arm just below the shoulder. He did it with no particular speed and yet somehow I could not react fast enough to stop him. And that touch, light though it was, paralysed my arm, leaving it withered and useless, even as it is today.

He put his drink down on the bar, and said, "Pick up my knapsack."

I did.

"Follow me."

So it was that without a word of farewell to my family or even a backward glance, I left New Auschwitz forever.

That night, over a campfire of eel grass and dried buffalo chips, we ate a dinner of refried beans and fatback bacon. It was a new and clumsy experience for me, eating one-handed. For a long time, neither one of us spoke. Finally I said, "Are you a magician?"

The stranger sighed. "Maybe so," he said. "Maybe I am."

"You have a name?"

"No."

"What do we do now?"

"Business." He pushed his plate toward me. "I cooked. It's your turn to wash."

Our business entailed constant travel. We went to Brinkerton with cholera and to Roxborough with typhus. We passed through Denver and Venice and Saint Petersburg and left behind fleas, rats, and plague. In Upper Black Eddy, it was ebola. We never stayed long enough to see the results of our work, but I read the newspapers afterwards, and it was about what you would expect.

Still, *on the whole*, humanity prospered. Where one city was decimated, another was expanding. The overspilling hospitals of one county created a market for the goods of a dozen others. The survivors had babies.

We walked to Tylersburg, Rutledge, and Uniontown and took wagons to Shoemakersville, Confluence, and South Gibson. Booked onto steam trains for Mount Lebanon, Mount Bethel, Mount Aetna, and Mount Nebo and diesel trains to McKeesport, Reinholds Station, and Broomall. Boarded buses to Carbondale, Feasterville, June Bug, and Lincoln Falls. Caught commuter flights to Paradise, Nickel Mines, Niantic, and Zion.The time passed quickly.

Then one shocking day my magician announced that he was going home.

"Home?" I said. "What about your work?"

"*Our* work, Daniel," he said gently. "I expect you'll do as good a job as ever I did." He finished packing his few possessions into a carpetbag.

"You can't!" I cried.

With a wink and a sad smile, he slipped out the door.

For a time – long or short, I don't know – I sat motionless, unthinking, unseeing. Then I leaped to my feet, threw open the door, and looked up and down the empty street. Blocks away, towards the train station, was a scurrying black speck.

Leaving the door open behind me, I ran after it.

I just missed the afternoon express to Lackawanna. I asked the stationmaster when was the next train after it. He said tomorrow. Had he seen a tall man carrying a carpetbag, looking thus and so? Yes, he had. Where was he? On the train to Lackawanna. Nothing more heading that way today. Did he know where I could rent a car? Yes, he did. Place just down the road.

Maybe I'd've caught the magician if I hadn't gone back to the room to pick up my bags. Most likely not. At Lackawanna station I found he'd taken the bus to Johnstown. In Johnstown, he'd moved on to Erie and there the trail ran cold. It took me three days' hard questioning to pick it up again.

For a week I pursued him thus, like a man possessed.

Then I awoke one morning and my panic was gone. I knew I wasn't going to catch my magician anytime soon. I took stock of my resources, counted up what little cash-money I had, and laid out a strategy. Then I went shopping. Finally, I hit the road. I'd have to be patient, dogged, wily, but I knew that, given enough time, I'd find him.

Find him, and kill him too.

The trail led me to Harper's Ferry, at the very edge of the oculus. Behind was civilization. Ahead was nothing but thousands of miles of empty chitin-lands.

People said he'd gone south, off the lens entirely.

Back at my boarding house, I was approached by one of the lodgers. He was a skinny man with a big mustache and sleeveless white T-shirt that hung from his skinny shoulders like wet laundry on a muggy Sunday.

"What you got in that bag?"

"Black death," I said, "infectious meningitis, tuberculosis. You name it."

He thought for a bit. "I got this wife," he said at last. "I don't suppose you could . . ."

"I'll take a look at her," I said, and hoisted the bag.

We went upstairs to his room.

She lay in the bed, eyes closed. There was an IV needle in her arm, hooked up to a drip feed. She looked young, but of course that meant nothing. Her hair, neatly brushed and combed, laid across the coverlet almost to her waist, was white – white as snow, as death, as finest bone china.

"How long has she been like this?" I asked.

"Ohhhh . . ." He blew out his cheeks. "Forty-seven, maybe fifty years?"

"You her father?"

"Husband. Was, anyhow. Not sure how long the vows were meant to hold up under these conditions: can't say I've kept 'em any too well. You got something in that bag for her?" He said it as casual as he could, but his eyes were big and spooked-looking.

I made my decision. "Tell you what," I said. "I'll give you forty dollars for her."

"The sheriff wouldn't think much of what you just said," the man said low and quiet.

"No. But then, I suppose I'll be off of the eye-lands entirely before he knows a word of it."

I picked up my syringe.

"Well? Is it a deal or not?"

Her name was Victoria. We were a good three days march into the chitin before she came out of the trance state characteristic of the interim zombie stage of Recovery. I'd fitted her with a pack, walking shoes, and a good stout stick, and she strode along head up, eyes blank, speaking in the tongues of angels afloat between the stars.

" – cisgalactic phase intercept," she said. "Do you read? *Das Uberraumboot zuruckgegenerinnernte. Verstehen?* Anadaemonic mesotechnological conflict strategizing. *Drei tausenden Affen mit Laseren!* Hello? Is anybody – "

Then she stumbled over a rock, cried out in pain, and said, "Where am I?"

I stopped, spread a map on the ground, and got out my pocket gravitometer. It was a simple thing: a glass cylinder filled with aerogel and a bright orange ceramic bead. The casing was tin, with a compressor screw at the top, a calibrated scale along the side, and the words "Flynn & Co." at the bottom. I flipped it over, watched the bead slowly fall. I tightened the screw a notch, then two, then three, increasing the aerogel's density. At five, the bead stopped. I read the gauge, squinted up at the sun, and then jabbed a finger on an isobar to one edge of the map.

"Right here," I said. "Just off the lens. See?"

"I don't – " She was trembling with panic. Her dilated eyes shifted wildly from one part of the empty horizon to another. Then suddenly, sourcelessly, she burst into tears.

Embarrassed, I looked away. When she was done crying, I patted the ground. "Sit." Sniffling, she obeyed. "How old are you, Victoria?"

"How old am . . . ? Sixteen?" she said tentatively. "Seventeen?" Then, "Is that really my name?"

"It was. The woman you were grew tired of life, and injected herself with a drug that destroys the ego and with it all trace of personal history." I sighed. "So in one sense you're still Victoria, and in another sense you're not. What she did was illegal, though; you can never go back to the oculus. You'd be locked into jail for the rest of your life."

She looked at me through eyes newly young, almost childlike in their experience, and still wet with tears. I was prepared for hysteria, grief, rage. But all she said was, "Are you a magician?"

That rocked me back on my heels. "Well – yes," I said. "I suppose I am."

She considered that silently for a moment. "So what happens to me now?"

"Your job is to carry that pack. We also go turn-on-turn with the dishes." I straightened, folding the map. "Come on. We've got a far way yet to go."

We commenced marching, in silence at first. But then, not many miles down the road and to my complete astonishment, Victoria began to *sing*!

We followed the faintest of paths – less a trail than the memory of a dream of the idea of one – across the chitin. Alongside it grew an occasional patch of grass. A lot of wind-blown loess had swept across the chitin-lands over the centuries. It caught in cracks in the carapace and gave purchase to fortuitous seeds. Once I even saw a rabbit. But before I could point it out to Victoria, I saw something else. Up ahead, in a place where the shell had powdered and a rare rainstorm had turned the powder briefly to mud, were two over-lapping tyre prints. A motorbike had been by here, and recently.

I stared at the tracks for a long time, clenching and unclenching my good hand.

The very next day we came upon a settlement.

It was a hardscrabble place. Just a windmill to run the pump that brought up a trickle of ichor from a miles-deep well, a refinery to process the stuff edible, and a handful of unpainted clapboard buildings and Quonset huts. Several battered old pickup trucks sat rusting under the limitless sky.

A gaunt man stood by the gate, waiting for us. His jaw was hard, his backbone straight and his hands empty. But I noted here and there a shiver of movement in a window or from the open door of a shed, and I made no mistake but that there were weapons trained upon us.

"Name's Rivera," the man said when we came up to him.

I swept off my bowler hat. "Daniel. This's Miss Victoria, my ward."

"Passing through?"

"Yessir, I am, and I see no reason I should ever pass this way again. If you have food for sale, I'll pay you market rates. But if not, why, with your permission, we'll just keep on moving on."

"Fair spoken." From somewhere Rivera produced a cup of water, and handed it to us. I drank half, handed the rest to Victoria. She shivered as it went down.

"Right good," I said. "And cold too."

"We have a heat pump," Rivera said with grudging pride. "C'mon inside. Let's see what the women have made us to eat."

Then the children came running out, whooping and hollering, too many to count, and the adult people behind them, whom I made out to be twenty in number. They made us welcome.

They were good people, if outlaws, and as hungry for news and gossip as anybody can be. I told them about a stump speech I had heard made by Tyler B. Morris, who was running for governor of the Northern Department, and they spent all of dinnertime discussing it. The food was good, too – ham and biscuits with red-eye gravy, sweet yams with butter, and apple cobbler to boot. If I hadn't seen their chemical complex, I'd've never guessed it for synthetic. There were lace curtains in the window, brittle-old but clean, and I noted how carefully the leftovers were stored away for later.

After we'd eaten, Rivera caught my eye and gestured with his chin. We went outside, and he led me to a shed out back. He unpadlocked the door and we stepped within. A line of ten people lay unmoving on plain-built beds. They were each catheterized to a drip-bag of processed ichor. Light from the door caught their hair, ten white haloes in the gloom.

"We brought them with us," Rivera said. "Thought we'd be doing well enough to make a go of it. Lately, though, I don't know, maybe it's the drought, but the blood's been running thin, and it's not like we have the money to have a new well drilled."

"I understand." Then, because it seemed a good time to ask, "There was a man came by this way probably less'n a week ago. Tall, riding a – "

"He wouldn't help," Harry said. "Said it wasn't his responsibility. Then, before he drove off, the sonofabitch tried to buy some of our food." He turned and spat. "He told us you and the woman would be coming along. We been waiting."

"Wait. He told you I'd have a woman with me?"

"It's not just us we have to think of!" he said with sudden vehemence. "There's the young fellers, too. They come along and all a man's stiff-necked talk about obligations and morality goes right out the window. Sometimes I think how I could come out here with a length of iron pipe and – well." He shook his head and then, almost pleadingly, said, "Can't you do something?"

"I think so." A faint creaking noise made me turn then. Victoria stood frozen in the doorway. The light through her hair made of it a white flare. I closed my eyes, wishing she hadn't stumbled across this thing. In a neutral voice I said, "Get my bag."

Then Rivera and I set to haggling out a price.

We left the settlement with a goodly store of food and driving their third-best pickup truck. It was a pathetic old thing and the shocks were scarce more than a memory. We bumped and jolted towards the south.

For a long time Victoria did not speak. Then she turned to me and angrily blurted, "You *killed* them!"

"It was what they wanted."

"How can you say that?" She twisted in the seat and punched me in the shoulder. Hard. "How can you sit there and . . . *say* that?"

"Look," I said testily. "It's simple mathematics. You could make an equation out of it. They can only drill so much ichor. That ichor makes only so much food. Divide that by the number of mouths there are to feed and hold up the result against what it takes to keep one alive. So much food, so many people. If the one's smaller than the other, you starve. And the children wanted to live. The folks in the shed didn't."

"They could go back! Nobody *has* to live out in the middle of nowhere trying to scratch food out of nothing!"

"I counted one suicide for every two waking adults. Just how welcome do you think they'd be, back to the oculus, with so many suicides living among them? More than likely that's what drove them out here in the first place."

"Well . . . nobody would be starving if they didn't insist on having so many damn children."

"How can you stop people from having children?" I asked.

There was no possible answer to that and we both knew it. Victoria leaned her head against the cab window, eyes squeezed tight shut, as far from me as she could get. "You could have woken them up! But no, you had your bag of goodies and you wanted to play. I'm surprised you didn't kill *me* when you had the chance."

"Vickie . . ."

"Don't speak to me!"

She started to weep.

I wanted to hug her and comfort her, she was so miserable. But I was driving, and I only had the one good arm. So I didn't. Nor did I explain to her why it was that nobody chose to simply wake the suicides up.

That evening, as usual, I got out the hatchet and splintered enough chitin for a campfire. I was sitting by it, silent, when Victoria got out the jug of rough liquor the settlement folks had brewed from ichor. "You be careful with that stuff," I said. "It sneaks up on you. Don't forget, whatever experience you've had drinking got left behind in your first life."

"Then *you* drink!" she said, thrusting a cup at me. "I'll follow your lead. When you stop, I'll stop."

I swear I never suspected what she had in mind. And it had been a long while since I'd tasted alcohol. So, like a fool, I took her intent at face value. I had a drink. And then another.

Time passed.

We talked some, we laughed some. Maybe we sang a song or two.

Then, somehow, Victoria had shucked off her blouse and was dancing. She whirled around the campfire, her long skirts lifting up above her knees and occasionally flirting through the flames so that the hem browned and smoked but never quite caught fire.

This wildness seemed to come out of nowhere. I watched her, alarmed and aroused, too drunk to think clearly, too entranced even to move.

Finally she collapsed gracefully at my feet. The firelight was red on her naked back, shifting with each gasping breath she took. She looked up at me through her long, sweat-tangled hair, and her eyes were like amber, dark as cypress swamp water, brown and bottomless. Eyes a man could drown in.

I pulled her towards me. Laughing, she surged forward, collapsing upon me, tumbling me over backwards, fumbling with my belt and then the fly of my jeans. Then she had my cock out and stiff and I'd pushed her skirt up above her waist so that it seemed she was wearing nothing but a thick red sash. And I rolled her over on her back and she was reaching down between her legs to guide me in and she was smiling and lovely.

I plunged deep, deep, deep into her, and oh god but it felt fine. Like that eye-opening shock you get when you plunge into a cold lake for the first time on a hot summer's day and the water wraps itself around you and feels so impossibly good. Only this was warm and slippery-slick and a thousand times better. Then I was telling her things, telling her I needed her, I wanted her, I loved her, over and over again.

I awoke the next morning with a raging hangover. Victoria was sitting in the cab of the pickup, brushing her long white hair in the rear-view mirror and humming to herself.

"Well," she said, amused. "Look what the cat dragged in. There's water in the jerrycans. Have yourself a drink. I expect we could also spare a cup for you to wash your face with."

"Look," I said. "I'm sorry about last night."

"No you're not."

"I maybe said some foolish things, but – "

Her eyes flashed storm-cloud dark. "You weren't speaking near so foolish then as you are now. You meant every damn word, and I'm holding you to them." Then she laughed. "You'd best get at that water. You look hideous."

So I dragged myself off.

Overnight, Victoria had changed. Her whole manner, the way she held herself, even the way she phrased her words, told me that she wasn't a child anymore. She was a woman.

The thing I'd been dreading had begun.

"Resistance is useless," Victoria read. "For mine is the might and power of the Cosmos Itself!" She'd found a comic book stuck back under the seat and gone through it three times, chuckling to herself, while the truck rattled down that near-nonexistent road. Now she put it down. "Tell me something," she said. "How do you know your magician came by this way?"

"I just know is all," I said curtly. I'd given myself a shot of B-complex vitamins, but my head and gut still felt pretty ragged. Nor was it particularly soothing having to drive this idiot truck one-armed. And, anyway, I couldn't say just how I knew. It was a feeling I had, a certainty.

"I had a dream last night. After we, ummmm, danced."

I didn't look at her.

"I was on a flat platform, like a railroad station, only enormous. It stretched halfway to infinity. There were stars all around me, thicker and more colourful than I'd ever imagined them. Bright enough to make your eyes ache. Enormous machines were every-where, golden, spaceships I suppose. They were taking off and landing with delicate little puffs of air, like it was the easiest thing imaginable to do. My body was so light I felt like I was going to float up among them. You ever hear of a place like that?"

"No."

"There was a man waiting for me there. He had the saddest smile, but cold, cruel eyes. Hello, Victoria, he said. How did you know my name, I asked. Oh, I keep a close eye on Daniel, he said, I'm grooming him for an important job. Then he showed me a syringe. Do you know what's in here? he asked me. The liquid in it was so blue it shone." She fell silent.

"What did you say?"

"I just shook my head. Mortality, he said. It's an improved version of the drug you shot yourself up with fifty years ago. Tell Daniel it'll be waiting for him at Sky Terminus, where the great ships come and go. That was all. You think it means anything?"

I shook my head.

She picked up the comic book, flipped it open again. "Well, anyway, it was a strange dream."

That night, after doing the dishes, I went and sat down on the pickup's sideboard and stared into the fire, thinking. Victoria came and sat down beside me. She put a hand on my leg. It was the lightest of touches, but it sent all my blood rushing to my cock.

She smiled at that and looked up into my eyes. "Resistance is useless," she said.

Afterwards we lay together between blankets on the ground.

Looking up at the night sky. It came to me then that being taken away from normal life young as I had been, all my experience with love had come before the event and all my experience with sex after, and that I'd therefore never before known them both together. So that in this situation I was as naive and unprepared for what was happening to us as Victoria was.

Which was how I admitted to myself I loved Victoria. At the time it seemed the worst possible thing that could've happened to me.

We saw it for the first time that next afternoon. It began as a giddy feeling, like a mild case of vertigo, and a vague thickening at the centre of the sky as if it were going dark from the inside out. This was accompanied by a bulging up of the horizon, as if God Himself had placed hands flat on either edge and leaned forward, bowing it upward.

Then my inner ear *knew* that the land which had been flat as flat for all these many miles was now slanting downhill all the way to the horizon. That was the gravitational influence of all that mass before us. Late into the day it just appeared. It was like a conjuring trick. One moment it wasn't there at all and then, with the slightest of perceptual shifts, it dominated the vision. It was so distant that it took on the milky backscatter colour of the sky and it went up so high you literally couldn't see the top. It was – I knew this now – our destination:

The antenna.

Even driving the pickup truck, it took three days after first sighting to reach its base.

On the morning of one of those days, Victoria suddenly pushed aside her breakfast and ran for the far side of the truck. That being the only privacy to be had for hundreds of miles around.

I listened to her retching. Knowing there was only one thing it could be.

She came back, pale and shaken. I got a plastic collection cup out of my bag. "Pee into this," I told her. When she had, I ran a quick diagnostic. It came up positive.

"Victoria," I said. "I've got an admission to make. I haven't been exactly straight with you about the medical consequences of your . . . condition."

It was the only time I ever saw her afraid. "My God," she said, "What is it? Tell me! What's happening to me?"

"Well, to begin with, you're pregnant."

There were no roads to the terminus, for all that it was visible from miles off. It lay nestled at the base of the antenna, and to look at the empty and trackless plains about it, you'd think there was neither reason for its existence nor possibility of any significant traffic there.

Yet the closer we got, the more people we saw approaching it. They appeared out of the everywhere and nothingness like hydrogen atoms being pulled into existence in the stressed spaces between galaxies, or like shards of ice crystallizing at random in supercooled superpure water. You'd see one far to your left, maybe strolling along with a walking stick slung casually over one shoulder and a gait that just told you she was whistling. Then beyond her in the distance a puff of dust from what could only be a half-track. And to the right, a man in a wide-brimmed hat sitting ramrod-straight in the saddle of a native parasite larger than any elephant. With every hour a different configuration, and all converging.

Roads materialized underfoot. By the time we arrived at the terminus, they were thronged with people.

The terminal building itself was as large as a city, all gleaming white marble arches and colonnades and parapets and towers. Pennants snapped in the wind. Welcoming musicians played at the feet of the columns. An enormous holographic banner dopplering slowly through the rainbow from infrared to ultraviolet and back again, read:

BYZANTIUM PORT AUTHORITY
MAGNETIC-LEVITATION MASS TRANSIT DIVISION
GROUND TERMINUS

Somebody later told me it provided employment for a 100,000 people, and I believed him.

Victoria and I parked the truck by the front steps. I opened the door for her and helped her gingerly out. Her belly was enormous by then, and her sense of balance was off. We started up the steps. Behind us, a uniformed lackey got in the pickup and drove it away.

The space within was grander than could have been supported had the terminus not been located at the cusp of antenna and forehead, where the proximate masses each canceled out much of the other's attraction. There were countless ticket windows, all of carved mahogany. I settled Victoria down on a bench – her feet were tender – and went to stand in line. When I got to the front, the ticket-taker glanced at a computer screen and said, "May I help you, sir?"

"Two tickets, first-class. Up."

He tapped at the keyboard and a little device spat out two crisp pasteboard tickets. He slid them across the polished brass counter, and I reached for my wallet. "How much?" I said.

He glanced at his computer and shook his head. "No charge for you, Mister Daniel. Professional courtesy."

"How did you know my name?"

"You're expected." Then, before I could ask any more questions, "That's all I can tell you, sir. I can neither speak nor understand your language. It is impossible for me to converse with you."

"Then what the hell," I said testily, "are we doing now?"

He flipped the screen around for me to see. On it was a verbatim transcript of our conversation. The last line was: I SIMPLY READ WHAT'S ON THE SCREEN, SIR.

Then he turned it back toward himself and said, "I simply read what's – "

"Yeah, yeah, I know," I said. And went back to Victoria.

Even at mag-lev speeds, it took two days to travel the full length of the antenna. To amuse myself, I periodically took out my gravito-meter and made readings. You'd think the figures would diminish exponentially as we climbed out of the gravity well. But because the antennae swept backward, over the bulk of the grasshopper, rather than forward and away, the gravitational gradient of our journey was quite complex. It lessened rapidly at first, grew temporarily stronger, and then lessened again, in the complex and lovely flattening sine-wave known as a Sheffield curve. You could see it reflected in the size of the magnetic rings we flashed through, three per minute, how they grew skinnier then fatter and finally skinnier still as we flew upward.

On the second day, Victoria gave birth. It was a beautiful child, a boy. I wanted to name him Hector, after my father, but Victoria was set on Jonathan, and as usual I gave in to her.

Afterwards, though, I studied her features. There were crow's-feet at the corners of her eyes, or maybe "laugh lines" is more appropriate, given Victoria's personality. The lines to either side of her mouth had deepened. Her whole face had a haggard cast to it. Looking at her, I felt a sadness so large and pervasive it seemed to fill the universe.

She was aging along her own exponential curve. The process was accelerating now, and I was not at all certain she would make it to Sky Terminus. It would be a close thing in either case.

I could see that Victoria knew it too. But she was happy as she hugged our child. "It's been a good life," she said. "I wish you could have grown with me – don't pout, you're so solemn, Daniel! – but other than that I have no complaints."

I looked out the window for a minute. I had known her for only – what? – a week, maybe. But in that brief time she had picked me up, shaken me off, and turned my life around. She had changed everything. When I looked back, I was crying.

"Death is the price we pay for children, isn't it?" she said. "Down below, they've made death illegal. But they're only fooling themselves. They think it's possible to live forever. They think there are no limits to growth. But everything dies – people, stars, the universe. And once it's over, all lives are the same length."

"I guess I'm just not so philosophical as you. It's a damned hard thing to lose your wife."

"Well, at least you figured that one out."

"What one?

"That I'm your wife." She was silent a moment. Then she said, "I had another dream. About your magician. And he explained about the drug. The one he called mortality."

"Huh," I said. Not really caring.

"The drug I took, you wake up and you burn through your life in a matter of days. With the new version, you wake up with a normal human lifespan, the length people had before the immortality treatments. One hundred fifty, two hundred years – that's not so immediate. The suicides are kept alive because their deaths come on so soon; it's too shocking to the survivors' sensibilities. The new version shows its effects too slowly to be stopped."

I stroked her long white hair. So fine. So very, very brittle. "Let's not talk about any of this."

Her eyes blazed "Let's *do*! Don't pretend to be a fool, Daniel. People multiply. There's only so much food, water, space. If nobody dies, there'll come a time when everybody dies." Then she smiled again, fondly, the way you might at a petulant but still promising child. "You know what's required of you, Daniel. And I'm proud of you for being worthy of it."

Sky Terminus was enormous, dazzling, beyond description. It was exactly like in Vickie's dream. I helped her out onto the platform. She could barely stand by then, but her eyes were bright and curious. Jonathan was asleep against my chest in a baby-sling.

Whatever held the atmosphere to the platform, it offered no resistance to the glittering, brilliantly articulated ships that rose and descended from all parts. Strange cargoes were unloaded by even stranger longshoremen.

"I'm not as excited by all this as I would've been when I was younger," Victoria murmured. "But somehow I find it more satisfying. Does that make sense to you?"

I began to say something. But then, abruptly, the light went out of her eyes. Stiffening, she stared straight ahead of herself into nothing that I could see. There was no emotion in her face whatsoever.

"Vickie?" I said.

Slowly, she tumbled to the ground.

It was then, while I stood stunned and unbelieving, that the magician came walking up to me.

In my imagination I'd run through this scene a thousand times: Leaving my bag behind, I stumbled off the train, towards him. He made no move to escape. I flipped open my jacket with a shrug of the shoulder, drew out the revolver with my good hand, and fired.

Now, though . . .

He looked sadly down at Victoria's body and put an arm around my shoulders.

"God," he said, "don't they just break your heart?"

I stayed on a month at the Sky Terminus to watch my son grow up. Jonathan died without offspring and was given an orbital burial. His coffin circled the grasshopper seven times before the orbit decayed and it scratched a bright meteoric line down into the night. The flare lasted about as long as would a struck sulfur match.

He'd been a good man, with a wicked sense of humour that never came from my side of the family.

So now I wander the world. Civilizations rise and fall about me. Only I remain unchanged. Where things haven't gotten too bad, I scatter mortality. Where they have I unleash disease.

I go where I go and I do my job. The generations rise up like wheat before me, and like a harvester I mow them down. Sometimes – not often – I go off by myself, to think and remember. Then I stare up into the night, into the colonized universe, until the tears rise up in my sight and drown the swarming stars.

I am Death and this is my story.

WAVES AND SMART MAGMA

Paul Di Filippo

This story was written especially for this anthology, but it's a sequel to an earlier story. When I was first checking out stories for this anthology, Paul sent me "Clouds and Cold Fires", originally published in 2003 in Live Without a Net, *edited by Lou Anders. It was a wonder-filled story set in a distant future where genetic engineering and the general manipulation of nature had reached an unprecedented extreme. The story ended on a positive note with the birth of a child, and I wanted to know what became of that child, and how he came to understand the world about him. So I challenged Paul to write that story. As ever, he was up to the challenge. You don't need to have read that earlier story as it's briefly summarized at the start of this one. But if you have read it, you'll be delighted to discover more about this remarkable future.*

Paul Di Filippo (b. 1954) is one of those annoyingly talented writers who seems to be able to write effortlessly and at will. I'm sure it's not like that, but his quirky and highly original, vivacious stories have been appearing at a relentless pace for over twenty years. A selection will be found in Ribofunk *(1996),* Fractal Paisleys *(1997),* Lost Pages *(1998),* Shuteye for the Timebroker *(2006) and a half-dozen other volumes. You'll find a lot more about him at* www.pauldifilippo.com.

SALT AIR STUNG STORM'S super-sensitive nose, although he was still several scores of kilometers distant from the coast. The temperate August sunlight, moderated by a myriad, myriad high-orbit pico-satellites, one of the many thoughtful legacies of the Upflowered, descended as a soothing balm on Storm's unclothed pelt. Several churning registers of flocculent clouds, stuffed full of the computational particles known as virgula and sublimula, betokened the watchful custodial omnipresence of the tropo-spherical mind. Peaceful and congenial was the landscape around him: a vast plain of black-leaved cinnabon trees, bisected by a wide, meandering river, the whole of which had once constituted the human city of Sacramento.

Storm reined to a halt his furred and feathered steed – the Kodiak Kangemu named Bergamot was a burly, scary-looking but utterly obedient bipedal chimera some three meters tall at its muscled shoulders, equipped with a high saddle and panniers – and paused for a moment of reflection.

The world was so big, and rich, and odd. And Storm was all alone in it.

That thought both frightened and elated him.

He felt he hardly knew himself or his goals, of what depths or heights he was capable. Whether he would live his long life totally independent of wardenly strictures, a rebel, or become an obedient part of the guardian corps of the planet. Hence this journey.

A sudden lance of light breaking through a bank of clouds brightened Storm's spirits – despite the distinct probability that the photons had been deliberately collimated by the tropospheric mind's manipulation of water molecules as a signal to chivvy him onward. Anything was possible, Storm realized. His destiny rested solely on the strength of his character and mind and muscles, and the luck of the Upflowered. Glory or doom, fame or ignominy, love or enmity . . . His fate remained unwritten.

And so far he had not done too badly, giving him confidence for his future.

The young warden had now travelled much further from home than he ever had in his short life; to barge in upon a perilous restoration and salvage mission whose members had known nothing of Storm's very existence until a short time ago. A gamble, to be sure, but one he had felt compelled to make. Perhaps his one and only chance for an adventure before settling down.

The death of Storm's parents, the wardens Pertinax and Chellapilla, had left him utterly and instantly adrift. Although by all rights and traditions, Storm should have stepped directly into their role as one of the several wardens of the Great Lakes bioregion, he had balked. The conventional lives his parents had led, in obedience to the customs and innate design of their species did not appeal to Storm's nature – at least not at this moment. Perhaps his unease with his assigned lot in life was due to the unusual conditions of his conception . . .

Some twenty years ago, five wardens, Storm's parents among them, had undertaken an expedition to the human settlement of "Chicago", one of the few places where those degraded *homo sap* remnants who had disdained the transcendence of the Upflowering still dwelled. During that dangerous enforcement action, which resulted in the destruction of the human village by the tropospheric mind, Storm had been conceived. Those suspenseful and tumultuous prenatal circumstances seemed to have left him predisposed to a characteristic restless thrill-seeking.

His conception and birth among the strictly reproductively regulated wardens had been sanctioned so that Storm might grow up to be a replacement for the elderly warden Sylvanus, who, at age 128, had already begun to ponder retirement.

And so Storm was raised in the cozy little prairie home – roofed with pangolin tiles, pots of greedy, squawking parrot tulips on the windowsill – shared by Pertinax and Chellapilla. His first two decades of life had consisted of education and play and exploration in equal measures. His responsibilities had been minimal.

Which explained his absence from the routine surveying expedition where his parents had met their deaths.

A malfunctioning warden-scent broadcaster had failed to protect their encampment from a migratory herd of galloping aurochs, and Storm's parents had perished swiftly at midnight in each other's arms in their tent.

Sylvanus, all grey around his muzzle and ear tufts, his once-sinewy limbs arthritic as he closed in on his second century, condoled with Storm.

"There, there, my poor boy, cry all you want. I know I've

drained my eyes already on the trip from home to see you. Your parents were smart and capable and loving wardens, and lived full lives, even if they missed reaching a dotage such as mine. You can be proud of them. They always honoured and fulfilled the burdens bestowed on our kind by the Upflowered."

At the mention of the posthumans who had spliced and redacted Storm's species out of a hundred baseline genomes, Storm felt his emotions flipflopping from sadness to anger.

"Don't mention the Upflowered to me! If not for them, my mother and father would still be alive!"

Sylvanus shook his wise old head. "If not for the Upflowered, none of our kind would exist at all, my son."

"Rubbish! If they wanted to create us, they should have done so without conditions."

"Are you not, then, going to step into my pawprints, so that I might lay down my own charge? You're fully trained now . . ."

Storm felt a burst of regret that he had to disappoint his beloved old "uncle". But the emotion was not strong enough to countervail his stubborn independence. He laid a paw-hand on Sylvanus's bony shoulder.

"I can't, uncle, I just can't. Not now, anyhow. And in fact, I'm leaving this bioregion entirely. I have to see more of the world, to learn my place in it."

Sylvanus recognized the futility of arguing with the headstrong youth. "So be it. Travel with my blessing, then, and try to return if you can before my passing, for a final farewell. I'll get Cimabue and Tanselle to breed my successor, while I hang in there for a while yet."

And so Storm had set out westward, across the vast continent, braving rain and heat, loneliness and fear, with no goal in mind other than to see what he could see. He and his trusty marsupial avian-ursine mount, Bergamot, foraged off the land, supplementing their herbivore diet with various nutriceuticals conjured up out of Storm's Universal Proseity Device.

Crossing the Rockies, he had encountered the tropospheric mind for the first time since his abdication. He had been deliberately avoiding this massive atmospheric intelligence due to its tendency to impose orders on all wardens. Storm feared chastisement for his rebellion. But travelling this high above sea level, there was no escaping the lower tendrils of the globally distributed artificial intelligence.

A chilly caplet of cloudstuff, rich in virgula/sublimula codec, had formed about his head, polling his thoughts by transcranial induction. Storm squirmed under the painless interrogation, irritated yet helpless to do anything.

A palm-sized high-res wetscreen formed in the air, and on it appeared the current chosen avatar of the tropospheric mind: a kindly sorcerer from some old human epic. (The tropospherical mind contained all the accumulated data of the Earth's digitized culture at the time of the Upflowering, a trove which the wardens frequently ransacked for their own amusement and edification.)

The sorcerer spoke. "You follow a lonely path, Storm. And a less-than-optimal one, so far as your own development is concerned."

Anticipating harsher rebuke, Storm was taken aback. "Perhaps. But it's my choice."

"Yet you might both extend your own growth and aid me and the world at the same time."

"How is that?"

"By joining a cohort of your fellows now assembling. As you work with them and bind together as a team, you might come to better appreciate your innate talents and how they could best benefit the planet under my direction."

"Your direction! That's always been my quarrel. We're just pawns to you! It was under your direction that my parents died."

Had the sorcerer denied this accusation, Storm would have definitely walked out on the mission. But the sorcerer had the good grace to look apologetic, sad and chagrined, although he did not actually accept responsibility for the deaths.

Mollified, Storm felt he could at least inquire politely about the mission. "What are these other wardens doing?"

"They are building a ship, and will embark from San Francisco Bay for the island of Hawaii, where they will confront my insane sister, Mauna Loa. She has already killed all the resident wardens there, as she seeks to establish her own dominion. No communications or diplomacy I have had with her have changed her plans. You think me a tyrant, but she wants utter control of all life around her."

Storm said, "Maybe she'll listen to reason from us."

"I sincerely doubt it. But you should feel free to try. In any case, I believe the odyssey will offer you the challenges you seek. Even a magnitude more."

Storm's curiosity was greatly piqued. Curse the weather mind! It was impossible to outwit or out-argue something that used a significant portion of the atmosphere as its computational reservoir. This was precisely why Storm had avoided speaking to the construct.

"If I agree to go on this journey with them, it does not mean I will fall right back into your tidy little schemes for me afterwards."

The sorcerer grinned. "Of course not."

Storm instantly regretted giving his tacit consent. But the lure of the dangerous mission was too strong to resist.

"Allow me," said the tropospheric mind, "to download your optimal route into your UPD."

Utility fog shrouded Storm's panniers, pumping information into his Proseity unit as he gee'd up and rode on.

Now, so close to his West Coast destination, Storm felt compelled to surrender his nostalgic ruminations for action. He kicked Bergamot into motion, and the biped surged in its odd loping fashion across the fruited plains that had once been covered by human urban blight.

As he passed beneath the cinnabon trees, Storm snatched a few dozen sweet sticky rolls from the branches overhead, filling a pannier with the welcome treats. He tossed several, one at a time, into the air ahead of him, where Bergamot snapped them up greedily with lightning reflexes. Gorging himself, eventually sated, Storm licked his paw-hands and muzzle clean.

Following the directions in his UPD, paralleling the Sacramento River for most of the journey, past the influx of its many tributaries, through its delta, Storm came in good time to the shores of San Pablo Bay. He continued west and south along that body of water, eventually reaching his ordained rendezvous point: the northern terminus of the roadless Golden Gate Bridge, anomalous in the manicured wilderness.

One of the select human artifacts preserved after the Upflowering for its utility and beauty, the span glistened with the essentially dumb self-repair virgula and sublimula that had maintained it against decay for centuries.

Storm admired the sight for a short time, then homed in on the scent of his fellow wardens. Following a steep path, he reached a broad stony beach. There he found ten wardens finishing the construction of their ship, and ten Kodiak Kangemus picking idly at drifts of seaweed and bivalves.

Six of the wardens worked around a composite UPD device. Their individual reconfigurable units had been slaved together in order to produce larger-than-normal output pieces. Three wardens fed biomass into the conjoined hopper, while three others handled the output, ferrying it to the workers on the ship. Those other four wardens, consulting printed plans, snapped the superwood pieces into place on the nearly completed vessel.

At first no one noticed Storm. But then he was spotted by a female, noteworthy for her unique piebald colouration.

"Ho! It's the supercargo!"

Storm bristled at the slight, but said nothing. He dropped down off Bergamot, shooing the beast towards its companions.

The ten wardens hastened to group themselves around Storm, in a not-unfriendly manner.

"You're Storm," said the pretty pinto female. Her voice was sweet and chirpy, her demeanour mischievous. "I'm Jizogirl. The weather mind told us you'd be here today. Just in time, too! Let me introduce everyone."

During the hellos, Storm uneasily sized up his new companions – all of whom were at least a few years older than he, and in some instances decades.

Pankey, Arp, Rotifero, Wrinkles and Bunter were males. Tallest of the ten, Pankey's bold mien bespoke a natural leadership. Arp managed to look bored and inquisitive simultaneously. Elegant Rotifero paid little attention to Storm, instead preferring to present his best profile to the ladies. Wrinkles plainly derived his name from his exaggerated patagium: the folds of flesh beneath a warden's arms that allowed brief aerial gliding. Bunter, plump as a pumpkin, was sniffing suspiciously in the direction of Storm's panniers.

Beyond the charming Jizogirl: Catmaul exhibited an athlete's lithe strength; Faizai echoed Rotifero's sexual preening; Shamrock was plainly itching to get back to work, as if looking to impress Pankey and secure the number-two slot; and Gumball shyly pondered her own paw-feet rather than make eye-contact with Storm.

"Pleased to meet you all," said Storm. "I'm anxious to learn more about our mission. I hope I'll be an asset."

Pankey spoke. "You are rather the 101st leg on a centipede, you know. We had a complete roster without you butting in."

"Pankey! For shame!" Jizogirl made up for her earlier quip about "supercargo" in Storm's eyes with this remonstrance, and he chose to appear unaffected by Pankey's gibe.

"I know I can be of some use. Just tell me what to do."

"Well, we want to sail at dawn, and we still have several hours of work to accomplish before dark. So if you could possibly pitch in – "

"Of course. Just point me towards a task."

"Why don't you collect biomass for now? It's the simplest chore."

Storm bit his tongue against a defence of his own abilities, and merely said, "Sure. Should I slave my UPD to the others?"

Pankey frowned. "I hadn't thought of that. Of course."

Storm did so. Then, removing a sharp, strong nanocellulose machete from his panniers (and also some cinnabons for everyone, much welcomed), he headed towards a stand of spartina. Soon, with energetic effort, he had accumulated a surplus of the tall grass, and so was able to take a break. He strolled onboard the ship to learn more about it. He saw that the superwood components were being grafted into place with various epoxies from the UPD.

Rotifero spied Storm and gestured grandly, eager to abandon his own work and act as tour guide. "The *Slippery Squid*! A sharp ship, isn't she? We should make it to the Sandwich Islands in just five days."

"So fast?"

Rotifero motioned for Storm to look over the side at the ship's unique construction. "The humans called this model the *hydroptère*. Multi-hulled, very fast. But here's the real secret."

Rotifero walked to the fore of the ship and kicked at a bundle of neatly sorted fabric and lines. "She's a kiteship. Once we get this scoop aloft, the weather mind provides an unceasing wind. We should average fifty knots. Old Tropo even keeps us on the proper heading. No navigation necessary. Which is fine by me, as I don't know a sextant from an astrolabe."

Storm nodded sagely, although the instruments named were unfamiliar to him. "And what do we do when we arrive in Hawaii?"

"Ah, I'd best let Pankey explain all that tonight. He's our leader, you know, and he rather resents anyone stepping on his lines. Say, what do you think of Fazai? Aren't her ears the perkiest and hairiest you've ever seen? You know what they say: 'Ears with tufts, can't get enough!'"

Storm felt hot blood flash beneath his furry face. Wardens lived solitary lives, each responsible for vast bioregions, meeting only infrequently. At such times, mating was lustily indulged in, with gene-regulated, reversible contraceptive locks firmly in place. In his two decades of family-centric life, Storm had not yet managed to meet a free female and mate. In fact, the unprecedented presence of so many of his kind in such proximity rather unnerved him.

"I – I wouldn't know."

Rotifero jabbed an elbow into Storm's ribs. "I realize the ten of us 're paired up evenly already, but don't worry. One of the does will probably take pity on you. If any of them have a spare minute!"

Storm's embarrassment flicked to hurt pride in an instant. "Thanks, I'm sure. But I'm used to Great Lakes does. They're much nicer in every way."

Pankey put a stop to any further amatory talk with a shouted, "Hey, you two, back to work!"

Storm spent the rest of the afternoon chopping and hauling spartina, and trying not to think of Faizai's ears.

Twilight brought successful completion of all their tasks. Sailing at dawn was assured, Pankey confirmed. A driftwood fire was kindled, tasty food was fabbed from spartina fed into the now separated UPDs (the same method by which the voyagers would sustain themselves at sea; the Proseity units could desalinate seawater as well), and everyone settled down around the flames on UPD-fabbed cushions laid over mattresses of dried seaweed. Conversation was casual, and Storm mainly listened. He soon deduced that the ten wardens all hailed from up and down the Pacific Coast, and knew each other to varying degrees.

When all had finished eating, Pankey stood, and the others, including Storm, snapped to attention.

"I will endeavour to bring our newest member up to speed," said the tall warden, grooming his muzzle somewhat self-consciously. "But this is a good time for anyone else to ask questions as well, if you're unsure of anything.

"We ten – excuse me, we eleven – have been constituted an ERT – an Emergency Response Team – by the tropospheric mind – Old Tropo, if he'll permit the familiarity – and given the assignment of straightening out the mess in Hawaii. All the wardens in that chain of islands have perished, assassinated by Mauna Loa, sister to Tropo, who wishes to enslave all the mobile entities of that biosphere.

"We are all familiar, I believe, with the phenomenon of 'rogue lobes', isolated colonies of virgula and sublimula which descend to the ground as star jelly. Usually, their lifetimes are extremely short and erratic, given their separation from the main currents of the weather mind. But in the case of Mauna Loa, we have an intelligent and self-sustaining organism, unfortunately quite deranged and exhibiting no signs of possessing any ethical constraints.

"As near as Tropo can determine, a rogue lobe hybridized with two types of extremophile microbe: an endolithic species and a hyperthermophilic species. The result is smart magma, centred in the active Mauna Loa volcano, with vast subterranean extensions throughout Hawaii's volcanic system and beyond. Mauna Loa's active tubes stretch far out to sea, in fact, and she appears to be trying to extend them to reach other landmasses in the Pacific Ring of Fire, to colonize them as well. Meanwhile, above ground, the magma's agents are local animal species controlled by transcranial inductive caps that consist of a kernel of smart magma insulated by a shell of inert, heat-absorptive material. It is these animal agents which slew our fellows."

Wrinkles stuck up a paw-hand, flaring his broad patagium, and asked a question that had been on Storm's mind.

"How did Mauna Loa ever capture animal agents in the first place?"

"Good question," Pankey said. "Tropo has reconstructed the

evolution of the non-fatal cold magma caps along these lines. Mauna Loa would throw out lariats of moderately hot smart magma – its necessarily high temperature downgraded by a radioactive component that served to keep the cooler substance plastic – at any animal that passed near an active flow. In ninety-nine point nine per cent of such attacks, the victim would die. But once a single victim, however damaged, survived with a magma patch on its epidermis, Mauna Loa had an agent. And once it recruited an agent with manipulative abilities – such as one of the many extant island simians – it had the ability to place the refined cold magma caps on a great numbers of recruits."

"So we can expect some hassle from these agents," said Jizogirl. Storm risked a glance towards her, admiring her understated bravado, and trying in the firelight to assess once again the degree of tuftedness of her ears.

"Yes. They will run interference to stop us from killing Mauna Loa."

This new talk of killing troubled Storm a bit. "Isn't there any way we might convince Mauna Loa to modify her bad behaviour, to fall in line with Tropo's leadership?"

Pankey emitted a derisive blurt. "Reason with a killer volcano! Good luck! I'd like to see you try!"

"Just watch me then!"

Pankey turned disdainfully away from Storm and directed his speech to the rest. "The saner members of the ERT will be employing logic bombs against Mauna Loa. The plan for the bomb has been uploaded to everyone's UPD – yes, Storm, yours as well. This goes a long way towards insuring that at least one of us should reach the volcano and be able to drop the bomb in. The bomb's antisense instructions will replicate and propagate rapidly through the siliceous medium, and shut down the magma mind."

"Do we have to deliver the bomb right to Mauna Loa herself?"

"No. We can attack Kilauea instead. It's a much smaller, lower, accessible target, and closer to the coast than Mauna Loa herself."

"Why can't we just dump the bomb into the first trickle of lava we see?"

Pankey began to manifest some irritation with Storm's persistent questions, even though he had invited them. "Because Mauna Loa has the ability to pinch off any small tendril of its body, and isolate the antisense wave. But Kilauea is too big and interconnected for that tactic to succeed."

Pankey paused, glaring a bit at Storm as if daring him to pose more stumpers. But Storm was satisfied that he had a grasp of their task. Pankey resumed a greater gravitas before next he spoke.

"And so we should all recognize, I believe, our true position. We stand now on the verge of a dangerous voyage, at the end of which we will face enemies who wish to stop us from crushing a brutal killer and tyrant. May Old Tropo guide our paws."

Concluding the lecture, this solemn invocation engendered a long and ponderous silence amongst the wardens, as they considered their chances for success, and the high stakes at play. Storm still debated internally whether Mauna Loa was really the unreasoning menace portrayed, or whether she could not be cajoled and reasoned with.

But their grim and thoughtful mood was ultimately leavened by a loud comment from Rotifero.

"Well, if I'm heading to my death, I intend to get in all the mating I can over the next five days! And I advise all my boon comrades to do the same!"

No sooner had this carnal activity been urged than the wardens began pairing off. Storm was disheartened to see Jizogirl beat out Shamrock in a bid for Pankey's attentions. Disgruntled but accepting, Shamrock settled for Arp instead, while Wrinkles and shy Gumball, Bunter and agile Catmaul hooked up.

Surprisingly, while most of the warden couples were already down on their mats, swiftly lost in petting and other foreplay, Rotifero and Faizai had not yet begun. Instead, the two, arms about each other's middles, approached Storm.

"Would you care to make it a threesome, Storm? I realize you hardly know us, and it's not much done. But under the circumstances, I thought . . ."

Storm hungrily drank in Faizai's allure, guttering flames glinting hotly in her liquid eyes. He gulped once, twice, then managed to speak.

"*Urk* – That is, not tonight, thank you. I'm very tired from my travels."

"Maybe some other time," Faizai slurred lusciously.

Storm made no reply, but instead dragged his mat away to lie with the Kodiak Kangemus, their musk and somnolent growls failing to fully mask the squeals and scents from his copulating comrades.

But at last he fell into a light, uneasy sleep.

"On three! One, two – three!"

The combined muscle power of all six males succeeded in tossing the bundle of the precisely packed kite a full five meters into the air, as the *Slippery Squid* floated just offshore. The kite began to unfurl. A perfectly timed wind sent by the tropospheric mind caught the MEMS fabric, belling it out to its full extent and lofting it higher, higher. The six tough composite lines fastened to the prow of the *Squid* tautened. The ship began to cut the pristine waters of San Francisco Bay, heading out to open sea.

A collective shout of triumph went up. The wardens hugged and slapped one another on the back. Jizogirl waved to the Kodiak Kangemus on the shore where they milled, reluctant to lose sight of their departing masters. Eventually, they would acknowledge the separation and find their way home.

"Goodbye, Slasher! See you soon!"

Arp said dourly, "You hope."

"Hey now, no defeatist talk," Pankey admonished.

Shamrock came up to the leader and said, "Shouldn't we erect the canopy now? Pretty soon it'll get hot, and we'll appreciate the shelter."

"Good idea. Wrinkles, Bunter, Catmaul, Faizai – get to it!"

Poles and a gaily striped awning soon shielded a large portion of the blonde superwood deck from the skies, and a few of the wardens took advantage of the shade to relax. Bunter was drawing a snack from his UPD. No one had gotten much sleep last night. But Storm stayed where he could see and admire the kite, a burnt-orange scoop decorated with the image of a sword-wielding paw and arm.

Jizogirl came up beside Storm. He nervously tightened his grip on the rail, then forced himself to relax. He looked straight at her, and admired the way the wind ruffled her patchwork fur.

"Do you like the picture on our kite, Storm? I designed it myself. No one else cared, but I thought we should have an emblem. I derived it from an old human saga. Lots of daring swordplay! So unlike our humdrum daily routines. The sweep of the action appealed to me. The humans were mad, of course, but so vibrant. I watched the show over and over. Once I played the video on a cloudscreen big as the horizon. Old Tropo indulged me, I guess. Shameful waste of computational power, but who cares. It was magnificent!"

Storm asked thoughtfully, "Are you okay with this mission? To kill a sentient being, even one accidentally born and malfunctioning?"

Jizogirl grew sober. "You didn't see the footage of the Hawaiian wardens being slaughtered, Storm. Horrible, just horrible. I don't think we have any choice . . ."

Jizogirl's sincere repugnance and sorrow was a strong argument in favour of the assassination of Mauna Loa, but Storm still felt a shard of uncertainty. He wished he could somehow speak to the rogue magma mind first.

Her natural sprightliness reasserting itself, Jizogirl resumed her light chatter. Grateful that the doe seemed content to conduct a monologue, Storm just smiled and nodded at appropriate places. He found her anecdotes charming. She moved from talk of her viewing habits into a detailed autobiography. She was thirty-two years old. Her assigned marches centred around old human Vancouver. Her father had died when a rotten Sequoia limb had fallen and crushed him, but her mother was still alive . . .

By the time the *Squid* was out of sight of land, Storm felt he knew Jizogirl as well as he knew old Sylvanus. But Sylvanus had never caused Storm's stomach to flutter, or his heart to thump so loudly.

In return for her story, Storm told his own – haltingly at first, then with a swelling confidence and excitement. Jizogirl listened appreciatively, her ears (distinctly less tufted than Faizai's) making continual microadjustments of attitude to filter out the *thwack* of waves, cries of gulls and cryptovolans, playful loud chatter of their fellow wardens. His story finally caught up with realtime, and Storm stopped, faintly chagrined. He had never talked about himself – about anything! – for such a stretch before. What would she think of such boasting?

Jizogirl smiled broadly, revealing big white shovel-like teeth.

"Why, I never could have made such a leap out of my rut when I was your age, Storm! You're so brave and daring. Imagine, travelling across half the continent on your own!"

Storm felt his head seemingly inflate, his vision fragment into sparkles. But Jizogirl's next words deflated his elation.

"If I had a little brother, I'd want him to be just like you!"

"Hey, Jizogirl, come look at this funny fish!" The voice belonged to Pankey, but a crumpled Storm could not even feel any twinge of jealousy when Jizogirl begged off and trotted over to see the latest specimen the wardens had caught for their continual cataloguing purposes. He remained at the rail, trying to estimate how long he could stay afloat alone, were he to jump, and why he would bother to prolong his miserable life.

That first day a-sea passed swiftly and easily. With no real duties (a rare condition for any warden), under the benevolent aegis of the weather mind, knowing their heading was correct and no doldrums or foul storms would ever bedevil them, the Emergency Response Team merely romped and rested, joked and petted, carefree as kits. All except Storm, who nursed his romantic disappointment alone.

As twilight swooped in from the east, the sea around the *Squid* came alive with luminescent dinoflagellates, pulsing with electric blue radiance. Storm watched the display for a while before an idea struck him.

The hasty construction of their ship had precluded any infrastructure, such as lights. Storm would provide some.

From his UPD he produced a dozen hollow, transparent spheres of biopolymer, each with a screw-on cap. He made a length of netting. Then he dipped each uncapped netted globe into the plankton flock, filling it to the brim. By the time he had dunked them all, darkness had thickened. But Storm's bioluminescent globes made spectral yet somehow comforting blue hollows in the night.

All his comrades thronged around Storm and his creations. "Brilliant!" "Just what we need!" "Let's get them hung up!"

More netting secured the globes beneath the canopy, and an exotic yet homey ambiance resulted. Arp got busy with his own UPD and produced the parts of a ukulele, which he quickly snapped together. He strummed a sprightly tune, and Catmaul commenced a sensuous dance, to much clapping and hooting.

Bunter concocted some kind of cocktail, which added considerably to the levity.

Storm watched with a blooming jubilation that received its greatest boost in the next moment. From the shadows, Jizogirl appeared to deliver unto Storm a quick hug and a kiss, before rejoining Pankey.

The second day of their voyage, the wardens were less sanguine. Hangovers reigned, and the prospect of entertaining themselves for another day seemed less like fun than a duty. Also, the further they drew from home, the larger loomed the grim struggle that awaited them.

Storm affected the most optimism and panache. His triumph last night – the invention of the light globes, the kiss – continued to sustain him. Standing at the bow, he tried to urge the *Slippery Squid* forward faster. He felt the urgent need to meet his destiny, to prove himself, to discover whether the action he had always imagined he craved truly suited him.

Studying the kite that pulled them onward, Storm had a sudden inspiration.

Pankey was scrolling through the headache-tablet templates on his UPD when Storm interrupted him.

"How are we going to fight?"

Pankey looked at Storm as if the youngster had spoken in an extinct human tongue. "Fight? You mean the animal agents Mauna Loa will throw at us? We can't possibly fight them. I counted on stealth. A midnight landing – "

"And if the enemy doesn't co-operate with your plans?"

Pankey waved Storm off. "I've considered everything. Go away now."

Storm retrieved his own UPD and called up the plans for his machete. He tinkered with them, then hit PRINT.

The scimitar-like sword necessarily emerged from the spatially restricted output port in three pre-epoxied pieces that locked inextricably together. The nanocellulose composite was stronger than steel and carried an exceedingly sharp edge.

Out on the open deck, Storm began energetically to practise thrusts, feints and parries alone. Soon he had attracted an audience. He added enthusiastic grunts and shouts to his routine.

Rotifero said, "I actually believe that such vigorous exercise might very well drive these demons out of one's head. Do you have another one of those weapons, Storm?"

Without stopping, Storm said, through huffs and puffs, "Just . . . hit . . . 'print' . . . on . . . my . . . . D . . ."

Soon all eleven wardens, even a grudging Pankey, were sparring vigorously. "Beware my unstoppable blade!" "Take that, foul fruitbat!" "I'll run you through!"

That night was spent mostly attending to various minor cuts and bruises.

Sword practice continued the next day, somewhat less faddishly, until just before noon came a cry of "Land ho!" from Catmaul.

Storm saw a small, heavily treed island at some distance off the port. "Is that Hawaii already?"

Pankey cupped the back of his own neck with one paw and massaged, as if to evoke insight. "Impossible . . ."

Bunter said, "Look how lush the vegetation is! We might find a species of nice fruit not templated in our UPDs, if we land."

The normally reticent Gumball now laughed and said, "I don't think we want to land on *that* 'island'."

"Why?" said Pankey.

"I'm surprised none of you have heard of the Terrapin Islands before. Down in Baja, we see them pass by all the time. Just watch."

As the *Squid* came abreast of the island at some remove, a patch of the ocean between island and ship began to bulge, water pouring off a rising humped form several times bigger than the *Squid*.

The gimlet-eyed scaled head of the gargantuan *Chelonioidea* regarded the vessel with cool reptilian disinterest. Sea grass draped from its jaws. Opening wide its horny mouth, working its tongue, the terrapin inhaled the masses of vegetation like a noodle.

Storm was secretly pleased to find his own nerves holding steady at the sight of the monster. The others reacted variously. Faizai shrieked, Arp clucked his tongue, Bunter gulped. Shamrock urged impossibly, "Get some more speed on here!" Gumball laughed.

"They're harmless! Don't worry!"

True to Gumball's reassurance, the *Squid* slipped past the mammoth grazing landscaped sea turtle without interference, and soon Terrapin Island lay below the horizon.

"And some claim the Upflowered had no sense of humour," Rotifero observed.

That night, long after his companions had passed satedly into deep sleep, Storm could be found awake at the rail, contemplating their luminescent wake.

He liked these people, bucks and does equally. Even Pankey's stern bossiness was fueled by pure and admirable motives. He enjoyed working with them, feeling part of a team. But did that mean he was ready completely to step into Old Tropo's harness? And what of their vengeful mission? Justified, or reprehensible?

The slick shadowy head of some marine creature broke the water then, and Storm jumped back. A dolphin! But capping its skull was a crust of magma! Here was one of Mauna Loa's captives.

The dolphin's precisely modulated squeaks were completely intelligible. "Stop! Don't run away! I just want to talk!"

"Mauna Loa . . . ?"

"Yes. I know who you are, and why you're coming. But you need not fear me. I only want to own a few islands, where I can practise my art. I want to mould life, just as the Upflowered did. Introduce novelty to the world. My tools are crude, though. Radiation mainly. You could help me gain access to better ones. Join me. Frustrate this mission. Turn it aside somehow."

"I – I don't know. I can't betray my friends. I have to think."

"Take your time then. I won't interfere. I'm harmless, really."

And with that promise, the dolphin was gone, leaving Storm to a troubled sleep.

Days four and five inched by tediously, as the wardens found all attractions equally stale, the monotony of the marine landscape infusing them with a sense of eternal stasis. Unspoken thoughts of the challenge awaiting them weighed them down. Storm tried to conceive of ways to convince his friends of the wrongness of their assault, but failed to come up with any dominant argument.

After their evening meal of the fifth day, Pankey gathered them together and said, "We should sight our destination some time tomorrow. It occurs to me that we should arm ourselves in advance with our logic bombs. Everyone make three apiece, and some sort of bandolier that can also hold your UPD."

Having complied, the wardens tested the fit of their bandoliers that cradled, across their furry muscled chests, the biopolymer eggs stuffed with antisense silicrobes, deadly only to the smart magma mind of Mauna Loa. Storm thought the UPD strapped to his back was a bulky and awkward feature, but refrained from questioning Pankey's orders. Pankey went around testing and tightening buckles before registering approval.

"Fine. Well done. Now, as to our chosen delivery method. We'll halt offshore by day and study our terrain maps one final time. We'll land under cover of darkness and split up, heading to Kilauea on pawfoot by a variety of routes. At any major vent near the summit caldera, feel free to bomb the living shit out of this volcano bitch!"

Pankey's curse-filled martial bravado rang false and antithetical to Storm, and he noted that the rough talk failed to inspire any signs of gung-ho enthusiasm in the rest.

Storm asked, "Can we expect any support from the weather mind? Maybe some storm coverage to shock the defenders?"

"I considered asking for that. But any bad weather will impede *us* just as much as it hurts Mauna Loa's slaves. No, stealth is our best bet."

"What about our swords?"

"Listen, Storm, all that swordplay onboard was good exercise and fun. It took our minds off our problems. But if you need to use those toothpicks on land, it'll be too late for you already. You'd best leave your sword behind. It's just extra weight that'll slow you down."

"I'm taking mine."

Pankey shrugged. "Junior knows best."

Storm noticed that Jizogirl appeared about to second Storm's objection to venturing forth unarmed. But then the doe relented, and said nothing.

Storm slept only fitfully, so angry was he at Pankey's rude dismissal of him. So when dawn was barely a rumour, Storm was already up, alone of the wardens, and defecating over the edge of the vessel.

Looking sleepily into the dark foaming waters that had swallowed his scat, Storm hoped for a return of the dolphin diplomat, for more talk that might help him decide whose side he was really on. But instead he saw a sleek grey hand and arm emerge to grip a ridge halfway up the hull.

He convulsively tumbled off his lavatory perch to the deck, then scrambled to his feet. A pair of hands now gripped the railing, then another pair, and another . . .

These were no innocent emissaries. Mauna Loa's promise not to interfere had been a lie. She had just been stalling, till she could outfit these attackers. Suddenly, Storm felt immense guilt at having kept the earlier visit a secret. The wardens could have been prepared for invasion by this route –

"Foes! Foes! Help! Attack!"

A wet torpedo face that seemed all teeth materialized between the first pair of hands. Gills flapped shut, and nostrils flared open.

Storm made a dive for his sword. The other wardens were stirring confusedly. Storm kicked them, slapped them with the flat of his blade.

"Swords! Swords! Get your swords!"

Turning back toward the rail, Storm faced the intruders fully.

The handsharks fused anthropoid and squaline designs into a bipedal monster all grey rugose hide and muscles. Neckless, their shark countenances thrust forward aggressively. Each wore the pebbled slave cap of the magma mind, clamped tight. A fishy carrion reek sublimed off them.

Involuntarily bellowing his anger and fear, Storm rushed forward, sword at the ready.

He got a deep resonant lick in on the ribs of a handshark at the same time he was batted powerfully across the chest. He went down and skidded on his butt across the wet deck. Leaping back to his feet, he confronted another monster – the same one? – and slashed out, blade landing with a squelch across its eyes.

Screams, battlecries, the thunk of blade into flesh. Storm could get no sense of the whole battle's tide, but only flail about in his little sphere of chaos.

Somehow he slaughtered without being slaughtered himself, until the battle was over.

Weeping, wiping blood from his face, his sword dripping gore, Storm reunited with his comrades.

Those who still lived.

That headless corpse was Bunter. The one with torn throat was Gumball. Half of Arp's torso was gone in a single bite. Faizai lay in several pieces. They never found Shamrock; perhaps a dying handshark had dragged her overboard.

Almost half their team dead, before they had even sighted their goal.

There could be no question now of where Storm must place his allegiance. All his doubt and conflicts had evaporated with the lives of his friends. Guilt plagued him as well. He knew the only way to make up for such a transgression was to carry forth the assault on Mauna Loa with all his wit and bravery. Although beyond the assassination attempt his future still floated mistily.

Only three handshark corpses littered the deck. Just one more attacker, and all the wardens would probably at this moment be dead.

Storm pulled a bloody, sobbing Jizogirl to him, clutched her tightly. He tried to imagine why he had ever sought adventure, and how he could instantly transport himself and Jizogirl and the others safely home. But hard as he pondered, throughout the sad task of creating winding sheets from the UPD, bundling up the bodies of their friends, and consigning them to the sea with a few appeals to the Upflowered, Storm could find no easy solutions.

Throughout the battle, and afterwards, their big-bellied kite had continued to pull the *Squid* onward, impelled by the insistent weather mind. The tropospheric intelligence seemed intent on throwing its agents against its rival without delay. And so by the time the surviving wardens had dumped the handshark corpses overboard, washed their clotted fur, disinfected their wounds and applied antibiotics and synthskin bandages, cleansed their swords, and sluiced the offal from the deck with seawater, the jade-green island of Hawaii had come dominantly into view, swelling in size minute by minute as their craft surged on.

Storm confronted Pankey. "You're not still thinking of hanging offshore till midnight, are you? Mauna Loa obviously knows we're here. We can't face another assault from more sharks."

Pankey appeared unsure and confused. "That plan can still work. We'll just need to put in to shore further away from Kilauea. Let's get the coastal maps . . ."

Storm's anger and anxiety boiled over. "Bugger that! The longer we have to travel overland, the more vulnerable we are!"

His expression ineffably sad, Faizai-bereft Rotifero said calmly, "I agree with our young comrade, Pankey. We need a different plan."

"All right, all right! But what!"

Jizogirl said, "Let's get in a little closer to shore anyhow. Maybe something we see will give us an idea."

Pankey said, "That makes sense."

Catmaul asked, "How will we get the weather mind to stop blowing us along?"

Normally, communication with the atmospheric entity was accomplished with programmed messenger birds that could fly high enough to have their brain states interpreted on the wing. But the wardens, overconfident about the parameters of their mission, had set out without any such intermediaries.

Pankey's voice conveyed less than total confidence. "Old Tropo is watching us. Surely he'll bring us to a halt safely."

Larger and larger Hawaii bulked. Details along the gentle sloping shore became more and more resolvable.

"Is that some kind of wall?"

"I – I'm not sure . . ."

As predicted and hoped, when the *Squid* had reached a point several hundred meters offshore, it came to a gradual stop. The weather mind had pinned the kite in a barometrically dead cell between wind tweezers that kept the parasail stationary but aloft.

With their extremely sharp eyes, the wardens stared landward, unbelieving.

Ranked along the beach was a living picket of animal slaves of the volcano queen. The main mass of the defence consisted of anole lizards. But not kawaii baseline creatures to be held with amusement in a paw. No, these anoles, unfamiliar to the main-landers, were evidently Upflowered creations, large as elephants. And atop each anole sat a simian carrying a crudely sharpened treebranch spear. Interspersed among the legs of the anoles were a host of lesser but still formidable toothed and clawed beasts. Blotches of stony grey atop the anoles were certainly slave caps, no doubt to be found on their companions as well. The huge gaudy dewlaps of the lizards flared and shrank, flared and shrank ominously, a prelude to attack.

"This – this is not good," murmured Wrinkles.

Pankey said, "We'll sail south or north, evade them – "

Storm grew indignant. He wanted to reach out and shake some sense into Pankey. "Are you joking? Those monsters can easily pace us on land, while we sail a greater distance than they need gallop."

Jizogirl interrupted the argument. "It's academic, my bucks! Look!"

The anoles and their riders were wading into the surf, making straight for the *Squid*.

"This – this is even worse," Wrinkles added – rather superfluously, thought Storm, in an uncanny interval of stunned calmness.

Catmaul began yanking on one of the half-dozen kite tethers. "We have to get away! Now! Why doesn't Tropo help us!"

Rotifero gently pulled the doe away from the cables. "Old Tropo is a stern taskmaster. He brought us here to do a job, and do it we must."

Storm looked up in vain at the unmoving kite.

The kite!

"I have a plan! But we need to ditch our UPDs first. They're too heavy for what I have in mind."

Suiting actions to words, Storm doffed his harness, detached the Proseity device, then redonned the bandolier with just logic bombs attached.

"Stash your swords in your harnesses, and follow me!"

Not waiting to see if they obeyed, Storm leaped onto the kite cables and began to climb. He felt a rightness and force to his actions, as he threw himself into battle without thought for his own safety, only that of his comrades, and the success of their necessary mission. Here, then, was the defining moment he had sought, ever since he left home.

The angle of the cables permitted a fairly easy ascent. Soon, Storm bellyflopped onto the wind-stuffed mattress of the kite. Seconds later, his five comrades joined him, with plenty of room to spare.

Below, the swimming anoles had closed half the distance to the ship.

"We have to do this just perfectly. We sever the four inner cables completely, and the two outer ones partially. Pankey and I will do the outer ones. Get busy!"

The composite substance of the cables was only a few Mohs softer than the sword blades, making for an arduous slog. But with much effort, Wrinkles, Jizogirl, Rotifero and Catmaul got the four inner cables completely separated – they fell gracefully, with an ultimate *splash*! – causing the parafoil configuration to deform non-aerodynamically, attached to the ship now only by a few threads at either end.

Storm spared a look down. The anoles were too big to clamber aboard the ship. But the simians weren't. And the apes were approaching the remaining two tethers linking kite and ship.

"Now!"

Storm and Pankey sawed frantically and awkwardly in synchrony from their recumbent positions –

Twin loud *pops* from the high-tensioned threads, and the kite was free. Instant winds sent by an alert weather mind grabbed it and pushed it toward land.

Storm allowed himself the tiniest moment of relief and triumph and relaxation. Then he sized up what awaited them.

The terrain below showed rampant greenery of cloud forest far off to every side. But the Kilauea caldera itself loomed off-centre in a barren zone of old and new lava flows: the Kau Desert. Twenty-four kilometers away, the mother volcano Mauna Loa reared almost four times higher.

"Can we ride this all the way?" shouted Pankey.

"I hope so!" Storm replied. "Maybe we can bomb one of the magma rifts from up here!"

But his optimism soon received a dual assault.

Several slave-capped gulls stalked their kite, relaying visual feeds to the magma mind. As the kite moved deeper inland, it met attacks.

From an artificially built-up stone nozzle, under concentrated pressure, a laser-like jet of magma shot up high as the kite, narrowly missing the wardens, but spattering them with painful droplets on its broken descent. The kite fabric received numerous smelly burn holes. At the same time a fumarole unleashed billowing clouds of opaque choking sulfurous gases, which the kite sailed blindly through, at last emerging into clear air.

Gasping for breath, wiping his reddened eyes, Storm finally found his voice again.

"We're a big easy target! We have to split up!"

Wrinkles got to his hands and knees. "Me first! I'm the best glider!"

Without any farewells, Wrinkles launched off the unsteady platform. He spread his unusually generous patagium and made graceful curves through the sky.

Jizogirl cried, "Go, Wrinkles, go!"

A lance of red-hot lava shot up from an innocuous spot, and incinerated Wrinkles' entire left side. With a wailing cry he plummeted to impact.

Storm felt gut-punched. "We all need to leap at once! Now! Find a rift and bomb it!"

The remaining five wardens flung themselves free of the kite.

Focused on his gliding, Storm could not keep track of the rest of the Fellowship. Heaven-seeking spears of hot rock burst into existence randomly, a gauntlet of fiery death. Deadly vog – the volcanic fog – stole his sight and breath. He lost track of his altitude, his goal. He thought he heard cries and screams –

Out of the vog he emerged, to see the tortured ground much too close, an eye-searing, writhing active rift bisecting the terrain. He braced for a landing.

His right paw-foot caught in a crevice, and he heard bones snap. The pain was almost secondary to his despair.

Working to free his paw-foot, he heard two thumps behind him.

Pankey and Jizogirl had landed, their fur smouldering, eyes cloudy and tearful.

Jizogirl came to help free Storm's paw-foot.

"Rotifero, Catmaul – ?"

Jizogirl just shook her head.

Meanwhile, Pankey had detached a logic bomb from his bandolier, and now darted in towards the living rift. Its incredible heat stopped him some distance away. He made to throw the bomb.

Overhead, the spy gulls circled low. One screeched just as Pankey threw.

A whip of lava caught the bomb in mid-air, incinerating it but prophylactically detaching from the parent flow, frustrating the spread of the released antisense agents backward along its interrupted length.

Pankey rushed back to his comrades. "It's no use. The bombs have to be delivered by hand. It's up to me!"

Jizogirl said, "And me!"

"No! Only if I fail. You and Storm – Just stay with him!"

Before either Storm or Jizogirl could protest, Pankey had taken off at a run.

Storm's nose could smell the scorched flesh of Pankey's paw-feet as the warden dodged one whip after another.

"Remember me – !" the leader of the team called, as he hurled himself and his remaining logic bombs into the rift.

The propagation of the antisense mind-killer agents was incredibly rapid, fueled by the high energies of the system. A deep subterranean rumble betokened the titanic struggle of intelligence against nescience. In a final spasm, the earth convulsed, rippling like a shaken sheet in all directions, tossing Jizogirl down beside Storm, then bouncing them both.

The quake lasted for what seemed minutes, before dying away. Even when the shaking at ground zero had stopped, rumbles and tremors continued to radiate outward into the surrounding ocean, as the antisense assault propagated. Storm could picture undersea lava tubes collapsing, tectonic plates shifting far out to sea –

Jizogirl got shakily to her paw-feet, and helped Storm stand on his one good leg.

"Is Mauna Loa dead?" she asked.

"I think so . . ."

Big menacing shapes moved in the vog around them.

"What now?" she asked hopelessly.

Out of the vog, several anoles and their riders emerged. But they no longer exhibited any direction or purpose or malice. One ape clawed at his slave cap and succeeded in ridding himself of it.

Jizogirl suddenly stiffened. "Oh, no! I just realized – We need to get inland, quickly! Up on the lizard!"

The tractable anole allowed Storm to climb onboard, with an assist from Jizogirl. His broken bones throbbed. She got up behind him, grabbing him around the waist.

"How do we make this buggered thing go?"

Storm pulled his sword out and jabbed it into the anole's shoulder. The lizard shot off, heading more or less into the interior.

"Can you tell me why this ride is necessary?"

"Tsunami! You prairie dwellers are so dumb!"

"But how?"

"The self-destruct information waves from the antisense bomb propagated faster than the physical collapse itself. When the instructions hit the furthest distal reaches of Mauna Loa out to sea, they rebounded back and met the oncoming physical collapse in mid-ocean. Result: tsunami!"

Up and up the anole skittered, leaving the Kau Desert behind and climbing the slopes of Mauna Loa. It stopped at last, exhausted, and no amount of jabbing could make it resume its flight.

Storm and Jizogirl dismounted and turned back toward the sea, the doe supporting the buck.

With the sea's recession, the raw steaming seabed lay exposed for several hundred meters out from shore. They saw the *Squid* sitting lopsided on the muck.

Then the crest of the giant wave materialized on the horizon, all spume and glory and destructive power.

"Are we far enough inland, high enough up?"

"Maybe. Maybe not."

The tsunami sounded like a billion lions roaring all at once.

Storm turned his face to Jizogirl's and said, "That kiss you gave me the other night – It was very nice. Can I have another?"

Jizogirl smiled and said, "If it's not our last, then count on lots more."

THE BLACK HOLE PASSES

John Varley

Back in 1975 I interested a British publisher in producing an annual selection of the year's best science fiction. No sooner had I signed the contract than there were changes at the publisher's, various editors moved on, and the idea for the annual series ceased. The first volume did appear, though a year late, as SF Choice '77. I mention it because that anthology included this story, which I rated as one of the best that appeared in 1975. I still think that. At the time, John Varley was still a new name, but he was rapidly making a reputation for himself and was soon regarded as one of the major new names of the seventies. I remember the same thrill in discovering his work as I did with that of Roger Zelazny's, ten years earlier. Varley's work just oozed sense of wonder. Some of his best early stories were collected in The Persistence of Vision *(1978), the title story of which won both the Hugo and Nebula awards. More recently, the retrospective* The John Varley Reader *(2004) appeared – essential reading for anyone who has not read the earlier collections. Unaccountably, the following story was not included in that compendium, and since I haven't reprinted it in over thirty years, it seems opportune to remind everyone what the excitement was all about.*

JORDAN LOOKED UP from the log of the day's transmissions and noted with annoyance that Treemonisha was lying with her legs half-buried in the computer console. He couldn't decide why that bothered him so much, but it did. He walked over to her and kicked her in the face to get her attention, his foot sailing right through her as if she wasn't there, which she wasn't. He waited, tapping his foot, for her to notice it.

Twenty seconds later she jumped then looked sheepish.

"You blinked," Jordan crowed. "You blinked. You owe me another five dollars." Again he waited, not even conscious of waiting. After a year at the station he had reached the point where his mind simply edited out the twenty-second time-lag. Given the frantic pace of life at the station, there was little chance he would miss anything.

"All right, so I blinked. I'm getting tired of that game. Besides, all you're doing is wiping out your old debts. You owe me . . . $455 now instead of $460."

"You liked it well enough when you were *winning*," he pointed out. "How else could you have gotten into me for that kind of money, with my reflexes?"

(Wait) "I think the totals show who has the faster reflexes. But I told you a week ago that I don't appreciate being bothered when I'm reading." She waved her fac-printed book, her thumb holding her place.

"Oh, listen to you. Pointing out to me what you don't like, while you're all spread out through my computer. You *know* that drives me up the wall."

(Wait) She looked down at where her body vanished into the side of the computer, but instead of apologizing, she flared up.

"Well, so what? I never heard of such foolishness; walking around chalk marks on the floor all the time so I won't melt into your precious furniture. Who ever heard of such . . ." She realized she was repeating herself. She wasn't good at heated invective, but had been getting practice at improving it in the past weeks. She got up out of the computer and stood glowering at Jordan, or glowering at where he had been.

Jordan had quickly scanned around his floor and picked out an area marked off with black tape. He walked over to it and stepped over the lines and waited with his arms crossed, a pugnacious scowl on his face.

"How do you like that?" he spat out at her. "I've been very scrupulous about avoiding objects in your place. Chalk marks, indeed. If you used tape like I told you, you wouldn't be rubbing them off all the time with that fat ass of yours." But she had started laughing after her eyes followed to where he was now standing, and it soon got out of control. She doubled over, threatened to fall down she laughed so hard. He looked down and tried to remember what it was that the tape marked off at her place. Was that where she kept the toilet . . . ?

He jumped hastily out of the invisible toilet and was winding up a scathing remark, but she had stopped laughing. The remarks about the fat ass had reached her, and her reply had crawled back at the speed of light.

As he listened to her, he realized anything he could say would be superfluous; she was already as angry as she could be. So he walked over to the holo set and pressed a switch. The projection he had been talking to zipped back into the tank, to become a ten-centimeter angry figure, waving her arms at him.

He saw the tiny figure stride to her own set and slap another button. The tank went black. He noticed with satisfaction just before she disappeared that she had lost her place in the book.

Then, in one of the violent swings of mood that had been scaring him to death recently, he was desolately sorry for what he had done. His hands trembled as he pressed the call button, and he felt the sweat popping out on his forehead. But she wasn't receiving.

"Great. One neighbor in half a billion kilometers, and I pick a fight with her."

He got up and started his ritual hunt for a way of killing himself that wouldn't be so grossly bloody that it would make him sick. Once again he came to the conclusion that there wasn't anything like that in the station.

"Why couldn't they think of things like that?" he fumed. "No drugs, no poison gas, no nothing. Damn air system has so goddam many safeties on the damn thing I couldn't raise the CO_2 count in here if my life depended on it. Which it *does*. If I don't find a painless way to kill myself, it's going to drive me to suicide."

He broke off, not only because he had played back that last rhetorical ramble, but because he was never comfortable hearing himself talk to himself. It sounded too much like a person on the brink of insanity.

"Which I *am!*"

It felt a bit better to have admitted it out loud. It sounded like a very sane thing to say. He gasped the feeling, built steadily on it until it began to feel natural. After a few minutes of deep breathing he felt something approximating calm. Calmly, he pressed the call button again, to find that Treemonisha was still not at home. Calmly, he built up spit and fired it at the innocent holo tank, where it dripped down obscenely. He grinned. Later he could apologize, but right now it seemed to be the right course to stay angry.

He walked back to the desk and sat down before the computer digest of the three trillion bits that had come over the Hotline in the last twenty-four hours. Here was where he earned his salary. There was an added incentive in the realization that Treemonisha had not yet started her scan of her own computer's opinions for the day. Maybe he could scoop her again.

Jordan Moon was the station agent for Star Line, Inc., one of the two major firms in the field of interstellar communication. If you can call listening in on a party line communication.

He lived and worked in a station that had been placed in a slow circular orbit thirteen billion kilometers from the sun. It was a lonely area; it had the sole virtue of being right in the center of the circle of greatest signal strength of the Ophiuchi Hotline.

About all that anyone had ever known for sure about the Ophiuchites was the fact that they had one hell of a big laser somewhere in their planetary system, 70 Ophiuchi. Aside from that, which they couldn't very well conceal, they were an extremely close-mouthed race. They never volunteered anything about themselves directly, and human civilization was too parsimonious to ask. Why build a giant laser, the companies asked when it was suggested, when all that lovely information floods through space for free?

Jordan Moon had always thought that an extremely good question, but he turned it around: why did the *Ophiuchites* bother to build a giant laser? What did they get out of it? No one had the slightest idea, not even Jordan, who fancied himself an authority on everything.

He was not far wrong, and that was his value to the company.

No one had yet succeeded in making a copyright stand up in court when applied to information received over the Hotline. The prevailing opinion was that it was a natural resource, like vacuum, and free to all who could afford the expense of maintaining a station in the cometary zone. The expense was tremendous, but the potential rewards were astronomical. There were fifteen companies elbowing each other for a piece of the action, from the giants like Star Line and HotLine, Ltd., down to several freelancers who paid holehunters to listen in when they were in the vicinity.

But the volume of transmissions was enough to make a board chairman weep and develop ulcers. And the aliens, with what the company thought was boorish inconsideration, insisted on larding the valuable stuff with quintillions of bits of gibberish that might be poetry or might be pornography or recipes or pictures or who-knew-what that the computers had never been able to unscramble and had given a few that chewed it over too long the galloping jitters. The essential problem was that ninety-nine percent of what the aliens thought worth sending over the Line was trash to humans. But that one per cent . . .

. . . the Symbiotic Spacesuits, that had made it possible for a human civilization to inhabit the Rings of Saturn with no visible means of support, feeding, respirating, and watering each other in a closed-ecology daisy chain.

. . . the Partial Gravitational Rigor, which made it possible to detect and hunt and capture quantum black holes and make them sit up and do tricks for you, like powering a space drive.

. . . Macromolecule Manipulation, without which people would die after only two centuries of life.

. . . Null-field and all the things it had made possible.

Those were the large, visible things that had changed human life in drastic amounts but had not made anyone huge fortunes simply because they were so big that they quickly diffused through the culture because of their universal application. The real money was in smaller, patentable items, like circuitry, mechanical devices, chemistry, and games.

It was Jordan's job to sift those few bits of gold from the oceans of gossip or whatever it was that poured down the Line every day. And to do it before Treemonisha and his other competitors. If possible, to find things that Treemonisha missed entirely. He was aided by a computer that tirelessly sorted and compared to dump the more obvious chaff before printing out a large sheet of things it thought might be of interest.

Jordan scanned that sheet each day marking out items and thinking about them. He had a lot to think about, and a lot to think with. He was an encyclopedic synthesist, a man with volumes of major and minor bits and pieces of human knowledge and the knack of putting it together and seeing how it might fit with the new stuff from the Line. When he saw something good, he warmed up his big laser and fired it off special delivery direct to Pluto. Everything else – including the things the computer had rejected as nonsense, because you never could tell what the monster brains on Luna might pick out of it on the second or third go-round – he recorded on a chip the size of a flyspeck and loaded it into a tiny transmitter and fired it off parcel post in a five-stage, high-gee message rocket. His aim didn't have to be nearly as good as the Ophiuchites; a few months later, the payload would streak by Pluto and squeal out its contents in the two minutes it was in radio range of the big dish.

"I wish their aim had been a *little* better," he groused to himself as he went over the printout for the fourth time. He knew it was nonsense, but he felt like grousing.

The diameter of the laser beam by the time it reached Sol was half a billion kilometers. The center of the beam was twice the distance from Pluto to the sun, a distance amounting to about twenty seconds of arc from 70 Ophiuchi. But why aim it at the sun? No one listening there. Where would the logical place be to aim a message laser?

Jordan was of the opinion that the aim of the Ophiuchites was better than the company president gave them credit for. Out here, there was very little in the way of noise to garble the transmissions. If they had directed the beam through the part of the solar system where planets are most likely to be found – where they all *are* found – the density of expelled solar gases would have played hob with reception. Besides, Jordan felt that none of the information would have been much good to planet-bound beings, anyway. Once humanity had developed the means of reaching the cometary zone and found that messages were being sent out there rather than to the Earth, where everyone had always expected to find them, they were in a position to utilize the information.

"They knew what they were doing, all right," he muttered, but the thought died away as something halfway down the second page caught his eye. Jordan never knew for *sure* just what he was seeing in the digests. Perhaps a better way to make cyanide stew, or advice to lovelorn Ophiuchites. But he could spot when something might have relevance to his own species. He was good at his work. He looked at the symbols printed there, and decided they might be of some use to a branch of genetic engineering.

Ten minutes later, the computer had lined up the laser and he punched the information into it. The lights dimmed as the batteries were called upon to pour a large percentage of their energy into three spaced pulses, five seconds apart. Jordan yawned, and scratched himself. Another day's work done; elapsed time, three hours. He was doing well – that only left twenty-one hours before he had anything else he needed to do.

Ah, leisure.

He approached the holo tank again and with considerable trepidation pressed the call button. He was afraid to think of what he might do if Treemonisha did not answer this time.

"You had no call to say what you said," she accused, as she appeared in the tank.

"You're absolutely right," he said, quickly. "It was uncalled for, and untrue. Tree, I'm going crazy, I'm not myself. It was a childish insult and you know it was without basis in fact."

She decided that was enough in the way of apology. She touched the projection button and joined him in the room. So beautiful, so alive, and so imaginary he wanted to cry again. Jordan and Treemonisha were the system's most frustrated lovers. They had never met in the flesh, but had spent a year together by holo projection.

Jordan knew every inch of Treemonisha's body, every pore, every hair. When they got unbearably horny, they would lie side by side on the floor and look at each other. They would strip for each other, taking hours with each garment. They developed the visual and oral sex fantasy to a pitch so fine that it was their own private language. They would sit inches apart and pass their hands close to each other, infinitely careful never to touch and spoil the illusion. They would talk to each other, telling what they would do when they finally got together in person, then they would sit back and masturbate themselves into insensibility.

"You know," Treemonisha said, "you were a lousy choice for this job. You look like shit, you know that? I worry about you, this isolation is . . . well, it's not good for you."

"Driving me crazy, right?" He watched her walk to one of the taped-off areas on his floor and sit; as she touched the chair in her room, the holo projector picked it up and it winked into existence in his world. She was wearing a red paper blouse but had left off the pants, as a reproach, he thought, and a reminder of how baseless his gibe had been. She raised her left index finger three times. That was the signal for a scenario – "Captain Future Meets the Black Widow," one of his favorites. They had evolved the hand signals when they grew impatient with asking each other "Do you want to play 'Antony and Cleopatra'?" one of *her* favourites.

He waved his hand, negating his opening lines. He was impatient with the games and fantasies. He was getting impatient with everything. Besides, she wasn't wearing her costume for the Black Widow.

"I think you're wrong," he said. "I think I was the perfect choice for this job. You know what I did after you shut off? I went looking for a way to kill myself."

For once, he noticed the pause. She sat there in her chair, mouth slightly open, eyes unfocused, looking like she was about to drool all over her chin. Once they had both been fascinated with the process by which their minds suspended operations during the time-lag that was such a part of their lives. He had teased her about how stupid she looked when she waited for his words to catch up to her. Then once he had caught himself during one of the lags and realized he was a slack-jawed imbecile, too. After that, they didn't talk about it.

She jerked and came to life again, like a humanoid robot that had just been activated.

"Jordan! Why did you do that?" She was half out of the chair in a reflex comforting gesture, then suppressed it before she committed the awful error of trying to touch him.

"The point is, I didn't. Try it sometime. I found nine dozen ways of killing myself. It isn't hard to do, I'm sure you can see that. But, you see, they have gauged me to a nicety. They know exactly what I'm capable of, and what I can never do. If I could kill myself painlessly, I would have done it three months ago, when I first started looking. But the most painless way I've doped out yet still involves explosive decompression. I don't have the guts for it."

"But surely you've thought of . . . ah, never mind."

"You mean you've thought of a way?" He didn't know what to think. He had been aware for a long time that she was a better synthesist than he; the production figures and several heated communications from the home office proved that. She could put nothing and nothing together and arrive at answers that astounded him. What's more, her solutions worked. She seldom sent anything over her laser that didn't bear fruit and often saw things he had overlooked.

"Maybe I have," she evaded, "but if I did, you don't think I'd tell you after what you just said. Jordan, I don't want you to kill yourself. That's not fair. Not until we can get together and you try to live up to all your boasting. After that, well, maybe you'll *have* to kill yourself."

He smiled at that, and was grateful she was taking the light approach. He *did* get carried away describing the delights she was going to experience as soon as they met in the flesh.

"Give me a hint," he coaxed. "It must involve the life system, right? It stands to reason, after you rule out the medical machines, which no one, *no* one could fool into giving out a dose of cyanide. Let's see, maybe I should take a closer look at that air intake. It stands to reason that I could get the CO_2 count in here way up if I could only . . ."

"No!" she exploded, then listened to the rest of his statement. "No hints. I don't know a way. The engineers who built these things were too smart, and they knew some of us would get depressed and try to kill ourselves. There's no wrenches you could throw into the works that they haven't already thought of and countered. You just have to wait it out."

"Six more months," he groaned. "What does that come to in seconds?"

"Twenty less than when you asked the question, and didn't that go fast?"

Looked at that way, he had to admit it did. He experienced no subjective time between the question and the answer. If only he could edit out days and weeks as easily as seconds.

"Listen, honey, I want to do anything I can to help you. Really, would it help if I tried harder to stay out of your furniture?"

He sighed, not really interested in that anymore. But it would be something to do.

"All right."

So they got together, and carefully laid out strips of tape on her floor marking the locations of objects in his room. He coached her, since she could see nothing of his room except him. When it was done, she pointed out that she could not get into her bedroom without walking through his auxiliary coelostat. He said that was all right as long as she avoided everything else.

When they were through, he was as depressed as ever. Watching her crawl around on her hands and knees made him ache for her. She was so lovely, and he was so lonely. The way her hair fell in long, ashen streams over the gathered materials of her sleeves, the curl of her toes as she knelt to peel off a strip of tape, the elastic give and take of the tendons in her legs . . . all the myriad tiny details he knew so well and didn't know at all. The urge to reach out and touch her was overpowering.

"What would you like to do today? she said when they were through with the taping.

"I don't know. Everything I *can't* do."

"Would you like me to tell you a story?"

"No."

"Would you tell *me* a story?" She crossed her legs nervously. She didn't know how to cope with him when he got in these unresponsive moods.

Treemonisha was not subject to the terrors of loneliness that were tearing Jordan apart. She got along quite well by herself, aside from the sometimes maddening sexual pressures. But masturbation satisfied her more than it did Jordan. She expected no problems waiting out the six months until they were rotated back to Pluto. There was even a pleasurable aspect of the situation for her: the breathless feeling of anticipation waiting for the moment when they would finally be in each other's arms.

Jordan was no good at all at postponing his wants. Those wants, surprisingly to him, were not primarily sexual. He longed to be surrounded by people. To be elbow to elbow in a crowd, to smell the human smell of them around him, to be jostled, even shoved. Even to be punched in the face if necessary. But to be *touched* by another human being. It didn't have to be Treemonisha, though she was his first choice. He loved her, even when he yelled at her for being so maddeningly insubstantial.

"All right, I'll tell you a story." He fell silent, trying to think of one that had some aspect of originality. He couldn't, and so he fell back on "The Further Exploits of the Explorers of the Pink Planet." For that one, Treemonisha had to take off all her clothes and lie on her back on the floor. He sat very close to her and put the trio of adventures through their paces.

Captain Rock Rogers, commander of the expedition, he who had fearlessly led the team over yawning wrinkles and around pores sunk deep into the treacherous surface of the pink planet. The conqueror of Leftbreast Mountain, the man who had first planted the flag of the United Planets on the dark top of that dangerously unstable prominence and was planning an assault on the fabled Rightbreast Mountain, home of the savage tribe of killer microbes. Why?

"Because it's there," Treemonisha supplied.

"Who's telling this story?"

Doctor Maryjane Peters, who single-handedly invented the epidermal polarizer that caused the giant, radioactive, mutated crab lice to sink into the epithelium on the trio's perilous excursion into the Pubic Jungle.

"I still think you made that up about the crab lice."

"I reports what I sees. Shut up, child."

And Trog, half-man, half-slime mold, who had used his barbarian skills to domesticate Jo-jo, the man-eating flea, but who was secretly a spy for the Arcturian Horde and was working to sabotage the expedition and the hopes of all humanity.

As we rejoin the adventurers, Maryjane tells Rock that she must again venture south, from their base at the first sparse seedlings of the twisted Pubic Jungle, or their fate is sealed.

"Why is that, my dear?" Rock says boyishly.

"Because, darling, down at the bottom of the Great Rift Valley lie the only deposits of rare musketite on the whole planet, and I must have some of it to repair the burnt-out de-noxifier on the overdrive, or the ship will never . . ."

Meanwhile, back at reality, Treemonisha caused her Left Northern Promontory to move southwards and rub itself lightly through the Great Rift Valley, causing quite an uproar among the flora and fauna there.

"Earthquake!" Trog squeaks, and runs howling back toward safety in the great crater in the middle of the Plain of Belly.

"Strictly speaking, no," Maryjane points out, grabbing at a swaying tree to steady herself. "It might more properly be called a Treemonisha-qua – "

"Treemonisha. Must you do that while I'm just getting into the story? It plays hell with the plot line."

She moved her hand back to her side and tried to smile. She was willing to patronize him, try to get him back to himself, but this was asking a lot. What were these stories for, she reasoned, but to get her horny and give her a chance to get some relief?

"All right, Jordan. I'll wait"

He stared silently down at her. And a tear trembled on the tip of his nose, hung there, and fell down toward her abdomen. And of course it didn't get her wet. It was followed by another, and another, and still she wasn't wet, and he felt his shoulders begin to shake. He fell forward onto the soft, inviting surface of her body and bumped his head hard on the deck. He screwed his eyes shut tight so he couldn't see her and cried silently.

After a few helpless minutes, Treemonisha got up and left him to recover in privacy.

Treemonisha called several times over the next five days. Each time Jordan told her he wanted to be alone. That wasn't strictly true; he wanted company more than he could say, but he had to try isolation and see what it did to him. He thought of it as destructive testing – a good principle for engineering but questionable for mental equilibrium. But he had exhausted everything else.

He even called up The Humanoid, his only other neighbor within radio range. He and Treemonisha had named him that because he looked and acted so much like a poorly constructed robot. The Humanoid was the representative of Lasercom. No one knew his name, if he had one. When Jordan had asked passing holehunters about him, they said he had been out in that neighborhood for over twenty years, always refusing rotation.

It wasn't that The Humanoid was unfriendly; he just wasn't much of anything at all. When Jordan called him, he answered the call promptly, saying nothing. He never initiated anything. He would answer your questions with a yes or a no or an I-don't-know. If the answer required a sentence, he said nothing at all.

Jordan stared at him and threw away his plan of isolating himself for the remainder of his stay at the station.

"That's me in six months," he said, cutting the connection without saying good-bye, and calling Treemonisha.

"Will you have me back?" he asked.

"I wish I could reach out and grab you by the ears and shake some sense back into you. Look," she pointed to where she was standing. "I've avoided your tape lines for five days, though it means threading a maze when I want to get to something. I was afraid you'd call me and I'd pop out in the middle of your computer again and freak you."

He looked ashamed; he *was* ashamed. Why did it matter?

"Maybe it isn't so important after all."

She lay down on the floor.

"I've been dying to hear how the story came out," she said. "You want to finish it now?"

So he dug out Rock Rogers and Maryjane and sent them into the bushes and, to enliven things, threw in Jo-jo and his wild mate, Gi-gi.

For two weeks, Jordan fought down his dementia. He applied himself to the computer summaries, forcing himself to work at them twice as long as was his custom. All it did was reconfirm to him that if he didn't see something in three hours, he wasn't going to see it at all.

Interestingly enough, the computer sheets were getting gradually shorter. His output dwindled as he had less and less to study. The home office didn't like it and suggested he do some work on the antennas to see if there was something cutting down on the quality of the reception. He tried it, but was unsurprised when it changed nothing.

Treemonisha had noticed it, too, and had run an analysis on her computer.

"Something is interfering with the signal," she told him after studying the results. "It's gotten bad enough that the built-in redundancy isn't sufficient. Too many things are coming over in fragmentary form, and the computer can't handle them."

She was referring to the fact that everything that came over the Hotline was repeated from ten to thirty times. Little of it came through in its totality, but by adding the repeats and filling in the blanks the computer was able to construct a complete message ninety percent of the time. That average had dropped over the last month to fifty per cent, and the curve was still going down.

"Dust cloud?" Jordan speculated.

"I don't think it could move in that fast. The curve would be much shallower, on the order of hundreds of years before we would really notice a drop-off."

"Something else, then." He thought about it. "If it's not something big, like a dust cloud blocking the signal, then it's either a drop-off in power at the transmitter, or it could be something distorting the signal. Any ideas?"

"Yes, but it's very unlikely, so I'll think about it some more."

She exasperated him sometimes with her unwillingness to share things like that with him. But it was her right, and he didn't probe.

Three days later Treemonisha suddenly lost a dimension. She was sitting there in the middle of his room when her image flattened out like a sheet of paper, perpendicular to the floor. He saw her edge-on and had to get up and walk around the flat image to really see it.

"I'll call it 'Nude Sitting in a Chair'," he said. "Tree, you're a cardboard cutout."

She looked up at him warily, hoping this wasn't the opening stanza in another bout with loneliness.

"You want to explain that?"

"Gladly. My receiver must be on the fritz. Your image is only two-dimensional now. Would you like to stand up?"

She grinned, and stood. She turned slowly, and the plane remained oriented the same way but different parts of her were now flattened. He decided he didn't like it and got out his tools.

Two hours of checking circuitry told him nothing at all. There didn't seem to be anything wrong with the receiver, and when she checked her transmitter, the result was the same. Midway through the testing she reported that his image had flattened out, too.

"It looks like there really is something out there distorting signals," she said. "I think I'll sign off now, I want to check something." And with that she cut transmission.

He didn't care for the abruptness of that and was determined that she wouldn't beat him to the punch in finding out what it was. She could only be searching for the source of the distortion, which meant she had a good idea of what to look for.

"If she can figure it out, so can I." He sat down and thought furiously. A few minutes later, he got up and called her again.

"A black hole," she said, when she arrived. "I found it, or at least a close approximation of where it must be."

"I was going to say that," he muttered. But he hadn't found it. He had only figured out what it must be. She had known that three days ago.

"It's pretty massive," she went on. "The gravity waves were what fouled up our reception, and now it's close enough to ruin our transmissions to each other. I thought at first I might be rich, but it looks far too big to handle."

That was why she hadn't said anything earlier. If she could locate it and get a track on it, she could charter a ship and come back to get it later. Black holes were fantastically valuable, if they were small enough to manipulate. They could also be fantastically dangerous . . .

"Just how big?" he asked.

"I don't know yet, except that it's too big to chase. I . . ."

Her image, already surreal enough from the flattening, fluttered wildly and dissolved. He was cut off.

He chewed his nails for the next hour, and when the call bell clanged, he almost injured himself getting to the set. She appeared in the room. She was three-dimensional again, wearing a spacesuit, and she didn't look too happy.

"What the hell happened? You didn't do that on purpose, did you? Because . . ."

"Shut up." She looked tired, like she had been working.

"The stresses . . . I found myself falling toward the wall, and the whole station shipped around it like *zzzip!* And all of a sudden everything was creaking and groaning like a haunted house. Bells clanging, lights . . . scared the *shit* out of me." He saw that she was shaking, and it was his turn to suffer the pain of not being able to get up and comfort her.

She got control again and went on.

"It was tidal strains, Jordan, like you read about that can wreck a holehunter if she's not careful. You don't dare get too close. It could have been a lot worse, but as it is, there was a slow blowout, and I only just got it under control. I'm going to stay in this suit for a while longer, because everything was bent out of shape. Not enough to see, but enough. Seams parted. Some glass shattered. Everything rigid was strained some. My laser is broken, and I guess every bit of precision equipment must be out of alignment. And my orbit was altered. I'm moving toward you slightly, but most of my motion is away from the sun."

"How fast?"

"Not enough to be in danger. I'll be in this general area when they get a ship out here to look for me. Oh, yes. You should get off a message as quick as you can telling Pluto what happened. I can't talk to them, obviously."

He did that, more to calm himself than because he thought it was that urgent. But he was wrong.

"I think it'll pass close to you, Jordan. You'd better get ready for it."

Jordan stood in front of the only port in the station, looking out at the slowly wheeling stars. He was wearing his suit, the first time he had had it on since he arrived. There had just been no need for it.

The Star Line listening post was in the shape of a giant dumbbell. One end of it was the fusion power plant, and the other was Jordan's quarters. A thousand meters away, motionless relative to the station, was the huge parabolic dish that did the actual listening.

"Why didn't they give these stations some means of movement?"

He was talking into his suit radio. Treemonisha's holo set had finally broken down and she could not patch it up. There were too many distorted circuits deep in its guts; too many resistances had been altered; too many microchips warped. He realized glumly that even if the passage of the hole left him unscathed he would not see her again until they were rescued.

"Too expensive," she said patiently She knew he was talking just to keep calm and didn't begrudge providing a reassuring drone for him to listen to. "There's no need under normal circumstances to move the things once they're in place. So why waste mass on thrusters?"

"'Normal circumstances,'" he scoffed. "Well, they didn't think of everything, did they? Maybe there *was* a way I could have killed myself. You want to tell me what it was, before I die?"

"Jordan," she said gently, "think about it. Isn't it rather unlikely for a black hole to pass close enough to our positions to be a danger? People hunt them for years without finding them. Who expects them to come hunting *you?*"

"You didn't answer my question."

"After the passage, I promise. And don't worry. You know how unlikely it was for it to pass as close as it did to me. Have some faith in statistics. It's surely going to miss you by a wide margin."

But he didn't hear the last. The floor started vibrating slowly, in long, accelerating waves. He heard a sound, even through the suit, that reminded him of a rock crusher eating its way through a solid wall. Ghostly fingers plucked at him, trying to pull him backwards to the place where the hole must be, and the stars outside the port jerked in dance rhythms, slowing, stopping, turning the other way, sashaying up and down, then starting to whirl.

He was looking for something to grab onto when the port in front of him shattered into dust and he was expelled with a monstrous whoosh as everything in the station that wasn't bolted down tried to fit itself through that meter-wide hole. He jerked his hands up to protect his faceplate and hit the back of his head hard on the edge of the port as he went through.

The stars were spinning at a rate fast enough to make him dizzy. Or were the stars spinning *because* he was dizzy? He cautiously opened his eyes again, and they were still spinning.

His head was throbbing, but he couldn't sync the throb-rate

with the pain. Therefore, he declaimed to himself, the stars *are* spinning. On to the next question. Where *am* I?

He had no answers and wished he could slip back into that comforting blackness. Blackness. Black.

He remembered and wished he hadn't.

"Treemonisha," he moaned. "Can you hear me?"

Evidently she couldn't. First order of business: stop the spin before my head unscrews. He carefully handled the unfamiliar controls of his suit jets, squirting streams of gas out experimentally until the stars slowed, slowed, and came to rest except for a residual drift that was barely noticeable.

"*Very* lonely out here," he observed. There was what must be the sun. It was bright enough to be, but he realized it was in the wrong place. It should be, now let's see, where? He located it, and it wasn't nearly as bright as the thing he had seen before.

"That's the hole," he said, with a touch of awe in his voice. Only one thing could have caused it to flare up like that.

The black hole that had wrecked his home was quite a large one, about as massive as a large asteroid. But with all that, it was much smaller than his station had been. Only a tiny fraction of a centimeter across, in fact. But at the "surface," the gravity was too strong to bear thinking about. The light he saw was caused by stray pieces of his station that had actually been swept up by the hole and were undergoing collapse into neutronium, and eventually would go even further. He wondered how much radiation he had been exposed to. Soon he realized it probably wouldn't matter.

There were a few large chunks of the station tumbling close to him, dimly visible in the starlight. He made out one of the three-meter rockets he used to send the day's output back to Pluto. For a wild second he thought he saw a way out of his predicament. Maybe he could work out a way of using it to propel him over to Treemonisha. Then he remembered he had worked all that out on the computer during one of his lonelier moments. Those rockets were designed for accelerating a pea-sized transmitter up to a tremendous velocity, and there was no provision for slowing it down again, or varying the thrust, or turning it on and off. It was useless to him. Even if he could rig it some way such that it would move him instead of drilling straight through his back, the delta-vee he could get from it was enough to let him reach Treemonisha in about three weeks. And that was far, far too long.

He started over to it, anyway. He was tired of hanging out there in space a billion kilometers from anything. He wanted to get close to it, to have something to look at.

He clanged onto it and slowly stopped its rotation. Then he clung to it tightly, like an injured monkey to a tree limb.

A day later he was still clinging, but he had thought of a better metaphor.

"Like a castaway clinging to a log," he laughed to himself. No, he wasn't sure he liked that better. If he cast loose from the rocket, nothing at all would happen to him. He wouldn't drown in salty seas or even choke on hard vacuum. He was like the monkey: very scared and not about to let go of the security that his limb afforded him.

". . . calling. Treemonisha calling Jordan, please answer quickly if you can hear me, because I have the radio set to . . ."

He was too astounded to respond at once, and the voice faded out. Then he yelled until he was hoarse, but there was no answer. He abandoned himself to despair for a time.

Then he pulled himself together and puzzled out with what wits he had left what it was she might doing. She was scanning the path of strewn debris with a tight radio beam, hoping he was one of the chunks of metal her radar told her was there. He must be alert and yell out the next time he heard her.

Hours later, he was trying to convince himself it hadn't been a hallucination.

". . . hear me, because – "

"Treemonisha!"

" – I have the radio set to scan the wreckage of your station, and if you take your time, I won't hear you. Treemonisha call . . ."

It faded again, and he jittered in silence.

"Jordan, can you hear me now?" The voice wavered and faded, but it was there. She must be aiming by hand.

"I hear you. I figured it out."

"Figured what out?"

"Your painless way of committing suicide. But you were wrong. It's true that if I had stepped outside the station wearing my suit, I would have died of CO_2 poisoning eventually, but you were wrong if you thought I could take this isolation. I would have jetted back to the station in just a few hours . . ." His voice broke as he forced himself to look again at the bottomless depths that surrounded him.

"You always take the hard way, don't you?" she said, in a voice so gentle and sympathetic that she might have been talking to a child. "Why would you have to step out?"

"Aaaaa . . ." he gurgled. One step ahead again. Why step outside, indeed? Because that's what you *do* in a spacesuit. You don't wear it inside the station, sealed off from the fail-safe systems inside unless you want to die when the oxygen in your tanks runs out.

"I'm not that dense, and you know it. You want to tell me why I didn't see that? No, wait, don't. Don't outfigure me in that, too. I'll tell you why. Because I didn't really want to kill myself, right? If I had been sincere, I would have thought of it."

"That's what I finally hoped was the case. But I still didn't want to take the chance of telling you. You might have felt pressured to go through with it if you knew there was a way."

Something was nagging at him. He furrowed his brow to squeeze it out in the open, and he had it.

"The time-lag's shorter," he stated. "How far apart are we?"

"A little over two million kilometers, and still closing. The latest thing I can get out of my computer – which is working in fits and starts – is that you'll pass within about 1.5 million from me, and you'll be going five thousand per, relative."

She cleared her throat. "Uh, speaking of that, how much reserve do you have left?"

"Why bother yourself? I'll just fade away at the right time, and you won't have to worry because you know how long I have to live."

"I'd still like to know. I'd rather know."

"All right. The little indicator right here says my recyclers should keep right on chugging along for another five days. After that, no guarantees. Do you feel better now?"

"Yes, I do." She paused again. "Jordan, how badly do you need to talk to me right now? I can stay here as long as you need it, but there's a lot of work I have to do to keep this place running, and I can't afford the power drain to talk to you continuously for five days. The batteries are acting badly, and they really do need constant attention."

He tried not to feel hurt. Of course she was fighting her own fight to stay alive – she still had a chance. She wouldn't be Treemonisha if she folded up because the going got rough. The rescue ship would find her, he felt sure, working away to keep the machines going.

"I'm sure I can get along," he said, trying his best to keep the reproach out of his voice. He was ashamed at feeling that way, but he did. The bleak fact was that he had felt for a brief moment that dying wouldn't be so hard as long as he could talk to her. Now he didn't know.

"Well, hang on, then. I can call you twice a day if my figures are right and talk for an hour without draining too much power for what I have to do. Are you *sure* you'll be all right?"

"I'm sure," he lied.

And he was right. He wasn't all right

The first twelve-hour wait was a mixture of gnawing loneliness and galloping agoraphobia.

About half one and half the other he commented during one of his lucid moments. They were rare enough, and he didn't begrudge himself the luxury of talking aloud when he was sane enough to understand what he was saying.

And then Treemonisha called, and he leaked tears through the entire conversation, but they didn't enter into his voice, and she never suspected. They were happy tears, and they wet the inside of his suit with his boundless love for her.

She signed off, and he swung over to hating her, telling the uninterested stars how awful she treated him, how she was the most ungrateful sentient being from here to 70 Ophiuchi.

"She could spare the power to talk just a few minutes longer," he raged. "I'm *rotting* out here, and she has to go adjust the air flow into her bedroom or sweep up. It's so damn important, all that housekeeping, and she leaves me all alone."

Then he kicked himself for even thinking such things about her. Why should she put her life on the line, wasting power she needed to keep breathing just to talk to him?

"I'm dead already, so she's wasting her time. I'll tell her the next time she calls that she needn't call back."

That thought comforted him. It sounded so altruistic, and he was uncomfortably aware that he was liable to be pretty demanding of her. If she did everything he wanted her to, she wouldn't have any time to do anything else.

"How are you doing, Rock Rogers?"

"Treemonisha! How nice of you to call. I've been thinking of you all day long, just waiting for the phone to ring."

"Is that sincere, or are you hating me again today?"

He sobered, realizing that it might be hard for her to tell anymore, what with his manic swings in mood.

"Sincere. I'll lay it on the line, because I can't stand not talking about it anymore. Have you thought of anything, *anything* I might do to save myself? I've tried to think, but it seems I can't think in a straight line anymore. I get a glimpse of something, and it fades away. So I'll ask you. You were always faster than me in seeing a way to do something. What can I do?"

She was quiet for a long time.

"Here is what you *must* do. You must come to terms with your situation and stay alive as long as you can. If you keep panicking like you've been doing, you're going to open your exhaust and spill all your air. Then all bets are off."

"If you were betting, would you bet that it matters at all how much longer I stay alive?"

"The first rule of survival is never give up. *Never.* If you do, you'll never take advantage of the quirks of fate that can save you. Do you hear me?"

"Treemonisha, I won't hedge around it any longer. Are you doing something to save me? Have you thought of something? Just what 'quirks' did you have in mind?"

"I have something that might work. I'm not going to tell you what it is, because I don't trust you to remain calm about it. And that's all you're getting from me."

"Haven't you considered that not knowing will upset me more than knowing and worrying about it?"

"Yes," she said, evenly. "But frankly, I don't want you looking over my shoulder and jostling my elbow while I try to get this together. I'm doing what I can here, and I just told you what *you* have to do out *there*. That's all I can do for you, and you won't change it by trying to intimidate me with one of your temper tantrums. Go ahead, sound off all you want, tell me I'm being unfair, that you have a right to know. You're not rational, Jordan, and *you* are the one who has to get yourself out of that. Are you ready to sign off? I have a lot of work to do."

He admitted meekly that he was ready.

Her next call was even briefer. He didn't want to remember it, but he had whined at her, and she had snapped at him, then apologized for it, then snapped at him again when he wheedled her for just a teeny tiny hint.

"Maybe I was wrong, not telling you," she admitted. "But I know this: if I give in and tell you now, the next phone call will be full of crap from you telling me why my scheme won't work. Buck up, son. Tell yourself a story, recite prime numbers. Figure out why entropy runs down. Ask yourself what The Humanoid does. But don't *do* what he does. That isn't your style. I'll see you later."

The next twelve hours marked the beginning of rising hope for Jordan, tinged with the first traces of confidence.

"I think I might be able to hold out," he told the stars. He took a new look at his surroundings.

"You aren't so far away," he told the cold, impersonal lights. It sounded good, and so he went on with it. "Why, how can I feel you're so far away when I can't get any perspective on you? You might as well be specks on my faceplate. You *are* specks." And they were.

With the discovery that he had some control of his environment, he was emboldened to experiment with it. By using his imagination, he could move the stars from his faceplate to the far-away distance, hundreds of meters away. That made the room he was in a respectable size, but not overwhelming. He turned his imagination like a focusing knob, moving the stars and galaxies in and out, varying the size of space as he perceived it.

When she called again, he told her with some triumph that he no longer cared about the isolation he was floating in. And it was true. He moved the stars back to their original positions, light-years away, and left them there. It no longer mattered.

She congratulated him tiredly. There was strain in her voice; she had been working hard at whatever mysterious labors had kept her from the phone. He no longer believed the story about maintenance occupying all her time. If that was true, when would she find time to work on rescuing him? The logic of that made him feel good all over.

He no longer clung to his bit of driftwood as an anchor against the loneliness. Rather, he had come to see it as a home base from which he could wander. He perched on it and looked out at the wide universe. He looked at the tiny, blinding spark that was the sun and wondered that all the bustling world of people he had needed so badly for so long could be contained in such a small space. He could put out his thumb and cover all the inner planets, and his palm took in most of the rest. Billions of people down there, packed solid, while he had this great black ocean to wallow around in.

Jordan's time was down to five hours. He was hungry, and the air in his helmet stank.

"The time," Treemonisha stated, "is fourteen o-clock, and all is well."

"Hmm? Oh, it's you. What is time?"

"Oh, brother. You're really getting into it, aren't you? Time is: the time for my twice-daily call to see how things are in your neck of space. How are you doing?"

"Wonderful. I'm at peace. When the oxygen runs out, I'll at least die a peaceful death. And I have you to thank for it."

"I always hoped I'd go kicking and screaming," she said. "And what's this about dying? I told you I had something going."

"Thank you, darling, but you don't need to carry on with that anymore. I'm glad you did, because for a time there if I hadn't thought you were working to save me, I never would have achieved the peace I now have. But I can see now that it was a device to keep me going, to steady me. And it worked, Tree, it worked. Now, before you sign off, would you take a few messages? The first one is to my mother. 'Dear mom . . .'"

"Hold on there. I refuse to hear anything so terribly personal unless there's a real need for it. Didn't I find a way for you to kill yourself after you had given it up? Don't I always pull more gold out of those transmissions than you do? *Haven't you noticed anything?*"

The time-lag!

Panic was rising again in his voice as he hoarsely whispered – "Where are you?"

And instantly:

"A thousand kilometers off your starboard fo'c'sle, mate, and closing fast. Look out toward Gemini, and in about thirty seconds you'll see my exhaust as I try to bring this thing in without killing both of us."

"This thing? What *is* it?"

"Spaceship. Hold on."

He got himself turned in time to see the burn commence. He knew when it shut off exactly how long the burn had been; he had seen it enough times. It was three and five-eighths seconds, the exact burn time for the first stage of the message rockets he had launched every day for almost a year.

"Ooh! Quite a few gees packed into these things," she said.

"But how . . . ?"

"Hold on a few minutes longer." He did as he was asked.

"Damn. Well, it can't be helped, but I'm going to go by you at about fifty kilometers per hour, and half a kilometer away. You'll have to jump for it, but I can throw you a line. You still have that rocket to push against?"

"Yes, and I have quite a bit of fuel in my backpack. I can get to you. That's pretty good shooting over that distance."

"Thanks. I didn't have time for anything fancy, but I . . ."

"Now you hush. I'm going to have to see this to believe it. Don't spoil it for me."

And slowly, closing on him at a stately fifty kilometers per, was . . . a thing . . . that she had off-handedly called a spaceship.

It was all rough-welded metal and ungainly struts and excess mass, but it flew. The heart of it was a series of racks for holding the message rocket first stages in clusters of ten. But dozens of fourth and fifth stages stuck out at odd angles, all connected by wire to Treemonisha's old familiar lounging chair. All the padding and upholstery had frozen and been carelessly picked off. And in the chair was Treemonisha.

"Better be ready in about fifty seconds."

"How did you do it? How long did it take you?"

"I just asked myself: 'What would Rock Rogers have done?' and started whipping this into shape."

"You don't fool me for an instant. You never cared for Rock. What would Maryjane Peters, superscientist, have done?"

He ould hear the pleased note in her voice, though she tried not to show it.

"Well, maybe you're right. I worked on it for three days, and then I had to go whether it was ready or not, because it was going to take me two days to reach you. I worked on it all the way over here, and I expect to nurse it all the way back. But I intend to *get* back, Jordan, and I'll need all the help I can get from my crew."

"You'll have it."

"Get ready. Jump!"

He jumped, and she threw the line out, and he snagged it, and they slowly spun around each other, and his arms felt like they would be wrenched off, but he held on.

She reeled him in, and he climbed into the awkward cage she had constructed. She bustled around, throwing away expended rocket casings, ridding the ship of all excess mass, hooking him into the big oxygen bottle she had fetched.

"Brace yourself. You're going to have bruises all over your backside when I start up."

The acceleration was brutal, especially since he wasn't cushioned for it. But it lasted only three and five-eighths seconds.

"Well, I've lived through three of these big burns now. One more to go, and we're home free." She busied herself with checking their course, satisfied herself, then sat back in the chair.

They sat awkwardly side by side for a long twenty seconds.

"It's . . . it's funny to be actually sitting here by you," he ventured.

"I feel the same way." Her voice was subdued, and she found it hard to glance over at him. Hesitantly, her hand reached out and took his. It shocked him to his core, and he almost didn't know what to do. But something took over for him when he finally appreciated through all the conditioned reflexes that it was *all right,* he could touch her. It seemed incredible to him that the spacesuits didn't count for anything; it was enough that they could touch. He convulsively swept her into his arms and crushed her to him. She pounded his back, laughing raggedly. He could barely feel it through the suit, but it was wonderful!

"It's like making love through an inflated tyre," she gasped when she calmed down enough to talk.

"And we're the only two people in the universe who can say that and still say it's great because, before, we were making love by postcard." They had another long hysterical laugh over that.

"How bad is it at your place?" he finally asked.

"Not bad at all. Everything we need is humming. I can give you a bath . . ."

"A bath!" It sounded like the delights of heaven. "I wish you could smell me. No, I'm glad you can't."

"I wish I could. I'm going to run the tub full of hot, hot water, and then I'm going to undress you and lower you into it, and I'm going to scrub all those things I've been staring at for a year and take my time with it, and then – "

"Hey, we don't need stories anymore, do we? Now we can do it."

"We need them for another two days. More than ever now, because I can't reach the place that's begging for attention. But you didn't let me finish. After I get in the tub with you and let you wash me, and before we head hand in hand for my bedroom, I'm going to get Rock Rogers and Maryjane Peters and The Black Widow and Marc Antony and Jo-jo and his wild mate and hold their heads under the water until they *drown*."

"No you don't. *I* claim the right to drown Rock Rogers."

THE PEACOCK KING

Ted White & Larry McCombs

Ted White (b. 1938) has a well-established reputation not only as a leading magazine editor and author, but also as a premier science-fiction fan, and a music columnist and aficionado. White edited science-fiction fanzines in the 1950s, and was able to make the step to editing professional magazines in 1968 with Amazing Stories *and* Fantastic. *Under his editorship the magazines published some of the most innovative material of the 1970s, but they were seriously underfunded and White eventually stood down as editor in 1978. He subsequently edited* Heavy Metal *and* Stardate. *He has written several novels, starting with* Invasion from 2500 *(1964) with Terry Carr, though perhaps his best work includes* By Furies Possessed *(1970) and the super-hero novel,* Doc Phoenix *(1977). "The Peacock King" was written early in his career based on a draft by fellow SF and music fan, Larry McCombs, who was at the time a physics teacher. It was published in* The Magazine of Fantasy and Science Fiction *but had previously been submitted to* Analog, *where the legendary editor, John W. Campbell, Jr., rejected it as scientifically inaccurate. White and McCombs were exploring a topic previously covered by Stanley G. Weinbaum and Arthur C. Clarke as to whether a human being could survive for a brief period unprotected in a vacuum. White also believes it was one of the first SF stories to legitimately incorporate psychedelic drugs. The combination of the two elements is a potent mix.*

THE FIRST SENSATION was like the initial nausea they'd known with the LSD. It was the nausea of total special disorientation, and worse. Before he'd lost touch with his body, Eric had felt it fragmenting, wrenched into disintegration. Then his last consciousness of the controls, the ship – and even his physical self – was gone, and there was no longer time nor space, but only their still-linked awareness of each other's spirits, freed into a void between motion and fixity.

Karen's touch was an emotional caress to which he readily responded. Their link, carefully built and fostered over the long months before, transcended the cleavage from physical reality that had come from the hyperspace jump.

They were *free!* Once again, their consciousness expanded out into the universe, this time with even greater exultation.

"We've been here before!" Was that Karen's thought or his own? He felt emotionally entwined with her; his thoughts were her thoughts. No matter whose, that thought voiced their mutual elation.

"Tao," was the reply.

There was no longer any boundary between their inner selves and the Outside, no boundary between them. All was Tao, all was now. Briefly they'd known this before, the uncrippling of release from the stunted senses of their bodies, the blossoming perception of *wholeness*. Now they experienced it to a far greater extent, feeling themselves unfolding, outward . . .

Then, suddenly, they were not. They were hanging in space, their skin-suited bodies joined by bare hands, pivoting on a common axis amid the empty stars. Eric had only just enough shocked awareness to hold his breath.

Where was the ship? Where was the Peacock?

Eric rolled over lazily and stretched. The auto-clock had gradually raised the lights in the room and wafted a fresh breeze across the sleeping floor to gently wake them. With a soft grin at the figure next to him, still stubbornly curled into a hedgehog curl, he waved a hand at the wall panel controlling the infrared lamps in the ceiling. As the cozy warmth died away, he ran a tender hand along Karen's bare back and tweaked her ear.

"Wake up, Porkypine. It's our big day."

With a great show of reluctance, Karen slowly rolled over and stretched out, rubbing and arching her back against the resilient plastic-covered foam floor like a friendly feline. Noting with pleasure Eric's continually fresh delight in the sight of her body, Karen wiggled provocatively. "Always interested in business, are you?"

"No time for that this morning," he replied decisively, digging a commanding finger into her navel. "Up and at 'em!" Suiting his actions to the words, he sprang limberly to his feet and made a mock grab for her hair.

"Okay, boss, okay. I'm coming."

Eric palmed a door open and stepped into the bathroom. While the walls sprayed him with alternating soapy and clear water, he washed his face and scalp clean of stubble with a depilitory cloth.

While blasts of hot air dried him, he felt his crown. "I still haven't gotten used to this bald head," he complained as he emerged into the bedroom again, where Karen had folded down the wall to cover the sleeping pad and reveal closets and drawers.

She took one wincing glance at her own reflection in a large vanity mirror, and turned to the bath. "Don't believe that stuff they give you about convenience for attaching the control electrodes," she said at the door. "It's just to keep us faithful to each other – no one else would take a second look at us! Romantically, anyhow!"

By the time Karen had emerged from the bathroom, Eric had slipped into the one-piece suit that fit him like a second skin. He remembered wryly the many almost embarrassing sessions of measurements and fittings that had gone into the making of the suit. Looking down his front, he announced in mock doubt, "I still feel like I ought to wear a pair of pants over this thing."

"What's the matter? Ashamed of it?" Karen wriggled her way into her own suit.

"No, but just don't make any provocative gestures in that thing before we're strapped in, or I may be embarrassed on nationwide television."

"It'll give the columnists something new to write about," Karen tossed back over her shoulder as she palmed another door and walked through it.

Eric followed her into the living room, where a breakfast sat steaming fragrantly on the low Japanese table. While Karen busied herself with the tea, he carefully chose a scroll from a rack hidden in a wall panel. He carefully unrolled it until it hung its full silken length against the rear wall of a tall recess opposite the breakfast table.

"For today, a special blessing from the Peacock King." The silk hanging depicted in faded subtle colors a six-armed figure seated upon the back of a peacock, whose many-eyed tail spread out as a background to the resplendent king. The scroll was an eleventh century Buddhist painting, and they'd fallen in love with it during one of their tours through Japan. No amount of money could persuade the monks of the Ninnaji temple to part with it, but with some reluctance they had finally agreed to loan it to these peculiar Americans who seemed so well to understand the beauty and meaning of the treasure.

As he seated himself cross-legged on the mat before the table, Eric brought his palms together in imitation of two of the king's hands and bowed to the scroll. "May the *Peacock* live up to its billing," he intoned, only half seriously.

Buddhist legend had it that the Peacock King removed the evil thoughts and passions from the minds of humans, while his peacock devoured the poisonous snakes, insects and plants in his path. The government had initially resisted their desire to name the ship the *Peacock*, but had finally given in to what some higher officials regarded as sheer frivolity.

Meantime Karen had taken the three perfect jonquils which lay on the breakfast tray and carefully arranged them in a jet black vase before the scroll. Their delicate fragrance blended with that of the tea.

They ate in silence, slowly savoring the good food, eyes and minds fixed upon the ominous and yet benevolent face before them. When they had finished, and swallowed one last ceremonious cup of tea, they rose and bowed towards the scroll, and then passed through a door which had thoughtfully slit open at their gesture.

The apartment which they were now leaving was cleverly designed to simulate the open grace of a Japanese pavilion. While its walls were not actually sliding screens, and indeed were loaded with automatic machinery, the basic design and decoration had skilfully suggested fresh air and sunshine lurking in the corners. This effect they'd contributed to with their own choice of furniture and hangings.

But there were no windows.

And this for a simple reason: the apartment was located in a vast government complex buried deep underground. Now that they had deserted the apartment, this fact was obvious. No pretense had been made with the long steel-grey corridor which stretched austerely before them. Their padded footsteps scraped loud echoes from the featureless walls.

They had taken perhaps twenty steps down the corridor when Eric suddenly stopped, snapping his fingers. "We almost forgot to consult the oracle."

"Not thinking of backing out now, are you?" Karen taunted lightly, but she followed him back into the apartment.

From another concealed shelf in the living room Eric removed a well-worn pair of black volumes and a handful of thin sticks. While Karen sat silently watching, Eric began casting the yarrow stalks.

It was a complex ritual, containing within it the rhythm and beauty of a dance. One could find justification enough in the action of the ritual itself, but at the end of each section of the dance, he made a mark on a piece of paper with a brush pen, until at last he had twelve symbols arranged in a pattern.

For a time he silently studied the pattern. Then he turned to the book. For a longer time he studied the pages related to the diagram he'd drawn. Finally he spoke softly, with a puzzled note to his voice.

"The symbol is Ming I, 'Intelligence Wounded'. The good and intelligent officer goes forth in the service of his country, notwithstanding the occupancy of the throne by a weak and unsympathising sovereign. In the circumstances it will be wise to realize the difficulty of the position and maintain firm correctness."

"It seems clear enough to me," Karen suggested. "The government still insists that we must claim any habitable planets for the United States and take whatever measures might be necessary to keep them from the knowledge of the Communist Bloc or the Chinese. We must 'maintain firm correctness' – do whatever seems right to us in the circumstances."

"Yes," Eric replied, "but I have two moving lines, in the second and sixth places. 'He is wounded in the left thigh. He saves himself by the strength of a swift horse. He is fortunate.' But in the sixth line, 'There is no light, only obscurity. He had at first ascended to the top of the sky. His future shall be to go into the earth.'"

For a few moments they pondered the reading in silence. Eric shrugged, and then a quiet belltone sounded. "We're late," he commented needlessly, and then quickly but respectfully replaced the *I Ching* and the yarrow stalks in their cabinet.

The corridor took them to an elevator, and when that disgorged them they were met by others, who escorted them, hand in hand, into the briefing room where a handful of reporters and a barrage of cameras and microphones waited for them. The air was faintly blue and stale; the refreshers were unable to cope with the concentration of nervously smoked cigarettes.

As they entered, the pool announcer was speaking suavely into the microphones, following an outline being held for him on cue cards by a grip behind the cameras.

". . . as you all know, culminates over a year of training and preparation for this trip. The *Peacock* represents the fifth in the experimental class of faster-than-light ships and is a last-ditch attempt to conquer the problems of interstellar flight. All four of the previous hyperspace ships are presumed lost, and the project would've been abandoned, had not Captain Arbogast of the *Lucifer II* managed to radio back a report on their transition to normal space just outside the orbit of Pluto. He reported that not only had the jump created a period of temporary insanity – analysis indicates extreme schizophrenia – but that his crewmate was missing. He then took the *Lucifer II* on the long jump to Alpha Centauri, never to regain contact with us or return. Since one more ship was ready, a radically new training program was instituted. Eric Bowman and Karen Hamblin, who are with us here now, have been thoroughly trained in all possible techniques of interpersonal communication, until they are able to function almost as a single person, and . . ."

A slight pressure from Karen's hand told Eric she was thinking the same thing. On the monitor screens behind the glittering lenses of the cameras and to one side he could see their images. Only their heads and shoulders showed; linked hands were discreetly ignored. As the announcer droned on, his mind wandered back over the preparation so briefly recapped . . .

They had originally been chosen among a thousand others in a test of intuitive abilities administered at colleges, universities and schools across the country. Eric had been a graduate student at Harvard, pursuing a course in the philosophy of science and delving into the interrelationships between oriental philosophy and modern physical science. He had taken the tests for the fun of it, and had almost laughed it all off when he was informed he'd been chosen for further testing.

Karen had been living with a jazz musician in Chicago and had heard about the tests at the University of Chicago, where she occasionally modelled for art classes. She'd taken the tests on a whim, having always suspected her intuition was more reliable than most, and on another strange whim, much to the disgust of her boyfriend, had decided to go to California for the further tests and training.

Eric and Karen had met soon after arrival, and had instantly been attracted to each other. The project was isolated in the high Sierras, almost ten miles beyond the end of the nearest paved road, and conducted in greatest secrecy. The secrecy was not so much due to any fear of sabotage or spying, but rather fear of public opinion and pressure, were news about the activities there to leak out. For, much to the dismay of the government authorities, the project had been put in the charge of a rather far-out philosopher who had written many books on the adaptation of Eastern mystic philosophies to the Western mind. While there was general higher echelon approval of Dr Tompkins' goals, there were many misgivings about his methods. Basically what was desired was a piloting team who could function together as a fully autonomous unit, and maintain their sanity when exposed to the mind-wrenching schizophrenia apparently experienced in hyperspace.

Little was known about hyperspace. Popularly it was referred to as a translation from one level of reality to another. One of its immediately obvious uses became apparent when it was discovered that in returning to normal space one could return to a different sector of it. The new reality of hyperspace bore a remarkable resemblance, Dr Tompkins decided, to descriptions in some Buddhistic writings of Nirvana. His decision was to crash-train his candidates to accept, at least temporarily, such a state.

After a few months of basic tutoring in Taoism, Zen, and – on their own, Tantrik Buddhism – Karen and Eric found themselves achieving a certain serenity and control over their own mental processes. And, because they had become lovers, they had found a closeness accented by their practice of *maithuna*, the yoga of love – reaching that rare state of love where they moved in complete awareness of each other. Meantime, the original thousand had been inconspicuously weeded down to about fifty of those who showed the most promise.

Along with the disciplines of Buddhism, drugs were also used. First, Eric and Karen took part in a group of fifteen who chewed the root bark of the Africantabernanthe iboga. This was one of the lesser known of the psychedelics, the so-called consciousness-expanding drugs.

The drug produced several hours of euphoric hallucinations, in which they took great delight. At first they watched, fascinated, as they became aware of familiar objects in new detail and marvelously glowing colors. There was a great deal of easy laughter among the fifteen, and Eric and Karen found themselves drawn into a deep affirmation of each other which rose and peaked upon the waves of their delight.

After the heady sensations had worn off, there followed almost twenty-four hours of sleeplessness during which time they found their brains highly sharpened. It was unlike the stimulation of such drugs as dexadrine; there was no nervousness or excitation. It was simply as though all the mental fog which normally obscures thought had been blown away and replaced by brilliantly illuminating sunshine. During this period they devoted themselves to the final digesting of all they had learned earlier. It would be impossible, Eric knew, to ever lose it now: the products of their momentary brilliance would always be with them.

When Dr Tompkins felt that they had been adequately prepared, he brought the last six survivors of the course together to take lysergic acid diethylamide, popularly known as LSD-25. This drug, the most potent of the psychedelics by far, could be used, when taken in a comparatively large dosage, to simulate schizophrenia. It was to be the final test.

The eight hours they spent together under that drug were a time that Eric and Karen would never forget. At first it went as before, a tingling euphoria bringing with it halucinatory powers. But while before they had felt some vestige of personal control, this time they did not. Eric felt himself slipping over a vast precipice, and knew he was powerless to halt himself.

The renewed colors seemed not quite so sharp this time, perhaps because they had each retained a little more sense of awareness after their previous psychedelic experience. But then they began to find themselves able to make things melt and change form before their eyes, simply by willing it – or even by suggestion from another. For some minutes (that might have been hours or seconds) they stared at each other. Eric was possessed by the knowledge that he had only to look into Karen's eyes to plumb the depths of her soul: all would be known to him. As he stared at her, and she at him, they saw a succession of demons and angels, age and youth, good and evil forms sliding across their faces. For a moment, Eric's heart froze as he saw on Karen's face the ugly vision of Evil Incarnate, then she shifted her position, the shadows changed, and it was gone, to be replaced by a look of loving acceptance.

At first they'd stayed with the others, participating in part in the group gestalt, finding ecstasies of meaning in the paintings and music. But as each of the six fell deeper into the experience, there was less communication between them and the others.

Eric had a vision then, of an unparted, fourth-dimensional figure of himself stretching back through adolescence, childhood, and early infancy to birth. *He had always been alone*, he realized. Man is born alone. Now each of them was experiencing this aloneness, each had withdrawn into himself.

But he was not lonely. As he grappled with this, he became aware of Karen again, aware of the depth of being which they shared. He found himself growing absorbed in her – and found her returning his response. Soon they quietly left the group to return to their room.

There they lost all consciousness of time or space, but became simply two spirits floating in a great sea of sensations – colors, sounds, feelings, smells, all heightened to a new and marvelous beauty. In the midst of *maithuna* lovemaking, they suddenly lost all awareness of having come from two bodies. Their heightened rapture seemed to transcend the physical, and there was between them only one great spirit occupying the entire room, even the entire universe. Eric was conscious of a wisp of thought, whose he did not know: "When this is all over, I wonder if we'll ever get sorted out into our own bodies again?"

They didn't. At first the somewhat uncomfortable insights into their own mental processes that the drug had given them left them with what Dr Tompkins assured them was a common sort of psychological hangover: for some days they were rather touchy and jumpy, their thoughts bound up in the problem of integrating all the new things they had learned about themselves.

But this initial period of reorientation passed, and they found a new awareness of each other. Most of their conversations were constantly being punctuated with the phrase, "I know." They found much less need for talking then – a simple look into each others' eyes could convey more than an hour's talking. Whether making love, or quietly strolling through the stunted sage under the close high clouds, they were startled to find that each could feel both the physical and emotional sensations in the other. If LSD was supposed to simulate conditions in hyperspace, they could hardly see why the concern; this was a new sort of heaven – not a hell of insanity.

"I never knew that schizophrenia was supposed to be like *that*," Karen confessed, puzzled, to Dr Tompkins.

"For you, apparently it wasn't a schizophrenic condition at all," replied Tompkins. "At least, not as we clinically define it. You found higher realities, while classically the schizophrenic condition represents a withdrawal from reality, or at least a retreat into a personal sort of reality which hasn't much in common with external reality.

"The difference seems to be in the way you approached the experience, the way in which you two had prepared yourselves emotionally."

"I understand one of the others had a bad time of it," said Eric.

"Yes, Reynolds. He had what we call 'the horrors'. When he got in deep enough he couldn't take it, he couldn't take the loneliness. Every man is an island – you know that now. We are each unique beings, born alone, living alone, dying alone. In one sense we will never cease being alone. This makes many lonely. There's a difference . . ."

"Yes," they chorused, and then looked at each other and laughed.

"The experience you went through strips away all the defenses. Most of us have sought to hide our aloneness from ourselves. Many simply can't face it. You did, and you transcended it. You accepted it, you affirmed it. You used it as a starting point, a jumping-off place.

"I don't think you'll have any trouble with the jump – and I've selected you to make it."

They had been so wrapped up in exploring their new mutual personality that they were almost startled at Tompkins' reminder of the project's ulterior purpose. They gazed into each others' eyes, hands tightly clasped, probing their emotions and intuition. Then Eric laughed delightedly. "Yes," he said, "we *will* go."

That had been just the beginning. They were given every opportunity to develop their growing love, living now in the apartment buried deep in the government complex, but the major part of this second phase of the project was a rigorous training program, spending so many hours in the mockup of the space ship cabin that it became – as intended – practically an extension of their bodies.

They were to pilot a unique kind of ship, for it could travel everywhere simply by translation into hyperspace. It had no need for rockets, no need to fly. But at the same time, it had to be equipped for space conditions, since their first jump would be a preliminary one to the edge of the solar system, and from there the big jump, across stars. Once in the Alpha Centauri system, they would have to hedgehop, looking each planet over before making any landings. And, once landed, they would not disembark, but would return immediately, directly to Earth. Computers would have carefully recorded and compiled the data from each of their jumps, carefully tracking their path. They would be able to backtrack automatically to any point they'd already touched upon; it was only the path ahead which needed to be picked out.

Once they'd recorded the way, it could be followed, automatically, in one direct jump, from Earth. Future trips would be closer to the old ideal of teleportation than space travel, and could be accomplished automatically. But for the initial exploration a great deal more was needed.

The controls would not be operated by their hands – although some auxiliary systems could be – but rather by direct mental impulse, transmitted through a maze of fine electrodes fitted to their shaven heads with a cybernetic helmet. By removing the gap in muscular reaction time in this fashion, a far more positive control could be assured.

During one of their brief vacations they had asked for the chance to travel to Japan for a visit to some of the temples and monasteries of the Buddhist religion, for they now considered themselves to represent a new synthesis of Buddhism. Its complex, yet simple rituals seemed to bring the mind to just that state of calmness needed for their mental unity. The government had acceded to the trip, after successfully arranging to conceal it as a public relations tour.

Now they were ready to board the *Peacock* for the trip that might bring mankind to the stars, or might end their lives within the next hour. The announcer beside them finished his speech with a smooth transition to the pair: ". . . and so mankind's dreams of stellar travel ride today with this fine young couple who are standing here at my side. How do you feel today, Eric and Karen?"

They looked at each other, tried to suppress a grin and failed, and then Karen said to the announcer, "We'll go."

He was somewhat startled, but managed a well-modulated appreciative chuckle. "Well, I'm sure everyone is relieved to hear that. Do you anticipate any trouble?"

This time Eric answered quickly. "Well, as a matter of fact, yes. We might get killed."

This was beyond the announcer's experience, and after an insistent signal from his director off camera he brought the interview to an end. "Well, Karen and Eric, the best wishes of the whole world ride with you today. We'll be praying for you."

Eric answered, suddenly serious. "We thank you," he said, nodding. Then he reached for Karen's hand just as she extended it, and they walked through the newsmen and were followed by their anonymous government escorts down another corridor.

The ship was nestled in the center of the great underground complex, a large sphere, the entrance port of which seemed simply another door at the end of the corridor. They clambered into the small control capsule, and for the next few minutes were completely engaged in the details of attaching the control helmets to their graphite-smeared heads, the sensors which monitored their physical reactions for ground control, and reading and checking over the instruments before them. The capsule did not smell quite as the mockup had; otherwise Eric could tell no difference. Eric reached out and met Karen's hand, and their fingers locked. Tests had borne out their insistence that physical touch was necessary for the optimum functioning of their mental-empathetic contact.

As the last minutes were counted off Eric reached over for a last hasty kiss, and they become so involved that they were only recalled to reality by the overhead speaker which insisted, "*Peacock* Control, signify ready!"

"Ready and willing," Karen snapped back with mock efficiency, and then with a laugh they settled into place.

The vacuum pumps outside the hull were rapidly fading in their monotonous throb as the air between the ship and the walls of the pocket it nested in was exhausted. The vacuum was necessary; otherwise their departure would create a sizeable implosion. It would be maintained until their return, for the same reasons.

As the last seconds ticked away, Eric and Karen found themselves fully alert, every sense tensed to the slightest reaction of the ship. They did not glance at each other, yet knew each others' feelings and fears completely.

"God bless you. Four. Three, Two. One. Jump," came the voice from Ground Control, and with the last word came a sudden wrench which threw the *Peacock* into hyperspace.

Something had thrown them back out again; something had precipitated them into normal space before it had been time. Naked of the Ship, they would die in minutes. Eric felt a cold tingling in his eyes, then noticed Karen's were shut. Quickly he closed his own.

That was better. *That's better,* he thought. Or was that his thought?

He felt a hand-squeeze. *Mine.* With his eyes closed, swinging in complete weightlessness, holding even his lungs motionless, he could feel the same special disorientation stealing over him again. His lungs seemed ready to burst, and he panicked. He exhaled with a shudder, and convulsively grabbed Karen's hand with crushing force. They were in space! *Alone, alone, alone.*

He would never again know true aloneness. In his mind's eye he still saw the cold unwinking stars wheeling about them. He was falling! – and there was no bottom!

Was this to be their fate, to perish alone and insignificant among the empty stars? Was this the meaning of the prophesy from the *I Ching*?

No. He felt Karen's reassuring grip. She squeezed, gently. '*His future shall be to go into the earth.*' Believe, Eric, *believe*.

There is a way, Karen tried to show him, pulling him, leading him. *Let yourself go free*.

Then he understood. Deliberately, he recalled into his mind the disciplines, carefully he began to relax himself, loose himself from the panicking fear. Slowly, he began to disassociate himself from physical sensation.

As a boy he'd sometimes laid upon a bed as motionless as possible. He used to call it "floating". After a time it would seem as though he was indeed floating; he'd no longer be able to feel his body, no longer even be able to tell the position of his limbs. He would spin in that narrow void until finally he became frightened and convulsively started, opened his eyes, and reasserted himself in the world of sensation.

It was like that now. They had to get out, out of physical reality – back into that otherwhen of hyperreality. Disassociation: that was the key. While he let himself spin out of his body, he tried to recall, to recreate the way they had done it before, with the LSD, and he let his spirit grope outwards, linking with Karen's, knowing and understanding – elsewards.

Their two bodies hung, dust motes in the vast starscape, for a long moment. Then they were gone.

There was no sensation of time. As soon as they'd re-established that transcendent contact, time ceased for them and they floated in an unbracketed infinity. For Eric it was also a period of insight and understanding; now he *knew*.

There was never any way of telling how long they'd hung together out there in space – much later the medicos told them that it could have been only a matter of a few seconds, but for Eric those had been long seconds indeed, even after he'd cut himself off from his body with its screaming lungs and frostbitten skin. And if they'd been, even for only a moment, alive in normal space, it had been for a finite amount of time, while afterwards, in non-space – call it *hyperspace*, another dimension, or nowhere – there was only infinity . . .

Then they, and the ship, were through, the jump completed. Eric was aware again of the touch of the electrodes clamped to his aching skull, his numbed feet and hands, his ringing ears and bleeding nose, and – most of all – the rasping breath shuddering up into his body.

He opened bloodshot eyes and stared into Karen's. Then they were laughing together.

"You're the Lost Weekend personified," she said.

"Hey, we did it!" he said at the same time. Then he reached overhead for the small gray mike, and pulled it down, the cord tense against its return spring, and repeated his words, this time for Earth.

His arm ached while he held the mike and waited. Finally the small speaker behind them spat twice and then crackled, "Congratulations on making the first leg. How was it?"

"A little bigger than we expected," Eric said, and exchanged a knowing grin with Karen.

They were still waiting for the reply to that one when, shifting his weight, Eric suddenly felt a sharp pain over the mass of lesser aches and pains in his left leg. There was a smooth furrow cutting a shallow groove through suit and skin. Blood still oozed into the gap.

After a moment of surprise, he realized the only possible explanation. "I must've been grazed by a tiny meteor or something while we were – out there," he told Karen. A cool chill blew through his mind as he momentarily recalled the vast majesty of the lost and fearfully empty space in which they'd hung. He shuddered. Then he was secure and confident again, nested in his awareness of Karen and the control capsule.

Karen looked startled, and then quoted softly: "'He is wounded in the left thigh. He saves himself by the strength of a swift horse. He is fortunate.'"

For Eric a laugh came quickly with his release of breath. "And the rest of it, then. It's not ominous at all. 'There is no light, only obscurity.' That was hyperspace. And, 'He had at first ascended to the top of the sky. His future shall be to go into the earth.' I think that augurs well for our safe return."

Karen paused, then said, "I wish I understood why that happened to us – I mean, our getting thrown back out into normal space like that. But at least now we know what happened to the other man who disappeared."

"There seems to be a lot more to the jump than just a matter of mechanics," Eric said, musing. "Once human beings are involved, an act of will seems to be involved. Hyperspace isn't another physical place; it's sort of like a state of mind – and our minds can apparently interact with it. Our mistake seems to have been in assuming that because we'd experienced something similar with drugs that we could expect the same sort of thing. We must not have handled it just right – because hyperspace is *not* an LSD experience, and once in it it appears we do have some measure of control over it. The others – who knows? Apparently the experience was beyond their capabilities. Some went crazy, others got halfway through, as we did, and came out too soon, without their ships. But we – "

Karen nodded. "We pulled ourselves through, we went from normal space back into hyperspace *by ourselves*. An 'act of will' . . . Do you suppose – ?"

"It's possible. I seemed to understand about that, after we went back in. It felt as though I was regaining something . . . some past knowledge. I felt a *familiarity*. I don't think we'll have any more trouble with our jumps, and – who knows? Perhaps in time, with experience, we won't need the ship at all."

"Teleportation – ?" Karen's eyes glistened.

Then the radio sputtered again and Ground Control asked, "Are you two sure you're ready? Everything ready for the big jump?"

"More than ready," Eric replied. And, maintaining firmness and correctness, mankind reached for the stars.

BRIDGE

James Blish

This is the oldest story in the anthology. It was first published in Astounding Science Fiction *(the forerunner of today's* Analog*) in February 1952. Yet, apart from some small points, I don't think it shows its age. In later years, James Blish (1921–75) would become better known for his adaptations and novelizations of* Star Trek *episodes, but in the 1950s he was one of the giants of science fiction. "Bridge" was one of a number of stories that were loosely bonded together by what became known as the "Okie" or "Spindizzy" series, the latter referring to a device that negated gravity and thus allowed whole cities (suitably protected, of course) to venture into space. The early stories were amalgamated in the book* They Shall Have Stars *in 1956, and the whole series was subsequently combined in the omnibus* Cities in Flight *(1970), one of the classic masterworks of science fiction. Among Blish's other classic works are* The Seedling Stars *(1957) and* A Case of Conscience *(1958). This story, which comes early in the series when they're still testing the invention, may not be quite so uplifting as others in this anthology, but the sheer scale of the concept – and remember this was written in 1951 – can't help but trigger that sense of wonder.*

1

A SCREECHING TORNADO was rocking the Bridge when the alarm sounded; it was making the whole structure shudder and sway. This was normal and Robert Helmuth barely noticed it. There was always a tornado shaking the Bridge. The whole planet was enswathed in tornadoes, and worse.

The scanner on the foreman's board had given 114 as the sector of the trouble. That was at the northwestern end of the Bridge, where it broke off leaving nothing but the raging clouds of ammonia crystals and methane, and a sheer drop thirty miles to the invisible surface. There were no ultraphone "eyes" at that end which gave a general view of the area – in so far as any general view was possible – because both ends of the Bridge were incomplete.

With a sigh Helmuth put the beetle into motion. The little car, as flat-bottomed and thin through as a bedbug, got slowly under way on its ball-bearing races, guided and held firmly to the surface of the Bridge by ten close-set flanged rails. Even so, the hydrogen gales made a terrific siren-like shrieking between the edge of the vehicle and the deck, and the impact of the falling drops of ammonia upon the curved roof was as heavy and deafening as a rain of cannon balls. As a matter of fact they weighed almost as much as cannon balls here, though they were not much bigger than ordinary raindrops. Every so often, too, there was a blast, accompanied by a dull orange glare, which made the car, the deck, and the Bridge itself buck savagely.

These blasts were below, however, on the surface. While they shook the structure of the Bridge heavily, they almost never interfered with its functioning, and could not, in the very nature of things, do Helmuth any harm.

Had any real damage ever been done, it would never have been repaired. There was no one on Jupiter to repair it.

The Bridge, actually, was building itself. Massive, alone, and lifeless, it grew in the black deeps of Jupiter.

The Bridge had been well planned. From Halmuth's point of view almost nothing could be seen of it, for the beetle tracks ran down the center of the deck, and in the darkness and perpetual storm even ultrawave-assisted vision could not penetrate more than a few hundred yards at the most. The width of the Bridge was eleven miles; its height, thirty miles; its length, deliberately unspecified in the plans, fifty-four miles at the moment – a squat, colossal structure, built with engineering principles, methods, materials, and tools never touched before —

For the very good reason that they would have been impossible anywhere else. Most of the Bridge, for instance, was made of ice: a marvellous structural material under a pressure of a million atmospheres, at a temperature of $-94°$C. Under such conditions, the best structural steel is a friable, talc-like powder, and aluminium becomes a peculiar, transparent substance that splits at a tap.

Back home, Helmuth remembered, there had been talk of starting another Bridge on Saturn, and perhaps still later, on Uranus, too. But that had been politicians' talk. The Bridge was almost five thousand miles below the visible surface of Jupiter's atmosphere, and its mechanisms were just barely manageable. The bottom of Saturn's atmosphere had been sounded at 16,878 miles, and the temperature there was below $-150°$C. There even pressure-ice would be immovable, and could not be worked with anything except itself. And as for Uranus . . .

As far as Helmuth was concerned, Jupiter was quite bad enough.

The beetle crept within sight of the end of the Bridge and stopped automatically. Helmut set the vehicle's eyes for highest penetration, and examined the nearby beams.

The great bars were as close-set as screening. They had to be, in order to support even their own weight, let alone the weight of the components of the Bridge. The whole web-work was flexing and fluctuating to the harpist-fingered gale, but it had been designed to do that. Helmuth could never help being alarmed by the movement, but habit assured him that he had nothing to fear from it.

He took the automatics out of the circuit and inched the beetle forward manually. This was only Sector 113, and the Bridge's own Wheatstone-bridge scanning system – there was no electronic device anywhere on the Bridge, since it was impossible to maintain a vacuum on Jupiter – said that the trouble was in Sector 114. The boundary of Sector 114 was still fully fifty feet away.

It was a bad sign. Helmuth scratched nervously in his red beard. Evidently there was really cause for alarm – real alarm, not just the deep, grinding depression which he always felt while working on the Bridge. Any damage serious enough to halt the beetle a full sector short of the trouble area was bound to be major.

It might even turn out to be the disaster which he had felt lurking ahead of him ever since he had been made foreman of the Bridge – that disaster which the Bridge itself could not repair, sending man reeling home from Jupiter in defeat.

The secondaries cut in and the beetle stopped again. Grimly, Helmuth opened the switch and set the beetle creeping across the invisible danger line. Almost at once, the car tilted just perceptibly to the left, and the screaming of the winds between its edges and the deck shot up the scale, sirening in and out of the soundless-dogwhistle range with an eeriness that set Helmuth's teeth on edge. The beetle itself fluttered and chattered like an alarm-clock hammer between the surface of the deck and the flanges of the tracks.

Ahead there was still nothing to be seen but the horizontal driving of the clouds and the hail, roaring along the length of the Bridge, out of the blackness into the beetle's fanlight, and onward into blackness again towards the horizon no eye would ever see.

Thirty miles below, the fusillade of hydrogen explosions continued. Evidently something really wild was going on on the surface. Helmuth could not remember having heard so much activity in years.

There was a flat, especially heavy crash, and a long line of fuming orange fire came pouring down the seething atmosphere into the depths, feathering horizontally like the mane of a Lipizzan horse, directly in front of Helmuth. Instinctively, he winced and drew back from the board, although that stream of flame actually was only a little less cold than the rest of the streaming gases, far too cold to injure the Bridge.

In the momentary glare, however, he saw something – an upward twisting of shadows, patterned but obviously unfinished, fluttering in silhouette against the hydrogen cataract's lurid light.

The end of the Bridge.

Wrecked.

Helmuth grunted involuntarily and backed the beetle away. The flare dimmed; the light poured down the sky and fell away into the raging sea below. The scanner clucked with satisfaction as the beetle recrossed the line into Zone 113.

He turned the body of the vehicle 180°, presenting its back to the dying torrent. There was nothing further that he could do at the moment on the Bridge. He scanned his control board – a ghost image of which was cast across the scene on the Bridge – for the blue button marked *Garage*, punched it savagely, and tore off his helmet.

Obediently, the Bridge vanished.

2

Dillon was looking at him.

"Well?" the civil engineer said. "What's the matter, Bob? Is it bad—?"

Helmuth did not reply for a moment. The abrupt transition from the storm-ravaged deck of the Bridge to the quiet, placid air of the control shack on Jupiter V was always a shock. He had never been able to anticipate it, let alone become accustomed to it; it was worse each time, not better.

He put the helmet down carefully in front of him and got up, moving carefully upon shaky legs; feeling implicit in his own body the enormous pressures and weights his guiding intelligence had just quitted. The fact that the gravity on the foreman's deck was as weak as that of most of the habitable asteroids only made the contrast greater, and his need for caution in walking more extreme.

He went to the big porthole and looked out. The unworn, tumbled, monotonous surface of airless Jupiter V looked almost homey after the perpetual holocaust of Jupiter itself. But there was an overpowering reminder of that holocaust – for through the thick quartz the face of the giant planet stared at him, across only 112,600 miles: a sphere-section occupying almost all of the sky except the near horizon. It was crawling with colour, striped and blotched with the eternal, frigid, poisonous storming of its atmosphere, spotted with the deep planet-sized shadows of farther moons.

Somewhere down there, 6,000 miles below the clouds that boiled in his face, was the Bridge. The Bridge was thirty miles high and eleven miles wide and fifty-four miles long – but it was only a sliver, an intricate and fragile arrangement of ice-crystals beneath the bulging, racing tornadoes.

On Earth, even in the West, the Bridge would have been the

mightiest engineering achievement of all history, could the Earth have borne its weight at all. But on Jupiter, the Bridge was as precarious and perishable as a snowflake.

"Bob?" Dillon's voice asked. "You seem more upset than usual. Is it serious?" Helmuth turned. His superior's worn young face, lantern-jawed and crowned by black hair already beginning to grey at the temples, was alight both with love for the Bridge and the consuming ardour of the responsibility he had to bear. As always, it touched Helmuth, and reminded him that the implacable universe had, after all, provided one warm corner in which human beings might huddle together.

"Serious enough," he said, forming the words with difficulty against the frozen inarticulateness Jupiter forced upon him. "But not fatal, as far as I could see. There's a lot of hydrogen vulcanism on the surface, especially at the northwest end, and it looks like there must have been a big blast under the cliffs. I saw what looked like the last of a series of fireballs."

Dillon's face relaxed while Helmuth was talking, slowly, line by engraved line. "Oh. Just a flying chunk, then."

"I'm almost sure that's what it was. The cross-draughts are heavy now. The Spot and the STD are due to pass each other some time next week, aren't they? I haven't checked, but I can feel the difference in the storms."

"So the chunk got picked up and thrown through the end of the Bridge. A big piece?"

Helmuth shrugged. "That end is all twisted away to the left, and the deck is burst to flinders. The scaffolding is all gone, too, of course. A pretty big piece, all right, Charity – two miles through at a minimum."

Dillon sighed. He, too, went to the window, and looked out. Helmuth did not need to be a mind reader to know what he was looking at. Out there, across the stony waste of Jupiter V plus 112,600 miles of space, the South Tropical Disturbance was streaming towards the great Red Spot, and would soon overtake it. When the whirling funnel of the STD – more than big enough to suck three Earths into deep-freeze – passed the planetary island of sodium-tainted ice which was the Red Spot, the Spot would follow it for a few thousand miles, at the same time rising closer to the surface of the atmosphere.

Then the Spot would sink again, drifting back towards the incredible jet of stress-fluid which kept it in being – a jet fed by no one knew what forces at Jupiter's hot, rocky, 22,000-mile core, under 16,000 miles of eternal ice. During the entire passage, the storms all over Jupiter became especially violent; and the Bridge had been forced to locate in anything but the calmest spot on the planet, thanks to the uneven distribution of the few permanent landmasses.

Helmuth watched Dillon with a certain compassion, tempered with mild envy. Charity Dillon's unfortunate given name betrayed him as the son of a hangover, the only male child of a Witness family which dated back to the great Witness Revival of 2003. He was one of the hundreds of government-drafted experts who had planned the Bridge, and he was as obsessed by the Bridge as Helmuth was – but for different reasons.

Helmuth moved back to the port, dropping his hand gently upon Dillon's shoulder. Together they looked at the screaming straw yellows, brick reds, pinks, oranges, browns, even blues and greens that Jupiter threw across the ruined stone of its innermost satellite. On Jupiter V, even the shadows had colour.

Dillon did not move. He said at last: "Are you pleased, Bob?"

"Pleased?" Helmuth said in astonishment. "No. It scares me white; you know that. I'm just glad that the whole Bridge didn't go."

"You're quite sure?" Dillon said quietly.

Helmuth took his hand from Dillon's shoulder and returned to his seat at the central desk. "You've no right to needle me for something I can't help," he said, his voice even lower than Dillon's. "I work on Jupiter four hours a day – not actually, because we can't keep a man alive for more than a split second down there – but my eyes and my ears and my mind are there, on the Bridge, four hours a day. Jupiter is not a nice place. I don't like it. I won't pretend I do.

"Spending four hours a day in an environment like that over a period of years – well, the human mind instinctively tries to adapt, even to the unthinkable. Sometimes I wonder how I'll behave when I'm put back in Chicago again. Sometimes I can't remember anything about Chicago except vague generalities, sometimes I can't even believe there is such a place as Earth – how could there be, when the rest of the universe is like Jupiter, or worse?"

"I know," Dillon said. "I've tried several times to show you that isn't a very reasonable frame of mind."

"I know it isn't. But I can't help how I feel. No, I don't think the Bridge will last. It can't last; it's all wrong. But I don't *want* to see it go. I've just got sense enough to know that one of these days Jupiter is going to sweep it away."

He wiped an open palm across the control boards, snapping all the toggles "Off" with a sound like the fall of a double-handful of marbles on a pane of glass. "Like that, Charity! And I work four hours a day, every day, on the Bridge. One of these days, Jupiter is going to destroy the Bridge. It'll go flying away in little flinders into the storms. My mind will be there, supervising some puny job, and my mind will go flying away along with my mechanical eyes and ears – still trying to adapt to the unthinkable, tumbling away into the winds and the flames and the rains and the darkness and the pressure and the cold."

"Bob, you're deliberately running away with yourself. Cut it out. Cut it out, I say!"

Helmuth shrugged, putting a trembling band on the edge of the board to steady himself. "All right. I'm all right, Charity. I'm here, aren't I? Right here on Jupiter V, in no danger, in no danger at all. The Bridge is 112,600 miles away from here. But when the day comes that the Bridge is swept away –

"Charity, sometimes I imagine you ferrying my body back to the cosy nook it came from, while my soul goes tumbling and tumbling through millions of cubic miles of poison. All right, Charity, I'll be good. I won't think about it out aloud; but you can't expect me to forget it. It's on my mind; I can't help it, and you should know that."

"I do," Dillon said, with a kind of eagerness. "I do, Bob. I'm only trying to help, to make you see the problem as it is. The Bridge isn't really that awful, it isn't worth a single nightmare."

"Oh, it isn't the Bridge that makes me yell out when I'm sleeping," Helmuth said, smiling bitterly. "I'm not that ridden by it yet. It's while I'm awake that I'm afraid the Bridge will be swept away. What I sleep with is a fear of myself."

"That's a sane fear. You're as sane as any of us," Dillon insisted, fiercely solemn. "Look, Bob. The Bridge isn't a monster. It's a way we've developed for studying the behaviour of materials under specific conditions of temperament, pressure, and gravity. Jupiter isn't Hell, either; it's a set of conditions. The Bridge is the laboratory we set up to work with those conditions."

"It isn't going anywhere. It's a bridge to no place."

"There aren't many *places* on Jupiter," Dillon said, missing Helmuth's meaning entirely. "We put the Bridge on an island in the local sea because we needed solid ice we could sink the caissons in. Otherwise, it wouldn't have mattered where we put it. We could have floated it on the sea itself, if we hadn't wanted to fix it in order to measure storm velocities and such things."

"I know that," Helmuth said.

"But, Bob, you don't show any signs of understanding it. Why, for instance, should the Bridge *go* any place? It isn't even, properly speaking, a bridge at all. We only call it that because we used some bridge-engineering principles in building it. Actually, it's much more like a travelling crane – an extremely heavy-duty overhead rail line. It isn't going anywhere because it hasn't any place interesting to go, that's all. We're extending it to cover as much territory as possible, and to increase its stability, not to span the distance between places. There's no point to reproaching it because it doesn't span a real gap – between, say, Dover and Calais. It's a bridge to knowledge, and that's far more important. Why can't you see that?"

"I can see that; that's what I was talking about," Helmuth said, trying to control his impatience. "I have as much common sense as the average child. What I was trying to point out is that meeting colossalness with colossalness – out here – is a mug's game. It's a game Jupiter will always win, without the slightest effort. What if the engineers who built the Dover–Calais bridge had been limited to broomstraws for their structural members? They could have got the bridge up somehow, sure, and made it strong enough to carry light traffic on a fair day. But what would you have had left of it after the first winter storm came down the Channel from the North Sea? The whole approach is idiotic!"

"All right," Dillon said reasonably. "You have a point. Now you're being reasonable. What better approach have you to suggest? Should we abandon Jupiter entirely because it's too big for us?"

"No," Helmuth said. "Or maybe, yes. I don't know. I don't

have any easy answer. I just know that this one is no answer at all – it's just a cumbersome evasion."

Dillon smiled. "You're depressed, and no wonder. Sleep it off, Bob, if you can – you might even come up with that answer. In the meantime – well, when you stop to think about it, the surface of Jupiter isn't any more hostile, inherently, than the surface of Jupiter V, except in degree. If you stepped out of this building naked, you'd die just as fast as you would on Jupiter. Try to look at it that way."

Helmuth, looking forward into another night of dreams, said: "That's the way I look at it now."

3

There were three yellow "Critical" signals lit on the long gang board when Helmuth passed through the gang deck on the way back to duty. All of them, as usual, were concentrated on Panel 9, where Eva Chavez worked.

Eva, despite her Latin name – such once-valid tickets no longer meant anything among Earth's uniformily mixed-race population – was a big girl, vaguely blonde, who cherished a passion for the Bridge. Unfortunately, she was apt to become enthralled by the sheer Cosmicness of it all, precisely at the moments when cold analysis and split-second decisions were most crucial.

Helmuth reached over her shoulder, cut her out of the circuit except as an observer, and donned the co-operator's helmet. The incomplete new shoals caisson sprang into being around him. Breakers of boiling hydrogen seethed 700 feet up along its slanted sides – breakers that never subsided, but simply were torn away into flying spray.

There was a spot of dull orange near the top of the north face of the caisson, crawling slowly towards the pediment of the nearest truss. Catalysis –

Or cancer, as Helmuth could not help but think of it. On this bitter, violent monster of a planet, even the tiny specks of calcium carbide were deadly. At these wind velocities, such specks imbedded themselves in everything; and at fifteen million pounds per square inch, pressure ice catalyzed by sodium took up ammonia and carbon dioxide, building protein-like compounds in a rapid, deadly chain of decay:

$$H_2NCHCO \cdot HNCHCO \cdot HNCHCO \cdot HN \ldots$$

with CaO, Ca, Ca branching below to

$$HNCHCO \cdot HNCHCO \cdot HNCHCO \cdot HN \ldots$$

with CaO, Ca, Ca branching below to

$$HNCHCO \cdot HNCHCO \cdot HN \ldots$$

For a second, Helmuth watched it grow. It was, after all, one of the incredible possibilities the Bridge had been built to study. On Earth, such a compound, had it occurred at all, might have grown porous, bony, and quite strong. Here, under nearly eight times the gravity, the molecules were forced to assemble in strict aliphatic order, but in cross-section their arrangement was hexagonal, as if the stuff would become an aromatic compound if it only could. Even here it was moderately strong in cross-section – but along the long axis it smeared like graphite, the calcium atoms readily surrendering their valence hold on one carbon atom to grab hopefully for the next one in line –

No stuff to hold up the piers of humanity's greatest engineering project. Perhaps it was suitable for the ribs of some Jovian jellyfish, but in a Bridge-caisson, it was cancer.

There was a scraper mechanism working on the edge of the lesion, flaking away the shearing aminos and laying down new ice. In the meantime, the decay of the caisson-face was working deeper. The scraper could not possibly get at the core of the trouble – which was not the calcium carbide dust, with which the atmosphere was charged beyond redemption, but was instead one imbedded sodium speck which was taking no part in the reaction – fast enough to extirpate it. It could barely keep pace with the surface spread of the disease.

And laying new ice over the surface of the wound was worthless. At this rate, the whole caisson would slough away and melt like butter, within an hour, under the weight of the Bridge above it.

* * *

Helmuth sent the futile scraper aloft. Drill for it? No – too deep already, and location unknown.

Quickly he called two borers up from the shoals below, where constant blasting was taking the foundation of the caisson deeper and deeper into Jupiter's dubious "soil". He drove both blind, fire-snouted machines down into the lesion.

The bottom of that sore turned out to be forty-five metres within the immense block. Helmuth pushed the red button all the same.

The borers blew up, with a heavy, quite invisible blast, as they had been designed to do. A pit appeared on the face of the caisson.

The nearest truss bent upward in the wind. It fluttered for a moment, trying to resist. It bent farther.

Deprived of its major attachment, it tore free suddenly, and went whirling away into the blackness. A sudden flash of lightning picked it out for a moment, and Helmuth saw it dwindling like a bat with torn wings being borne away by a cyclone.

The scraper scuttled down into the pit and began to fill it with ice from the bottom. Helmuth ordered down a new truss and a squad of scaffolders. Damage of this order took time to repair. He watched the tornado tearing ragged chunks from the edges of the pit until he was sure that the catalysis had stopped. Then, suddenly, prematurely, dismally tired, he took off the helmet.

He was astounded by the white fury that masked Eva's big-boned, mildly pretty face.

"You'll blow the Bridge up yet, won't you?" she said evenly, without preamble. "Any pretext will do!"

Baffled, Helmuth turned his head helplessly away; but that was no better. The suffused face of Jupiter peered swollenly through the picture-port, just as it did on the foreman's desk.

He and Eva and Charity and the gang and the whole of satellite V were falling forward towards Jupiter; their uneventful cooped-up lives on Jupiter V were utterly unreal compared to the four hours of each changeless day spent on Jupiter's ever-changing surface. Every new day brought their minds, like ships out of control, closer and closer to that gaudy inferno.

There was no other way for a man – or a woman – on Jupiter V to look at the giant planet. It was simple experience, shared by all of them, that planets do not occupy four-fifths of the whole sky, unless the observer is himself up there in that planet's sky, falling, falling faster and faster –

"I have no intention," he said tiredly, "of blowing up the Bridge. I wish you could get it through your head that I want the Bridge to stay up – even though I'm not starry-eyed to the point of incompetence about the project. Did you think that rotten spot was going to go away by itself when you'd painted it over? Didn't you know that – "

Several helmeted, masked heads nearby turned blindly towards the sound of his voice. Helmuth shut up. Any distracting conversation or activity was taboo, down here in the gang room. He motioned Eva back to duty.

The girl donned her helmet obediently enough, but it was plain from the way her normally full lips were thinned that she thought Helmuth had ended the argument only in order to have the last word.

Helmuth strode to the thick pillar which ran down the central axis of the shack, and mounted the spiralling cleats towards his own foreman's cubicle. Already he felt in anticipation the weight of the helmet upon his own head. Charity Dillon, however, was already wearing the helmet; he was sitting in Helmuth's chair.

Charity was characteristically oblivious of Helmuth's entrance. The Bridge operator must learn to ignore, to be utterly unconscious of anything happening around his body except the inhuman sounds of signals; must learn to heed only those senses which report something going on thousands of miles away.

Helmuth knew better than to interrupt him. Instead, he watched Dillon's white, blade-like fingers roving with blind sureness over the controls.

Dillon, evidently, was making a complete tour of the Bridge – not only from end to end, but up and down, too. The tally board showed that he had already activated nearly two-thirds of the ultraphone eyes. That meant that he had been up all night at the job; had begun it immediately after last talking to Helmuth.

Why?

With a thrill of unfocused apprehension, Helmuth looked at the foreman's jack, which allowed the operator here in the cubicle to communicate with the gang when necessary, and which kept him aware of anything said or done at gang boards.

It was plugged in.

Dillon sighed suddenly, took the helmet off and turned.

"Hello, Bob," he said. "Funny about this job. You can't see, you can't hear, but when somebody's watching you, you feel a sort of pressure on the back of your neck. ESP, maybe. Ever felt it?"

"Pretty often, lately. Why the grand tour, Charity?"

"There's to be an inspection," Dillon said. His eyes met Helmuth's. They were frank and transparent. "A mob of Western officials, coming to see that their eight billion dollars isn't being wasted. Naturally, I'm a little anxious to see that they find everything in order."

"I see," Helmuth said. "First time in five years, isn't it?"

"Just about. What was that dust-up down below just now? Somebody – you, I'm sure, from the drastic handiwork involved – bailed Eva out of a mess, and then I heard her talk about your wanting to blow up the Bridge. I checked the area when I heard the fracas start, and it did seem as if she had let things go rather far, but – What was it all about?"

Dillon ordinarily hadn't the guile for cat-and-mouse games, and he had never looked less guileful now. Helmuth said carefully, "Eva was upset, I suppose. On the subject of Jupiter we're all of us cracked by now, in our different ways. The way she was dealing with the catalysis didn't look to me to be suitable – a difference of opinion, resolved in my favour because I had the authority, Eva didn't. That's all."

"Kind of an expensive difference, Bob. I'm not niggling by nature, you know that. But an incident like that while the commission is here – "

"The point is," Helmuth said, "are we to spend an extra ten thousand, or whatever it costs to replace a truss and reinforce a caisson, or are we to lose the whole caisson – and as much as a third of the whole Bridge along with it?"

"Yes, you're right there, of course. That could be explained, even to a pack of senators. But – it would be difficult to have to explain it very often. Well, the board's yours, Bob. You could continue my spot-check, if you've time."

Dillon got up. Then he added suddenly, as if it were forced out of him:

"Bob, I'm trying to understand your state of mind. From what Eva said, I gather that you've made it fairly public. I . . . I don't think it's a good idea to infect your fellow workers with your own pessimism. It leads to sloppy work. I know that regardless of your own feelings you won't countenance sloppy work, but one foreman can do only so much. And you're making extra work for yourself – not for me, but for yourself – by being openly gloomy about the Bridge.

"You're the best man on the Bridge, Bob, for all your grousing about the job, and your assorted misgivings. I'd hate to see you replaced."

"A threat, Charity?" Helmuth said softly.

"*No.* I wouldn't replace you unless you actually went nuts, and I firmly believe that your fears in that respect are groundless. It's a commonplace that only sane men suspect their own sanity, isn't it?"

"It's a common misconception. Most psychopathic obsessions begin with a mild worry."

Dillon made as if to brush that subject away. "Anyhow, I'm not threatening; I'd fight to keep you here. But my say-so only covers Jupiter V; there are people higher up on Ganymede, and people higher yet back in Washington – and in this inspecting commission.

"Why don't you try to look on the bright side for a change? Obviously the Bridge isn't ever going to inspire you. But you might at least try thinking about all those dollars piling up in your account every hour you're on this job, and about the bridges and ships and who knows what-all that you'll be building, at any fee you ask, when you get back down to Earth. All under the magic words, 'One of the men who built the Bridge on Jupiter!'"

Charity was bright red with embarrassment and enthusiasm. Helmuth smiled.

"I'll try to bear it in mind, Charity," he said. "When is this gaggle of senators due to arrive?"

"They're on Ganymede now, taking a breather. They came directly from Washington without any routing. I suppose they'll make a stop at Callisto before they come here. They've something new on their ship, I'm told, that lets them flit about more freely than the usual uphill transport can."

An icy lizard suddenly was nesting in Helmuth's stomach, coiling and coiling but never settling itself. The room blurred. The persistent nightmare was suddenly almost upon him – already.

"Something . . . new?" he echoed, his voice as flat and noncommittal as he could make it. "Do you know what it is?"

"Well, yes. But I think I'd better keep quiet about it until – "

"Charity, nobody on this deserted rock-heap could possibly be a Soviet spy. The whole habit of 'security' is idiotic out here. Tell me now and save me the trouble of dealing with senators; or tell me at least that you know I know. *They have antigravity!* Isn't that it?"

One word from Dillon, and the nightmare would be real.

"Yes," Dillon said. "How did you know? Of course, it couldn't be a complete gravity screen by any means. But it seems to be a good long step towards it. We've waited a long time to see that dream come true – But you're the last man in the world to take pride in the achievement, so there's no sense exulting about it to you. I'll let you know when I get a definite arrival date. In the meantime, will you think about what I said before?"

"Yes, I will." Helmuth took the seat before the board.

"Good. With you, I have to be grateful for small victories. Good trick, Bob."

"Good trick, Charity!"

4

Instead of sleeping – for now he knew that he was really afraid – he sat up in the reading chair in his cabin. The illuminated microfilm pages of a book flipped by across the surface of the wall opposite him, timed precisely to the reading rate most comfortable for him, and he had several weeks' worry-conserved alcohol and smoke rations for ready consumption.

But Helmuth let his mix go flat, and did not notice the book, which had turned itself on, at the page where he had abandoned it last, when he had fitted himself into the chair. Instead, he listened to the radio.

There was always a great deal of ham radio activity in the Jovian system. The conditions were good for it, since there was plenty of power available, few impeding atmosphere layers, and those thin, no Heaviside layers, and few official and no commercial channels with which the hams could interfere.

And there were plenty of people scattered about the satellites who needed the sound of a voice.

" . . . anybody know whether the senators are coming here? Doc Barth put in a report a while back on a fossil plant he found here, at least he thinks it was a plant. Maybe they'd like a look at it."

"They're supposed to hit the Bridge team next." A strong voice, and the impression of a strong transmitter wavering in and out; that would be Sweeney, on Ganymede. "Sorry to throw the wet blanket, boys, but I don't think the senators are interested in our rock-balls for their own lumpy selves. We could only hold them here three days."

Helmuth thought greyly: *Then they've already left Callisto.*

"Is that you, Sweeney? Where's the Bridge tonight?"

"Dillon's on duty," a very distant transmitter said. "Try to raise Helmuth, Sweeney."

"Helmuth, Helmuth, you gloomy beetle-gooser! Come in, Helmuth!"

"Sure, Bob, come in and dampen us."

Sluggishly, Helmuth reached out to take the mike, where it lay clipped to one arm of the chair. But the door to his room opened before he had completed the gesture.

Eva came in.

She said, "Bob, I want to tell you something."

"His voice is changing!" the voice of the Callisto operator said. "Ask him what he's drinking, Sweeney!"

Helmuth cut the radio out. The girl was freshly dressed – in so far as anybody dressed in anything on Jupiter V – and Helmuth wondered why she was prowling the decks at this hour, halfway between her sleep period and her trick. Her hair was hazy against the light from the corridor, and she looked less mannish than usual. She reminded him a little of the way she had looked when they first met.

"All right," he said. "I owe you a mix, I guess. Citric, sugar, and the other stuff is in the locker . . . you know where it is. Shot-cans are there, too."

*   *   *

The girl shut the door and sat down on the bunk, with a free litheness that was almost grace, but with a determination which Helmuth knew meant that she had just decided to do something silly for all the right reasons.

"I don't need a drink," she said. "As a matter of fact, lately I've been turning my lux-R's back to the common pool. I suppose you did that for me by showing me what a mind looked like that is hiding from itself."

"Eve, stop sounding like a tract. Obviously, you've advanced to a higher, more Jovian plane of existence, but won't you still need your metabolism? Or have you decided that vitamins are all-in-the-mind?"

"Now you're being superior. Anyhow, alcohol isn't a vitamin. And I didn't come to talk about that. I came to tell you something I think you ought to know."

"Which is?"

She said, "Bob, I mean to have a child here."

A bark of laughter, part sheer hysteria and part exasperation, jack-knifed Helmuth into a sitting position. A red arrow bloomed on the far wall, obediently marking the paragraph which, supposedly, he had reached in his reading, and the page vanished.

"*Women!*" he said, when he could get his breath back. 'Really, Evita, you make me feel much better. No environment can change a human being much, after all.'

"Why should it?" she said suspiciously. "I don't see the joke. Shouldn't a woman want to have a child?"

"Of course she should," he said, settling back. The flipping pages began again. "It's quite ordinary. All women want to have children. All women dream of the day they can turn a child out to play in an airless rock-garden, to pluck fossils and get quaintly star-burned. How cosy to tuck the little blue body back into its corner that night, promptly at the sound of the trick-change bell! Why, it's as natural as Jupiter-light – as Earthian as vacuum-frozen apple pie."

He turned his head casually away. "As for me, though, Eva, I'd much prefer that you take your ghostly little pretext out of here."

Eva surged to her feet in one furious motion. Her fingers grasped him by the beard and jerked his head painfully around again.

"You reedy male platitude!" she said, in a low grinding voice. "How you could see almost the whole point and make so little of it – *Women*, is it? So you think I came creeping in here, full of humbleness, to settle our technical differences."

He closed his hand on her wrist and twisted it away. "What else?" he demanded, trying to imagine how it would feel to stay reasonable for five minutes at a time with these Bridge-robots. "None of us need bother with games and excuses. We're here, we're isolated, we were all chosen because, among other things, we were judged incapable of forming permanent emotional attachments, and capable of such alliances as we found attractive without going unbalanced when the attraction diminished and the alliance came unstuck. None of us have to pretend that our living arrangements would keep us out of jail in Boston, or that they have to involve any Earth-normal excuses."

She said nothing. After a while he asked, gently, "Isn't that so?"

"Of course it's so. Also it has nothing to do with the matter."

"It doesn't? How stupid do you think I am? *I* don't care whether or not you've decided to have a child here, if you really mean what you say."

She was trembling with rage. "You really don't, too. The decision means nothing to you."

"Well, if I liked children, I'd be sorry for the child. But as it happens, I can't stand children. In short, Eva, as far as I'm concerned you can have as many as you want, and to me you'll *still* be the worst operator on the Bridge."

"I'll bear that in mind," she said. At this moment she seemed to have been cut from pressure-ice. "I'll leave you something to charge your mind with, too, Robert Helmuth. I'll leave you sprawled here under your precious book . . . what is Madame Bovary to you, anyhow, you unadventurous turtle? . . . to think about a man who believes that children must always be born into warm cradles – a man who thinks that men have to huddle on warm worlds, or they won't survive. A man with no ears, scarcely any head. A man in terror, a man crying Mamma! *Mamma!* all the stellar days and nights long!"

"Parlour diagnosis!"

"Parlour labelling! Good trick, Bob. Draw your warm woolly blanket in tight about your brains, or some little sneeze of sense might creep in, and impair your – efficiency!"

The door closed sharply after her.

A million pounds of fatigue crashed down without warning on Helmuth's brain, and he fell back into the reading chair with a gasp. The roots of his beard ached, and Jupiters bloomed and wavered away before his closed eyes. He struggled once, and fell asleep.

Instantly he was in the grip of the dream.

It started, as always, with commonplaces, almost realistic enough to be a documentary film-strip – except for the appalling sense of pressure, and the distorted emotional significance with which the least word, the smallest movement was invested.

It was the sinking of the first caisson of the Bridge. The actual event had been bad enough. The job demanded enough exactness of placement to require that manned ships enter Jupiter's atmosphere itself: a squadron of twenty of the most powerful ships ever built, with the five-million-ton asteroid, trimmed and shaped in space, slung beneath them in an immense cat's cradle.

Four times that squadron had disappeared beneath the clouds; four times the tense voices of pilots and engineers had muttered in Helmuth's ears; four times there were shouts and futile orders and the snapping of cables and someone screaming endlessly against the eternal howl of the Jovian sky.

It had cost, altogether, nine ships and 231 men, to get one of five laboriously shaped asteroids planted in the shifting slush that was Jupiter's surface. Helmuth had helped to supervise all five operations, counting the successful one, from his desk on Jupiter V; but in the dream he was not in the control shack, but instead on shipboard, in one of the ships that was never to come back –

Then, without transition, but without any sense of discontinuity either, he was on the Bridge itself. Not *in absentia*, as the remote guiding intelligence of a beetle, but in person, in an ovular, tank-like suit the details of which would never come clear. The high brass had discovered antigravity, and had asked for volunteers to man the Bridge. Helmuth had volunteered.

Looking back on it in the dream, he did not understand why he had volunteered. It had simply seemed expected of him, and he had not been able to help it, even though he had known what it would be like. He belonged on the Bridge, though he hated it – he had been doomed to go there, from the first.

And there was . . . something wrong . . . with the antigravity. The high brass had asked for its volunteers before the scientific work had been completed. The present antigravity fields were weak, and there was some basic flaw in the theory. Generators broke down after only short periods of use, burned out, unpredictably, sometimes only moments after testing up without a flaw – like vacuum tubes in waiting life.

That was what Helmuth's set was about to do. He crouched inside his personal womb, above the boiling sea, the clouds raging about him, lit by a plume of hydrogen flame, and waited to feel his weight suddenly become eight times greater than normal. He knew what would happen to him then.

It happened.

Helmuth greeted morning on Jupiter V with his customary scream.

5

The ship that landed as he was going on duty did nothing to lighten the load on his heart. In shape it was not distinguishable from any of the long-range cruisers which ran the legs of the Moon–Mars–Belt–Ganymede trip. But it grounded its huge bulk with less visible expenditures of power than one of the little inter-satellary boats.

That landing told Helmuth that his dream was well on its way to coming true. If the high brass had had a real antigravity, there would have been no reason why the main jets should have been necessary at all. Obviously, what had been discovered was some sort of partial screen, which allowed a ship to operate with far less jet action than was normal, but which still left it subject to a sizeable fraction of the universal stress of space.

Nothing less than a complete and completely controllable antigravity would do on Jupiter.

He worked mechanically, noting that Charity was not in evidence. Probably he was conferring with the senators, receiving what would be for him the glad news.

Helmuth realized suddenly that there was nothing left for him to do now but to cut and run.

There could certainly be no reason why he should have to re-enact the entire dream, helplessly, event for event, like an actor committed to a play. He was awake now, in full control of his own senses, and still at least partially sane. The man in the dream had volunteered – but that man would not be Robert Helmuth. Not any longer.

While the senators were here, he would turn in his resignation. Direct, over Charity's head.

"Wake up, Helmuth," a voice from the gang deck snapped suddenly. "If it hadn't been for me, you'd have run yourself off the end of the Bridge. You had all the automatic stops on that beetle cut out."

Helmuth reached guiltily and more than a little too late for the controls. Eva had already run his beetle back beyond the danger line.

"Sorry," he mumbled. "Thanks, Eva."

"Don't thank me. If you'd actually been in it, I'd have let it go. Less reading and more sleep is what I recommend for you, Helmuth."

"Keep your recommendations to yourself," he snapped.

The incident started a new and even more disturbing chain of thought. If he were to resign now, it would be nearly a year before he could get back to Chicago. Antigravity or no antigravity, the senators' ship would have no room for unexpected passengers. Shipping a man back home had to be arranged far in advance. Space had to be provided, and a cargo equivalent of the weight and space requirements he would take up on the return trip had to be deadheaded out to Jupiter.

A year of living in the station on Jupiter V without any function – as a man whose drain on the station's supplies no longer could be justified in terms of what he did. A year of living under the eyes of Eva Chavez and Charity Dillon and the other men and women who still remained Bridge operators, men and women who would not hesitate to let him know what they thought of his quitting.

A year of living as a bystander in the feverish excitement of direct, personal exploration of Jupiter. A year of watching and hearing the inevitable deaths while he alone stood aloof, privileged, and useless. A year during which Robert Helmuth would become the most hated living entity in the Jovian system.

And, when he got back to Chicago and went looking for a job – for his resignation from the Bridge gang would automatically take him out of government service – he would be asked why he left the Bridge at the moment when work on the Bridge was just reaching its culmination.

He began to understand why the man in the dream had volunteered.

When the trick-change bell rang, he was still determined to resign, but he had already concluded bitterly that there were, after all, other kinds of hells besides the one on Jupiter.

He was returning the board to neutral as Charity came up the cleats. Charity's eyes were snapping like a skyful of comets. Helmuth had known that they would be.

"Senator Wagoner wants to speak to you, if you're not too tired, Bob," he said. "Go ahead; I'll finish up there."

"He does?" Helmuth frowned. The dream surged back upon him. *No.* They would not rush him any faster than he wanted to go. "What about, Charity? Am I suspected of unWestern activities? I suppose you've told them how I feel."

"I have," Dillon said, unruffled. "But we're agreed that you may not feel the same after you've talked to Wagoner. He's in the ship, of course. I've put out a suit for you at the lock."

Charity put the helmet over his head, effectively cutting himself off from further conversation, or from any further consciousness of Helmuth at all.

Helmuth stood looking at him a moment. Then, with a convulsive shrug, he went down the cleats.

Three minutes later, he was plodding in a spacesuit across the surface of Jupiter V, with the vivid bulk of Jupiter splashing his shoulders with colour.

A courteous Marine let him through the ship's air lock and deftly peeled him out of the suit. Despite a grim determination to be uninterested in the new antigravity and any possible consequence of it, he looked curiously about as he was conducted up towards the bow.

But the ship was like the ones that had brought him from

Chicago to Jupiter V – it was like any spaceship: there was nothing in it to see but corridor walls and stairwells, until you arrived at the cabin where you were needed.

Senator Wagoner was a surprise. He was a young man, no more than sixty-five at most, not at all portly, and he had the keenest pair of blue eyes that Helmuth had ever seen. He received Helmuth alone, in his own cabin – a comfortable cabin as spaceship accommodations go, but neither roomy nor luxurious. He was hard to match up with the stories Helmuth had been hearing about the current Senate, which had been involved in scandal after scandal of more than Roman proportions.

Helmuth looked around. "I thought there were several of you," he said.

"There are, but I didn't want to give you the idea that you were facing a panel," Wagoner said, smiling. "I've been forced to sit in on most of these endless loyalty investigations back home, but I can't see any point in exporting such religious ceremonies to deep space. Do sit down, Mr Helmuth. There are drinks coming. We have a lot to talk about."

Stiffly, Helmuth sat down.

"Dillon tells me," Wagoner said, leaning back comfortably in his own chair, "that your usefulness to the Bridge is about at an end. In a way, I'm sorry to hear that, for you've been one of the best men we've had on any of our planetary projects. But, in another way, I'm glad. It makes you available for something much bigger, where we need you much more."

"What do you mean by that?"

"I'll explain in a moment. First, I'd like to talk a little about the Bridge. Please don't feel that I'm quizzing you, by the way. You're at perfect liberty to say that any given question is none of my business, and I'll take no offence and hold no grudge. Also, 'I hereby disavow the authenticity of any tape or other tapping of which this statement may be part.' In short, our conversation is unofficial, highly so."

"Thank you."

"It's to my interest; I'm hoping that you'll talk freely to me. Of course my disavowal means nothing, since such formal statements can always be excised from a tape; but later on I'm going to tell you some things you're not supposed to know, and you'll be able to judge by what I say then that anything you say to me is privileged. Okay?"

A steward came in silently with the drinks, and left again. Helmuth tasted his. As far as he could tell, it was exactly like many he had mixed for himself back in the control shack, from standard space rations. The only difference was that it was cold, which Helmuth found startling, but not unpleasant after the first sip. He tried to relax. "I'll do my best," he said.

"Good enough. Now: Dillon says that you regard the Bridge as a monster. I've examined your dossier pretty closely, and I think perhaps Dillon hasn't quite the gist of your meaning. I'd like to hear it straight from you."

"I don't think the Bridge is a monster," Helmuth said slowly. "You see, Charity is on the defensive. He takes the Bridge to be conclusive evidence that no possible set of adverse conditions ever will stop man for long, and there I'm in agreement with him. But he also thinks of it as Progress, personified. He can't admit – you asked me to speak my mind, senator – that the West is a decadent and dying culture. All the other evidence that's available shows that it is. Charity likes to think of the Bridge as giving the lie to that evidence."

"The West hasn't many more years," Wagoner agreed, astonishingly. "Still and all, the West has been responsible for some really towering achievements in its time. Perhaps the Bridge could be considered as the last and the mightiest of them all."

"Not by me," Helmuth said. "The building of gigantic projects for ritual purposes – doing a thing for the sake of doing it is the last act of an already dead culture. Look at the pyramids in Egypt for an example. Or an even more idiotic and more enormous example, bigger than anything human beings have accomplished yet, the laying out of the 'Diagram of Power' over the whole face of Mars. If the Martians had put all that energy into survival instead, they'd probably be alive yet."

"Agreed," Wagoner said.

"All right. Then maybe you'll also agree that the essence of a vital culture is its ability to defend itself. The West has beaten off the Soviets for a century now – but as far as I can see, the Bridge is the West's 'Diagram of Power', its pyramids, or what have you.

All the money and the resources that went into the Bridge are going to be badly needed, *and won't be there*, when the next Soviet attack comes."

"Which will be very shortly, I'm told," Wagoner said, with complete calm. 'Furthermore, it will be successful, and in part it will be successful for the very reasons you've outlined. For a man who's been cut off from the Earth for years, Helmuth, you seem to know more about what's going on down there than most of the general populace does."

"Nothing promotes an interest in Earth like being off it," Helmuth said. "And there's plenty of time to read out here." Either the drink was stronger than he had expected, or the senator's calm concurrence in the collapse of Helmuth's entire world had given him another shove towards nothingness; his head was spinning.

Wagoner saw it. He leaned forward suddenly, catching Helmuth flat-footed. "*However,*" he said, "it's difficult for me to agree that the Bridge serves, or ever did serve, a ritual purpose. The Bridge served a huge practical purpose which is now fulfilled – the Bridge, as such, is now a defunct project."

"Defunct?" Helmuth repeated faintly.

"Quite. Of course we'll continue to operate it for a while, simply because you can't stop a process of that size on a dime, and that's just as well for people like Dillon who are emotionally tied up in it. You're the one person with any authority in the whole station who has already lost enough interest in the Bridge to make it safe for me to tell you that it's being abandoned."

"But why?"

"Because," Wagoner went on quietly, "the Bridge has now given us confirmation of a theory of stupendous importance – so important, in my opinion, that the imminent fall of the West seems like a puny event in comparison. A confirmation, incidentally, which contains in it the seeds of ultimate destruction for the Soviets, whatever they may win for themselves in the next fifty years or so."

"I suppose," Helmuth said, puzzled, "that you mean anti-gravity?"

For the first time, it was Wagoner's turn to be taken aback. "Man," he said at last, "do you know *everything* I want to tell you? I hope not, or my conclusions will be mighty suspicious. Surely Charity didn't tell you we had antigravity; I strictly enjoined him not to mention it."

"No, the subject's been on my mind," Helmuth said. "But I certainly don't see why it should be so world-shaking, any more than I see how the Bridge helped to bring it about. I thought it had been developed independently, for the further exploitation of the Bridge, and would step up Bridge operation, not discontinue it."

"Not at all. Of course, the Bridge has given us information in thousands of different categories, much of it very valuable indeed. But the one job that *only* the Bridge could do was that of confirming, or throwing out, the Blackett-Dirac equations."

"Which are – ?"

"A relationship between magnetism and the spinning of a massive body – that much is the Dirac part of it. The Blackett equation seemed to show that the same formula also applied to gravity. If the figures we collected on the magnetic field strength of Jupiter forced us to retire the Dirac equations, then none of the rest of the information we've gotten from the Bridge would have been worth the money we spent to get it. On the other hand, Jupiter was the only body in the solar system available to us which was big enough in all relevant respects to make it possible for us to test those equations at all. They involve quantities of enormous orders of magnitudes.

"And the figures show that Dirac was right. *They also show that Blackett was right.* Both magnetism *and* gravity are phenomena of rotation.

"I won't bother to trace the succeeding steps, because I think you can work them out for yourself. It's enough to say that there's a drive-generator on board this ship which is the complete and final justification of all the hell you people on the Bridge gang have been put through. The gadget has a long technical name, but the technies who tend it have already nicknamed it the spindizzy, because of what it does to the magnetic moment of any atom – *any* atom – within its field.

"While it's in operation, it absolutely refuses to notice any atom outside its own influence. Furthermore, it will notice no other strain or influence which holds good beyond the borders of that field. It's so snooty that it has to be stopped down to almost nothing when it's brought close to a planet, or it won't let you land. But in deep space . . . well, it's impervious to meteors and such trash, of course; it's impervious to gravity; and – it hasn't the faintest interest in any legislation about top speed limits."

"You're kidding," Helmuth said.

"Am I, now? This ship came to Ganymede directly from Earth. It did it in a little under two hours, counting manoeuvring time."

Helmuth took a defiant pull at his drink. "This thing really has no top speed at all?" he said. "How can you be sure of that?"

"Well, we can't," Wagoner admitted. "After all, one of the unfortunate things about general mathematical formulas is that they don't contain cut-off points to warn you of areas where they don't apply. Even quantum mechanics is somewhat subject to that criticism. However, we expect to know pretty soon just how fast the spindizzy can drive an object, if there is any limit. We expect you to tell us."

"I?"

"Yes, Helmuth, you. The coming débâcle on Earth makes it absolutely imperative for us – the West – to get interstellar expeditions started at once. Richardson Observatory, on the Moon, has two likely-looking systems picked out already – one at Wolf 359, another at 61 Cygni – and there are sure to be hundreds of others where Earth-like planets are highly probable. We want to scatter adventurous people, people with a thoroughly indoctrinated love of being free, all over this part of the galaxy, if it can be done.

"Once they're out there, they'll be free to flourish, with no interference from Earth. The Soviets haven't the spindizzy yet, and even after they steal it from us, they won't dare allow it to be used. It's too good and too final an escape route.

"What we want you to do . . . now I'm getting to the point, you see . . . is to direct this exodus. You've the intelligence and the cast of mind for it. Your analysis of the situation on Earth confirms that, if any more confirmation were needed. And – there's no future for you on Earth now."

"You'll have to excuse me," Helmuth said, firmly. "I'm in no condition to be reasonable now; it's been more than I could digest in a few moments. And the decision doesn't entirely rest with me, either. If I could give you an answer in . . . let me see . . . about three hours. Will that be soon enough?"

"That'll be fine," the senator said.

"And so, that's the story," Helmuth said.

Eva remained silent in her chair for a long time.

"One thing I don't understand," she said at last. "Why did you come to me? I'd have thought that you'd find the whole thing terrifying."

"Oh, it's terrifying, all right," Helmuth said, with quiet exultation. "But terror and fright are two different things, as I've just discovered. We were both wrong, Evita. I was wrong in thinking that the Bridge was a dead end. You were wrong in thinking of it as an end in itself."

"I don't understand you."

"All right, let's put it this way: the work the Bridge was doing was worthwhile, as I know now – so I was wrong in being frightened of it, calling it a bridge to nowhere.

"But you no more saw where it was going than I, and you made the Bridge the be-all and end-all of your existence.

"Now, there's a place to go to; in fact there are places – hundreds of places. They'll be Earth-like places. Since the Soviets are about to win Earth, those places will be more Earth-like than Earth itself, for the next century or so at least!'

She said, "Why are you telling me this? Just to make peace between us?"

"I'm going to take on this job, Evita, if you'll go along?"

She turned swiftly, rising out of the chair with a marvellous fluidity of motion. At the same instant, all the alarm bells in the station went off at once, filling every metal cranny with a jangle of pure horror.

"*Posts!*" the speaker above Eva's bed roared, in a distorted, gigantic version of Charity Dillon's voice. "*Peak storm overload! The STD is now passing the Spot. Wind velocity has already topped all previous records, and part of the land mass has begun to settle. This is an A-1 overload emergency.*"

Behind Charity's bellow, the winds of Jupiter made a spectrum of continuous, insane shrieking. The Bridge was responding with monstrous groans of agony. There was another sound, too, an almost musical cacophony of sharp, percussive tones, such as a dinosaur might make pushing its way through a forest of huge steel tuning-forks. Helmuth had never heard that sound before, but he knew what it was.

The deck of the Bridge was splitting up the middle.

After a moment more, the uproar dimmed, and the speaker said, in Charity's normal voice, "Eva, you too, please. Acknowledge, please. This is it – unless everybody comes on duty at once, the Bridge may go down within the next hour."

"Let it," Eva responded quietly.

There was a brief, startled silence, and then a ghost of a human sound. The voice was Senator Wagoner's, and the sound just might have been a chuckle.

Charity's circuit clicked out.

The mighty death of the Bridge continued to resound in the little room.

After a while, the man and the woman went to the window, and looked past the discarded bulk of Jupiter at the near horizon, where there had always been visible a few stars.

ANHEDONIA

Adam Roberts

Adam Roberts (b. 1965), when not writing books about Dickens, Tennyson, Browning or other literary coves, and when not teaching English Literature and Literary Criticism, somehow finds time to write science fiction and fantasy. His books include such impressively varied novels with thankfully easily memorized titles as Salt *(2000),* Stone *(2002) and* The Snow *(2004) and the equally memorable parodies* The Soddit *(2002),* The Sellamillion *(2004) and* The Da Vinci Cod *(2005). None of this, though, prepares you for this story, which marks its first appearance here, and which starts with a "bang" and takes you somewhere you didn't expect to go.*

W RITE IT OUT THREE TIMES. Where are you going? And through *this* porthole we have – Mars, of course. The view from the MMA base (Mars May Amaze, the crew used to say, and they don't say *that* any more). Mars itself, whose oceans of blood have long since coagulated into frozen boulders and desiccated to rust. The window is set in a rough-edged roseate wall, extruded from a paste made of this same dust. The carpet underfoot is a brighter red, for *you* are *special*. A solitary bot going through and through its hoovering program: inching forward, head down, as if looking for a contact lens. Where are you going?

"What's that?'

Where are you going, Macro?

This muffling of all sounds. That's an unexpected part of it. Walking about Mars with the sound turned down. A sense of

insulating foam, or *wadding* inside the hollow space of my skull.
It's Ann, and she is talking to him, and the polite thing to do is to
reply.

"I'm going to talk to the Hitchers."

Again?

Again.

And you think that'll do any good?

That's a strange way of putting it, though, isn't it? Good is a
strange word to use. "I've got my orders," he says, padding down
the corridor. The fibres of the carpet tickle his bare feet. There's no
pleasure for him in the sensation. It could be broken glass. It could
just as well be vacuum and *néant* and nothing at all. You're lying
back on the slab, and they've put the coins over your eyes, and you
think: with a proper flow of tears I could wash these disks quite
away. But the tears won't come. These tears will never now come.
Naturally the world continues to think you're dead. And perhaps
you *are* dead. Perhaps we all are. Nobody lives through their own
death. Think of it! *That* would be a contradiction in terms.

The aliens, when they came, promised us the technologies to travel
from star to star. We believed them. We didn't properly understand them. But – to the *stars*? How could we turn down such an
offer? Macro's first experience of interacting with them had been
awe-tinged. But awe is a sort of pleasure, and that was long gone.
And, you know? It is hard, even, to *see* them correctly. MMA had
built a large dome, deep blue and gold on the inside like an
undersea grotto, or like Dante's vision of heaven – and low
ambient light; and a high concentration of methane in the atmosphere, just as they liked it. But to go through the lock into that
space was only to find it, at the beginning, empty; or so you
thought. You had to find the right spot, and stand still. Only by
standing still, often for a long period, could you begin to see them:
a bundle of ribbons and spreading for metres, or a flicker of
something starfishy, or starbursty, or rah-rah, with a twitch of
sudden tightening. I can't tell you exactly what they're like. You
can look right at them. With eyes or with lenses. And they're never
quite exactly in focus.

Macro put on the breather and the goggles, and went through
the lock. The inside was royal blue that was scratched with gold:

deep-evening coloured, and perfectly empty. He went to the middle and sat down crosslegged. Apart from the kit on his head he was naked, because by this stage – you know, why not? I did not realize before, Keedwell once said to me, that the pleasure we took in wearing clothes was not in their external cut or colour, but simply in the logic of what they *covered up*. Since we now take no pleasure in the naked human body there's no joy to be had in covering up the nakedness either.

He sat for a long time, blank-minded. Eventually he began to see them. How they come and go, from their craft (whatever their craft is – if in Mars orbit then we can't locate it) into the dome and back, we don't know.

"Hello," he said. They speak English, of course. Of course they do: they're inside our heads. But they speak it in a queer way. It's as if they're joking, and at the same time as if they don't understand what a *joke* is. They say: "have you come again to discover our techniques of interstellar travel?"

"Are you ready to give them to us?'

"Are you ready," they say, "to take them?"

"That's not why I've come, actually," he says. "I've come to ask once more about the anhedonia."

And then he shifts in my posture, and they vanish from perception. He has to sit perfectly still, and meditate himself back into communication.

"The anhedonia," he repeats, to pick up the thread of conversation.

"What about it?" The voice sounds different now. Who knows why? Maybe it's a different Hitcher; maybe it's the same one in a different mood; maybe the difference is entirely in your head.

"How much longer?" he asks.

"How much longer?" they echo.

There have been studies published on the Hitcher habit of repeating what is said to them. Sometimes they simply echo us, and sometimes they spin back what we say with some small alteration.

Macro had been discussing this very topic with Ann the previous night. "Why do they echo so much of what we say?" he asked her. "Maybe they have nothing original to say for themselves," she said. "Ever think of that?" The two of them had had sex, but with the usual result. Macro's penis got hard, but as usual the end of it felt like the end of his thumb. Ann lay there with her legs tucked up and her knees pressed against her breasts and he slammed away for a while. She had on this peculiar expression of intense concentration, as if she were trying to remember exactly where she had mislaid her apprehension of sensual pleasure. He came, and it felt, as it always does, like spitting.

I know how he felt; it's how I always feel. It's how we all feel since the anhedonia.

"I don't know why we carry on," said Ann, afterwards.

"It doesn't do any harm," he said, getting his breath back. "Good to keep in practice." "In case what?" she said, wearily. "In case what?" In case the Hitchers decide to give us back our ability to feel pleasure, he was going to say; but he didn't. "In case," she pressed, "*this* time it miraculously *works*?" No, he wanted to say. No. He wasn't sure what he wanted to say. It might have been this: in case, by pursuing this most ancient and most intense form of human pleasure, despite knowing that no pleasure could be found that way, we achieved a mental stillness sufficient suddenly to comprehend *how* the aliens were messing with our heads.

I know all about the conversation they had that night.

"Morale is very low in the base," Macro told the Hitchers. The golden scintillations in the dark blue of the dome twinkled into new constellations, as they have been programmed to do. A domed-ceiling festooned with artificial stars. A decoration. A former version of Macro would have found it pleasurable. "It is not natural for human beings to live without pleasure. Without any pleasurable apprehension at all. Some of the people here are, you know, calling it torture." *You know?* They knew.

"Torture," says the Hitcher.

"Torture," Macro repeats. But the word lacks savour. Existing as it does, here, free of intensities either of pleasure or pain it was a whey-word. A blank.

"Torture.'

"You promised us the use of technologies of interstellar travel," he said, in a grey tone.

"We were once promised the use of those same technologies," the Hitcher says.

"Yes! *You* promised *we* could become like *you*. But – months ago, that was months, and since then all you have done is . . ."

But he shuffled a little, in his posture, in his exasperation, and he lost them. This wasn't what he'd come to talk about. This wasn't what he'd been ordered to tell them.

Long minutes of settling himself.

"Hello again," he said.

"Hello." A different voice again: high-pitched.

"I've been ordered to ask you . . ." he said. "How much *longer* are you going to impose this quarantine on our ability to experience pleasure?"

"We can end it, if you like," said the Hitcher.

"When, though?"

"End it now if you like. But if we do that," the merest pause, "then we cannot pass on the technologies."

"See," said Macro, straining inwardly to remain still, to complete the conversation: "that's what we don't understand – right there. *Why* is it one-or-the-other? We've been looking into what's happening. Happening inside our heads I mean. At first we thought it was a dopamine depletion. We thought you'd somehow got into our heads and interfered with the chemistry. But it's not the chemistry, is it? It's purely neural."

"It's purely neural, is it?" the Hitchers said.

"It is,"

"It is purely neural. Is it?"

"We've all taken a turn at speculating, all through the base," said Macro. "Can you at least tell us how the interstellar travel be accomplished? I don't mean the specifics of the technology. I mean the general principle. Is it something to do with hyperspace?"

"What is hyperspace?" the Hitcher asks.

Most conversations with the Hitchers went round and round like this. Here's another. Macro was trying to get at answers. He wanted to know, as we all did: was the faster-than-light travel in some sense neural? Was that why the Hitchers had messed about with our neural capacity? He spoke slowly, and put the sentence together one brick upon another. It was a question we were eager to have answered: "Is it that the technologies of travel are such that our organic neural network needs to be reworked, or reconfigured, before it can operate? Is *that* it?"

"It," trilled the Hitcher. They were behind him now. He snuffed the urge to turn his head and look. "It. It."

"I was ordered to ask you," he said.

Then the Hitcher said, in a voice like temptation: "Do *you* want to travel?"

"Me, personally?" he replied, rapidly. "Or – in the sense of humanity? Of all of us?" And then, to cover the baseness of his initial reaction: "The answer's the same either way. The answer's yes – you're in our heads, you *know* that."

"How *much* do you want to travel?"

For a moment he thought he understood. "Like – like – enough to be prepared to sacrifice our sense of pleasure? Is *that* what it is? That's what some of the staff think. They think the anhedonia is some kind of test. Okay, Okay, so you're testing us. You're seeing if we're worthy. Okay. Well, and how long until we *pass* the test? When does it end – when do we get to send some people to other stars, as you promised?" He was actually asking: *how long until I get my orgasms back*. They knew that. They were inside his head.

"You are speaking," the Hitcher said. "You are speaking, perhaps, on behalf of everybody on Earth?"

"On Mars," he said, quickly. "Don't try this on Earth, please. If you enforced anhedonia there as you've done here – if you robbed the whole Earth population of – " Oh God, if that.

"If?"

"There would be riots," he said, although that wouldn't be the half of it, and he knows that wouldn't be the half of it.

"People on Earth would riot?"

"I think people would push themselves that far, yes."

"No riots here."

"We're all trained. We're military, most of us. We're used to the discipline. But on Earth, if people lost their ability to feel pleasure all at once they'd freak out. There would be a lot of deaths. You don't want to be responsible for a lot of deaths, do you?"

"Are people on Earth such hedonists?" the Hitcher asked.

"Not – not saying that," he stuttered, "I'm not saying that human beings are nothing but hedonists. There's more to homo sapiens than just . . . hedonism." But what if it is the truth? They are inside our heads; they can tell. "In the sense," he went on, "that pleasure is the *only* thing they care about. Pleasure is important, but it's not the only thing." But even as he said this he was pondering the pleasure-shaped hole inside his soul. What did the hole leave, if not a thin and flaking shell? "It's certainly an *important* part of being human. It is an important part of working, and loving."

"Breeding?"

"That too. It is just – important." So now pleasure had become it. An evasion? A euphemism? "We want to travel to other stars because it's in our nature. It's part curiosity, part . . . part urge. But in either case, there's *pleasure* involved. What I mean is that not all pleasures are merely physical. There's the pleasure of finding new stuff out. Without the *pleasure* of discovery it's going to seem to a lot of people there's no point in going in the first place. Do you see? It's a double bind. It's like a deliberate paradox: you can have the pleasure of discovering new stars, but not the technology to get there. Or you can have the technology to discover new stars, but not the pleasure when you do so."

This thought had crossed all our minds, of course. We had all wondered whether the Hitcher's point was precisely that they were *testing* us. Giving us a double bind and seeing what we did. Except that they didn't work in such a calculated manner. They were evasive, but curiously ingenuous at the same time.

This is what they offered: to *show*. Not to tell. We had a meeting, Keedwell in the chair. Once upon a time (Why *upon*? Do we really tell children that events sit *upon* time like scum on a pond? Like human settlement upon Mars?) – once upon a time, we had tried to hold meetings in camera, secret meetings, to keep the Hitchers from knowing what we were discussing. But they were in our heads. The feeling was: they would have destroyed us by now if they wanted to destroy us. They certainly had that capacity. The feeling was they were playing some complex long game. At the same time there were those who felt they were as benign and child-like as they sometimes appeared. Keedwell put before us the results of his team. "It is chemical, the anhedonia, but only in response to neurological stimulus. The dopamine imbalance, the rewiring of the seratonin uptake cascade – it's almost fractal, it's very complex. But the Hitchers are not the proximate cause of this. The proximate cause is in the sub-brain. The stem, we think. The spine, we think." Dosing with dopamine, or SSRI, or any of the usual strategies had no effect whatsoever.

"And they're doing this – " Philps asked, "*how*?"

Of course we wanted to know that. Almost as much as we wanted to know *why*.

Half a dozen volunteers had submitted to various experimental procedures and there had been no positive outcome except in the case of Militiaman Kawa who had experienced sharp tinges of non-localized *pain* upon the application of modulated electrostimulation to the mid-spine in combination with a drug regimen of sopamphetamine, 2.1mg in . . .

"We can all feel *pain*," interrupted Philps. Pain was not as intense as once it was.

"Nonlocalized pain, not as the result of any . . ."

"But could he feel any *pleasure*?"

No. No. Write it out three times. No.

"There are probably neuropsychiatric experts with the electrochemical expertise to take this research further in Old Europe . . ." Keedwell said, in a weary voice.

We all spoke with weary voices, of course.

"Don't even," said Li. "Don't even . . ."

This was, of course, out of the question.

"I asked them," Macro reminded us, "whether they had plans to enforce the anhedonia upon Earth as well."

"They didn't exactly answer you," said Philps. She was scratching under her left armpit.

"I don't think they plan that."

"We need to know why they're doing it to *us*?"

This went without saying. "We don't know what they're planning," said Keedwell.

Macro was the one sent in to speak to them because he was better at reaching them. There's a stillness to him. Ann says so, for instance. She says it in a necessarily bored tone of voice.

He began like this. "We are concerned that if the anhedonia becomes general, across the human species, then we'll cease to breed." We'd raised this matter with them before, but there didn't seem any harm in repeating it. It was always possible, as some said, that the Hitchers didn't understand the necessary human relationship between pleasure and conception.

"You can still breed," they said.

"We're still physiologically *capable* of it," he agreed. "Erection, emission and so forth. But pleasure has been the major evolutionary motor for procreation for millions of years. Not just for us, but for all the higher life forms on our planet. If you take that out, then, then well we think there's a good chance . . ."

"It doesn't."

"What doesn't?"

"It doesn't happen that way." A new voice: a different Hitcher, or the same one putting on a new tone. "Decouple pleasure from procreation and procreation slows; but it don't stop altogether. And your people have been using contraception precisely to limit procreation for centuries."

This was an unusually lengthy and information-rich speech for the Hitchers.

We, who were watching the exchange on the relay, held our breaths.

"Is this a *standard* thing?" Macro asked. Then: "Did it happen to *you*?"

"Did it happen to us?"

"Did it happen to you?" Macro pressed. "In your history."

A weird little singsong oo-oo-oo.

"You've said," Macro pressed, "that you didn't develop these technologies of interstellar travel yourselves. You said you were gifted them. Was this part of the deal? Were you offered the same deal that you are now offering us?"

The gold swirls washed and sparkled like slow fireworks through the blue of the roof. Dark blue. Oceanic.

"Deal?" said a Hitcher voice, a different one again, or the same one adopting a higher register.

"We understand econo-ethics," Macro assured them. "We understand that this is a universal principle. There's no such thing as a free lunch." They were in his head; they would understand this. "Nothing for nothing. If the Gifters grant you this benefit – the ability to travel to the stars – they expect you to give up something in return. *Hence* the anhedonia? Is that it? Was it that way for you?"

"Way?"

This had happened before; like a software malfunction the

Hitchers would sometimes fall back on single words, and repeat those back at their questioners.

"Please!" Macro urged.

"Way?" And again: "Way?"

"You call yourself Hitchers," he said. "You're hitching a ride on some older species' technology. Please tell us this – was your encounter with *them* run along the same lines as *our* encounter with *you*?"

"Hitch?"

"You're the only aliens we've encountered," Macro pointed out. "You're all we have to go on. Are all alien species like you?"

"And *why*," (a deeper, yet other Hitcher voice this; or the same Hitcher ventriloquizing another voice) "have you never encountered another alien race?"

They knew what our answer would be to this question. To any question. But Macro answered it anyway: "that's an old question for us. There was a human called Fermi . . ."

"The Old Fermi," said the Hitcher.

"Yes, so it used to run, like: if there are other alien races why haven't we met them? Now it's: *we know* there are other alien races. So why have we not encountered any until now? Why are you guys the first? Why haven't the others approached us?"

"What are their reasons?" said the Hitchers.

Macro persevered. "So, so, for instance: what are *your* reasons for approaching us? Well, maybe to do what you've offered: to give us the technological wherewithal to join the galactic club."

"And why would they do that?"

"Why are *you* doing it?"

"And why would *they* do that?"

Macro breathed in, breathed out. "There could be other reasons for aliens wanting to contact us. Conquest, for instance."

"You think aliens might come to conquer you?"

But he was becoming frustrated, and had to focus to stay still, not to lose them. "We. Here on Mars. We're predominantly a military base. We understand that the universe is a battleground. We're not naive. There are plenty who don't trust *your* motives, for instance. Who think this is all an elaborate passive-aggressive alien invasion."

"Why would we invade?"

"Same reason anybody makes war on anybody. Power."

"And why power?"

It took him a moment to parse this question. "What do you mean *why*? Sentient creatures enjoy power. They just do. That's just the way life is." I mean, come *on*.

"There you go," a different Hitcher voice – definitely different. Not only pitched differently, but more fluid; almost breathy. "There's your false step. *Enjoy* is the false step. There is the mistake you are making in your formulation of the paradoxes of alien encounter – the Old Fermi."

That was the end of the exchange.

It took a while before we began to see that this was indeed a significant breakthrough in our dealings with the Hitchers. Sifting in amongst the recordings of the exchange, it dawned on us that we had uncovered an important alien datum.

Outside the base was the landscape of Mars, as cold as strawberry ice-cream – no! much much colder than that! The dust was colder than ice, and the boulders were colder than ice. The stones had been cleared away from a two-hectare patch in front of the camp buildings, and a field had been excavated where GE-Grass and Clover and FlogiWheat was growing. But from every other perspective, from any other window or porthole in the base, the view was of a flat rust-coloured plain scattered with large, maroon-coloured boulders. The boulders were surprisingly regularly spaced, and of a surprising uniformity of size. I always thought so, at any rate. And here we were, like ants in a frozen Zen garden, except that ants have the internal chemical and neurological wherewithal to feel ant-pleasure.

We convened a meeting.

This was Keedwell's view: "I don't believe they're enforcing our anhedonia as a punishment."

"Speculation," groaned somebody. "You're guessing."

Keedwell was not one to be sidetracked. "I don't believe," he repeated, doggedly, "they're enforcing our anhedonia as a punishment. I don't believe, either, that they're doing it as the down payment, as it were, for our acquisition of interstellar technologies. I believe that neither of those theories is correct."

As if I care, I thought to myself. As if any of us do! What's the point? What's the point? I didn't say this.

Various members of the base spoke up on behalf of one or other of these two theories, in a desultory manner that now characterized our interchanges. Ten minutes or so of chat. Let's not simply dismiss the idea that it would be a punishment, said Li. It surely feels like a punishment. And why, said Kawa, mightn't they not be testing us? Seeing how we handle hardship – giving us a chance to prove that we're worthy of being given this secret? But after a quantity of half-hearted chatter, Keedwell came back to his point.

"I want to revisit the Lagosse hypothesis," he said. Lagosse was an Earth-based analyst, and he had theorized that the imposed anhedonia was in effect sacramental for the Hitchers. "What," said Keedwell, "if anhedonia is, like, a *religious* thing for them? What if it is a virtue in itself? What if they're the new Puritans? What if we're just the unlucky Native Americans who happen to have a first-encounter with stuck-up Puritans who consider our ability to enjoy ourselves to be like a kind of god-cursed naked-ness? Or heathenness? Or. Or. I don't know."

There was a fan inset in the ceiling of the room, and it ground round and round, with a scratchy relentlessness. The air was stirred and circulated. We continued breathing.

This was one use for our breath: we talked round and round this possibility, without any great engagement or passion, and Keedwell kept coming back to: "but think what they said at the end of the last communication." He met all objections with this.

Macro had once asked them about religious belief and they had denied having any. No Gods, no God. And on another occasion, he had asked whether our first-encounter with them was going to follow the model with which we, as humans, were familiar from the Diasporic Age on our own world; and they had said . . . they had said *not at all. By no means. No no no.* To this Keedwell only said, "but perhaps they mean something different by religion to what we mean by the word. Maybe they don't understand our concept of culture shock."

The obscure, foundational work of my psyche ground round, and I found myself distantly angry, in an underpowered sort of way. I couldn't tell you why. Ann used to be my partner – *me* – how comical! Going out on Mars meant stepping into the most hostile environment! We hardly ever *went out*! That's what robots are for! The very idea!

Ann is a Canadian by birth, though I suppose she's a Martian now. That she grew up in the world of wolves and snow and cold desert seems right, somehow. There has always been a loose, poised quality to her. Her body is suited to this low-gravity environment. Her legs and arms are long, and although her torso is shorter than you might expect, she does not look disproportionate. Her face is long and lean and her nose sharp. Her black hair is fixed by a clip at the back of her head, the strands pulled up tight above her high, scholar's brow. Her eyes are grey the way rainfall is grey, or the way silver is grey. Or, her eyes *were* grey like that until the Hitchers came and they became the same hopeless grey of everything else in the base. Her lips are thin, and her backside is muscular, with a small concavity where each thigh meets its buttock. Despite this leanness of limb and torso she has rounded protruding breasts that sit much better in Martian gravity than they ever did on Earth. When we were first arrived, and when she and I were still lovers, she used to joke that women must originally have come from Mars, the gravity here suited the female form much better – where men (she meant me) must have originated on Venus, whose crushing heat and pressure shaped the intensity of misery in our being. She meant I was on the edge of becoming obsessive about her. She meant that we must guard against the claustrophobia of our environment turning a simple love affair into a dangerous duo-religion of sex and self. The ground plan of the base was 7,000 square metres of enclosed ground, and the team on the base was eighty-people strong. It was a village, and for Ann our relationship was a village fling.

I said to her: I am in love with you.

My feelings were very intense, painfully so. But as I have since discovered most of the pain we feel is grounded in our pleasure, such that when the pleasure is taken away the pain recedes to a mere nervous reflex and you are left with the sense only of something missing.

So, I told her: I love you.

She said to me: that means a lot to me. That was, of course, her way of saying: I don't love you back.

We went about our duties, and each Martian day clocked round and days aggregated into elongated Martian weeks, and I tried to get on with other things, but I was stupidly and intensely in love with her. Keedwell called me to a personal meeting, one-to-one, and told me to rein myself in. This was an order, he told me. This was a direct order. But the intensity of my pleasure in anticipating having sex with Ann was greater even than the pleasure of having sex with her. I thought about her all the time. I thought about her all the time. Her skin was smooth as oil. Her extraordinary black hair. Her mithril-grey eyes. I proposed marriage repeatedly, and took a greater pain-pleasure in her refusals than I ever would have done in any acceptance. I begged, and promised. I humiliated myself.

I thought about her all the time.

The Hitchers came. They promised us the technology to travel to the stars.

Then we woke up to our collective anhedonia.

Shortly after this Ann broke up with me – it seems to me, even today, as I type this out, just *crazy* that this adolescent phrase ("broke up with me") could be applied to something as grand and significant as our love affair. She began seeing Macro. I was not happy, but neither was I profoundly sad. But I was jealous.

As communications officer I was able to observe her, intimately.

I am not saying that I hated Macro, because after all, as we all now know, hatred is fuelled by its dark supply of sheer pleasure, and its motor runs sputtery without that fuel. There are, perhaps, few things as intensely pleasurable as full-throated hatred. Hatred is not the right word for the way I was emotionally oriented towards Macro.

Ann informed me she would have broken up with me sooner or later anyway. It wasn't the Hitcher's fault. It wasn't Macro's fault. She spoke without emphasis, and I didn't especially care. Neither did she. Except, I suppose, there was *some* sort of scorpion inside my cranium when I thought of Macro. If I cannot call it hatred, then I must log it as some akin, bleached version of the same feeling. It crawled. Round and round it went.

Now, it is different of course. Now I can hate him again. There's a sheer relief in that, believe me.

What I am saying is that this has to do with something more

than simple jealousy. This was the situation the Hitchers had placed us in. They asked, in effect, a question. It was an important and straightforward question: what happens to love when pleasure is excised from it? It is a straightforward question without being a simple one, because the majority sharehold we all take in love – in *our being in love*, I mean – is our own dignity. None of us wants to believe that our love for another human being is only a sort of puffed-up and habitual hedonism. We like to think on the contrary that our love is selfless; self-sacrificing; dedicated, pure. Anhedonia puts those beliefs to the test. What we want to believe is that our own pleasure is vindicated by being predicated on the pleasure of the other. What I discovered, on Mars, was the hollowness of this fiction. If we feel no pleasure in ourself, then it is next to impossible to care one way or another about the pleasure of our partner. It's the other way about. The truth is that the pleasure of the other is always predicated on our own ecstasy.

I don't suppose Macro was really any different, and yet he and Ann persevered in their relationship. The anhedonia did not kill it, or if it killed it then they refused to let go of it. They did this not because their love for one another was so elevated as to transcend pleasure. Rather they did so because they were military. They had been trained up in the logic of discipline, and to have abandoned their relationship simply because neither party was enjoying it very much would have seemed to them a failure in discipline. With me it was different. There was, it transpired, nothing to my feelings for Ann apart from self-pleasure. I am not saying, here, that it was envy that made me hate Macro. It was something else. Because, after all, discipline, military or otherwise, is only a manifestation of a deeper, or larger, human impulse – *impulse* in the "science of mechanics" sense of the word, as something that imparts momentum. The word for this is *will*. I did not envy Macro his intimacy with Ann. I envied him his strength of will.

Sometimes I spoke to the Hitchers. I told nobody about this. I spoke to the Hitchers through the com-system. They were capricious, and sometimes they tuned themselves into one or other com. I listened to them, and they listened to me – only sometimes. "Give us back our pleasure," I begged. I asked them once.

"Are you ready for it?" they replied.

I stared at the plastic-coated wall on the other side of my desk. I might have been looking at a canvas by Rubens, or a superb dust-filtered strawberry sunset, or a sheet of pale blue plastic-covered dividing wall. It was all the same.

"Please," I said. "Please – put an end to the anhedonia."

"Should you even be talking to us?" they replied. They liked this sort of exasperating statement. "Should you? Isn't Macro the ambassador."

So I thought of Macro. I had him on a screen – I was looking right of him. I thought of the capacity of pleasure in his cranium, blocked by the Hitchers. I thought of him going through the motions of fucking Ann, as if it were a strenuous and rather dull exercise routine. "Please," I asked, for the third time. "Please: give *him* back his ability to feel pleasure."

"Him? Macro?"

"He's the one."

Either I said this to them, or I fantasized about saying it, or I dreamt it, in a moment of sheer wish-fulfillment. There was no pleasure in dreaming any more. Had there ever been?

The next thing that happened was that Macro got his pleasure back.

This is how he described it: "one minute I was listening to some music as I exercised in the tension rack. And the next thing I felt a tingle in my scalp, and the hairs on the back of my neck stood up. I almost fell over with astonishment. I had forgotten what it was to take pleasure in a piece of music. I rushed to a larderspout and drank some chocolate milkshake, and it tasted fucking *delicious*."

The first thing he did was to go straight to Ann. She was in her room staring blankly at her screen, doing some work without enthusiasm or resentment. "Can you feel it?" he asked her. "Is it back for you too?"

It wasn't back for her. Nor for me neither, and I was watching them both.

In her anhedonic state, lacking highs or lows, Ann could not feel overly disappointed; but she felt, she later said, a *little* disappointed for all that. They fucked on her bed. Macro came – a shuddery siphoning of joy through mind and penis – and she lay beneath him almost motionless. He kept apologizing to her, but couldn't keep the laughter from his voice. He was laughing with sheer pleasure.

Word spread through the village, of course. Mars amazes again. A command meeting was convened. Macro was tested immediately; the usual dopamine pathways in the brain were functioning as before, although nobody seemed to know how the change had been effected. It was, I heard, an awkward debrief, because Macro kept bursting into laughter.

"*They've* done this," Keedwell said with a sour face.

This also struck Macro as wonderfully funny. The unadulterated pleasure of *being* with these people. These *guys*!

"I mean," Keedwell announced, to a meeting of all key personnel. His face was grey. "It's not a malfunction, or the end of the phenomenon's natural term or anything. *They* have chosen, for whatever reason, to do this to you. They took away, they gave back."

It was reported to Earth, of course; and the fact that Earth had placed us in effective quarantine, and had held back permission – for three months now – for any of the station staff to return home after their stint, rankled in me for the first time. Macro announced that he found himself angry at their irrational fear – as if we were polluted? We were not polluted. He was having, he said, difficulty, in fact, holding onto his anger. He was like a toddler.

We had questions: why Macro? Were they now going to rescind the anhedonia from all of us? Some of us? Just him? Why *him*?

So Macro went to talk to them once more. It was harder than usual to concentrate. The dome was now a space of wonder and glory to him: a womb of delight. The gold shone like happiness itself. The Hitchers manifested like angels, or starbursts.

"I don't understand why you did it," he said to the empty chamber. "But I'm sure *glad* you did."

Eventually he settled himself, and the extraordinary filaments of an alien form of life – a being from the other side of the galaxy! *Imagine* it! – came into view. There were tears in his eyes, and the words they spoke, at first, didn't register fully. The weight of them. The importance of them didn't register, not at first.

This is what these glorious beings, these spirits, these demigods, were saying: "we shall take you to another star. We shall punch you through the cowl of dark matter that hoods this portion of the galaxy and show you the cosmos as it truly is."

He wept.

It was everything he had ever wanted, tumbling upon him now, now, now. "Thank you," he gabbled. "Thank you." Do you know what he thought? He thought to himself: this has been a test.

This is what he realized: they came to our solar system, and saw that humanity, mostly, was a slave to pleasure. Our hedonism had kept us low, at the level of beasts. We shall *test* them, quoth the Hitchers. We shall deprive them of their sense of pleasure for three months and see if they can become higher beings – see how they survive, see what they do. They *were* testing us, and we *have* passed the test. And now the reward will be ours, and – Macro thought – mine first of all.

He had never known a purer joy. "What must I do?" he begged. "Tell me what to do!"

"Let your people know how you feel."

"Just that?"

"Just that."

But nothing was easier than this, because as a matter of course all his communications with the Hitchers were recorded. I was the communications officer; I had set it up. A catch-all was set into the skin of his scalp, just above the hairline over my left ear. Everything he said, and everything that was said to him, was recorded. The Hitchers knew this, of course, because they were inside our heads.

He found the faces of his colleagues a joy, and a bliss in his eyes; and we looked wearily and dolefully back upon him. "They've rescinded *my* anhedonia," he reminded everybody. "It won't be long before they do the same for you all. I believe it to have been a test, you see."

"What did they mean – punching through?" Keedwell asked.

"Punching through?"

"Punch you through the cowl of dark matter that hoods this portion of the galaxy," I quoted, for I had the video transcript right there.

"Dark matter does clump," said Beyman. "We all know about that. There are areas of relative baryonic density, and areas of attenuation. But I'm not sure what it means to suggest that our system is *hooded* by it. Baryonic matter in a – hood?"

"Does it matter?"

"We don't know what matters."

We fitted him with a new range of catch-alls and instruments; some embedded in his skin, some worn about him on belts and in pockets. A running feed, open mike, visuals, electrographic and so on. Then we gave him back to the Hitchers. He was to be the first human to travel between the stars. He was suitably excited. He was excited enough for all of us.

"You hope to decode the mystery of the method of travel itself," said a Hitcher. Because of course it was exactly why we had festooned him with such a wealth of scientific instrumentation. "This won't help you," the Hitcher added.

"I'll keep up a running commentary," he said.

Of course.

And here. He asked the Hitchers how he should prepare himself – what to wear, whether safety gear was needful – a hard shell? a supply of oxygen? food? – but they were as playfully evasive as ever they are; so we covered our bases. "I am wearing an elastic vacuum-suit, with a pack on my back the size of a laptop computer, and a belt around my hips containing supplies and water." For the record.

He went to the meeting area, but the Hitchers didn't seem to be there. After an hour of meditative sitting he gave up and wandered the corridors of the base. The underpowered Martian gravity gave a spring to his step. He teetered on the edge of anticlimax. The buzz, the buzz, the intense pleasure of anticipation. "I am going to another star."

"Having experienced the anhedonia," he told Ann, sipping a little ceramic thimble of ersatz coffee, very dark brown, very sweet, "and now having *recovered* my capacity for pleasure again . . ."

"Bully for you," said Ann, passionlessly.

"I know! I'm sorry! But having lost it and recovered it, I find I am a more *anxious* person than I was before."

They were in the mess. Small porthole windows gave out over desert sown only with stone conkers that would never seed or sprout. The sky was pink.

"You're anxious," she suggested, "that the Hitchers might take away your ability to feel pleasure again."

"That," he conceded. "But also, there's a more general nonspecific anxiety." He drained his coffee. "For instance, an anxiety that I might find myself stalking uselessly about the base for days, dressed up like a vacuum cowboy. They said they'd take me to the stars; but maybe that was just another example of their caprice. You know? Anxiety," he said, understanding belatedly why he felt that way, "about my *looking foolish*, you know?"

"I used to be very self-conscious," said Ann, sitting opposite him in a low soft chair naked, unwashed, with her legs apart. "That doesn't seem to be a problem any more."

"I'm going to the stars!" he declared, with a whoop. "I'm going *all the way*!"

"We might . . ." she began.

"It's all to do with – " he interrupted her. But then there was an alien in the mess. The place was deserted except for Macro, and Ann, and for me, and then this spread of brilliance and ribbony force. They had never before been seen outside the blue-gold dome. It was astonishing. For Macro there was a leaven of sheer pleasure – of excitement – in his astonishment.

"Where would you like to go?" asked the alien.

"I," he said, caught off-guard. "I don't know. Centauri?"

"Do you think that's far enough?"

"Galactic centre!" he sang. "Or would the black hole swallow us?"

"No," said the Hitcher, in a different voice. "It won't do that."

And down he went.

He was plumbed in, wired up, and we followed him the whole journey. Travel is effected by a sort of process of *elaboration*. He is in the middle, and two Hitchers are on either side. They are making a first – I'm tempted to call it a *jump*, but jump is not the right word at all. Our imaginations have been infected by science fiction in that respect. They didn't step through a door into hyper-space, or subspace, or anything like that. The relationship is not really spatial. It is, rather, a circumvention of the logic of dimensionality. No, not that. So, it is not an instantaneous journey, and nor is it a journey constrained by Einstein. If a diver comes up from the deep deeps she is constrained by the physics of decompression, and must stop, and wait, and delay. But if those chemical constraints were circumvented, then the distance from the bottom of the ocean to the top is only a few miles. You can run a few miles in minutes. That's what they are doing. He understands this. You don't need to shrink *space* to change the relationship between the ocean bed and the surface from *days* to *minutes*. You don't need to step into a rival dimension.

He says to them: I can't see anything.

They say: you're not looking.

And that's right, because now he looks, and he *can* see. He sees hundreds of thousands of stars. He sees them feelingly, as it were, like luminiferous Braille on a black page. White, amber, sherry-coloured, scarlet like a car's backlights, brown as timber, more blue than oceans and deeper. A profound blue in which we might easily lose ourselves. *Life*, it's beautiful. God, it's beautiful!

Because now he looks and he can see this rapidly spinning star is mottled in jewel-white and turquoise, and it is rotating with sublime rapidity. A sensual jet of molten matter spears from its two poles. We slip past. Clouds, or densities, or clumps of obscurity pool, spill, and suddenly we – as the Hitchers promised we would – we punch through. Hundreds of thousands of stars are suddenly millions of stars.

Dark matter clumps and stretches, says the Hitcher. There's a new tone to its voice. It takes him a moment to realize that it is sorrow. He had not realized they were capable of that emotion.

Dark matter, Macro repeats.

From your position in the galaxy it is hard for you to understand the extent to which you are cowled-about with it, said the Hitcher.

He can barely concentrate upon these words. My God it's beautiful. My Life it's beautiful. The range of stars! The *variety*. The gorgeous intricacy of this galactic flank. Its vastness. He can feel it pregnant with movement, Will itself in material form, Force on an inhumanely beautiful scale. And the colours! A paprika of the heavens. Fireworks and sparks in every millimetre of its stretching light years above, below, before, behind, left-hand, right-hand. The quality of the light; the wavefront superb turbulence of it. The excess of it. My *Life* it's beautiful. My *God* it's beautiful.

A small black sun, darker than any vacuum-black. And a great ring of shining matter light-years in circumference. Glitter, glitter.

An eminence front of forty million stars, fixed in staggering profusion and range and glory.

"There's a fantastic . . . superb . . . *throb* in the texture of things," Macro says, and his voice is recorded for us all to wonder about for years afterwards. "Not a throb exactly, not a physical sensation, but a brimming intensity, or a kind of . . . tranquillity of Sublime . . . there's a piercing quality . . ."

Here is a rush of stars, and the rustling of background static like all the dead leaves in all the world's forests. Black, black, blue, searing white. This pulsar spins 40,000 times a second; to call it a blur would understate it comically.

And here we are, through the vast hanging tapestry of pearlescent stars, and spacetime itself bows under, or stretches inward on itself, at the central mass of the galaxy. Macro's words are failing him. It is no longer appropriate to talk in terms of colour, or dimension, or quality: this is a sphere thousands of light-years across that draws the principle of extension and attribute and even thought down – or along – or in upon itself. He doesn't seem to be able to articulate what he is seeing. "It's amazing," he is saying. "The size of it! The size! The colours have all gone away, but light is still . . ."

The visuals here are of a drop of ink the size of infinity. The visuals are of a perfect sphere trillions of trillion-trillion kilometres across. It is so dense that the conventional mathematical descriptions of spherical matter (four-thirds? r? and so on) no longer apply. "It's," Macro is saying, as if breathing is hard for him. The stars all about it! Suns enormously more massive than our sun and enormously more numerous than can be seen from any Earthly sky, reduced to a foggy incandescence about this vast central black-hole sun. A mist rising behind the infinite equator. A curve so huge it is a straight line.

Then Macro's last words, recorded for us all to ponder afterwards: *Its. Ah! It is. It's –*

Ah!
Then, this: *only shield from full intensity of.*
That's all that's left now; the reedy, almost inaudible voice of – we assume – one of the two attendant Hitchers. There's nothing more from Macro. There are some images. We've downloaded a whole

bunch of really interesting images from his machinery. Some of these do seem to show aspects of the cosmos from radically new angle. It seems true what the Hitchers say, that by chance the solar system exists in a semisphere of space, perhaps a thousand light years across, that is arced about by a curving wall of fairly densely accumulated dark matter. This protects us from, as the Hitcher puts it, the full intensity.

We picked up all this stuff after they returned, of course. We piece the elements together. Macro was no better than a child. No better? Much worse. He was a broken-down consciousness. He eats, he sleeps, he stares at the wall. The only thing the camp doctors are agreed upon is that, whilst it's possible the psychotropic pharmacies of Earth might be able to help him, the limited facilities available here on Mars are not up to the job.

A whole bunch of vocal outrage from various Earthly individuals about how the Hitchers sucked out Macro's brain – or poisoned his consciousness – that they made war upon us, in effect, by depriving us of the two things that make us human: *viz.*, our ability to experience pleasure, and our ability to think cogently. Not that there's anything we can do about it. Even the most hawkish of hawks knows that launching a strike against the Mars base, whilst it is certain to kill the human staff, will leave the Hitchers unharmed. They would blip away just before the missiles fell, to who knows where.

He sleeps, and eats, and sits in a man-nappy staring at the wall.

We had assumed that desire transforms us. But actually only the death of desire can transform us. We thought, for a while, that Macro was unusually blessed; but the truth is quite otherwise. In another man this might have diluted the hatred. I did not realize, on Mars, that hatred was the right term; but on the shuttle to Earth, looping around a fern-curl trajectory in company of my rival, my pleasure came back to me. And with it came the realization that hatred for Macro had reorganized my psyche almost wholly around its line of force. The greatest pleasure of all, of course, was knowing that his mind is destroyed. That is a continual refreshing mountain stream of joy inside my soul.

We know, now, where we stand. This is how I reported it to the UN council. We know the Hitchers, like us, originated in a portion of the galaxy swaddled about with enough dark matter to protect them from the fullest awe-blast of the naked sky. They, like us, evolved in a sort of galactic microclimate. This is not to say that life can only evolve intelligence in such places – quite the reverse, in fact. It transpires that there is a staggering wealth and variety of other forms of alien life; but almost all of them grew to species maturity in the waterfall blast of the sense of wonder. Accordingly they developed a particular form of consciousness: as a sea-shrimp evolves able to endure the intense pressures of the ocean floor so they evolved a pleasure-protected mind. The Hitchers were different, though, in the exact manner in which we are different. Because of their galactic environment they evolved a pleasure-sensitive consciousness of delicate intensities. It could not endure the awe-pressure of the naked cosmos. I think they made the choice to shed their hedonia long ago. I think that all that remains is a sort of residual curiosity, or even perhaps nostalgia, for a lost mode of being – as a grown man, in a suit, walking past a copse of trees on his way to work might feel a flicker of simian desire to toss everything aside and clamber into the boughs and branches. Other intelligent species would no more offer humanity the means to travel from star to star than we would give a boat to a man allergic to seawater. Than we would give a hang-glider to a man allergic to *air*. But the Hitchers have their reasons for wanting, at least, to give us the *choice*.

How badly, then, do we *want* to travel to the stars? Is the answer to that question: *badly enough to be prepared to sterilize our sense of wonder*?

Of course, the sense of wonder is why we've always wanted to go in the first place. We can have our desire to go, and never survive the trip; or we can fit the emotional prophylactic necessary for survival and lose the desire to go in the first place.

Perhaps we should castrate (as it were) a self-selected corps of explorers, travellers and traders; enable them to go on our vicarious behalf. But this travel will not require elaborate fleets of exclusive spacecraft. It will open the door to everybody. If they are still prompted by their hunger of wonder, how many will heed warnings not to rush through? These are big and important questions. Oh, they pass me by. My hatred, and its dumb idiotic object, is too important for me now to be prepared to give it up. I shall stay, and relish. My hatred remains, and I take a solace in that. Because it a pure hatred. It endured when unsupported by pleasure. I hated him despite the fact that it gave me no pleasure to do so, back on Mars. Nothing is purer.

TIGER BURNING

Alastair Reynolds

Though Welsh born, and having spent his formative years in Cornwall and Scotland, Alastair Reynolds (b. 1966) moved to the Netherlands in 1991 where he spent the next twelve years working for the European Space Agency until taking the plunge to become a full-time writer in 2004. He is best known for his Revelation Space sequence of novels that began with Revelation Space *in 2000. All of Reynolds' work boasts an understanding and conviction about the future of technology and that can be found in miniature in this story which was written in homage to that glorious 1950s movie,* Forbidden Planet.

IT WAS NOT THE FIRST TIME that Adam Fernando's investigations had taken him this far from home, but on no previous trip had he ever felt quite so perilously remote; so utterly at the mercy of the machines that had copied him from brane to brane like a slowly randomizing Chinese whisper. The technicians in the Office of Scrutiny had always assured him that the process was infallible; that no essential part of him was being discarded with each duplication, but he only ever had their word on the matter, and they *would* say it was safe, wouldn't they? Memory, as always, gained foggy holes with each instance of copying. He recalled the precise details of his assignment – the awkward nature of the problem – but he couldn't for the life of him say why he had chosen, at what must have been the very last minute, to assume the physical embodiment of a man-sized walking cat.

When Fernando had been reconstituted after the final duplication, he came to awareness in a half-open metal egg, its inner surface still slick with the residue of the biochemical products from which he had been quickened. He pawed at his whorled, matted fur, then willed his retractile claws into action. They worked excellently, requiring no special effort on his part. A portion of his brain must have been adapted to deal with them, so that their unsheathing was almost involuntary.

He stood from the egg, taking in his surroundings. His colour vision and depth perception appeared reassuringly human-normal. The quickening room was a grey-walled metal space under standard gravity, devoid of ornamentation save that provided by the many scientific tools and instruments that had been stored here. There was no welcoming party, and the air was a touch cooler than conventional taste dictated. Scrutiny had requested that he be allowed embodiment, but that was the only concession his host had made to his arrival. Which could mean one of two things: Doctor Meranda Austvro was doing all that she could to hamper his investigation, without actually breaking the law, or that she was so blissfully innocent of any actual wrongdoing that she had no need to butter him up with formal niceties.

He tested his claws again. They still worked. Behind him, he was vaguely aware of an indolently swishing tail.

He was just sheathing his claws when a door whisked open in one pastel-grey wall. An aerial robot emerged swiftly into the room: a collection dull metal spheres orbiting each other like clockwork planets in some mad, malfunctioning orrery. He bristled at the sudden intrusion, but it seemed unlikely that the host would have gone to the bother of quickening him only to have her aerial murder him immediately afterwards.

"Inspector Adam Fernando, Office of Scrutiny," he said. No need to prove it: the necessary authentication had been embedded in the header of the graviton pulse that had conveyed his resurrection profile from the repeater brane.

One of the larger spheres answered him officiously. "Of course. Who *else* might you have been? We trust the quickening has been performed to your general satisfaction?"

He picked at a patch of damp fur, suppressing the urge to shiver.

"Everything seems in order. Perhaps if we moved to a warmer room . . ." His voice sounded normal enough, despite the alterations to his face: maybe a touch less deep than normal, with the merest suggestion of feline snarl in the vowels.

"Naturally. Doctor Austvro has been waiting for you."

"I'm surprised she wasn't here to greet me."

"Doctor Austvro is a busy woman, Inspector; now more than ever. I thought someone from the Office of Scrutiny would have appreciated that."

He was about to mention something about common courtesies, then thought better of it: even if she wasn't listening in, there was no telling what the aerial might report back to Austvro.

"Perhaps we'd better be moving on. I take it Doctor Austvro can find time to squeeze me into her schedule, now that I'm alive?"

"Of course," the machine said sniffily. "It's some distance to her laboratory. It might be best if I carried you, unless you would rather locomote."

Fernando knew the drill. He spread his arms, allowing the cluster of flying spheres to distribute itself around his body to provide support. Small spheres pushed under his arms, his buttocks, the padded black soles of his feet, while others nudged gently against chest and spine to keep him balanced. The largest sphere, which played no role in supporting him, flew slightly ahead. It appeared to generate some kind of aerodynamic air pocket. They sped through the open door and down a long, curving corridor, gaining speed with each second. Soon they were moving hair-raisingly fast, dodging round hairpin bends and through doors that opened and shut only just in time.

Fernando remembered his tail and curled it out of harm's way.

"How long will this take?" he asked.

"Five minutes. We shall only be journeying a short distance into the inclusion."

Fernando recalled his briefing. "What we're passing through now: this is all human built, part of Pegasus Station? We're not seeing any KR-L artifacts yet?"

"Nor shall you," the aerial said sternly. "The actual business of investigating the KR-L machinery falls under the remit of the Office of Exploitation, as you well know. Scrutiny's business is confined only to peripheral matters of security related to that investigation."

Fernando bristled. "And as such . . ."

"The word was 'peripheral', Inspector. Doctor Austvro was very clear about the terms under which she would permit your arrival, and they did not include a guided tour of the KR-L artifacts."

"Perhaps if I ask nicely."

"Ask whatever you like. It will make no difference."

While they sped on – in silence now, for Fernando had decided he preferred it that way – he chewed over what he knew of the inclusion, and its significance to the Metagovernment.

Hundreds of thousands of years ago, humanity had achieved the means to colonize nearby branes: squeezing biological data across the hyperspatial gap into adjacent realities, then growing living organisms from those patterns. Now the Metagovernment sprawled across 30,000 dense-packed braneworlds. Yet in all that time it had only encountered evidence of one other intelligent civilization: the vanished KR-L culture.

Further expansion was unlikely. Physics changed subtly from brane to brane, limiting the possibilities for human colonization. Beyond 15,000 realities in either direction, people could only survive inside bubbles of tampered spacetime, in which the local physics had been tweaked to simulate homebrane conditions. These "inclusions" became increasingly difficult to maintain as the local physics grew more exotic. At five kilometres across, Meranda Austvro's inclusion was the smallest in existence, and it still required gigantic support machinery to hold it open. The Metagovernment was happy to shoulder the expense because it hoped to reap riches from Austvro's investigations into the vanished KR-L culture.

But that investigation was supposed to be above-top-secret: the mere existence of the KR-L culture officially deniable at all levels of the Metagovernment. By all accounts Austvro was close to a shattering discovery.

And yet there were leaks. Someone close to the operation – maybe even Austvro herself – was blabbing.

Scrutiny had sent Fernando in to seal the leak. If that meant shutting down Austvro's whole show until the cat could be put back into the bag (Fernando could not help but smile at the metaphor) then he had the necessary authorization.

How Austvro would take it was another thing.

The rush of corridors and doors slowed abruptly, and a moment later Fernando was deposited back on his feet, teetering slightly until he regained his balance. He had arrived in a much larger room than the one where he had been quickened, one that felt a good deal more welcoming. There was plush white carpet on the floor, comfortable furniture, soothing pastel decor, various homely knick-knacks and tasteful *objets d'art*. The rock-effect walls were interrupted by lavish picture windows overlooking an unlikely garden, complete with winding paths, rock pools and all manner of imported vegetation, laid out under a soothing green sky. It was a convincing simulacrum of one of the more popular holiday destinations in the low-thousand branes.

Meranda Austvro was reclining in a silver dress on a long black settee. Playing cards were arranged in a circular formation on the coffee table before her. She put down the one card that had been in her hand and beckoned Fernando to join her.

"Welcome to Pegasus Station, Inspector," she said. "I'm sorry I wasn't able to greet you sooner, but I've been rather on the busy side."

Fernando sat himself down on a chair, facing her across the table. "So I see."

"A simple game of Clock Patience, Inspector, to occupy myself while I was waiting for your arrival. Don't imagine this is how I'd rather be spending my afternoon."

He decided to soften his approach. "Your aerial did tell me you'd been preoccupied with your work."

"That's part of it. But I must admit we botched your first quickening, and I didn't have time to wait around to see the results a second time."

"When you say 'botched' . . ."

"I neglected to check your header tag more carefully. When all that cat fur started appearing . . ." She waved her hand dismissively. "I assumed there'd been a mistake in the profile, so I aborted the quickening, before you reached legal sentience."

The news unnerved him. Failed quickenings weren't unknown,

though, and she'd acted legally enough. "I hope you recycled my remains."

"On the contrary, Inspector: I made good use of them." Austvro patted a striped orange rug, spread across the length of the settee. "You don't mind, do you? I found the pattern quite appealing."

"Make the most of me," Fernando said, trying not to sound as if she had touched any particular nerve. "You can have another skin when I leave, if it means so much to you."

She clicked her fingers over his shoulder, at the aerial. "You may go now, Caliph."

The spheres bustled around each other. "As you wish, Doctor Austvro."

When Fernando had heard the whisk of the closing door, he leaned an elbow on the table, careful not to disturb the cards. He brought his huge whiskered head close to Austvro's. She was an attractive woman, despite a certain steely hauteur. He wondered if she could smell his breath; how uniquely, distastefully feline it was. "I hope this won't take too much time, for both our sakes. Scrutiny wants early closure on this whole mess."

"I'm sure it does. Unfortunately, I don't know the first thing about your investigation." She picked up a card from one part of the pattern, examined it with pursed lips, then placed it down on top of another one. "Therefore I'm not sure how I can help you."

"You were informed that we were investigating a security hole."

"I was informed, and I found the suggestion absurd. Unless I am the perpetrator." She turned her cool, civil eyes upon him. "Is that what you think, Inspector? That I am the one leaking information back to the homebrane, risking the suspension of my own project?"

" I know only that there are leaks."

"They could be originating from someone in Scrutiny, or Exploitation. Have you considered that?"

"We have to start somewhere. The operation itself seems as good a place as any."

"Then you're wasting your time. Return down-stack and knock on someone else's door. I've work to do."

"Why are you so certain the leaks couldn't be originating here?"

"Because – firstly – I do not accept that there *are* leaks. There are merely statistical patterns, coincidences, which Scrutiny has latched onto because it has nothing better to do with its time. Secondly, I run this show on my own. There is no room for anyone else to be the source of these non-existent leaks."

"Your husband?"

She smiled briefly and extended a hand over the coffee table, palm down. A figure – a grave, clerical-looking man in black – appeared above the table's surface, no larger than a statuette. The man made a gesture with his hands, as if shaping an invisible ball, then said something barely audible – Fernando caught the phrase "three hundred" – then vanished again, leaving only the arrangement of playing cards.

Austvro selected another, examined it once more and returned it to the table.

"My husband died years ago, Inspector. Edvardo and I were deep inside the KR-L machinery, protected by an extension of the inclusion. My husband's speciality was acausal mechanics . . ." For a moment, a flicker of humanity interrupted the composure of her face. "The extension collapsed. Edvardo was on the other side of the failure point. I watched him fall into KR-L spacetime. I watched what it did to him."

"I'm sorry," Fernando said, wishing he had paid more attention to the biographical briefing.

"Since then I have conducted operations alone, with only the machines to help me. Caliph is the most special of them: I place great value on his companionship. You can question the machines if you like, but it won't get you anywhere."

"Yet the leaks are real."

"We could argue about that."

"Scrutiny wouldn't have sent me otherwise."

"There must be false alarms. Given the amount of data Scrutiny keeps tabs on – the entire informational content of meta-humanity, spread across 30,000 reality layers – isn't *any* pattern almost guaranteed to show up eventually?"

"It is," Fernando conceded, stroking his chin tufts. "But that's why Scrutiny pays attention to context, and to clustering. Not simply to exact matches for sensitive keywords, either, but for suspicious similarities: near-misses designed to throw us off the scent. Miranda for Meranda; Ostrow for Austvro, that kind of thing."

"And you've found these clusters?"

"Nearly a dozen, at the last count. Someone with intimate knowledge of this research project is talking, and we can't have that."

This amused her. "So the Metagovernment does have its enemies after all."

"It's no secret that there are political difficulties in the high branes. Talk of secession. Exploitation feels that the KR-L technology may give the Metagovernment just the tools it needs to hold the stack together, if the dissidents try to gain the upper hand."

Austvro sneered. "Tools of political control."

"An edge, that's all. And obviously matters won't be helped if the breakaway branes learn about the KR-L discoveries, and what we intend to do with them. That's why we need to keep a lid on things."

"But these clusters . . ." Austvro leaned back into the settee, studying Fernando levelly. "I was shown some of the evidence – some of the documents – before you arrived, and, frankly, none of it made much sense to me."

"It didn't?"

"If someone – some mole – was trying to get a message through to the breakaway branes, why insist on being so cryptic? Why not just come out and say whatever needs to be said, instead of creating jumbled riddles? Names mixed up . . . names altered . . . the context changed out of all recognition . . . some of these keywords even looked like they were embedded in some kind of play."

"All I can say is that Scrutiny considered the evidence sufficiently compelling to require immediate action. It's still investigating the provenance of these documents, but I should have word on that soon enough."

Austvro narrowed her flint-grey eyes. "Provenance?"

"As I said, the documents are faked: made to appear historical, as if they've always been present in the data."

"Which is even more absurd than there being leaks in the first place."

He smiled at her. "I'm glad we agree on something."

"It's a start."

He tapped his extended claws against the coffee table. "I appreciate your scepticism, Doctor. But the fact is I can't leave here until I have an explanation. If Scrutiny isn't satisfied with my findings – if the source of the leaks can't be traced – they'll have no option but to shut down Pegasus, or at least replace the current set-up with something under much tighter government control. So it's really in your interests to work with me, to help me find the solution."

"I see," she said coldly.

"I'd like to see more of this operation. Not just Pegasus Station, but the KR-L culture itself."

"Unthinkable. Didn't Caliph clarify where your jurisdiction ends, Inspector?"

"It's not a question of jurisdiction. Give me a reason to think you haven't anything to hide, and I'll focus my enquiries somewhere else."

She looked down, fingering the striped orange rug she had made of his skin.

"It will serve no purpose, Inspector: except to disturb you."

"I'll edit the memories before I pass them back down the stack. How does that sound?"

She rose from the settee, abandoning her card game. "Your call. But don't blame me when you start gibbering."

Austvro led him from the lounge, back into a more austere part of the station. The hem of her silver dress swished on the iron-grey flooring. Now and then an aerial flashed past on some errand, but in all other respects the station was deserted. Fernando knew that Exploitation had offered to send more expertise, but Austvro had always declined assistance. By all accounts she worked efficiently, feeding a steady stream of titbits and breakthroughs back to the Metagovernment specialists. According to Fernando's dossier, Austvro didn't trust the stability of anyone who would actually volunteer to be copied this far up-stack, knowing the protocols. It was no surprise that she treated him with suspicion, for he was also a volunteer, and only his memories would be going back home again.

Presently they arrived at an oval aperture cut into one wall. On the other side of the aperture, ready to dart down a tunnel, was a two-seater travel pod.

"Are you sure about this, Inspector?"

"I'm perfectly sure."

She shrugged – letting him know it was his mistake, not hers – and then ushered him into one of the seats. Austvro took the other one, facing him at right angles to the direction of travel. She applied her hand to a tiller and the pod sped into motion. Tunnel walls zipped by in an accelerating blur.

"We're about to leave the main body of the inclusion," Austvro informed him.

"Into KR-L spacetime?"

"Not unless the support machines fail. The inclusion's more or less spherical – in so far as one can talk about 'spherical' intrusions of one form of spacetime into another – but it sprouts tentacles and loops into interesting portions of the surrounding KR-L structure. Maintaining these tentacles and loops is much harder than keeping the sphere up, and I'm sure you've heard how expensive and difficult *that* is."

Fernando felt his hairs bristling. The pod was moving terrifically fast now; so swiftly that there could be no doubt that they had left the main sphere behind already. He visualized a narrow, delicate stalk of spacetime jutting out from the sphere, and him as a tiny moving mote within that stalk.

"Was this where your husband died, Doctor?"

"A similar extension; it doesn't matter now. We've made some adjustments to the support machinery, so it shouldn't happen again." Her expression turned playful. "Why? You're not *nervous*, are you?"

"Not at all. I just wondered where the accident had happened."

"A place much like here. It doesn't matter. My husband never much cared for these little jaunts, anyway. He much preferred to restrict himself to the main inclusion."

Fernando recalled the image of Austvro's husband, his hands cupping an imaginary ball, like a mime, and something of the gesture tickled his interest.

"Your husband's line of work: acausal signalling, wasn't it: the theoretical possibility of communication through time, using KR-L principles?"

"A dead-end, unfortunately. Even the KR-L had never made *that* work. But the Metagovernment was happy with the crumbs and morsels he sent back home."

"He must have thought there was something in it."

"My husband was a dreamer," Austvro said. "His singular failing was his inability to distinguish between a practical possibility and an outlandish fantasy."

"I see."

"I don't mean to sound harsh. I loved him, of course. But he could never love the KR-L the way I do. For him these trips were always something to be endured, not relished."

He watched her eyes for a glimmer of a reaction. "And after his accident – did you have misgivings?"

"For a nanosecond. Until I realized how important this work is. How we must succeed, for the sake of the homebrane." She leaned forward in her seat and pointed down the tunnel. "There. We're approaching the interface. That's where the tunnel cladding becomes transparent. The photons reaching your eyes will have originated as photon-analogues in KR-L spacetime. You'll see their structures, their great engines. The scale will astound you. The mere geometry of these artifacts is . . . deeply troubling, for some. If it disconcerts you, close your eyes." Her hand remained hard on the tiller. "I'm used to it, but I'm exposed to these marvels on a daily basis."

"I'm curious," Fernando said. "When you speak of the aliens, you sometimes sound like you're saying three letters. At other times . . ."

"Krull, yes," she said, dismissively. "It's shorthand, Inspector: nothing more. "Long before we knew it had ever been inhabited, we called this the KR-L brane. K and R are the Boltzmann and Rydberg constants, from nuclear physics. In KR-L spacetime, these numbers differ from their values in the homebrane. L is a parameter that denotes the degree of variation."

"Then Krull is . . . a word of your own coining?"

"If you insist upon calling it a word. Why? Has it appeared in these mysterious keyword clusters of yours?"

"Something like it."

The pod swooped into the transparent part of the stalk. It was difficult to judge speed now. Fernando assumed there was some glass-like cladding between him and the inclusion boundary, and somewhere beyond that (he was fuzzy on the physics) the properties of spacetime took on alien attributes, profoundly incompatible with human biochemistry. But things could still live in that space-time, provided they'd been born there in the first place. The KR-L had evolved into an entire supercivilization, and although they were gone now, their great machines remained. He could see them now, as huge and bewildering as Austvro had warned. They were slab-sided, round-edged, ribbed with flanges and cooling grids, surmounted by arcing spheres and flickering discharge cones. The structures glowed with a lilac radiance that seemed to shade into ultraviolet. They receded in all directions – more directions, in fact, than seemed reasonable, given the usual rules of perspective. Somewhere low in his throat he already felt the first queasy constriction of nausea.

"To give you an idea of scale . . ." Austvro said, directing his unwilling attention towards one dizzying feature, " . . . that structure there, if it were mapped into our spacetime, and built from our iron atoms, would be larger than a Jupiter-class gas giant. And yet it is no more than a heat dissipation element, a safety valve on a much larger mechanism. That more distant machine is almost three light-hours across, and it too is only one element in a larger whole."

Fernando fought to keep his eyes open. "How far do these machines extend?"

"At least as far as our instruments can reach. Hundreds of light-hours in all directions. The inclusion penetrates a complex of KR-L machinery larger than one of our solar systems. And yet even then there is no suggestion that the machinery ends. It may extend for weeks, months, of light-travel time. It may be larger than a galaxy."

"Its function?" Seeing her hesitation, he added: "I have the necessary clearance, Doctor. It's safe to tell me."

"Absolute control," she said. "Utter dominance of matter and energy, not just in this brane, but across the entire stack of realities. With this instrumentality, the KR-L could influence events in any brane they selected, in an instant. This machinery makes our graviton pulse equipment – the means by which you arrived here – look like the hamfisted workings of a brain-damaged caveman."

Fernando was silent for a moment, as the pod sped on through the mind-wrenching scenery.

"Yet the KR-L only ever occupied this one brane," he said. "What use did they have for machinery capable of influencing events in another one?"

"Only the KR-L can tell us that," Austvro said. "Yet it seems likely to me that the machinery was constructed to deal with a threat to their peaceful occupation of this one brane."

"What could threaten such a culture, apart from their own bloody-minded hubris?"

"One must presume: another culture of comparable sophistication. Their science must have detected the emergence of another civilization, in some remote brane, hundreds of thousands or even millions of realities away, that the KR-L considered hostile. They created this great machinery so that they might nip that threat in the bud, before it spilled across the stack towards them."

"Genocide?"

"Not necessarily. Is it evil to spay a cat?"

"Depends on the cat."

"My point is that the KR-L were not butchers. They sought their own self-preservation, but not at the ultimate expense of that other culture: whoever *they* might have been. Surgical intervention was all that was required."

Fernando looked around again. Some part of his mind was finally adjusting to the humbling dimensions of the machinery, for his nausea was abating. "Yet they're all gone now. What happened?"

"Again, one must presume: some fatal hesitancy. They created this machinery, but, at what should have been their moment of greatest triumph, flinched from using it."

"Or they did use it, and it came back and bit them."

"I hardly think so, Inspector."

"How many realities have we explored? Eighty, ninety thousand layers in either direction?"

"Something like that," she said, tolerantly.

"How do we know what happens when you get much further out? For that matter, what could the KR-L have known?"

"I'm not sure I follow you."

"I'm just wondering . . . when I was a child I remember someone – I think it was my uncle – explaining to me that the stack was like the pages of an infinitely thick book, a book whose pages reached away to an infinite distance in either direction: reality after reality, as far as you could imagine, with the physics changing only slightly from page to page."

"As good an explanation as the layman will ever grasp."

"But the same person told me there was another theory of the stack: taken a bit less seriously, but not completely discredited."

"Continue," Austvro said.

"The theory was that physics kept changing, but after a while it flattened out again and began to converge back to ours. And that by then you were actually coming back again, approaching our reality from the other direction. The stack, in other words, was circular."

"You're quite right: that theory is taken a bit less seriously."

"But it isn't discredited, is it?"

"You can't discredit an untestable hypothesis."

"But what if it is testable? What if the physics does begin to change less quickly?"

"Local gradients tell you nothing. We'd have to map millions, tens of millions of layers, before we could begin . . ."

"But you already said the KR-L machinery might have had that kind of range. What if they were capable of looking all the way around the stack, but they didn't realize it? What if the hostile culture they thought they were detecting was actually themselves? What if they turned on their machinery and it reached around through the closed loop of realities and nipped *them* in the bud?"

"An amusing conceit, Inspector, but no more than that."

"But a deadly one, should it happen to be true." Fernando stroked his chin tufts, purring quietly to himself as he thought things through. "The Office of Exploitation wishes to make use of the KR-L machinery to deal with another emerging threat."

"The Metagovernment pays my wages. It's up to *it* what it does with the results I send home."

"But as was made clear to me when I arrived, you are a busy woman. Busy because you are approaching your own moment of greatest triumph. You understand enough about the KR-L machinery to make it work, don't you. You can talk to it through the inclusion, ask it do your bidding."

Her expression gave nothing away. "The Metagovernment expects results."

"I don't doubt it. But I wonder if the Metagovernment has been fully appraised of the risks. When they asked you what happened to the KR-L, did you mention the possibility that they might have brought about their own extinction?"

"I confined my speculation to the realm of the reasonably likely, Inspector. I saw no reason to digress into fancy."

"Nonetheless, it might have been worth mentioning."

"I disagree. The Metagovernment is intending to take action against dissident branes within its own realm of colonization, not some barely-detected culture a million layers away. Even if the topology of the layers *was* closed . . ."

"But even if the machinery was used, it was only used once," Fernando said. "There's no telling what other side-effects might be involved."

"I've made many local tests. There's no reason to expect any difficulties."

"I'm sure the KR-L scientists were equally confident, before they switched it on."

Her tone of voice, never exactly confiding, turned chill. "I'll remind you once again that you are on Scrutiny business, not working for Exploitation. My recollection is that you came to investigate leaks, not to question the basis of the entire project."

"I know, and you're quite right. But I can't help wondering whether the two things aren't in some way connected."

"I don't even accept that there are leaks, Inspector. You have some way to go before you can convince me they have anything to do with the KR-L machinery."

"I'm working on it," Fernando said.

They watched the great structures shift angle and perspective as the pod reached the apex of its journey and began to race back towards the inclusion. Fernando was glad when the shaft walls turned opaque and they were again speeding down a dark-walled tunnel, back into what he now thought of as the comparable safety and sanity of Pegasus Station. Until he had recorded and transmitted his memories down the stack, self-preservation still had a strong allure.

"I hope that satisfied your curiosity," Austvro said, when they had disembarked and returned to her lounge. "But as I warned you, the journey was of no value to your investigation."

"On the contrary," he told her. "I'm certain it clarified a number of things. Might I have access to a communications console? I'd like to see if Scrutiny have come up with anything new since I arrived."

"I'll have Caliph provide you with whatever you need. In the meantime I must attend to work. Have Caliph summon me if there is anything of particular urgency."

"I'll be sure to."

She left him alone in the lounge. He fingered the tiger skin rug, repulsed and fascinated in equal measure at the exact match with his own fur. While he waited for the aerial to arrive, he swept a paw over the coffee table, trying to conjure up the image of Austvro's dead husband. But the little figure never appeared.

It hardly mattered. His forensic memory was perfectly capable of replaying a recent observation, especially one that had seemed noteworthy at the time. He called to mind the dead man, dwelling on the way he shaped an invisible form: not, Fernando now realized, a ball, but the ring-shaped stack of adjacent branes in the closed-loop of realities. "Three hundred and sixty degrees," he'd been saying. Meranda Austvro's dead husband had been describing the same theoretical meta-reality of which Fernando's uncle had once spoken. Did that mean that the dead man believed that the KR-L had been scared by their own shadow, glimpsed at some immense distance into the reality stack? And had they forged this soul-crushingly huge machinery simply to strike at that perceived enemy, not realizing that the blow was doomed to fall on their own heads?

Perhaps.

He looked anew at the pattern of cards, untouched since Austvro had taken him from this room to view the KR-L machinery. The ring of cards, arranged for Clock Patience, echoed the closed-loop of realities in her husband's imagination.

Almost, he supposed, as if Austvro had been dropping him a hint.

Fernando was just thinking that through when Caliph appeared, assigning one of his larger spheres into a communications console. Symbols and keypads brightened across the matte grey surface. Fernando tapped commands, claws clicking as he worked, and soon accessed his private data channel.

There was, as he had half-expected, a new message from Scrutiny. It concerned the more detailed analysis of the leaks that had been in motion when he left on his investigation.

Fernando placed a direct call through.

"Hello," said Fernando's down-brane counterpart, a man named Cook. "Good news, bad news, I'm afraid."

"Continue," Fernando purred.

"We've run a thorough analysis on the keyword clusters, as promised. The good news is that the clusters haven't gone away: their statistical significance is now even more certain. There's clearly been a leak. That means your journey hasn't been for nothing."

"That's a relief."

"The bad news is that the context is still giving us some serious headaches. Frankly, it's disturbing. Whoever's responsible for these leaks has gone to immense trouble to make them look as if they've always been part of our data heritage."

"I don't understand. I mean, I *understand*, but I don't get it. There must be a problem with your methods, your data auditing."

Cook looked pained. "That's what we thought, but we've been over this time and again. There's no mistake. Whoever planted these leaks has tampered with the data at a very deep level; sufficient to make it seem as if the clusters have been with us long before the KR-L brane was ever discovered."

Fernando lowered his voice. "Give me an example. Austvro mentioned a play, for instance."

"That would be one of the oldest clusters. *The Shipwreck*, by a paper-age playwright, around 001611. No overt references to the KR-L, but it does deal with a scholar on a haunted island, an island where a powerful witch used to live . . . which could be considered a metaphorical substitute for Austvro and Pegasus Station. Contains a Miranda, too, and . . ."

"Was the playwright a real historical figure?"

"Unlikely, unless he was almost absurdly prolific. There are several dozen other plays in the records, all of which we can presume were the work of the mole."

"Mm," Fernando said, thoughtfully.

"The mole screwed up in other ways too," Cook added. "The plays are riddled with anachronisms; words and phrases that don't appear earlier in the records."

"Sloppy," Fernando commented, while wondering if there was something more to it than mere sloppiness. "Tell me about another cluster."

"Skip to 001956 and we have another piece of faked drama: something called a 'film'; some kind of recorded performance. Again, lots of giveaways: Ostrow for Austvro, Bellerophon – he's the hero who rode the winged horse Pegasus – the KR-L themselves . . . real aliens, this time, even if they're confined to a single planet, rather than an entire brane. There's even – get this – a tiger."

"Really," Fernando said dryly.

"But here's an oddity: our enquiries turned up peripheral matter which seems to argue that the later piece was in some way based upon the earlier one."

"Almost as if the mole wished to lead our attention from one cluster to another." Fernando scratched at his ear. "What's the next cluster?"

"Jump to 002713: an ice opera performed on Pluto Prime, for one night only, before it closed due to exceptionally bad notices. Mentions 'entities in the 83,000th layer of reality'. This from at least 6,000 years before the existence of adjoining braneworlds was proven beyond doubt."

"Could be coincidence, but . . . well, go on."

"Jump to 009655, the premier of a Tauri-phase astrosculpture in the Wenlock star forming region. Supplementary text refers to 'the aesthetic of the doomed Crail' and 'Mirandine and Kalebin'."

"There are other clusters, right up to the near-present?"

"All the way up the line. Random time-spacing: we've looked for patterns there, and haven't found any. It must mean something to the mole, of course . . ."

"If there is a mole," Fernando said.

"Of course there's a mole. What other explanation could there be?"

"That's what I'm wondering."

Fernando closed the connection, then sat in silent contemplation, shuffling mental permutations. When he felt that he had examined the matter from every conceivable angle – and yet still arrived at the same unsettling conclusion – he had Caliph summon Doctor Austvro once more.

"Really, Inspector," she said, as she came back into the lounge. "I've barely had time . . ."

"Sit down, Doctor."

Something in the force of his words must have reached her. Doctor Austvro sank into the settee, her hands tucked into the silvery folds of her dress.

"Is there a problem? I specifically asked . . ."

"You're under arrest for the murder of your husband, Edvardo Austvro."

Her face turned furious. "Don't be absurd. My husband's death was an accident: a horrid, gruesome mistake, but no more than that."

"That's what you wished us all to think. But you killed him, didn't you? You arranged for the collapse of the inclusion, knowing that he would be caught in KR-L spacetime."

"Ridiculous."

"Your husband understood what had happened to the KR-L: how their machinery had reached around the stack, through 360 degrees, and wiped them out of existence, leaving only their remains. He knew exactly how dangerous it would be to reactivate the machinery; how it could never become a tool for the Metagovernment. You said it yourself, Meranda: he feared the machinery. That's because he knew what it had done; what it was still capable of doing."

"I would never have killed him," she said, her tone flatly insistent.

"Not until he opposed you directly, not until he became the only obstacle between you and your greatest triumph. Then he had to go."

"I've heard enough." She turned her angry face towards the aerial. "Caliph: escort the Inspector to the dissolution chamber. He's in clear violation of the terms under which I agreed to this investigation."

"On the contrary," Fernando said. "My enquiry is still of central importance."

She sneered. "Your ridiculous obsession with leaks? I monitored your recent conversation with the homebrane, Inspector. The leaks are what I've always maintained: statistical noise, meaningless coincidences. The mere fact that they appear in sources that are incontrovertibly old . . . what further evidence do you need, that the leaks are nothing of the sort?"

"You're right," Fernando said, allowing himself a heavy sigh. "They aren't leaks. In that sense I was mistaken."

"In which case admit that your mission here was no more than a wild goose chase, and that your accusations concerning my husband amount to no more than a desperate attempt to salvage some . . ."

"They aren't leaks," Fernando continued, as if Austvro had not spoken. "They're warnings, sent from our own future."

She blinked. "I'm sorry?"

"It's the only explanation. The leaks appear in context sources that appear totally authentic . . . because they are."

"Madness."

"I don't think so. It all fits together quite nicely. Your husband was investigating acausal signalling: the means to send messages back in time. You dismissed his work, but what if there was something in it after all? What if a proper understanding of the KR-L technology allowed a future version of the Metagovernment to send a warning to itself in the past?"

"What kind of warning, Inspector?" she asked, still sounding appalled.

"I'm guessing here, but it might have something to do with the machinery itself. You're about to reactivate the very tools that destroyed the KR-L. Perhaps the point of the warning is to stop that ever happening. Some dreadful, unforeseen consequence of turning the machinery against the dissident branes . . . not the extinction of humanity, obviously, or there wouldn't be anyone left alive to send the warning. But something nearly as bad. Something so awful that it must be edited out of history, at all costs."

"You should listen to yourself, Inspector. Then ask yourself whether you came out of the quickening room with all your faculties intact."

He smiled. "Then you have doubts."

"Concerning your sanity, yes. This idea of a message being sent back in time . . . it might have some microscopic degree of credibility if your precious leaks weren't so hopelessly cryptic. Who sends a message and then scrambles the facts?"

"Someone in a hurry, I suppose. Or someone with an imperfect technique."

"I'm sure that means something to you."

"I'm just wondering: what if there wasn't time to get it right? What if the sending of the message was a one-shot attempt, something that had to be attempted even though the method was still not fully understood?"

"That still doesn't explain why the keywords would crop up in . . . a *play*, of all things."

"Perhaps it does, though. Especially if the acausal signalling involves the transmission of patterns directly into the human mind, across time, in a scattergun fashion. The playwright . . ."

"What about him?" she asked, with a knowingness that reminded him she had listened in on his conversation with Cook.

"The man lived and died before the discovery of quantum mechanics, let alone braneworlds. Even if the warning arrived fully-formed and coherent in his mind, he could only have interpreted it according to his existing mental framework. It's no wonder things got mixed up, confused. His conceptual vocabulary didn't extend to vanished alien cultures in adjacent reality stacks. It did extend to islands, dead witches, ghosts."

"Ridiculous. Next you'll be telling me that the other clusters . . ."

"Exactly so. The dramatized recording – the 'film' – was made a few centuries later. The creators did the best they could with their limited understanding of the universe. They knew of space travel, other worlds. Closer to the truth than the playwright, but still limited by the mental prison of their contemporary world-view. The same goes for all the other clusters, I'm willing to bet."

"Let me get this straight," Austvro said. "The future Meta-government resurrects ancient KR-L time-signalling machinery, technology that it barely understands. It attempts to send a message back in time, but it ends up spraying it through history, back to the time of a man who probably thought the Sun ran on coal."

"Maybe even earlier," Fernando said. "There's nothing to say there aren't other clusters, lurking in the statistical noise . . ."

Austvro cut him off. "And yet despite this limited understanding of the machinery, the – as you said – scattershot approach – they still managed to score direct hits into the heads of playwrights, dramatists, sculptors . . ." She shook her head pityingly.

"Not necessarily," Fernando said. "We only know that these people became what they were in our timeline. It might have been the warning itself that set these individuals on their artistic courses . . . planting a seed, a vaguely-felt anxiety, that they had no choice but to exorcise through creative expression, be it a play, a film, or an ice-opera on Pluto Prime."

"I'll give you credit, Inspector: you really know how to take an argument beyond its logical limit. You're actually suggesting that if the signalling hadn't taken place, none of these works of art would ever have existed?"

He shrugged. "If you admit the possibility of time messages . . ."

"I don't. Not at all."

"It doesn't matter. I'd hoped to convince you – I thought it might make your arrest an easier matter for both of us – but it's really not necessary. You understand now, though, why I must put an end to your research. Scrutiny and Exploitation can decide for themselves whether there's any truth in my theory."

"And if they don't think there is – then I'll be allowed to resume my studies?"

"There's still the small matter of your murder charge, Meranda."

She looked sad. "I'd hoped you might have forgotten."

"It's not my job to forget."

"How did you guess?"

"I didn't guess," he said. "You led me to it. More than that: I think some part of you – some hidden, subconscious part – actually wanted me to learn the truth. If not, that was a very unfortunate choice of card game, Meranda."

"You're saying I wanted you to arrest me?"

"I can't believe that you ever hated your husband enough to kill him. You just hated the way he opposed your research. For that reason he had to go, but I doubt that there's been a moment since when what you did hasn't been eating you from inside."

"You're right," she said, as if arriving at a firm decision. "I didn't hate him. But he still had to go. And so do you."

In a flash her hand had emerged from the silvery folds of her dress, clutching the sleek black form of a weapon. Fernando recognized it as a simple blaster: not the most sophisticated weapon in existence, but more than capable of inflicting mortal harm.

"Please, Doctor. Put that thing away, before you do one of us an injury."

She stood, the weapon wavering in her hand, but never losing its lock on him.

"Caliph," she said. "Escort the Inspector to the dissolution chamber. He's leaving us."

"You're making a mistake, Meranda."

"The mistake would be in allowing the Metagovernment to close me down, when I'm so close to success. Caliph!"

"I cannot escort the Inspector, unless the Inspector wishes to be escorted," the aerial informed her.

"I gave you an order!"

"He is an agent of the Office of Scrutiny. My programming does not permit . . ."

"Walk with me, please," Fernando said. "Put the gun away and we'll say no more about it. You're in enough trouble as it is."

"I'm not going with you."

"You'll receive a fair trial. With the right argument, you may even be able to claim your husband's death as manslaughter. Perhaps you didn't mean to kill him, just to strand him . . ."

"It's not the trial," she snarled. "It's the thought of stepping into that *thing* . . . when I came here I never intended to leave. I won't go with you."

"You must."

He took a step towards her, knowing even as he did it that the move was unwise. He watched her finger tense on the blaster's trigger, and for an instant he thought he might cross the space to her before the weapon discharged. Few people had the nerve to hold a gun against an agent of Scrutiny; even fewer had the nerve to fire.

But Meranda Austvro was one of those few. The muzzle spat rapid bolts of self-confined plasma, and he watched in slow-motion horror as three of the bolts slammed into his right arm, below the elbow, and took his hand and forearm away in an agonizing orange fire, like a chalk drawing smeared in the rain. The pain hit him like a hammer, and despite his training he felt the full force of it before mental barriers slammed down in rapid succession, blocking the worst. He could smell his own charred fur.

"An error, Doctor Austvro," he grunted, forcing the words out.

"Don't take another step, Inspector."

"I'm afraid I must."

"I'll kill you." The weapon was now aimed directly at his chest. If her earlier shot had been wide, there would be no error now.

He took another step. He watched her finger tense again, and readied himself for the annihilating fire.

But the weapon dropped from her hand. One of Caliph's smaller spheres had dashed it from her grip. Austvro clutched her hand with the other, massaging the fingers. Her face showed stunned incomprehension. "You betrayed me," she said to the aerial.

"You injured an agent of Scrutiny. You were about to inflict further harm. I could not allow that to happen." Then one of the larger spheres swerved into Fernando's line of sight. "Do you require medical assistance?"

"I don't think so. I'm about done with this body anyway."

"Very well."

"Will you help me to escort Doctor Austvro to the dissolution chamber?"

"If you order it."

"Help me, in that case."

Doctor Austvro tried to resist, but between them Fernando and Caliph quickly had the better of her. Fernando kicked the weapon out of harm's way, then pulled Austvro against his chest with his left arm, pinning her there. She struggled to escape, but her strength was nothing against his, even allowing for the shock of losing his right arm.

Caliph propelled them to the dissolution chamber. Austvro fought all the way, but with steadily draining will. Only at the last moment, when she saw the grey hood of the memory recorder, next to the recessed alcove of the dissolution field, did she summon some last reserve of resistance. But her efforts counted for nothing. Fernando and the robot placed her into the recorder, closing the heavy metal restraining buckles across her body. The hood lowered itself, ready to capture a final neural image; a snapshot of her mind that would be encoded into a graviton pulse and relayed back to the homebrane.

"Meranda Austvro," Fernando said, pushing the blackened stump of his arm into his chest furs, "I am arresting you on the authority of the Office of Scrutiny. Your resurrection profile will be captured and transmitted into the safekeeping of the Metagovernment. A new body will be quickened and employed as a host for these patterns, and then brought to trial. Please compose your thoughts accordingly."

"When they quicken me again, I'll destroy your career," she told him.

Fernando looked sympathetic. "You wouldn't believe how many times I've heard that before."

"I should have skinned you twice."

"It wouldn't have worked. They'd have sent a third copy of me."

He activated the memory recorder. Amber lights flickered across the hood, stabilizing to indicate that the device had obtained a coherent image and that the relevant data was ready to be committed to the graviton pulse. Fernando issued the command, and a tumbling hourglass symbol appeared on the hood.

"Your patterns are on their way home now, Meranda. For the moment you still have a legal existence. Enjoy it while you can."

He'd never said anything that cruel before, and almost as soon as the words were out he regretted them. Taunting the soon-to-be-destroyed had never been his style, and it shamed him that he had permitted himself such a gross lapse of professionalism. The only compensation was that he would soon find himself in the same predicament as Doctor Austvro.

The hourglass vanished, replaced by a steady green light. It signified that the homebrane had received the graviton pulse, and that the resurrection profile had been transmitted without error.

"Former body of Meranda Austvro," he began, "I must now inform you . . ."

"Just get it over with."

Fernando and Caliph helped her from the recorder. Her body felt light in his hands, as if some essential part of it had been erased or extracted during the recording process. Legally, this was no longer Doctor Meranda Austvro: just the biological vehicle Austvro had used while resident in this brane. According to Metagovernment law, the vehicle must now be recycled.

Fernando turned on the pearly screen of the dissolution field. He tested it with a stylus, satisfied when he saw the instant actinic flash as the stylus was wrenched from existence. Dissolution was quick and efficient. In principle the atomic fires destroyed the central nervous system long before pain signals had a chance to reach it, let alone be experienced as pain.

Not that anyone ever *knew*, of course. By the time you went through the field, your memories had already been captured. Anything you experienced at the moment of destruction never made it into the profile.

"I can push you into the field," he told Austvro. "But by all accounts you'll find it quicker and easier if you run at it yourself."

She didn't want it to happen that way. Caliph and Fernando had to help her through the field. It wasn't the nicest part of the job.

Afterwards, Fernando sat down to marshal and clarify his thoughts. In a little while he too would be consumed by fire, only to be reborn in the homebrane. Scrutiny would be expecting a comprehensive report into the Pegasus affair, and it would not do to be woolly on the details. Experience had taught him that a little mental preparation now paid dividends in the long run. The recording and quickening process always blurred matters a little, so the clearer one could be at the outset, the better.

When he was done with the recorder, when the green light had reported safe receipt of his neural patterns, he turned to Caliph. "I no longer have legal jurisdiction here. The 'me' speaking to you is not even legally entitled to call itself Adam Fernando. But I hope you won't consider it improper of me to offer some small thanks for your assistance."

"Will someone come back to take over?" Caliph asked.

"Probably. But don't be surprised if they come to shut down Pegasus. I'm sure my legal self will put in a good word for you, though."

"Thank you," the aerial said.

"It's the least I can do."

Fernando stood from the recorder, and – as was his usual habit – took a running jump at the dissolution field. It wasn't the most elegant of ends – the lack of an arm hindered his balance – but it was quick and efficient and the execution not without a certain dignity.

Caliph watched the tiger burn, the stripes seeming to linger in the air before fading away. Then it gathered its spheres into an agitated swarm and wondered what to do next.

THE WIDTH OF
THE WORLD

Ian Watson

*Ian Watson (b. 1943) is one of those wonderful maver-
icks of science fiction. He doesn't follow the rule book –
rather he bends the rules to suit his purpose. The ideas in
his stories and novels are always radical, frequently
bizarre and invariably fascinating. I have wondered,
from time to time, whether some of this is because
Watson experienced at an early age various other
cultures. He worked in Africa and Japan before he began
to sell stories to the British SF magazines and produced
his first novel,* The Embedding *in 1973. Amongst his
many intriguing novels are such inventive works as*
Deathhunter *(1981),* Queenmagic, Kingmagic *(1986)
and the Black Current sequence that began with* The
Book of the River *(1984). Some of his most unusual
story ideas will be found in his early collections,* The
Very Slow Time Machine *(1979) and* Slow Birds *(1985),
which included this story.*

THERE WERE FOUR of us in Dave Bartram's office at GeoGraphics
that afternoon: Dave himself, puffing his pipe, Sally-Ann from
design, Maggie from marketing, and myself from the computer
graphics side.

After hours of gentle gloomy rain, the sun had finally come out
over Launchester. The steeply pitched slate roofs of the town out-

side were shimmering blue and green as though slicked with oil, while the stone of the cathedral glowed almost golden.

And I was scrapping with Maggie, as usual.

This time it was over the idea I'd had that we ought to expand the Mappamundi to include optional programs for maps of imaginary worlds – Tolkien's Middle Earth, Donaldson's the Land, that sort of thing. I wasn't exactly winning the argument, but I had certainly managed to rile Maggie.

"For heaven's sake, we're just about to launch the Mappamundi! The thing's a surefire bestseller as it is – for the whole educational market, *and* for the mums and dads. And that's because it's an *accurate* record of what the world was like in the past. Your idea would turn it into" – she searched for a suitable term of abuse – "into a video game!"

"I'm betting that we could expand the appeal enormously."

"No takers, Alan. Mappamundi's a serious project."

A brief reprieve, by buzzer. Dave flicked his intercom, and we heard Dorothy sing out from Reception:

"Mr MacNamara called from Heathrow, sir. He said not to bother you in conference, but his flight was late from New York. So he won't be at your house till about seven." Dan MacNamara was our American marketing agent for Mappamundi; this visit mattered to us.

"Right," said Dave. "Call Mrs B, will you? Dinner at eight, to be on the safe side."

In a sense, of course, Maggie was quite right. For Mappamundi – as the brochure boasted – was the ultimate teaching aid: a home computer package displaying on your own TV screen the changing map of the world from the Paleozoic through to modern times. You could zoom in on any million-square-kilometer section; that's roughly the size of France. You could overlay appropriate animated graphics which were just as good as movie footage: of dinosaurs grazing or fighting, of primitive hominids bashing flints together, of the *Niña, Pinta,* and *Santa Maria* sailing to discover America, of Napoleon marching on Moscow . . .

"Apparently a lot of other planes were late, sir."

"Tut tut."

I myself had been hooked on geography, as a boy, by something much more vulgar: an adventure magazine, long defunct, called *Wide World*. I still had a stack of these at home, and every once in a while I hauled them out for a nostalgic chuckle. What lurid covers! And what tall tales inside! Seven-foot-long anacondas out-racing galloping horses; six weeks alone on a raft in the shark-infested South Seas . . .

By the time I grew up, alas, the job of geography was somewhat different. It didn't involve drawing pirate charts with X marking where the sea chest lay buried.

Dave was champing impatiently at his pipe, and it seemed to have gone out.

"Well, Alan?"

"Look, if we include a stylus and digitizing tablet, and modify the software slightly, we can even let people design their own maps – of their own imaginary worlds . . ."

"No," said Maggie flatly.

"But, Dave, don't you think we should keep a trick up our sleeves?"

Our chairman read the auspices in the hot dottle of his pipe bowl.

"Hmm, hmm, hmm," he said.

"I'm willing to work up a presentation in my spare time." Oh, yes, Sarah should *love* that . . . I'd been eating and breathing Mappamundi for the best part of two years now . . .

"Spare time?" said Maggie archly. "I trust you weren't thinking of taking a holiday right now?"

"Whatever for? They don't schedule flights to El Dorado."

"What a weird remark."

"There be no dragons on our maps."

"And a good thing too!"

"We'd better wind this up," said Dave, consulting his watch. "Listen, Alan, your idea *might* have merits. Nothing ventured, eh? So why don't you go ahead and work up something for us to get our teeth into?"

Maggie grinned at me, conceding tactical defeat. But she would make sure, by next time, that she had her teeth sharpened.

It's a twelve-mile drive home over the moors to Ferrier Malvis. The Volvo always got me back there in just under twenty minutes, and

I'd long since stopped paying much conscious heed to the business of steering, or to the sheep grazing amidst heather and bracken.

But this time, just as I was zipping along smartly past a certain ruined dry-stone barn, an alarm bell went off in my head. Because I had left GeoGraphics exactly as usual . . . and I ought to have been home already.

A glance at my watch confirmed this; twenty minutes had passed.

"The world's been stretched," I thought ridiculously. "It's been inflated, like a balloon. The surface looks the same, but there's farther to go."

It didn't seem very likely.

I arrived at Ferrier Malvis fifteen minutes late, and Sarah's green Renault wasn't parked outside the house. She must be late home too, from the craft shop in Forby.

En route to the kitchen, I flipped on a Vivaldi cassette. I poured some chilled wine from the fridge, then opened my briefcase on the pine table, to work in the golden light of the westering sun.

Maybe I was heading for a nervous breakdown? Could the weird stretching of the journey home be a warning sign from my psyche – a shot across the bows?

Presently a car door thumped outside.

"Kitchen, love!"

Silver Sarah looked distraught, as though she had been combing her blond hair with her fingers.

"Hullo, Silver."

"Haven't you been listening to the radio, Alan?"

"No, I was listening to *The Four Seasons*. Should I have been?"

She darted back toward the lounge, presumably to kill the Vivaldi, but checked herself.

"Faster to tell you, my mappaholic husband! The latest planes from the States are landing up to three hours overdue at Heathrow."

"So?"

"One of them just barely got down at Shannon, out of fuel. A jumbo from Brazil has ditched off Lisbon. It's the same all over. It took me *far* too long to drive home."

"Oh, my God, I thought it was just me. Hell, I don't know what I thought it was!"

"Those planes aren't leaking, you know. They're using their fuel. They're still traveling at the same speed."

"And yet there's farther to go – "

"Miles and miles farther."

"I'll get you a drink, love."

"Scotch. Neat."

As I went through to the lounge for the Famous Grouse, *The Four Seasons* was just over. The tape ran on for a moment. Then click, and silence. Silver Sarah followed me.

"So how do you explain it?" She sounded accusatory – as if I had programmed untold square kilometers of blank space into the Mappamundi and these had suddenly sprung into being in the real world.

I poured a few fingers of the noble bird for both of us.

"Something must be happening to space," I said lamely.

"Space?"

"I mean the nature of space. The universe is expanding, isn't it? So space is expanding too. And now the space between places is getting bigger into the bargain. It takes longer to get from A to B." I laughed.

Four hours later – after several more fingers of the bird, a scratch meal and much TV-viewing – we knew that space was just the same today as it had been yesterday. The moon hadn't moved one inch farther away from Earth. Satellite data confirmed that the earth's circumference was exactly the same as usual.

Nevertheless, radar and laser fixes from orbit upon jets sent up specially showed that these aircraft certainly weren't covering the distances as measured by airspeed and fuel consumption. There was much talk that night – to little effect – of lasers and the speed of light and trigonometry, and how photons are massless particles . . .

When we went to bed eventually, all airports around the world were closed, and all flights grounded. Apparently the "distance effect" was still on the increase.

Next morning, when the alarm clock grabbed me out of the middle of some silly dream, the radio was repeating the same bulletin – with minor updates – every fifteen minutes.

The distance effect seemed to have stabilized overnight. Imagine a graph with a curve on it, rising gently at first, then ever more steeply. Distances of up to fifty miles were now doubled. A journey of a hundred miles was in the region of five hundred. And the distance between London and New York, say – measured by radio-wave delays – was something on the order of a hundred thousand miles. It might be as far as a million miles from England to Australia, unless the distance effect followed a bell curve, though no one was certain. The American government, in consultation with the Russians, intended to test-fire an ICBM with an instrument package in place of its warhead from Nevada across the Pacific toward Guam . . .

"Wouldn't they just?" exclaimed Silver. "All they can think about is whether they can still fight a nuclear war! Just try flying a B-1 bomber to Russia now – "

"Or a Backfire bomber from Russia over here."

"Which is why they're going to test a missile, of course! Because a missile leaves the atmosphere."

"It's just to measure the extent of the phenomenon."

"Oh, yes. Of course."

Power transmission through the National Grid was down by some eight per cent, due to loss over extra distances; so consumers were being asked to be sparing in their use of power . . .

"I suppose we'd better do without toast, Silver. How about cornflakes?"

"For goodness' sake!"

"Well, we have to eat."

"Don't you realize anything, Alan? What about fuel? Oil! Raw materials. Imported food. What price New Zealand lamb, coming from a million miles away? The ship would have to carry nothing but fuel. The crew would be old men by the time they docked."

I worked it out in my head. "No, actually it would take the ship about ten years. But I see what you mean."

"I'm *glad* you do. Oh, we'll still be able to hear the news, from a hundred thousand miles away. As Japan grinds to a halt. As people die in famines that no one can reach with food aid. People *like us*, Alan dear."

"God, we'll never see a banana again . . ." Curiously, it was this which popped into my head, rather than the wholesale demise of civilization. Or perhaps as an example of it.

"It'll be like living on Mars. And dying on Mars."

The radio advised commuters with journeys of less than thirty miles to proceed to work normally, but allowing extra time and fuel.

"That's stupid," said Silver. "How long is there going to be any fuel in the filling stations?"

"Do you suggest we walk? I suppose it's possible. Twelve miles to Launchester? In the old days, some kids used to walk twelve miles to school."

"Just what would you be going to Launchester for? Instead of, say, digging up the back lawn quickly – to plant vegetables *tout de suite*? And getting hold of some good egg-laying hens, before everyone realizes?"

"Well, for one thing Dan MacNamara's due at GeoGraphics today."

"What for?"

"The Mappamundi – what did you think?"

"And you're going to be able to export this TV toy a hundred thousand miles to the Land of the Free, in time for Christmas?"

"Look, we shouldn't assume this distance effect is going to continue. It sprang up in a few hours yesterday. It stabilized overnight. It could fade away just as fast. Still I'd better phone Dave to check that Big Mac made it. Let's have orange juice rather than coffee, hmm? And it *isn't* a TV toy, Silver."

Though, come to think of it, with my proposed extras it *could* come to resemble one . . . Maybe Maggie's taunt was on target.

Heading for the phone in my pajamas, I lit a stick of my favorite Algerian camel dung, alias Disque Bleu; and I wondered how far away the factories of the Régie Française de Tabac were today.

Big Mac had indeed reached Dave's house – about three hours late – and Dave agreed with me about the sense of coming in to GeoGraphics. So after a rather fraught, cold breakfast I departed, Volvo-borne, toward Launchester, leaving Silver vowing that she was going to dig up the lawn all by herself and sow carrot or cabbage seed or something, if she could get hold of seed packets at the village shop in Hornton, down the road.

*   *   *

We had all got in to work, but it was a somewhat chastened team which met Big Mac in Dave's office. Redheaded Dan MacNamara was acting in a bluffly amiable way, though I couldn't help noticing a persistent line of sweat along his upper lip, which he wiped away frequently.

After a while, the sales conference ran out of steam.

"Oh, hell," said Big Mac. "Let's stop pretending. It's okay for you guys. You live here."

"And here we may very well starve, too," said I. "Britain isn't self-sufficient. So my wife's busy digging up the lawn right now, to plant cabbages . . . We've *got* to assume that this business is going to reverse itself. And soon."

Maggie drummed her fingers on a brochure.

"Or find some way out. Some way round the phenomenon. We're supposed to be the hotshot cartographers. So how about thinking our way out of this, Alan, instead of ignoring it?"

A challenge. Even with the whole world inflating exponentially, she had managed to sharpen her teeth – as other ladies might find time to powder their noses during an earthquake.

"*Think* our way out of it? Maybe it *is* in the mind? Maybe it's an illusion?" I was just talking off the top of my head.

"If that's so," objected Big Mac, "and we're just imagining it, you'd get planes stalling in midair and autos in the wrong gear, and all."

"True. We've *got* to be covering extra space – but the space has no content. It doesn't contain anything. Because . . ." – and I searched around – "because we can only see the world that's here."

We couldn't see the Wide World of childhood: the world of El Dorado and King Solomon's Mines. Because the map of the world was full up with roads and railways, oil rigs and megalopoli. There was no room left for "Here Be Dragons" or sea serpents. So . . . what if the map of the world had mysteriously expanded to include all of these other things – at precisely the moment when every last geographical detail had at last been calibrated and computerized, including even prehistoric geography? But no one saw anything new. People were just grossly delayed in their travels. *Was* it possible to see something extra, something new, in the interstices of the world? Was it not space which had betrayed us – but vision?

No, it wasn't quite that . . .

The world was overfilled with people: people who all shared a collective unconscious, a dream mind.

When a hive becomes too crowded with bees, the bees know instinctively when to swarm; and away fly half of them to find another hive. But we only had one single hive, one world. So when the urge to swarm came, there was no other space to fly off into . . .

"Penny for them," demanded Maggie. "Penny for your thoughts."

"Oh, I was just wondering how many disappearances have been reported to the police. Missing persons. Dave, you play golf with the chief constable, don't you?"

"Once in a blue moon, lad. What's that got to do with anything?"

"Just a hunch. Would you do me a big favor, and phone him to ask? Please. It'll only take a moment."

In fact, it took many moments to get through, but that was Dorothy's department. Shortly after Dave did finally get to pose the question, he covered the mouthpiece, giving me a peculiar look.

"There are quite *a lot* of people reported missing. He wants to know how *we* knew. At first they thought it was just a case of people not reaching their destinations."

"Oh, they're reaching those, all right!"

"Getting delayed. Running out of petrol, that kind of thing. But a lot of people have promised to phone home, and haven't. There's no sign of them. Here, you'd better talk to him."

I took the handset.

"One thing I *can* tell you," I was saying to the chief constable a little later, "is that you're going to he snowed under with missing person calls by tonight."

"I'll bear this in mind, Mr – ?"

"Roxbury. Alan Roxbury."

"I'll definitely bear you in mind." He rang off unceremoniously, and I could see that Dave was embarrassed by the episode.

"Would you mind going through that again, for us dummies?" asked Big Mac angrily.

"It's like this," I said to him. "Mind constructs reality. Our thoughts make the world – "

"Oh, in a sense!" protested Sally-Ann, with a toss of her brown curls. "In a sort of philosophical sense. But" – and she thumped her hand down hard on Dave's desk – "thus I refute you. Flesh and wood. Solid stuff."

"But what if the mind really does construct reality? And the world has got too small for us. Breakfast in London, second breakfast in New York. We put a girdle round the earth in forty minutes. And every square inch is filled up solid with detail. The world has been shrinking for the last hundred years, faster and faster. Now here comes the bounce-back at last. Or rather, here's where we swarm. As soon as enough people have found the way out, distances should return to normal."

"The way out?" echoed Maggie, incredulous.

"Into the extra spaces."

"Obviously you're under a lot of strain, Alan. Why don't you go home and have a rest?"

"Why don't we *all* go – and look for the way out ourselves? And try to come back again? Of course, there'll be millions of exit points – and by tonight millions of people will have found these, of their own accord. The invisible boundaries. Well, we'll pinpoint one of these. We'll map it. That *was* your bright idea, wasn't it, Maggie? Use our minds. Market the thing."

I hadn't really expected that Dave would want to do anything other than feast Big Mac royally at Launchester's only *Good Food Guide* restaurant, the Sorrento, and sink a few bottles to take all our minds off the collapse (or, rather, the expansion) of the world which we had been so sure of yesterday. Well, he did – and he didn't. Or else he drank more than I noticed. For halfway through the *tagliatelle al prosciutto* he suddenly said, "Okay, lad, we'll give it a try. Nothing ventured, eh?"

And outside, afterward, he handed me the keys to his Jag.

"You drive, lad. Seeing as you know the way."

"Which way?" demanded Maggie.

"Just let him drive. Spontaneously." And Dave jammed his pipe into his mouth.

Pragmatic Sally-Ann would have nothing to do with this charade, and insisted on being dropped back at GeoGraphics; but Maggie was determined to enjoy this proof of my insanity, while

Big Mac was filled with sudden wanderlust, since he was now effectively a prisoner in the Launchester area. (I suppose, similarly, one's immediate response to the threat of starvation could well be a bout of gluttony!) So off we went, and I took the most spontaneous, unconscious route I knew – which happened to be the road home to Ferrier Malvis. We kept our eyes peeled.

Some fifty minutes later I swung the Jaguar into our driveway. Silver's Renault was absent, so she must have driven the two miles (or four miles) to Hornton to buy cabbage seed. If indeed one does grow cabbages from seed . . .

And nothing at all had happened. Except that the journey had taken twice as long as usual.

"You'd better all come in or a drink," I said. "I want to see what Sarah's done to the lawn."

"Good job someone in the family's got their head screwed on." Maggie couldn't resist it. "Oh, by the way, you do realize that you'll have to drive all the way back with us?"

"Eh?"

"To pick up your own car."

God help me . . . ! "So maybe something'll happen on the way back!" I snapped.

Maggie simply laughed.

We went inside, where I told them to help themselves to drinks, while I went through to the kitchen.

Out on the lawn a patch ten yards long by a yard wide had been stripped of its turf – the same turf which we had brought in so expensively a couple of years earlier. Sods were piled in a dirty mass on the patio. The spade was stuck in the upturned soil, upright.

How long would this have taken her? Half an hour. Less than an hour, anyway. Whereupon Silver had decided that I could damn well finish the job. Alternatively, she had panicked about a possible rush on cabbage seed, and driven off to Hornton.

Hours ago. Well before lunch. Now it was three-thirty.

I hurried back to the lounge, where gin was glugging into glasses.

"Got any ice, Alan?"

"Fridge. I have to make a phone call."

I found the number of the Hornton shop in Silver's own neat hand in the red book by the phone.

And Mrs What's-her-name told me that Silver had indeed been in, buying packets of seed – about ten o'clock in the morning. Then she had driven straight back in the direction of Ferrier Malvis.

A distance of two miles. (Or four.) Five hours ago.

I turned to the others. "My wife's gone missing. Sarah's disappeared. She found one of the ways out."

But, of course, as I realized when I returned the Jag and passengers to Dave's personal parking space outside GeoGraphics, the reason why *we* couldn't find any of these exit points was that we were looking for them. We were searching for one in full consciousness of what they were. We *knew*. But it was the unconscious of the world which was at work . . .

Recovering the Volvo, I drove homeward recklessly, pushing my registered speed higher and higher so that (as I imagined) I might take all the longer over the journey. All too soon, it seemed to me, I arrived home.

Fixing myself a stiff shot of the bird – as a gesture toward unconsciousness – I switched on the TV and watched for an hour.

There were missing-persons reports galore by now. An epidemic of them. A veritable Hamelin – with hundreds of thousands of people in these British Isles alone somehow following this Pied Piper of the extra spaces, away into somewhere else. A lot of people had only needed to go for a walk around the corner. Or potter down to the bottom of the garden . . .

Drunk, I took the Volvo out several times that evening to race toward Hornton and back again. But, drunk as I was, I still knew exactly what I was doing.

Finally I slept alone, crying maudlin tears into the pillow for a little while, before the bird put me soddenly to sleep . . .

. . . to wake at dawn, sweaty with the alcohol, to the bright carillon of other birds: finches, blackbirds, thrushes; and to thumb the radio on.

". . .clear signs that the distance effect has been growing steadily less during the past few hours," was what I heard.

"Silver!" I cried – though there was no one to hear me.

Hauling my clothes and shoes on, I raced downstairs unwashed and uncombed. A couple of minutes later, and I was on the road driving hell for leather toward the sharp bends leading up onto the moors.

For the next three hours I drove back and forth between Ferrier Malvis and Launchester, hearing the car radio tell me with increasing optimism that the space anomaly (for such it was being renamed) really was receding as rapidly and inexplicably as it had first arisen.

Silver! Silver! *Where?*

I sped with all the mad possession of the last old rat out of Hamelin – and it was I who was left behind while the anomaly closed up seamlessly.

Eventually the Volvo ran out of fuel, by the same tumbled dry-stone barn. I started to walk home. Then I began to run as fast as I could, hoping that by exhausting my body I might entrance myself, and so gain entrance Still. Soon, with a terrible stitch in my side, I had to drop back to walking pace. The pain felt rather like a broken heart.

We are decimated, at the very least. Perhaps one tenth of the human race disappeared during the anomaly, overall. The effect was more severe in highly populated areas. Such as Britain.

Now, six months later, a sort of emotional anesthesia seems to affect our memories of that time – an inability, in retrospect, to focus clearly on what happened, as great as that of the Australian aborigines who reputedly paid no attention whatever to Captain Cook's proud sailing ship when it first anchored off their shores, for the simple reason that there was nothing in their previous experience as huge as it. Like animals we mourned our losses: lowing piteously for a few days, then walking on and forgetting. And at the same time, we're all rather glad to see each other – we who remain. We greet each other joyfully.

Not I, though. Because I failed – by knowing.

The jets fly from Heathrow to New York in exactly the same time as ever they did before. Yet when I drive back from Launchester over the moors, I know that Silver is somewhere out there – except that I can't see her or reach her. She's somewhere in the extra spaces.

Oh, Silver!

Maybe in another ten years' time – or twenty – when the population again reaches swarming density, the seams will open up again, and there'll be a second exodus.

Today I resigned from GeoGraphics. A foolish mistake, said Dave – just at the moment when Mappamundi is really taking off, worldwide, selling in the millions beyond our wildest hopes. It seems that something has triggered, deeply, people's interest in cartography. Hearing of my decision, Maggie brought her teeth together in a satisfied, crocodilian snap. I didn't care.

Tomorrow I shall burn all my old copies of *Wide World Magazine,* out on the strip of soil which Silver cleared. The stainless steel spade still stands upright there, just as she left it – a good test of the manufacturer's boast about weather resistance. I couldn't bear to touch the spade till now. But tomorrow I will, once all the tales of El Dorado and the poison darts of pygmies in the Belgian Congo have been burned. However hard the ground is this winter, I'll dig the ashes in.

I'm going to take over Silver's old job at the craft shop in Forby. I"ll forget about running a Volvo and smoking Disque Bleu and drinking the juice of the bird. In the evenings, come the spring, I'll dig up the rest of the lawn and turn the whole garden over to vegetables, to feed myself cheaply. The hens I'll buy should be good enough company for me.

And I'll wait, till the world widens out again. Then I'll be the first person to walk around the corner. Or to stroll down to the bottom of the garden.

OUR LADY OF THE SAUROPODS

Robert Silverberg

There's no way I can summarize Robert Silverberg's career in one short paragraph. He is amongst science fiction's most prolific and most accomplished writers, producing a stream of highly readable but chiefly formulaic stories in the late 1950s before reinventing himself in the early 1960s to produce another stream of powerfully original award-winning stories and novels. There came a point, though, in the mid-1970s, when Silverberg (b. 1935), grew tired of the trends and marketing within science fiction that was publishing material of little merit, while the more challenging and innovative work, including his own, barely stayed in print. Silverberg announced his retirement from the field, though he continued to write non-fiction and columns. But a writer of Silverberg's achievements was not going to stay quiet for long. He returned a third time in the 1980s to produce another stream of remarkable and varied material. The first story he completed in this latest guise was the following, "Our Lady of the Sauropods", published in Omni, the glossy pop-science companion to Penthouse, that published a considerable amount of highly original material. You might think this story bears some similarity to Michael Crichton's Jurassic Park, but that novel wasn't published until 1990. Silverberg's story appeared ten years earlier and reached a very different finale.

21 August. 0750 hours. Ten minutes since the module meltdown. I can't see the wreckage from here, but I can smell it, bitter and sour against the moist tropical air. I've found a cleft in the rocks, a kind of shallow cavern, where I'll be safe from the dinosaurs for a while. It's shielded by thick clumps of cycads, and in any case it's too small for the big predators to enter. But sooner or later I'm going to need food, and then what? I have no weapons. How long can one woman last, stranded and more or less helpless, aboard Dino Island, a habitat unit not quite fifteen hundred meters in diameter that she's sharing with a bunch of active hungry dinosaurs?

I keep telling myself that none of this is really happening. Only I can't quite convince myself of this.

My escape still has me shaky. I can't get out of my mind the funny little bubbling sound the tiny powerpak made as it began to overheat. In something like fourteen seconds my lovely mobile module became a charred heap of fused-together junk, taking with it my communicator unit, my food supply, my laser gun, and just about everything else. But for the warning that funny little sound gave me, I'd be so much charred junk, too. Better off that way most likely.

When I close my eyes, I imagine I can see Habitat Vronsky floating serenely in orbit a mere one hundred twenty kilometers away. What a beautiful sight! The walls gleaming like platinum, the great mirror collecting sunlight and flashing it into the windows, the agricultural satellites wheeling around it like a dozen tiny moons. I could almost reach out and touch it. Tap on the shielding and murmur, "Help me, come for me, rescue me." But I might just as well be out beyond Neptune as sitting here in the adjoining Lagrange slot. There's no way I can call for help. The moment I move outside this protective cleft in the rock I'm at the mercy of my saurians, and their mercy is not likely to be tender.

Now it's beginning to rain – artificial, like practically everything else on Dino Island. But it gets you just as wet as the natural kind. And just as clammy. Pfaugh.

Jesus, what am I going to do?

0815 hours. The rain is over for now. It'll come again in six hours. Astonishing how muggy, dank, thick the air is. Simply breathing is hard work, and I feel as though mildew is forming on my lungs. I miss Vronsky's clear, crisp, everlasting springtime air. On previous trips to Dino Island I never cared about the climate, But of course I was snugly englobed in my mobile unit, a world within a world, self-contained, self-sufficient, isolated from all contact with this place and its creatures. Merely a roving eye, traveling as I pleased, invisible, invulnerable. Can they sniff me in here?

We don't think their sense of smell is very acute. And the stink of the burned wreckage dominates the place at the moment. But I must reek with fear signals. I feel calm now, but it was different when I got out of the module. Scattered pheromones all over the place, I bet.

Commotion in the cycads. *Something's coming in here!* Long neck, small birdlike feet, delicate grasping hands. Not to worry. Struthiomimus, is all – dainty dino, fragile, birdlike critter barely two meters high. Liquid golden eyes staring solemnly at me. It swivels its head from side to side, ostrichlike, click-click, as if trying to make up its mind about coming closer to me. *Scat!* Go peck a stegosaur. Let me alone.

It withdraws, making little clucking sounds. Closest I've ever been to a live dinosaur. Glad it was one of the little ones.

0900 hours. Getting hungry. What am I going to eat?

They say roasted cycad cones aren't too bad. How about raw ones? So many plants are edible when cooked and poisonous otherwise. I never studied such things in detail. Living in our antiseptic little L5 habitats, we're not required to be outdoors-wise, after all. Anyway, there's a fleshy-looking cone on the cycad just in front of the cleft, and it's got an edible look. Might as well try it raw, because there's no other way. Rubbing sticks together will get me nowhere.

Getting the cone off takes some work. Wiggle, twist, snap, tear – *there*. Not as fleshy as it looks. Chewy, in fact. It's a little like munching on rubber. Decent flavor, though. And maybe some useful carbohydrate.

The shuttle isn't due to pick me up for thirty days. Nobody's apt to come looking for me, or even to think about me, before then. I'm on my own. Nice irony there: I was desperate to get out of Vronsky and escape from all the bickering and maneuvering, the endless meetings and memoranda, the feinting and counterfeinting, all the ugly political crap that scientists indulge in when they turn into administrators. Thirty days of blessed isolation on Dino Island! An end to that constant dull throbbing in my head from the daily infighting with Director Sarber. Pure research again! And then the meltdown, and here I am cowering in the bushes, wondering which comes first, starving or getting gobbled by some cloned tyrannosaur.

0930 hours. Funny thought just now. Could it have been sabotage?

Consider. Sarber and I, feuding for weeks over the issue of opening Dino Island to tourists. Crucial staff vote coming up next month. Sarber says we can raise millions a year for expanded studies with a program of guided tours and perhaps some rental of the island to film companies. I say that's risky for the dinos and for the tourists, destructive of scientific values, a distraction, a sellout. Emotionally the staff's with me, but Sarber waves figures around, shows fancy income projections, and generally shouts and blusters. Tempers running high, Sarber in lethal fury at being opposed, barely able to hide his loathing for me. Circulating rumors – designed to get back to me – that if I persist in blocking him, he'll abort my career. Which is malarkey, of course. He may outrank me, but he has no real authority over me. And then his politeness yesterday (*Yesterday?* An eon ago!) Smiling smarmily, telling me he hopes I'll rethink my position during my observation tour on the island. Wishing me well. Had he gimmicked my powerpak? I guess it isn't hard, if you know a little engineering, and Sarber does. Sorne kind of timer set to withdraw the insulator rods? Wouldn't be any harm to Dino Island itself, just a quick, compact, localized disaster that implodes and melts the unit and its passenger. So sorry, terrible scientific tragedy, what a great loss! And even if by some fluke I got out of the unit in time, my chances of surviving here as a pedestrian for thirty days would be pretty skimpy, right? Right.

It makes me boil to think that someone would be willing to murder you over a mere policy disagreement. It's barbaric. Worse than that, it's tacky.

1130 hours. I can't stay crouched in this cleft forever. I'm going to explore Dino Island and see if I can find a better hideout. This one simply isn't adequate for anything more than short-term huddling. Besides, I'm not as spooked as I was right after the meltdown. I realize now that I'm not going to find a tyrannosaur hiding behind every tree. And even if I do, tyrannosaurs aren't going to be much interested in scrawny stuff like me.

Anyway I'm a quick-witted higher primate. If my humble mammalian ancestors seventy million years ago were able to elude dinosaurs well enough to survive and inherit the earth, I should be able to keep from getting eaten for the next thirty days. And, with or without my cozy little mobile module, I want to get out into this place whatever the risks. Nobody's ever had a chance to interact this closely with the dinos before.

Good thing I kept this pocket recorder when I jumped from the module. Whether I'm a dino's dinner or not I ought to be able to set down some useful observations.

1830 hours. Twilight is descending now. I am camped near the equator in a lean-to flung together out of tree-fern fronds – a flimsy shelter – but the huge fronds conceal me, and with luck I'll make it through to morning. That cycad cone doesn't seem to have poisoned me yet, and I ate another one just now, along with some tender new fiddleheads uncoiling from the heart of a tree fern. Spartan fare, but it gives me the illusion of being fed.

In the evening mists I observe a brachiosaur, half grown but already colossal, munching in the treetops. A gloomy-looking triceratops stands nearby, and several of the ostrichlike struthiomimids scamper busily in the underbrush, hunting I know not what. No sign of tyrannosaurs all day. There aren't many of them here, anyway, and I hope they're all sleeping off huge feasts somewhere in the other hemisphere.

What a fantastic place this is!

I don't feel tired. I don't even feel frightened – just a little wary. I feel exhilarated, as a matter of fact.

Here I sit, peering out between fern fronds at a scene out of the dawn of time.

What a brilliant idea it was to put all the Olsen-process dinosaur reconstructs aboard a little L5 habitat of their very own and turn them loose to re-create the Mesozoic! After that unfortunate San Diego event with the tyrannosaur it became politically unfeasible to keep them anywhere on Earth, I know, but, even so, this is a better scheme. In just a little more than seven years Dino Island has taken on an altogether convincing illusion of reality. Things grow so fast in this lush, steamy, high-CO_2 tropical atmosphere! Of course we haven't been able to duplicate the real Mesozoic flora, but we've done all right using botanical survivors, cycads and tree ferns and horsetails and palms and ginkgos and auracarias, and thick carpets of mosses and selaginellas and liverworts covering the ground. Everything has blended and merged and run amok. It's hard now to recall the bare and unnatural look of the island when we first laid it out. Now it's a seamless tapestry in green and brown, a dense jungle broken only by streams, lakes, and meadows, encapsulated in spherical metal walls some five kilometers in circumference.

And the animals, the wonderful, fantastic, grotesque animals.

We don't pretend that the real Mesozoic ever held any such mix of fauna as I've seen today, stegosaurs and corythosaurs side by side, a triceratops sourly glaring at a brachiosaur, struthiomimus contemporary with iguanodon, a wild unscientific jumble of Triassic, Jurassic, and Cretaceous, a hundred million years of the dinosaur reign scrambled together. We take what we can get. Olsen-process reconstructs require sufficient fossil DNA to permit the computer synthesis, and we've been able to find that in only some twenty species so far. The wonder is that we've accomplished even that much: to replicate the complete DNA molecule from battered and sketchy genetic information millions of years old, to carry out the intricate implants in reptilian host ova, to see the embryos through to self-sustaining levels. The only word that applies is *miraculous*. If our dinos come from eras millions of years apart, so be it: we do our best. If we have no pterosaur and no allosaur and no archaeopteryx, so be it: we may have them yet. What we already have is plenty to work with. Someday there may be separate Triassic, Jurassic, and Cretaceous satellite habitats, but none of us will live to see that, I suspect.

Total darkness now. Mysterious screechings and hissings out there. This afternoon, as I moved cautiously but in delight from the wreckage site up near the rotation axis to my present equatorial camp, sometimes coming within fifty or a hundred meters of living dinos, I felt a kind of ecstasy. Now my fears are returning, and my anger at this stupid marooning. I imagine clutching claws reaching for me, terrible jaws yawning above me.

I don't think I'll get much sleep tonight.

22 August. 0600 hours. Rosy-fingered dawn comes to Dino Island, and I'm still alive. Not a great night's sleep, but I must have had some, because I can remember fragments of dreams. About dinosaurs, naturally. Sitting in little groups, some playing pinochle and some knitting sweaters. And choral singing, a dinosaur rendition of *The Messiah* or Beethoven's Ninth, I don't remember which. I think I'm going nuts.

I feel alert, inquisitive, and hungry. Especially hungry. I know we've stocked this place with frogs and turtles and other small-size anachronisms to provide a balanced diet for the big critters. Today I'll have to snare some for myself, grisly though I find the prospect of eating raw frog's legs.

I don't bother getting dressed anymore. With rain showers programmed to fall four times a day, it's better to go naked anyway. Mother Eve of the Mesozoic, that's me! And without my soggy tunic I find that I don't mind the greenhouse atmosphere of the habitat half as much as I did.

Out to see what I can find.

The dinosaurs are up and about already, the big herbivores munching away, the carnivores doing their stalking. All of them have such huge appetites that they can't wait for the sun to come up. In the bad old days when the dinos were thought to be reptiles, of course, we'd have expected them to sit there like lumps until daylight got their body temperatures up to functional levels. But one of the great joys of the reconstruct project was the vindication of the notion that dinosaurs were warm-blooded animals, active and quick and pretty damned intelligent. No sluggardly crocodilians, these! Would that they were, if only for my survival's sake.

1130 hours. A busy morning. My first encounter with a major predator.

There are nine tyrannosaurs on the island, including three born in the past eighteen months. (That gives us an optimum predator-to-prey ratio. It the tyrannosaurs keep reproducing and don't start eating each other, we'll have to begin thinning them out. One of the problems with a closed ecology – natural checks and balances don't fully apply.) Sooner or later I was bound to encounter one, but I had hoped it would be later.

I was hunting frogs at the edge of Cope Lake. A ticklish business: calls for agility, cunning, quick reflexes. I remember the technique from my girlhood – the cupped hand, the lightning pounce – but somehow it's become a lot harder in the last twenty years. Superior frogs these days, I suppose. There I was kneeling in the mud, swooping, missing, swooping, missing; some vast sauropod snoozing in the lake, probably our diplodocus; a corythosaur browsing in a stand of ginkgo trees, quite delicately nipping off the foul-smelling yellow fruits. Swoop. Miss. Swoop. Miss. Such intense concentration on my task that old T. rex could have tiptoed right up behind me and I'd never have noticed. But then I felt a subtle something, a change in the air, maybe, a barely perceptible shift in dynamics. I glanced up and saw the corythosaur rearing on its hind legs, looking around uneasily, pulling deep sniffs into that fantastically elaborate bony crest that houses its early-warning system. *Carnivore alert!* The corythosaur obviously smelled something wicked this way coming, for it swung around between two big ginkgos and started to go galumphing away. Too late. The treetops parted, giant boughs toppled, and out of the forest came our original tyrannosaur; the pigeon-toed one we call Belshazzar, moving in its heavy, clumsy waddle, ponderous legs working hard, tail absurdly swinging from side to side. I slithered into the lake and scrunched down as deep as I could go in the warm, oozing mud. The corythosaur had no place to slither. Unarmed, unarmored, it could only make great bleating sounds, terror mingled with defiance, as the killer bore down on it.

I had to watch. I had never actually seen a kill before.

In a graceless but wondrously effective way the tyrannosaur dug its hind claws into the ground, pivoted astonishingly, and, using its massive tail as a counterweight, moved in a ninety-degree arc to knock the corythosaur down with a stupendous sidewise swat of its huge head. I hadn't been expecting that. The corythosaur dropped and lay on its side, snorting in pain and feebly waving its limbs. Now came the coup de grace with hind legs, and then the rending and tearing, the jaws and the tiny arms at last coming into play. Burrowing chin-deep in the mud, I watched in awe and weird fascination. There are those among us who argue that the carnivores ought to be segregated – put on their own island – that it is folly to allow reconstructs created with such effort to be casually butchered this way. Perhaps in the beginning that made sense, but not now, not when natural increase is rapidly filling the island with young dinos. If we are to learn anything about these animals, it will only be by reproducing as closely as possible their original living conditions. Besides, would it not be a cruel mockery to feed our tyrannosaurs on hamburger and herring?

The killer fed for more than an hour. At the end came a scary moment: Belshazzar, blood-smeared and bloated, hauled himself ponderously down to the edge of the lake for a drink. He stood no more than ten meters from me. I did my most convincing imitation of a rotting log, but the tyrannosaur, although it did seem to study me with a beady eye, had no further appetite. For a long while after he departed I stayed buried in the mud, fearing he might come back for dessert. And eventually there was another crashing and bashing in the forest – not Belshazzar this time, though, but a younger one with a gimpy arm. It uttered a sort of whinnying sound and went to work on the corythosaur carcass. No surprise: we already knew from our observations that tyrannosaurs had no prejudices against carrion.

Nor, I found, did I.

When the coast was clear, I crept out and saw that the two tyrannosaurs had left hundreds of kilos of meat. Starvation knoweth no pride and also few qualms. Using a clamshell for my blade, I started chopping away at the corythosaur.

Corythosaur meat has a curiously sweet flavor – nutmeg and cloves, dash of cinnamon. The first chunk would not go down. You are a pioneer, I told myself, retching. You are the first human ever to eat dinosaur meat. *Yes, but why does it have to be raw?* No choice about that. Be dispassionate, love. Conquer your gag reflex or die trying. I pretended I was eating oysters. This time the meat went down. It didn't stay down. The alternative, I told myself grimly is a diet of fern fronds and frogs, and you haven't been much good at catching the frogs. I tried again. Success!

I'd have to call corythosaur meat an acquired taste. But the wilderness is no place for picky eaters.

* * *

23 August. 1300 hours. At midday I found myself in the southern hemisphere, along the fringes of Marsh Marsh, about a hundred meters below the equator. Observing herd behavior in sauropods: five brachiosaurs, two adult and three young, moving in formation, the small ones in the center. By *small* I mean only some ten meters from nose to tail tip. Sauropod appetites being what they are, we'll have to thin that herd soon, too, especially if we want to introduce a female diplodocus into the colony. *Two* species of sauropods breeding and eating like that could devastate the island in three years. Nobody ever expected dinosaurs to reproduce like rabbits – another dividend of their being warm-blooded, I suppose. We might have guessed it, though, from the vast quantity of fossils. If that many bones survived the catastrophes of a hundred-odd million years, how enormous the living Mesozoic population must have been! An awesome race in more ways than their mere physical mass.

I had a chance to do a little herd thinning myself just now. Mysterious stirring in the spongy soil right at my feet, and I looked down to see triceratops eggs hatching. Seven brave little critters, already horny and beaky, scrabbling out of a nest, staring around defiantly. No bigger than kittens, but active and sturdy from the moment they were born.

The corythosaur meat has probably spoiled by now. A more pragmatic soul very likely would have augmented her diet with one or two little ceratopsians. I couldn't bring myself to do it.

They scuttled off in seven different directions. I thought briefly of catching one and making a pet out of it. Silly idea.

25 August. 0700 hours. Start of the fifth day. I've done three complete circumambulations of Dino Island. Slinking around on foot is fifty times as risky as cruising around in a module, and fifty thousand times as rewarding. I make camp in a different place every night. I don't mind the humidity any longer. And despite my skimpy diet I feel pretty healthy. Raw dinosaur, I know now, is a lot tastier than raw frog. I've become an expert scavenger – the sound of a tyrannosaur in the forest now stimulates my salivary glands instead of my adrenals. Going naked is fun, too. And I appreciate my body much more, since the bulges that civilization put there have begun to melt away.

Nevertheless, I keep trying to figure out some way of signaling Habitat Vronsky for help. Changing the position of the reflecting mirrors, maybe, so I can beam an SOS? Sounds nice, but I don't even know where the island's controls are located, let alone how to run them. Let's hope my luck holds out another three and a half weeks.

27 August. 1700 hours. The dinosaurs know that I'm here and that I'm some extraordinary kind of animal. Does that sound weird? How can great dumb beasts *know* anything? They have such tiny brains. And my own brain must be softening on this protein-and-cellulose diet. Even so, I'm starting to have peculiar feelings about these animals. I see them *watching* me. An odd, knowing look in their eyes, not stupid at all. They stare, and I imagine them nodding, smiling, exchanging glances with each other, discussing me. I'm supposed to be observing them, but I think they're observing me, too, somehow.

No, that's just crazy. I'm tempted to erase the entry. But I suppose I'll leave it as a record of my changing psychological state, if nothing else.

28 August. 1200 hours. More fantasies about the dinosaurs. I've decided that the big brachiosaur – Bertha – plays a key role here. She doesn't move around much, but there are always lesser dinosaurs in orbit around her. Much eye contact. *Eye contact between dinosaurs?* Let it stand. That's my perception of what they're doing. I get a definite sense that there's communication going on here, modulating over some wave that I'm not capable of detecting. And Bertha seems to be a central nexus, a grand totem of some sort, a – a switchboard? What am I talking about? What's happening to me?

30 August. 0945 hours. What a damned fool I am! Serves me right for being a filthy voyeur. Climbed a tree to watch iguanodons mating at the foot of Bakker Falls. At the climactic moment the branch broke. I dropped twenty meters. Grabbed a lower limb or I'd be dead now. As it is, pretty badly smashed around. I don't think anything's broken, but my left leg won't support me and my back's in bad shape. Internal injuries, too? Not sure. I've crawled into a little rock shelter near the falls. Exhausted and maybe feverish. Shock, most likely. I suppose I'll starve now. It would have been an honor to be eaten by a tyrannosaur, but to die from falling out of a tree is just plain humiliating.

The mating of iguanodons is a spectacular sight, by the way. But I hurt too much to describe it now.

31 August. 1700 hours. Stiff, sore, hungry, hideously thirsty. Leg still useless, and when I try to crawl even a few meters, I feel as if I'm going to crack in half at the waist. High fever.

How long does it take to starve to death?

1 September. 0700 hours. Three broken eggs lying near me when I awoke. Embryos still alive – probably stegosaur – but not for long. First food in forty-eight hours. Did the eggs fall out of a nest somewhere overhead? Do stegosaurs make their nests in trees, dummy?

Fever diminishing. Body aches all over. Crawled to the stream and managed to scoop up a little water.

1330 hours. Dozed off. Awakened to find haunch of fresh meat within crawling distance. Struthiomimus drumstick, I think. Nasty sour taste, but it's edible. Nibbled a little, slept again, ate some more. Pair of stegosaurs grazing not far away, tiny eyes fastened on me. Smaller dinosaurs holding a kind of conference by some big cycads. And Bertha Brachiosaur is munching away in Ostrom Meadow, benignly supervising the whole scene.

This is absolutely crazy.

I think the dinosaurs are taking care of me. But why would they do that?

2 September. 0900 hours. No doubt of it at all. They bring me eggs, meat, even cycad cones and tree-fern fronds. At first they delivered things only when I slept, but now they come hopping right up to me and dump things at my feet. The struthiomimids are the bearers – they're the smallest, most agile, quickest hands. They bring their offerings, stare me right in the eye, pause as if waiting for a tip. Other dinosaurs watching from the distance. This is a coordinated effort. I am the center of all activity on the island, it seems. I imagine that even the tyrannosaurs are saving choice cuts for me. Hallucination? Fantasy? Delirium of fever? I feel lucid. The fever is abating. I'm still too stiff and weak to move very far, but I think I'm recovering from the effects of my fall. With a little help from my friends.

1000 hours. Played back the last entry. Thinking it over. I don't *think* I've gone insane. If I'm sane enough to be worried about my sanity, how crazy can I be? Or am I just fooling myself? There's a terrible conflict between what I think I perceive going on here and what I know I ought to be perceiving.

1500 hours. A long, strange dream this afternoon. I saw all the dinosaurs standing in the meadow, and they were connected to one another by gleaming threads, like the telephone lines of olden times and all the threads centered on Bertha. As it she's the switchboard, yes. And telepathic messages were traveling through her to the others. An extrasensory hookup, powerful pulses moving along the lines. I dreamed that a small dinosaur came to me and offered me a line and, in pantomime, showed me how to hook it up, and a great flood of delight went through me as I made the connection. And when I plugged it in, I could feel the deep and heavy thoughts of the dinosaurs, the slow, rapturous philosophical interchanges.

When I woke, the dream seemed bizarrely vivid, strangely real, the dream ideas lingering as they sometimes do. I saw the animals about me in a new way. As if this is not just a zoological research station but a community, a settlement, the sole outpost of an alien civilization – an alien civilization native to Earth.

Come off it. These animals have minute brains. They spend their days chomping on greenery except for the ones that chomp on other dinosaurs. Compared with dinosaurs, cows and sheep are downright geniuses. I can hobble a little now.

3 September. 0600 hours. The same dream again last night, the universal telepathic linkage. Sense of warmth and love flowing from dinosaurs to me.

And once more I found fresh tyrannosaur eggs for breakfast.

*   *   *

5 September. 1100 hours. I'm making a fast recovery. Up and about, still creaky but not much pain left. They still feed me. Though the struthiomimids remain the bearers of food, the bigger dinosaurs now come close, too. A stegosaur nuzzled up to me like some Goliath-sized pony and I petted its rough, scaly flank. The diplodocus stretched out flat and seemed to beg me to stroke its immense neck.

If this is madness, so be it. There's a community here, loving and temperate. Even the predatory carnivores are part of it. Eaters and eaten are aspects of the whole, yin and yang. Riding around in our sealed modules, we could never have suspected any of this.

They are gradually drawing me into their communion. I feel the pulses that pass between them. My entire soul throbs with that strange new sensation. My skin tingles.

They bring me food of their own bodies, their flesh and their unborn young, and they watch over me and silently urge me back to health. Why? For sweet charity's sake? I don't think so. I think they want something from me. More than that. I think they need something from me.

What could they need from me?

6 September. 0600 hours. All this night I have moved slowly through the forest in what I can only term an ecstatic state. Vast shapes, humped, monstrous forms barely visible by dim glimmer, came and went about me. Hour after hour I walked unharmed, feeling the communion intensify. I wandered, barely aware of where I was, until at last, exhausted, I have come to rest here on this mossy carpet, and in the first light of dawn I see the giant form of the great brachiosaur standing like a mountain on the far side of Owen River.

I am drawn to her. I could worship her. Through her vast body surge powerful currents. She is the amplifier. By her are we all connected. The holy mother of us all. From the enormous mass of her body emanate potent healing impulses.

I'll rest a little while. Then I'll cross the river to her.

0900 hours. We stand face to face. Her head is fifteen meters above mine. Her small eyes are unreadable. I trust her and I love her.

Lesser brachiosaurs have gathered behind her on the riverbank. Farther away are dinosaurs of half a dozen other species, immobile, silent.

I am humble in their presence. They are representatives of a dynamic, superior race, which but for a cruel cosmic accident would rule the earth to this day, and I am coming to revere them, to bear witness to their greatness.

Consider: they endured for a hundred forty million years in ever-renewing vigor. They met all evolutionary challenges, except the one of sudden and catastrophic climatic change, against which nothing could have protected them. They multiplied and proliferated and adapted, dominating land and sea and air, covering the globe. Our own trifling, contemptible ancestors were nothing next to them. Who knows what these dinosaurs might have achieved if that crashing asteroid had not blotted out their light? What a vast irony: millions of years of supremacy ended in a single generation by a chilling cloud of dust. But until then – the wonder, the grandeur . . .

Only beasts, you say? How can you be sure? We know just a shred of what the Mesozoic was really like, just a slice, literally the bare bones. The passage of a hundred million years can obliterate all traces of civilization. Suppose they had language, poetry, mythology, philosophy? Love, dreams, aspirations? No, you say they were beasts, ponderous and stupid, that lived mindless, bestial lives. And I reply that we puny hairy ones have no right to impose our own values on them. The only kind of civilization we can understand is the one we have built. We imagine that our own trivial accomplishments are the determining case, that computers and spaceships and broiled sausages are such miracles that they place us at evolution's pinnacle. But now I know otherwise. Humans have done marvellous, even incredible, things, yes. But we would never have existed at all, had this greatest of races been allowed to live to fulfill its destiny.

I feel the intense love radiating from the titan that looms above me. I feel the contact between our souls steadily strengthening and deepening.

The last barriers dissolve.

And I understand at last.

I am the chosen one. I am the vehicle. I am the bringer of rebirth, the beloved one, the necessary one. Our Lady of the Sauropods am I, the holy one, the prophetess, the priestess.

Is this madness? Then it is madness, and I embrace it.

Why have we small hairy creatures existed at all? I know now. It is so that through our technology we could make possible the return of the great ones. They perished unfairly. Through us, they are resurrected aboard this tiny globe in space.

I tremble in the force of the need that pours from them.

I will not fail you, I tell the great sauropods before me and the sauropods send my thoughts reverberating to all the others.

20 September. 0600 hours. The thirtieth day. The shuttle comes from Habitat Vronsky today to pick me up and deliver the next researcher.

I wait at the transit lock. Hundreds of dinosaurs wait with me, each close beside the next, both the lions and the lambs, gathered quietly their attention focused entirely on me.

Now the shuttle arrives, right on time, gliding in for a perfect docking. The airlocks open. A figure appears. Sarber himself! Coming to make sure I didn't survive the meltdown, or else to finish me off.

He stands blinking in the entry passage, gaping at the throngs of placid dinosaurs arrayed in a huge semicircle around the naked woman who stands beside the wreckage of the mobile module. For a moment he is unable to speak.

"Anne?" he says finally "What in God's name – "

"You'll never understand," I tell him. I give the signal. Belshazzar rumbles forward. Sarber screams and whirls and sprints for the airlock, but a stegosaur blocks the way.

"No!" Sarber cries as the tyrannosaur's mighty head swoops down. It is all over in a moment.

Revenge! How sweet!

And this is only the beginning. Habitat Vronsky lies just one hundred twenty kilometers away. Elsewhere in the Lagrange belt are hundreds of other habitats ripe for conquest. The earth itself is within easy reach. I have no idea yet how it will be accomplished, but I know it will be done and done successfully, and I will be the instrument by which it is done.

I stretch forth my arms to the mighty creatures that surround me. I feel their strength, their power, their harmony. I am one with them, and they with me. The Great Race has returned, and I am its priestess. Let the small hairy ones tremble!

INTO THE MIRANDA RIFT

G. David Nordley

Here's our second novella – almost a short novel, at
25,000 words. And I'm sure you'll find you've never read
25,000 words so quickly. Taking its cue from Jules
Verne's Journey to the Centre of the Earth, Nordley
considers how explorers are going to survive and escape
if they find themselves trapped under the surface of
Uranus's mini-moon, Miranda.

Gerald David Nordley (b. 1947) trained as an airman,
but his subsequent career has been mostly as an astro-
nautical engineer, managing satellite operations,
engineering, and advanced propulsion research, and
rising to the rank of Major. His stories began to appear
in the SF magazines, chiefly Analog, in 1991, soon after
his retirement. His work is pure hard-tech SF and has
included several related stories taking our explorers to
some of the most hostile environments of the solar
system. But this one beats all. Surprisingly only a handful
of Nordley's stories have appeared in book form, and
those were a series involving the colonization of Mars,
After the Vikings (2001). This story and the related
stories "The Protean Solution", "Dawn Venus" and
"Crossing Chao Meng Fu" are screaming out for a
collection, but until that happens, we can enjoy this one.

I

THIS STARTS AFTER WE had already walked, crawled, and clawed our way fifty-three zig-zagging kilometres into the Great Miranda Rift, and had already penetrated seventeen kilometres below the mean surface. It starts because the mother of all Miranda-quakes just shut the door behind us and the chances of this being rescued are somewhat better than mine; I need to do more than just take notes for a future article. It starts because I have faith in human stubbornness, even in a hopeless endeavour; and I think the rescuers will come, eventually. I am Wojciech Bubka and this is my journal.

Miranda, satellite of Uranus, is a cosmic metaphor about those things in creation that come together without really fitting, like the second try at marriage, ethnic integration laws, or a poet trying to be a science reporter. It was blasted apart by something a billion years ago and the parts drifted back together, more or less. There are gaps. Rifts. Empty places for things to work their way in that are not supposed to be there; things that don't belong to something of whole cloth.

Like so many great discoveries, the existence of the rifts was obvious after the fact, but our geologist, Nikhil Ray, had to endure a decade of derision, several rejected papers, a divorce from a wife unwilling to share academic ridicule, and public humiliation in the pop science media – before the geology establishment finally conceded that what the seismological network on Miranda's surface had found had, indeed, confirmed his work.

Nikhil had simply observed that although Miranda appears to be made of the same stuff as everything else in the Uranian system, the other moons are just under twice as dense as water while Miranda is only one and a third times as dense. More ice and less rock below was one possibility. The other possibility, which Nikhil had patiently pointed out, was that there could be less of *every-thing*; a scattering of voids or bubbles beneath.

So, with the goat-to-hero logic we all love, when seismological results clearly showed that Miranda was laced with substantial amounts of nothing, Nikhil became a minor solar system celebrity, with a permanent chair at Coriolis, and a beautiful, high strung, young renaissance woman as a trophy wife.

But, by that time, I fear there were substantial empty places in Nikhil, too.

Like Miranda, this wasn't clear from his urbane and vital surface when we met. He was tall for a Bengali, a lack of sun had left his skin with only a tint of bronze, and he had a sharp face that hinted at an Arab or a Briton in his ancestry; likely both. He moved with a sort of quick, decisive, energy that nicely balanced the tolerant good-fellow manners of an academic aristocrat in the imperial tradition. If he now distrusted people in general, if he kept them all at a pleasantly formal distance, if he harboured a secret contempt for his species, well, this had not been apparent to Catherine Ray, MD, who had married him after his academic rehabilitation.

I think she later found the emptiness within him and part of her had recoiled, while the other, controlling, part found no objective reason to leave a relationship that let her flit around the top levels of Solar System academia. Perhaps that explained why she chose to go on a fortnight of exploration with someone she seemed to detest; oh, the stories she would tell. Perhaps that explained her cynicism. Perhaps not.

We entered the great rift three days of an age ago, at the border of the huge chevron formation: the rift where two dissimilar geologic structures meet, held together by Miranda's gentle gravity and little else. Below the cratered, dust-choked surface, the great rift was a network of voids between pressure ridges; rough wood, slap-glued together by a lazy carpenter late on a Saturday night. It could, Nikhil thinks, go through the entire moon. There were other joints, other rifts, other networks of empty places – but this was the big one.

Ah, yes, those substantial amounts of nothing. As a poet, I am fascinated by contradiction and I find a certain attraction to exploring vast areas of hidden emptiness under shells of any kind.

I fill voids, so to speak. I am an explicit rebel in a determinedly impressionist literary world of artful obscurity which fails to generate recognition or to make poets feel like they are doing anything more meaningful than the intellectual equivalent of masturbation – and pays them accordingly. The metaphor of Miranda intrigued me; an epic lay there beneath the dust and ice. Wonders to behold there must be in the biggest underground system of caverns in the known universe. The articles, interviews, and talk shows played out in my mind. All I had to do was get there.

I had a good idea of how to do that. Her name was Miranda Lotati. Four years ago, the spelunking daughter of the guy in charge of *Solar System Astrographic*'s project board had been a literature student of mine at Coriolis university. When I heard of the discovery of Nikhil's mysterious caverns, it was a trivial matter to renew the acquaintance, this time without the impediments of faculty ethics. By this time she had an impressive list of caves, mountains, and other strange places to her credit, courtesy of her father's money and connections, I had thought.

She had seemed a rough edged, prickly woman in my class, and her essays were dry condensed dullness, never more than the required length, but which covered the points involved well enough that honesty had forced me to pass her.

Now, armed with news of the moon Miranda's newly discovered caverns, I decided her name was clearly her destiny. I wasn't surprised when an inquiry had revealed no current relationship. So, I determined to create one and bend it toward my purposes. Somewhat to my surprise, it worked. Worked to the point where it wasn't entirely clear whether she was following my agenda, or I, hers.

Randi, as I got to know her, was something like a black hole; of what goes in, nothing comes out. Things somehow accrete to her orbit and bend to her will without any noticeable verbal effort on her part. She can spend a whole evening without saying anything more than "uh-huh". Did you like the Bach? Nice place you have. Are you comfortable? Do you want more? Did you like it? Do you want to do it again tomorrow?

"Uh-huh."

"Say, if you go into Miranda someone should do more than take pictures, don't you think? I've thrown a few words around in my time, perchance I could lend my services to chronicle the expedition? What do you think?".

"Uh-huh."

My contract with her is unspoken, and is thus on her terms. There is no escape. But we are complementary. I became her salesman. I talked her father into funding Nikhil, and talked

Nikhil into accepting support from one of his erstwhile enemies. Randi organized the people and things that started coming her way into an expedition.

Randi is inarticulate, not crazy. She goes about her wild things in a highly disciplined way. When she uses words, she makes lists: "Batteries, CO_2 Recyclers, Picks, Robot, Ropes, Spare tightsuits, Tissue, Vacuum tents, Medical supplies, Waste bags, etc."

Such things come to her through grants, donations, her father's name, friends from previous expeditions, and luck. She worked very hard at getting these things together. Sometimes I felt I fit down there in "etc", somewhere between the t and the c, and counted myself lucky. If she had only listed "back door," perhaps we would have had one.

As I write, she is lying beside me in our vacuum tent, exhausted with worry. I am tired, too.

We wasted a day, sitting on our sausage-shaped equipment pallets, talking, and convincing ourselves to move on.

Nikhil explained our predicament: Randi's namesake quivers as it bobs up in down in its not quite perfect orbit, as inclined to be different as she. Stresses accumulate over ages, build up inside and release, careless of the consequences. We had discovered, he said, that Miranda is still shrinking through the gradual collapse of its caverns during such quakes. Also, because the gravity is so low, it might take years for a series of quakes and aftershocks to play itself out. The quake danger wouldn't subside until long after we escaped, or died.

We had to make sure the front door was closed. It was – slammed shut: the wide gallery we traversed to arrive at this cavern is now a seam, a disjoint. A scar and a change of colour remain to demarcate the forcible fusion of two previously separate layers of clathrate.

Sam jammed all four arms into the wall, anchored them with piton fingers, pressed part of its composite belly right against the new seam, and pinged until it had an image of the obstructed passage. "The closure goes back at least a kilometre," it announced.

The fibre-optic line we have been trailing for the last three days no longer reached the surface either. Sam removed the useless line from the comm set and held it against the business end of its laser radar. "The break's about fifteen kilometres from here," it reported.

"How do you know that?" I asked.

"Partial mirror." Randi explained on Sam's behalf. "Internal reflection."

Fifteen kilometres, I reflected. Not that we really could have dug through even one kilometre, but we'd done some pretending. Now the pretence ceased, and we faced reality.

I had little fear of sudden death, and in space exploration, the rare death is usually sudden. My attitude toward the risks of our expedition was that if I succeeded, the rewards would be great, and if I got killed, it wouldn't matter. I should have thought more about the possibility of enduring a long, drawn-out process of having life slowly and painfully drain away from me, buried in a clathrate tomb.

Then the group was silent for a long time. For my part, I was reviewing ways to painlessly end my life before the universe did it for me without concern for my suffering.

Then Nikhil's voice filled the void. "Friends, we knew the risks. If it's any consolation, that was the biggest quake recorded since instruments were put on this moon. By a factor of ten. That kind of adjustment," he waved his arms at obvious evidences of faults in the cavern around us, "should have been over with a hundred million years ago. Wretched luck, I'm afraid."

"Perhaps it will open up again?" his wife asked, her light features creased with concern behind the invisible faceplate of her helmet.

Nikhil missed the irony in her voice and answered his wife's question with an irony of his own. "Perhaps it will. In another hundred million years." He actually smiled.

Randi spoke softly; "Twenty days, CO_2 catalyst runs out in twenty days. We have two weeks of food at regular rations, but can we stretch that to a month or more. We have about a month of water each, depending on how severely we ration it. We can always get more by chipping ice and running it through our waste reprocessors. But without the catalyst, we can't make air."

"And we can't stop breathing," Cathy added.

"Cathy," I ask, "I suppose it is traditional for poets to think this way, so I'll ask the question. Is there any way to, well, end this gracefully, if and when we have to?"

"Several," she replied a shrug. "I can knock you out first, with anaesthetic. Then kill you."

"How?" I ask.

"Does it matter?"

"To a poet, yes."

She nodded, and smiled. "Then, Wojciech, I shall put a piton through your heart, lest you rise again and in doing so devalue your manuscripts which by then will be selling for millions." Cathy's rare smiles have teeth in them.

"My dear," Nikhil said, our helmet transceivers faithfully reproducing the condescension in his tone, "your bedside manner is showing."

"My dear," Cathy murmured, "what would you know about anything to do with a bed?"

Snipe and countersnipe. Perhaps such repartee held their marriage together, like gluons hold a meson together until it annihilates itself.

Sam returned from the 'front door'. "We can't go back that way, and our Rescuers can't come that way in twenty days with existing drilling equipment. I suggest we go somewhere else." A robot has the option of being logical at times like this.

"Quite right. If we wait here," Nikhil offered, "Miranda may remove the option of slow death, assisted or otherwise. Aftershocks are likely."

"Aftershocks, cave-in, suffocation," Randi listed the possibilities, "or other exits."

Nikhil shrugged and pointed to the opposite side of the cavern. "Shall we?"

"I'll follow you to hell, darling," Cathy answered.

Randi and I exchanged a glance which said; thank the lucky stars for *you*.

"Maps, such as they are," Randi began. "Rations, sleep schedule, leadership, and so on. Make decisions now, while we can think." At this she looked Nikhil straight in the eye, "While we care."

"Very well then," Nikhil responded with a shrug. "Sam is a bit uncreative when confronted with the unknown, Cathy and Wojciech have different areas of expertise, so perhaps Randi and I should take turns leading the pitches. I propose that we don't slight ourselves on the evening meal, but make do with minimal snacks at other times . . ."

"My darling idiot, we need protein energy for the work," Cathy interrupted. "We will have a good breakfast, even at the expense of dinner."

"Perhaps we could compromise on lunch," I offered.

"Travel distance, energy level, sustained alertness."

"On the other hand," I corrected, "moderation in all things . . ."

By the time we finally got going, we were approaching the start of the next sleep period, and Randi had effectively decided everything. We went single file behind the alternating pitch leaders. I towed one pallet, Cathy towed the other and Sam brought up the rear.

There was a short passage from our cavern to the next one, more narrow than previous ones.

"I think . . . I detect signs of wind erosion," Nikhil sent from the lead, wonder in his voice.

"Wind?" I said, surprised. What wind could there be on Miranda?

"The collisions which reformed the moon must have released plenty of gas for a short time. It had to get out somehow. Note the striations as you come through."

They were there, I noted as I came through, as if someone had sandblasted the passage walls. Miranda had breathed, once upon a time.

"I think," he continued, "that there may be an equilibrium between the gas in Miranda's caverns and the gas torus outside the ring system. Miranda's gravity is hardly adequate to compress that very much. But a system of caverns acting as a cold trap and a rough diffusion barrier . . . hmm, maybe."

"How much gas?" I wondered.

He shook his head. "Hard to tell that from up here, isn't it?"

We pushed half an hour past our agreed stop time to find a monolithic shelter that might prove safe from aftershocks. This passage was just wide enough to inflate our one-metre sleeping tubes end to end. We ate dinner in the one Randi and I used. It was a spare, crowded, smelly, silent meal. Even Nikhil seemed depressed. I thought, as we replaced our helmets to pump down to let the Rays go back to their tent, that it was the last one we would eat together in such circumstances. The ins and outs of vacuum tents took up too much time and energy.

We repressurized and I savoured the simple pleasure of watching Randi remove her tightsuit and bathe with a damp wipe in the end of the tent. She motioned for me to turn while she used the facility built into the end of our pallet, and so I unrolled my notescreen, slipped on its headband, and turned my attention to this journal, a process of clearly subvocalizing each word that I want on the screen.

Later she touched my arm indicating that it was my turn, kissed me lightly and went to bed between the elastic sheets, falling asleep instantly. My turn.

Day four was spent gliding through a series of large, nearly horizontal caverns. Miranda, it turns out, *is* still breathing. A ghost breath to be sure, undetectable except with such sensitive instruments as Sam contains. But there appears to be a pressure differential; gas still flows through these caverns out to the surface. Sam can find the next passage by monitoring the molecular flow.

We pulled ourselves along with our hands, progressing like a weighted diver in an underwater cave; an analogy most accurate when one moves so slowly that lack of drag is unremarkable.

As we glided along, I forgot my doom, and looked at the marbled ice around me with wonder. Randi glided in front of me and I could mentally remove her dusty coveralls and imagine her hard, lithe, body moving in its skin-hugging shipsuit. I could imagine her muscles bunch and relax in her weight-lifter's arms, imagine the firm definition of her neck and forearms. A poet herself, I thought, who could barely talk, but who had written an epic in the language of her body and its movement.

Sam notified us that it was time for another sounding and a lead change. In the next kilometre, the passage narrowed, and we found ourselves forcing our bodies through cracks that were hardly large enough to fit our bones through.

My body was becoming bruised from such tight contortions, but I wasn't afraid my tightsuit would tear; the fabric is slick and nearly invulnerable. On our first day, Randi scared the hell out of me when by taking a hard-frozen, knife-edged sliver of rock and trying to commit hara-kiri with it, stabbing herself with so much force that the rock broke. She laughed at my reaction and told me that I needed to have confidence in my equipment.

She still has the bruise, dark among the lighter, older blemishes on her hard-used body. I kiss it when we make love and she says "Uh-huh. Told you so." Randi climbed Gilbert Montes in the Mercurian antarctic with her father and brother carrying a full vacuum kit when she was thirteen. She suffered a stress fracture in her ulna and didn't tell anyone until after they reached the summit.

The crack widened and, to our relief, gave onto another cavern, and that to another narrow passage. Randi took the lead, Nikhil followed, then me, then Cathy, then Sam.

Sam made me think of a cubist crab, or maybe a small, handle-less lawn mower, on insect legs instead of wheels. Articulate and witty with a full range of simulated emotion and canned humour dialogue stored in its memory, Sam was our expert on what had been. But it had difficulty interpreting things it hadn't seen before, or imagining what it had never seen, and so it usually followed us.

By day's end we had covered twenty-eight kilometres and are another eighteen kilometres closer to the centre. That appeared to be where the road went, though Nikhil said we were more likely to be on a chord passing fifty kilometres or so above the centre, where it seems that two major blocks came together a billion years ago.

This, I told myself, is a fool's journey, with no real chance of success. But how much better, how much more human, to fight destiny than to wait and die.

We ate as couples that night, each in our own tents.

II

On day five, we became stuck.
Randi woke me that morning exploring my body, fitting various

parts of herself around me as the elastic sheets kept us pressed together. Somehow, an intimate dream I'd been having had segued into reality, and I felt only a momentary surprise at her intrusion.

"You have some new bruises," I told her after I opened my eyes. Hers remained closed.

"Morning," she murmured and wrapped herself around me again. Time slowed as I spun into her implacable, devouring, wholeness.

But of course time would not stop. Our helmets beeped simultaneously with Sam's wake up call, fortunately too late to prevent another part of me from becoming part of Randi. Sam reminded us, that, given our fantasy of escaping from Miranda's caverns, we had some time to make up.

Randi popped out of the sheets, spun around airborne, in graceful athletic move and slowly fell to her own cot in front of me, exuberantly naked, stretching like a sensual cat, staring right into my enslaved eyes.

"Female display instinct; harmless, healthy, feels good."

Harmless? I grinned and reminded her: "But it's time to spelunk."

"Roger that," she laughed, grabbed her tightsuit from the ball of clothes in the end of the tent, and started rolling it on. They go on like a pair of pantyhose, except that they are slick on the inside and adjust easily to your form. To her form. I followed suit, and we quickly depressurized and packed.

It took Sam an hour to find the cavern inlet vent, and it was just a crack, barely big enough for us to squeeze into. We spent an hour convincing ourselves there was no other opportunity, then we wriggled forward through this crack like so many ants, kits and our coveralls pushed ahead of us, bodies fitting any way we could make them fit.

I doubt we made a hundred yards an hour. Our situation felt hopeless at this rate, but Sam assured us of more caverns ahead.

Perhaps it would have been better if Nikhil had been on lead. Larger than Randi and less inclined to disregard discomfort, he would have gone slower and chipped more clathrate, which, as it turned out, would have been faster.

Anyway, as I inched myself forward with my mind preoccupied

with the enigma of Randi, Miranda groaned – at least that's what it sounded like in my helmet, pressed hard against the narrow roof of the crack our passage has become. I felt something. Did the pressure against my ribs increase? I fought panic, concentrating on the people around me and their lights shining past the few open cracks between the passage and their bodies.

"I can't move." That was Cathy. "And I'm getting cold."

Our tightsuits were top of the line "Explorers," twenty layers of smart fibre weave sandwiched with an elastic macromolecular binder. Despite their thinness, the suits are great insulators, and Miranda's surrounding vacuum is even better.

Usually, conductive losses to the cryogenic ice around us are restricted to the portions of hand or boot that happens to be in contact with the surface and getting *rid* of our body heat is the main concern. Thus, the smart fibre layers of our suits are usually charcoal to jet black. But if almost a square metre of you is pressed hard against a cryogenic solid, even the best million atom layer the Astrographic Society can buy meets its match, and the problem is worse, locally.

The old expression, "colder than a witch's tit" might give you some idea of Cathy's predicament.

"I can't do much," I answered, "I'm almost stuck myself. Hang in there."

"Sam," Cathy gasped, her voice a battleground of panic and self-control, "wedge yourself edge up in the crack. Keep it from narrowing any more."

"That's not going to work, Cathy," it replied. "I would be fractured and destroyed without affecting anything."

"Remember your laws!" Cathy shrieked. "You have to obey me. Now do it, before this crushes my ribs! Nikhil, make the robot obey me!"

"Cathy, dear," Nikhil asks, "I sympathize with your discomfort, but could you hold off for a bit. Let us think about this."

"I'll be frozen solid in minutes and you want to think. Damnit, Nikhil, it hurts. Expend the robot and save me. I'm your doctor."

"Cathy," Sam says, "We will try to save you, but we have gone only a hundred kilometres since the quake, and there may be a thousand to go. If we encounter such difficulties every hundred kilometres, there may be on the order of ten of them yet to come. And you only have one robot to expend, as you put it. Sacrificing me now places the others in an obviously increased risk. Nothing is moving now, so thinking does not entail any immediate increased risk."

"DAMN YOUR LOGIC. I'M GETTING FROSTBITE. GET ME OUT OF HERE"

Embarrassed silence slammed down after this outburst, no one even breathing for what seemed like a minute. Then Cathy started sobbing in short panicky gasps, which at least let the rest of us know she was still alive.

Randi broke the silence. "Can the rest of you move forward?"

"Yes," Nikhil answers, "a little."

"Same here," I add.

"Sam," Randi ordered. "Telop bug. Rope."

"I have these things."

"Uh-huh. Have your telop bug bring the rope up to me, around Cathy. When I've got it, put a clamp on it just behind Cathy's feet."

"Yes, Randi," Sam acknowledged its orders. "But why?" It also requested more information.

"So Cathy's feet can . . . grab – uh – get a foothold on it." Randi's voice showed her frustrations with speech, but no panic. "Can you model that? Make an image? See what will happen?"

"I can model Cathy standing on a clamp on the rope, then rotate horizontal like she is, then put the passage around her . . . I've got it!" Sam exclaimed. "The telop's on its way."

"Please hurry," Cathy sobs, sounding somewhat more in control now.

I felt the little crab-like telop scuttling along through the cracks between my flesh and rock. The line started to snake by me, a millimetre Fullerene fibre bundle that could support a dinosaur in Earth gravity, a line of ants marching on my skin. I shivered just as the suit temperature warning flashed red in my visor display. The telop's feet clicked on my helmet as it went by. I waited for what seemed hours that way.

"Grab the line." Randi commanded and we obeyed. "Feet set, Cathy?"

"I can't . . . can't feel the clamp."

"Okay. I'll take up some of the, the slack . . . Okay now, Cathy?"

"It's there. Oh, God I hope this works."

"Right," Randi answered. "Everyone. Grab. Heave."

I set my toe claws and gave it my best effort forward. Nothing seemed to move much.

"Damn!" Randi grunted.

"Use the robot, I'm freezing," Cathy sobbed.

"Dear," Nikhil muttered, "she *is* using the robot. She's just not *being* one."

I started to get cold myself. My toes were dug in, but I couldn't bend my knees, so everything was with the calves. If I could just get my upper legs into it, I thought . . . If I just had a place to stand. Of course, that was it.

"Randi," I asked, "If Cathy grabbed the rope with her hands, stood on Sam and used all of her legs? Wouldn't that make a difference."

Her response was instantaneous. "Uh-huh. Sam, can you, uh, move up under Cathy's feet and, uh, anchor yourself."

"Do you mean under, or behind so that she can push her feet against me?"

"I meant behind, Sam. Uh," Randi struggled with words again. "Uh, Rotate model so feet are down to see what I see, er, imagine."

"Yes . . . I can model that. Yes, I can do that, but Cathy's knees cannot bend much."

"Roger, Sam. A little might be enough. Okay, Cathy, understand?"

"Y – Yes, Randi." Seconds of scraping, silence, then "Okay, I've got my feet on Sam."

"Then let's try. Pull on three. One, two, three."

We all slid forward a bit this time, but not much. Still it was much more progress than we'd made in the last half hour.

"Try again." I feel her take up the slack. "One, two, three."

That time it felt like a cork coming out of the bottle.

Over the next hour, we struggled forward on our bellies for maybe another 110 metres. Then Randi chipped away a final obstruction and gasped.

Haggard and exhausted as I am, my command of the language is inadequate to my feelings as I emerged from the narrow passage, a horizontal chimney actually, onto the sloping, gravelly, ledge of the first great cavern. Involuntarily, I groaned; the transition from claustrophobia to agoraphobia was just too abrupt. Suddenly, there was this immense space with walls that faded into a stygian blackness that swallowed the rays of our lights without so much as a glimmer in return.

My helmet display flashed red numbers which told me how far I would fall, some 600 metres; how long I would fall, just over two minutes, and how fast I would hit, almost ten metres per second; a velocity that would be terminal for reasons not involving air resistance. Think of an Olympic 100-metre champion running full tilt into a brick wall. I backed away from the edge too quickly and lost my footing in Miranda's centigee gravity.

In slow frustration, I bounced; I couldn't get my clawed boots down to the surface, nor reach anything with my hands. Stay calm, I told myself, I could push myself back toward the cavern wall on the next bounce. I waited until I started to float down again and tried to reach the ledge floor with my arm, but my bounce had carried me out as well as down. A look at the edge showed me that my trajectory would take me over it before I could touch it. There was nothing I could do to save myself – my reaction pistol was in a pallet. Visions of Wiley Coyote scrambling in air trying to get back to the edge of a cliff went through my mind, and I involuntarily tried to swim through the vacuum – not fair; at least the coyote had air to work with.

The helmet numbers went red again as I floated over the edge. Too desperate now to be embarrassed, I found my voice and a sort of guttural groan emerged. I took another breath, but before I could croak again, Cathy grabbed my arm and clipped a line to my belt. She gave my hand a silent squeeze as, anchored firmly to a piton, I pressed my back against the wall of the cavern to get as far as I could from the edge of the ledge. I shook. Too much, too much.

I cancelled any judgment I'd made about Cathy. Judge us by how far, not how, we went.

Sam told us the cavern is twenty-seven kilometres long and slants severely downhill. Our ledge topped a 600-metre precipice that actually curved back under us. We gingerly made our camp on the ledge, gratefully retreated to our piton-secured tents, and ate a double ration silently, unable to keep our minds off of the vast inner space which lay just beyond the thin walls of our artificial sanity. Sleep will be welcome.

Day six. The inner blackness of sleep had absorbed my thoughts the way the cavern absorbed our strobes and I woke aware of no dreams. After a warm, blousy, semiconscious minute, the cold reality of my predicament came back to me and I shivered. It had taken a full day to complete the last ten kilometres, including five hours of exhausted unconsciousness beneath the elastic sheets. We would have to make much better time than that.

That morning, Randi managed to look frightened and determined at the same time. No display behaviour this morning – we dressed efficiently, packed our pallet and turned on the recompressors minutes after waking. Breakfast was ration crackers through our helmet locks.

I stowed the tent in the pallet and turned to find Randi standing silent at the edge. She held the Fullerene line dispenser in one hand, the line end in the other, snapped the line tight between them, and nodded. We had, I remembered, fifty kilometres of Fullerene line.

"Randi, you're not considering . . ."

She turned and smiled at me the way a spider smiles to a fly. Oh, yes she was.

"Preposterous!" was all Nikhil could say when Randi explained what she had in mind. Cathy, docile and embarrassed after yesterday's trauma, made only a small, incoherent, frightened, giggle.

And so we prepared to perform one of the longest bungee jumps in history in an effort to wipe out the entire length of the passage in, as it were, one fell swoop. Nikhil drilled a hole through a piece of the cavern wall that looked sufficiently monolithic and anchored the line dispenser to that. Sam, who was equipped with its own propulsion, would belay until we were safe, then follow us.

Randi stretched a short line segment between two pitons and showed us how to use it to brace ourselves against the wall in Miranda's less-than-a-milligee gravity. We held our fly-like position easily and coiled our legs like springs.

"Reaction pistols?" Randi asked.

"Check." Nikhil responded.

"Feet secure?"

Three "Checks" answered.

"Line secure."

Sam said "check."

Randi cleared her throat. "On three now. One, two, *three*."

We jumped out and down, in the general direction of Miranda's centre. After a brief moment of irrational fear, we collected ourselves and contemplated the wonders of relativity as we sat in free fall while the "roof" of the cavern flashed by. It was a strange experience; if I shut my eyes, I felt just like I would feel floating outside a space station. But I opened my eyes and my light revealed the jagged wall of the cavern whipping by a few dozen metres away. It was, I noted, getting closer.

Judiciously taking up the slack in our common line, Nikhil, who was an expert at this, used the reaction pistol to increase our velocity and steer us slightly away from the roof. A forest of ice intrusions, curved like elephant tusks by eons of shifting milligravity, passed by us too close for my comfort as the minuscule gravity and the gentle tugs of the reaction pistol brought us back to the centre of the cavern.

We drifted. Weight came as a shock: our feet were yanked behind us and blood rushed to our heads as the slack vanished and the line started to stretch. Randi, despite spinning upside down, kept her radar pointed "down". We must have spent twenty seconds like that, with the pull on our feet getting stronger with every metre further down. Then, with surprising quickness cavern wall stopped rushing past us. Randi said "Now!" and released the line, leaving us floating dead in space only a kilometre or so from the cavern floor.

I expended a strobe flash to get a big picture of the cavern wall floating next to us. It looks like we are in an amethyst geode; jumbles of sharp crystals everywhere and a violet hue.

"Magnificent," Cathy says with a forced edge in her voice. Trying to make contact with us, to start to put things back on a more normal footing after yesterday, I thought.

"Time to keep our eyes down, I should think," Nikhil reminded her, and the rest of us. "Wouldn't want to screw up again, would we?"

There was no rejoinder from Cathy so I glanced over at her. Her visor was turned towards the crystal forest and apparently frozen in space. A puff from my reaction pistol brought me over to her and my hand on her arm got her attention. She nodded. The crystals were huge, and I wondered at that, too.

I check my helmet display – its inertial reference function tells me I'm fifty kilometres below the surface and the acceleration due to Miranda's feeble gravity is down to seven centimetres per second squared so when we touched down to the rugged terrain a kilometre below in just under three minutes . . . we'd hit it at eleven metres per second – another sprint into a brick wall.

"Randi, I think we're too high." I tried to keep my voice even. This was the sort of thing we left to Sam, but he wasn't with us just now.

As if in answer, she shot a lined piton into the wall next to us, which was starting to drift by at an alarming rate.

"Swing into the wall feet first, stop, fall again," she said.

"Feet towards the wall!" Nikhil echoed as the tension started to take hold, giving us a misleading sense of down. The line gradually pulled taut and started to swing us toward the wall. Then it let go, leaving us on an oblique trajectory headed right towards the forest of crystals. Piton guns are neat, but no substitute for a hammer.

"No problems" Nikhil says. "We dumped a couple of metres per second. I'll try this time."

He shot as Randi reels her line in.

Eventually we swing into the wall. Cathy seemed rigid and terrified, but bent her legs properly and shielded her face with her arms as the huge crystals rushed to meet us.

They shattered into dust at our touch, hardly even crunching as our boots went through them to the wall.

"What the . . ." I blurted, having expected something a little more firm.

"Deposition, not extrusion?" Randi offered, the questioning end of her response clearly intended for Nikhil.

"Quite so. Low gravity hoarfrost. Hardly anything to them, was there?"

"You, you, knew didn't you?" Cathy accused, her breath ragged.

"Suspected," Nikhil answered without a trace of feeling in his voice, "but I braced just like the rest of you. Not really certain then, was I?"

"Hello everyone, see you at the bottom," Sam's voice called out, breaking the tension. Three of us strobe and spot the robot free-falling past us.

The wall on which we landed curved gently to the lower end of the cavern, so we covered the remaining distance in 100-metre leaps, shattering crystals with each giant step, taking some sort of vandalistic delight in the necessity of destroying so much beauty. We caught up to Sam laughing.

"This way," it pointed with one of its limbs at a solid wall, "there is another big cavern, going more or less our way. It seems to be sloped about one for one instead of near vertical."

Our helmet displays reproduced its seismologically derived model which was full of noise and faded in the distance, but clearly showed the slant down.

After a couple of false leads we found a large-enough crack leading into the new gallery. Cathy shuddered as she squeezed herself in.

That cavern was a mere three kilometres deep – we could see the other end. We shot a piton gun down there, and cheered when it held; using the line to keep us centred, we were able to cross the cavern in ten minutes.

Cathy dislodged a largeish boulder as she landed, and it made brittle, tinkling, ice noises as it rolled through some frost crystals.

"Hey," I said when the significance of that got through to me. "I heard that!"

"We have an atmosphere, mostly methane and nitrogen. It's about ten millibars and nearly a hundred Kelvins," Sam answered my implied question. Top-of-the-line robot, Sam.

It occurred to me then that, should we all die, Sam might still make it out. Almost certainly would make it out. So someone will read this journal.

The next cavern went down as well and after that was another. We kept going well past our planned stopping time, almost in a daze. Our hammers made echoes now, eerie high-pitched echo rattling around in the caverns like a steelie marble dropped on a metal plate.

We made camp only 170 kilometres above Miranda's centre, eighty-five below the surface. Nikhil told us that if the rift continued, like this, along a cord line bypassing the centre itself, we were more than one-third of the way through, well ahead of schedule.

Randi came over to me as I hammered in the piton for a tent line and put a hand on my arm.

"Psyche tension; Cathy and Nikhil, danger there."

"Yeah. Not much to do about it, is there?"

"Maybe there is. Sleep with Cathy tonight. Get them away from each other. Respite."

I looked at Randi, she was serious. They say tidal forces that near a black hole can be fatal.

"Boys in one tent, girls in the other?"

"No. I can't give Cathy what she needs."

"What makes you think I can?"

"Care about her. Make her feel like a person."

Honestly, I was not that much happier with Cathy's behaviour than Nikhil's. Though I thought I understood what she was going through and made intellectual allowances, I guess I saw her as being more of an external situation than a person to care about. What Randi was asking wouldn't come easy. Then, too, there was the other side of this strange currency.

"And you? With Nikhil?"

"Skipped a week of classes at Stanford once. Went to a Nevada brothel. Curious. Wanted to know if I could do that, if I needed to, to live. Lasted four days. Good lay, no personality." She tapped the pocket of my coveralls where my personal electronics lived, recording everything for my article. "You can use that if we get out. Secrets are a headache." She shrugged. "Dad can handle it."

"Randi . . ." I realized that, somehow, it fit. Randi seems to be in a perpetual rebellion against comfort and normalcy, always pushing limits, taking risks, seeking to prove she could experience and endure anything. But unlike some mousy data tech who composes sex thrillers on the side, Randi has no verbal outlet. To express herself, she has to live it.

"Randi, I can see that something has to be done for Nikhil and Cathy, but this seems extreme."

"Just once. Hope." She smiled and nestled herself against me.

"Just be nice. Don't worry about yourself. Let her lead. Maybe just hugs and kisses, or listening. But whatever, give. Just one night, okay? So they don't kill themselves. And us."

It took me a minute or so to digest this idea. Another thought occurred to me. Randi and I were single – not even a standard cohab file – but Nikhil and Cathy . . . "Just how are you going to suggest this to them?" I asked.

Randi shook her head and looked terrified. "Not me!"

I don't think I'm going to be able to finish the journal entry tonight.

III

Day seven. Last night was an anticlimax. Nikhil thought the switch was jolly good fun, in fact, he seemed relieved. But Cathy . . . Once her nervousness had run its course, she simply melted into my arms like a child and sobbed. I lay there holding her as she talked.

Born to a wealthy Martian merchant family, she'd been an intellectual rebel, and had locked horns with the authoritarian pastoral movement there, which eventually gave rise to the New Reformation. When she was fifteen, she got kicked out of school for bragging about sleeping with a boy. She hadn't, but: "I resented anyone telling me I couldn't so much that I told everyone that we did."

Her parents, caught between their customers and their daughter, got out of the situation by shipping her off to the IPA space academy at Venus L1. She met Nikhil there as an instructor in an introductory Paleontology class. She got her MD at twenty-two and plunged into archaeo-immunology research. A conference on fossil disease traces linked her up with Nikhil again, who had been ducking the controversy about Miranda's internal structure by using p-bar scans to critique claims of panspermia evidence in Triton sample cores. His outcast status was an attraction for her. They dated.

When he became an instant celebrity, she threw caution to the wind and accepted his proposal. But, she found, Nikhil kept sensual things hidden deep, and there was a cold, artificial hollowness where his sense of fun should be. Cathy said they had their first erudite word fight over her monokini on their honeymoon and they had been "Virginia Woolfing" it ever since.

"Damn dried-up stuffed-shirted bastard's good at it," she muttered as she wrapped herself around me that night. "It stinks in here, you know?" Then she fell asleep with tears in her eyes. She was desirable, cuddly, and beyond the stretch of my conscience.

That morning, when our eyes met and searched each other, I wondered if she had any expectations, and if, in the spirit of friendship, I should offer myself. But I decided not to risk being wrong, and she did nothing but smile. Except, possibly, for that brief look, we were simply friends.

Randi didn't say anything about her night in Nikhil's tent; I didn't expect her to. She gave me a very warm and long hug after she talked to Cathy. We were all very kind to each other as we broke camp and began casting ourselves along a trail of great caverns with the strides of milligee giants.

Cathy passed out the last of our calcium retention pills that morning. In a week or so we would start to suffer some of the classic low-gravity symptoms of bone loss and weakness. It didn't worry us greatly – that was reversible, if we survived.

At day's end, I was not physically exhausted, but my mind was becoming numb with crystal wonders. Where are these crystals coming from? Or rather where had they come from; Sam and Nikhil concur that the existing gas flow, though surprising in its strength, is nowhere near enough to deposit these crystal forests in the few hundred million years since Miranda's remaking.

We were 150 kilometres deep now and Nikhil says these rocks must withstand internal pressures of more than ninety atmospheres to hold the caverns open. Not surprisingly, the large caverns don't come as often now, and when they do, the walls are silicate rather than clathrate; rock slabs instead of dirty ice. I thought I could hear them groan at a higher pitch last night.

"It's after midnight, universal time," Cathy announced. She seemed recovered from her near panic earlier, and ready to play her doctor role again. But there seemed something brittle in her voice. "I think we should get some sleep now." She said this as we pushed our baggage through yet another narrow crack between the Rift galleries Sam kept finding with his sonar, so Randi and I had a chuckle at the impossibility of complying with the suggestion just then. But she has a point. We had come one-half of the way through Miranda in five of our twenty days – well ahead of schedule.

Nikhil on lead, missed her humour and said: "Yes, dear, that sounds like a very good idea to me. Next gallery, perhaps."

"You humans will be more efficient if you're not tired," Sam pointed out in a jocular tone that did credit to its medical support programmers but, I thought, this feigned robot chauvinism probably did not sit well with Cathy.

"We," I answered, "don't have a milligram of antihydrogen in our hearts to feed us."

"Your envy of my superior traits is itself an admirable trait, for it recognizes . . ."

"Shiva!" Nikhil shouted from the head of our column.

"What is it?" Three voices asked, almost in unison.

"Huge. A huge cavern. I . . . you'll have to see it yourselves."

As we joined him, we found he had emerged on another ledge looking over another cavern. It didn't seem to be a particularly large one to start – our lights carried to the other side – just another crystal cathedral. Then I looked down – and saw stars. Fortunately, my experience in "Randi's Room" kept my reaction in check. I did grab the nearest piton line rather quickly, though.

"Try turning off your strobes," Nikhil suggested as we stuck our heads over the ledge again.

The stars vanished, we turned the strobes on again, and the stars came back. The human eye is not supposed to be able to detect time intervals so small, so perhaps it was my imagination. But it seemed as though the "stars" below came on just after the strobe flashed.

"Ninety kilometres," Sam said.

"Ninety kilometres!?" Nikhil blustered in disbelief, his composure still shaken. "How is this possible? Clathrate should not withstand such pressure."

Randi anchored herself, dug into the supply pallet I'd been towing, and came up with a geologists pick. She took a swing at the ledge to which the gentle three and a half centimetres per second local gravity had settled us and a sharp pink made its way to my ears, presumably through my boots.

"Nickel iron?" Nikhil asked.

"Uh-huh. Think so," Randi answered. "Fractured, from here down."

"Maybe this is what broke Miranda up in the first place," Cathy offered.

"Pure supposition," Nikhil demurred. "Friends, we must move on."

"I know. Take samples, analyse later." Randi said. "Got to move."

"Across or down?" I asked. This wasn't a trivial question. Our plan was to follow the main rift, which, presumably, continued on the other side. But down was an unobstructed ninety-kilometre run leading to the very core of the moon. I thought of Jules Verne.

"We need to get out of this moon in less than two weeks," Nikhil reminded us. "We can always come back."

"Central gas reservoir, chimneys, connected." Randi grunted.

After a nonplussed minute, I understood. If we went down the chimney, our path would leave the chord for the centre. The Rift is along the chord; Sam could see it in his rangings. But, not being a gas vent, it wouldn't be well enough connected to travel. We had to find another back door.

"Oh, of course," Nikhil said. "All roads lead to Rome – which also means they all go *from* Rome. The outgassing, the wind from the core, is what connected these caverns and eroded the passages enough to let us pass through. She means our best chance is to find another chimney, and the best place to do that at the core, isn't it."

"Uh-huh," Randi answered.

No one said anything, and, in the silence I swore I could hear dripping, and beneath that a sort of dull throbbing that was probably my pulse. At any rate, the pure dead silence of the upper caverns was gone. I risked another peak down over the edge. What was down there?

"We have a problem," Cathy informed us. "Poison gas. The nitrogen pressure is up to a twentieth of a bar, and that's more than there was on old Mars. It's enough to carry dangerous amounts of aromatics – not just methane, but stuff like cyanogen. I don't know if anyone else has noticed it, but this junk is starting to condense on some of our gear and stink up our tents. It might get worse near the core, and I can't think of any good way to decontaminate."

"Uh, rockets," Randi broke the silence. "Sam's rockets. Our reaction pistols. Try it first."

So we did. We figured out how far to stand from the jets, how long to stand in them – enough to vaporize anything on the surface of our coveralls and equipment, but not long enough to damage it – and how many times we could do it. Sam had enough fuel for 120 full decontaminations – more than we'd ever live to use. Cathy volunteered to be the test article, got herself blasted, then entered a tent and emerged saying it smelled just fine.

We decided to go for the core.

This close to the centre of Miranda, gravitational acceleration was down to just over five centimetres per second squared, about one three-hundredth of earth normal. Five milligees. Release an object in front of you, look away while you count 1001, and look back again: it will have fallen maybe the width of a couple of fingers – just floating. So you ignore it, go about other things and look back after ten minutes. It's gone. It has fallen ten kilometres and is moving three times as fast as a human can run; over thirty metres per second. That's if it hasn't hit anyone or anything yet. Low gravity, they drill you over and over again, can be dangerous.

That's in a vacuum, but we weren't in a vacuum any more. Even with the pallet gear apportioned, we each weighed less than ten newtons – about the weight of a litre of vodka back in Poland, I thought, longingly – and we each had the surface area of a small kite; we'd be lucky to maintain three metres per second in a fall at the start, and at the bottom, we'd end up drifting like snowflakes.

For some reason, I thought of butterflies.

"Could we make wings for ourselves?" I asked.

"Really, wings?" Nikhil's voice dripped with scepticism.

"Wings!" Cathy gushed, excited.

"Sheets, tent braces, tape, line. Could do," Randi offered.

"We are going to be very, very, sorry about this," Nikhil warned.

Four hours later, looking like something out of a Batman nightmare, we were ready.

Randi went first. She pushed herself away from the precipice with seeming unconcern and gradually began to drift downward.

Biting my lip and shaking a bit, I followed. Then, came a stoic Nikhil and a quiet Cathy.

Ten minutes after jumping, I felt a tenuous slipstream and found I could glide after a fashion – or at least control my attitude. After some experimentation, Randi found that a motion something like the butterfly stroke in swimming seemed to propel her forward.

Half an hour down, and we found we could manage the airspeed of a walk with about the same amount of effort. Soon we were really gliding, and could actually gain altitude if we wanted.

After drifting down for another hour we came to the source of the dripping sound I had heard the night before. Some liquid had condensed on the sides of the chimney and formed drops the size of bowling balls. These eventually separated to fall a kilometre or so into a pool that had filled in a crack in the side of the chimney. The Mirandan equivalent of a waterfall looked like a time-lapse splash video full of crowns and blobs, but it was at macroscale and in real time.

"Mostly ethane," Sam told us. Denser and more streamlined than we were, the robot maintained pace and travelled from side to side with an occasional blast from a posterior rocket: a "roam fart" it called it. If I ever get out of this, I will have to speak to its software engineers.

"Wojciech, come look at this!" Cathy called from the far side of the chimney. I sculled over, as did Randi and Nikhil.

"This had better be important," Nikhil remarked, reminding us of time. I needed one, having been mesmerized by drops that took minutes to fall and ponds that seemed to oscillate perpetually.

Cathy floated just off the wall, her position maintained with a sweep of her wings every three or four seconds. As we joined her, she pointed to a bare spot on the wall with her foot. Sticking out near the middle of it was a dirty white "T" with loopholes in each wing.

"It's a piton. It must be."

What she left unsaid was the fact that it certainly wasn't one of ours.

"Sam, can you tell how old it is?"

"It is younger than the wall. But that, however, looks to be part of the original surface of one of Miranda's parent objects. Do you see the craters?"

Now that he pointed it out, I did. There were several, very normal minicraters of the sort you find tiling the fractal surface of any airless moon, except 200 kilometres of rock and clathrate lay between these craters and space. I had the same displaced, eerie feeling I had when, as a child, I had explored the top of the crags on the north rim of the Grand Canyon of the Colorado on Earth, over 2,000 metres above sea level – and found seashells frozen in the rock.

"The piton," Sam added, "is younger than the hoar crystals, because the area was first cleared."

Something clicked in for me then. The crystals surrounding the bare spot were all about a metre long. "Look at the length of the nearby crystals," I said, excited with my discovery. "Whatever cleared the immediate area must have cleared away any nearby crystal seeds, too. But just next to the cleared area it must have just pushed them down and left a base from which the crystals could regenerate. So the height of the crystals just outside the cleared area is the growth since then."

"But what do you think that growth rate is?" Nikhil asked. "We can't tell, except that it is clearly slow now. I regret to say this, because I am as interested as anyone else, but we must move on. Sam has recorded everything. If we regain the surface, other expeditions can study this. If we do not – then it does not matter. So, shall we?"

Without waiting for assent from the others, Nikhil rotated his head down and started taking purposeful wingstrokes towards the centre of Miranda.

"Damn him," Cathy hissed and flew to the piton and, abandoning one wing sleeve, grabbed the alien artifact. So anchored, she put her feet against the wall it protruded from, grasped it with both hands and pulled. Not surprisingly, the piton refused to move.

"Other expeditions. We'll come back," Randi told her.

Cathy gasped as she gave up the effort, and let herself drift down and away from the wall. We drifted with her until she started flying again. We made no effort to catch up to Nikhil, who was by this time a kilometre ahead of us.

The air, we could call it that now, was becoming mistier, foggier. Nikhil, though he still registered in my helmet display, was hidden from view. Sam's radar, sonar, filters and greater spectral range made this a minor inconvenience for him, and he continued to flit from side to side of this great vertical cavern, gathering samples. When we could no longer see the walls, we gathered in the centre. Incredibly, despite the pressure of the core on either side, the chimney widened.

"This stuff is lethal," Cathy remarked. "Everyone make sure to maintain positive pressure, but not too much to spring a leak; oxygen might burn in this. If this chimney were on Earth, the environmental patrol would demolish it."

A quick check revealed my suit was doing okay – but the pressure makeup flow was enough that I would think twice about being near anything resembling a flame. Our suits were designed, and programmed, for vacuum, not chemical warfare; we were taking them well beyond their envelope.

"Chimney needs a name," Randi said. "Uh-huh. Job for a poet, I think."

That was my cue. But the best thing I could come up with on the spot was "Nikhil's Smokestack." This was partly to honour the discoverer and partly a gentle dig at his grumpiness about exploring it. Cathy laughed, at least.

Having nothing else to look at, I asked Sam for a three-dimensional model of the chimney, which it obligingly displayed on my helmet optics. A three-dimensional cut-away model of Miranda reflected off my transparent face plate, appearing to float several metres in front of me. Our cavern was almost precisely aligned with Miranda's north pole, and seemed to be where two great, curved, 100-kilometre chunks had come together. Imagine two thick wooden spoons, open ends facing.

These slabs were hard stuff, like nickel-iron and silicate asteroids. Theories abound as to how that could be; radioactivity and tidal stress might have heated even small bodies enough to become differentiated; gravitational chaos in the young solar system must have ejected many main belt asteroids and some might well have made it to the Uranian gravitational well; or perhaps the impact that had set Uranus to spinning on its side had released a little planetesimal core material into its moon system.

My body was on autopilot, stroking my wings every ten seconds or so to keep pace with Randi while I daydreamed and played astrogeologist, so I didn't notice the air start to clear. The mist-cloud seemed to have divided itself to cover two sides of the chimney, leaving the centre relatively free. Then, they thinned – and through gaps, I could see what looked to be a river running . . . beside? above? below?

"Randi, I think I can see a river."

"Roger, Wojciech."

"But how can that be? How does it stay there?"

"Tides."

"Yes," Nikhil added. "The chimney is almost three kilometres wide now. One side is closer to Uranus than Miranda's centre of mass and moving at less than circular orbital velocity for its distance from Uranus. Things there try to fall inward as if from the apoapsis, the greatest distance, of a smaller orbit. The other side is further away than the centre and moving at greater than orbital velocity. Things there try to move outward.

"The mass of Miranda now surrounds us like a gravitational equipotential shell, essentially cancelling itself out, so all that is left is this tidal force. It isn't much – a few milligees, but enough to define up and down for fluids. In some ways, this is beginning to resemble the surface of Titan, though it's a bit warmer and the air pressure is nowhere near as high."

"Is that water below us?" Cathy asked

"No," Sam answered. "The temperature is only 200 Kelvins, some seventy degrees below the freezing point of water. Water ice is still a hard rock here."

At the bottom, or end, of Nikhil's smokestack was a three-kilometre rock, which had its own microscopic gravity field. The centre of Miranda, we figured, was some 230 metres below us. Close enough; we were effectively weightless. We let Sam strobe the scene for us, then set up our tents. Decontamination was a bit nervy, but most of the bad stuff was settled on either side of the tidal divide, and the air here was almost all cold dry nitrogen.

Nonetheless, set up took until midnight, and we all turned in immediately.

It has been a very long day.

Nikhil and Cathy forgot last night that, while they were in a vacuum tent, the tent was no longer in a hard vacuum. Much of

what we heard was thankfully faint and muffled but what came
through in the wee small hours of the morning of day eight clearly
included things like:

". . . ungrateful, arrogant, pig . . ."

". . . have the self discipline of a chimp in heat . . ."

". . . so cold and unfeeling that . . ."

". . . brainless diversions while our lives are in the balance . . ."

Randi opened her eyes and looked at me, almost in terror, then
threw herself around me and clung. It might seem a wonder that
this steely woman who could spit in the face of nature's worst
would go into convulsions at the sound of someone else's marriage
falling apart, but Randi's early childhood had been filled with
parental bickering. There had been a divorce, and I gathered a
messy one from a six-year-old's point of view, but she had never
told me much more than that.

I coughed, loud as I could, and soon the sound of angry voices
was replaced by the roar of distant ethane rapids.

Randi murmured something.

"Huh?" Was she going to suggest another respite?

"Could we be married? Us?"

It was her first mention of the subject. I'd developed my relationship with her with the very specific intention of creating and
reporting this expedition, and had never, never, hinted to her I had
any other designs on her person or fortune. I'd been pretty sure
that the understanding was mutual.

"Uh, Randi. Look, I'm not sure we should think like that.
Starving poets trying to fake it as journalists don't fit well in your
social circle. Besides, that," I tossed my head in the direction of the
other tent, "*that* doesn't seem to put me in the mood for such
arrangements. Why – "

"Why is: you don't do that." Randi interrupted me. This was
startling; she never interrupted, except in emergencies – she was
the most non-verbal person I knew.

Okay, I thought. This was an emergency of sorts. I kissed her on
the forehead, then stifled a laugh. What a strange wife for a poet
she would be! She sat there fighting with herself, struggling to put
something in words.

"*Why* . . . is sex, working together, adventure, memories of this,
not being afraid, not *fighting*."

My parents had had their usual share of discussions and debates, but raised voices had been very rare. The Rays' loud argument had, apparently, opened some old wounds for Randi. I held her and gave her what comfort I could. Finally, curiosity got the better of me.

"Your parents fought?"

"Dad wouldn't go to parties. Didn't like social stuff. Didn't like mom's friends. His money." Randi looked me in the eye with an expression somewhere between anger and pleading. "So. She had him shot. Hired someone."

I'd never heard anything like that, and anything that happened to papa Gaylord Lotati would have been big news. "Huh?"

"Someone Mom knew knew someone. The punk wasn't up to it. Non-fatal chest wound. Private doctor. Private detective. Real private. A settlement. Uncontested divorce. I was six. All I knew then was dad sick in the hospital for a week. Later mom just didn't come home from one of her trips. A moving van showed up and moved . . . moved some stuff. One of the movers played catch with me. Another van came and moved dad and me to a smaller house. And there was no more yelling, never, and no more mom. So you know now. When you hold me, that kind of goes away. I feel secure, and I want that feeling, forever."

What in a freezing hydrocarbon hell does one say to that? I just rocked her gently and stared at the wall of the tent, as if it could give me an answer. "Look, I care about you, I really do," I finally told her. "But I need to find my own 'whys'. Otherwise, the relationship would be too dependent." I grinned at her. "We should be more like Pluto and Charon, not like Uranus and Miranda."

"Who gets to be Pluto and who gets to be Charon?" she asked, impishly, eyes sparkling through embryonic tears, as she began devouring me. One does not escape from a black hole, and once I fell beneath her event horizon and we merged into a singularity, the question of who is Pluto and who is Charon, to the rest of the universe, mattered not. Nor did whatever noise we made.

We re-entered the real universe late for our next round of back-door searching; Cathy and Nikhil were almost finished packing their pallet when we emerged from our deflated tent. We stared at each other in mutual embarrassment. Nikhil put his hand on his wife's shoulder.

"Sorry. Bit of tension is all, we'll be right." He waved at Miranda around us. "Now, shall we have another go at it?"

"Any ideas of where to look?" I asked.

"Ethane outlet?" Randi inquired.

Yes, I thought, those rivers had to go somewhere. I had, however, hoped to avoid swimming in them.

"There is," Sam announced, "a large cavern on the other side of this siderophilic nodule."

"This what?" Cathy started.

"This bloody three-kilometre nickel iron rock you're standing on," Nikhil snapped before Sam could answer, then he caught himself and lamely added, "dear."

She nodded curtly.

Randi took a couple of experimental swings at the nodule, more, I thought, in frustration than from doubting Sam. "No holes in this. Best check edges," she suggested. We all agreed.

After five hours of searching, it was clear that the only ways out were the ethane rivers.

"Forgive me if I now regret giving in on the rift route," Nikhil had to say. Cathy was in reach, so I gave her hand a pat. She shrugged.

We had a right-left choice, a coin flip. Each side of the tidal divide had it's own ethane river and each river disappeared. Sam sounded and sounded around the ethane lakes at the end of Nikhil's Smokestack. The inner one, on the side toward Uranus, appeared to open into a cavern five kilometres on the other side of "Cathy's Rock," as we called the central nodule. The other one appeared to go seven kilometres before reaching a significant opening, but that opening appeared to lead in the direction of the rift. No one even thought to question Nikhil this time.

Now that the route was decided, we had to face the question of how to traverse it.

"Simple," Cathy declared. "Sam carries the line through, then we all get in a tent and he pulls us through."

"Unfortunately, I cannot withstand ethane immersion for that period of time," Sam said. "And you will need my power source, if nothing else, to complete the journey."

"Cathy," Randi asked. "Ethane exposure, uh, how bad?"

"You don't want to breathe much of it – it will sear your lungs."

"Positive pressure."

"Some could still filter in through your tightsuit pores."

She was right. If moisture and gas from your skin could slowly work its way out of a tightsuit, then ethane could probably work its way in.

Randi nodded. "Block tightsuit pores?"

A loud "What?" escaped me when I realized she was considering. Tightsuits worked because they let the skin exhale – sweat and gasses could diffuse slowly through the porous, swollen, fabric. Stopping that process could be very uncomfortable – if not fatal. But Cathy Ray, MD, didn't seem to be in a panic about it. Apparently, it was something one could survive for a while.

"Big molecules. Got any, Cathy?"

"I have some burn and abrasion coating, semi-smart fibres. The brand name is Exoderm, what about it Sam?"

"Exoderm coating will not go through tightsuit pores. But it has pores of its own, like the tightsuits, and may allow some ethane to work its way in after a while. A few thousand molecules a second per square metre."

Randi shrugged. "And a tightsuit with pores blocked will cut that way down. Too little to worry about."

"I'm going with you," I announced, surprising myself.

Randi shook her head. "You try the outer passage if I don't make it. Get the gook, Cathy."

Cathy opened up one of the pallets and produced a spray dispenser. I started unpacking a vacuum tent.

"This is going to be a little difficult to do in a tent," Cathy mused.

"Wimps. Is it ready?" Randi asked.

Cathy nodded and gave an experimental squirt to her arm. For a moment, the arm looked like it was covered with cotton candy, but the fluff quickly collapsed to a flat shiny patch. Cathy pulled the patch off and examined it. "It's working just fine, all I need is some bare skin and a place to work."

Randi answered by hyperventilating, then before anyone could stop her, she dumped pressure, fluidly removed her helmet, deactivated her shipsuit seals and floated naked before us.

Cathy, to her credit, didn't let shock stop her. "Breathe out, not in, no matter how much you want," she told Randi, and quickly started spraying Randi's back while Randi was still stepping out of the boots. In less than a minute, Randi was covered with the creamy grey stuff. Calmly and efficiently, Randi rolled her tightsuit back on over the goo, resealed, checked and rehelmeted. It was all done in less than three minutes. Nikhil was speechless and I wasn't much better.

"You okay?" I asked, though the answer seemed obvious.

Randi shrugged. "One tenth atmosphere, ninety below, no wind, no moisture, no convection, air stings a bit. Bracing. No problem – goo handles stings. Can hold breath five minutes."

"You . . . you'd best get on with it, now," Cathy said, struggling to maintain a professional tone in her voice. "Your skin will have as much trouble breathing out as the ethane has getting in."

Randi nodded. "Line dispenser. Clips. Piton gun."

I got my act together and dug these things out of the same pallet where Cathy had kept the Exoderm. Randi snapped the free end of the line to her belt, took it off, double-checked the clip, and snapped it back on again.

"Three tugs, okay? Wait five minutes for you to collect yourselves, then I start hauling. Okay?"

We nodded. Then she reached for my helmet and held it next to hers.

"I'll do it. If not, don't embarrass me, huh?"

I squeezed her hand in an extremely inadequate farewell, then she released her boot clamps, grabbed her reaction pistol, and rocketed off to the shore of the ethane lake 1,500 metres away.

There was, I thought, no reason why one couldn't weave a fibre-optic comm line into the test line, and use it for communications as well as for hauling, climbing, and bungee jumping. But ours weren't built that way, and we lost radio with Randi shortly after she plunged into the lake. The line kept snaking out, but, I reminded myself, that could just be her body being carried by the current. I wondered whether there had been a line attached to the alien piton we'd found above, and how long it had hung there.

Assuming success, we prepared everything for the under-ethane trip. Tents were unshipped, and pallets resealed. I broke out another line reel and looped its end through a pitoned pulley on Cathy's Rock, just in case someone did come back this way.

"I doubt that will be needed," Nikhil remarked, "but we'll

be thankful if it is. You're becoming quite proficient, Mr Bubka."

"Thanks."

I kept staring at the dispenser, fighting back the irrational desire to reel her back.

Cathy grabbed the packed pallets and moved them nearer to the shore, where the changed orientation of the milligee fields left her standing at right angles to Nikhil and myself. She chose to sit there and stare at the lake where Randi had vanished.

I stayed and puttered with my pulleys.

Nikhil came up to me. "I don't think of myself as being Bengali, you know," he said out of the blue. "I was ten when my parents were kicked out of Bangladesh. Politics, I understand, though the details have never been too clear to me. At any rate, I schooled in Australia and Cambridge, then earned my doctorate at Jovis Tholus."

I knew all this, but to make conversation, responded. "J.T.U. is New Reformationist, isn't it?"

"It's officially non-sectarian, state supported, you know. The council may lean that way, but the influence is diffuse. Besides, there is no such thing as New Reformationist geology, unless you're excavating the Face of Mars." Nikhil waved his hand in a gesture of dismissive toleration. "So you see, I've lived in both worlds; the cool, disciplined, thoughtful British academic world, and the eclectic, compulsive, superstitious Bengali hothouse."

No question of which one he preferred. I thought, however, to find a chink in his armour. "You are an Aristotelian then?"

"I won't object to the description, but I won't be bound by it."

"Then the golden mean must have some attraction for you, the avoidance of extremes."

"Quite."

"Okay, Nikhil. Consider then, that within rational safeguards, that the spontaneity may be useful. A safety valve for evolutionary imperatives. A shortcut to communication and ideas. Creativity, art. A motivation for good acts; compassion, empathy."

"Perhaps." He gave me a wintry smile. "I am not a robot. I have these things . . ." disgust was evident in the way he said "things", ". . . within me as much as anyone else. But I strive to hold back unplanned action, to listen to and analyse these biochemical rumblings before responding. And I *prefer* myself that way."

"Does Cathy?"

I regretted that as soon as I said it, but Nikhil just shook his helmeted head.

"Cathy doesn't understand the alternative. I grew up where life was cheap and pain commonplace. I saw things in Dum Dum, horrifying things . . . but things that nevertheless have a certain fascination for me." The expression in his unblinking brown eyes was contradictory and hard to read – perhaps a frightened but curious seven-year-old peered at me from beneath layers of adult sophistication. But did those layers protect him from us, or us from him? What had Randi's night with him been like?

"Well," he continued, "Cathy will never experience that sort of thing as long as I keep a grip on myself. She means too much to me, I owe her too much." He shook his head. "If she just would not ask for what I dare not give . . . Between us, fellow?"

I'm not sure how I should have answered that, but just then Sam told us the line had stopped reeling out, I nodded briskly to him and we glided "down" to the ethane river shore to wait for the three sharp tugs that would signal us to follow.

They didn't come. We pulled on the line. It was slack. So we waited again, not wanting to face the implications of that. I update my journal, trying not to think about the present.

IV

It was almost the end of the schedule day when I finally told Cathy to get ready to put the Exoderm on me. There was no debate; we'd probably waited longer than we should have. "Don't embarrass me," Randi had said. Grimly, I determined to put off my grief, and not embarrass her. The fate, I recalled, of many lost expeditions was to peter out, one by one. Damn, I would miss her.

The plan had been to take the other outlet, but we silently disregarded that: I would go the same way, just in case there was any chance of a rescue. I needed that little bit of hope, to keep going.

By the laws of Murphy, I was, of course, standing stark freezing naked in ethane laced nitrogen half-covered with spray gook and holding my breath when the original line went taut. Three times. Cathy and Nikhil had to help seal me back in. I was shaking so hard, almost fatally helpless with relief.

We had to scramble like hell to get Sam, Cathy and Nikhil bagged in an uninflated tent. Since I was ready for immersion, and Randi had apparently survived said immersion, I would stay on the outside and clear us around obstacles. I was still double-checking seals as Randi started hauling. By some grace of the universe, I had remembered to clip my pulley line to the final pallet, and it trailed us into the ethane lake.

It was cold, like skinny-dipping in the Bering Sea. The ethane boiled next to my tightsuit and the space between it and my cover-alls became filled with an insulating ethane froth. With that and the silvery white sheen of maximum insulation, my suit was able to hold its own at something like 290 Kelvins. I shivered and deliberately tensed and relaxed every muscle I could think about, as we slipped through the ethane.

There wasn't much to see, the passage was wide, broadened perhaps by eons of flow. Strobes revealed a fob of bubbles around me, otherwise the darkness smothered everything.

The line drew us up? down? to the inside of the passage, out of the current. I grabbed the line and walked lightly against the tension of the pulling line as if I were rappelling on a low-gravity world. The tent with my companions and our pallets were thus spared bumping along the rough surface.

I asked for the time display, and my helmet told me we'd been under for an hour.

We rounded a corner and entered a much narrower passage. I became so busy steering us around various projections that I forgot how cold I was. But I noted my skin starting to itch.

Then I caught a flash of light ahead. Did I imagine it?

No. In much less time than I thought, the flash repeated, showing a frothy hole in the liquid above us. Then we were at the boiling surface and Randi was waving at us as she pulled us to shore.

I flew out of the water with a kick and a flap of my hands and was in her arms. A minute must have passed before I thought to release the rest of the expedition from their tent cum submarine.

"No solid ground at the end of the main branch. I came up in a boiling sea, full of froth and foam, couldn't see anything. Not even a roof. Had to come back and take the detour." She trembled. "I have to get in a tent quick."

But with all our decontamination procedures, there was no quick about it, and it was 0300 universal on day ten before we were finally back in our tubular cocoons. By that time, Randi was moaning, shivering and only half-conscious. The Exoderm came off as I peeled her tightsuit down and her skin was a bright angry red, except for her fingers and toes, which were an ugly yellow-black. I linked up the minidoc and called Cathy, who programmed a general tissue regenerative, a stimulant, and directed that the tent's insulation factor be turned up.

By 0500, Randi was sleeping, breathing normally, and some of the redness had faded. Cathy called and offered to watch the minidoc so I could get some sleep.

The question I fell asleep with was, that with everyone's lives at stake, could *I* have pushed myself so far?

Day ten was a short one. We were all exhausted, we didn't get started until 1500 hours.

Randi looked awful, especially her hands and feet, but pulled on her back-up tight suit without a complaint. My face must have told her what I was thinking because she shot me a defiant look.

"I'll do my pitch."

But Cathy was waiting for us and took her back into the tent, which repressurized. Nikhil and I shrugged and busied ourselves packing everything else. When the women reappeared, Cathy declared, very firmly, that Randi was to stay prone and inactive.

Randi disagreed. "I do my pitch . . . I, I, have to."

My turn. "Time to give someone else a chance, Randi. Me for instance. Besides, if you injure yourself further, you'd be a liability."

Randi shook her head. "Can't argue. Don't know how. I don't . . . don't want to be baggage."

"I'd hardly call it being baggage," Nikhil sniffed. "Enforced rest under medical orders. Now, if you're going to be a professional in your own right instead of Daddy's little indulgence, you'll chin up, follow medical orders, and stop wasting time."

"Nikhil, dear," Cathy growled, "get your damn mouth out of my patient's psyche."

Nikhil was exactly right, I thought, but I wanted to slug him for saying it that way.

"Very well," Nikhil said, evenly ignoring the feeling in Cathy's voice, "I regret the personal reference, Randi, but the point stands. Please don't be difficult."

Lacking support from anyone else, Randi's position was hopeless. She suffered herself to be taped onto a litter improvised from the same tent braces, sheets, and tape we had used earlier to make her wings.

This done, Nikhil turned to me. "You mentioned leading a pitch?"

Fortunately, the route started out like a one-third scale version Nikhil's Smokestack. It wasn't a straight shot, but a series of vertical caverns, slightly offset. Sam rocketed ahead with a line, anchored himself, and reeled the rest of us up. The short passages between caverns were the typical wide, low, cracks and I managed them without great difficulty, though it came as a surprise to discover how much rock and ice one had to chip away to get through comfortably. It was hard work in a pressure suit, and my respect for Nikhil and Randi increased greatly.

At the end of the last cavern, the chimney bent north, gradually narrowing to a funnel. We could hear the wind blow by us. At the end was a large horizontal cavern, dry, but full of hoar crystals. The rift was clearly visible as a fissure on its ceiling. That was for tomorrow.

The ethane level was down enough for us to forego decontamination, and before we turned in we congratulated ourselves for traversing sixty percent of the rift in less than half our allotted time.

As we turned in, Randi said she had feeling in her fingers and toes again. Which meant she must have had no feeling in them when she was demanding to lead the pitch this afternoon.

She's sleeping quietly, it's only midnight, and I am going to get my first good night's sleep in a long time.

Day eleven is thankfully over, we are all exhausted again, and bitterly disappointed.

The day started with a discovery that, under other circumstances, would have justified the entire expedition; the mummified remains of aliens, presumably those who had left the strange piton. There were two large bodies and one small, supine on the cavern floor, lain on top of what must have been their pressure suits. Did they run out of food, or air, and give up in that way? Or did they die of something else, and were laid out by compatriots we might find elsewhere?

They were six-limbed bipeds, taller than us and perhaps not as heavy in life, though this is hard to tell from a mummy. Their upper arms were much bigger and stronger than their lower ones and the head reminded me vaguely of a Panda. They were not, to my memory, members of any of the five known spacefaring races, so, in any other circumstances, this would have been a momentous event. As it was, I think I was vaguely irritated at the complication they represented. Either my sense of wonder wasn't awake yet, or we'd left it behind, a few geode caverns back.

"How long?" Cathy asked Sam in a hushed voice. She, at least, was fascinated.

"If the present rate of dust deposition can be projected, about 230,000 years, with a sigma of 10,000."

"Except for the pressure suits, they didn't leave any equipment," Nikhil observed. "I take that to mean that this cavern is *not* a dead end – as long as we do press on. You have your images, Sam? Good. Shall we?"

We turned to Nikhil, away from the corpses.

"The vent," he said, looking overhead, "is probably up there."

"The ceiling fissure is an easy jump for me," Sam offered. "I'll pull the rest of you up."

We got on our way, but the rift quit on us.

Once in the ceiling caves, we found there was no gas flowing that way, the way where Sam's seismological soundings, and our eyes, said the rift was. We chanced the passage anyway, but it quickly narrowed to a stomach-crawling ordeal. Three kilometres in, we found it solidly blocked and had to back our way out to return to the cavern. Another passage in the ceiling proved equally unpromising.

"Quakes," Nikhil said. "The rift must have closed here, oh, a hundred million years ago or so – from the dust." So, when dinosaurs ruled the Earth, Miranda had changed her maze, no doubt with the idea of frustrating our eventual expedition in mind.

Finally, Sam found the outlet airflow. It led back to the north.

"I hereby dub this the Cavern of Dead Ends," I proclaimed as we left, with what I hoped was humorous flourish.

Surprisingly, Nikhil, bless his heart, gave me one short "ha!"

Randi was not to be denied today, and took the first pitch out in relief of Nikhil. But she soon tired, according to Cathy, who was monitoring. I took over and pushed on.

The slopes were gentle, the path wide with little cutting to do, and we could make good time tugging ourselves along on the occasional projecting rock and gliding. We took an evening break in a tiny ten-metre bubble of a cavern and had our daily ration crackers, insisting that Randi have a double ration. No one started to make camp, a lack of action that signified group assent for another evening of climbing and gliding.

"We are," Sam said, showing us his map on our helmet displays, "going to pass very close to the upper end of Nikhil's Smokestack." No one said anything, but we knew that meant we were backtracking, losing ground.

There was a final horizontal cavern, and its airflow was toward the polar axis. We could pretty much figure out what that meant, but decided to put off the confirmation until the morning. I'd once read a classic ancient novel by someone named Vance about an imaginary place where an accepted means of suicide was to enter an endless maze and wander about, crossing your path over and over again until starvation did you in. There, you died by forgetting the way out. Here, we did not even know there *was* a way out.

The beginning of day twelve thus found us at the top of Nikhil's Smokestack again, on a lip of a ledge not much different than the one about a kilometre away where we had first seen it. We were very quiet, fully conscious of how much ground we had lost to the cruel calendar. We were now less than halfway through Miranda, with less than half our time left.

Sam circled the top of the Smokestack again, looking for outlets other than the one we had come through. There were none. Our only hope was to go back down.

"Do we," I asked, "try the inner river, or try the other branch of Randi's River and fight our way through the Boiling Sea?"

Nikhil, though he weighed less than three newtons, was stretched out on the ledge, resting. His radio voice came from a still form that reminded me in a macabre way of the deceased aliens back in the Cavern of Dead Ends.

"The Boiling Sea," he mused, "takes the main flow of the river, so it should have an outlet vent. It is obviously in a cavern, so it has a roof. Perhaps we could just shoot a piton up at it, blindly."

But I thought of Nikhil's Smokestack – a blind shot could go a long way in something like that.

"Sam could fly up to it," I offered. "If we protect it until we reach the Boiling Sea's surface, it could withstand the momentary exposure. Once at the ceiling, it could pull the rest of us up."

Cathy nodded and threw a rock down Nikhil's Smokestack, and we watched it vanish relatively quickly. Dense, I thought, less subject to drag. As it turned out, I wasn't the only one with that thought.

"Look what I have," Randi announced.

It was a large boulder, perhaps two metres across, and loose; Randi could rock it easily, though it must have had a mass of five or six tonnes. "Bet *it* doesn't fall like a snowflake," she said as she hammered a piton into it.

Even in the low gravity, it took two of us to lift it over the edge. Two hours later, about a kilometre above Cathy's Rock, we jumped off into the drag of the slipstream and watched the boulder finish its fall. It crashed with a resounding thud, shattered into a thousand shards, most of which rebounded and got caught in the chimney walls. We soon reached local terminal velocity and floated like feathers in the dust back to the place we had first departed three days ago.

Cathy decided that Randi was in no shape for another immersion and didn't think I should risk it either. I did have a few red patches, though I'd spent nowhere near as much time in the ethane as Randi. We looked at Nikhil, who frowned.

Cathy shook her head. "My turn, I think." But her voice quavered. "I'm a strong swimmer and I don't think Nikhil's done it for years. You handle the spray, Wojciech. You don't have to cover every square centimetre, the fibres will fill in themselves, but make sure you get enough on me. At least fifteen seconds of continuous spray. Randi – I can't hold my breath as long as you. You'll have to help me get buttoned up again, fast."

When all was ready, she took several deep breaths, vented her helmet and stripped almost as quickly as Randi had. This, I thought as I sprayed her, was the same woman who panicked in a tight spot just over a week ago. The whole operation was over in 100 seconds.

The pulley I'd left was still functional, but that would only get us to the branch in the passage that led to the Cavern of Dead Ends. From there on, Cathy would have to pull us.

It was not fun to be sealed in an opaque, uninflated, tent and be bumped and dragged along for the better part of an hour with no control over anything. The return of my minuscule weight as Sam winched us up to the roof of the Boiling Sea cavern was a great relief.

Randi, Nikhil, and I crawled, grumbling but grateful, out of the tent onto the floor of the cave Sam had found a couple of hundred yards from the centre of the domed roof of the cavern. The floor sloped, but not too badly, and with a milligee of gravity it scarcely mattered. I helped Nikhil with the tent braces and we soon had it ready to be pressurized. Sam recharged the pallet power supplies and Randi tacked a glowlamp to the wall. Cathy then excused herself to get the Exoderm out of her tightsuit while we set up the other tent.

Work done, we stretched and floated around our little room in silence.

I took a look out the cave entrance; all I could see of the cavern when I hit my strobe was a layer of white below and a forest of yellow and white stalactites, many of them hundreds of metres long, on the roof. The far side, which Sam's radar said was only a couple of kilometres away, was lost in mist.

Then I noticed other things. My tightsuit, for instance, didn't feel as tight as it should.

"What's the air pressure in here?"

"Half a bar," Sam responded. "I've adjusted your suits for minimum positive pressure. It's mostly nitrogen, methane, ethane, and ammonia vapour, with some other volatile organics. By the way, the boiling sea is mainly ammonia; we are up to 220 Kelvins here. The ethane flashes into vapour as it hits the ammonia – that's why all the boiling."

Miranda's gravity was insufficient to generate that kind of pressure, and I wondered what was going on.

"Wojciech," Randi whispered, as if she were afraid of waking something. "Look at the walls."

"Huh?" The cave walls were dirty brown like cave walls anywhere – except Miranda. "Oh, no hoar crystals."

She rubbed her hand on the wall and showed me the brown gunk.

"I'd like to put this under a microscope. Sam?"

The robot came quickly and held the sample close to its lower set of eyes. I saw what it saw, projected on the inside of my helmet.

"This has an apparent cellular structure, but little, if any structure within. Organic molecules and ammonia in a kind of jell."

As I watched, one of the cells developed a bifurcation. I was so fascinated, I didn't notice that Cathy had rejoined us. "They must absorb stuff directly from the air." she theorized. "The air is toxic, by the way, but not in low concentrations. Something seems to have filtered out the cyanogens and other really bad stuff. Maybe this."

"The back of the cave is full of them," Randi observed. "How are you?"

"My skin didn't get as raw as yours, but I have a few irritated areas. Physically, I'm drained. We're going to stop here tonight, I hope."

"This is one of the gas outlets of the Cavern of the Boiling Sea," Sam added. "It seems to be a good place to resume our journey. The passage is clear of obstructions as far as I can see, except for these growths, which are transparent to my radar."

"They impede the airflow," Nikhil observed, "which must contribute to the high pressure in here. I think they get the energy for their organization from the heat of condensation."

"Huh?" I wracked my memories of bonehead science.

"Wojciech, when a vapour condenses, it undergoes a phase change. When ethane vapour turns back into ethane, it gives off as much heat as it took to boil it in the first place. That heat can make some of the chemical reactions this stuff needs go in the right direction."

"Are they alive?" I asked.

"Hard to say," Cathy responded. "But that's a semantic discussion. Are hoar crystals alive? There's a continuum of organization and behaviour from rocks to people. Any line you draw is arbitrary and will go right through some grey areas."

"Hmpf," Nikhil snorted. "Some distinctions are more useful than others. This stuff breeds, I think. Let's take some samples, but we need to get some rest, too."

"Yes, dear." Cathy yawned in spite of herself.

In the tent, Randi and I shared our last regular meal; a reconstituted chicken and pasta dish we'd saved to celebrate something. The tent stank of bodies and hydrocarbons, but we were used to that by now, and the food tasted great despite the assault on our nostrils. From now on, meals would be crackers. But we were on our way out now, definitely. We had to be. Randi felt fully recovered now and smiled at me as she snuggled under her elastic sheet for a night's rest.

It must have been the energy we got from our first good meal in days. She woke me in the middle of our arbitrary night and gently coaxed me into her cot for lovemaking, more an act of defiance against our likely fate than an act of pleasure. I surprised myself by responding, and we caressed each other up a spiral of intensity which was perhaps fed by our fear as well.

There are the tidal forces near Randi's event horizon; she is not just strong for a woman, but strong in absolute terms; stronger than most men I have known including myself. I had to half-seriously warn her to not crack our low gravity-weakened ribs. This made her giggle and squeeze me so hard I couldn't breathe for a moment, which made her giggle again.

When we were done, she gestured to the tent roof with the middle finger of her right hand and laughed uncontrollably. I joined her in this as well, but I felt momentarily sad for Nikhil and Cathy.

It was another of those polite mornings, and we packed up and were on our way with record efficiency. We looked around for the vent and Sam pointed us right at the mass of brown at the rear of the cave.

"The gas goes into that, right through it," it said.

We called the stuff "cryofungus". It had grown out from either side of the large, erosion-widened vertical crack that Sam found in the back of our cave until it met in the middle. However the cryofungus colonies from either side didn't actually fuse there, but just pressed up against each other. So, with some effort, we found we could half-push, half-swim, our way along this seam.

We had pushed our way through five kilometres of "cryofungus" before a macabre thought occurred to me. The rubbery brown stuff absorbed organics through the skin of its cells. Did said organic stuff have to be gas? I asked Cathy.

"I did an experiment. I fed my sample a crumb of ration cracker."

"What happened?"

"The cracker sort of melted into the cryofungus. There are transport molecules all over the cell walls."

I thought a second. "Cathy, if we didn't have our suits on . . ."

"I'd think water would be a little hot for them, but then again water and ammonia are mutually soluble. If you want to worry, consider that your tightsuit is porous. It might," I could see her toothy smile in my mind, "help keep you moving."

"Nice, dear," Nikhil grumbled. "That gives a whole new meaning to this concept of wandering through the bowels of Miranda."

A round of hysterical laughter broke whatever tension remained between us, and resolved into a feeling of almost spiritual oneness among us. Perhaps you have to face death with someone to feel that – if so, so be it.

At the ten-kilometre point, the cryofungus started to loose its resiliency. At twelve, it started collapsing into brown dust, scarcely offering any more resistance than the hoar crystals. This floated along with the gas current as a sort of brown fog. I couldn't see, and had Sam move up beside me.

After three kilometres of using Sam as a seeing-eye dog, the dust finally drifted by us and the air cleared. It was late again, well past time to camp. We had been underground thirteen days, and had, by calculation, another eight left. According to Sam, we were still 215 kilometres below the surface. We decided to move on for another hour or two.

The passageway was tubular and fairly smooth, with almost

zero traction. We shot pitons into the next curve ahead, and pulled ourselves along.

"Massive wind erosion," Nikhil remarked as he twisted the eye of a piton to release it. "A gale must have poured through here for megayears before the cryofungus choked it down."

Each strobe revealed an incredible gallery of twisted forms, loops, and carved rocks, many of which were eerily statuesque, saints and gargoyles. This led us into a slightly uphill kilometre-long cavern formed under two megalithic slabs, which had tilted against each other when, perhaps, the escaping gas had undermined them. After the rich hoarcrystal forest of the inbound path, this place was bare and dry. Sam covered the distance with a calculated jump carrying a line to the opposite end. We started pulling ourselves across. We'd climbed enough so that our weight was back to twenty newtons – minuscule, yes, but try pumping twenty newtons up and down for eighteen hours .

"I quit," Cathy said. "My arms won't do any more. Stop with me, or bury me here." She let go of the line, and floated slowly down to the floor.

It was silent here, no drippings, no whistling, reminiscent of the vacuum so far above. I tried to break the tension by naming the cavern. "This was clearly meant to be a tomb, anyway. The Egyptian Tomb, we can call it."

"Not funny, Wojciech," Nikhil snapped. "Sorry, old boy, a bit tired myself. Yes, we can make camp, but we may regret it later."

"Time to stop. We worked out the schedule for maximum progress," Randi said. "Need to trust our judgment. Won't do any better by over-pushing ourselves now."

"Very well," Nikhil conceded, and dropped off as well. He reached Cathy and put his arm around her briefly, which I note because it was the first sign of physical affection I had seen between them. Randi and I dropped the pallets, and followed to the floor. We landed harder than we expected – milligee clouds judgment almost as badly as free-fall, I thought. Worse perhaps, because it combines a real up and down with the feeling that they don't matter.

We were very careful and civilized in making camp. But each of us was, in our minds, trying to reach an accommodation with the idea that, given what we had been through so far, the week we had left would not get us to the surface.

Before we went into our separate tents, we all held hands briefly. It was spontaneous – we hadn't done so before. But it seemed right, somehow, to tell each other that we could draw on each other that way.

V

That last was for day thirteen, this entry will cover days fourteen and fifteen. Yes, my discipline in keeping the journal is slipping.

We'd come to think of Randi as a machine – almost as indestructible and determined as Sam, but last night, at the end of day fourteen that machine cried and shook.

Low rations and fatigue are affecting all of us now. We let Sam pull us through the occasional cavern, but it has mostly been wriggling through cracks with a human in the lead. We changed leads every time we hit a place that's wide enough, but once that was six hours. That happened on Randi's lead. She didn't slack but when we finally reached a small cavern, she had rolled to the side with her face to the wall as I went by. We heard nothing from her for the next four hours.

We ended up at the bottom of a big kidney-shaped cavern 160 kilometres below the surface; almost back to the depth of the upper end of Nikhil's Smokestack. We staggered through camp set up, with Sam double-checking everything. We simply collapsed on top of the stretched sheets in our coveralls and slept for an hour or so, before our bodies demanded that we take care of other needs. Washed, emptied, and a bit refreshed from the nap, Randi had snuggled into my arms, then let herself go. Her body was a mass of bruises, old and new. So was mine.

"You're allowed a safety valve, you know," I told her. "When Cathy feels bad, she lets us know outright. Nikhil gets grumpy. I get silly and started telling bad jokes. You don't have to keep up an act for us."

"Not for you, for, for me. Got to pretend I can do it, or I'll get left behind, with Mom."

I thought about this. A woman that would attempt to murder her husband to gain social position might have been capable of other things as well.

"Randi, what did that mean? Do you want to talk?"

She shook her head. "Can't explain."

I kissed her forehead. "I guess I've been lucky with my parents."

"Yeah. Nice people. Nice farm. No fighting. So why do you have to do this stuff."

Why indeed? "To have a real adventure, to make a name for myself outside of obscure poetry outlets. Mom inherited the farm from her father, and that was better than living on state dividends in Poland, so they moved. They actually get to do something useful, tending the agricultural robots. But they're deathly afraid of losing it because real jobs were so scarce and a lot of very smart people are willing to do just about anything to get an Earth job. So they made themselves very, very nice. They never rock any boats. Guess I needed something more than nice."

"But you're, uh, nice as they are."

"Well-trained, in spite of myself." Oh, yes, with all the protective responses a non-conformist learns after being squashed time and time again by very socially correct, outwardly gentle, and emotionally devastating means. "By the way, Randi, I hate that word."

"Huh?"

"Nice."

"But you use it."

"Yeah, and I hate doing that, too. Look, are you as tired as I am?" I was about to excuse myself to the questionable comforts of my dreams.

"No. Not yet. I'll do the work."

"Really . . ."

"Maybe the last time, way we're going." We both knew she was right, but my body wasn't up to it, and we just clung to each other tightly, as if we could squeeze a little more life into ourselves. I don't remember falling asleep.

Day fifteen was a repeat, except that the long lead shift fell on Cathy. She slacked. For seven hours, she would stop until she got cold, then move forward again until she got tired. Somehow we reached a place where I could take over.

What amazed me through all of that was how Nikhil handled it. There was no sniping, no phony cheeriness. He would simply ask if she was ready to move again when he started getting cold.

We ended the day well past midnight. For some reason, I am having trouble sleeping,

Today the vent finally led us to a chain of small caverns, much like the rift before we encountered the top of Nikhil's Smokestack. We let Sam tow us most of the way and had only two long crack crawls. The good news is our CO_2 catalyst use is down from our passivity, and we might get another day out of it.

The bad news is that Randi had to cut our rations back a bit. We hadn't been as careful in our counting as we should have been, thinking that because the CO_2 would get us first, we didn't have a problem in that area. Now we did. It was nobody's fault, and everyone's. We'd all had an extra cracker here and there. They add up.

We ended up, exhausted as usual, in a 500-metre gallery full of jumble. I called it "The Junk Yard". Sam couldn't find the outlet vent right away, but we made such good progress that we thought we had time to catch up on our sleep.

Where are we? It's day eighteen. We have gained a total of fifteen kilometres in radius over the past two days. "The Junk Yard" was a dead end, at least for anything the size of a human being. There was some evidence of gas diffusing upward through fractured clathrate, but it was already clear that it wasn't the main vent, which appeared to have been closed by a Miranda quake millions of years ago.

We had to go all the way back to a branch that Sam had missed while it was towing us through a medium-sized chimney. Logic and experience dictated that the outlet would be at the top of the chimney, and there was a hole there that led onward. To "The Junk Yard". Miranda rearranges such logic.

We spotted the real vent from the other side of the chimney as we rappelled back down.

"A human being," Cathy said when she saw the large vertical crack that was the real vent, "would have been curious enough to check that out. It's so deep."

"I don't know, dear," Nikhil said, meaning to defend Sam, I suppose, "with the press of time and all, I might not have turned aside, myself."

We were all dead silent at Nikhil's unintentional self-identification with a robot. Then Randi giggled and soon we were all laughing hysterically again. The real students of humour, I recall, say that laughter is not very far from tears. Then Nikhil, to our surprise, released his hold to put his arms around his wife again. And she responded. I reached out and caught them before they'd drifted down enough centimetres for their belt lines to go taut. So at the end of day seventeen, we had covered sixty kilometres of caverns and cracks, and come only fifteen or so nearer the surface.

By the end of day eighteen, we'd done an additional fifteen kilometres of exhausting crack crawling, found only one large cavern, and gave in to exhaustion, camping in a widening of the crack just barely big enough to inflate the tents.

What occurred today was not a fight. We didn't have enough energy for a fight.

We had just emerged into a ten-metre long, ten-metre wide, two-metre high widening gallery in the crack we were crawling. Cathy was in the lead and had continued on through into the continuing passage when Nikhil gave in to pessimism.

"Cathy," he called, "stop. The passage ahead is getting too narrow, it's another bloody dead end. We should go back to the last large cavern and look for another vent."

Cathy was silent, but the line stopped. Randi, sounding irritated, said "No time," and moved to enter the passage after Cathy.

Nikhil yawned and snorted. "Sorry, little lady. I'm the geologist and the senior member, and not to be too fine about it, but I'm in charge." Here he seemed to loose steam and get confused, muttering "You're right about no time – there's no time to argue."

No one said anything, but Randi held her position.

Nikhil whined, "I say we go back, an', this time, back we go."

My mind was fuzzy; we still had four, maybe five days. If we found the right chain of caverns we could still make the surface. If we kept going like this, we weren't going to make it anyway. He might be right I thought. But Randi wouldn't budge.

"No. Nikhil. You owe me one, Nikhil, for, for, two weeks ago. I'm collecting. Got to go forward now. Air flow, striations, Sam's soundings, and, and my money, damn it."

So much for my thoughts. I had to remember my status as part of Randi's accretion disk.

"Your *daddy's* money," Nikhil sniffed, then said loudly and with false jollity, "But never mind. Come on everyone, we'll put Randi on a stretcher again until she recovers . . . her senses." He started reaching for Randi, clumsy fumbling really. Randi turned and braced herself, boots clamped into the clathrate, arms free.

"Nikhil, back off," I warned. "You don't mean that."

"Ah appreciate your expertise with words, old chap." His voice was definitely slurred. "But these are mine and I mean them. I'm too tired to be questioned by amateurs anymore. Back we go. Come on back, Cathy. As for you . . ." He lunged for Randi again. At this point I realized he was out of his mind, and possibly why.

So did Randi, for at the last second instead of slapping him away and possibly hurting him, she simply jerked herself away from his grasping fingers.

And screeched loudly in pain.

"What?" I asked, brushing by the startled Nikhil to get to Randi's side.

"Damn ankle," she sobbed. "Forgot to release my boot grapples. Tired. Bones getting weak. Too much low gee. Thing fucking hurts."

"Broken?"

She nodded, tight-lipped, more in control. But I could see the tears in her eyes. Except for painkillers, there was nothing I could do at the moment for her. But I thought there might be something to be done for Nikhil. Where was Cathy?

"Nikhil," I said as evenly as I could. "What's your O_2 partial?"

"I beg your pardon?" he drawled.

"Beg Randi's. I asked you what your O_2 partial is."

"I've been conserving a bit. You know, less O_2, less CO_2. Trying to stretch things out."

"What . . . is . . . it?"

"Point one. It should be fine. I've had a lot of altitude experience . . ."

"Please put it back up to point two for five minutes, and then we'll talk."

"Now just a minute, I resent the implication that . . ."

"Be reasonable Nikhil. Put it back up for a little, please. Humour me. Five minutes won't hurt."

"Oh perhaps not. There. Now just what is it you expect to happen?"

"Wait for a bit."

We waited, silently. Randi sniffed, trying to deal with her pain. I watched Nikhil's face slowly grow more and more troubled. Finally I asked:

"Are you back with us?"

He nodded silently. "I think so. My apologies, Randi."

"Got clumsy. Too strong for my own bones. Forget it. And you don't owe me, either. Dumb thing to say. It was my choice."

What was? Two weeks ago, in his tent?

"Very well," Nikhil replied with as much dignity as he could muster.

Who besides Randi could dismiss a broken ankle with "forget it"? And who besides Nikhil would take her up on that? I shook my head.

Randi couldn't keep the pain out of her voice as she held out her right vacuum boot. "This needs some work. Tent site. Cathy." Nothing would show, of course, until it came off.

"Quite," Nikhil responded. "Well, you were right on the direction. Perhaps we should resume."

I waved him off for a moment and found a painkiller in the pallet for Randi, and she ingested it through her helmet lock, and gagged a bit.

"Still a little ethane here," she gave a little laugh. "Woke me up. I'll manage."

"Let me know." I was so near her event horizon now that everything I could see of the outside world was distorted and bent by her presence. Such were the last moments my freedom, the last minutes and the last seconds that I could look on our relationship from the outside. My independent existence was stretched beyond the power of any force of nature to restore it. Our fate was to become a singularity.

It was a measure of my own hunger and fatigue that I half-seriously considered exterminating Nikhil; coldly, as if contemplating a roach to be crushed. A piton gun would have done nicely. But, I thought, Cathy really ought to be in on the decision. She might want to keep him as a pet. Cathy, of course, was on the lead pitch. That meant she was really in charge, something Nikhil had forgotten.

"Cathy," I called, laying on the irony. "Randi has a broken ankle. Otherwise, we are ready to go again."

There was no answer, but radio didn't carry well in this material – too many bends in the path and something in the clathrate that just ate our frequencies like stealth paint. So I gave two pulls on our common line to signal okay, go.

The line was slack.

Cathy, anger with Nikhil possibly clouding her judgment, had enforced her positional authority in a way that was completely inarguable: by proceeding alone. At least I fervently hoped that was all that had happened. I pulled myself to where the passage resumed, and looked. No sign of anything.

"Sam, take the line back up to up to Cathy and tell her to wait up, we're coming."

Sam squeezed by me and scurried off. Shortly, his monitors in my helmet display blinked out; he was out of radio range as well –

Again, we waited for a tug on a line in a silence that shouted misery. Nikhil pretended to examine the wall, Randi stared ahead as if in a trance. I stared at her, wanting to touch her, but not seeming to have the energy to push myself over to her side of the little cave.

Both hope and dread increased with the waiting. The empty time could mean that Cathy had gone much further than our past rate of progress had suggested, which would be very welcome news. But it could also mean that some disaster ahead that had taken both her and Sam. In which case, we were dead as well. Or, like Randi's detour from the Boiling Sea, it could mean something we had neglected to imagine.

"Wojciech, Nikhil," Randi asked in her quiet, anticipatory, tone, "would you turn off your lamps?"

I looked at Nikhil, and he stared off in space, saying as much as that he could not care less. But his light went out. I nodded and cut mine. The blackness was total at first, then as my pupils widened, I realized I could sense a grey-green contrast, a shadow. My shadow.

I turned around to the source of the glow. It was, of course, the crack behind me, through which Cathy and Sam had vanished. As my eyes adapted further, it became almost bright. It was white, just tinged with green. The shadows of rocks and ice intrusions made the crack look like the mouth of some beast about to devour us.

"Is there," I asked, "any reason why we should stay here?"

We left. The crack widened rapidly, and after an hour of rather mild crack-crawling, we were able to revert to our distance eating hand-hauling routine. We covered ten kilometres, almost straight up this way. With the sudden way of such things the crack turned into a tubular tunnel, artificial in its smoothness, and this in turn gave into a roughly teardrop-shaped, 100-metre diameter cavern with slick ice walls, and a bright circle at the top. I was about to use my piton gun when Randi tugged my arm and pointed out a ladder of double-looped pitons, set about three metres apart, leading up to the circle.

We were thus about to climb into Sphereheim when Cathy's line grew taut again.

That was, by the clock, the end of day nineteen. We were, it seems, both too exhausted and too excited to sleep.

The cavern above was almost perfectly spherical, hence the name we gave it, and was almost fifteen kilometres in diameter. A spire ran along its vertical axis from the ceiling to the floor, littered like a Christmas tree with the kind of cantilevered platforms that seventy-five milligees permits.

By now, we had climbed to within forty kilometres of the surface, so this was all in a pretty good vacuum, but there were signs that things had not always been this way.

"Cathy?" Nikhil called, the first words he had spoken since the fight.

"Good grief, you're here already. We waited until we thought it was safe."

"We saw the light."

"It came on as soon as I got in here. Sam's been looking for other automatic systems, burglar protection, for instance."

"There," Sam interjected, "appear to be none. The power source is two-stage – a uranium radionic long duration module, and something like a solid state fuel cell that works when it's warmed up. The latter appears to be able to produce almost a kilowatt."

"Good," I said, wondering if Sam's software could discern the contrary irritation in my voice. "Cathy, Randi has a broken ankle." Even in less than a hundredth of gee, Randi wouldn't put any weight on it.

"Oh, no! We need to get a tent up right away. Sam, break off and come down here, I need you. And you!" she pointed at Nikhil. "This is a medical emergency now, and what I say goes. Do you have a problem with that?" The edge in Cathy's voice verged on hysteria.

Nikhil simply turned away without saying anything and began setting up the tent.

Randi reached for Cathy. "Cathy, Nikhil cut his oxygen too thin, trying to save CO_2 catalyst for all of us. He wasn't himself. Ankle hurts like hell, but that was my fault. I'd feel better if you weren't so, uh, hard on him. Okay?"

Cathy stood quietly for a couple of seconds then muttered. "All right, all right. Give me a minute to collect things, and we'll get in the tent. I'll see what I can do. Wojciech?"

"Yes Cathy?"

"As I guess everyone knows, I just blew it with my husband, and I can't fix things right now because I have to fix Randi's ankle. He's in a blue funk." She pulled the velcro tab up on one of her pockets, reached in and produced a small, thin, box. "Give him one of these and tell him I'm sorry."

I looked at her. She seemed on the brink of some kind of collapse, but was holding herself back by some supreme effort of will. Maybe that's what I looked like to her.

"Sorry, Wojciech," she whispered, "best I can do."

I gave her hand a squeeze. "We'll make it good enough, okay? Just hang in there, Doc."

She gave me a quick, tear-filled smile, then grabbed the minidoc and followed Randi into the tent, which inflated promptly.

Nikhil was sitting on the other pallet and I sat next to him. "Look, Nikhil, the way I see it, none of this stuff counts. All that counts is that the four of us get out of this moon alive."

He looked at me briefly, then resumed looking at the ground. "No, no. Wojciech, it counts. Do you understand living death? The kind where your body persists, but everything that you thought was you has been destroyed? My reputation . . . they'll say

Nikhil Ray cracked under pressure. It got too tough for old Nikhil. Nikhil beats up on women. It's going to be bloody bad."

I remembered the box Cathy gave me, pulled it out and opened it. "Doctor's orders, Nikhil. She cares, she really does."

He gave me a ghastly grin and took a caplet envelope, unwrapped it and stuck it through his helmet lock. "Can't say as I approve of mind altering drugs, but it wouldn't do to disappoint the doctor any more, now would it? I put her through medical school, did you know. She was eighteen when we met. Biology student studying evolution, and I was co-lecturing a paleontology section. Damn she was beautiful, and no one like that had ever . . ." he lifted his hands as if to gesture, then set them down again. "I broke my own rule about thinking first, and I have this to remind me, every day, of what happens when you do that."

"Look, Nikhil. She doesn't mean to hurt you." I tried to think of something to get him out of this, to put his mind on something else. "Say, we have a few minutes. Why don't we look around, it may be the only chance we get. Soon as Cathy's done with Randi, we'll need to get some sleep, then try to make it to the surface. We've forty kilometres to go, and only two days before our catalyst runs out."

"My line, isn't that? Very well." He seemed to straighten a bit. "But it looks as if the visitors packed up pretty thoroughly when they left. Those platforms off the central column are just bare honeycomb. Of course, it would be a bit odd if they packed *everything* out."

"Oh?"

"Field sites are usually an eclectic mess. All sorts of not-immediately-useful stuff gets strewn about. If the strewers don't expect the environmental police to stop by, it usually just gets left there by the hut site – the next explorer to come that way might find something useful."

"I see. You think there might be a dump here, somewhere."

"It seems they had a crypt. Why not a dump?"

What kind of alien technology might be useful to us, I didn't know. It would take a lot longer than the two days we had to figure out how to do anything with it. But the discussion has seemed to revive Nikhil a bit, so I humoured him.

We found the junkyard. It was in a mound about 100 metres

from the tower base, covered with the same colour dust as every-thing else. A squirt from my reaction pistol blew some of the dust away from the junk.

And it was just that. Discarded stuff. Broken building panels, A few boxes with electrical leads. What looked like a busted still. A small wheeled vehicle that I would have taken for a kid's tricycle, an elongated vacuum helmet with a cracked visor. Other things. I'd been rummaging for five minutes before I noticed that Nikhil hadn't gone past the still.

"Nikhil?"

"It is within the realm of possibility that I might redeem myself. Look at that."

The most visible part was a big coil of what looked to be tubing. There were also things that looked like electric motors, and several chambers to hold distilled liquids.

"The tubing, Wojciech."

"I don't understand."

"If we breathe through it, at this temperature, the CO_2 in our breath should condense."

Oh! We could do without the CO_2 catalyst.

"It wouldn't be very portable."

"No, it wouldn't," Nikhil nodded slowly, judiciously. "But it doesn't have to be. Cathy and Randi can remain here while you, Sam and I take the remaining catalyst and go for help."

Did I hear him right? Then I thought it through. Randi was disabled, Cathy, by strength and temperament, was the least suited for the ordeal above us. It made sense, but Randi would . . . no, Randi would have to agree if it made sense. She was a pro.

"We'd better see if it works first," I said.

VI

An hour later, our still was working. Tape, spare connectors, the alien light source, and Sam's instant computational capabilities yielded something that could keep two relatively quiescent people alive. They'd have to heat it up to sublimate the condensed CO_2 every other hour, or the thing would clog, but it worked.

Randi's ankle was a less happy situation.

"Randi's resting now," Cathy told us when she finally emerged from the vacuum tent, exhausted. "It's a bad break, splintered. Her bones were weak from too much time in low gravity, I think. Anyway, the breaks extend into the calcaneus and her foot is much too swollen to get back into her vacuum boots. Had to put her in a rescue bag to get out of the tent." Cathy shot a look of contempt at her husband who stared down. "The swelling will take days to go down, and she should have much more nourishment than we have to give her."

"I . . ." Nikhil started, then, in a moment I shall remember forever, he looked confused. "I?" Then he simply went limp and fell, much like an autumn leaf in the gentle gravity of Miranda, to the cavern dust. We were both too surprised to catch him even though his fall took several seconds.

"No, no . . ." Cathy choked.

I knelt over Nikhil and straightened his limbs. I couldn't think of anything else to do.

"Stroke?" I asked Cathy.

She seemed to shake herself back into a professional mode. I heard her take a breath.

"Could be. His heart telemetry's fine. Or he may have just fainted. Let's get the other tent set up."

We did this only with Sam's help. We made errors in the set-up, errors which would have been fatal if Sam hadn't been there to notice and correct them. We were tired and had been eating too little food. It took an hour. We put Nikhil in the tent and Cathy was about to follow when she stopped me.

"The main med kit's in Randi's tent. I'll need it if I have to operate. She'll have gotten out of the rescue bag to sleep after I left. You'll have to wake her, get her back in the bag and depressure . . ."

I held up a hand. "I can figure it out, and if I can't, she can. Cathy, her foot's busted, not her head."

Cathy nodded and I could see a bit of a smile through her faceplate.

"Randi," I called, "Sorry to wake you, but we've got a problem."

"I heard. Comsets are dumb, guys. Can't tell if you talk *about* someone instead of *to* someone. Be right out with the med kit."

"Huh?" Cathy sounded shocked. "No, Randi don't try to put that boot on. Please don't."

"Too late," Randi answered. We watched the tension go out of the tent fabric as it depressurized. Randi emerged from the opening with the med kit and a sample bag. Cathy and I immediately looked at her right boot – it seemed perfectly normal, except that Randi had rigged some kind of brace with pitons and vacuum tape.

Then we looked at the sample bag. It contained a blue-green swollen travesty of a human foot, severed neatly just above the ankle, apparently with a surgical laser. I couldn't think of anything to do or say.

"Oh, no, Randi," Cathy cried and launched herself toward Randi. "I tried Randi, I tried."

"You didn't have time." The two women embraced. "Don't say anything," Randi finally said, "to him," she nodded at Nikhil's tent. "Until we're all back and safe. Please, huh?"

Cathy stood frozen, then nodded slowly, took the sample bag and examined the foot end of the section. "Looks clean, anyway. At least let me take a look at the stump before you go, okay?"

Randi shook her head. "Bitch to unwrap. Cauterized with the surgical laser. Plastiflesh all over the stump. Sealed in plastic. Plenty of local. Don't feel anything. I did a good enough job, Cathy."

I finally found my voice. "Randi . . . why?"

"Nikhil's gone. Got to move. It's okay, Wojciech. They can regenerate. You and I got to get going."

"Me? Now?" I was surprised for a moment, then realized the need. Cathy had to stay with Nikhil. And I'd already seen too many situations where one person would have been stopped that we'd managed to work around with two. Also, our jury-rigged CO_2 still's capacity was two people, max.

"Now. Go as long as we can, then sleep. Eat everything we have left. Push for the surface. Only way."

Cathy nodded. She handed Randi's foot to me, almost absent-mindedly, and went into the tent to attend to Nikhil. Randi laughed, took the foot from me, and threw it far out of sight towards Sphereheim's junk pile. In the low gravity, it probably got there.

I tried not to think about it as Randi and I packed, with Sam's help. Moving slowly and deliberately, we didn't make that many errors. What Randi had to draw on, I didn't know. I drew on her. In an hour, we were ready to go and said our farewells to Cathy.

She would have to wait there, perhaps alone if Nikhil did not recover, perhaps forever if we did not succeed. What would that be like, I wondered. Would some future explorers confuse her with the beings who had built the station in this cavern? Had we already done that with the corpses we found in the Cavern of the Dead Ends?

I wished I had made love to Cathy that night we spent together – I felt I was leaving a relationship incomplete; a feeling, a sharing, uncommunicated. Here, even a last embrace would have been nice, but she was in her tent caring for her husband, and out of food, low on time, Randi and I had to go, and go now. In the dash to the surface, even minutes might be critical.

Tireless Sam scaled the alien tower, found the vent in the magnificent, crystal lined dome of the cavern roof, and dropped us a line. I was suspended among wonders, but so tired I almost fell asleep as Sam reeled us up. The experience was surreal and beyond description.

Of most of the next few days, I have little detailed memory. Sam dragged us through passages, chimneys vents and caverns. Occasionally, it stopped at a problem that Randi would somehow rouse herself to solve.

On one occasion, we came to a wall a metre thick which had cracked enough to let gas pass through. Sam's acoustic radar showed a big cavern on the other side, so, somehow, we dug our way through. For all its talents, Sam was not built for wielding a pick. I leave this information to the designers of future cave exploration robots.

Randi and I swung at that wall in five-minute shifts for a three-hour eternity, before, in a fit of hysterical anaerobic energy, I was able to kick it through. We were too tired to celebrate – we just grabbed the line as Sam went by and tried to keep awake and living as it pulled us through another cave and another crack.

In one of a string of ordinary crystal caverns, we found another alien piton. Randi thought it might be a different design that the one we had found before, and had Sam pull it out and put it in a sample bag, which we stored on Sam – the most likely to survive.

I mentioned this because we were near death and knew it, but could still do things for the future. Everyone dies, I thought, so we all spend our lives for something. The only thing that matters at the end is: for what? In saving the piton, we were adding one more bit to the tally of "for what?"

This was almost certainly our last "night" in a tent. I think we both stank, but I was too far gone to tell for sure. We'd gone for thirty-seven hours straight. Sam says we are within three kilometres of the surface, but the cavern trail lies parallel to this surface, and refuses to ascend.

In theory, our catalyst was exhausted, but we continued to breathe.

Another quake trapped me.

Randi was in front of me. Somehow, she managed to squeeze aside and let Sam by to help. Sam chipped clathrate away from my helmet, which let me straighten my neck.

As this happened, there was another movement, a big slow one this time, and the groan of Miranda's tortured mantle was clearly audible as my helmet was pressed between the passage walls again. I could see the passage ahead of me close a little more with every sickening wave of ground movement, even as I could feel the pressure at my spot release a bit. But the passage ahead – if it closed with Randi on this side, we were dead.

"Go!" I told Randi. "It's up to you now." As if it hadn't always been so. I was pushed sideways and back again as another train of s-waves rolled through. Ice split with sharp retorts.

Sam turned sideways in the passage, pitting its thin composite against billions of tons of rock.

Randi vanished forward. "I love you," she said, "I'll make it."

"I know you will. Hey, we're married, okay?"

"Just like that?"

"By my authority as a man in a desperate position."

"Okay. Married. Two kids. Deal?"

"Deal."

"I love you again."

Sam cracked under the pressure, various electronic innards spilling onto the passage floor. I couldn't see anything beyond him.

"Sam?" I asked. Useless question.

"Randi?"

Nothing.

For some strange reason I felt no pressure on me now. Too worried for Randi, too exhausted to be interested in my own death, I dozed.

There was definitely CO_2 in my helmet when I woke again. It was pitch black – the suit had turned off my glowlamp to conserve an inconsequential watt or two. Groggy, I thought turning on my back would help my breathing, vaguely thinking that the one percent weight on my lungs was a problem. To my surprise, I could actually turn.

In the utter dead black overhead, a star appeared. Very briefly, then I blinked and it vanished.

I continued to stare at this total darkness above me for minutes, not daring to believe I'd seen what I thought I'd seen, and then I saw another one. Yes, a real star.

I thought that could only mean that a crack to the surface had opened above me; incredibly narrow, or far above me, but open enough that now and then a star drifted by its opening. I was beyond climbing, but perhaps where photons could get in, photons could get out.

Shaking and miserable, I started transmitting.

"Uranus Control, Uranus Control, Wojciech Bubka here. I'm down at the bottom of a crack on Miranda. Help. Uranus Control, Uranus Control . . ."

Something sprayed on my face, waking me again. Air and mist as well.

I opened my eyes and saw that a tube had cemented itself to my faceplate and drilled a hole through it to admit some smaller tubes. One of these was trying to snake its way into my mouth. I opened up to help it, and got something warm and sweet to swallow.

"Thanks," I croaked, around the tube.

"Don't mention it," a young female voice answered, sounding almost as relieved as I felt.

"My wife's in this passage, somewhere in the direction my head is pointed. Can you get one of these tubes to her?"

There was a hesitation.

"Your wife."

"Miranda Lotati," I croaked. "She was with me. Trying to get to the surface. Went that way."

More hesitation.

"We'll try, Wojciech. God knows we'll try."

Within minutes, a tiny version of Sam fell on my chest and scuttled past Sam's wreckage down the compressed passage in her direction trailing a line. The line seemed to run over me forever. I remember reading somewhere that while the journey to singularity is inevitable for someone passing into the event horizon of a black hole, as viewed from our universe, the journey can take forever.

What most people remember about the rescue is the digger; that vast thing of pistons, beams, and steel claws that tore through the clathrate rift like an anteater looking for ants. What *they* saw, I assure you, was in no way as impressive, or scary, as being directly under the thing.

I was already in a hospital ship bed when they found Randi, eleven kilometres down a passage that had narrowed, narrowed, and narrowed.

At its end, she had broken her bones forcing herself through one more centimetre at a time. A cracked pelvis, both collarbones, two ribs, and her remaining ankle.

The last had done it, for when it collapsed she had no remaining way to force herself any further through that crack of doom.

And so she had lain there and, minute by minute, despite everything, willed herself to live as long as she could.

Despite everything, she did.

They got the first tubes into her through her hollow right boot and the plastiflesh seal of her stump, after the left foot had proven to be frozen solid. They didn't tell me at first – not until they had convinced themselves she was really alive.

* * *

When the rescuers reached Cathy and Nikhil, Cathy calmly guided the medic to her paralyzed husband, and as soon as she saw that he was in good professional hands, gave herself a sedative, and started screaming until she collapsed. She wasn't available for interviews for weeks. But she's fine now, and laughs about it. She and Nikhil live in a large university dome on Triton and host our reunions in their house, which has no roof – they've arranged for the dome's rain to fall elsewhere.

Miranda my wife spent three years as a quadruple amputee, and went back into Miranda the moon that way, in a powered suit, to lead people back to the Cavern of Dead Ends. Today, it's easy to see where the bronze weathered flesh of her old limbs ends and the pink smoothness of her new ones start. But if you miss it, she'll point it out with a grin.

So, having been to Hades and back, are the four of us best friends? For amusement, we all have more congenial companions. Nikhil is still a bit haughty, and he and Cathy still snipe at each other a little, but with smiles more often than not. I've come to conclude that, in some strange way, they need the stimulation that gives them, and a displacement for needs about which Nikhil will not speak.

Cathy and Randi still find little to talk about, giving us supposedly verbally challenged males a chance. Nikhil says I have absorbed enough geology lectures to pass doctorate exams; so maybe I will do that someday. He often lectures me towards that end, but my advance for our book was such that I won't have to do anything the rest of my life, except for the love of it. I'm not sure I love geology.

Often, on our visits, the four of us simply sit, say nothing, and do nothing but sip a little fruit of the local grape, which we all enjoy. We smile at each other and remember.

But don't let this studied diffidence of ours fool you. The four of us are bound with something that goes far beyond friendship, far beyond any slight conversation, far beyond my idiot critiques of our various eccentric personalities or of the hindsight mistakes of our passage through the Great Miranda Rift. These are the table crumbs from a feast of greatness, meant to sustain those who follow.

The sublime truth is that when I am with my wife, Nikhil, and

Cathy, I feel elevated above what is merely human. *Then* I sit in the presence of these demigods who challenged, in mortal combat, the will of the universe – and won.

THE REST IS SPECULATION

Eric Brown

When I first sent out enquiries to authors regarding this anthology, Eric Brown was the first to respond with a new story. He took my requirements of "sense of wonder", "positive and uplifting" and "awe-inspiring" to heart, producing this magnificent Wellsian-like homage to the last days of Earth. It inspired the illustration on this book's cover.

Brown (b. 1960) has written over twenty books and eighty short stories, since his first collection The Time-Lapsed Man *(1990). His first novel was* Meridian Days *(1992). Recent works include* The Fall of Tartarus *(2005) and* The Extraordinary Voyage of Jules Verne *(2005). He has twice won the BSFA short story award, in 2000 and 2002. I also had the pleasure of collaborating with him in compiling* The Mammoth Book of New Jules Verne Adventures *(2005).*

THE DEAD CITY THRUST itself from the escarpment above the vanished sea, its soaring towers and minarets a lament in stone for the race that aeons past had lifted it, block by block, towards the heavens. Something about its vaulting design might have inspired awe long ago, but now evoked mere sadness. And the great scoop of the drained ocean, which fell away from the city to a desiccated seabed split by chasms and fissures miles below, was just as monumentally tragic.

I know that I was born and that I died, but the rest is speculation. My death I recall but dimly: my passing had about it an odd elusive sense of déjà-vu, as if I had been travelling towards this familiar place all my life. I was surrounded by loved ones, I think, and I was not in pain; death was a sadness, not so much a longing for more but a desire to have it all again; death was a diminishing of the senses, a dwindling towards a beckoning darkness.

And then came the light.

"Where am I?"

After my initial panic and confusion I was flooded by a sense of calm.

"Be easy. You are well. We welcome you."

I was in a vast chamber seared with sunlight that fell *en bloc* from a far window, and an odd creature confronted me.

"You are," I said, "a crab."

The crab waved one of its four large pincers, as if conducting an orchestra. "I am a member of the race known as the Ky[20], and my name is Replenish-362."

"And my name," I said, as if constrained by a reciprocal formality, "is . . ." But for the life of me I could not recall my name.

"It is of little matter," said Replenish-362. The words came from a small silver box slung beneath the chitinous letterbox of its unmoving mouth. I too wore a similar device about my neck. "You may call me Rep. I will call you . . . Channon, I think."

"Channon . . ." I repeated. I knew I was not dreaming: the experience had the clarity of reality. "Rep, what am I doing here?"

"In time," said Rep. "In time."

"But am I on Earth?" I persisted.

Rep waved a pincer. "You are on Earth," it replied.

Then I noticed we were not alone.

A figure vaguely human-shaped stood behind Rep, and a little to one side. It was twice as tall as an average human, and silver, and across the surface of its face passed a series of evanescent features, as if it were cycling through a sequential amalgam of every human face that had ever been. I did not know whether this being was male or female, but from it I sensed an emanation of such peace and tranquillity that I almost wept.

"I am Kamis," said the silver being. "Or, rather, that is the name given me by Rep." Its lips moved, but out of synchronization with its words, which issued instead from its own silver box. "I am from the race which translates in your language as the shimmer-folk."

Then the ceiling moved, or I thought it did. Startled, I stared up (only then realizing that I lay on a surface canted at a forty-five degree angle) and saw that what descended was not the ceiling but another creature, this one like a manta-ray, a flat golden hovering thing with four eyes set in its underside between an array of waving cilia.

"And Rep calls me Cheth," it said, "of the villicent people. I greet you, Channon."

As it lowered itself and levitated beside Kamis, I saw that the creature called Cheth was perhaps five metres broad, and as many long.

I leaned forward, and the surface on which I rested tipped me to my feet. I stood with surprise, and another surprise awaited me as I looked down the length of my naked body. Dimly I recalled my former body, but gone was the stringy, wasted, pain-wracked frame of old. I seemed forty again, trim and well-muscled.

I looked at the three very different creatures before me and said, "Where am I? How did I get here?"

"You are," said Replenish-362, "in the year 2,405,355,223, by your reckoning of these things."

"Two . . .." I just could not comprehend the scale.

Kamis inclined its silver head, and I saw a procession of smiles decorate its face "Call it two billion, plus a few hundred million years," it said.

"But how . . . ?" I gestured towards the chamber, the sunlight behind the trio.

Rep stepped forward, legs ticking upon the floor. "You would not understand the science of the process, Channon," it said. "Suffice to say that we accessed your DNA-identity, and enabled you, and brought you to fruition."

Kamis gestured with a silver hand. "Just as my identity was accessed, and enabled, and brought to fruition. I too am like you, though from an age long after yours. Almost ten million years after, which itself seen from this age seems ancient history indeed."

Rep said, "Cheth hails from a more recent age."

The manta-ray spoke. "I am from Earth of just three million five hundred thousand years ago," it said. "We were the dominant species on the planet for almost four million years, and that time was a time of peace and prosperity, of learning and high culture. It ended," Cheth went on, "it ended, as all things must do."

"Four million years," I said. Then, "And do you know how long *Homo sapiens* walked the planet?"

"From the time when you began to keep records," Rep said, "to your extinction, was but 400,000 years."

"Which," said Kamis, "might seem a long time, but is just an eye-blink in the long history of our planet. My people had records of your reign on Earth. You were, if you will pardon me, a primitive species. You . . . fought, waged war, despoiled the Earth."

"But," Rep put in, "too they were inventive, and artistic, and philosophically inclined."

"That I acknowledge," Kamis said, inclining its argent head.

I smiled. "I have little memory of who I was, of who my people were."

Kamis said, "Cheth and I, too, came to fruition with little knowledge of our identities, our histories."

"You underwent," Rep said, "extensive trauma in being enabled; of course you will experience certain . . . shall we say . . . cognitive dysfunctions, for a time."

I looked at the crab-like being. "And can you tell me why I was accessed, enabled, and brought to fruition?"

The crab did a little dance, or what looked like a dance; a quick skittering jig with much chitinous tattooing on the marble floor. Quickly, without replying, it moved around the surface on which I had lain and tiptoed towards an aperture which slid open upon its approach.

"Kamis, Cheth," it called.

The two creatures complied, moved towards the door; in parting, Cheth said, "Rep will not impart the reason for our arrival in this age, my friend. It says, 'In time, in time'."

They joined Rep, who swivelled and said to me, "In one hour we begin our journey, Channon. Your provisions will be brought. Until then . . ." It gestured with a pincer, then left the chamber with Kamis and Cheth.

I stood, alone, bathed in sunlight.

I moved towards a vast window, which bulged out from the room. I saw the great mountain range on either hand, serried peaks falling gradually towards what I guessed was a dried up seabed. I later learned that I was right; that once this was indeed a mighty ocean. The mountains seemed silver, and so the seabed was split with dark fissures like the photographic negative of a lightning storm.

I stopped at the edge of the room, where the marble tiles segued seamlessly into the transparent material of the window.

I gasped, for a city fell away at my feet. It was as if I were levitating in the air, and was gazing upon a series of alleys and stairways as they fell down the shelving slope of the mountainside. I saw buildings like beehives, and towers which speared past where I stood, and a million windows looking out over the desiccated seabed – but I beheld not one figure in all the sprawling, falling cityscape, not one being to suggest that this perpendicular metropolis harboured life. It seemed as dead as the silver, dried up seabed far below.

Then I looked up and saw the sun, and I almost sobbed.

It filled the breadth of the horizon, and was bisected by that far away line of land, a great red fulminating dome that pulsed with life – or rather a semblance of life: magnificent molten eject, spuming geysers, looping strands of liquid fire. I laughed in awe at the sight, and knew it for the most wondrous thing I had ever witnessed.

I heard a sound behind me and turned quickly. Where nothing had stood before, in the centre of the chamber, now reposed upon a silver disc a pile of clothing and what looked like a stylized backpack. I left the window to inspect these things – the provisions, no doubt, which Rep had promised.

The clothing comprised a silver suit fashioned from a material so soft and light that I stood fondling it for minutes, smiling in wonder. The backpack was of a like material, and contained canisters holding what I guessed might be water. There were other objects in the pack: something like a pen, which I could not work, and a silver ball which defied my comprehension.

I pulled on the one-piece overall, which quickly shrank to hug my body and head, with a diaphanous membrane before my face. I looked up, attracted by something, and made out hovering above my head what looked like a halo; I smiled at the thought.

Rep had mentioned a journey; and was I now fully equipped? My curiosity was piqued. A journey, presumably, outside, in that harsh and sun-scorched landscape? And for what purpose? And this, in turn, brought my thoughts to the reason for my . . . what had Rep called it? . . . my fruition? At any rate, my presence in this wondrous age?

I shook my head and moved, as if compelled, towards the bulging window again, and stared out at the ancient Earth tortured by the engorged sun, and wondered what awaited me out there.

The aperture swished open and Rep jigged in on tiptoe, followed by the tall and striding Kamis; behind them, Cheth furled its wings to accommodate its passage into the chamber.

Rep said, "Ah, I see you have prepared yourself."

"For what, I would like to know," I said.

"For a journey to the end of the Earth," Rep said, "with many a wonder upon the way."

"Which," said Kamis with a hint of humour, "is as much as our crustacean friend has deigned to tell us, despite our constant questions."

"How long have you both been . . . enabled?" I asked.

The giant manta-ray known as Cheth replied, "Two days, no more."

"A day for me," answered Kamis. "A day of wonders enough, without promise of more."

Rep was leading the way towards the bulging window; we followed. As the crab-being approached, the transparent material opened like a clam-shell, hinged up to give access to a precipitous flight of stairs wide enough to accommodate even Cheth. I followed Rep, with Kamis by my side and Cheth bringing up the rear.

I had expected fierce heat, a searing wind. The reality was that the atmosphere without differed not in the slightest from that within the chamber. I breathed cool air, was aware of no hot wind.

We moved down the stairs away from the jutting chamber. Ahead, as if discerning my puzzlement, Rep twisted an eye-stalk and regarded me with a black orb. It said, "The suit you wear is equipped to equalize the temperature, to shield you from the worst of this world's inclemencies."

I pointed. "And the halo?"

"You might call it a . . . a solar panel," Rep said, "or at least a solar collector. At any rate, it gives power to your suit."

I looked at Kamis. "You wear no suit . . ." I began.

Something like a million different smiles chased themselves across the creature's face. "In my time the sun, though not this size, was almost beyond the tolerance of most living creatures. We adapted, suited our forms to the solar radiation."

"And you, Cheth?" I asked.

"Likewise," it replied. "My tegument is adapted, armoured. I use to my advantage that which many creatures would find inimical."

I smiled. "I am a primitive indeed," I said.

The humane Kamis said, "The happenstance of your genealogy does not preclude your potentiality, my friend."

I smiled and nodded and gave my attention to the descent.

It was my guess that the city was not built by human beings, or rather by any human beings that might have conformed to my approximate dimensions. For one thing the steps were too high, suggesting architects with longer legs than mine; for another, the apertures leading from the steps to the dwellings on either side were tall and attenuated: I would have had to turn sideways to gain entry. I imagined a city peopled by a race of long-legged giants.

Seconds later I heard a distant rumble, followed by a tremor; I staggered. It was as if for an instant my legs had turned to jelly.

Rep explained, "The Earth is old, and suffers quakes from time to time."

Kamis, beside me, asked Rep, "And this city? Is it a redundancy to ask if it is no longer inhabited?"

"Its last guardians left its shelter and took refuge underground some half a million years gone," Rep said. "They became extinct long ago."

"Guardians? But they were not the beings who built the city?" Cheth asked.

"No. The last inhabitants were spider creatures, living here like vermin and hardly sentient, we think."

"But do you know who did build the city?" I asked.

"A race known as the Effectuators," Rep told us. "They were a hallowed people, a philosopher race. Their artifacts can be found all over the surface of this old planet."

"And the stars," I said to myself. "In two billions years, the stars would have been conquered."

"Legions of races have left the refuge of planet Earth and gone among the stars, in search of knowledge and wisdom, adventure. And aliens," Rep went on, "stop by from time to time, with stories of their wanderings, and even tales of the many Terran races they have happened upon out there."

"And you?" Kamis asked. "Are your people, the Ky[20], a star-faring race?"

Replenish-362 raised two pincers in an indecipherable gesture. "We have never left the cradle of our birth, my friend. We leave adventuring to more daring species."

Cheth asked, "If this, then, is not your city – where do you dwell?"

"We are a subterranean species," Rep replied. "We live in vast excavated caverns in the cool far underground."

"But what," I said, "is the reason for your venturing out on this quest, if I might ask?"

The crab waved four pincers. "That will become apparent in time, in time," it said.

Beside me, Kamis smiled.

We had passed though a series of shelved dwellings, and now approached an escarpment. To either side were terraced ellipses, which once, in far earlier times, might have been gardens. Now they were parched furrows, from which even the soil had been dried to dust and stolen by the wind.

We stopped before what appeared to be a sheer drop, and Rep gestured with its largest pincer. "Behold."

The dehydrated seabed stretched away before us like some lifeless lunar landscape, magnificent not only in its size but in its silence, its grandeur made all the more impressive by the backdrop of the apoplectic sun.

At first I thought its only features the cracks and rills that striated its surface; but then I made out tiny specks of wrecked vessels canted and embedded in the silt, and here and there scattered about the shattered plain I glimpsed what might once have been former dwelling places, agglomerations of bubble-domes and things like termite mounds, cracked and crumbled now. The landscape was as bereft of colour as of life: a dozen shades of grey predominated, from dull pewter to silver. I looked about for signs of vegetation, but saw only sporadic, stunted bindweed, ground hugging and the colour of straw.

Indeed the only real colour provided was the bloody hue of the sun, which filled the air with a light like wine.

Rep gestured towards the ruined domes. "Long ago the Kleem took to the sea, and became in time aquatic. They raised great submarine cities, and for aeons were the dominant species on the planet. Their days passed, however, and their cities fell to ruin."

"When did this race prosper?" I asked.

"The Kleem were relatively recent, approximately nine million years gone. Some say they went to the stars aboard vast water-filled arks, when the seas of Earth began to dry, but that is only apocryphal."

We were standing on an apron of stone jutting out above the canyon, and I could see no steps leading the rest of the way.

Kamis said, "We will cross the bottom of this vanished sea?"

"We will," Rep answered.

"I see no means of descent," I said.

Rep waved a humorous pincer. "Our means is amongst us," it said, and gestured towards Cheth.

The manta-ray being descended and prostrated itself across the sun-blasted stones, like some vast and living mat of silver. "Step aboard," it said, voice muffled.

I glanced at Kamis, who gestured that I should go first.

Rep said, "Move to the middle and be seated. I assure you that you will be safe."

"And I second that assurance," came the modulated response from the ray's hidden mouth.

Tentatively, I took a step, and then another, across the flesh of the being, which gave like the surface of some liverish trampoline. I expected cries of surprise or pain from my host, but it was silent as I lowered myself and sat cross-legged on the broad back. I reached out and felt its skin: it was cold and rough, like frozen sandpaper.

Kamis sat beside me and Rep took up position ahead of us, eye-stalks peering forward as we lifted and floated out over the void.

The experience was as I guessed it must be like to ride a flying carpet. Cheth moved slowly at first, the edges of its wings scrolled to ensure our safety. There was no sensation of vertigo – the extent of Cheth's back was such that we had no sheer vision of the drop beneath us – or even danger; what I felt was a heady exhilaration as we picked up speed and descended in a great swooping parabola towards the seabed.

I looked up and back, and saw the city move away from us with surprising speed. It presented an aged face, blasted by the sun, and I wondered how mighty it had been aeons ago, fully populated by its builders, abustle with life unimaginable to me. I looked ahead and wondered at our destination.

I was skewered then by a fierce lancing stab of regret, and I tried to source it. I sensed the feelings I had felt for . . . loved ones, and I knew that much of the joy of my previous life, so long ago, had been because I had been able to share my experiences with them. How much more, I felt, I would appreciate what was happening now if only these faceless, nameless people were by my side to share this wondrous ride.

I tried to recapture lost memories, but experienced only abstractions, wellings of love as evanescent as lost dreams, and no more.

At one point we were side-swiped by a fierce wind, and rocked a little, and Kamis reached out with a silver hand and steadied me. The touch was a revelation. Whatever I had expected, it was not this: that its touch should communicate the essence of its humanity – a feeble word to use of a being not even human. It was as if it had communicated directly with my brain, as if its touch was all I needed to know that Kamis was good.

In time we came to the surface of the seabed, and hovered along perhaps two metres above the drifted silver sands. We passed close by the shattered domes, among which stood monuments of the Kleem – their great and good, no doubt – with wasted bodies and bulbous heads, and fins instead of limbs. There was something ineffably sad about the ruins, the canted broken statues and the domes half-buried in scintillating drifts, as if we were passing through not the remains of a city but a graveyard. Indeed, I thought, that was what planet Earth had become in this advanced age two billion years from my own time, an august graveyard of the many races that had lived and died in ignorance of what might succeed them.

It was a sobering thought as we left behind the once-submarine city and headed towards the roiling hemisphere of the swollen sun.

"Does it ever set?" I asked.

Rep said, "The rotation of planet Earth has slowed considerably over the millennia. A day now lasts almost a week, in your reckoning; a year lasts five of your years. The seasons are correspondingly protracted. We are in winter now."

"Winter?" Kamis said, surprised. "If this is winter, then what must summer be like?"

"A time of solar storms when the surface of the planet is uninhabitable, and all creatures burrow deep underground. A minute on the surface in high summer spells certain death."

"So that is why," said Cheth beneath us, "we are making this voyage now, in winter?"

Rep inclined an eye-stalk. "That is why indeed."

The silence stretched as we waited for Rep to continue; it deigned not to, and we did not press it.

Beside me, Kamis raised a hand and touched its temple. I said, "You are in pain?"

"Not pain," it said, a smile racing across its varied features. "I had a sudden . . . a fleeting return of memory. And yet . . . the memory is vague, though hauntingly strong, if that is not a contradiction. I recall a time in my childhood, when I accompanied my clan on a pilgrimage to the sea. It was the annual time of rejoicing in the fecundity of nature."

"Tell us," said Cheth.

The tall silver man sat up straight and looked ahead, into the sun. "There is little to tell, sadly. I recall great happiness, and safety. I was with my siblings, all thirty-odd of them, and we knew with the certainty of youth that the future held wondrous and miraculous events in store for us. I . . . I can sense more, feelings of tragedy, of elation, but it is as if these might belong to another person, so nebulous are they." It paused, then said, "And you, Cheth? What do you recall?"

The manta-ray replied, "Like you, my recollections are vague, abstract. As to specific instances of my life – these I find impossible to place, to pin down." It stopped there, then continued. "I receive the impression that we were like creatures in a small pond, which dreamed of the life that might exist out there, but which could only think within the narrow remit of the pond containing that life." It paused, then said, "And you, Channon?"

I shook my head. "I have no recollections, other than maddening abstractions. I do know that those of my race were short-lived compared to yourselves. We lived perhaps seventy, eighty, ninety years in total."

"So little time!" Rep said, aghast.

"No time," Kamis went on, "to assess one's suitability for . . . for *anything*."

I smiled. "In retrospect, I think we humans spent so much time mired in regret, wishing things were . . . different. Perhaps that's the corollary of living such short lives."

I considered my words, then said tentatively, "Kamis, Cheth, do either of you recall loved ones, family?"

A silence greeted my words, and then Kamis said, "I recall lovers . . . I think. In a lifetime of a thousand years, we would have perhaps thirty or forty partners, often concurrently. But the depth of our love for each other was not diminished by this fact. And yet . . ." A frown chased itself across its shimmering face. "And yet I recall no specific mates."

"Cheth?" I asked.

"Unlike the shimmer-folk, we villicents had but one lover in a lifetime, to whom we were devoted until death. But for the life of me, sadly, I do not recall the specifics of a mate."

A silence fell. Were we three thinking the same thing? That this absence, this lacunae in our memories, was a common link between us.

We rode on in silence.

Perhaps an hour passed before Rep said, "I think perhaps the time has arrived to pause for refreshments."

Duly Cheth slowed and came to rest a foot above the silver sands. We stepped off, into hot silt that lapped about our ankles, and Cheth rose so that it could regard us with the eyes which adorned its underside.

From our backpacks we took the canisters, all except Cheth; it was without provisions, and at my enquiry it explained, "The sunlight is enough, my friend, to provide all my bodily needs."

I watched Rep as it deftly unscrewed the lid from its canister and tipped it towards its letter-box mouth. A foamy liquid poured out. Kamis, tentatively, did likewise, then nodded. "Quite wonderful," it opined.

"A nutrient which will provide you with strength," Rep said.

I opened my canister and drank. The liquid frothed and spangled upon my palate, leaving me feeling both refreshed and satisfied.

"And these?" I asked, taking out the silver ball and the pencil-like implement.

"The sphere is a protector," Rep said. "It maintains a field about your person which repels any predators which might be lurking."

"Predators?"

"Strange beasts patrol the torrid wastes," Rep said.

"And the sticks?" Kamis asked.

"Keys," said Rep.

A silence, then we all three asked in concert, "Keys, for what?"

Its eye-stalks moved from Kamis to Cheth to me. "For what comes next, my friends," it said with maddening taciturnity.

"And that might be?" I ventured.

Its eye-stalks swivelled until they were regarding the sun. It gestured with a pincer and said, "Look, our bellicose primary has loosed a supra-flare."

We looked, and beheld, emerging from the bloated belly of the sun, a quick lick of flame racing through space towards the planet.

"But what," said Cheth, "has this to do with the keys we carry?"

"In time, in time," said the damnable crab. "Follow me. The flare will arrive in perhaps one hour, and it would be well if we were far below the surface when it blasts the land."

It minced towards an outcropping of rock, and we followed.

As it approached what appeared to be a slab of fractured basalt, a circular aperture in its flank irised to reveal a hovering disk of flat metal, perhaps five metres across. Rep stepped onto it, and we joined it. Instantly we were aboard, it dropped. I cried out in consternation and reached out to Kamis, who steadied me. The hovering Cheth gave a cry of surprise and dropped with us.

A minute later the disk slowed its rapid descent, and I stepped off it into a chamber that staggered my senses with its dimensions.

It was v-shaped, perhaps a hundred metres tall, constructed of some brilliant white ceramic substance, and it diminished into the distance for as far as the eye could see. Its sloping sides were scored with galleries, and on the ground floor and on each gallery – and I counted twenty of them before the distance defeated my eyesight – dozens of crabs like Replenish-362 worked at banks of consoles.

Their activity was frantic as they skittered back and forth, tapping at surfaces, adjusting panels, conferring together and then parting in great haste.

Kamis voiced what I was thinking, "What is happening here?"

"These are scientists," Rep said. "They are carrying out the work of the Effectuators."

"What work? Kamis asked.

The reticent crab kept its own counsel and its eye-stalks peered ahead as it led us along the chamber.

I recalled mention of the keys. "Our keys have some function down here?" I asked as we pursued the skittering crab.

We came to a canted series of consoles, etched with arcane hieroglyphs and indented with several slots. At the sight of us, three crabs working at the consoles backed off, eye-stalks turned our way, and watched us as we approached with Rep.

"If each of you takes a console, and inserts the key into the appropriate aperture . . ."

Hastily, Kamis and I unfastened our packs and withdrew the pen-like implement. Rep stirred a pincer in its own pack, and withdrew a stick which it passed to Cheth, who manoeuvred its cilia to accept it.

I stepped forward, towards the console, and slipped the pen point first into the appropriate slot. It was tugged from my grip in a rush . . . and I have no explanation for what happened next.

It was as if the chamber ceased to exist. I was in a white limitless area, and out of the opalescence which surrounded me coalesced a series of images, a rapid procession of incidents which I knew – somehow – to be the history of planet Earth.

And then I beheld a hundred creatures, a thousand, and with each one I was granted its name, its place in history, its significance. And I knew the planet Earth to be a wondrous place which over billions of years had played host to all manner of sentient lifeforms, races and species which had spanned hundreds of thousand of years before passing into oblivion, or a million years before disappearing from evolution's stage: but whatever the race, and however long they ruled the planet, their fate was certain: they would one day hand the flame of the planet's stewardship onto another emergent race.

And then I was looking upon a creature I knew, somehow, to be an Effectuator: a bipedal ant-like being with a human's swollen cranium. It turned and regarded me, and then smiled, and an exquisite sensation of well-being flooded my senses. I had the sudden knowledge, then, as he peered at me, that I was being assessed by this being, judged even, but for what I could not guess.

I had a dozen questions, more, but at that instant I was whisked from the opalescent realm and I found myself back in the chamber surrounded by the scurrying crabs, with Kamis and Cheth by my side and Rep standing before me, regarding us with its eye-stalks.

Kamis was the first to gather its thoughts, and I knew from what it said that it had experienced much the same as I. "And what," it said, "became of the Effectuators?"

Rep said, "They . . . ascended, stepped up, and employed us, the humble species known as Ky[20], to do their bidding."

"Which is?" Kamis said.

"And what," I asked, "do they want with us? I felt I was being . . . *judged* – but for what?"

Instead of replying, Rep moved away from the consoles, back towards the aperture which housed the elevator disc. It stepped upon it, and we had little option but to follow.

Rep was silent as we rode to the surface of the planet and stepped out into the scorched landscape.

Much was as it had been, but for twists and torques of fire scattered about the seabed, combustible material ignited by the errant supra-flare.

Rep gestured, and Cheth descended. We accommodated ourselves upon its back, and it rose and flew towards the sun.

We travelled for hours, and the sun expanded to fill fully half the sky. I dozed, and dreamed, lucid images of men and women, golden humans who radiated greatness, and I was filled by an inexpressible surge of joy, of ineffable rapture. The intensity was such that it brought me awake, and for seconds I was disconcerted to find myself riding upon the back of a strange creature, across a dying earth, towards a boiling sun.

I closed my eyes and attempted to recapture the images, to access memories so far denied me. I failed to recall specific instances of my life before, but I did come upon nebulous feelings, maddeningly elusive: feelings of love and hope, upwellings of basic emotion. They were so general they might have belonged to any human at any time in history.

We were travelling high above the seabed obscured by drifting sands. I thought I saw, to my left, a mountainside shiver and collapse. I blinked, and the movement of my travelling companions, as they turned and watched the looming peak crumble and slide into the seabed, alerted me to the fact that I was not hallucinating.

"What is happening?" asked Kamis.

"The Earth," Rep replied, "suffers stress from time to time; the pressure of the sun . . ." It was silent for a time, then said, "These are the last years of the planet."

We greeted its words with silence, such was the enormity of the concept.

"The last years," I echoed.

"The sun's gravitational force is tearing the planet apart, and has been doing so for millennia; but now has come the time when the integrity of the world will bear no more, and Earth will be torn to pieces. Already the moon has crumbled to dust . . ."

Cheth said, "To think! The end of the world which has harboured so many great races, so much grand history. The planet has been an arena, upon which has been played out the destiny and fate of countless optimistic races."

It was a humbling thought.

"And this," said Kamis, "is why we were brought here, to the end of time?"

Instead of replying, Rep turned a claw towards the earth below. The sandstorm had abated, to reveal a flat expanse of shimmering sand. I saw, far below, and made minuscule by our elevation, a procession of . . . at first I thought them vehicles, but on closer inspection I made out groups of individuals making their way towards the sun at speed.

Cheth banked, and we glided towards the seabed, and the individuals resolved themselves into all manner of strange and wondrous creatures. I beheld a great segmented insects scurrying alongside a creature as golden and proud as a lion, but bi-pedal and clad in robes. I saw something like a jellyfish pulsing along through the air, its polychromatic innards strobing through the spectrum in what might have been some form of arcane language; I saw beings like birds the size of pterosaurs, and rolling balls of sinew that conformed to no life-form I had ever beheld. Among these varied beings I made out familiar figures: crab-beings like Rep running hither and yon as if shepherding the crowds.

Kamis laughed. "But there are hundreds of them! Thousands!"

Across the wide breadth of the seabed, the cavalcade of beings was drawn like iron fillings as if by some invisible magnet towards the beauteous attractor of the dying sun.

"But not all are from Earth?" Cheth said.

"You are correct," Rep said. "Some hail from Mars and the moons of Jupiter, Saturn and Uranus, and beyond. All are races which once dwelled proudly in the solar system."

"And they, too," Kamis asked, "have been accessed, enabled and brought to fruition?"

Rep waved an acknowledging claw. "That is so."

I said, "So, then, has every sentient being that has ever lived been brought to fruition to witness the end of planet Earth and the solar system?"

There was a pause before Rep said, "Not every being, my friend. Merely . . . representatives."

We all three allowed this statement to sit in the air, before Cheth said, "But by what right, or by what stroke of fortune, was it deemed that *I* should represent my race?"

It was the question which had sprung to my mind, too. Rep was silent. At last Kamis prompted, "Well? I think Cheth's query is valid."

"I will explain very soon," was all the crab would say.

I gazed down at the throng, and saw that it was added to all the time by the arrival of more beings from every direction, escorted by their Ky[20] guides. Then I beheld, among the teeming life down there, something almost human. It was small and ape-like, though walked upright with a noble bearing. I gestured to Rep and said, "A human being, like me?"

Rep responded, "A being which came to sentience on Earth a million years before *Homo sapiens*, but of a different species."

I thought of the scientists working away in the underground bunker, and said, "The scientists we saw – what exactly were they doing?"

Rep tuned an eye-stalk my way. "They were bringing about a rift in space and time."

I gasped, and thought I had an answer. "Our summons here, the scientists . . . they – you – are sending us back in time to warn our races of the doom that awaits the planet?"

Rep made a sound like laughter. "Such a rationalistic theory, my friend. But what might that achieve? The end of Earth is a fact, an immutable law which cannot be averted. It is, indeed, to be celebrated."

"Ah ha!" said Kamis. "So that is what this great pilgrimage is – a celebration?"

"Not," said Rep, "as such."

"Then what?" asked Cheth.

Instead of replying, Rep spoke hurriedly to Cheth, and in response Cheth dropped so that we were flying low above the seabed, just above the heads – and other appendages – of the marching assembly.

I looked upon the varied life that had shared the solar system, and marvelled.

Ahead, the seabed came to an end, dipped and formed a vast amphitheatre. Gathered within this declivity, washed with the light of the ailing primary, sat, stood, and hovered a myriad curious individuals. We came to a halt, hovering above the heads of the crowd, and stared.

And as we stared, a remarkable thing happened high above the amphitheatre; it was as if the air before the sun had finally succumbed to the great heat and split, for the sky was torn from horizon to zenith to reveal an ellipse of such blinding luminescence that it dazzled the gaze to look upon it. I turned my head and beheld, to either side of the rent, great silver machines the size of planets with claws which reached out and held open the sides of the blinding ellipse.

Rep gestured. "The last gesture of the Effectuators," it said, "aided by our humble selves."

"But what . . . ?" I managed.

"They were masters of space and time," it said, "and we their mere minions, slaves if you like, to do their bidding. But what bidding!"

"Tell us," said Cheth.

"We have helped to open a rift in the fabric of the continuum; we gaze now upon the fundament, the essence that underpins all reality."

"And our presence here?" I asked.

Rep turned to me, and regarded me with its eye-stalks, and paused before saying, "I implied earlier that you represent your race, my friend."

Kamis said, "And we wondered why us, why we of all the millions, the billions, of our race . . . why we should be selected for this . . . honour."

And Rep said, "When I said represent your race, that is exactly what I meant." It paused before continuing, "You are not individuals, as such, but distillations of the essences of your respective races."

I felt a welling sadness within me, almost like despair. "But my memories . . . my loved ones . . . The love I felt, the love I feel!"

Rep said, "It is valid, my friend, but does not refer to specific individuals. Instead, it is something far greater – the incarnation of the goodness that made your race great."

"And we were brought here for what reason?" asked Kamis. "Surely, not just to witness the end of the Earth?"

Rep waved a claw. "The Effectuators were perhaps the greatest of all the races that ever graced the solar system, and they foresaw an end to all things, not just our sun – but the universe itself."

Something stirred within me at these words, some premonition of what all this was about, and I felt a fluttering sensation within my chest.

"They worked to defy entropy, to abnegate the draconian laws of the universe – the laws which state that all things must end."

"And?" I asked, my voice a tremor.

"And," said Rep, waving towards th
succeeded. Behold the entrance to another th

We stared, but comprehension eluded us.

Before we could question Rep, there was a stirring
beneath us, a surge forward, and I looked ahead and saw
the distant horizon, the amphitheatre was emptying of its asse
bled species, draining like water from a dam.

They were giving themselves to the rent in the space-time
continuum.

And we too were moving towards it.

Rep said, "You contain, within you, the essences of your races,
the life-force of the universe."

"And you, my friend?" I asked.

"I am a mere guide," Rep said. "I go no further, but will live out
my last years among my kind, secure in the knowledge that we
have fulfilled the desire of the Effectuators."

"And they?" I Kamis asked.

"They dwell in the universe as beings of energy," Rep said.
"Now . . . go!"

We left Rep, and moved swiftly towards the light, and it was
blinding.

And I cried out, reaching for memories. I felt great sadness that
I was no more than an illusion, and then a welling of rapture that
everything I was should amount to such greatness, for I knew then
that I – and Kamis and Cheth and the countless others with me –
were seeds.

We moved towards the rent, towards the beginning of a myriad
new universes, and I gave thanks.

And fell into the light.

...rd, Gerald Nordley and several others ...logy, Geoffrey Landis (b. 1955) is a science-fic... ...ter who also gets his hands very dirty as a practising scientist. He has worked for NASA and the Ohio Aerospace Institute and specializes in photovoltaics, which is about harnessing the power of the sun. He has been writing science fiction for over twenty years and has won two Hugo Awards and a Nebula for his short fiction. His books include the novel Mars Crossing (2000) and the collection Impact Parameter (2001).

I had originally intended that Eric Brown's story would close this anthology, but this one kept niggling at the back of my mind. It just would not fit anywhere else in the anthology, and just had to come at the end. You'll soon see why, as it's quite short, and will leave you wondering in classic "Lady and the Tiger" tradition. I hope, by now, your sense of wonder is fully restored.

> "...the vacuum state must contain many particles
> in a state of transient existence
> with violent fluctuations ...
> The total energy of the vacuum is infinite ..."

P. A. M. Dirac, *Quantum Mechanics*

YOU OPEN THE DOOR hesitantly, then walk into the laboratory where the two scientists wait for you. They seem to know you. Perhaps you are a science writer, well known for your ability to convey a sense of the excitement of even the most arcane scientific discoveries. Or perhaps you are merely a friend, someone who knows both of them from long ago. It doesn't matter.

The older scientist smiles as she sees you. She is a world-renowned physicist, and justly so, an iconoclast who laughingly destroyed the world-view of her predecessors and rebuilt the universe to match her own view of beauty. Some say that now, older, she has grown conservative, less open to speculation. Her hair is clipped short, just beginning to grey. Call her Celia. Whatever else she may be, she is a friend. Between you no titles or last names are needed.

And the younger scientist, barely out of grad school, with an infectious enthusiasm and boundless energy; the new iconoclast, the barbarian storming the walls of the citadel of knowledge, already being compared to the young Einstein or Dirac. Perhaps he is tall and lanky, with unruly black hair, wearing a grey sweatshirt emblazoned with a cartoon picture of Schrödinger's cat. Or maybe he wears a three-piece suit; such an incongruity would appeal to his sense of humour.

You were there when they first met. Perhaps you even introduced them, in the hopes of seeing sparks fly. If so, you were disappointed, since their conversation had quickly shifted to another language, a language of Hilbert spaces and contravariant derivatives. Perhaps the very language, you muse, of the Word spoken in the Beginning, before the world began.

But sparks indeed flew, could you but have seen. And one of them had caught fire.

"I came," you say, "as soon as I could."

The younger scientist – perhaps his name is David? – takes your hand and shakes it vigorously. "Yes, yes, yes, yes," he says, "I knew you would. I trust you are ready to see something, well – " he grins, "Earth-shaking?"

"What do you know about guts?" says the older scientist.

"Yes," you say, speaking to the scientist whose name is perhaps David, and "GUTs? Grand Unification Theories? Just the barest bones," you say to the other.

"But you do know that the quantum vacuum is quite full of energy?" she asks, in her slightly British accent. "That, according to quantum mechanics, even empty space must have a large 'zero point energy'?"

"Alive with virtual particles," he interjects, "bursting with the energies of creation; constantly afroth and aboil with the boundless, countless, infinite dance of creation and annihilation below the Heisenberg limit."

"Yes," you say, slowly. You've tried to understand quantum mechanics before. Somehow, though, the vital essence has always managed to elude you. "But it's not *real* energy, is it?"

"Indeed," she says, "most respectable (she pronounces the word as if it were somehow dirty) physicists will tell you that zero-point energy is just a mathematical artifact, a figment of the formalism."

"So goes the conventional wisdom," he says. "But it's there, never the less."

"Maybe," she says dryly, "you should show the apparatus."

"Yes, of course. This way." He turns and walks with a bounce across the room, not even looking to see if you are behind him. You follow him into an adjoining room where a large, complicated piece of experimental apparatus fills most of the available space. "What do you think?"

You hate to admit it, but all physics experiments look alike to you. A shiny stainless-steel vacuum chamber, large storage tanks of liquid nitrogen and helium, racks of digital meters, an oscilloscope or two, with brightly coloured wires strung all about and the ubiquitous computer sitting in front. "Very pretty," you say, hoping he won't notice your indifference. Experimenters all think that their apparatus is beautiful. "What is it?"

"A device to extract energy from the vacuum," she says.

"What?"

"An endless energy source," he says. "A rabbit that pulls itself out of a hat. A perpetual motion machine, if you will."

"Oh." You are impressed. "Does it work?"

The two scientists look at each other. David sighs. "We haven't tried it."

"Why not?"

"There is a question we disagree about, and we thought we'd ask your opinion," Celia says, slowly. For a moment you think this is funny; there is no way that you could hope to answer a question that they could not. Then it seems less funny, then not funny at all.

So you hold your silence. "A philosophical question: if we take energy out of the vacuum, what do we have left?"

"Nothing!" he interjects, barely waiting for her to finish speaking. "That's the symmetry of the vacuum. Since the zero-point energy is infinite, no matter how much energy is extracted there is always an infinite amount left."

"So goes conventional wisdom," she replies softly. "But the infinity is a renormalized infinity, and that the only thing of importance is differences in energy. If we remove energy, what is left must be a vacuum with lower energy.

"Therefore, if we can extract energy, the physical vacuum must be a false vacuum."

She makes this pronouncement seem portentous, as if it were the most important thing in the world. "True vacuum?" you say. "False vacuum?"

"Right," she says. "It's simple. A 'true vacuum' by definition is the lowest energy state of empty space. If you put anything into it – remember, mass has energy! – the energy must increase, and it's no longer the true vacuum."

You plop yourself down onto a lab stool, a spidery metal thing with a round metal seat, slickly enamelled in nondescript light brown. Through your jeans you feel it cool against your buttocks. You swivel slightly, back and forth, like a compass needle uncertain of true north.

"The GUTS theory postulates that when the universe was young there existed a vacuum that was just as empty of matter, but had higher energy. This 'false' vacuum decayed into our 'true' vacuum by a process we call spontaneous breaking of symmetry."

Her colleague leans back against a rack of equipment, smiling slightly. He seems willing to let her do the explaining. She glances at her watch. "We don't have a whole lot of time, so please pay careful attention.

"Here's an example. Consider a beaker of perfectly pure liquid water. The water has perfect symmetry, which means if you start from one water molecule, you have just as much likelihood of finding another water molecule in one direction as any other. Now, cool the water down. Cool it past the freezing point, and keep cooling it. If it's really pure water, it won't freeze. Instead, it supercools. That's because ice has lower symmetry than liquid water, all directions are *not* the same. Some directions are along the crystal axis, others aren't. Since pure water doesn't have any way to "pick" a preferred direction to orient the crystals, it can't crystalize.

"Now drop in a tiny crystal of ice. One little seed of ice, no matter how tiny, and whamo! Suddenly the whole mass of water crystallizes, releasing energy in the process. Explosive crystalization, it's called.

"That's symmetry breaking.

"Now, symmetries exist in empty space as well, although a bit more abstract ones. According to GUTs, the big bang itself was caused by symmetry breaking. In the beginning, the universe was unthinkably small, and unimaginably hot, but empty. Everything was supersymmetric, all the four forces were the same, and all particles were alike. The universe cooled, and then supercooled. After a while the supersymmetric vacuum wasn't the true vacuum any more, but a false vacuum, laden with potential energy. Nobody knows what triggered the crystallization, but suddenly it happened, and the universe flipped over into one of the lower energy states.

"A lot of energy was released. Everything that is, was created from that explosive transition to a lower energy vacuum."

"Oh," you say, since you can't think of anything else.

"Sometimes I dream of it," she says. "Perhaps before the big bang, there were intelligent creatures in the universe. What they were like we couldn't possibly imagine. Their world was hot, and dense, and tiny; their entire universe would have been smaller than the point of a pin, and they would have lived a trillion generations in the shortest time we can measure. Perhaps one of them realized that the vacuum they were living in was a false vacuum, and that they could create energy from nothing. Perhaps one of them tried it. One tiny seed, no matter how small . . ."

Your head is spinning, trying to imagine little tiny scientists before the big bang. You picture them as something like ants, but smaller, and moving so fast that they're like blurs. And hot, don't forget hot. You give up trying to picture it, and go back to listening. She is saying something about cubic potentials, comparing the universe to a marble on top of a hill – if the marble is right exactly at the top, it doesn't know which way to roll.

"The question is," she continues, "if energy can be extracted from the vacuum, why doesn't it happen spontaneously, all by itself? The answer has to be, because some symmetry forbids it. But if that symmetry is broken . . .

"Since the big bang, the universe has cooled a lot. Perhaps *our* vacuum has cooled out of the lowest energy state. If the symmetry is broken, all the energy of the vacuum would be released at once. It would be the end, not only of the Earth, but of the universe as we know it.

"And now David, here, wants to do exactly that."

"As it turns out, her worries are pointless," he says. "There are plenty of energetic objects in the universe that would trip such a transition. Quasars, black holes, Seyfert galaxies. If the universe were a false vacuum, it would have transitioned billions of years ago."

"Have you ever wondered about the Fermi paradox?" she asks. "How it is that we've never seen any signs of other intelligent life in the universe? I can tell you the answer. If any alien civilizations more advanced than ours existed, they would have already found the secret to extracting vacuum energy. Sooner or later, they'd try it, and, wham! The end of the universe. So the universe wouldn't exist, unless we're the first."

You notice that they are both waiting for you to say something. You scuffle your feet against the rough concrete floor. You've figured out why they called you here, and are desperately trying to thing of what to say. "So you have cold feet? You want me to tell you whether you should do the experiment?"

"No," he tells you. "We already have started the experiment." He gestures at a digital read-out. "I turned it on when you first walked in the door. The field is building up now. When it hits ten thousand tesla, the generator is programmed to flip on automatically." You look at the LED indicator. 9.4, it tells you, in a cheerful cherry-red glow.

"But," says the other.

"But?" you say. David takes your hand, and wraps it around the handle of a switch, a large old-fashioned knife switch, the kind that you privately think of as a "Frankenstein switch". You briefly pretend that you are the obsessed doctor, with life and death subjugated to your power. You've watched too many old monster movies. "This turns it off?"

"In a matter of speaking," he says.

"I doubt anybody else will reproduce what we found," she says. "This may sound like boasting, but it took a few pretty radical insights – and more than a bit of luck – and it's not at all the direction that other theoretical physicists are searching. Not the idea of getting energy from the vacuum – plenty of people could think of that. It's our way to do it that's the trick."

"I disagree. What one person discovers, no matter how esoteric, another will duplicate. Maybe not for a long time, maybe not in our lifetimes, but sooner or later, it will happen."

She smiles. "Again, it's a question of philosophy. I've been playing the game long enough to know that real science doesn't work the way the science books pretend. It's not like making a map, unless you think of it as creating the land as we map it. The very shape of science is created by the scientists who first make it. We think in their metaphors; we see what they chose to look at. If we let go of this discovery, it won't be duplicated in our lifetimes, and by then the flow of science will be elsewhere."

"In any case," he says, "there isn't enough money in the grant for us to do it again.

"The switch you're holding breaks the circuit in the superconducting magnets. There's about a thousand amps running through the coils now. Quench the magnet and the superconductors heat up, transition back into ordinary metal. In other words, they become resistors. All that current . . . it'll create a lot of heat. Throw that switch, and ten million dollars worth of equipment melts into a puddle of slag."

"Not to worry too much, though," Celia adds cheerfully. "It's only grant money."

Suddenly your lips are dry. You run the tip of your tongue over them. "And you want *me* to . . ."

"We've agreed on this much," she says, exasperated. "If you stop the experiment, we'll abide by your decision. We won't publish. Nor even hint."

"But why me?" you ask. "Why not bring in an expert?"

"We *are* the experts," he says. "What we need is somebody from outside, somebody with an unbiased opinion."

"Don't be silly," she says, speaking to you. "We wanted somebody who *couldn't* understand the details. If we called in a bunch of experts, do you think they could possibly keep it secret, after?"

"And besides," he adds, "committees are always conservative. We all know what they'd say: wait, let's study it some more. Well, damn, we've *already* studied it. If she'd told me we need to have a committee discuss it, I'd have just snuck in one midnight and run it myself. No, we have to do it this way. Whatever you decide, that's it. No dithering. No second thoughts. We go for it right now, or forget it."

"If I'm right," he continues, "then the stars are ours. The *universe* is ours. Humanity will be immortal. When the sun burns out, we'll create our own suns. We will have all the energy of creation at our fingertips."

"And if he's wrong," she says, "then this is the end. Not just the end of us. The end of the universe."

"Except that I'm not wrong."

"If you are, we'll never know. Either way."

"Still, I'd risk it all. This is the key to the universe. It's worth the risk. It's worth any risk."

She looks back at you. "So there you have it."

He raises an eyebrow. "On the one hand, infinity. On the other, the end of everything."

He looks over at the digital readout, and your eye follows his. As you watch, it flicks from 9.8 to 9.9. The handle of the switch is warm, faintly slick with sweat. In your hand it seems almost to vibrate.

She looks at you. You look at him. He looks at the switch. You look at her. They both look at you.

"You'd best decide quickly," he says, softly.